# THE MAN IN THE IRON MASK

# THE MAN IN
# THE IRON MASK

Alexandre Dumas

*Introduction and Notes by*
KEITH WREN
*University of Kent at Canterbury*

WORDSWORTH CLASSICS

For my husband
**ANTHONY JOHN RANSON**
with love from your wife, the publisher.
Eternally grateful for your unconditional love.

Readers who are interested in other titles from
Wordsworth Editions are invited to visit our website at
www.wordsworth-editions.com

First published in 2002 by Wordsworth Editions Limited
8B East Street, Ware, Hertfordshire SG12 9HJ

ISBN 978 1 84022 435 1

Wordsworth Editions
is the company founded in 1987 by
**MICHAEL TRAYLER**

Typeset in Great Britain by Antony Gray
Printed and bound by Clays Ltd, Elcograf S.p.A.

# GENERAL INTRODUCTION

Wordsworth Classics are inexpensive editions designed to appeal to the general reader and students. We commissioned teachers and specialists to write wide ranging, jargon-free introductions and to provide notes that would assist the understanding of our readers rather than interpret the stories for them. In the same spirit, because the pleasures of reading are inseparable from the surprises, secrets and revelations that all narratives contain, we strongly advise you to enjoy this book before turning to the Introduction.

*General Adviser*
KEITH CARABINE
*Rutherford College*
*University of Kent at Canterbury*

# INTRODUCTION

As early as the middle of the first chapter, it is clear that *The Man in the Iron Mask* is a very odd novel indeed. Within the first paragraph we are shown 'a house that may be recognised as the same which . . . had been besieged by d'Artagnan as elsewhere recorded' (p. 3) – but where recorded? and who exactly is d'Artagnan? A couple of pages later, the mysterious duchess is talking about the strange death of a Franciscan and a conversation in a cemetery – and if it then occurs to her (as it does) 'that we had scarcely told each other anything' (p. 4), prior to her referring familiarly to a character called Marie Michon whose first and last appearance in the novel this is (but whose ghost has forgotten nothing), it similarly occurs to *us* that no one has told us anything at all, and – frankly – what the devil is going on?

In fact, *The Man in the Iron Mask* is not a novel at all. It is, loosely speaking, the third section of *The Vicomte de Bragelonne*, Alexandre Dumas's immensely long sequel to the first two novels of what we may term the *Musketeers* cycle. After the huge success of *The Three Musketeers* in 1844 and *Twenty Years After* in 1845, Dumas embarked between 1847 and 1850 on the publication in serialised form of the third and last novel in the sequence. When published in English translation, this blockbuster (it runs to well over 2000 pages in a recent French paperback edition) is normally (if arbitrarily) divided into three segments, entitled *The Vicomte de Bragelonne*, *Louise de la Vallière* and *The Man in the Iron Mask*. However, there is no agreement as to where one segment ends and the next begins, with the confusing consequence that different editions of *The Man in the Iron Mask* pick up the narrative in different places. For example, the recent Penguin version released to coincide with the 1998 film of the book, starring Leonardo di Caprio, starts with the chapter entitled 'The Prisoner', whereas the current edition, in common with that issued in the Oxford World's Classics series, opens a good deal further back in the proceedings with 'A Pair of Old Friends'.[1] However, as we have already seen, there are problems for the reader no matter which point of embarkation is preferred.

Serial fiction was hugely popular in France at the time Dumas was writing. It was a relatively recent phenomenon, dating back to 1836, when two rival newspapers, *La Presse* and *Le Siècle*, were able to cut their cover price by some fifty per cent thanks to the simple wheeze of accepting commercial advertising. In those days, newspapers depended for sales on a subscription system: the consequence of the dramatic price reduction was an equally dramatic increase in the number of subscribers.[2] The proprietors then had to devise ways of hanging on to their new readers, and, although they did not initially see serial fiction as the trump card it rapidly turned out to be, they did see the value of including regular features to keep the punters coming back for more. By 1838, *Le Siècle* had already developed the nineteenth-century equivalent of the modern trailer, boasting of the coming fictional attractions in store for the public, and the serial-fiction juggernaut was in the process of developing an unstoppable momentum.

1 Sadly, irrespective of the starting point, any similarity between book and film is almost entirely coincidental.

2 David Coward notes in his edition of *The Vicomte de Bragelonne* (World's Classics, Oxford 1995) that the number of newspaper subscribers rose as a result of this development from 70,000 throughout France in 1835 to 200,000 in Paris alone in 1836.

Dumas quickly realised the potential of this new genre, as, given his past history and credentials, we might reasonably expect him to have done. Born in 1802 in Villers-Cotterêts, some fifty miles north-east of Paris, the son of a career soldier in Napoleon's army and an innkeeper's daughter, he migrated to the capital in 1823, where he quickly became involved in literary activity, initially as a dramatist, with a string of stage successes from the late 1820s onwards. However, by the mid 1830s his playwright's star was beginning to fade and the moment was ripe for him to change direction. He was quite at home with the public's enthusiasm for historical fiction (it has been calculated that around half of the serials published in the two main newspapers had settings that were at least ostensibly historical). Inspired, like most of the rest of Europe's budding literary talent, by the novels of 'the wizard of the North', Sir Walter Scott, he had set many of his plays in a historical context, and already in July 1836 he was setting the pace in *La Presse* for the new craze.[3]

Dumas thought traditional textbook history was boring, but took (at least for public consumption) a somewhat prudishly moralistic view of pure fiction. His compromise solution was to opt for a narrative version of a rather odd (and unsurprisingly ephemeral) dramatic form that had been popular for some years in France. This was the *scène historique*, supposedly unadulterated history in dialogue form (for reasons not difficult to divine, these *scènes* were never staged). Dumas, never averse to self-congratulation, argued that his adaptation of this genre to a narrative form brought history to life whilst not contaminating it with the base fictions of the novel, thus avoiding the pitfalls of both genres 'since truth would be rigorously adhered to as well as acquiring substance and spirit, and no invented characters would be mixed in with authentic historical figures, who alone would play out the drama of the past.'[4]

Doubtless entirely laudable, this endeavour was never entirely convincing, and by the 1840s, Dumas had changed tack somewhat. It is fortunate for us that he did so, since with the best will in the world, the nail-biting suspense of Edward III's preparations for the Hundred Years' War hardly seems quite on a par with the exploits

3 His first dramatic success, *Henri III et sa cour* (1829), was set against the background of the sixteenth-century Wars of Religion in France: arguably his best play, *Charles VII chez ses grands vassaux* (1831), has its setting a century earlier.

4 quoted in Y. Knibiehler and R. Ripoll, 'Les Premiers pas du feuilleton: chronique historique, nouvelle, roman', *Europe*, 542, June 1974, pp. 7–19

of the immortal (but essentially fictitious) musketeers in defence of honour, land and lady.

For with *The Three Musketeers* in 1844 Dumas struck a rich vein (indeed, 1844 was something of an *annus mirabilis* for him, since it was also the date when the serialisation of *The Count of Monte Cristo* began). His readership clamoured for more, and a fortnight before the day of the last instalment, the paper announced the imminent serialisation of *Twenty Years After*.[5] Nine months later, rejoicing (somewhat prematurely, as it transpired) at having secured Dumas's agreement to write *The Vicomte de Bragelonne*, it lauded the two previous novels of its star contributor to the skies:

> M. Alexandre Dumas's talent shines forth brilliantly in these productions, where he has demonstrated signal qualities of which the combination is so rare at any time in history: compelling interest, involving verve, wit, charm, vigour, a fruitful imagin-ation, extensive erudition, comic spirit, picturesque and sparkling literary style.[6]

Of course, one should never repose total confidence in advertising copy. There had arguably been a good deal less verve, wit and sparkle in *Twenty Years After* than in its predecessor – Dumas had got rather bogged down in the complexities of the Fronde rebellion – and although these qualities are far from absent in *The Vicomte de Bragelonne*, the Dumas of 1850 was on the whole a sadder, wiser man than his predecessor of 1844. Robert Louis Stevenson, who included the novel among his favourites (claiming to have read it 'either five or six' times), defined its attributes thus:

> I was asked the other day if Dumas ever made me laugh or cry. Well, in this my late fifth reading . . . I did laugh once . . . and to make up for it, I smiled continually. But for tears, I do not know . . . above all, in this last volume, I find a singular charm of spirit. It breathes a pleasant and a tonic sadness . . . Upon the crowded, noisy life of this long tale, evening gradually falls; and the lights are extinguished, and the heroes pass away one by one.[7]

---

5 The last episode of *The Three Musketeers* appeared in *Le Siècle* on 14 July 1844; on 30 June, the newspaper had announced that it was already in possession (which it manifestly was not) of the first three volumes of *Twenty Years After*.

6 quoted in A. Dumas, *Vingt Ans Après*, ed. C. Samaran, Paris 1962, p. xxvii

7 R. L. Stevenson, *Works*, ed. E. Gosse, Cassell, London 1905, Vol. IX, p. 144

*The Man in the Iron Mask* is at least partially a novel about old men, and a lament for vanished glories – 'never glad confident morning again!' The musketeers are all in their fifties or sixties, and although the story makes fleeting reference to the famous oath of *The Three Musketeers* ('all for one and one for all'), this is shown to be an aspiration rather than a reality. For Athos, Porthos, Aramis and d'Artagnan are not only constantly at odds with each other, but – more significantly – are never once in the entire novel seen all together. In the cold, hard, cruelly efficient world they now inhabit, Dumas's musketeers are anachronisms – or at least, three of them are. The case of Aramis is rather different, as I shall hope to show.

Set against the musketeers and the heroic values of the past that they embody is the figure of Louis XIV, King of France. The Sun King, as he has come to be known to posterity, is portrayed here as a rather unpleasant customer whose sole aim in life is personal and political self-gratification elevated to the status of a creed. Dumas hints at the psychological damage inflicted on him when a boy by his humiliation during the Fronde (pp. 254–5).[8] His subsequent resolve to achieve both absolute power and absolute invulnerability are revealed in his resentment of his minister, Fouquet, who ultimately (and ironically) pays the penalty for releasing his king from the Bastille. Louis's personal imperatives (p. 128) dovetail neatly with the politics lesson he gives d'Artagnan towards the end of the novel:

> I am founding a state in which there shall be but one master. I promised you this long ago, and the moment has come for the promise to be kept. You think you can be allowed to thwart my plans and shield my enemies according to your own preferences or friendships? I will break you or I will get rid of you. [p. 552]

His complete success in all he has set out to do is illustrated in the closing pages of the novel (the Epilogue).

There is, however, a price to be paid. Dumas uses the musketeers to enshrine a series of challenges to Louis's authority and the nature of his vision. In three cases out of four, these challenges are moral or ideological, and, for historical reasons, foredoomed to failure. If Dumas had moved some distance from his initial premise of dramatising the past without misrepresenting it, he was still a historical romancer rather than a historical fantasist. Just as, in *Twenty Years*

---

8 In Chapter 54 of *Twenty Years After*, Louis, then aged ten, is paraded, much to his resentment, before the rebellious populace of Paris to prove that the king has not abandoned his people.

*After*, he had been unable to allow the musketeers to save Charles I of England from execution, so now he could not change the character or the policies of Louis XIV. Athos, Porthos and d'Artagnan, one by one, (fairly) effortlessly achieve the moral high ground in their explicit or implicit opposition to the king. But fine words butter no parsnips. Louis still comes out on top.

The least successful of the challenges is that posed by Athos and his son Raoul, the eponymous Vicomte de Bragelonne.[9] This is not because of the nature of the challenge itself, since Athos is arguably the only character (apart, that is, from Louis) to possess a clearly developed ideology. This is most lucidly enunciated in *Twenty Years After*: Athos, probably speaking for Dumas himself, states that 'the king is but man; royalty is the spirit of God', and subsequently berates Louis for failing to live up to this somewhat metaphysical conception of his role.[10] But Athos, 'sacred relic of the ancient glories of France' (p. 570) though he may be, is none the less a prig, and Raoul is a complete dead loss. The cloying relationship between father and son results from Dumas's misplaced desire to depict an implausibly idealised version of his difficult relationship with his own adored son (also named Alexandre).[11] This goes beyond the point where it is implied that father and son are twin souls (p. 429) and founders in a glutinous sea of sentiment when the spirit of the mercifully deceased Raoul rises Christ-like to heaven in a vision, leading his gently grieving papa with him through the pearly gates. Stevenson (for some inexplicable reason) thought highly of this scene, and French critics go into raptures about it, but it is sadly emetic stuff for all that.

Porthos is an individual of an altogether different kidney, a far cry from odour of sanctity and *Songs of Praise*. He is a brilliant

---

9 Jean-Yves Tadié notes that Dumas's choice of title originally symbolised the coming of age of a new generation, the young superseding the old (*Le Vicomte de Bragelonne*, Gallimard, Paris 1997, p. 20). In the completed novel, however, where Raoul is presented as the spiritual inheritor of the musketeers, the symbolism is slightly different, the older generation defeated in its younger representative as Raoul loses Louise de la Vallière to the king.

10 *Twenty Years After*, ed. D. Coward, World's Classics, Oxford 1993, p. 224

11 Even Dumas's English hagiographer-in-chief, A. Craig Bell, notes sniffily of Athos that 'his relationship with his son is an amalgam of old-world parental strictness and over-emotional affection which today's reader must find both repellently sentimental and improbable' ('*Le Vicomte de Bragelonne* [*The Man in the Iron Mask*]', Merlin, Braunton [Devon] 1995, p. 2).

combination of Frank Spencer, Hyacinth Bucket and the Incredible
Hulk. He has not the first idea what is going on most of the time –
what little brain power he ever had (in *The Three Musketeers*), age
seems to have eroded completely. Much of the comedy in the novel
centres on his character and his actions. He acts as Raoul's second in a
challenge to a duel, although he has not a clue what the duel is about,
and he breaks a chair simply by sitting on it (but then, they don't make
chairs like they used to). He is the coachman who drives the kid-
napped Louis XIV to the Bastille, because Aramis persuades him that
the king is not the king, but a usurper – and poor Porthos never
tumbles to what is going on here, because in a body the size of
Godzilla's, he has a brain the size of a pea. And he is the most
appalling snob – witness his refusal to be measured for a court suit,
because to be so, a mere tailor's boy would actually have to touch him,
which would be 'humiliating, degrading . . . disgusting and repugnant
to the feelings of a gentleman' (p. 206). But he is sublime in his
innocence and unquestioning loyalty, his 'simple greatness of soul' (p.
497), dying for his friend in stark contrast to the way in which Louis
XIV effectively (in his treatment of Fouquet) allows his friend to die
for him. When Dumas came to write Porthos's death scene, his son
found him slumped in his armchair and dissolved in tears.[12] Certainly
the pages devoted to the event have a heartfelt (if slightly bombastic)
eloquence somewhat reminiscent of the death of Sydney Carton in
Dickens's almost contemporary novel *A Tale of Two Cities*.[13]

D'Artagnan is in many respects a more complex case. He, like the
others, can be seen to embody aspects of his creator – if Athos
represents the paternal Dumas, and Porthos is Dumas the trencherman, then d'Artagnan is the acquisitive Dumas, the Dumas who is
reputed to have told his son 'don't let anything go without getting
money for it'.[14] At the end of *The Three Musketeers*, Richelieu buys

12  'I found you sitting sadly in your big armchair . . . your eyes red. "You've
been crying. What's the matter?" I can still hear your answer: "I'm very
unhappy. Porthos is dead. I've just killed him. I can't prevent myself
mourning him. Poor Porthos!"' (quoted in *Les Trois Mousquetaires. Vingt Ans
Après*, ed. C. Schopp, Robert Laffont, Paris 1991, p. lviii, note 5).

13  Dumas wrote to his collaborator Auguste Maquet in December 1849:
'I want Porthos's death to have as much grandeur as possible' (quoted in
*Le Vicomte de Bragelonne*, ed. C. Schopp, Robert Laffont, Paris 1991, Vol. II,
p. 774, note). *A Tale of Two Cities* was serialised in *All the Year Round* during
the second half of 1859.

14  quoted in H. Clouard, *Alexandre Dumas*, Albin Michel, Paris 1955, p. 370

d'Artagnan with a lieutenant's commission; at the end of *The Man in the Iron Mask*, Louis XIV buys d'Artagnan with the implicit promise of the baton of a Marshal of France. This is logical, in a way: d'Artagnan is a professional soldier, dependent on the income of soldiering, just as Dumas was a professional author, dependent on the income of authoring. Athos and Porthos have private incomes; Aramis has the untold financial reserves of the Society of Jesus at his disposal. D'Artagnan has neither of these, and must do the best he can. Oddly enough, despite Dumas's frequent references to his shrewdness, he is, for once in the cycle, rather out of his depth. Though he manages to persuade the king to release Athos from the Bastille, he cannot save Fouquet, he is outfoxed by Aramis, and, in the end, out-thought by Louis. He is an enthusiastic teller of home truths to the king:

> Do you prefer those who love you, or those who only fear you? If you prefer servility, duplicity, and cowardice, only say so, sire, and we will go away – we, who are the sole remnant . . . of a pre-existent chivalry . . . If you refuse to listen to the plain speaking of d'Artagnan, you are not a good king, and, tomorrow, may be a poor one.                              [p. 246]

But he runs out of steam. His ultimate secret weapon against the king is his resignation as captain of the musketeers, but, like the boy who cried wolf, he uses it once too often, and the king calls his bluff. D'Artagnan's belief that he can engineer a pardon for his friends Aramis and Porthos simply because (in the final analysis) they are his friends is shown to be incompatible with the workings of Louis's vision of the modern state. His insistence on getting the king's signature for everything he is asked to do plays into the hands of the monarch, who uses the weapon against him, tying his hands and preventing him from being more than a spectator of the final apocalypse. In the regime that Louis is constructing, only one person is indispensable – and that one person is not d'Artagnan, but Louis himself. 'You also must humble your pride,' he tells d'Artagnan, 'or else choose such exile as will suit you best' (p. 555). And d'Artagnan 'remained lost in mute bewilderment . . . he had at last found an adversary worthy of his steel' (ibid.). The d'Artagnan of the Epilogue is no foppish courtier, certainly, but he knows his place, and the concluding aspirations of his life are not to give the king lessons on how to govern, but to make sure that he gets his marshal's baton firmly in his knapsack before he shuffles off his mortal coil.

Which leaves us with Aramis, by some way the most intriguing of the four in this part of the cycle, and the only one to remain alive at its conclusion. His role is integrally bound up with that of the man in the iron mask, a historically-attested character whom Dumas makes into Philippe, the apocryphal twin brother of Louis XIV. It was Voltaire who, some hundred years earlier, had, in his *Century of Louis XIV*, first given wide currency to this putative identity of the masked prisoner, and Dumas, who shared the Romantic fascination for doomed heroes, was not the only nineteenth-century French writer to exploit the legend. Alfred de Vigny (1797–1863) had in 1819 written a very fine narrative poem called 'La Prison' on the topic (though he may have been inspired as much by Byron's *The Prisoner of Chillon* as by the story of the Iron Mask himself). Victor Hugo (1802–85) had in 1839 partly written then abandoned a verse drama entitled *Les Jumeaux* (The Twins) which Dumas may also have had access to. Both Dumas and Hugo, at all events, acknowledged a debt to Paul Lacroix's *The Man in the Iron Mask*, which appeared in 1838.[15] In addition, Francis Wey (1812–82) had in 1839 provided *La Presse* with a short serial entitled *The Three Prisoners of Pignerol*, of whom the second was Fouquet, and the third the Iron Mask himself, again depicted as Louis XIV's identical twin brother. Dumas had previously touched on the matter in his volumes of historical popularisation entitled *Louis XIV and His Century* (1844), as well as developing a sequence of so-called 'systems' as to the real identity of the masked figure.[16] Whatever this might have been, Dumas had far too much of an eye for a good plot-line to pass up the opportunity of following the example of his illustrious literary predecessors and introducing him into the novel as the Sun King's twin.[17]

Popular prejudice (doubtless not unaffected in this respect by Hollywood's view of the matter) holds that the virtuous Philippe is substituted for his wicked brother and rules gloriously and justly in his stead. Dumas, though not above tinkering with history for the purposes of his narrative, baulked at taking such extensive liberties,

15 Lacroix is more commonly known by his pseudonym, Le Bibliophile Jacob (Jacob the Bibliophile); he lived from 1807 until 1884.

16 In 1841, writing in *Le Siècle* (19 and 21 February), Dumas had stated the existence of nine 'systems' in relation to the man in the iron mask. By 1844, in *Louis XIV and His Century*, the number had risen to 'more than twelve'.

17 A bewildering variety of possible identities have been advanced: these are helpfully (if briefly) reviewed in David Coward's edition of *The Man in the Iron Mask*, World's Classics, Oxford 1991, pp. xvii–xxiii.

with the result that Philippe becomes an innocent pawn in the devious and demonic game that Aramis is playing. That he does have a genuine claim to the throne is clear, even though he was born some hours later than Louis. Aramis stresses that in such cases 'both doctors and lawyers maintain that there is a doubt whether the child who happens to be the first-born of twins is in reality the elder by the laws of heaven and of nature' (p. 196), and his patron Fouquet, himself a jurist, agrees that this is so. Fouquet similarly accepts Aramis's contention that Louis is a usurper, in that he has seized the entire inheritance of his father, Louis XIII, whereas he is only legally entitled to half of it. But Aramis is essentially uninterested in the justice of Philippe's cause, nor is he really, as he subsequently protests, attempting to effect the substitution in the interests of his patron Fouquet, whom Louis XIV is determined to ruin. With Philippe on the throne, Aramis intends first to ensure that he is made a cardinal, secondly (like Cardinals Richelieu and Mazarin before him) to take over the government of France from Fouquet, and finally to employ Philippe's influence to have himself elected Pope.

Philippe therefore becomes the sacrificial lamb caught in the toils of Aramis's Mephistophelean endeavours. At various points in the novel Dumas purposely stresses Aramis's diabolical attributes: his eyes are 'two blades of fire' (p. 176), and he invites Fouquet to 'hold fast to my cloak' (p. 73) and be transported to safety (just as Mephistopheles invites Faust).[18] An 'angel of death' (p. 236) with a 'sepulchral voice' (p. 532), he uses Philippe as the instrument of his ambition, abandoning him with barely a second thought when his plans go awry. More than once he is explicitly referred to as 'the tempter' (most notably in the title of Chapter 37). In this guise, he seduces Philippe just as Satan attempts to seduce Christ: 'he sheweth him all the kingdoms of the world, and the glory of them' (Matthew 4:8). Lacking Christ's willpower, Philippe passes up the opportunity of the Edenic refuge in Poitou that Aramis offers as an alternative (just as Aramis had gambled that he would), only to find himself at the end of the novel imprisoned for ever in a parody of Eden, the prison governor's garden on the Ile Sainte-Marguerite. Aramis, on the other hand, gets away scot-free, to reappear in the Epilogue as the Duc d'Alameda, Spain's ambassador to the French court.

18 Aramis's involvement with the Prince of Darkness is signalled as early as Chapter 8 in *Twenty Years After*: 'in Aramis one finds Simara, which is the name of a demon'.

So *The Man in the Iron Mask* projects a rather gloomy view of the human condition that seems light years removed from the swashbuckling, devil-may-care heroics of *The Three Musketeers*, although that is not to say that such an upshot is not fleetingly prefigured even there. The young d'Artagnan had yielded to Richelieu just as the old d'Artagnan yields to Louis XIV. Athos withdraws – temporarily in *The Three Musketeers*, definitively in *The Man in the Iron Mask* – taking his dispiriting offspring with him. Porthos dies. Philippe, born to rule, 'every whit as much a king as his brother' (p. 373) in d'Artagnan's view, ends up doubly imprisoned, incarcerated on the Ile Sainte-Marguerite and inside a mask of iron. Aramis, having spent the entire novel trying to subvert the system that Louis is devoting all his efforts to creating, suddenly changes tack and announces to the unsurprisingly bewildered inhabitants of Belle-Isle-en-Mer that 'the king is master in his kingdom. The king is God's chosen instrument. God and the king have smitten M. Fouquet' (p. 514). It is possible that he does this in part with the intention of saving their rebellious skins from the king's troops, but in reality he too accepts the principle of the system, albeit ideally under somewhat different management. It is therefore certainly symbolic that, in the closing lines of the novel, d'Artagnan looks forward to being reunited with Athos and Porthos, but bids Aramis an eternal farewell. As General of the Jesuits, Aramis wields a power at least as absolute as Louis XIV's: significantly, he is the only one of the four musketeers to survive beyond the end of the novel, and Dumas may even have been thinking of bringing him back (presumably on a Zimmer frame) in an unwritten sequel, *Le Comte de Vermandois*.[19]

The reasons for the tone of disillusionment are not far to seek. By the time he completed *The Man in the Iron Mask* (the last instalment was published on 12 January 1850), Dumas was heading for bankruptcy. The glory days of the 1840s, when he appeared to have the

19 In *Louis XIV and His Century*, Dumas's review of the 'systems' relating to the man in the iron mask had included the suggestion that he might be the Comte de Vermandois, a natural son of Louis XIV and Louise de la Vallière. A letter to Maquet, dated March 1851, indicates that Dumas intended to write a novel with this title. However, nothing came of it, and in January 1854 he announced a sequel to *The Vicomte de Bragelonne* called *Le Maréchal-Ferrant* (The Blacksmith). This, too, failed to materialise, and it was left to an imitator of Dumas called Paul Mahalin to polish off Aramis in a spurious sequel to the *Musketeers* cycle entitled *The Son of Porthos; or the Death of Aramis* (first published in 1883). (I am very grateful to Jonathan Snowdon for alerting me to the existence of this text.)

Midas touch, were gone for ever. The Théâtre Historique, set up in
1847 under the sponsorship of the king's son, the Duc de
Montpensier, to perform plays by Dumas and his friends, was
folding, a victim of the 1848 Revolution and Dumas's lack of business
acumen. The ludicrously lavish Château de Monte Cristo that he had
built for himself at Marly-le-Roi, just outside Paris, had been mortgaged in a vain attempt to rescue the theatre. His aspirations to play a
political role in the new order had come to nothing as a consequence
of repeated defeats at the polls. Rather like his illustrious predecessor
Walter Scott, he was writing to pay his debts and keep his creditors at
bay. In such an atmosphere, it is hardly surprising that he should have
reflected ruefully on the heady days of the 1830s and the 1840s, and
that the overriding impression given by the novel should be one of
sadness and of opportunities lost, of regret for a gallant, colourful,
chivalrous past set against the depressing greyness of a regulated and
regimented present. Dumas is ultimately too honest not to admit that
the new regime achieved what it set out to do, and the Epilogue
shows how Louis XIV, having got a grip on himself and his country,
would go on to dominate Europe in precisely the way that Aramis
envisaged the combined forces of Philippe and himself doing (Chapter 37). He is similarly too honest to deny that such a regime offered
worthwhile prospects for a particular type of public servant (witness
the transformation of Colbert in the closing chapters of the novel).
But all this is achieved at a cost that Dumas cannot but regret.

   If the tone is darker than in the earlier novels of the cycle, the
trademarks of the master craftsman are none the less apparent.
There are of course the inevitable inconsistencies deriving from the
fact that, given the insatiable demands of serial publication, Dumas
was writing, as always, at tremendous speed. But does it really
matter that he forgets whether Philippe has spent six or eight years
in the Bastille, whether his co-prisoner Seldon is Scots or Irish,
whether the mask he wears on the Ile Sainte-Marguerite is made of
iron or of steel? We may be slightly puzzled, but we are not greatly
bothered – we are reading a historical romance, not the *Encyclopae-
dia Britannica*. Harder to forgive, perhaps, is his catastrophic
misjudgement in respect of the emotional intrigues involving characters representing the younger generation. Dumas had observed to
his collaborator Auguste Maquet in respect of *Twenty Years After*
that 'the absence of a love intrigue will be a drawback' and detrimental to the success of the novel: readers had, he later argued,
greatly enjoyed the tensions created in *The Three Musketeers* by the
clandestine relationship between Anne of Austria and the Duke of

Buckingham.[20] But his young lovers are anaemic in the extreme. The ostensible hero of the whole saga (the eponymous vicomte) is Athos's son Raoul, the unlikely by-blow of his father's improbable one-night stand with Mme de Chevreuse (an old flame of Aramis's): a paragon of knightly virtue, he is a character of quite surpassing dullness. Whilst not all critics have been as extreme in their deprecation as Paul Morand ('Let Raoul de Bragelonne go off and get himself killed, we really couldn't care less!'), rarely has any character in literature received such a uniformly and continuously bad press.[21] Louise de la Vallière, Raoul's childhood sweetheart, is not much better: she falls in love with Louis XIV (and he – inexplicably – with her), and subsequently spends so much time dissolved in tears and 'fainting in coils' as to leave us profoundly bored and irritated with her antics. The best that can be said is that these two uniquely dismal tyros are rather less in evidence here than in the two previous sections of the novel.

But other characters are boldly, if brashly, drawn – and serial fiction is after all hardly the place to go for psychological refinement, especially when we remember that Dumas had no time to review and revise his work for publication in book form. A whole gallery of them is impressively memorable. Among the musketeers, Aramis in particular merits a mention. In his unscrupulous scheming for world domination, and in the way that, despite our better instincts, we half hope he may succeed – or at least live to fight another day – he is reminiscent of more contemporary villains such as the Mekon in *Dan Dare* or the Master in *Dr Who*. Even among the minor characters, those who make an appearance for a few chapters then vanish for ever, or those who pop up sporadically throughout the narrative, there are some undoubted successes. Here is Dumas's telling – and witty – description of Fouquet's nemesis, Colbert:

> Close behind the king came Monsieur Colbert, who had waylaid his majesty in the corridor and now followed him like a dark and watchful shadow. Monsieur Colbert, with his square-shaped head and his untidy though rich dress, reminded one somewhat of a Flemish gentleman after a more than usually prolonged interview with a beer-jug.                    [p. 113]

20 quoted in *Les Trois Mousquetaires. Vingt Ans Après*, ed. C. Schopp, Robert Laffont, op. cit., p. xxv.

21 quoted in *Le Vicomte de Bragelonne*, ed. J.-Y. Tadié, Gallimard, Paris 1997, Vol. I, p. xxxii.

Fouquet, too, sticks in the mind – a characterisation in defiance both of historical veracity and of natural common sense (though very much like Dumas himself in many of his attributes). This is the man who seals his own fate because, in spite of his recognition of the justice of Philippe's cause, he cannot bear the thought that the hospitality of his own house has been violated by the abduction of Louis XIV to the Bastille. This is the man who entertains his friends flanked by his 'two guardian angels', his devoted wife on one side and his devoted mistress on the other. This, finally, is the man who gets off his horse and allows d'Artagnan to arrest him, when d'Artagnan's own mount, foundered in the pursuit, has collapsed beneath him. 'Oh, monsieur,' cries d'Artagnan, 'the man who is really a king for true nobility is not Louis at the Louvre, nor Philippe at Sainte-Marguerite – it is you, the condemned outlaw!' (p. 477).

And there are some wonderful set pieces too, such as only Dumas could write them. The above incident is thrillingly narrated in the chapter 'White Horse and Black Horse', but Dumas does not just do horseback chases – he does pursuits in barges, too, as Colbert tails Fouquet all the way down the Loire from Orléans to Nantes. I personally feel that he slightly muffs the climactic confrontation scene between Philippe, the bird in borrowed plumage, and his identical twin, hotfoot from a night in the Bastille, but arguably the build-up has been so remorseless that the tension is difficult to maintain and extend convincingly. In any case, he redeems himself superbly with the extraordinary sequence that narrates the heroic death of Porthos, into which he self-evidently channels so much emotion and commitment. The tone is unashamedly epic, and cosmic and mythological imagery abounds. Porthos is the Destroying Angel, the barrel of gunpowder hurled at his enemies is compared to 'a shooting star across the heavens', prior to exploding and creating 'the very pit of hell'. 'One man had made all this chaos, worse confounded than the chaos that reigned ere ever God spake the word and brought forth light out of darkness' (p. 536) – Porthos, 'a giant in the midst of giants', 'the genius of ancient chaos', the Titan who finally cannot himself resist the unrelenting cascade of boulders that buries him alive in 'a giant's sepulchre befitting his gigantic frame' (p. 538). It is fabulous, riveting, spellbinding stuff, Dumas writing his heart out. No wonder he needed a few days' grace after burying this friend of six years' standing, and this despite the protestations of the paper's proprietor and the chagrin of the subscribing public.[22]

22  He wrote, at once apologetically and rhetorically, to Louis Perrée, the

'Does Dumas make us think?' asked one of his biographers, the French novelist André Maurois. 'Not very often. Dream? Never. Go on turning the pages? Always.'[23] It is without doubt the epitaph our writer would have wanted.

KEITH WREN
*University of Kent at Canterbury*

director of *Le Siècle*: 'You are scolding me for taking a few days' rest, and you are right, since this rest, as you are kind enough to tell me, is detrimental to the pleasure of your subscribers. But . . . one does not part with a friend of six years' standing . . . without an anguish of heart and spirit that leaves one temporarily devoid of strength . . . ' (quoted in *Le Vicomte de Bragelonne*, ed. C. Schopp, Robert Laffont, op. cit., Vol. II, p. 884).

23  A. Maurois, *Three Musketeers*, Jonathan Cape, London 1957, p. 183

# THE BACKGROUND TO THE NOVEL

New readers of the novel may like to begin by reading this Note, which provides a brief account of the historical context in which it is set, and an explanation of its place in Dumas's cycle of *Musketeers* novels, with particular reference to the three-part saga of which it is the concluding section. (The Notes at the end of this volume provide additional elucidation.)

Dumas sets *The Vicomte de Bragelonne* (of which *The Man in the Iron Mask* constitutes the third and final section) in 1660–1, at the beginning of the personal rule of Louis XIV, the Sun King, and the triumph of absolute monarchy.[1] This triumph had been gradually prepared over the centuries by the patient erosion of the power and authority of the great nobles of France. By the middle of the previous century, kings such as François I (1509–47) and Henri II (1547–59) had achieved a considerable measure of control over the country, but this was all but destroyed by the Wars of Religion (1563–93), a sequence of civil conflicts pitting Catholics against Protestants (Huguenots). In 1589, the Catholic Henri III was assassinated and the crown reverted to the Huguenot Henri, King of Navarre. Henri converted to Catholicism in 1593 (famously remarking that 'Paris is well worth a mass') and formally brought the religious wars to an end in 1598 by promulgating the Edict of Nantes. This period of peace allowed Henri and his ministers to concentrate on reasserting the crown's control over the devastated country. In 1610, Henri was assassinated in his turn and the crown passed to his young son Louis XIII (1601–43), a boy of nine. A further period of chaos ensued during the regency of his mother, Marie de Médicis, as the nobility tried once more to reassert itself against the power of the monarchy. The turning point in the fortunes of the latter was the appointment in 1624 of Cardinal Richelieu (1585–1642) as the king's first minister.

Richelieu was determined to consolidate the position of France against both internal and external enemies and to render the country pre-eminent in Europe. He rapidly confronted the Huguenots who, during the period of Louis XIII's minority, had effectively created a

[1] Except for the Epilogue, set in 1665, and the concluding chapter, presumably set in the following spring, although the event it recounts dates historically from 1673.

state within a state. The fall of La Rochelle, one of their major fortified towns, in 1628, was instrumental in breaking their power. Externally the main obstacles were the Spanish, and Richelieu's policy was therefore hostile to Spain's interests, although he did not declare war until 1635. This conflict was not finally resolved (in France's favour) until the Treaty of the Pyrenees in 1659. Although he did not put in place a strongly centralised government machine, Richelieu's reputation for ruthlessness (derived not just from the clinical efficiency with which he punished conspiracies, but from his rigorous implementation of the law) ensured that his opponents were kept firmly in check.

Internally, Richelieu was never secure. He was constantly threatened by plots, involving (at various times, and among others) the queen, the queen mother, the king's brother Gaston d'Orléans, and numerous members of the aristocracy. He died in 1642, having fulfilled his aspiration of making France the leading power in Europe. Louis XIII died the following year, to be succeeded by his five-year-old son Louis XIV, for whom his mother, Anne of Austria (1601–66), became regent, supported by Richelieu's successor, Cardinal Mazarin (1602–61). A reaction by all classes against Richelieu's tyrannical style of rule resulted in what was to be the last concerted effort to prevent the imposition of the absolute power of the crown: this was the civil conflict known as the Fronde, which continued on and off between 1648 and 1653. Although twice forced out of France during this time, Mazarin's devious policy of playing his opponents off against each other ultimately paid dividends, and the war petered out, leaving the monarchy strongly placed. The minister then ruled France unchallenged until his death, at which point Louis XIV, aged twenty-three, announced his attention of ruling alone.

The *Musketeers* cycle begins with *The Three Musketeers* (1844). The novel opens in 1625, when the young Gascon d'Artagnan, arriving in Paris, forms an alliance with three members of King Louis XIII's regiment of musketeers – Athos (the Comte de la Fère), Porthos (Monsieur du Vallon) and Aramis (the Chevalier d'Herblay). A sequence of adventures pits them against King Louis XIII's Machiavellian minister Cardinal Richelieu, and Richelieu's demonic female agent, Milady. In the course of these adventures, they preserve the queen, Anne of Austria, from disgrace and humiliation at Richelieu's hands, by retrieving a set of diamond studs from her would-be English lover, the Duke of Buckingham, whom Milady subsequently causes to be assassinated. The musketeers, after a successful interlude at the siege of La Rochelle, bring Milady (who turns out to be Athos's faithless and presumed defunct wife) to justice for her crimes. The novel concludes with the reconciliation of d'Artagnan and Richelieu, whilst Athos withdraws to his estates near Blois, Porthos marries a rich widow and Aramis takes holy orders. Only d'Artagnan remains a musketeer.

The second novel, *Twenty Years After* (1845), opens in 1648. Louis XIII has been succeeded by his son, the boy king Louis XIV. Anne acts as regent, in close association with Richelieu's successor, Cardinal Mazarin, whom she has secretly married. France is in the early stages of civil war (the Fronde), and d'Artagnan and his erstwhile musketeer colleagues are on different sides: d'Artagnan and Porthos support (albeit somewhat reluctantly) Louis, Anne and Mazarin, whilst Athos and Aramis back the rebels. Sinking their differences, however, they travel to England in an abortive attempt to rescue the doomed Stuart king, Charles I. They are foiled by Milady's son Mordaunt, a protégé of Oliver Cromwell, who yields nothing to his mother in fiendishness. He pursues d'Artagnan and his friends back to France but is killed by them *en route*. At the end of the novel, the friends once again disperse, to be (to some extent) reunited in the third and last novel of the sequence, *The Vicomte de Bragelonne* (1847–50).

This is so long that it is usually subdivided into three parts, entitled *The Vicomte de Bragelonne*, *Louise de la Vallière* and *The Man in the Iron Mask*. It opens in 1660 and chronicles the beginning of Louis XIV's personal rule, dating from the death of Mazarin in 1661. The eponymous hero is Raoul de Bragelonne, the illegitimate son of Athos and Madame de Chevreuse. He is passionately in love (and has been since his teenage years, featured in the previous novel) with Louise de la Vallière, who is now a lady-in-waiting to Henriette d'Orléans, the newly wed wife of the king's younger brother. D'Artagnan and his friends play a relatively episodic role in the earlier sections of this novel. D'Artagnan resigns his position as captain of the king's musketeers and he and Athos go back (independently of each other) to England to negotiate with Cromwell's successor, General Monk, the restoration to the throne of Charles II. This is finally brought about when d'Artagnan kidnaps Monk and takes him off to the Low Countries to negotiate with Charles face to face. On their return to France, d'Artagnan is reinstated, and Athos again retires to his estates. Meanwhile Porthos nourishes ambitions to be made a duke and Aramis, now Bishop of Vannes, is conspiring against the young Louis XIV on behalf of his patron Fouquet, the Minister of Finance. The epicentre of the novel, however, is the royal court, where Louis, egged on by Colbert, a disciple of the deceased Mazarin, is moving against Fouquet, as well as discovering the delights of infidelity. He neglects his queen, Marie-Thérèse, and is attracted to Henriette – as is she to him. To throw the court gossip factory off the scent, his courtiers spread the rumour that he is in love with Louise (who, since meeting the king, has been carrying a torch for him). Louis accidentally overhears her confess her passion for him and promptly complicates matters by falling in love with her in earnest. He gets Raoul out of the way by packing him off to the English court (ostensibly in conformity with the desires of Athos, who is not enthusiastic about his son's infatuation with Louise). At the point where *The Man in the Iron Mask* begins, Raoul has just been summoned back to France, both by Henriette and by his friend Guiche, to learn of Louise's 'betrayal', whilst Aramis, recently elected General of the Jesuit Order, is about to put the finishing touches to his conspiracy against the king.

# BIBLIOGRAPHY

Dumas has recently been rediscovered by the French critical establishment (always something of a mixed blessing), but there is still relatively little written about him in English. The best introduction is the critical biography by F.W.J. Hemmings, *The King of Romance* (Hamish Hamilton, London 1979). This may be supplemented, for those who are more interested in what Dumas wrote, by Richard Stowe's *Alexandre Dumas père* (Twayne, Boston 1976). Claude Schopp's biography *Alexandre Dumas – Genius of Life* (Franklin Watts, Toronto 1988) is more recent, but poorly translated. (Schopp is also responsible for the excellent French two-volume critical edition of *Le Vicomte de Bragelonne* [Robert Laffont, Paris 1991], which may be supplemented by Jean-Yves Tadié's three-volume edition (Paris 1997) for Gallimard.) André Maurois's *Three Musketeers* (Jonathan Cape, London 1957) is dated, but eminently readable. David Coward's edition of *The Man in the Iron Mask* (World's Classics, Oxford 1991) has an engaging introduction and very full notes, to which I have been much indebted in preparing my own. Those who are interested in a rather fuller account of 'the story so far' than I am able to provide will find it in A. Craig Bell's critical study *'The Vicomte de Bragelonne (The Man in the Iron Mask)'*, (Merlin, Braunton [Devon] 1995). For the historical and social background to seventeenth-century France, most useful is Robin Briggs, *Early Modern France* (University Press, Oxford 1998).

There are useful websites on Alexandre Dumas at http://www.acamedia.fr/dumas (the more complete version is in French, but there is an English alternative); and http://www.cadytech.com/dumas. A useful digest of the Iron Mask legend with brief commentaries on the possible identities of the masked prisoner may be found at http://www.royalty.nu/legends/IronMask.html.

# THE MAN IN THE IRON MASK

CHAPTER I

# A pair of old friends

LEAVING EVERYONE AT COURT occupied with his own affairs, we will follow a man who, avoiding the gaze of passers-by, is repairing to a secret rendezvous at a house situated at the back of the Place de Grève – a house that may be recognised as the same which, during a popular rising, had been besieged by d'Artagnan, as elsewhere recorded.[1] The principal entrance was in the Place Baudoyer. It was a moderately large house, surrounded by gardens, and enclosed by cutlers' shops which hid it from the gaze of prying eyes and listening ears. Thus it was isolated by a triple rampart, the noise of the grindstones, the walls of the shops and the belt of verdure – like a mummy enclosed within its triple casings.

The man of whom we speak walked with a firm step, although past the prime of life. His dark cloak and the long sword, which, carried horizontally, raised the cloak behind, plainly revealed the seeker of adventures; and if one had noticed the rakish curl of his moustaches, the delicate, smooth skin visible beneath his broad sombrero, it would have seemed impossible to doubt that he was engaged upon an adventure of gallantry. As the cavalier entered the house, eight o'clock sounded on the chimes of Saint-Gervais. Ten minutes later, a lady, followed by an armed attendant, approached the same door and knocked. The door was opened immediately by an ancient woman-servant. The lady raised her veil as she entered. She was no longer beautiful; still, she was well preserved, for she had by no means lost her feminine coquetry; she was not young, but she was still active and of imposing presence. Beneath a rich toilette in the most exquisite taste, she concealed an age which Ninon de l'Enclos[2] alone could have carried off smilingly. Scarcely had she gained the entrance-hall ere the cavalier, whose features we have but roughly portrayed, advanced to meet her, holding out his hand.

'Dear duchess,[3] how charmed I am to see you,' said he.

'Charmed, my dear Aramis!' replied the duchess.

Aramis conducted her into an elegantly furnished saloon, whose high windows stood out from the darkness of the room, as the last rays of departing day filtered through the dusky crests of the tall fir trees without. They sat down side by side. Neither of them had any idea of calling for lights; they buried themselves in the gloom as though they wished to surround themselves with the shades of oblivion.

'Chevalier,' said the duchess, suddenly, 'you have given no further sign of existence since the occasion of our interview at Fontainebleau,[4] and I confess that your presence in thé Franciscan's death-chamber, and your initiation into certain secrets, gave me the greatest surprise I have ever received in my life.'

'I can give you an explanation, both of my presence and of my initiation,' said Aramis.

'But, before we speak of anything else,' said the duchess, quickly, 'let us speak of ourselves. You do not forget our long-standing friendship?'

'No, madame; and, please God, we shall remain friends, not merely for a long time, but for ever.'

'That is certain, chevalier, and my visit tonight is a proof of it.'

'We have no longer the same interests as formerly, duchess,' said Aramis, permitting himself to smile openly, for, in the gloom, he had no occasion to fear that his smile would appear less pleasant than it had been in days gone by.

'Ah, yes, chevalier, today our interests are different. Every period of life has its own; and since today we are able to understand one another by conversing as well as we used to do in former days without speaking a word, why, let us talk.'

'Duchess, I am at your disposal. By the way, how did you find my address? – and why?'

'Why? I have told you – out of curiosity. I wished to know what you were to that Franciscan, with whom I also had dealings, and who died in so strange a manner. You remember that at our interview at Fontainebleau, in the cemetery, at the foot of that tomb so recently filled in,[5] our emotion prevented both of us from confiding anything of importance.'

'True, madame.'

'Ah well, I had no sooner left you than I began to feel regret. I have always had a thirst for knowledge – you know that Madame de Longueville[6] resembles me in that respect, do you not?'

'I hardly know,' replied Aramis, discreetly.

'It occurred to me,' continued the duchess, 'that we had scarcely told each other anything while we were in the cemetery – you did not tell me how you stood with the Franciscan at whose burial you had assisted, nor did I tell you what dealings I had had with him. Now all this struck me as unworthy of such old friends as we are, and I sought an opportunity of meeting you, in order to give you this information, and to assure you that Marie Michon[7] – dead and gone, poor soul! – has left behind her a ghost who has forgotten nothing.'

Aramis bent over the hand of the duchess and kissed it gallantly.

'No doubt you had some difficulty in finding me,' said he.

'Oh no,' cried the duchess, provoked by Aramis's persistency in turning the conversation towards what he wished to learn. 'I knew, of course, that you were a friend of Monsieur Fouquet, and, equally of course, I went to him.'

'Friend?' cried the chevalier; 'oh, one can hardly say that, madame. I am but a poor priest full of gratitude and fidelity towards a generous benefactor – that is all I can claim to be with regard to Monsieur Fouquet.'

'He gave you a bishopric?'

'Yes, duchess.'

'A fitting occupation for the retirement of a bold musketeer.'

'Just as you employ yourself in political intrigue,' thought Aramis. Then aloud, 'So then, you made enquiries of Monsieur Fouquet?' he added.

'Naturally. You had been in his company at Fontainebleau, and had made a little excursion to your diocese – I think it is Belle-Isle-en-Mer[8] – am I right?'

'By no means, madame. My diocese is Vannes.'

'Ah, Vannes! – that is what I meant to say. Only I had an idea that Belle-Isle-en-Mer – '

'Monsieur Fouquet owns an estate there, that is all.'

'Ah, I remember. Somebody told me that Belle-Isle had been fortified, and as I know you for a distinguished soldier – '

'I have quite forgotten all such things since I entered the church,' replied Aramis, somewhat curtly.

'To be sure. Well, I was saying that I heard you had returned from Vannes, and I sent to a friend of ours, the Comte de la Fère.'

'Ah,' exclaimed Aramis.

'He is a model of discretion; he told me he did not know your address.'

'How like Athos,' thought the bishop; 'but there, good blood will always out.'

'Then I met – By the way, you know that I dare not show myself here, for the queen mother still thinks she has a grievance[9] against me.'

'Yes, I know that – it is very strange.'

'Oh, there are plenty of reasons for it. But to proceed. I am obliged to remain out of sight; but, by good luck, I happened to meet Monsieur d'Artagnan – an old friend of yours, is he not?'

'And still a friend of mine, duchess.'

'He was able to put me on the right track; he told me to apply to Monsieur de Baisemeaux,[10] governor of the Bastille.'

Aramis started angrily, and a fierce light came into his eyes, which, notwithstanding the darkness, his companion saw or rather divined.

'Monsieur de Baisemeaux!' cried he. 'Why on earth did d'Artagnan send you to him?'

'Ah, that I can't tell you.'

'What is all this leading to?' thought the bishop, summoning all the powers of his mind in order to sustain the combat in a manner worthy of his keen intellect.

'Monsieur de Baisemeaux was indebted to you for some good office – at least, that is what d'Artagnan told me.'

'Very true.'

'And one generally knows a creditor's address quite as well as that of a debtor?'

'Of course. So then, Baisemeaux told you – '

'To go to Saint-Mandé, whence a letter could reach you.'

'I have the letter here,' said Aramis, 'and it has a value in my eyes, since I am indebted to it for the pleasure of seeing you once more.'

The duchess, relieved at having overcome without mishap the difficulties of an awkward situation, now felt more at her ease. Aramis, however, felt anything but comfortable: 'We were speaking of your visit to Baisemeaux,' said he.

'No,' replied the duchess, with a laugh, 'we had advanced further than that.'

'Well then, we were speaking about your enmity towards the queen mother.'

'Further still,' said she, 'much further – we had settled all that. You are aware,' continued the duchess, making her decision, 'you are aware that I am living with Monsieur de Laicques?'

'Yes, madame.'

'Almost husband and wife, in fact.'

'So I have heard.'

'In Brussels.'

'Yes.'

'You know that my children have ruined me – plundered me of all I possessed.'

'Dear duchess, what a terrible thing!'

'Dreadful, is it not? I was obliged to use my wits in order to live, and especially to avoid vegetating.'

'That can be easily understood.'

'I had old hatreds to avenge; old friendships to serve; and I had neither protectors nor credit.'

'And you, too, who have acted as protector to so many!' cried Aramis, in a tone of suave commiseration.

'Ah, chevalier, it is always the way. At that time I went to see the King of Spain.'

'Ah!'

'He had just nominated a General of the Jesuits, according to custom.'

'Is that the custom?'

'Did you not know it?'

'Forgive me, I was thinking of something else.'

'Really, you ought to know it – you who were on such intimate terms with the Franciscan.'

'With the General of the Jesuits, you mean to say?'

'Exactly. Well, I saw the King of Spain. He was well disposed towards me, but could do little or nothing. However, he gave me some letters of recommendation for Flanders, for Laicques and myself, and a pension out of the funds belonging to the order.'

'Of the Jesuits?'

'Yes. The Franciscan – I mean the general – was sent to me, and, in order to conform with the statutes of the society, they assumed that I was in a position to render services to the order.'

'Is that the rule?'

Madame de Chevreuse paused to look at Aramis; but darkness had already fallen.

'Oh yes, it is the rule,' she rejoined. 'They had to make it appear that I could be of some use to them. I proposed that I should travel in the interests of the society, and my name was placed upon the list of travellers affiliated to the order. You understand, of course, that it was a mere formality.'

'Undoubtedly.'

'By this means I am enabled to draw my pension, which, as you may suppose, is very acceptable.'

'Great heavens, duchess! what you tell me fills me with sorrow. Can it be possible that you – *you*, are reduced to accepting a pension from the Jesuits?'

'Nay, chevalier, from Spain.'

'Except as a saving scruple, duchess, you will not deny that it is much the same thing.'

'No, no; not at all.'

'But, tell me, of all the wealth you enjoyed, surely something remains?'

'I still possess Dampierre, that is all.'

'A pretty considerable estate, though.'

'Yes; but the property is encumbered – eaten up with mortgages – Dampierre is nearly a ruin, like its owner.'

'And the queen mother, can she see all this unmoved?' asked Aramis, his curious glance baffled by the darkness.

'Yes; she has forgotten everything.'

'Am I right in saying, duchess, that you have made an attempt to re-enter her good graces?'

'Yes; but through a freak of heredity almost incredible, it happens that the little king inherited all the dislike his dear father used to display towards me. Ah, perhaps you will tell me I am one of those women who are instinctively hated, not one of those whom people love.'

'Dear duchess, pray tell me quickly what it is you have to say, for I believe we can be of some use to one another.'

'That is what I thought. I had a double object in going to Fontainebleau. In the first place, I was summoned by that Franciscan whom you know of. By the way, how did you come to know him? I have told you my story, but you have told me nothing of yours.'

'It is very simple, duchess. I studied theology with him in Parma; we became friends, but afterwards we were separated – business, travels – and then the war, you understand.'

'But you knew he was General of the Jesuits?'

'I had some idea of it.'

'But, tell me, by what strange chance did you happen to be present at the inn where the meeting of affiliated travellers[11] was held?'

'Oh,' said Aramis, calmly, 'it was pure chance. I happened to be going to visit Monsieur Fouquet at Fontainebleau in order to obtain an audience of the king. I was passing – quite unknown, of course – and I saw the poor man dying by the wayside, and recognised him. You know the rest. He died in my arms.'

'Yes; and bequeathed to you such unlimited power, both spiritual and temporal, that you are able to issue high commands in his name.'

'He certainly did leave me several commissions to attend to.'

'And did he mention me?'

'I have told you. I was to pay you a sum of twelve thousand livres.[12]

I think I have supplied you with the documents necessary to draw the money. Have you not had it?'

'Yes, yes. Ah, my dear bishop, I am told that you bestow these orders with so much mystery and in such a majestic manner that you are generally credited with being the successor of the dear departed.' Aramis reddened with impatience. The duchess continued, 'I made enquiries at the Court of Spain, and some of my doubts on this matter were cleared up. Every General of the Jesuits is, and must be, according to the statutes of the society, a Spanish subject at the time of his nomination. You are not a Spaniard, and therefore you cannot have been nominated by the King of Spain.'

Aramis contented himself with replying, 'You see then, duchess, that you were mistaken, since the King of Spain has himself told you.'

'True, my dear Aramis, but there was something else I thought of.'

'What is that?'

'You know I have some ideas about most things.'

'Yes, indeed, duchess.'

'Do you happen to know the Spanish language?'

'Every Frenchman who had anything to do with the Fronde knows something of the language.'

'You have lived in Flanders?'[13]

'Three years.'

'And you have been in Madrid?'

'I was there fifteen months.'

'You are in a position, then, to become a naturalised Spaniard whenever you please.'

'Is that really a fact?' exclaimed Aramis, in such a tone of simplicity that the duchess was deceived.

'Undoubtedly. Two years' residence and a knowledge of the language are the qualifications necessary. You have three years and a half to your credit – fifteen months beyond what is necessary.'

'Dear lady, tell me, what are you driving at?'

'I will tell in a few words: my credit with the King of Spain is good.'

'My own is not bad,' thought Aramis.

'Do you wish me to ask the king to confer upon you the office which the Franciscan held?'

'Oh, duchess!'

'Perhaps you hold it already?'

'No, upon my honour.'

'Well, I am in a position to render you this service.'

'Then why did you not render Monsieur de Laicques the service you offer me? He is a man of great gifts, and moreover, a man whom you love.'

'Yes, no doubt, but there are obstacles. Come now, leaving de Laicques out of the question, do you agree?'

'Thank you, duchess, no.'

Madame de Chevreuse was silent. 'He has been nominated,' she thought. After a pause, she continued, 'In refusing me thus, you give me very little encouragement to ask a favour from you.'

'Oh, pray ask. What can I do?'

'What use, if you have not the power to accord it?'

'However poor my abilities may be, I have the will, so ask me, in any case.'

'I am in need of a sum of money to enable me to restore Dampierre.'

'Ah!' replied Aramis, coldly, 'you want money? Come, duchess, how much do you require?'

'Oh, a good round sum.'

'That is unfortunate. You know, of course, I am not rich?'

'You, personally, may not be wealthy, but the order! Now, if you had been the general – '

'But you know I am not the general.'

'In any case, you have a friend who is wealthy – Monsieur Fouquet.'[14]

'Monsieur Fouquet! Why, madame, he is more than half ruined!'

'So I was told, but I was unwilling to believe it.'

'Why?'

'Because I have several letters from Cardinal Mazarin[15] in my possession – I mean to say, Laicques has them – which reveal some extraordinary financial methods.'

'What do you mean?'

'Oh, with regard to farming the taxes, loans, I scarcely know what. But they seem to establish the fact, vouched for by Mazarin's own signature, that the minister of finance has appropriated some thirty million out of the royal Treasury. The matter is serious.'

Aramis bit his lip. 'What!' said he, 'you possess such documents as those, and you say nothing to Monsieur Fouquet about them?'

'Oh, things of this sort one keeps in reserve. When one is in difficulties is the time for them to be brought out.'

'And that time has come?' said Aramis.

'Yes, dear friend.'

'So you are going to show these letters to Monsieur Fouquet?'

'I should prefer to speak to you about them.'

'You must indeed be urgently in need of money, my poor duchess, to have recourse to such shifts as these, you, who always had such a paltry opinion of Mazarin's lucubrations.'

'The fact is, I *am* in need of money.'

'And again,' continued Aramis, with ironical sympathy, 'you do violence to your own nature in adopting this resource: it is cruel.'

'Oh, if I had wished to act cruelly,' said Madame de Chevreuse, 'instead of asking the General of the Jesuit Order – instead of thinking of applying to Monsieur Fouquet for the half million livres I have need of – '

'Half a million livres!'

'No more. Do you consider it a large sum? To restore Dampierre would require that amount, at least. I was saying, then, instead of asking for this money, I should have gone to my old friend, the queen mother; the letters of her lamented husband, Signor Mazarini, would have served as an introduction, and I should have asked her for this bagatelle thus: "Madame, I wish to have the honour of receiving your majesty at Dampierre; permit me to put Dampierre in a fit state." ' Aramis made no reply. 'Well,' she continued, 'what is running in your head?'

'Merely a little mental addition,' said Aramis.

'Ah, yes; and Monsieur Fouquet can do the subtraction. For my part, I am doing my best to attend to the multiplication. What splendid mathematicians we are, to be sure! How charmingly we understand one another!'

'Will you permit me time to consider?' asked Aramis.

'I scarcely think so. For an offer of this sort, among people like ourselves, the answer should be yes or no, and that without hesitation.'

'It is a trap,' thought the bishop. 'Such a woman would never be received by Anne of Austria.'

'Well?' cried the duchess.

'Well, madame, I should be much surprised if Monsieur Fouquet could at present see his way to disposing of five hundred thousand livres.'

'Then there is no more to be said,' replied the duchess, 'and Dampierre must contrive to get restored as best it can.'

'Oh, surely, you are not embarrassed to that extent?'

'No, I am never embarrassed.'

'And the queen will certainly do for you,' continued Aramis, 'what Monsieur Fouquet is unable to do.'

'Why, of course. By the way, you don't wish me, I suppose, to speak to Monsieur Fouquet himself about these letters?'

'With regard to that, duchess, you will suit your own convenience entirely. But there are two alternatives: either Monsieur Fouquet feels himself to be guilty, or he does not. In the former case, I know him to be too proud to admit it; in the latter, he will consider the offer as a direct insult.'

'Your reasoning was always forcible, dear Aramis.'

The duchess rose.

'Then you intend to denounce Monsieur Fouquet to the queen?' said Aramis.

' "Denounce!" Oh, that is a very ugly word. I do nothing so crude, my dear friend; you are too well versed in politics not to know how such matters are arranged; I shall take the side opposed to Monsieur Fouquet, that is all.'

'You are right.'

'And, in party warfare, any weapon will serve.'

'Undoubtedly.'

'My former footing once regained with the queen mother, I may be dangerous.'

'You have the right to be, duchess.'

'And I shall avail myself of it, my dear friend.'

'I suppose you are not unaware that Monsieur Fouquet is upon the best of terms with the King of Spain?'

'Oh, I had supposed that was the case.'

'If you engage in party warfare in opposition to Monsieur Fouquet, he will reply in the same way.'

'Well, well, that cannot be helped.'

'You will admit that he, also, has the right?'

'Certainly.'

'And as his credit with Spain is high, he will make use of it as a weapon against you.'

'You mean to say that he stands well with the General of the Society of Jesus, my dear Aramis.'

'That may be the case, duchess.'

'And consequently the pension I receive from the order will be cancelled.'

'I am very much afraid you are right.'

'I shall find consolations. Ah, my dear friend, after having battled successfully with Richelieu – after having survived the Fronde and exile – what can have terrors for Madame de Chevreuse?'

'You must remember that the pension amounts to forty-eight thousand livres.'

'Alas! I am well aware of it.'

'Moreover, when one is engaged in party warfare, one does not spare the friends of one's opponent.'

'Ah, you mean that they will make poor Laicques suffer?'

'It is scarcely to be avoided, duchess.'

'Oh, it would be paltry – his pension only amounts to twelve thousand livres.'

'Yes, but the King of Spain is powerful; if requested by Monsieur Fouquet, he might imprison Monsieur Laicques in some fortress.'

'I have no great fear of that, my good friend, because when once I am reconciled to Anne of Austria, I can beg her to intercede for poor Monsieur Laicques.'

'That is true; but then there is another thing you have to fear.'

'What is that?' cried the duchess, with an ironically assumed accent of surprise and terror.

'You know, or you will discover, that once affiliated to the order, one does not easily leave it. The secrets which one has learned become unwholesome, for they carry within them the germs of misfortune for whoever may reveal them.'

The duchess reflected for a moment. 'That is a more serious matter,' said she, after a pause. 'I will think it over.'

And, notwithstanding the perfect darkness, Aramis felt the look of concentrated malevolence which she darted at him. Could she have killed him with a look, he would have died there and then. As it was, Aramis slipped his hand beneath his coat and grasped the poniard concealed there, holding himself on the alert: 'To sum the matter up – ' he began.

'Yes, yes; short accounts, you know, make long friends.'

'First, the suppression of your pension – '

'Forty-eight thousand livres, and Laicques' twelve thousand, make sixty thousand livres; that is what you mean, is it not?'

'Exactly, and I am still waiting to hear what you can find to counterbalance that.'

'The five hundred thousand livres I shall get from the queen.'

'Perhaps you will not get them.'

'I know a means of obtaining them,' said the duchess, taken off her guard.

These words caused the chevalier to prick up his ears. After this slip on the part of his adversary he increased the advantage which his self-control had given him, whilst she continued to lose ground.

'For the sake of argument,' said Aramis, 'we will take it that you get this half-million; it cannot bring you in more than thirty thousand at the outside – the half of what your pension amounts to.'

'You are forgetting that I shall only be deprived of my pension for as long as Monsieur Fouquet retains the ministry – a period I estimate at two months. You will perceive that I am frank with you.'

'Thanks, duchess; but you are mistaken in supposing that, after Monsieur Fouquet's downfall, the society will resume payment of your pension.'

'I know a means of making the order pay, just as I know a means of causing the queen to contribute.'

'In that case, duchess, you force us all to lower our flags before you. The victory is yours, and I give you joy of it. Let the paeans be sounded! But as you are strong, so you should be merciful.'

'Why on earth,' resumed the duchess, ignoring Aramis's irony, 'should you shy at a paltry half-million, when it is a question of sparing yourself – pardon me, your friend I mean to say – all the unpleasant consequences which arise from party contests?'

'I will tell you, duchess. After you had got your half-million, Monsieur de Laicques would demand his share; and that would be another half-million, would it not? And when his demands were satisfied, there would be those of your children, and then your pensioners – in short, there would be no end to it all. However compromising the letters may be, they can scarcely be worth three or four million. Deuce take it, duchess, these wretched screeds signed by Mazarin can hardly be worth the diamonds of the Queen of France, and yet, if you remember, these did not cost a fourth part of what you are asking for those documents of yours!'

'True, true; but the seller is always at liberty to set his own price upon his wares, and it rests with the buyer to accept or to refuse them.'

'Stop a moment, duchess, shall I tell you why I am not anxious to purchase your letters?'

'By all means.'

'Your letters purporting to be signed by Mazarin are forgeries.'

'Nonsense!'

'Undoubtedly they are; for it would be strange, to say the least, if you had succeeded in establishing intimate relations with Mazarin after he had prevailed upon the queen to quarrel with you. It would certainly seem to indicate a very queer state of affairs between you – perhaps you acted as his spy, or was it a case of infatuation? You have always been an attractive woman, and possibly you were – but I scarcely like to make use of the word – '

'Oh, out with it!'

'Complaisant.'

'All that is very true; and the statements contained in these letters are no less true.'

'You may take my word for it, duchess, the queen will have no use for your letters.'

'Oh, will she not, indeed! I shall know how to make them of use to her!' said the duchess, venomously.

'Oh, very well!' thought Aramis. 'Hiss, viper! Screech on, old hag!'

But the duchess had no more to say, she made towards the door.

Aramis had still another discomfiture in store for her.

He rang the bell, and the servant appeared with lights. The bishop advanced to the circle of brightness which lit up the drawn haggard features of the duchess. Aramis gazed fixedly with an ironical expression at her shrunken cheeks, at the crow's-feet round her rheumy eyes, which still shone with an evil gleam, at her withered lips, tightly compressed to hide the few remaining, discoloured teeth. He even took the trouble to strike an attitude in order to make the contrast between them the more noticeable; he displayed his shapely leg and his well-poised, handsome head; he smiled in order to exhibit his even teeth, which gleamed in the light of the candles. The superannuated coquette understood his mocking smile; she was standing exactly in front of a large mirror which revealed the decrepitude she had attempted so carefully to conceal. Choking with impotent rage and spite, she hobbled away as fast as she could, her haste only serving to accentuate the uncertainty of her gait, and without the least acknowledgment of the easy and graceful bow which Aramis made her, worthy of the elegant young musketeer of former days. Aramis sprang lightly after her, and conducted her gallantly to the door.

The Duchesse de Chevreuse made a sign to her tall footman, who, shouldering his musket, followed her as she hastened away from the house where the two old and faithful friends had failed to come to an understanding, and this for a very good reason, because they knew each other only too well.

## CHAPTER 2

### *Which shows that if you cannot drive a bargain with one person you can with another*

ARAMIS HAD JUDGED CORRECTLY, for, upon leaving the house in the Place Baudoyer, the Duchesse de Chevreuse ordered her coachman to drive straight home.

Fearing she might be followed, she thus sought to give an innocent appearance to her proceedings, but no sooner had she entered her house, and assured herself that she had arrived there unobserved, than she made her way to Monsieur Colbert's[16] residence in the Rue Croix-des-Petits-Champs by means of a garden door which gave access to a back street. We have already said that the time was evening; by this time night had fallen – night thick and black. Paris, her equanimity regained, hid under the same friendly mantle of obscurity the high-born duchess engaged in political intrigue and the humble citizen's wife, who, having lingered unduly over the delights of a supper in town, was now hurrying, upon the arm of a lover, along the road to the conjugal mansion. Madame de Chevreuse was too old a political hand not to know that a minister is, at any hour, accessible, in his own house, to young and pretty women disinclined to face the noise and dust of a public office, or to crafty old ladies afraid lest an echo of their doings might be heard outside the walls of official premises.

Upon her arrival, the duchess met with a none too courteous reception at the hands of a manservant, who, after a glance at her face, did not scruple to intimate pretty plainly that neither the lateness of the hour nor the age of the lady would justify him in disturbing Monsieur Colbert, who was still engaged in finishing up his work for the night.

But Madame de Chevreuse, nothing dismayed, calmly wrote, upon a leaf of her tablets, her name, that dread name which had so often made the ears of Louis XIII and of the great cardinal tingle unpleasantly. She inscribed her name in the big, uncultured hand-writing common amongst the aristocracy of the period, folded the paper in a manner peculiar to herself, and handed it to the man without a word, but with so imperious a gesture that the fellow, who knew his book, at once scented a princess, and, with a low obeisance, hurried off to Monsieur Colbert.

Upon opening the paper, the minister could not repress a slight exclamation which was sufficient to make obvious to the servant the importance of the mysterious visit, and to cause him to hurry off at best speed to usher in the duchess.

She leisurely ascended the staircase, and, pausing for a moment upon the landing-place to take breath, presented herself to the gaze of Monsieur Colbert who, himself, held open the folding doors which led to his apartment. The duchess halted upon the threshold, and subjected the man with whom she had to deal to a short but sharp scrutiny. At first sight, the heavy bullet-head, the thick eyebrows, and the generally ungracious expression of a face surmounted by a head-covering such as is worn by priests, if they promised the duchess small difficulty as regards the negotiations she had in view, afforded little hope of any interest in the discussion of details; for, judging from appearances, this gross nature would be insensible to the allurements either of refined revenge, or of the contemplation of humbled ambition.

But when, upon closer inspection, the duchess took notice of the little piercing black eyes, the line across the prominent forehead, and the almost imperceptible trembling of the lips, which certainly gave no hint of a tendency towards austerity, a fresh complexion was put upon the matter, and Madame de Chevreuse said to herself: 'I have come to the right man.'

'To what am I indebted for the honour of this visit, madame?' asked the Secretary of Finance.

'The want I have of you, monsieur, and the want you have of me.'

'I am charmed with the first reason, madame, but, as regards the second – '

Madame de Chevreuse sat down in an armchair which Colbert wheeled towards her.

'Monsieur Colbert, you are Secretary of Finance?'

'Yes, madame.'

'And you hope to become minister?'

'Madame!'

'Nay, don't deny it; to do so would only unnecessarily prolong our conference; besides, it is useless.'

'Nevertheless, madame, however full I may be of goodwill, and of desire to be obliging to so distinguished a lady as yourself, I must really draw the line at confessing that I seek to supplant my chief.'

'I am not speaking of *supplanting*, Monsieur Colbert. Did I, inadvertently, make use of the word? I think not. The word *replace* is less objectionable, and more correct, from a grammatical point of view, as Monsieur de Voiture[17] would say. Let us say, then, that you hope to *replace* Monsieur Fouquet.'

'The position of Monsieur Fouquet, madame, is one not easily to be assailed. He is the Colossus of Rhodes of the present century, and ships pass beneath him without overturning him.'

'An admirable comparison! Yes, Monsieur Fouquet plays the role of Colossus of Rhodes, but I seem to remember hearing it related by Monsieur Conrart[18] – an academician, I think – that the Colossus having fallen, the merchant by whom it was wrecked – a simple merchant mind you – carried off four hundred camel-loads of wreckage.'

'Madame, permit me to assure you that I shall never be the means of wrecking Monsieur Fouquet.'

'Well, well, Monsieur Colbert, since you persist in playing the sentimentalist with me, as if you were unaware that my name is de Chevreuse, and that I am no longer young, which is equivalent to saying that you have to do with a woman who has had dealings with Monsieur de Richelieu, and who has no time to waste; since, I say, you persist in treating me thus, I must seek others less blind to their own interests, and more eager to take the tide of fortune at the flood.'

'In what way, madame, in what way?'

'Upon my word, you give me but a sorry notion of modern astuteness. In my time, let me tell you, that if a woman had gone to Monsieur de Cinq-Mars[19] – and he was not particularly brilliant – and had told him about the cardinal what I have come to tell you about Monsieur Fouquet, Monsieur de Cinq-Mars would have had his irons in the fire before she had finished speaking.'

'A little patience, madame, I implore of you.'

'Aha! so then you *are* willing to replace Monsieur Fouquet ?'

'By all means, should the king dispense with his services.'

'One word more. It is quite obvious that if you have not already succeeded in bringing about Monsieur Fouquet's dismissal, it is only because it has not been in your power to bring it about, and I should be a poor creature indeed, if, now that I have come to you, I fail to bring you your heart's desire.'

'It distresses me to appear unconvinced, madame,' said Colbert, after a pause which enabled the duchess to gauge the depth of his dissimulation, 'but I would point out that during the last six years denunciation upon denunciation has been heaped upon the head of Monsieur Fouquet and that his position still remains unshaken.'

'All in good time, Monsieur Colbert, and understand that those by whom the accusations have been made are not entitled to call themselves *de Chevreuse*, neither have they been possessed of such proofs as six letters from Monsieur de Mazarin establishing the misdemeanour.'

'The misdemeanour!'

'Well, the crime, if you prefer the expression.'

'Crime! and committed by Monsieur Fouquet?'

'Just so. How strange it is, Monsieur Colbert, that your countenance, usually so calm and impassive, should so suddenly brighten up.'

'A crime!'

'I am pleased to see that the intelligence has caused you some sort of emotion.'

'Oh, it is because the word embraces so many possibilities, madame.'

'It implies a brevet of minister of finance for you and exile or the Bastille for Monsieur Fouquet.'

'Forgive me, madame, but it seems almost incredible that Monsieur Fouquet should be sent into exile; surely imprisonment, with its attendant disgrace, would be an all-sufficient punishment.'

'Oh, I know what I am talking about,' replied the duchess, coolly. 'I don't live so far from Paris but that I know what goes on there. The king is not very fond of Monsieur Fouquet, and would willingly ruin him, did an opportunity present itself.'

'The reason would have to be a powerful one.'

'Quite so; and I estimate its value to me at five hundred thousand livres.'

'How is that, madame?'

'I mean to say that, holding as I do the key to the situation in my own hands, I do not intend to let it pass into yours for less than the sum I have just indicated.'

'Very good, madame, I understand you perfectly. But, since you have named your price, it would be well to know what you have for sale.'

'Oh, the least thing in the world: six letters from Monsieur Mazarin, as I have already told you. I hardly think they can be considered dear at the price, since they furnish irresistible proof that Monsieur Fouquet has wrongfully appropriated to his own use large sums of the public money.'

'Irresistible proof!' exclaimed Fouquet, his eyes beaming with delight.

'Absolutely,' replied the duchess. 'Perhaps you would like to read the letters.'

'I should much like to do so. They are merely copies, I presume.'

'Copies, of course,' said the duchess, and she drew forth from the bosom of her dress a small flat packet. 'Read,' she said.

Colbert eagerly seized the packet and devoured its contents with his eyes.

'Marvellous!' he exclaimed.

'Clear enough, isn't it?'

'Yes, indeed, madame. There seems to be no doubt that Monsieur de Mazarin has entrusted Monsieur Fouquet with certain sums of money, but the question is what money?'

'Ah, exactly, *what* money? If we come to a satisfactory arrangement, I shall add to the six letters which you hold in your hand, a seventh, which will supply you with that last piece of information.'

Colbert considered. 'And the original letters?' he asked.

'That is an absurd question. It is as though I should ask you whether the money-bags which you will give me will be full or empty.'

'Well, well, madame, let it pass.'

'Is it a bargain?'

'Not yet.'

'How is that?'

'There is one point that neither you nor I have taken into consideration.'

'Tell me what it is.'

'Monsieur Fouquet's downfall could be accomplished only through an impeachment.'

'Yes.'

'And that implies a public scandal.'

'Well, what then?'

'Simply, it would be impossible to have him arraigned, or publicly disgraced.'

'And why?'

'Because he is Procureur-Général to the Parlement; because in France all branches of the administration – military, legal, commercial – are bound together by a bond of goodwill which is known as *esprit de corps*, and the Parlement would never allow its chief to be dragged before a tribunal of justice; and, were he to be arraigned even at the king's command, he would never be convicted.'

'Perhaps so, Monsieur Colbert; still, that does not concern me.'

'I am aware of that, madame; but it concerns me very greatly, and, moreover, diminishes the value of what you offer me. Of what use to me is the proof of a crime if I cannot make use of it to ensure a conviction?'

'But, at the least, Monsieur Fouquet would have to resign.'

'Ah, and what a grand thing that would be!' cried Colbert, whose sombre features suddenly lit up, as a feeling of hatred and revenge took possession of him.

'Really, Monsieur Colbert,' said the duchess, 'I had no idea you were so impressionable. It is quite gratifying. However, since it seems that I am unable to supply all that you ask for, there can be no good reason for continuing the discussion.'

'Nay, madame, let us continue it by all means; only, as your wares seem to have declined in value, I trust you will see the propriety of making a corresponding reduction in their price?'

'You would haggle, then?'

'It is one of the necessities of fair dealing, madame.'

'How much, then, do you offer?'

'Two hundred thousand livres.'

The duchess laughed in his face; then, all at once: 'Wait a moment,' she said.

'You agree to my terms?'

'Not yet. I have another proposition to make.'

'Say on.'

'You shall give me three hundred thousand livres.'

'No, no!'

'Well, take it or leave it. And then, that is not all.'

'What, more ? Really, madame, you are impossible!'

'Less so than you suppose. It is now no longer money that I demand.'

'What then?'

'A service. You are aware that I have always regarded the queen with the tenderest affection.'

'Well?'

'Well, I wish for an interview with her majesty.'

'With the queen?'

'Yes, Monsieur Colbert, with the queen. It is true that she has long since ceased to be my friend, but she might easily renew her friendship if opportunity were afforded her for doing so.'

'Her majesty receives no one, madame; she is a great sufferer, and the paroxysms of her illness occur with increasing frequency.'

'That is precisely why I am so anxious to obtain an interview with her. The malady from which she suffers is quite common with us in Flanders.'

'Cancer? It is a terrible and incurable complaint.'

'The Flemish peasant is a somewhat coarse animal, and the woman to whom he is married more his slave than his wife. She labours whilst he smokes his pipe; it is she who draws the water from the well, and loads the mule or ass, not sparing her own shoulders. She puts by little for a rainy day, is buffeted from pillar to post, and not unfrequently beaten black and blue. A cancer, as you are aware, is often the result of a contusion.'

'That is true.'

'But the Flemish women don't die for all that. When the pain becomes insupportable they look about for a remedy. The Béguines[20] of Bruges are excellent doctors for all sorts of diseases. They have wonderful waters and all kinds of specifics. They give the patient a bottle of medicine and a wax taper, thus, at the same time, benefiting the clergy and doing God service by the sale of their nostrums. I will take the queen a bottle of water from the Béguinage at Bruges. Her majesty will be cured, and can burn as many wax candles as she pleases. You see, then, Monsieur Colbert, that to prevent me from seeing the queen is almost to be guilty of the crime of regicide.'

'Madame, you are a woman of infinite resource, and quite over-whelm me. At the same time, I make a shrewd guess that beneath this grand display of affection for the queen runs a tiny thread of personal interest.'

'Why should I be at the trouble of concealing it, monsieur? The interest is very great, as I will prove to you presently. Get me admitted to the queen's presence, and I will content myself with the three hundred thousand livres I have demanded; otherwise, I keep my letters unless you are prepared to pay down five hundred thousand for them forthwith.' Then, having pronounced this ultimatum, the duchess rose from her seat, leaving Monsieur Colbert in a very awkward dilemma. On the one hand, any further attempt at bargaining would appear to be useless; whilst, on the other, to let the matter drop would entail so great a loss that Monsieur Colbert went cold at the bare thought of it.

'Madame,' said he, 'I shall have the pleasure of handing over to you one hundred thousand crowns.'

'Oh!' said the duchess.

'But how am I to obtain the original letters?'

'In the simplest manner in the world, my dear Monsieur Colbert. In whom do you place confidence?'

At this question the stolid financier chuckled inwardly, causing his heavy black eyebrows to rise and fall like the wings of a bat above his yellow countenance.

'In no one,' he said.

'Oh! but surely you make an exception in your own favour, Monsieur Colbert.'

'Why naturally, madame.'

'Well, then, if you will take the trouble to accompany me, the letters shall be placed in your own hands. You can then verify and make what use you please of them.'

'That would be quite satisfactory.'

'You will be good enough to bring with you a hundred thousand crowns, because, for my part, I have ceased to trust anyone.'

Monsieur Colbert coloured to the roots of his hair. Like all men skilled in the use of figures, his probity was of the aggressive and mathematical order.

'I will bring with me, madame,' he said, 'the sum agreed upon in two drafts on my treasury. Will that be satisfactory to you?'

'I only wish the drafts were for two million, monsieur. And now shall I have the honour to show you the way?'

'Let me order my carriage to be got ready.'

'Nay! I have a coach ready and waiting below, Monsieur Colbert.'

Colbert coughed irresolutely. It suddenly struck him that the duchess might have been laying a trap for him; that she might even have someone waiting for him at the door; nor was it impossible that the secret which she had just sold to him for a hundred thousand crowns might have been previously offered to Fouquet for the same sum. Whilst he yet hesitated, the duchess looked him straight in the face.

'Possibly you prefer your own carriage?' she said.

'I must admit that I should prefer it, madame.'

'You suspect that I am trying to entrap you?'

'Madame, you have a reputation for being occasionally somewhat frivolous, whilst I am credited with a character which is serious and deliberate. A joke might compromise me.'

'Ah! I see how it is; you are afraid. Well, then, take your own carriage and as many attendants as you please. Only remember that what we do must be known to our two selves alone. To admit a third into the secret would be to publish it to the whole world. After all, I don't make a point of it; my carriage can follow your own, and I shall be quite content to be driven in your carriage to pay my visit to the queen.'

'To visit the queen!'

'Have you already forgotten a clause in our agreement which is of such immense importance to me? It seems to be but a small thing to you. Had I known it, I would have demanded double the sum that I have asked for.'

'Upon consideration, madame, I shall not accompany you.'

'Really! and, pray, why not?'

'Because I have unbounded confidence in you.'

'You overwhelm me; but as regards the hundred thousand crowns, how shall I obtain them?'

'They are here,' said Colbert, and writing a few words upon a piece of paper he handed it to the duchess. 'You are paid,' he said.

'This confidence is a touching trait in your character, Monsieur Colbert,' said the duchess, laughingly, 'and I will take care that it receives appropriate recognition.'

The laugh of Madame de Chevreuse was not pleasant to listen to. To any man who could feel youth, faith, love, and life throbbing in his heart, tears were preferable to that sardonic cachinnation.

The duchess unfastened the bodice of her dress, and drew forth from her bosom, which had lost something of its pristine fairness, a small packet of papers tied together with flame-coloured ribbon. The fastenings of her dress had given way under the nervous clutch of her fingers, and her skin, chafed from contact with the papers, was revealed to the gaze of Monsieur Colbert, who was, to say the truth, somewhat taken aback at these unexpected preliminaries.

'Here,' said the duchess, still laughing, 'are the original letters of Monsieur de Mazarin. They are now your own, and, moreover, you have had the privilege of seeing the Duchess de Chevreuse undress before you, as if you had been – but I will not mention the names which self-complacency or jealousy might suggest to you. Now, Monsieur Colbert,' she continued, rapidly rearranging her dress, 'your fortune is made; come with me to the queen.'

'No, madame; were you to get into fresh disgrace with her majesty at the Palais-Royal, and it were known that I had a hand in gaining your admission to her presence, the queen would never forgive me as long as she lived. There are people at the Palais-Royal who are devoted to my interests, and through them you can gain admission without compromising me.'

'Just as you please, provided that I *am* admitted.'

'What is the name you give to those devout women of Bruges who cure maladies?'

'Béguines.'

'Then, you must be a Béguine.'

'So be it; but I cannot play the part for ever.'

'That is your affair.'

'But I don't wish to run any risk of being refused admittance.'

'That, again, is entirely your affair, madame. I shall give instructions to the chief valet to the gentleman in waiting on her majesty to admit a Béguine, who brings a remedy which will alleviate the queen's suffering. You will be the bearer of a letter from me, and to you must be left the application of the remedy, together with all necessary explanations. I recognise the Béguine, but have no knowledge whatever of Madame de Chevreuse.'

'That will suffice.'

'Here, then, is your letter of introduction, madame.'

## CHAPTER 3

## *The bear's skin*

COLBERT HANDED THE LETTER to the duchess, quietly removing the chair behind which she had taken up her position, and, with a slight inclination of the head, Madame de Chevreuse took her departure.

Colbert, who had recognised Mazarin's handwriting and counted the letters, rang for his secretary and instructed him to go in search of Monsieur Vanel, Counsellor of Parlement. The secretary replied that Monsieur Vanel, according to his wont, was at that moment entering the house for the purpose of reporting to his chief the principal details of the business which had been transacted during the day's session of Parlement.

Colbert, approaching the lamp, reread the letters of the deceased cardinal, and smiled more than once as he recognised the value of the papers which Madame de Chevreuse had just given to him; then, burying his head in his hands, he pondered deeply for several minutes.

Meanwhile a large-framed man, with prominent cheekbones, steady eyes and a hooked nose, had entered the room with an air of modest assurance which indicated a character at once supple and stern – supple towards the master who could throw him a bone, but truculent towards other dogs who might be likely to dispute with him the possession of it.

Monsieur Vanel carried under his arm a voluminous bundle of papers which he deposited upon the table close to the elbows which supported Monsieur Colbert's head.

'Good-day, Monsieur Vanel,' said the latter, rousing himself from his meditation.

'Good-day, monseigneur,' replied Vanel, in a natural tone of voice.

'You should say "monsieur", ' corrected Colbert, gently.

'Ministers are addressed as "monseigneur", ' replied Vanel, with inimitable coolness; 'and you are a minister.'

'Not yet.'

'But you are practically, and, therefore, I call you monseigneur. If you object to being so addressed before the world, at least permit me to give you the title in private.'

Colbert raised his head to the light, and read, or tried to read, in Vanel's countenance how much sincerity there might be in this protestation of devotion. But the counsellor knew well how to bear the brunt of a look, even were it directed at him by one having undoubted right to the title by which he had addressed him. Colbert sighed. Vanel's face told him nothing. The man might be sincere, after all. Colbert reflected that this so-called inferior, was, in one respect, at all events, superior to himself in that he had an unfaithful wife.[21] Whilst he dwelt upon this man's lot with a feeling akin to compassion, Vanel calmly took from his pocket a perfumed note sealed with Spanish wax, and this he handed to the monseigneur.

'What have we here, Vanel?'

'A letter from my wife, monseigneur.'

Colbert coughed. He took the letter, opened it, read it, and consigned it to his pocket, whilst Vanel placidly turned over and arranged the papers which he had brought with him.

'Vanel,' said Colbert suddenly to his protégé, 'you work hard, do you not?'

'I do, monseigneur.'

'Twelve hours a day would not frighten you?'

'I work fifteen hours a day.'

'Is it possible? A counsellor should not work more than three hours for Parlement.'

'Oh, I am preparing some financial statements for a friend who is in the accounts department, and, as I have still some time left on my hands, I study Hebrew.'

'You are highly thought of in Parlement, Vanel.'

'I venture to think so, monseigneur.'

'You must not become rooted to your counsellor's seat.'

'How am I to prevent it, monseigneur?'

'By purchasing a post.'

'But which one?'

'Any one, so that it is important. Small ambitions are always the most difficult to satisfy.'

'Small purses, monseigneur, are the most difficult to fill.'

'Well, what place have you in view,' said Colbert.

'Truly, none whatever.'

'I can tell you of one, but the king alone is rich enough to buy it; but again, I hardly think that his majesty covets the post of Procureur-Général.'

On hearing these words, Vanel turned to Colbert with a diffident and spiritless expression of face, which made the latter wonder if he had made himself understood.

'Are you speaking, monseigneur, of the post of Procureur-Général to the Parlement ? I only know of the one which is held by Monsieur Fouquet.'

'Exactly so, my dear counsellor.'

'You are not fastidious, monseigneur; but it seems to me that, before an article can be bought, it must be offered for sale.'

'It is my belief, Monsieur Vanel, that this post will be for sale in a very short time.'

'What! Monsieur Fouquet's post for sale?'

'So it is whispered.'

'The post which renders him invulnerable for sale! Oh, oh!' and Vanel laughed at the idea.

'Would you be afraid to accept the position?' asked Colbert, seriously.

'Afraid? assuredly not.'

'And would you like to have it?'

'Monseigneur is poking fun at me,' replied Vanel. 'As if any counsellor would not jump at the prospect of becoming Procureur-Général.'

'Then, Monsieur Vanel, since I tell you that this post will, before long, be in the market – that is to say, if current rumour may be relied on – '

'I repeat that it is incredible that any man would throw away the buckler behind which he shields his honour, his fortune, and his life.'

'Oh, now and again one meets with a fool who fancies himself superior to all malign influence.'

'True, monseigneur; but I am afraid that it is not for the advantage of the poor Vanels of this world that such idiots commit their follies.'

'And why not?'

'Simply because these Vanels are poor.'

'No doubt Monsieur Fouquet's post would fetch a large sum. What would you bid for it, Monsieur Vanel?'

'All that I possess, monseigneur – some three or four hundred thousand livres; whereas it is really worth a million and a half at the lowest estimate.'

'Indeed, I know that a million seven hundred thousand livres has been offered; and that this sum even has been insufficient to tempt Monsieur Fouquet. Now, if by any chance it should happen that he is willing to sell, which I don't for a moment believe, notwithstanding anything that may be said to the contrary – '

'Ah! then someone *has* spoken to you on the subject. Who was it?'

'Monsieur Gourville, Monsieur Pélisson;[22] oh, the rumour is in the air.'

'Well, then, assuming that Monsieur Fouquet is willing to sell?'

'I certainly could not buy at once. The superintendent will sell only for ready money, and, I suppose, no one is prepared to pay down a million and a half in a lump sum.'

The counsellor was, at this point, stopped by Colbert with an imperious gesture. Once again he began to reflect.

Having regard to the serious attitude of his chief, and to his evident intention to continue the conversation temporarily interrupted, Monsieur Vanel thought it advisable to exercise patience rather than to force the discussion.

'Give me your idea,' said Colbert, presently, 'of the privileges attached to the post of Procureur-Général.'

'The right of impeaching any French subject who is not of the blood royal; the power of nullifying all accusations brought against a Frenchman who is neither king nor prince. The Procureur-Général is the right hand of the king wherewith to punish the guilty, and it is in his power to stay the course of justice. Through his influence with the Parlement, Monsieur Fouquet can hold his own even against the king himself; whilst, with the help of Monsieur Fouquet, the king can ensure the enforcement of his edicts in face of all opposition. Thus the Procureur-Général becomes a powerful instrument either for good or evil.'

'Will you become Procureur-Général, Vanel?' said Colbert, suddenly, with a softened expression of look and voice.

'I!' exclaimed Vanel. 'Have I not just had the honour to explain to you that I lack the means of gratifying any such ambition?'

'But you could borrow the money from your friends?'

'Alas! Monseigneur, my friends are no richer than myself.'

'At all events, Vanel, you are perfectly ingenuous.'

'I wish everyone else were of the same opinion as you.'

'Well, it is *my* opinion, and that is enough; and, as to the money, I will guarantee it if necessary.'

'Remember the proverb, monseigneur.'

'Which proverb?'

' "He who is answerable for another has to pay." '

'It does not apply in the present case.'

Vanel rose from his seat, quite overcome by this offer so spontaneously made by a man who regarded the most trivial affairs of life from a serious point of view.

'Surely, monseigneur,' he said, 'you do not trifle with me?'

'Let us see, Monsieur Vanel; I understand you to say that Monsieur Gourville has already approached you on the subject of Monsieur Fouquet's post.'

'Yes, and Monsieur Pélisson as well.'

'Officially, or not?'

'This is what was said: "These men of the Parlement are rich and ambitious; they ought to form themselves into a syndicate, and subscribe two or three million for Monsieur Fouquet, their leader and protector." '

'And what did you say to that?'

'I said that, for my part, I would subscribe six million livres, if it were necessary.'

'Ah! then you admire Monsieur Fouquet?' cried Colbert, with a look full of venom.

'Not at all; but Monsieur Fouquet is Procureur-Général, he is in debt, he is in deep water, and it is our duty to save him.'

'And that is the reason why, so long as he sticks to his post, Monsieur Fouquet will always be safe and sound.'

'Whereupon,' continued Vanel, 'Monsieur Gourville added: "To suggest to Monsieur Fouquet that he should become the recipient of charity, would be to offer him an affront which he would resent." No; let the members buy outright the post of Procureur-Général, and thus save the honour of the body without wounding the self-respect of Monsieur Fouquet.'

'That would be a preliminary step.'

'I think so too, monseigneur.'

'Very good, Monsieur Vanel; then you will be good enough at once to go in search of either Monsieur Gourville or Monsieur Pélisson. Do you know any other friend of Monsieur Fouquet?'

'I know Monsieur de La Fontaine very well.'

'La Fontaine, the rhymester?'

'The same; he dedicated some verses to my wife at the time when we were on friendly terms with Monsieur Fouquet.'

'Endeavour, then, to obtain, through him, an interview with

Monsieur Fouquet.'

'I will do so willingly; but the money?'

'At the time fixed for the appointment, Monsieur Vanel, you will be provided with the necessary sum. Don't let that worry you.'

'Ah, monseigneur, what munificence! You eclipse the king; you surpass Monsieur Fouquet.'

'One moment; let us not misunderstand one another. I am not making you a present of fourteen hundred thousand livres; I have children to provide for.'

'Then you will lend them to me, monseigneur? That will do equally well.'

'Yes, I will lend them to you.'

'Ask whatever interest, whatever security you please, I shall be prepared with them, and your slightest wish shall be respected. You have only to name your own conditions.'

'Repayment within eight years.'

'Oh, by all means.'

'A mortgage upon the post itself.'

'Certainly; anything else?'

'Wait a moment. I reserve to myself the right of relieving you of the post at a profit to yourself of a hundred and fifty thousand livres, provided that, in the conduct of business, you fail to act strictly in the king's interests, and in furtherance of my own projects.'

'H'm!' said Vanel, slightly taken aback.

'Is there anything in these conditions which displeases you?' enquired Colbert, icily.

'Oh, dear me, no; not at all,' replied Vanel, with great alacrity.

'Very good; then we can sign and complete the transaction as soon as you please. And now, be off, find Monsieur Fouquet's friends, and make arrangements for the interview. Don't refuse to make any reasonable concessions, and when once you have come to an understanding – '

'I will obtain Monsieur Fouquet's signature.'

'*You will do nothing of the kind.* Be careful not to breathe a word to Monsieur Fouquet about signatures or deeds. Don't even ask him to give you his word. To do so would be to ruin everything.'

'But what am I to do, then, monseigneur? The position is a terribly difficult one.'

'Get him to give you his hand on the bargain. Now go.'

## CHAPTER 4

# *The queen mother*

THE QUEEN MOTHER was in her bedchamber at the Palais-Royal with Madame de Motteville and the Señora Molina. The king, who had been expected all day, had failed to make his appearance, and the anxious queen had sent in search of news of him at frequent intervals.

The weather threatened to be stormy, and courtiers and ladies took refuge in antechambers and corridors to avoid being drawn into the discussion of compromising subjects. Monsieur had joined the king's hunting-party in the morning, whilst Madame[23] had stayed at home, out of temper with everybody. The queen mother, having said her prayers in Latin, chatted in pure Castilian upon everyday topics with her two friends. Madame de Motteville, who understood Castilian perfectly, carried on her share of the conversation in French.

When the three ladies had exhausted every form of polite verbal ingenuity in conveying to each other that the king's behaviour was driving the queen, the queen mother, and all his kindred to the verge of despair; when, in elegant language, every sort of imprecation had been fulminated against Mademoiselle de la Vallière, the queen mother brought her recriminations to an end with the following characteristic words. 'Estos hijos!' (These children!) she said to La Molina. Portentous words in the mouth of a mother; words of terrible import in the mouth of a queen, within whose gloomy soul lay hidden many a dark and sinister secret.

'Yes, indeed,' acquiesced La Molina; 'these children! for whom every mother makes a sacrifice of herself.'

'For whom,' said the queen, 'a mother has sacrificed everything.'

She did not finish her phrase. It seemed to her, as she raised her eyes to the full-length portrait of pale Louis XIII, that a light once again blazed in her husband's lack-lustre eyes, and that his nostrils dilated with anger. The portrait came to life, and, although it spoke not, it menaced.

The queen's last words were followed by a deep silence. La Molina began to turn over the lace and ribbons in a large work-basket. Madame de Motteville, surprised at the glance of intelligence which flashed between mistress and confidante, cast down her eyes like a discreet woman, and, whilst seeking to see nothing, listened with all her ears. She was rewarded, however, with nothing beyond a single, 'Hum,' in the voice of that model of circumspection, the Spanish duenna, and the sound of a sigh wrung from the bosom of the queen.

She raised her head immediately. 'You are in pain,' she said.

'No, indeed, Motteville. What makes you say that?'

'I fancied I heard your majesty groan.'

'You are right,' said the queen; 'and, as a matter of fact, I am suffering slightly.'

'Monsieur Valot[24] is here, with Madame, I believe.'

'With Madame? Is anything the matter with her?'

'She is suffering from an attack of the vapours, I fancy.'

'A fashionable complaint! But Monsieur Valot has no right to be with Madame when another doctor would cure her.'

Madame de Motteville again raised her eyes in surprise.

'Another doctor would cure Madame,' she said. 'What can you mean?'

'Occupation, Motteville – occupation. Ah! if anyone is ill, it is my poor daughter.'

'And your majesty also.'

'I am less ill than usual this evening.'

'Do not be too confident, madame.'

And, as if to justify the caution of Madame de Motteville, a sharp spasm cut the queen to the heart, causing her to turn pale as death, and to sink into an armchair in a fainting condition.

'Fetch me my drops,' she murmured.

'Tut, tut!' said La Molina, and, leisurely crossing the room, she took from a cabinet of gilded tortoiseshell a flask of rock crystal, and brought it to the queen. Having taken the restorative, the queen sighed, and said in a low voice: 'It is in one of these attacks that I shall die; but God's holy will be done.'

'It does not follow that a fainting-fit will cause your majesty's death,' replied La Molina, as she replaced the flask in the cabinet.

'Does your majesty feel better now?' enquired Madame de Motteville presently.

'A little better, thank you,' returned the queen, enjoining, with a finger to her lips, discretion on the part of her favourite.

'It is very strange,' continued Madame de Motteville, after a short silence.

'What is very strange?' asked the queen.

'Does not your majesty recollect the day when this pain attacked you for the first time?'

'I remember that it was a day of bitter sorrow, Motteville.'

'And yet your majesty's recollection of that time should not be altogether sad.'

'Why not?'

'Because twenty-three years previously, at that very hour, was born your glorious son his majesty the king.'

The queen uttered a cry, covered her face with her hands, and appeared, for some minutes, to be overcome with emotion.

Was this caused by painful remembrance, or was it due to a fresh access of physical suffering? Señora Molina cast a furious look at Madame de Motteville, which the poor lady was quite at a loss to interpret. Before, however, she had time to ask for an explanation, Anne of Austria, having recovered herself, rose from her seat.

'The 5th of September,' she said. 'Yes, my sufferings began on the 5th of September. One day of supreme happiness, followed by one of intense grief – grief which I bore in atonement for too pure a joy.' And from that moment Anne of Austria, having apparently exhausted all her mental faculties, sank into a state of utter despondency.

'We had better put her to bed,' said La Molina.

'Presently, Molina.'

'Let us leave the queen to herself,' added the uncompromising Spaniard.

Madame de Motteville rose accordingly, whilst heavy teardrops glistened in the eyes and ran down the pale face of the queen; and Molina, perceiving her thus overcome, looked at her with a keen and penetrating glance.

'Yes, yes; leave us, Motteville,' said the queen, wearily. 'Go.'

The word *us* sounded unpleasantly in the ear of the French favourite. It implied that an interchange of secrets and recollections was about to take place in which it was not desired that she should have any share.

'Will the Señora Molina's unaided services be sufficient for your majesty?' she asked.

'Quite sufficient,' answered the queen.

Madame de Motteville bent her head in submission. Then suddenly an aged tire-woman, dressed in the fashion of the Spanish court of 1620, entered the room, finding the queen in tears, and Madame de Motteville in the act of retiring.

'A remedy! a remedy!' she cried triumphantly, as, without ceremony, she approached the group.

'What remedy, *Chica*?' asked Anne of Austria.

'For your majesty's complaint,' she replied.

'And who brings it?' demanded Madame de Motteville, sharply. 'Monsieur Valot?'

'No; a lady from Flanders.'

'A lady from Flanders! Is she Spanish?' asked the queen.

'I don't know.'

'By whom is she sent here?'

'By Monsieur Colbert.'

'What is her name?'

'She has given none.'

'Of what rank is she?'

'That she must tell you herself.'

'What is she like?'

'She wears a mask.'

'These enquiries are futile,' came from the other side of the tapestry, in a quiet but stern voice – a voice which made the queen shudder, and the others shake in their shoes; and, at the same moment, a masked woman showed herself in the opening between the curtains.

Before the queen had time to utter a word, the unknown lady explained that she came from the Béguinage at Bruges, and that she was the bearer of a remedy with which she hoped to effect the queen's restoration to health. No one spoke, nor did the Béguine make any further advance into the room.

'Well, say what you have to say,' said the queen at length.

'Not until we are alone,' replied the Béguine.

Anne of Austria made a sign to her companions to withdraw, and they retired at once. The Béguine then took three steps in the direction of the queen, and bowed her head reverently. The queen looked mistrustfully at the woman, whose bright eyes were fixed on her through the holes in her mask.

'The Queen of France must be ill indeed,' said Anne of Austria, 'when it is known at the Béguinage at Bruges that she stands in need of a remedy.'

'Your majesty's malady, thanks be to God, is not incurable.'

'How is it that you are so well acquainted with my condition?'

'Your majesty has friends in Flanders.'

'And it is these friends who have sent you here?'

'Yes, madame.'

'Tell me who they are.'

'It would be useless for me to tell you, madame, since your own heart has not revived your recollection.'

Anne of Austria leant forward, seeking to pierce through the disguise of this mysterious visitor who addressed her so unceremoniously. Then, all at once, as if in scorn of giving way to a curiosity so little in harmony with the natural pride of her character: 'Madame,' she said haughtily, 'you appear to be unaware that it is not customary to appear masked in the presence of royalty.'

'I entreat you to excuse me, madame,' replied the Béguine, humbly.

'I cannot excuse you, but I will pardon you if you will remove your mask.'

'I am under a vow, madame, to render aid to afflicted and suffering persons without allowing them to see my face. I can afford comfort to you both in body and soul, but, since your majesty declines my services, permit me to take my departure. Adieu, madame, adieu.'

The gentle and respectful tone in which these words were uttered allayed the queen's indignation and mistrust, but without diminishing her curiosity.

'You are right,' she said; 'it ill-becomes sufferers to despise the consolations which are sent to them by God. Try, then, to give some relief to my tortured body. Alas! I fear that God has prepared a terrible ordeal for me.'

'Let us speak a little of the mind, madame,' replied the Béguine, 'of your mind which, I feel sure, suffers also.'

'The mind?'

'There are gnawing cancers whose action is invisible. They allow the skin to retain its ivory whiteness, and they marble not the flesh with their disfiguring veins. The physician, as he bends over the chest of his patient, does not hear, beneath the flow of the blood, the insatiable tooth of these monsters gnawing its way into the muscles. Neither knife nor cautery has ever been able to kill or even to scotch the rage of these mortal scourges. They live in the mind and contaminate it; they grow in the heart, causing it to swell until it bursts. Such, madame, are the cancers which prove fatal to queens. Tell me, are you not a prey to them?'

Anne slowly raised an arm, as white and as perfectly formed as in the days of her youth.

'These evils of which you speak,' she said, 'form part of the conditions under which we exist – we, the great ones of the earth, whom God has endowed with the higher order of intelligence. We may rely upon the Lord to lighten our burdens, if we are penitent, when they become too heavy for us to bear; and it is always permitted to us to lay them down before the tribunal of penitence. But do not forget that this same Sovereign Lord never overtaxes the strength of His creatures, and, for my part, I am able to sustain the weight of the burden which He has imposed upon me. As for the secrets of others, let them be left in the hands of God; as to my own, I am content to rely on the discretion of my confessor.'

'I find that you are still as brave as ever in the face of your enemies, madame, but I feel that you have not much confidence in your friends.'

'Queens have no friends. If you think yourself a prophetess inspired of heaven, I pray you withdraw, for I regard the future with apprehension.'

'I should have thought,' pursued the Béguine, remorselessly, 'that you have greater reason to fear the past.'

Scarcely had she uttered these words than the queen rose and stood erect.

'Speak!' she said, in a tone of command, 'speak! Explain yourself shortly, quickly and completely, otherwise – '

'Pray do not use threats, your majesty,' interrupted the Béguine, gently. 'I approach you with a heart full of respect and compassion. I come here on the part of a friend.'

'Prove it, then,' said the queen. 'Try to comfort, instead of irritating me.'

'That is easily done; and your majesty shall judge who is your friend.'

'Well, we shall see.'

'What misfortunes have happened to your majesty during the last three and twenty years?'

'Oh, great misfortunes; for instance, I have lost the king.'

'I desire to ask whether, since the birth of your son the king, the indiscretion of any friend has caused your majesty uneasiness?'

'I do not understand you,' answered the queen, setting her teeth to conceal her emotion.

'I will endeavour to make myself intelligible. Your majesty will recollect that the king was born on the 3rd of September 1638, at a quarter past eleven.'

'Yes,' assented the queen.

'At half-past twelve, the dauphin, who had been baptised by the Bishop of Meaux in the king's and in your own presence, was proclaimed heir to the throne of France, and the king attended the chapel of the old Château of Saint-Germain, and heard the *Te Deum.*'

'That is perfectly correct,' murmured the queen.

'Your majesty's confinement took place in the presence of Monsieur the king's late uncle, of the princes, and of the ladies of the court. The king's physician Bouvard and the surgeon Honors were in attendance in the antechamber. Your majesty afterwards slept from about three o'clock until seven o'clock. Was not that the case?'

'Undoubtedly; but you are simply stating what all the world knows as well as ourselves.'

'I am coming, madame, to what very few people know. Few, did I say? I may say two persons only, for originally only five were in the secret, and those who played the principal parts in the drama have been dead for many years. The king sleeps with his fathers, the midwife Péronne is dead also, and Laporte[25] is forgotten long ago.'

The queen made an effort to reply; she felt, with the ice-cold hand which she carried to her face, a burning perspiration break out upon her forehead.

'It was eight o'clock,' continued the Béguine; 'the king took supper, and was in boisterous spirits, and the air resounded with shouts and exclamations of joy. The populace cheered under the balconies, and the Swiss Guards and the musketeers strolled about the town, or were triumphantly carried shoulder high by the intoxicated students. These loud indications of popular enthusiasm awakened the future king of France, who was placidly sleeping in the arms of Madame de Hausac his nurse, and who might, as he opened his eyes, have observed two crowns at the foot of his cradle. Suddenly your majesty uttered a piercing cry, and Madame Péronne hastened to the bedside. The medical men were dining in an apartment at some little distance from the sick room, and, owing to the general excitement which prevailed, the palace was left practically unguarded. The midwife, having carefully examined your majesty's condition, uttered an exclamation of surprise, and, supporting you in her arms, sent Laporte to inform the king that your majesty wished to see him at once. Now, Laporte, as you will no doubt recollect, madame, was a very self-possessed and resourceful person, and he knew better than to deliver his message in such a way as to alarm the king; nor, indeed, was his errand of a very alarming nature, after all. He, therefore, approached the king with a smiling face, and said, "Sire, the queen is very happy, but would be still more so if your majesty would condescend to pay her a visit."

'At that moment Louis XIII would have given away even the crown itself to any poor devil as a thank-offering to God, and he cheerfully left the table, saying, in a tone which reminded one of Henri IV, "Gentlemen, I am going to see my wife."

'He reached your majesty's bedside just in time to receive, at the hands of Madame Péronne, a second son, as lusty and as beautifully proportioned as the first-born prince. "Sire," said she, "it is evident that it is not the intention of the Almighty that the kingdom of France shall be ruled under a distaff;" and the king, in an access of joy, took the child in his arms, exclaiming, "My God, I thank Thee!" '

The Béguine, observing how acutely the queen was suffering, at this point in her story came to a pause. Anne of Austria threw herself back in her chair, and with outstretched neck and starting eyes, listened without seeming to understand, whilst, from the convulsed twitching of her lips, it seemed that either she prayed to heaven, or muttered imprecations against the woman who tormented her.

'But do not believe,' cried the Béguine, 'that although there is but one dauphin in France, and that although the queen has allowed this second child to vegetate far removed from his proper surroundings, she deserves to be stigmatised as a heartless mother. Oh no! There are those who know of the bitter tears she has shed; there are those who have taken note of the passionate kisses which she has bestowed upon this innocent child, as the sole recompense she could make to him for the wretched and gloomy life to which state policy has condemned the twin brother of Louis XIV.'

'My God! my God!' faintly murmured the queen.

'When the king,' continued the Béguine, 'found himself with two sons, equal both in age and pretensions, he trembled for the safety of France and the tranquillity of the state. Then it was that he took counsel with Cardinal Richelieu, who, after considering the matter for upwards of an hour in his majesty's cabinet, pronounced the following sentence: "A king has been born to succeed his majesty, and it has pleased heaven to cause a second to be born to succeed the first. We have, however, need only of one – the first-born. Let us, therefore, conceal from France the birth of the second. One prince means peace and security for the state; two princes, having rival claims, mean civil war and anarchy." '

The queen rose suddenly from her seat, with bloodless cheeks and clenched hands.

'You know too much,' she said, in a suppressed tone of voice, 'since you profess to be acquainted with state secrets. As for the friends from whom you have derived this precious information, they are dastardly and false, and you have made yourself an accomplice in the crime which is being committed today. And now, away with your mask, or I will have you arrested by the captain of my guards. Oh, your secret does not terrify me. You have buried it, and must now unearth it. Neither your secret nor your life is your own any longer;' and Anne of Austria, with threatening aspect, strode towards the Béguine.

'Learn, then,' said the latter, 'to recognise fidelity, honour and secrecy in the person of a discarded friend.'

With these words she threw off her mask.

'Madame de Chevreuse!' cried the astonished queen.

'The only person, besides your majesty, to whom the secret is known.'

'Embrace me, duchess,' said Anne of Austria. 'You kill your friend by thus wantonly playing upon her feelings.' And, leaning her head upon the shoulder of the aged duchess, the queen burst into a flood of bitter tears.

'You are very young still,' said the duchess; 'you can actually weep.'

CHAPTER 5

## Two dear friends

THE QUEEN looked haughtily at Madame de Chevreuse.

'I think,' she remarked, 'that in speaking of me you made use of the word *happy*. Until the present moment, duchess, I should have believed it impossible for any human being to be less happy than the Queen of France.'

'Madame, you have, indeed, suffered deeply. But, by the side of these great misfortunes, of which we, two old friends unhappily estranged through the unworthy conduct of men, have just been speaking, you have many pleasures, insignificant perhaps in your own estimation, but such as would, nevertheless, excite the envy of the world at large.'

'What pleasures?' said Anne of Austria, bitterly. 'How can you make use of such a word, duchess? You who know so well that neither in mind nor in body am I ever granted a moment's respite from pain.'

Madame de Chevreuse collected herself a moment.

'Truly,' she murmured, 'kings are far removed from ordinary beings.'

'What do you mean by that?'

'I mean that they are so far removed from commonplace existence, that they forget that less favoured mortals sometimes lack the bare necessities of life. In the same way, he who lives upon the verdant table-land of an African mountain, which is watered by rivulets of melted snow, does not understand that on the sun-dried plains at his feet, his less fortunate brother is dying of hunger and thirst.'

The queen coloured slightly. She was beginning to understand.

'I feel,' she said, 'that I ought not to have forsaken you.'

'Ah, madame, the king has, I fear, inherited the hatred which his father bore me. Did he but know that I was at the Palais-Royal, he would have me turned out.'

'I cannot pretend that the king is very well disposed towards you; but, nevertheless, I might, perhaps, manage secretly – '

The duchess smiled with a disdain that caused some uneasiness to the queen, who hastened to add: 'At any rate, you were quite right to come here, if only to show that there was no foundation for the report of your death.'

'Has it really been reported that I was dead?'

'Everywhere.'

'My children, nevertheless, have not gone into mourning.'

'Well, you see, duchess, the court moves about a good deal; we see little of the Messieurs d'Alberts de Luynes, and, in the bustle and hurry of the life we lead, a great many things escape notice.'

'Your majesty, surely, did not believe the report of my death?'

'Why not? Alas! we are all mortal, and you cannot but see that I, your little sister, as you used to call me in the days that are gone by, already tremble upon the verge of the grave.'

'If your majesty really believed me to be dead, were you not surprised at receiving no direct news of me?'

'Death often takes us unawares, duchess.'

'Oh, your majesty, those whose minds are troubled with such weighty secrets as those of which we have been talking, are never free from the desire to unburden their consciences; and it is the duty of those about to die to take care that their papers are left in proper order.' The queen shuddered. 'And when the time comes,' continued the duchess, 'your majesty will assuredly receive incontestable evidence of my death.'

'How shall I be certain of it?'

'Because your majesty will receive, on the following day, in a carefully secured packet, the whole of the private correspondence that has ever passed between us.'

'You have not destroyed my letters?' cried Anne, in alarm.

'Oh, your majesty, traitors only would dream of destroying royal correspondence.'

'Traitors?'

'Yes; or rather, whilst pretending to destroy it, they would either keep or sell it. Trustworthy allies, on the contrary, would carefully conceal such precious documents in a secure hiding-place. Then, someday, they might go to their queen, and say, "Madame, I am growing old, and my health is failing me. It is dangerous for me any longer to keep in my possession papers which might compromise your majesty. Take them, therefore, and destroy them yourself." '

'Compromising papers? Which are they?'

'To be precise, I have actually only one; but it is one of a highly dangerous character.'

'Oh, duchess, tell me what it is!'

'It is a letter, dated 2 August 1644, in which you invite me to go to Noisy-le-Sec, to see that beloved and unhappy child. There it is, madame, in your own handwriting, "that unhappy child".'

Both were silent for a time. The queen was thinking of the past; Madame de Chevreuse was speculating on her chances of success.

'Yes, unhappy, most unhappy,' murmured Anne of Austria. 'How cruel was the life he led, and how sad its end!'

'Is he dead, then?' asked the duchess, so sharply that the queen could not fail to observe how keen was the curiosity which prompted the question.

'He died of consumption, and his death is forgotten. He faded away like the flowers which a lover gives to his mistress, who leaves them to wither in a drawer in which she has hid them from the world.'

'Dead!' repeated the duchess, with an air of concern which would have gratified the queen had it not been tempered by a shadow of doubt. 'He died at Noisy-le-Sec?'

'Yes, in the arms of his tutor, poor, honest fellow, who did not long survive him.'

'That is easy to understand; the combined weight of his secret and the poignancy of his grief was more than he could bear.'

The queen taking no notice of the irony concealed in this observation, Madame de Chevreuse continued: 'To be candid, madame, I made enquiry, some years ago, at Noisy-le-Sec, as to the fate of this unhappy child, and it was certainly the impression there that he was not dead. For this reason I did not at once condole with your majesty; for, had I really believed him to be dead, I would not on any account have reawakened your majesty's legitimate grief by any allusion to so painful a subject.'

'You say that, at Noisy, the child is not believed to be dead?'

'No, madame.'

'What did they say about it, then?'

'They said – but, no doubt, they were mistaken.'

'Never mind, tell me.'

'They said that, one evening about the year 1645, a distinguished-looking lady, whose undoubtedly high rank it was impossible for her mask and cloak to conceal, came in a carriage to the turning in the road at the corner of which, you may remember, I waited for news of the young prince when your majesty did me the honour to send me there.'

'Well?'

'The child's tutor took him to this lady, and, next day, both tutor and child had disappeared from the neighbourhood.'

'Well, you may judge what truth there is in the statement, since, as a matter of fact, the child was struck down by one of those sudden attacks which, according to the doctors, cause the life of a young child to hang by a thread.'

'What your majesty says is quite true: no one knows it better than you; no one believes it more firmly than I. Still, observe the singularity – '

'What! is there more to come?' said the queen to herself.

'The person who made me acquainted with these details, who had made enquiry as to the child's health, this person – '

'Surely you did not depute that duty to another person! Oh, duchess!'

'Someone as silent as your majesty, as dumb as myself; let us suppose that it *was* myself, madame. This person, I say, who was travelling some time afterwards through Touraine, recognised tutor and child, or, I would say, believed that she recognised them, both alive, and, apparently, in excellent health and spirits – the one having attained a green old age, the other being in the full vigour of youth. Judge, after that, what is the value of rumours which are noised abroad, and don't doubt the possibility of anything happening in this world. But I fatigue your majesty; permit me, therefore, to take my leave with the renewed assurance of my respectful devotion.'

'Stay, duchess, let us speak a little of yourself.'

'Of *me*, madame? I would not have your majesty carry your condescension to that length.'

'Why not? Are you not my oldest friend? I have not given you offence, duchess?'

'Offended *me*? How can your majesty make such a suggestion? Had I a grievance, should I have intruded myself into your majesty's presence?'

'Duchess, old age is gaining on us both. We should endeavour to give each other courage and strength to meet the inevitable end.'

'Madame, your gracious words overpower me.'

'No one has ever loved me so well, and served me so faithfully as yourself, duchess.'

'Your majesty is not unmindful of my services?'

'I shall never forget them. Duchess, will you give me a proof of your friendship?'

'I am altogether devoted to your majesty.'

'Then ask something of me.'

'Ask?'

'Oh, I know how disinterested you are, and how noble, how truly royal is your character.'

'You praise me too highly, madame,' said the duchess, slightly disconcerted.

'I do not praise you more highly than you deserve.'

'Age and misfortunes bring about changes in most people, madame.'

'I am glad that it is so, for the duchess of former days – the beautiful, proud, and adored Chevreuse – might have answered me ungraciously, "I want nothing at your hands." Welcome misfortune, then, if it has so changed you as to lead you to answer, "I accept your offer!" '

At these words the asperity of the duchess's manner became somewhat modified; she felt as if under a spell, and had no longer the power to dissemble.

'Speak, dearest,' said the queen. 'What shall I do for you?'

'It is necessary that I should explain.'

'Well, do so, then, without further ceremony.'

'It is in your majesty's power to make me ineffably happy.'

'Yes; but we must not forget,' said the queen, who was feeling slightly nervous as to what was coming next. 'We must not forget that I am quite as much under the control of my son as I was formerly under that of my husband.'

'I shall not be very exacting, my beloved queen.'

'Call me Anne, as you used to do; it will sound like a sweet echo of childhood.'

'Well, then, beloved mistress, dearest Anne – '

'You understand Spanish?'

'Perfectly.'

'Then ask your favour of me in that language.'

'It is this: honour me by spending a few days with me at Dampierre.'

'Is that all?' cried the queen, in astonishment.

'Absolutely all,' replied the duchess. 'Great heaven! did you imagine that I was about to ask any immense favour of you? If your majesty thought that, you little know me. Do you consent?'

'Oh yes, with all my heart.'

'Ah! thank you, thank you.'

'And I shall be much gratified,' continued the queen, not without a shadow of mistrust, 'if my presence prove useful to you in any way.'

'Useful?' cried the duchess, with a smile. 'Useful? No, no. But inexpressibly sweet and charming? Yes, yes, a thousand times. Is it a promise?'

'I give you my solemn promise,' said the queen.

The duchess seized the queen's hand and covered it with kisses.

'She is a kind-hearted woman, after all,' said the queen to herself.

'Your majesty, however, must give me a fortnight's grace,' stipulated the duchess, after a pause.

'By all means; but why?'

'Because,' said the duchess, 'knowing me to be in disgrace, no one would lend me the hundred thousand crowns which will be required for putting Dampierre into a proper state of repair; but, when it is known that I am about to entertain your majesty, all the money in Paris will be at my disposal.'

'A hundred thousand crowns!' said the queen, making a sign of intelligence with a slight movement of the head. 'Will it cost as much as that to restore Dampierre?'

'Oh, quite as much.'

'And no one will lend you the money?'

'Not a soul.'

'Then I will lend it to you, if you like, duchess.'

'Oh, I should be afraid to accept the offer.'

'Then you would be wrong.'

'Really?'

'On my honour as a queen; besides, a hundred thousand crowns is not such an enormous sum, after all.'

'Is it not?'

'No. Oh, I am well aware that you have never put a sufficiently high estimate upon your fidelity and discretion. Now, push that table over here, and I will write you a draft upon Monsieur Colbert – no, upon Monsieur Fouquet; he is by far the more pleasant man to deal with.'

'But will he honour it?'

'If he does not pay, I will; but this will be the first time that he has ever refused me.'

The queen wrote, handed her the draft, and, with a warm and tender embrace, dismissed her.

CHAPTER 6

## Shows how Jean de La Fontaine came to write his first tale

ALL THESE INTRIGUES are now exhausted. The human mind, so variable in its developments, has been enabled readily to depict itself upon the three canvasses[26] with which our story has supplied it. In the course of what follows, politics and intrigue may again, perhaps, be forced upon our notice; but the springs which govern their action will be so well concealed that nothing besides painting and flowers will be visible, as at a country theatre, where some grisly monster appears upon the scene, moved and governed by the tiny limbs of a child concealed within its bulk:

We will return to Saint Mandé,[27] where the superintendent, according to his custom, is receiving the cream of Epicurean society.

For some time past, the minister had been going through a terrible ordeal, and everyone in the house shared in his anxiety of mind. No more extravagant entertainments were given. 'They cost too much money,' had been Fouquet's excuse for their discontinuance; but, as Gourville remarked, no excuse could have been more transparently ridiculous. There had never been a vestige of any ready money about the place at all. Monsieur Vatel did his best to sustain the reputation of the establishment. Nevertheless, the gardeners who supplied the kitchens complained bitterly of arrears in payments, and the merchants who supplied the Spanish wines found that their oft-rendered accounts remained unnoticed. The fishermen employed by the minister along the coasts of Normandy computed that, when they received what was due to them, they would be able to retire from business and live in comfort for the rest of their days; and fish, which was destined in the end to be the death of Vatel, gradually ceased to arrive at all.

Nevertheless, upon the regular reception day, Monsieur Fouquet's adherents appeared upon the scene in unusual numbers. Gourville and the Abbé Fouquet discussed finance – that is to say, the abbé borrowed some money from Gourville, whilst Pélisson, reclining at his ease, concluded the peroration of a speech with which it was intended that Monsieur Fouquet should reopen the Parlement. And this speech was a masterpiece, for Pélisson, having written it for his friend, had put into it a great deal more than he would have taken the trouble to think out for himself. Presently, discussing the niceties of versification, Loret and La Fontaine[28] arrived from the far end of the garden. Painters and musicians made the best of their way to the supper-room, knowing that, at the stroke of eight, an attack would be made on the provisions. It was half-past seven; the minister was always punctual, and appetite had begun to assert itself.

When the guests had assembled, Gourville went straight to Pélisson, roused him from his reverie, and drew him into a room, the doors of which he closed.

'Well,' he said, 'what is the news?'

'I have borrowed,' replied Pélisson, 'twenty-five thousand livres from my aunt. Here is the money in bank drafts.'

'Good,' said Gourville; 'we only now require a hundred and ninety-five thousand livres to enable us to make the first payment.'

'The first payment of what?' asked La Fontaine, in the casual tone of voice in which he might have enquired what day of the week it was.

'Absent-minded as ever,' exclaimed Gourville. 'Why, it was you who told us that the little estate at Corbeil was about to be sold by one of Monsieur Fouquet's creditors, and suggested that a subscription should be got up amongst the minister's friends. You even expressed your intention of selling a corner of your own property in order to furnish your share; and now you come to us and coolly ask, "First payment of what?"'

A general laugh greeted this speech, and made La Fontaine colour up to the tips of his ears.

'Pardon, pardon,' he said; 'I had not really forgotten. Oh, dear me, no! Only – '

'Only you didn't recollect,' hazarded Loret.

'That is quite true, and, in fact, he is quite right. There is a wide distinction to be drawn between forgetting and failing to recollect.'

'No doubt, then,' said Pélisson, 'you have brought with you the sum for which you sold your corner of land.'

'But I haven't sold it. My wife wouldn't let me.' And at this there was another laugh.

'And yet you went to Château-Thierry for the purpose, did you not?'

'I did, and on horseback, too. I rode eight different horses on the journey, and a fine bucketing they gave me, I can assure you.'

'What devoted friendship! However, it is fortunate that, having arrived, you were able to rest.'

'Rest, did you say? Oh yes, very much so! Let me tell you that, when I got home, I found a nice piece of work cut out for me.'

'Why, how was that?'

'Oh, when I reached home, I found that my wife had been compromising herself with the very man I wanted to sell the land to, and, damn the fellow! I had to call him out.'

'Good,' said the poet; 'and so you fought?'

'It would seem not.'

'Then what took place?'

'Oh, my wife and her relations must needs have a finger in the pie. I stood for a quarter of an hour with my sword in my hand, but I was not wounded.'

'And your adversary?'

'Neither was he, for the simple reason that he did not put in an appearance on the ground.'

'Capital!' cried everyone. 'What a towering rage you must have been in!'

'I should think so, indeed, for I caught an abominable cold, and, when I re-entered the house, my wife abused me, and threw a great loaf of bread at my head.'

'And what did you do then?'

'Oh, I overturned the table on top of her, upset all her guests, mounted my horse and here I am.'

No one could keep his countenance at the relation of this farcical anecdote, which was greeted with a perfect storm of laughter and applause.

'So that is all you have brought us?' they said to La Fontaine, when something like order had been restored.

'Oh no! I have conceived an excellent idea.'

'Well, out with it.'

'You have, no doubt, remarked the large number of naughty books which are written in France?'

'Most certainly,' replied those present.

'And you are also aware,' continued La Fontaine, 'that very few of them are ever printed.'

'Well, as to that, the law is very stringent.'

'That is true. In my opinion, however, whatever is rare, is bound to command a high price. And that is why I have been at some pains to make my book as objectionable as possible. I have used exceedingly plain and uncompromising language, and have not hesitated to call a spade a spade.'

His audience were convulsed with laughter at hearing this description of the poet's work.

'Yes,' continued La Fontaine, 'and I flatter myself that I have surpassed anything that such authors as Boccaccio and Aretino[29] have attempted in the same direction.'

'Well, well,' cried Pélisson, 'your book will most certainly be suppressed.'

'You think so?' asked the poet. 'Well, let me tell you that I have not written it so much on my own account as in the interests of Monsieur Fouquet.'

This remarkable assertion appeared to afford those present the liveliest satisfaction.

'I have sold the first edition of the book for eight hundred livres,' cried La Fontaine, chuckling with satisfaction, 'and I will wager that a religious work would not fetch more than half that amount.'

'In that case,' said Gourville, laughing, 'perhaps it would have been better to have produced two works of a serious character.'

'It would have taken too long, and there would not have been enough fun in it,' replied La Fontaine. 'However, here are the eight hundred livres in this bag, and I beg leave to offer them as my contribution to the fund.' And he placed the money in the treasurer's hands.

Then it came to the turn of Loret, who contributed a hundred and fifty livres, whilst the rest gave whatever they had been able to scrape together. The whole amounted, in the aggregate, to forty thousand livres.

Never had more freely given offerings been poured into the divine scales, where love balances kind hearts and good intentions against the spurious coin[30] of the self-righteous Pharisee.

Scarcely had the money been handed over, than the minister, who had overheard everything that had taken place, silently entered the room. And then this large-hearted and fertile-brained man who had, in his time, accumulated so many millions, this plutocrat who had devoured the substance, both moral and material, of the first kingdom in the world, crossed the room with tear-bedimmed eyes, and passed through his trembling fingers the pieces of gold and silver with which his partisans had presented him.

'Poor little sum,' he said, in a voice full of emotion. 'You will take up but little space in my empty coffers; but you have filled to overflowing my grateful heart. Thank you, my dear friends, thank you,' and, not being able conveniently to embrace everyone in the room, he made La Fontaine the recipient of that attention, saying at the same time, 'My poor fellow, it is for my sake that you have been beaten by your wife, and censured by your confessor.'

'That is of little consequence,' replied the poet; 'and, provided that your creditors will wait a couple of years, I will write books enough to free you entirely from debt.'

CHAPTER 7

## La Fontaine as a man of business

FOUQUET pressed La Fontaine's hand warmly.

'My dear friend,' said he, 'I trust you will write a hundred more books, not only for the sake of the money they will bring in, but in order that our language may be enriched with the gems of a hundred masterpieces.'

'Oh, it must not be supposed,' said La Fontaine, pluming himself, 'that an idea and eighty pistoles are the only things I bring to the minister.'

'Just listen to that!' cried everyone. 'Monsieur de La Fontaine must be in funds today.'

'Welcome the idea!' cried Fouquet, cheerfully, 'if only it supplies me with a million or two.'

'Exactly,' said the poet.

'Explain!' cried the assembly.

'Be careful,' said Pélisson in La Fontaine's ear; 'you have scored brilliantly up to the present. Don't mar your success by going too far.'

'Not a bit of it, Monsieur Pélisson; and I am sure that you, as a man of taste, will be the first to approve of everything.'

'But this is a question of millions,' said Gourville.

'I have here, Monsieur Gourville,' said La Fontaine, tapping his chest, 'fifteen hundred thousand livres.'

'To the devil with this Gascon[31] from Château-Thierry!' cried Loret.

'It is not his pocket he should have touched, but his head,' said Fouquet.

'Why, look there,' cried La Fontaine, 'you are not Procureur-Général; you are a poet!'

'That is true,' cried Loret; 'he is Conrart and all the rest of the men of letters combined.'

'You are,' repeated La Fontaine, 'a poet, a painter, a sculptor and a patron of all the arts and sciences; but I think you will admit that you are no lawyer.'

'Yes, I certainly admit that,' answered Fouquet, smiling.

'If you were offered a membership of the Academy, would you not refuse it?'

'I think I should, with all deference to the Academicians.'

'Then why, if you are unwilling to belong to the Academy, do you permit yourself to serve in Parlement?'

'Oh,' said Pélisson, 'the conversation is taking a political turn.'

'What I want to know is,' pursued La Fontaine, 'whether the black robe does or does not suit Monsieur Fouquet.'

'There is no question as to a robe at all,' returned Monsieur Pélisson, somewhat nettled at observing the smiles of his audience.

'On the contrary, that is exactly what *is* in question,' said Loret.

'Discard the Procureur-Général's robe,' said Conrart, 'and Monsieur Fouquet still remains to us. We have no ground for complaint against him, but, since he cannot be Procureur-Général without his robe, we will agree with Monsieur de La Fontaine, that, decidedly, that garment is a bugbear.'

'*Fugiunt risus leporesque*,'[32] said Loret.

'The smiles and the graces,' said a scholar who was present.

'That is not how *I* translate *lepores*,' said Pélisson, gravely.

'How do you render it, then?' asked La Fontaine.

'Thus: "The hares run away when they see Monsieur Fouquet!" '

This raised a laugh, in which Fouquet himself joined.

'Why do you say *hares*?' said Conrart, a little piqued.

'Simply because the hares are amongst those who will be very sorry to see Monsieur Fouquet in the trappings which are the outward and visible sign of his greatness in Parlement.'

'It seems to me,' said Conrart, 'impossible to reconcile *Quo non ascendam* with the robe of a Procureur-Général.'

'And to *me*, it seems impossible *without* it,' replied Pélisson, obstinately. 'What is your opinion, Gourville?'

'Oh, I think that the robe is all very well,' answered the latter; 'but, for my own part, I should prefer a million and a half.'

'And I agree with Gourville,' cried Fouquet, thus cutting short a discussion which threatened to become wearisome.'

'A million and a half,' growled Pélisson; 'that reminds me of an Indian fable which I have heard.'

'Tell it,' said La Fontaine. 'I should like to hear it, too.'

'Well, there was once a tortoise, who was, of course, provided with a shell, and within this shell he used to hide for protection against the attacks of his enemies. One day, someone said to him, "You must find it very hot inside there in the summertime. Besides, when you are hidden, no one can admire your bodily perfections. Now, here is a serpent who will give you a million and a half for your shell." '

'Good!' said Monsieur Fouquet, laughing.

'So the tortoise sold his shell, and had to go about unprotected. He was discovered by a vulture, who, feeling hungry, broke his back with a blow of his beak, and had him for dinner.'

' "Ὁ μῦθος δηλοῖ?' ('And the parable proves?') said Conrart.

'Oh, the moral is that Monsieur Fouquet had better take care not to part with his robe.'

La Fontaine took the tale seriously. 'You forget Aeschylus,' he said to his opponent.

'What of him?'

'Why, Aeschylus had a bald head, and one day a vulture – *your* vulture probably – who was very fond of tortoise, being high up in the air, mistook his cranium for a white stone, and dropped a tortoise, who was tucked up in his shell, on the top of it.'

'By the Lord! La Fontaine is right!' exclaimed Fouquet, thoughtfully. 'Every vulture who hankers after tortoise can find a means of breaking the shell. Thrice happy the tortoise who meets with a serpent able and willing to give him a million and a half for his roof. If anyone will bring me a snake who will make me as handsome an offer as did the fellow mentioned in your fable, Pélisson, he shall certainly have *my* shell.'

' "*Rara avis in terris*," '[33] quoted Conrart.

' "And very like a black swan." Is not that how the line runs?' added La Fontaine. 'Yes, exactly; a bird quite black, and very rare. I have found one.'

'Do you mean that you have found someone who will buy my post of Procureur-Général?'

'Yes, I have.'

'But the minister has never yet intimated that it is for sale,' remarked Pélisson.

'Pardon me, but you have spoken of it yourself,' said Conrart.

'I can corroborate that statement,' said Gourville.

'He alludes to the interesting fable which has just been told us,' said Fouquet, with a laugh. 'And now, touching this purchaser, La Fontaine?'

'He is a bird entirely black, a counsellor of Parlement, and really a most estimable person.'

'What is his name?'

'Vanel.'

'What! Vanel, the husband of – '

'Precisely so, *her* husband; yes, monsieur.'

'And does this charming individual aspire to become Procureur-Général?'

'His one desire is to imitate you in everything,' said Gourville.

'How very interesting! Tell us how it happened, La Fontaine.'

'It is very simple. I meet him from time to time. A short time ago only I saw him loitering about the Place de la Bastille, as I was on my way to take the coach for Saint-Mandé.'

'Perhaps he was watching his wife,' suggested Loret.

'Oh dear no!' said Fouquet innocently; 'he is not a bit jealous.'

'He pounced upon me,' continued La Fontaine, 'carried me off to the Image-Saint-Fiacre tavern, and regaled me with a recital of his troubles.'

'He has troubles, then?'

'Yes; his wife tries to stir up his ambition.'

'And he told you – '

'That he had been spoken to about a post in the Parlement; that Monsieur Fouquet's name had been mentioned; that, for a long time, Madame Vanel has been dreaming that she was Madame la Procureuse-Générale, and invariably awakens from such dreams disappointed and out of humour.'

'Poor woman!' said Fouquet.

'Wait a minute. Conrart always tells me that I have no capacity for business. Now you shall see how I am managing this affair.'

'Well, let us hear.'

'Do you know,' said I to Vanel, 'that to purchase a post such as Monsieur Fouquet's would be a very expensive business?'

'How much do you think it would cost?' he asked.

'Well, I know that Monsieur Fouquet has refused seventeen hundred thousand livres for it.'

'My wife,' said Vanel, 'reckons it at about fourteen hundred thousand.'

'Ready money?' said I.

'Yes; she has sold some property in Guienne, and has received the money for it.'

'A nice little sum to lay hands on in a lump,' remarked the Abbé Fouquet, who had not previously spoken.

'Poor Madame Vanel!' murmured Fouquet.

Pélisson shrugged his shoulders. 'That woman is a fiend!' he whispered to Fouquet.

'That may be so; still it would not be a bad idea to make use of this fiend's money to repair an injury which an angel has done me.'

Pélisson looked at Fouquet with an air of surprise; but the latter had, from that moment, a fresh end in view.

'Well, what think you of my negotiation?' asked La Fontaine.

'Admirable! my dear poet.'

'Yes,' said Gourville; 'but a man may want to buy a horse, and yet not have enough money to pay for the bridle.'

'If Vanel were taken at his word, he would probably draw back,' said the Abbé Fouquet.

'I don't think so,' said La Fontaine.

'Why do you say that?'

'Because you have not heard the end of my story.'

'Well, if there is any important sequel to it, why beat about the bush?' said Gourville.

'*Semper ad adventum*;[34] is that right?' said Fouquet, with the air of a great personage who has permitted himself the use of a barbarism. The Latinists present loudly applauded.

'The climax,' said La Fontaine, 'is that Vanel, knowing that I was on my way to Saint-Mandé, besought me to take him with me, and to present him to monseigneur.'

'And the result?'

'That he is, at this moment, cooling his heels upon the lawn outside. What say you to that, Monsieur Fouquet?'

'I think that the husband of Madame Vanel must not be allowed to run the risk of catching cold, and, since you know where he is, La Fontaine, you had better send for him.'

'I will go myself,' said La Fontaine.

'And I will go with you,' said the abbé. 'I can carry the money-bags.'

'Let us have no unseemly joking,' said Monsieur Fouquet, severely. 'If this is a matter of business, let us deal with it seriously. But, in the first place, let us show that we are hospitable. Make my excuses, La Fontaine, to this gentleman, and say that, had I been informed of his arrival, he should not have been kept waiting.'

La Fontaine set out at once, and, fortunately, Gourville went with him, for the poet, entirely absorbed in his own calculations, had taken the wrong road, and was hurrying, as fast as his legs could carry him, towards Saint-Maur. A quarter of a hour later, Monsieur Vanel was ushered into the minister's cabinet,[35] which has already been described at the commencement of our story. Fouquet, on seeing him approach, called Pélisson to him, and whispered a few words in his ear.

'Listen attentively to what I am going to say,' said he. 'See that all the gold and silver plate, as well as all the jewels, are carefully packed and put in the carriage before you start on the return journey. You had better have the black horses. You will bring the jeweller back with you; and order supper to be put back until Madame de Bellière[36] arrives.'

'Will it be necessary to inform Madame de Bellière?' asked Pélisson.

'No; I will attend to that myself.'

'Very good.'

'And now, go, my friend.'

Pélisson thereupon took his departure, apprehensive of trouble, but having full confidence in the wisdom of his chief. And therein lies the value of true friendship. Distrust is bred only in inferior natures.

Vanel bowed respectfully to the minister, and prepared to state his business.

'Take a seat, sir,' said Fouquet, politely. 'Well, it seems that you wish to buy my post. How much will you give for it?'

'It is for you, monseigneur, to fix the price. I am aware that you have had several offers already.'

'I am told that Madame Vanel values it at fourteen hundred thousand livres.'

'It is all we have in the world, monseigneur.'

'Could you pay down that sum at once?'

'Well, I haven't it in my pocket at the present moment,' answered Vanel, naïvely, astonished at the simple manner in which the business was being transacted, for he had anticipated that the negotiation would entail the use of much finesse and diplomacy.

'When will you have it?'

'When monseigneur pleases.' And he trembled lest Fouquet might not really be in earnest.

'If it were not for giving you the trouble of returning to Paris, I would say, at once.'

'Oh, monseigneur!'

'But,' interrupted the minister, 'we can sign and complete the transaction at six o'clock tomorrow morning.'

'At six o'clock,' repeated Vanel.

'Goodbye, then, sir, and pray make my compliments to Madame Vanel,' said Fouquet, as he rose from his seat.

The blood rushed to Vanel's head, and his brain became slightly bewildered.

'Monseigneur,' he said earnestly, 'will you give me your word on this transaction?'

Fouquet turned his head. 'Why, bless my soul!' said he, 'I might ask you the same question.'

Vanel hesitated, and then timidly put out his hand. Fouquet frankly held out his own, and his loyal hand was, for a moment, in contact with Vanel's hypocritical palm.

'Goodbye, again,' said the minister, as he gently withdrew his hand.

Vanel backed to the door, reached the vestibule, and hurried off at full speed.

CHAPTER 8

## Madame de Bellière's plate and diamonds

No sooner had Vanel taken his departure than Fouquet sat down for a few moments' reflection.

'It is impossible,' said he, 'to do too much for a woman whom I once loved. Marguerite wishes to be Procureuse-Générale, and why should not her wish be gratified? And, now that the most exacting conscience can reproach me with nothing, I may surely be permitted to give a little thought to the woman who loves me at the present time. By this time, Madame de Bellière should be there;' and he gave a glance in the direction of the secret door.

Having shut himself in, he proceeded along the subterranean passage which led from his dwelling to the house at Vincennes. He had not thought it necessary to apprise his friend of his approach by the customary ringing of a bell, feeling assured that she would not fail to keep her engagement; and, indeed, the marquise had already arrived, and was waiting to receive him. The noise which he made announced that he was at hand, and she hastened to possess herself of the note which he had pushed under the door. This note merely contained these words: 'Come, marquise, we are waiting supper for you.'

Happy, and full of life and activity, the marquise quickly reached the carriage which was waiting for her in the Avenue de Vincennes, and gave her hand to Gourville, who, in order to please his master, had constituted himself her escort. She did not notice Monsieur Fouquet's black horses which, smoking and flecked with foam, had just brought back to Saint-Mandé Pélisson and the same jeweller to whom she had sold her plate and jewellery.

Pélisson brought this man to Monsieur Fouquet, who was still in his cabinet. The minister hastened to thank the jeweller for having looked upon these treasures in the light of a deposit simply, notwithstanding that he had a perfect right to sell them, and he then looked at the total of the account, which amounted to thirteen hundred thousand livres. Then he sat down at his table and wrote a draft on his treasury for fourteen hundred thousand livres, payable at sight before twelve o'clock next day.

'A hundred thousand livres profit!' cried the jeweller. 'Ah, monseigneur! you are too generous.'

'Not at all, not at all,' answered Fouquet, tapping him on the shoulder; 'there are some acts of courtesy which it is impossible to repay. The profit amounts to about what you would have made, and there yet remains the interest on your money to be considered.'

So saying, he detached from his sleeve a diamond button, which the jeweller himself had often valued at three thousand pistoles.

'Accept this,' he said, 'as a remembrance of me, and goodbye. You are a good fellow.'

'And you, monseigneur,' said the jeweller, much affected, 'are a gentleman.'

Fouquet dismissed the worthy jeweller by a private door, and then went to receive Madame de Bellière, who was already surrounded by the rest of the guests.

The marquise, who was always beautiful, seemed, upon this occasion, to be more lovely than ever.

'Do you not think, gentlemen,' asked Fouquet, 'that madame looks inexpressibly sweet this evening? Do you know why?'

'Because madame is absolutely the most beautiful of women,' replied someone.

'No; it is because she is the *best*. Nevertheless – '

'Nevertheless, what?' said the marquise, smiling.

'All the jewels which she is wearing this evening are false stones.'

The marquise blushed scarlet.

'Ha, ha!' laughed several voices, 'that is a fine thing to say about a lady whose diamonds are the finest in Paris.'

'Well?' enquired Fouquet of Pélisson, in a whisper.

'Oh, well, I understand at last,' replied the latter, 'and I think you have done well.'

'I am glad to hear you say so,' said the minister, with a smile.

'Monseigneur, supper is on the table,' announced Vatel, pompously.

With less dignity than is usually observed at ministerial receptions, the guests made their way to the dining-room, and there a magnificent spectacle awaited them.

Upon the sideboards, side-tables, as well as upon the supper-table itself, glittered the most dazzling display of gold and silver plate that can be imagined – relics of the works of art which the Florentine artists, introduced by the Medici, had sculptured, chased and cast, in the days when yet there was gold in France. These hidden treasures, which had been buried during the civil wars, had, from time to time, made a timid reappearance in the intervals of that war of good taste known as the Fronde, in which noblemen fighting against noblemen slew their adversaries but scorned to pillage. All this plate was engraved with the arms of Madame de Bellière.

'Look,' cried La Fontaine, 'a P and a B.'

But perhaps the most striking sight of all was a pyramid of precious stones which was heaped up in front of the seat which had been assigned to Madame de Bellière. This was composed of a vast quantity of diamonds, sapphires, emeralds, and antique cameos; sardonyx stones cut by the ancient Greeks of Asia Minor and set in Mysian gold; curious mosaics of ancient Alexandria mounted in silver; whilst massive Egyptian bracelets of the time of Cleopatra filled a huge platter of Palissy ware, supported, in its turn, by a tripod of gilt bronze, sculptured by Benvenuto Cellini.

The marquise turned pale at beholding what she had never thought to see again, and a profound silence reigned in the banqueting-room, whilst Fouquet made no sign in dismissal of the gorgeously attired servants who swarmed like bees about the huge buffets and side-tables.

'Gentlemen,' he said, 'this plate which you see was once the property of Madame de Bellière, who, seeing one of her friends in distress, sent to the goldsmith's all this gold and silver, together with the heap of precious stones now in front of her. This act of devoted friendship will, I feel sure, be readily appreciated by such friends as yourselves. Happy is the man who finds himself so greatly beloved. Let us drink to the health of Madame de Bellière.'

These words evoked a tremendous outburst of applause, and poor Madame de Bellière sank back in her chair in an almost fainting condition.

'And next,' cried Pélisson, who was easily touched by any good action as he was charmed by anything beautiful, 'let us drink to him who inspired this noble conduct, for such a man is worthy of all the affection that can be lavished on him.'

Then came the turn of the marquise. Pale and yet smiling, with an effort she rose from her seat and held out her glass with unsteady hand until her trembling fingers touched those of Monsieur Fouquet, whilst she sought to read in his eyes all the love for her with which his tender heart overflowed.

Having begun in this gallant fashion, the supper soon became a fête whereat none had occasion to force his wit, for witty speeches rose spontaneously to the lips of all. La Fontaine forgot his beloved Gorgny wine, and allowed Vatel to fill his glass with wines from the Rhone and with those of Spain; and the Abbé Fouquet melted to such a degree that Gourville said to him: 'Have a care, Monsieur l'Abbé; if you become much more *tender*, we shall be tempted to eat you.'

The hours passed so quickly and pleasantly that, contrary to his general custom, Monsieur Fouquet did not rise from the table until after dessert. He beamed upon his friends in that state of pleasurable excitement when the heart, rather than the head, is affected, and, for the first time that evening, he looked at the clock. Suddenly, above the buzz of conversation, the sound was heard of a carriage entering the courtyard.

Fouquet pricked up his ears, and turned his head towards the antechamber. He seemed to be aware of a footstep which, instead of touching the ground, trod heavily upon his heart. Instinctively he withdrew his foot with which he was gently pressing that of Madame de Bellière.

'Monsieur d'Herblay, Bishop of Vannes,' announced the usher, and the dark and pensive face of Aramis appeared in the doorway, between two wreaths of which the connecting thread had been destroyed by the flame of a lamp.

CHAPTER 9

*Monsieur Mazarin's receipt*

FOUQUET was about to utter an exclamation of joy at the appearance of another friend, but the grave aspect of Aramis checked his enthusiasm. Collecting himself, however, he greeted the new arrival, saying: 'If the noise we are making is not too much for you, perhaps you will sit down and take some refreshment.'

'Monseigneur,' replied Aramis, courteously, 'I must offer you my apologies for intruding upon your convivial party; but I must ask you to grant me, at your convenience, a few minutes' conversation upon a matter of importance.'

'Business before everything, Monsieur d'Herblay,' answered Fouquet. 'I consider that we are very fortunate when business demands attention only at the end of a feast.'

As he spoke, he gave his hand to Madame de Bellière, who was looking at him with something of uneasiness, and conducted her into an adjoining apartment, where he left her in the care of two or three of the least riotous of his companions. Then, taking Aramis by the arm, he led him into his cabinet. Once there, Aramis cast aside all formality, and, throwing himself into a chair, said abruptly: 'Whom do you think I have seen this evening?'

'My dear chevalier, whenever you begin a conversation in this manner, I feel sure that you have something disagreeable to say to me.'

'This time, at all events, you are not mistaken, my dear friend.'

'Don't keep me in suspense,' added Fouquet, apathetically.

'Well, then, I have seen Madame de Chevreuse.'

'The old duchess?'

'Yes.'

'You are sure it was not her ghost?'

'Oh no; it was the old she-wolf in the flesh.'

'Without teeth?'

'Possibly; but certainly not without claws.'

'Well, she cannot want to rend me with them. I am not miserly as regards women who are not prudes. That is a quality which always commends itself, even to the woman who no longer seeks to inspire love.'

'Madame de Chevreuse knows quite well that you are no miser, and, in fact, her object is to get some money out of you.'

'But under what pretext?'

'Oh, pretexts are never hard to find. Listen to hers.'

'I am all attention.'

'It seems,' continued Aramis, 'that Madame de Chevreuse is in possession of some letters from Monsieur Mazarin.'

'That does not cause me the least surprise; the prelate was quite a ladies' man.'

'Yes, but these particular letters do not relate to his love-affairs. They deal with financial matters.'

'That is still less interesting.'

'Do you mean to say that you have no suspicion of what I am going to tell you?'

'Not the least.'

'Have you never heard of a man being accused of misappropriating the public money?'

'Yes, of course; hundreds of times. Why, since I have been in office, I have heard of nothing else. Even you yourself, my dear M. d'Herblay, are reproached, as a bishop, for impiety, and, as a musketeer, for want of courage; whilst a minister of finance is for ever under suspicion of having embezzled the public funds.'

'But, according to the duchess, Monsieur Mazarin brings definite charges.'

'Let us hear what he has to say.'

'He says that you would find it difficult to account for the expenditure of something like thirteen million.'

'Thirteen million!' said Fouquet, leaning back in his chair, the more conveniently to stare at the ceiling. 'Thirteen million! How on earth am I to distinguish them from all the rest of the money which I am accused of having stolen?'

'Pray, do not treat it as a joke, my dear sir, it is a very serious matter. It is certain that the duchess is in possession of these letters, and it is equally clear that they are genuine and compromising, since she is asking five hundred thousand livres for them.'

'Oh, one can have a very pretty scandal hatched up for a sum like that,' replied Fouquet; 'and now I think I understand what you are driving at,' and he indulged in a hearty laugh.

'So much the better,' said Aramis, slightly reassured.

'The story of those thirteen million comes back to me. Yes, certainly, I remember all about it distinctly.'

'I am delighted to hear you say so. Let us see.'

'Well, then, this is what happened. Signor Mazarin – God rest his soul – upon a certain occasion, made a profit of thirteen million upon a concession of disputed lands in the Valtellina;[37] he caused this sum to be cancelled in the record of receipts, had it sent to me, and then obtained it again from me for the expenses of the war.'

'In that case, the expenditure of the money is sufficiently accounted for.'

'No; the cardinal had the money placed to my account, and sent me a receipt for it.'

'Which receipt you still have?'

'Of course,' said Fouquet, rising and unlocking a drawer in a huge bureau inlaid with gold and mother-of-pearl.

'What I admire in you,' said Aramis, much impressed, 'is, first, your wonderful memory; next, your perfect imperturbability; and, lastly, the perfect order which prevails in your method of conducting business. You, too, who are a poet before everything.'

'Yes,' replied Fouquet, 'but I am orderly simply because I am lazy, for, when I can lay my hand upon everything, I am saved the trouble of hunting about for what I want. For instance, I know that Mazarin's receipt is in this drawer – number three, under letter M. I simply open the drawer, and there it is. I could find it in the dark.' And without a moment's hesitation he selected a bundle of papers from amongst those in the drawer. 'Moreover,' he said, 'I can remember the kind of paper upon which the receipt was written; it was thick, somewhat crumpled, was gilt edged, and the cardinal dropped a blot of ink upon one of the figures in the date. H'm,' he continued, turning over the papers, 'one would think that the receipt knows that I am looking for it, and is hiding itself out of sheer contrariness.'

Aramis was on his legs in a moment.

'It is certainly very strange,' said Fouquet.

'Perhaps your memory is at fault, my dear sir. Suppose you examine another bundle.'

Fouquet ran, once more, through the papers in his hand; then, the blood left his cheeks.

'Don't be so positive as to that particular packet,' said Aramis, 'look through some of the others.'

'It would be quite useless; I am never mistaken. No one but myself has the handling of papers of this kind, and no one else knows how to open this drawer, which is, as you see, a secret one.'

'What conclusion do you arrive at?' asked Aramis, much concerned.

'That Mazarin's receipt has been stolen from me. Madame de Chevreuse is right, chevalier. I have embezzled the public money. I have stolen thirteen million from the state coffers. I am very much afraid that I am a thief, Monsieur d'Herblay.'

'Sir, I beg of you to be calm.'

'How can I help being agitated, chevalier; have I not good cause to be so? Legal proceedings will be instituted; I shall be impeached and convicted, and then your friend, the minister of finance, will follow to Montfaucon his colleague Enguerrand de Marigny, and his predecessor Samblançay.'[38]

'Not so fast,' said Aramis, smiling.

'How, not so fast! What do you suppose Madame de Chevreuse will do with the letters? You have refused to buy them, have you not?'

'Yes, I refused point-blank. Well, I suppose she will try to sell them to Monsieur Colbert.'

'Very likely; we shall see.'

'I said *suppose*, but I might have said *I am sure*, because, when she left me, I had her followed. First she returned to her own house, and, from thence, by a back door, she went to Monsieur Colbert's residence in the Rue Croix-des-Petits-Champs.'

'And then will follow impeachment, scandal and dishonour. The whole will fall upon me like a thunderbolt, blindly, cruelly, pitilessly.'

Aramis walked across to Fouquet, who sat trembling in his chair opposite the open drawers, and, placing his hand on his shoulder, said kindly: 'Do not forget that Monsieur Fouquet's position is entirely different from that of Samblançay and Marigny.'

'In what way?' asked Fouquet.

'The ministers in question were arrested, tried, convicted and sentenced; whereas, in your case, nothing of the kind will happen.'

'How can that be? Surely a peculator must always be a criminal.'

'Criminals who find their way to a "city of refuge" have nothing to fear.'

'Am I, then, to fly the country?'

'I am not suggesting it; but you seem to forget that proceedings of this kind are instituted by Parlement on the advice of the Procureur-Général, and that you happen to be Procureur-Général yourself. Well, now, unless you are anxious to prosecute yourself – '

'Damnation!' roared Fouquet, dashing down his fist upon the table.

'Why, whatever is the matter?'

'The matter is that I am no longer Procureur-Général.'

It was now the turn of Aramis to grow pale; he became perfectly livid; he wrung his hands in his agitation, and turned upon Fouquet a wan and haggard look.

'Do I understand you to say that *you are no longer* Procureur-Général?' he asked, speaking slowly, and laying stress on each separate syllable.

'Yes.'

'Since when?'

'Four or five hours ago.'

'For heaven's sake be careful,' said Aramis. 'I think you cannot be in possession of your right senses; collect yourself, my friend.'

'I tell you,' said Fouquet, seriously, 'that, but a few hours since, someone, who was introduced to me by my friends, offered me fourteen hundred thousand livres for my post, and that I sold him the appointment.'

Aramis was absolutely dumbfounded; his intelligent and cynical face assumed an aspect of mournful surprise and dismay which had more effect upon Fouquet than could have been produced by any expressions of expostulation or reproach.

'Are you in want of money, then?' he asked, after a pause.

'Yes, to pay a debt of honour;' and he related to Aramis, in a few words, the story of Madame de Bellière's generous conduct, and of the manner in which he felt himself bound to recompense her for her act of devotion.

'It shows a fine trait in your character,' said Aramis, 'but it must have cost you a large sum of money?'

'Exactly the price of my post,' said Fouquet, 'fourteen hundred thousand livres.'

'And you accepted that sum without a moment's reflection? Oh, the imprudence of it, my friend!'

'I have not actually received the money yet, but I shall have it tomorrow.'

'Then, the transaction is not positively completed?'

'Practically it is, since I have given the goldsmith a draft upon my treasury payable at noon tomorrow, and the purchaser's money will be in my hands between six and seven o'clock in the morning.'

'Heaven be praised!' cried Aramis, clapping his hands, 'nothing is finally settled since you have not yet been paid.'

'But the jeweller?'

'You will receive the fourteen hundred thousand livres from me at a quarter to twelve tomorrow.'

'One moment; six o'clock tomorrow is the hour appointed for me to sign the deed of sale.'

'Well, you will simply decline to sign it; that's all.'

'But I have given my word, chevalier.'

'Then, you will take your word back again, and the incident will be closed.'

'And you counsel *me*, *Fouquet*, to break my word!'

'Why, sir!' returned Aramis, almost angrily, 'I believe I have some pretensions to be called a man of honour. As a soldier, I have risked my life five hundred times, and, as a priest, I have rendered still greater services to God, to the state, and to mankind. The value of a man's word is commensurate with the worth of the man who gives it. When he keeps it, it is pure gold, and when he does not choose to keep it, it is a trenchant blade. With it he defends his life as with an honourable weapon, considering that, when he breaks it, he is in danger of death, and runs more risks than his adversary gains profits. Then, sir, he appeals to heaven, and the justice of his cause.'

Fouquet bowed his head. 'I am,' he said, 'but a humble, if self-opinionated, Breton; I recognise that your intelligence is superior to my own, and feel a respect for it which is not unmingled with awe. I do not pretend that I keep my word solely at the dictates of my conscience. To do so has become habitual to me; and the habit is one which even commonplace individuals may be single-minded enough to regard with approval. It is my sole virtue; do not try to rob me of it.'

'Then you seriously intend to ratify the sale of this appointment in the full knowledge that you are parting with an absolute protection against the schemes of your enemies?'

'Yes, I shall sign.'

'And you will give yourself up, bound hand and foot, for a false sentiment of honour which the strictest casuists would not hesitate to disregard?'

'I shall, certainly, sign.'

With a deep sigh, Aramis glared around with the look of a man who wanted to smash something.

'There is one way still left,' he said, 'and I earnestly hope you will not refuse to avail yourself of it.'

'Assuredly not, so it be honourable, as everything is which is proposed by you, my friend.'

'I see nothing dishonourable in repudiating the whole transaction. Is the intending purchaser a friend?'

'Certainly, but – '

'But, if you will only allow me to manage the business, I don't despair of being able to arrange matters satisfactorily.'

'Oh! I will leave the business entirely in your hands.'

'Who and what is this man with whom you have been in negotiation?'

'I don't know whether you are acquainted with the Parlement?'

'I know most of the members. Is your friend one of the presidents?'

'No, merely a counsellor.'

'What is his name?'

'Vanel.'

Aramis turned purple with indignation. 'What!' he shouted, 'Vanel! the husband of Marguerite Vanel?'

'Exactly.'

'The husband of your former mistress?'

'Yes, my dear friend. She has long wanted to be called Madame la Procureuse-Générale. I think I owe as much as that to poor Vanel; besides which I shall be a gainer, since I shall confer a pleasure upon his wife.'

Aramis walked straight up to Fouquet, and held out his hand.

'Do you know,' he said, 'the name of Madame Vanel's present lover?'

'Oh! has she a new lover? I was not aware of it. No, I've no idea who it is.'

'It is Jean Baptiste Colbert. He is Secretary of Finance; he lives in the Rue Croix-des-Petits-Champs, and Madame de Chevreuse went there this evening to try to sell him Mazarin's letters.'

'Good heavens!' said Fouquet, mopping his forehead, down which a stream of perspiration was running.

'Now you begin to understand, don't you?'

'That I am utterly ruined – yes.'

'And do you still think it worth while to be so particular about keeping your word?'

'No,' said Fouquet, 'I do not.'

'One cannot help admiring these obstinate people, after all,' said Aramis to himself.

Fouquet held out his hand.

At that moment a handsome tortoiseshell clock, ornamented with gilt figures, which stood upon a console table opposite the fireplace, struck the hour of six in the morning, and, at the same time, a door in the vestibule was heard to open.

'Monsieur Vanel,' said Gourville, at the door of the cabinet, 'has arrived and wishes to know if monseigneur will receive him.'

Fouquet turned away his eyes from those of Aramis.

'Let Monsieur Vanel be admitted,' he said.

CHAPTER 10

## *Monsieur Colbert's rough draft*

VANEL, who entered the room at this point in the conversation, represented, so far as Aramis and Fouquet were concerned, the full stop which ends a sentence. But, for Vanel, the presence of Aramis in Monsieur Fouquet's cabinet had another signification altogether.

At his first step into the room, his attention was at once attracted by the clear-cut and firm features of the Bishop of Vannes, and his look, at first one of curiosity simply, quickly became one of keen scrutiny. Fouquet himself, a true diplomat, and perfectly self-possessed, had already, through sheer strength of will, caused every trace of the emotion which the revelation of Aramis had called up to disappear from his face. He was no longer a man overwhelmed by misfortune and obliged to resort to expedients; he stood with head erect, and with a courteous gesture signed to Vanel to come in. He was the prime minister at home. Aramis knew the minister well, and no sensibility or breadth of mind which he might display had any power to astonish him. For the present, he held himself in reserve, intending, however, presently to take a more active part in the conversation – a difficult role for a man to play who looks on and listens with a view to learn and make himself master of the situation.

Vanel was evidently extremely nervous; he walked into the middle of the room, and seemed to bow, in a bewildered manner, to everything as well as to everybody.

'I have come,' said he.

'You are punctuality itself, Monsieur Vanel,' replied Fouquet.

'In business, monseigneur,' said Vanel, 'I consider punctuality to be a virtue.'

'You are quite right, sir.'

'Pardon me,' interrupted Aramis, 'but is not this the gentleman who is anxious to buy an appointment?' And he indicated Vanel with a careless motion of the hand.

'It is I,' replied Vanel, somewhat taken aback at the arrogant manner in which Aramis put the question. 'But may I venture to ask to whom I have the honour – '

'You can address me as monseigneur,' replied Aramis, in freezing tones.

Vanel bowed.

'Now, gentlemen, now,' said Fouquet, 'have done with ceremony. Let us proceed to business.'

'Monseigneur may observe,' said Vanel, 'that I only await his pleasure.'

'On the contrary, it is I who am waiting,' replied Fouquet.

'For what is monseigneur waiting?'

'I am thinking that, perhaps, you may have something to suggest to me.'

'Oho,' thought Vanel, 'he has been reflecting, and the game is up;' but, pulling himself together, he said aloud, 'No, monseigneur, I have nothing to say beyond what I said yesterday, and am ready to repeat today.'

'To be perfectly frank, Monsieur Vanel, does not this arrangement handicap you rather heavily?'

'Well, certainly, monseigneur, fourteen hundred thousand livres is a large sum of money.'

'So large, indeed,' said Fouquet, 'that I have reflected.'

'You have reflected, monseigneur?' cried Vanel, sharply.

'Yes, I have reflected that you may not be in a position to find so much money.'

'But, indeed, monseigneur – '

'Don't let it distress you, Monsieur Vanel. I am the last person in the world to find fault with a man who does not meet an obligation if it is really out of his power to do so.'

'In this case, monseigneur, you might blame me with perfect justice, for a man who makes engagements which he is unable to meet is either culpably reckless, or a fool, pure and simple; and I have always considered that a bargain, when it is once agreed to, is as good as carried out.'

Fouquet coloured up, and Aramis gave vent to a grunt of dissatisfaction.

'It will not do, however, to unduly exaggerate such ideas as these, monsieur,' said the minister, 'for the mind of man is changeable, and prone to little caprices which may be not only quite excusable, but sometimes even commendable; and a man may have wished for yesterday, something that today he no longer desires.'

Vanel broke into a cold perspiration.

'Monseigneur!' he stammered out; whilst Aramis, delighted that Fouquet was holding his own so stoutly, rested an elbow upon a marble console, and began to play with a small gold knife with a malachite handle.

Fouquet did not hurry himself, but, after a short silence, said: 'Come, my dear Monsieur Vanel, let me explain the situation to you.'

Vanel shook with apprehension.

'You are a good fellow, and, like myself, a man of the world. Yesterday, I wished to sell.'

'Monseigneur did more than that; he actually sold.'

'But, today, I ask you as a favour to let me off the bargain.'

'You have given me your hand on it, monseigneur.'

'I admit it,' said Fouquet, 'and that is why I entreat you, as a favour, not to insist upon the arrangement being carried out.'

Fouquet stopped short, for the mere utterance of the words *I entreat you* nearly choked him, and he did not, for the moment, perceive the effect they had produced; whilst Aramis, still playing with his knife, fixed a look upon Vanel which seemed to penetrate to the inmost recesses of his heart.

'Monseigneur,' said Vanel, with a low bow, 'I am deeply conscious of the honour you do me in consulting me upon a matter which is already completed, but – '

'Do not say *but*, dear Monsieur Vanel.'

'I am sorry, monseigneur, but I have brought the whole of the money with me,' replied Vanel, as he unfastened a large pocket-book.

'Observe, monseigneur,' he continued. 'Here is a deed relating to the sale of some property which I have just effected on behalf of my wife; and here is a draft bearing the necessary signatures, and payable at sight – that is to say, here is the ready money. In a word, then, the business is settled.'

'My dear Monsieur Vanel, there is no business in the world, however important it may be, which cannot be cancelled in order to oblige a man who, by this means, may be made a sincere friend.'

'No doubt,' grumbled Vanel.

'And the more important the service so rendered, the more binding does the friendship become. I hope I make myself understood; and now let me hear your decision.'

Vanel held his peace.

Meanwhile Aramis had still continued his scrutiny. Vanel's thin face, his sunken eyes and arched eyebrows had revealed to the Bishop of Vannes a type of man at once greedy and ambitious. To use one passion as a weapon against the other was the method employed by Aramis. He saw that Fouquet was beaten and demoralised, and, thus newly armed, he threw himself into the thick of the fight.

'Pardon me,' he said, 'if I point out that Monsieur Vanel's interests are directly opposed to the cancelling of the agreement.'

Vanel looked at the bishop in wonder, little expecting a backer to spring from such a quarter, and Fouquet also regarded him with mild surprise.

'You see, monseigneur,' said Aramis, 'that, in order to raise the purchase money of this appointment, Monsieur Vanel has been compelled to dispose of some property belonging to his wife. Well that, in itself, is a serious matter, because a man cannot realise fourteen hundred thousand livres at a moment's notice, except at a considerable sacrifice, and possibly great inconvenience.'

'That is quite true,' assented Vanel, eagerly; and the keen eyes of Aramis read the secret which lay in the depths of his soul.

'Such inconvenience,' continued Aramis, 'sometimes takes the form of forced expenditure, in which case the sum thus disbursed should be the first thing to be taken into consideration.'

'Yes, yes,' said Fouquet, who began to see what Aramis was driving at.

Vanel said not a word, for he, too, now understood. Aramis took note of his stolid demeanour.

'Oho! old ugly-mug,' he said to himself; 'I see how the land lies. You're waiting to learn how much we're going to offer you. But don't be afraid; I shall fire such a volley of crown-pieces into you that you will be obliged to strike your colours.'

'We really ought to beg Monsieur Vanel's acceptance of a hundred thousand crowns at once,' said Monsieur Fouquet, impulsively.

It was a very handsome offer, with which even a prince might have been satisfied. A hundred thousand crowns, at that period, was a dowry for a king's daughter. Still Vanel made no sign.

'We have caught a Tartar,' thought the bishop; 'the rascal is standing out for the whole fourteen hundred thousand livres, and we shall have to give it him.' And he signed to Fouquet accordingly.

'I fear you must have spent considerably more than the sum I mentioned just now, Monsieur Vanel,' said Fouquet, taking the hint; 'and, besides, money is very dear. Yes, you must be a good round sum out of pocket by this sale of property. Bless my soul! what could I have been thinking of? *Five* hundred thousand livres is what I should have said; and even then I shall consider myself your debtor.'

Vanel remained utterly dumb and impassive. There was not so much as the twitch of a muscle in his stolid face. Aramis gave Fouquet a look full of meaning; then he darted at Vanel, and seized him by the lapels of his coat.

'Look here, Monsieur Vanel,' he said; 'it is neither the worry, nor the money, nor the sale of your property that is troubling you. I know what it is; therefore listen attentively to what I am going to say to you.'

'Yes, monseigneur,' answered Vanel; and he trembled before Aramis, whose piercing eyes seemed to be burning a hole in him.

'I offer you, then, in the name of the minister, not *three*, nor *five* hundred thousand livres, but *a million. A million!* Do you understand that?'

'A million!' repeated Vanel, turning pale.

'Yes, a million; that is to say, at the current rate of interest, an income of sixty-five thousand livres.'

'I think, monsieur,' said Fouquet, 'that you will hardly refuse such an offer as that. Say, then, do you accept?'

'It is impossible,' murmured Vanel.

Aramis bit his lips, and a sort of white cloud seemed to pass over his face – a cloud behind which it was easy to imagine thunder. He still retained his hold upon Vanel.

'You have bought this appointment for fourteen hundred thousand livres – is not that so? Very well, that sum shall be given to you, and, in addition, you are offered a million, so that, having paid a visit to Monsieur Fouquet and been permitted to touch his hand, you will be just upon a million and a half in pocket. Honour and profit at the same time, Monsieur Vanel.'

'I cannot do it,' said Vanel, in a hollow voice.

'Very good,' replied Aramis, letting go his hold upon the coat so suddenly that Vanel staggered back a few paces – 'very good. Your refusal makes the object with which you came here perfectly obvious.'

'Perfectly plain,' assented Fouquet.

'But – ' stammered Vanel, endeavouring to regain his composure before these two honourable gentlemen.

'The fellow has found his voice, I believe!' said Aramis, with the tone of an emperor.

'Fellow!' repeated Vanel.

'Scoundrel, I should have said,' replied Aramis, with his customary self-possession. 'Come, let us see this precious deed of sale. I presume you have it in your pocket, in readiness, in the same way in which an assassin carries a pistol or dagger hidden beneath his cloak.'

Vanel uttered some inarticulate sound.

'That will do,' cried Fouquet. 'Produce the deed.'

Vanel, after fumbling in his pocket with trembling hand, at length produced his pocket-book, from which, as he handed the deed to

Fouquet, another paper escaped, and fell to the floor, and upon this document, Aramis, who recognised the handwriting upon it, immediately pounced.

'It is only the rough draft of the deed,' said Vanel, in explanation.

'So I see,' replied Aramis; 'and I see, also,' he added, with a smile about as sweet as a cut from a whip, 'that it is in the handwriting of a no less distinguished personage than Monsieur Colbert. Look at it, monseigneur.'

He handed the paper to Fouquet, who at once recognised the handwriting. Covered with erasures, corrections and marginal notes, this document bore witness to Monsieur Colbert's conspiracy, and revealed the whole plot to his victim.

'The devil!' exclaimed Fouquet; and Vanel, utterly dumfounded, seemed to be looking for a hole to hide in.

'Well,' said Aramis, 'if your name were not Fouquet, and that of your enemy Colbert, and if this dirty thief were not standing before us, I should counsel you to repudiate the whole business, for such a proof of treachery is ample to absolve you from your promise, but these ruffians who think you were afraid, and would fear you less than they do now; therefore I say *sign*.' And he handed him a pen.

Fouquet pressed his friend's hand, but instead of taking Vanel's deed, he took Colbert's rough draft of it.

'No, not that paper,' said Aramis, quickly; 'this is the one. The other is too valuable to part with.'

'No, no,' replied Fouquet. 'I will sign the paper which is in Monsieur Colbert's own handwriting, and, moreover, I will mark it, "Handwriting approved".' He signed it. 'Here it is, Monsieur Vanel,' he said.

Vanel took the paper, put the money on the table, and turned to leave the room.

'Stop a moment,' said Aramis; 'are you quite sure that the amount is correct? Money should always be counted, Monsieur Vanel, especially when Monsieur Colbert gives money to ladies. The excellent Colbert is not nearly so generous as Monsieur Fouquet.' And Aramis, spelling over every word, and examining each letter of the order for payment, distilled all his rage and contempt, drop by drop, upon the wretched Vanel, who spent a very uncomfortable quarter of an hour under the process. Aramis then intimated that he might go, not by word of mouth, but with a gesture such as he would have used to dismiss a beggar or order a servant from his presence. When Vanel had gone, the minister and the bishop stood for a moment looking at each other in silence.

'Well,' said Aramis, who was the first to speak, 'what do you think of a man who, being about to fight an enemy who is well armed and furiously incensed against him, comes upon the ground unprotected, throws down his arms, and kisses his hand to his adversary? Upon my word, Monsieur Fouquet, it is a weapon that rogues often use against honest men, and it pays them well to do it. Men of honour, therefore, would be quite justified if they acted in bad faith when opposed to such scoundrels. You would see what power it would give them, without depriving them of the right to be called honourable men.'

'Such conduct would be regarded as disgraceful,' replied Fouquet.

'Not a bit of it,' said Aramis; 'it would be looked upon merely as playing the coquette with probity. However, since you have finished with this fellow Vanel, since you have deprived yourself of the gratification of making him bite the dust by repudiating your obligation, and have placed in his hands, to be used against you, the only thing that can ruin you – '

'Oh, my friend,' interrupted Fouquet, sadly, 'you remind me of the philosophical tutor of whom La Fontaine was telling us the other day. He saw his little pupil drowning, and at once proceeded to deliver a discourse to him under three headings.'

Aramis smiled, and replied, 'Philosopher – yes, drowning child – yes; but you shall presently see the child whose life it was possible to save. But, first of all, let us speak of business.'

Fouquet looked at him with an air of astonishment.

'Did you not once,' continued Aramis, 'confide in me a project which you entertained of giving a fête at Vaux?'[39]

'Ah!' sighed Fouquet; 'that was in my prosperous days.'

'A fête to which, I think, the king did you the honour to invite himself of his own accord?'

'No, my dear bishop, a fête to which the king was advised by Monsieur Colbert to invite himself.'

'Ah, quite so, in order that it might thus be made so costly an affair as to ruin you.'

'Yes, that was the idea. Well, in my prosperous days, as I was saying just now, I was seized with a desire to dazzle the eyes of my enemies with the wealth of my resources. I cherished the notion of striking them with astonishment by making millions where they could foresee nothing but bankruptcy. But now I must set my affairs in order, and render an account of my stewardship to the state and to the king. I must adopt cheese-paring tactics. I shall have to show the world that I know how to manipulate deniers as well as how to deal with bags of pistoles, and from tomorrow, with my carriages and horses sold, my estates mortgaged, and my personal expenses cut down to the lowest possible figure – '

'From tomorrow, my dear friend,' interrupted Aramis, 'you will give your undivided attention to the preparations for this splendid fête at Vaux, which will one day be spoken of as being, perhaps, the most magnificent incident in your career.'

'Really, you must be mad, Chevalier d'Herblay.'

'What, I? Oh, I'm sure you know better than that.'

'But just consider what it would cost to give a fête, even the simplest one, at Vaux. From four to five million!'

'I am not talking about the simplest one, my dear Fouquet.'

'But since the fête would be given in honour of the king,' said Fouquet, who quite misunderstood the meaning of Aramis, 'it could not possibly be a simple one.'

'Quite so; it would have to be on a scale of the utmost splendour.'

'In which case, I should have to spend between ten and twelve million.'

'You will spend twenty million, if necessary,' replied Aramis, with the utmost coolness.

'But where on earth should I get the money from?' cried Fouquet.

'That is my affair, my dear Monsieur Fouquet, and need not occasion you a moment's uneasiness. The money will be at your disposal before you have time to countermand your orders for the fête.'

'Chevalier, chevalier!' said Fouquet, feeling faint and giddy, 'whither would you lead me?'

'To the other side of the chasm upon the brink of which you stand,' replied the Bishop of Vannes. 'Hold fast to my cloak, and don't be frightened.'

'Why did you not say all this sooner, Aramis? The time has passed when a million would have been my salvation.'

'And the time has now come when I can offer you twenty,' said the bishop. 'That is the state of the case, and the explanation is very simple. At the time to which you refer, I had not the necessary million at my disposal, but today I can easily raise twenty million.'

'May heaven hear you, and save me!'

'Oh, heaven always listens to me,' replied Aramis, with the inscrutable smile that was habitual to him.

'Well, I place myself entirely in your hands,' said Fouquet.

'Oh, I don't understand things at all in that way,' replied Aramis. 'It is I who am altogether at *your* service. In a business of this kind you are, I consider, by far the more capable man of the two, and you shall, therefore, have the arrangement of the fête down to its smallest details. Only – '

'Ah! *only*,' said Fouquet, who was quite alive to the possible value of the condition to be imposed.

'Well, whilst you issue your commands, I reserve to myself the right of seeing that they are properly carried out; that is to say, you will constitute me, for the occasion, your major-domo and general factotum – something between captain of the guards and chief steward. I shall see that everything is properly done, and shall have the keys of the doors. You will, of course, give your orders, but you will give them to me only, and I shall convey them to the proper quarters. You understand?'

'Not very clearly, I am afraid,' said Fouquet.

'Anyhow, you agree?'

'Oh, certainly.'

'Thank you; that is enough. Now go and make out your list of invitations.'

'Whom shall I invite?'

'Everyone.'

## CHAPTER II

### *In which the author deems it is high time to return to the Vicomte de Bragelonne*

IN THE COURSE of this history, as our readers will have observed, the adventures of a past and of a new generation have been allowed to develop side by side. To the former belongs the reflection of the glory of a bygone time, and the bitter experiences of life, together with that peace which pervades the heart and suffers the blood to flow tranquilly beneath scars which once were gaping wounds. To the latter, the conflicts between love and self-love, grievous disappointments and joys ineffable: to them is life itself, in place of the recollection of it. If, therefore, considerable variety has been presented to the reader of the episodes related, the cause will be found in the diversity of tints offered by the twofold palette from which have been painted these two pictures, in which bright and sombre hues blend harmoniously. The repose of the one is in agreeable contrast to the emotion induced by the other. After taking counsel with the grey-beards, to romp with the children is a pleasant relief.

Again, if the chapter upon which we are now engaged does not, at first sight, appear to have any direct connection with some of those which have preceded it, we shall trouble ourselves no more about the apparent incongruity than did Ruysdael,[40] who would paint an autumn sky with the same brushes used for depicting a scene of springtime.

We will ask our readers, therefore, to take up the thread of our story at the point where we last left Raoul de Bragelonne.[41]

In a state of utter mental disorder, with no power to concentrate his thoughts, and without any definite idea as to his future line of action, Raoul fled from the scene which had just come to an end in La Vallière's apartment. The king, Montalais, Louise, that room, that unaccountable exclusion, Montalais's terror and the fury of the king, all seemed to unite in foreboding calamity. But of what kind? He had left London upon learning that there was danger in the air, and had found, upon his arrival, incontestable evidence that the rumour was not without foundation. Was not this enough for any ordinary lover? Undoubtedly; but it was not enough to intimidate Raoul, whose brave heart was dismayed at no danger to be encountered in defence of the woman he loved. Raoul did not adopt the course which jealous or less diffident lovers than himself might have taken. He did not go to La Vallière and say, 'Louise, do you no longer love me? Do you love another?' Courageous, and as staunch in friendship as he was true in love; punctilious respecter of his own word, and placing unquestioning confidence in the word of another, he said to himself, 'De Guiche wrote to warn me; de Guiche must understand what is going on. I will go and ask him what he knows, and tell him what I have seen.'

It was not a long journey to take. Two days since, de Guiche had been conveyed from Fontainebleau to Paris. He was recovering from his wound, and could already move a little about his room.

He uttered an exclamation of pleasure as Raoul's friendly face greeted him from the doorway.

Raoul, on the other hand, could not conceal the distress he felt at the suffering which his friend had evidently gone through. A word, and the gesture with which he declined the assistance of his friend's arm, were sufficient to inform Raoul of what had happened.

'Ah! it is always thus,' said Raoul, taking a seat by the side of his friend; 'one loves, and dies.'

'No, not always,' replied de Guiche, with a smile. 'Not in my case, at all events. See, I can walk without assistance, and can press you in my arms.'

'Ah! but, in spite of that, I understand.'

'And I understand also. You think that I am unhappy, Raoul?'

'I fear so.'

'But I am not; I am the happiest of men. It is true that I suffer in my body, but not in my heart or mind. Oh, if you only knew! I swear to you that I am the happiest man alive.'

'Well, so much the better,' replied Raoul. 'I only hope that your happiness may last.'

'Oh! I have already tasted happiness enough to last my lifetime.'

'Yes, that may be, so far as you are concerned; but what of *her*?'

'Look here, my friend, I love her, and – but you are not listening.'

'I really beg your pardon.'

'I see that you are preoccupied.'

'Well, yes, I am slightly. In the first place, your state of health – '

'Oh, it isn't that.'

'My dear fellow, I don't think *you* have any right to question what I say in this manner;' and he laid such stress on the word *you* that his friend at once guessed the nature of his malady, and saw how difficult it would be to find a remedy for it.

'You say that, Raoul, with reference to what I wrote to you.'

'Well, yes; but we will discuss that subject when you have finished telling me your own story.'

'My dear friend, I am altogether at your disposal, and at once.'

'Many thanks. As for me, I am in a frantic hurry – I am positively on fire. I have come here from London in half the time that the state couriers usually allow themselves for the journey. Now, tell me, what was your object in sending for me?'

'Nothing, my dear fellow, except that I was dying to see you.'

'Well, here I am.'

'Then all is well.'

'I think you must have had some other motive.'

'No, really.'

'De Guiche!'

'On my honour.'

'But, surely, you have not torn all hope out of my heart – you have not exposed me to the wrath of the king for an infraction of his commands – you have not, in a word, inspired me with jealousy, merely to say to me, "All is well; you may rest in peace!" '

'I do not tell you to rest in peace; but be assured that I neither can, nor will, tell you anything to the contrary.'

'My dear fellow, what do take me for?'

'I don't understand you.'

'If you know anything, why hide it from me? If you know nothing, what induced you to write me that warning letter?'

'There is a good deal in what you say. I admit that I was wrong, and I am very sorry, Raoul. It does not seem much to write to a friend and say, "Come;" but to meet him face to face, and to witness his agitation as he breathlessly awaits news that I dare not give him is quite another thing.'

'*Dare* not! I, at least, have courage, if you have none,' said Raoul, desperately.

'Now you are doing me an injustice, and appear to forget that you are speaking to a wounded man, and to one who loves you. For heaven's sake, be calm. I ask you to come, and you are here, but pray refrain from pressing me any further.'

'You told me to come, hoping that I should find out the rest for myself. Is it not so?'

'But – '

'Well, I have found out, or, at least, I think I have.'

'Ah! that is it; you only *think* you have; and if you feel any doubt about it yourself, what remains for me to do?'

'I have seen La Vallière in distress, Montalais terrified, and the king – '

'The king?'

'Yes. Ah! you no longer look me in the face. Therein lies the danger, does it not? It is the king!'

'I do not say so.'

'Ah! yes, you say it a thousand times over. For mercy's sake, my friend, my only friend, let me know the truth. My heart is torn to pieces. I am dying of despair!'

'If that is so, my dear Raoul, it removes a great weight from my own heart, and I will tell you all, because I am sure that the knowledge of it will be positive consolation in comparison with what you feel now.'

'Pray go on; I am all attention.'

'Well, I can only tell you what you might learn from the first person you meet.'

'Is that so? Then the matter must be talked about.'

'Before saying that it is talked about,' said de Guiche, 'let us see whether there is much to talk about, after all. I declare to you that I believe there is nothing that does not admit of a most innocent explanation; perhaps a walk – '

'What! a walk with the king?'

'Well, what of that? The king frequently walks with the ladies of the court, without anything – '

'I tell you, de Guiche, that, if nothing unusual had taken place, you would not have written to me as you did.'

'I think it would have been better for the king to have taken shelter from the storm, than to have stood before La Vallière with uncovered head; but then, the king is so courteous – '

'Oh! de Guiche. You break my heart.'

'Then let us speak no more of it.'

'No, go on; I suppose this walk was followed by others?'

'Well, no – that is to say, yes – there was, of course, that little episode of the oak tree,[42] if that is what you mean; but I know nothing about it.'

Raoul stood up, and de Guiche, in spite of his weakness, followed his example.

'Look here,' said the latter; 'I will not say another word. Already I have said either too much or too little. You must make further enquiries elsewhere. It was my duty to warn you, and I have performed it. You must now take the matter in hand yourself.'

'Make enquiry of others? De Guiche, you are no friend of mine when you speak like that,' said the young man, disconsolately. 'The first person of whom I might enquire would not improbably be either a liar or a fool; the one would only add to my suffering, and the other would do worse. My good fellow, within the course of two hours, I might very well encounter ten liars, and find myself involved in as many duels. Tell me all; is it not best that I should know the worst at once?'

'But I know nothing, I tell you. I have been wounded, and prostrated by fever. I was, for a time, unconscious, and have only the slightest recollection of what took place. But what a pair of idiots we are to stand talking here, when the very man who can help us is within a stone's throw of us. Is not d'Artagnan one of your friends?'

'Why, of course he is.'

'Go to him, then. He is the man who will help you, and, at the same time, spare your feelings as much as possible.'

At this juncture, a servant entered the room.

'What is it?' said de Guiche.

'A visitor desires to see monseigneur in the Cabinet des Porcelaines.'

'Very well. You will excuse me, dear Raoul? You don't know how proud I feel at being able to walk alone.'

'I would gladly offer you my arm, my dear fellow, but I have a shrewd suspicion that your visitor is a lady.'

'I shall not be greatly surprised if I find that you are right,' replied de Guiche, with a smile, as he left Raoul.

Raoul stood motionless, crushed under the weight of his own sorrowful reflections, like a miner upon whom the roof of an underground gallery has fallen, wounded, bleeding, and only partially conscious, yet who makes a desperate effort to gather his wits together and save his life.

After a few minutes Raoul succeeded in collecting his thoughts, and had already recovered the thread of his ideas when, through the open door, he thought he recognised the voice of Montalais in the Cabinet des Porcelaines.

'Montalais!' he exclaimed. 'Yes, certainly it is her voice. Here is a woman who can tell me the truth; but I can hardly intrude upon her when it is evident that she does not want me to know that she is here; and, no doubt, Madame has sent her. Never mind, I can see her at her own lodging, as soon as d'Artagnan has inspired me with sufficient courage to listen to her revelations. Madame herself is a coquette, but, at the same time, a coquette who has a love affair of her own. I believe her to be as uncertain as life or death; nevertheless, she has contrived to make de Guiche feel that he is the happiest of men. He, at any rate, is on velvet. And now, let me be off.'

So saying, he hurried away, and reproaching himself as he went with having talked with de Guiche solely about his own affairs, quickly reached d'Artagnan's quarters.

## CHAPTER 12

# De Bragelonne pursues his investigations

THE CAPTAIN was at home; he had just come off duty, and Raoul found him buried in the recesses of a large leathern armchair, his sword between his knees, and engaged in reading a big budget of letters and twirling his moustaches.

D'Artagnan gave a cordial welcome to his friend's son.

'Halloa! Raoul, my boy,' he cried; 'what good wind has blown you hither? Has the king recalled you?'

This question seemed to the young man a somewhat awkward one to answer, and, taking a seat, he replied: 'Upon my word, I cannot tell you. All that I know is that I have come back.'

'Hum,' said d'Artagnan, refolding his letters, and casting a sharp look at his companion. 'The king has not recalled you, and yet you are here! I can't understand that at all.'

Raoul, who had already turned pale, could do nothing but twiddle his hat round in his fingers.

'What the devil are you doing. Can't you speak?' roared the captain. 'Are these glum manners what you have learnt in England? I have been there myself, but I came back as lively as a cricket. Say something, for heaven's sake.'

'I have only too much to say.'

'Oho!' said d'Artagnan. 'Well, how is your father?'

'Forgive me, my dearest friend, but that is the very question I was about to put to you.'

D'Artagnan increased the scrutiny of his look, from which no secret could be successfully hidden.

'You are in trouble?' he said, interrogatively.

'Yes, and you know it as well as I do, Monsieur d'Artagnan.'

'I know it?'

'Undoubtedly; please don't pretend to be astonished.'

'I don't pretend anything of the sort, my friend.'

'My dear captain, I know that you are my master, both in strength, and at the game of *finesse*. At the present moment I am simply a fool, an idiot. I have neither strength of will, nor force of arm. Nevertheless, I hope that you will not despise, but rather help me, for I am the most miserable devil on the face of the earth.'

'Why, how is that?' said d'Artagnan, as, with an encouraging smile, he unbuckled his waist-belt.

'It is because Mademoiselle de la Vallière is deceiving me.'

D'Artagnan moved not a muscle of his face. Then he said: 'Those are big words, young fellow. Who makes use of them?'

'Everybody.'

'Well, if everybody says so, there would seem to be some truth in them. I, myself, when I see smoke, look out for fire. A silly idea, perhaps, but so it is.'

'Then you believe it yourself?' cried de Bragelonne, sharply.

'Oh, you mustn't try to drag me into it.'

'But what else can I do?'

'You know perfectly well, my good boy,' replied d'Artagnan, 'that I never allow myself to become involved in affairs of this kind.'

'But for a friend – a son?'

'Exactly; if you were a stranger I might tell you. As you are not, I will tell you nothing at all. Have you heard of Porthos lately?'

'Oh, sir,' cried Raoul, seizing d'Artagnan's hand, ' for the sake of the great friendship which exists between you and my father – '

'Oh, the devil!' said d'Artagnan. 'You are indeed sick – with curiosity.'

'Not with curiosity, but with love.'

'Good! that's another big word. If you were really in love, my dear Raoul, it would be a very different thing.'

'I don't understand you, sir.'

'I mean that if your love was of that serious nature that I could believe that I was speaking to your heart – but it is impossible.'

'I swear to you that I love Louise desperately.'

D'Artagnan's eyes penetrated to the bottom of the young man's heart.

'It is impossible, I tell you. You are like all the rest of the young people – you are crazy.'

'Well, and supposing that it is as you say.'

'No man can be lucid or amenable to reason if his brain has lost its balance in the slightest degree. I have been out of my senses a hundred times in the course of my life. You would listen without hearing me; you would hear me without understanding; and, even if you understood me, you would not take my advice.'

'Only try me.'

'I will say, moreover, that if I were unlucky enough to know anything, and if I were fool enough to tell it to you – You regard me as a friend, I think you said?'

'Oh yes, indeed.'

'Well, then, we should quarrel. You would never forgive me for having disillusioned you, as people say when they speak of love-affairs.'

'Monsieur d'Artagnan, you know everything; yet you leave me bewildered and in despair. You drive me to death itself. It is horrible.'

'My good boy, don't make an ass of yourself.'

'I never make a fuss, as you know. And, since God and my father would never pardon me, were I to blow out my brains, I will ask the first man I meet for the information which you refuse to give me. Then I will tell him that he lies – '

'And you will kill him. What a fine exploit!'

'So much the better. What does it matter to me?'

'Kill away, my friend, kill away, if it will afford you any gratification. You are like people who have the toothache, and say, "Oh, what agony I suffer; I could bite a bar of iron in two." I always answer, "Bite away, my friends, but you won't get rid of the tooth, for all that." '

'I shall kill no one,' said Raoul, gloomily.

'Then I suppose you mean that you will allow someone to kill you. That would be funnier still. How I shall mourn for you! I shall go about all day long saying, "What a delightful young idiot was this poor little Bragelonne! What a double-distilled jackass. I have wasted half a lifetime in teaching him to use a sword, with the result that he deliberately goes and gets himself spitted like a lark." Well, go, Raoul, and get yourself spitted by all means. I don't know of whom you learnt logic, but, damme, as the English say, whoever the fellow may have been, he robbed your father of his money.'

Raoul buried his face in his hands, and groaned aloud.

'I have not a solitary friend,' he murmured.

'Oh, nonsense!' said d'Artagnan. 'Don't talk such foolishness.'

'I meet with none but unfeeling people who ridicule me.'

'Rubbish, I do not laugh at you, Gascon though I be. And unfeeling! If I were that, I should have told you to go to the devil a quarter of an hour ago. You are enough to damp the spirits of the most cheerful-minded man, and to make a fellow of a melancholy temperament feel inclined to hang himself. You are asking me to put you out of conceit with your mistress, and to give you a distaste for all womankind, who constitute the joy and delight of human existence.'

'Oh, sir! tell me what you know, and I shall be for ever grateful.'

'My dear boy, is it possible that you imagine that my head is filled with the escapades of the carpenter[43] or the painter, or that I know all about the staircase and the portrait, and a thousand other things of like importance?'

'Carpenter, carpenter – what do you mean by carpenter?'

'I mean nothing; only that I have heard it said that a carpenter was employed to cut a hole through the floor.'

'In La Vallière's apartment?'

'Oh, I don't know where.'

'In the king's?'

'Excellent! If it were in the king's room I should naturally blab it all out to you; shouldn't I?'

'Where was it, then?'

'Bless me! for the last hour I have done nothing but repeat that I know nothing at all about it.'

'But the painter, and the portrait you spoke of?'

'It seems that the king had a portrait painted of one of the ladies of the court.'

'La Vallière's portrait?'

'Why is La Vallière's name for ever in your mouth? Who said anything about La Vallière?'

'But if it was not *her* portrait, what makes you think that it concerns me?'

'I don't suggest that it concerns you. Simply, you ask questions, and I reply to them. You want to know all the court scandal; well, I supply you with it, and much good may it do you.'

Raoul struck his forehead with impatience.

'This will kill me,' he said.

'You said that before.'

'You are right;' and Raoul took a step in the direction of the door.

'Where are you going?' asked d'Artagnan.

'I am going to find someone who will tell me the truth.'

'Who is that?'

'A woman.'

'Mademoiselle de la Vallière herself, I suppose,' said d'Artagnan, with a grin. 'Well, that really is a famous idea. You need consolation, and you go at once to get it. She is not likely to give herself away. Well, be off with you.'

'You are mistaken, sir; the person to whom I am going will probably tell me a great deal.'

'Then, I'll bet that you are going to Montalais.'

'Yes, I am.'

'To her friend, who, on that very account, will be likely to exaggerate all that she knows, whether for good or for evil. Don't go to Montalais, my dear Raoul.'

'But that is not the sole reason which urges you to keep me away from her.'

'I admit it. But why should I play with you as a cat does with a mouse? You distress me, Raoul. If I do not wish you to talk with Montalais just now, it is because you would give away your secret and put it in her power to make an unfair use of it. Wait a bit, if you can.'

'I cannot.'

'So much the worse. Look here, Raoul, if I had any suggestion to offer – but I have none.'

'Give me the assurance of your sympathy, my dear friend, and I shall be satisfied. Then leave me to get out of my difficulty as best I can.'

'So that you may flounder still deeper in the mire. That would be a clever thing to do. No; sit down at that table and take a pen.'

'For what purpose?'

'To write, asking Montalais to give you an appointment.'

'Ah!' said Raoul, seizing the pen which the captain offered him.

At that moment the door opened, and a musketeer, approaching d'Artagnan, said: 'Mademoiselle de Montalais, captain, would like to speak with you.'

'To *me*,' muttered d'Artagnan. 'Show her in; then I shall soon see,' he added, 'whether it is with me that she wants to speak.'

The wily captain's doubt was fully justified.

Montalais, as soon as she entered the room, and caught sight of Raoul, exclaimed: 'Monsieur, monsieur! – I beg your pardon, Monsieur d'Artagnan.'

'Not at all, Mademoiselle,' replied d'Artagnan. 'I know that, at my time of life, people don't come to me unless I can be of use to them.'

'I was looking for Monsieur de Bragelonne,' said Montalais.

'How strange, he was just going in search of you. Raoul, perhaps you will accompany Mademoiselle?'

'With much pleasure.'

'Go, then,' said d'Artagnan; and, having gently pushed Raoul outside the door, he took Montalais by the hand.

'Be kind to him,' he said, in a low tone, 'and do the best you can both for him and her.'

'Oh!' she replied; 'it is not I who desire to talk to him. It is Madame who has sent me to look for him.'

'Nothing could be better,' said d'Artagnan. 'Since it is Madame, the poor boy will be cured in an hour.'

'Or dead,' said Montalais, compassionately. 'Goodbye, Monsieur d'Artagnan;' and she hastened to rejoin Raoul, who was waiting at a short distance from the door, slightly bewildered, and rendered somewhat uneasy by this dialogue, which, apparently, foreboded no good to him.

## CHAPTER 13

## A double jealousy

LOVERS are always tenderly disposed towards everything connected, however slightly, with the object of their adoration, and Raoul no sooner found himself alone with Montalais, than he seized her hand and covered it with kisses.

'Gently, gently,' said the girl. 'You are wasting your kisses, dear Monsieur Raoul, and I fear they will never bear you any interest.'

'How? what? Pray explain what you mean, my dear Aure!'

'Oh, Madame will, no doubt, give you every necessary explanation. It is she to whom I am taking you.'

'To Madame?'

'Hush! and don't look so horrified. Remember that the windows here have eyes and the walls ears. Oblige me by not looking at me, and speak, in an audible voice, about the rain or the fine weather, or tell me about the pleasant time you spent in England.'

'In short – '

'Mind! I warn you that, in some quarter or another, I cannot tell in which, Madame will surely have a vigilant eye and an attentive ear employed in her service. I am not anxious, as you may suppose, to receive my dismissal, nor to be sent to the Bastille; so let us chatter to one another, or, better still, let us not speak at all.'

Raoul pulled himself together, and assumed the firm step and bearing of a brave man; but it was the bearing of a brave man on his way to the rack. Montalais, well on the alert but with careless demeanour and a saucy poise of the head, walked in front of him.

Raoul was at once shown into Madame's apartments.

'Ah, well,' he said to himself, 'I suppose this day is destined to pass without my learning anything. De Guiche showed too much consideration for me. He is in league with Madame, and they have agreed, no doubt with the kindest motives, to withhold from me the solution of the problem in which I take so overwhelming an interest. Why have I not a good honest enemy? – that serpent de Wardes,[44] for instance. He would probably bite, but I should not hesitate again. To hesitate – to doubt – better to die.'

In another minute he stood in Madame's presence. Henrietta, more charming than ever, was reclining in an easy-chair, her tiny feet resting on an embroidered cushion; she played with a little, silky-furred kitten, which bit her fingers and clung to the guipure round her neck.

She was in deep meditation, and it took the voice of Montalais, as well as that of Raoul, to rouse her from her reverie.

'Your highness sent for me,' Raoul ventured to remark for the second time.

Madame looked at him with an air of having just awakened from sleep.

'Good-morning, Monsieur de Bragelonne,' she said. 'Yes, I sent for you. I see that you have come back from England.'

'At your royal highness's service.'

'You are very good. You may leave us, Montalais.'

Montalais withdrew.

'You can spare a few minutes of your time, I trust, Monsieur de Bragelonne.'

'My whole life is at the service of your royal highness,' replied Raoul, who felt, with a vague uneasiness, that something serious lay beneath the surface of these polite introductory remarks on the part of Madame. The feeling, however, did not cause him much alarm, since he was convinced that there was a certain unanimity of sentiment between her and himself, whilst her capricious imagination and despotic will were well known to all those at court who had at any time come within the range of her influence.

Madame had been immensely flattered[45] by the attentions of the king; she had got herself talked about, and inspired the queen with a mortal jealousy, which is the worm that gnaws at the roots of feminine happiness. Madame, in a word, in trying to cure a wounded pride, had fallen hopelessly in love.

We know what Madame had done in order to bring about the return of Raoul, who had been sent out of the way by Louis XIV. Raoul knew nothing about the letter to Charles II, although d'Artagnan had guessed to what it had reference. This inexplicable mixture of love and vanity, these marvellous exhibitions of extreme tenderness and of the greatest duplicity, who shall explain them? No one; not even the malignant spirit who kindles the flame of coquetry in the heart of woman.

'Monsieur de Bragelonne,' said the princess, after a pause, 'have you come back satisfied?'

De Bragelonne saw that Madame Henrietta had turned pale with the effort of concealing what she was burning to express.

'Madame,' said he, 'what is there for me to be satisfied or dissatisfied with?'

'What would be likely to cause satisfaction or the reverse of it to a man of your years and appearance?'

'She is not losing any time,' thought Raoul, becoming alarmed. 'With what can she be trying to inspire my heart?'

He trembled with apprehension at what he might have to listen to, and tried to put off for a time that moment so fateful, yet so anxiously looked forward to, when everything would be made clear to him.

'Madame,' he said, 'I left a very dear friend in good health, and, on my return, find him very ill.'

'Do you allude to Monsieur de Guiche?' asked Henrietta, imperturbably. 'He is said to be a very close friend of yours.'

'Yes, madame.'

'It is true that he has been wounded, but he is recovering from his wound. Oh, I don't think Monsieur de Guiche has much to complain of,' she said quickly. Then she added, 'Has he complained? Has he, do you think, any cause for dissatisfaction of which we are unaware?'

'I am alluding only to his wound, madame.'

'I am glad to hear it, for, otherwise, Monsieur de Guiche seems to be happy enough; at all events, he is always in excellent spirits. As for you, Monsieur de Bragelonne, I feel convinced that if you, like him, were suffering only from a wounded body, you could be well content to bear the pain. For, after all, what matters a wound of that kind?'

Raoul shivered. 'She is coming back to it again,' he thought, but he held his peace.

'What did you say?' asked she.

'I said nothing, madame,' replied Raoul.

'You said nothing. That means that you don't agree with me. Are you, then, contented with the present state of affairs?'

Raoul drew a step nearer to her. 'Madame,' said he, 'I feel that your royal highness has something to tell me, and that your natural kindness of heart prompts you to say it as delicately as possible. I would, however, beg your highness to tell me the plain truth. I am strong enough to bear it, whatever it may be, and am all attention.'

'What, then,' asked Henrietta, 'do you know at the present moment?'

'Precisely what your royal highness wishes me to understand.'

As he said these words, Raoul trembled in spite of himself.

'As a matter of fact,' said the princess, in a low tone of voice, 'it is rather cruel, but since I have begun – '

'Yes, madame, since your highness has condescended to begin, deign, at least, to finish.'

Henrietta rose from her seat, and began to pace the room backwards and forwards.

'What has Monsieur de Guiche told you?' she asked suddenly.

'Nothing, madame.'

'He has told you nothing. Ah! that is like him.'

'No doubt he wished to spare my feelings, madame.'

'And this is what is called friendship beween friends! But Monsieur d'Artagnan, whom you have just left, surely he has told you something?'

'Not a word more than de Guiche, madame.'

Henrietta made a gesture of impatience.

'At least,' she said, 'you have heard what is said at court?'

'I know nothing at all, madame.'

'Nothing of the scene in the storm?'

'No, madame.'

'Nor of the *tête-à-tête* in the forest?'

'No, madame.'

'Nor of the flight to Chaillot?'[46]

Raoul resembled a cut flower as he bent his head, for a moment, over the vacant chair; then, after a desperate effort to smile, he replied, with the utmost gentleness: 'I have had the honour to assure your royal highness that I know absolutely nothing. I am but a poor exile newly arrived from England. Between my friends here and myself has raged so turbulent a sea that no whisper of what your highness has been speaking of has been able to reach my ear.'

The princess was touched by his pitiable condition, as well as by the courage he had shown, but her dominant wish, at that moment, was to learn with what kind of feeling he now regarded her who had treated him so cruelly, and caused him so much suffering.

'Monsieur de Bragelonne,' she said, 'what your friends have declined to do for you, I will do, for I esteem and like you very much. Look upon me as your friend. You hold your head high like a brave and honourable man, and I should be sorry to see you bend it beneath the weight of ridicule, and perhaps, later on, of contempt.'

'Ha!' exclaimed Raoul; 'has it gone so far as that, then?'

'If you do not know,' said the princess, 'I see that you guess what has happened. You were engaged to Mademoiselle de la Vallière, were you not?'

'Yes, madame.'

'That being the case, it is only right that you should be put in possession of the whole truth; especially as, sooner or later, I shall have to relieve Mademoiselle de la Vallière from attendance upon me.'

'Dismiss La Vallière!' exclaimed de Bragelonne.

'Undoubtedly. Do you suppose that I am, for ever, to be annoyed by the tears and lamentations of the king? No, I will no longer allow my house to be made use of for such practices as these. But you are terribly agitated.'

'No, madame; it is nothing,' said de Bragelonne, struggling to recover his composure. 'I thought for the moment that I was about to die, that is all. Your royal highness has done me the honour to tell me that the king has wept and implored.'

'Yes, but in vain.'

And she told Raoul of the scene at Chaillot, and the despair of the king upon his return; she told him also of his gracious behaviour towards herself, and of the fierce expression with which the outraged princess, the humiliated coquette, had extinguished the royal anger.

Raoul bent his head.

'What are you thinking of?' she said.

'The king loves her,' he replied.

'And you think that all the love is on one side?'

'Alas, alas! I was thinking of the time when she loved me.'

Henrietta could not help feeling a momentary admiration for this sublime incredulity; then, with a shrug of her shoulders, she said: 'I see you do not believe me. Oh! how much you must love her, to doubt that she loves the king.'

'Pardon me, your highness, but she gave me her word. I believe her to be true and loyal, and I will not doubt her in the absence of proof.'

'You want proof?' said the princess. 'Very well, be it so; come with me.'

## CHAPTER 14

# A domiciliary visit

PRECEDING RAOUL, the princess led him across the courtyard to that part of the building in which La Vallière was lodged, and, mounting the same staircase which Raoul himself had ascended but a few hours previously, she halted before the door of the room where the young man had been so mysteriously received by Montalais.

The time was well chosen for accomplishing the project which Madame Henrietta had conceived. The château was deserted, for the king, courtiers and ladies of the court had taken their departure for Saint-Germain. Madame Henrietta, alone, in anticipation of de Bragelonne's return, and thinking of the advantage which his presence might gain for her, had feigned indisposition, and remained behind. She was sure, therefore, of finding the respective apartments of La Vallière and Saint-Aignan[47] unoccupied. She drew a master-key from her pocket, and opened the door of her maid of honour's apartment.

De Bragelonne took in all the details of the room, which he recognised at a glance, and the impression produced upon him was the first of the tortures that awaited him. The princess watched him carefully, and, with practised eye, saw what was passing in the young man's mind.

'You have demanded proofs,' she said; 'do not be surprised when I give them to you; but, if you don't feel strong enough to bear the ordeal, there is yet time to withdraw.'

'Thank you, madame,' answered de Bragelonne, 'but I have come here to satisfy myself, and you have undertaken to convince me. I pray you, then, to do so.'

'Come in, then,' said Madame, 'and shut the door after you.'

De Bragelonne did as he was told, and, turning to the princess, questioned her by a look.

'You know where you are?' asked Henrietta.

'To the best of my belief, madame, I am in Mademoiselle de la Vallière's apartment.'

'You are quite right.'

'But I crave permission to point out to your highness, that it is simply an apartment, and not a proof.'

'Wait a moment.'

The princess moved towards the foot of the bed, and, after removing a folding-screen which stood there, bent down over the floor.

'Now, come here,' she said; 'stoop down, and raise this trap-door yourself.'

'This *trap-door*!' cried Raoul, in surprise, for he remembered his conversation with d'Artagnan, and had a vague recollection of hearing him use this very word.

Raoul searched carefully, but could find no crack in the flooring to indicate that it could be opened, nor could he find any ring with which to pull up a trap-door, supposing one to be there.

'Ah! true,' said Madame Henrietta. 'I forgot the secret spring. It is in the fourth plank of the flooring. Press the place where there is a knot in the wood; so say the instructions. Press the knot yourself, Vicomte; look, here is the place.'

Raoul, pale as death, applied his thumb to the spot indicated, and immediately the spring worked, and the trap opened of itself.

'How exceedingly ingenious,' said the princess; 'and observe that the contriver of this arrangement must have foreseen that it would not improbably be made use of by a not over-powerful person, for you see that the trap-door opens, as it were, of its own accord.'

'A staircase!' cried Raoul.

'And a very elegant one, too,' said the princess. 'You see, Vicomte, that it is provided with a handrail to enhance the safety of the delicate creatures who risk its descent, as I am about to do. Follow me.'

'Before following you, madame, I should like to know whither this staircase leads?'

'Ah! quite true. I forgot to tell you.'

'I am all anxiety to hear, madame,' said Raoul, hardly daring to breathe.

'You may be aware that, at one time, Monsieur Saint-Aignan's rooms almost immediately adjoined those of the king?'

'Yes, madame, I remember that they were so situated at the time of my departure, and, more than once, I have had the honour of visiting him there.'

'Well, he obtained the king's permission to exchange that spacious and handsome apartment for the two little rooms to which this staircase gives access, and which are twice as inconvenient as the old ones, and ten times farther off the king, to be in juxtaposition to whom is usually considered a great privilege by the gentlemen of the court.'

'So far, so good, madame; but pray go on, for I hardly yet see the drift of what you are telling me.'

'Well, it happens that these new rooms are situated beneath the apartments of my ladies, and exactly under the room occupied by La Vallière.'

'But for what purpose were this trap-door and this staircase constructed?'

'Oh! good gracious, how should I know? Suppose we go down the stairs, and see if any explanation offers itself.' And setting the example, Madame descended at once.

Raoul, with a sigh, followed her. With every stair creaking beneath his weight, de Bragelonne at length entered the mysterious apartment, the atmosphere of which seemed yet to breathe the subtle perfume of La Vallière's presence, and every breath he drew served to assure him that she had been there very recently; whilst the impression was confirmed by the presence of the particular flowers and books which she affected. Had a single doubt remained in Raoul's mind, it would have been promptly dispelled by the subtle manner in which evidence of La Vallière's presence was made manifest even in the commonest surroundings of everyday life; for La Vallière's spirit lived in the furniture, the choice of the hangings, and even, as it seemed to de Bragelonne, in the highly polished surface of the floor.

Mute, and overwhelmed with grief, he felt that there was nothing left for him to learn, and he followed his pitiless conductress as the victim follows the executioner.

Madame, her nerves now strung up to the highest point of tension, was determined, on the other hand, to spare him no single detail.

It must be admitted, however, that, notwithstanding his dazed state of mind, none of these points would have escaped Raoul's observation, even had he been by himself. The happiness of the woman he loves, when it comes to her in the shape of a rival, is torture to the man of jealous temperament, but to a lover like Raoul, whose heart was now, for the first time, filled with gall and wormwood, the happiness of Louise meant shameful death – death of body and soul.

In his mind's eye he could see the lovers standing with clasped hands in front of the mirror, into which they gazed again and again, that the recollection of those happy moments might be for ever imprinted on their memories. This luxury; this solicitous care taken to shield the beloved object from discomfort or to cause her agreeable surprise; this power of love, augmented by the power of royalty, struck Raoul as with a mortal blow. If the pangs of jealousy can be tempered at all, it may be in the reflection that the preferred rival is inferior to oneself, but, with the knowledge that youth, beauty and grace are on his side, comes unspeakable torment. It is a moment when even heaven itself seems to take part against the discarded lover.

A final shaft was yet to be launched at the heart of the unfortunate Raoul. Madame Henrietta raised a silk curtain and disclosed a portrait of La Vallière – a portrait of La Vallière, young, radiant, beautiful, drinking in life at every pore; for, at the age of eighteen, life means love.

'Louise,' murmured de Bragelonne, 'it is true, then! Had you ever loved me, you could not look at me like that.' He felt that his heart was broken.

Madame Henrietta looked at him almost with a feeling of envy, although she knew well enough that there was nothing to be envious of, seeing that de Guiche was quite as infatuated with her as poor de Bragelonne was with La Vallière.

Raoul intercepted her look. 'Pray forgive me,' he said; 'I know that I ought to exercise more self-control in your highness's presence. May you never feel such a blow as I have just been struck, for, being a woman, I fear you would not have strength to support it. Yet, pardon me, for I am but a simple gentleman, whilst you are sprung from a proud and all-powerful race, from the elect – '

'Monsieur de Bragelonne,' interrupted Henrietta, 'such a heart as your own is worthy of the respect and sympathy of a queen. I am your friend, monsieur, and I will not suffer your life to be poisoned by perfidy, nor embittered by ridicule. It is I who, more courageous than any of your friends, except Monsieur de Guiche, caused your return from London; it is I who have furnished you with the painful truths necessary for your cure; and cured you will be if, as I believe, you are a brave man and not a snivelling poltroon. Nay, do not thank me; blame me, if you will; and do not serve the king less zealously on account of what has happened.'

Raoul smiled bitterly. 'Ah!' he said, 'I had forgotten, for the moment, that the king is my master.'

'Remember that your liberty, perhaps your life, is at stake.'

A sharp and penetrating look from Raoul showed the princess that she had committed a mistake, and that her last argument was one of the least likely to have any effect upon the young man.

'Beware, Monsieur de Bragelonne,' said she, 'lest, by not duly weighing every future action, you provoke the wrath of a prince of ungovernable temper, and plunge your family and friends in grief; and remember that your safety can be assured only by absolute submission.'

'I thank you, madame,' replied Raoul. 'I assure you that I fully appreciate the value of the advice which your highness has given me, and I will do my best to follow it; but may I say one word more?'

'By all means.'

'Well then, if it would not be indiscreet to ask, I should much like to know how your highness discovered the secret of this trap-door, staircase and portrait.'

'Oh, nothing could be more simple. In order to exercise proper supervision over these young girls, for whose discretion I consider myself to be morally responsible, I provided myself with duplicate keys to their apartments. Now, it struck me as being very strange that La Vallière should seclude herself so long, and so often, in her own room. I could not understand why Monsieur de Saint-Aignan changed his apartments, nor why the king visited him every day; and I could not but remark that all these changes had taken place since your departure. I object to being made use of by the king as a screen for his love affairs, especially as, when he is tired of La Vallière, who is always in tears, he will make love to the laughter-loving Montalais, and, after her, to Tonnay-Charente,[48] who sings from morning till night. It is beneath my dignity to accept such a position. Therefore I hushed any scruples of conscience that I might have had, and discovered the secret. I have deeply wounded you, for which I ask your forgiveness, but I had a duty to fulfil and I fulfilled it. That is all. You are now forewarned; the storm will break. It remains for you to take measures for your own protection.'

'But you expect something to happen, nevertheless, madame,' said de Bragelonne, firmly; 'for you surely do not imagine that I shall tamely submit to all the shame and duplicity of which I have been the victim.'

'You will, of course, take what action you think proper, Monsieur Raoul; but I beg you not to divulge the source of your inspiration. That is all I require of you. It is the sole reward I ask for the service I have rendered you.'

'Have no apprehension on that head, madame,' replied de Bragelonne, with a bitter smile.

'For my part, I bribed the locksmith who was employed to do the work; there is no reason why you should not have obtained your information by similar means, is there?'

'No, madame. I understand that your royal highness imposes no

restriction whatever upon my course of action, provided that you are
not compromised by it?'

'No other restriction whatever.'

'Then I shall ask your royal highness's permission to remain here
for a few minutes.'

'Do you mean that you wish to be alone?'

'Oh no, madame; what I have to do can be very well done in your
presence. I only wish to write a short note.'

'It is rather dangerous, Monsieur de Bragelonne; pray be careful.'

'No one can possibly know that it was your royal highness who
brought me here. Besides, I shall sign what I write.'

'Do so, monsieur.'

Raoul drew forth his tablets and hurriedly wrote the following
words upon a blank leaf:

> MONSIEUR LE COMTE – Do not be surprised at receiving this note
> signed by me before one of my friends, whom I will at once send
> to your residence, has had the honour of explaining the object of
> my visit.
>
> VICOMTE RAOUL DE BRAGELONNE

He rolled up the paper, and slid it into the keyhole in the door of the
room which was sacred to the lovers, and, after satisfying himself
that it was so placed that it could not escape the eye of Saint-Aignan
when he should return, he rejoined the princess, who had already
reached the top of the staircase. They separated on the landing
outside, Raoul affecting to feel gratitude towards her highness, and
Henrietta herself, feeling, or pretending to feel, sincere pity for the
unfortunate young man whom she had just condemned to the most
acute suffering.

'Oh!' she said, as he walked away with pale face and bloodshot
eyes, 'if I had only known, I really think I should have refrained from
enlightening him.'

## CHAPTER 15

## *Porthos's* [49] *plan of action*

IN THE COURSE of this lengthy history it has been necessary to introduce to our readers so many different characters that each of them has, in turn, to remain in the background until the exigencies of the story require his or her presence on the scene, and it is thus that we have been compelled to lose sight of our friend Porthos since his return from Fontainebleau.

The honours which the king had bestowed upon him had, in no sense, changed the genial nature of this excellent fellow, although he carried his head a trifle higher than before and his general bearing had inclined towards the majestic since he had had the honour of dining at the king's table. The very aspect of the royal dining-room was not without its effect upon Porthos; and the Seigneur de Bracieux et de Pierrefonds loved to recall the vast number of servants and officials of the court who were on duty during the dinner, and who gave a tone to the proceedings and adorned the room.

It was the intention of Porthos to place Monsieur Mouston[50] in a dignified and responsible position, to establish his household upon a kind of feudal system, and to become the founder of a warlike clan. There was not, however, much originality in the idea, many of the great captains of the time having already adopted the system, whilst, in the preceding century, were to be remarked, in association with it, the names of Monsieurs de Tréville, de Schomberg, de la Vieuville, to say nothing of Monsieurs de Richelieu, de Condé and de Bouillon-Turenne.

And he, Porthos, a friend of the king and of Monsieur Fouquet, a baron, an engineer,[51] and heaven knows what else, why should not he enjoy the privileges to which large possessions and sterling worth so clearly entitled him?

Temporarily forsaken by Aramis (whose time, as we know, was now fully taken up in attending to Monsieur Fouquet's business, somewhat neglected, owing to the exigencies of duty, by d'Artagnan) and wearied of Trüchen and Planchet,[52] Porthos lapsed into a dreamy condition for which he could not account; although had anyone said to him, 'Porthos, is there anything which you want?' he would most assuredly have answered 'Yes.'

After one of those dinners, at which Porthos never failed to reproduce, to the best of his ability, the details of the royal banquet, as his spirits rose under the influence of good wine, or became depressed as he thought of his yet unrealised ambitions, and, finally, as he was dropping off into a doze, a servant announced the arrival of Monsieur de Bragelonne. Porthos passed into the next room, where he found his young friend in the same disconsolate frame of mind as when we last left him. Raoul hastened to press his hand, and Porthos, surprised at the solemnity of the other's manner, offered him a seat.

'Dear Monsieur Du Vallon,' said Raoul, 'I have a favour to beg of you.'

'You are just in the nick of time, my young friend, for I have had eight thousand livres sent to me this very morning from Pierrefonds, so if you are short of money – '

'Many thanks, most excellent of friends, but it is not money.'

'So much the worse. I have always heard it said that the service of providing a friend with money is, at once, the most valuable and the easiest to render. The saying impressed me, and I am fond of quoting sayings that strike me.'

'You are as kind-hearted as you are full of common sense and wisdom.'

'You are very good to say so. You will dine with me, of course?'

'Thank you, no. I have no appetite.'

'Good gracious! what a dreadful country England is.'

'Oh no, but – '

'I tell you this; if it were not for the fish, and the general excellence of the living there, the country would be unendurable.'

'Perhaps. Well, I have come to – '

'Yes, go on; I am listening. But, in the first place, I propose that we have a drink. The food in Paris makes a man devilish thirsty,' said Porthos, as he proceeded to open a bottle of champagne. Having filled his friend's and his own glass, he took a mighty draught, and, having slaked his thirst, he continued. 'Now I shall be better able to give your business proper consideration. I am all attention. What is it, my dear Raoul? What can I do for you?'

'Give me your opinion on quarrels in general, my dear friend.'

'My opinion? My dear fellow, pray be a little more explicit,' said Porthos, rubbing his forehead.

'Well then, what attitude would you assume in the case of a serious misunderstanding between one of your friends and a stranger? A good-natured one?'

'Oh, of course, I am always good-natured,' said Porthos.

'Very good; but what action would you take?'

'Oh, when any friend of mine gets into a row of that kind I always act on one principle only.'

'And that is?'

'Well, I hold that to lose time is absolutely to waste it. Depend upon it, an affair can never be arranged so satisfactorily as when both men are hot with indignation.'

'Oh, indeed, is that your principle?'

'Yes; and therefore, when two fellows quarrel, I lose no time in bringing them together.'

'Oh, indeed.'

'Yes; don't you see that, in this way, the affair simply arranges itself.'

'I should have thought,' said Raoul, rather taken aback, 'that, by that means, the affair would be more likely to develop into – '

'Not a bit of it. Why, I myself have, in the course of my life, been concerned in from a hundred and eighty to a hundred and ninety such matters, without reckoning impromptu fights and chance encounters.'

'That is a very pretty total,' said Raoul, smiling in spite of himself.

'Oh, that is nothing; as a matter of fact, I am really too easy going. Look at d'Artagnan! Why, he reckons his duels by the hundred. It is true that he is rather touchy. I have often told him so.'

'I presume, then,' said Raoul, 'that you generally succeed in arranging any quarrels which your friends may confide to you.'

'I have never, in a single instance, failed to do so,' answered Porthos, with a suavity and assurance which quite startled the other.

'But,' said he, 'the arrangement you come to is, at least, honourable?'

'You may be sure of that,' was the reply; 'and now I may as well explain to you another principle which I adopt. When once my friend has placed his honour in my hands, this is how I go to work. I lose not a moment in finding his adversary, and I assume the punctiliously polite and self-possessed manner which are indispensable to the occasion.'

'And it is that, I suppose, which makes you feel so confident of arranging the matter quickly,' said Raoul, somewhat tartly.

'Quite so. Well, having found my man, I say to him, always with the greatest courtesy, my dear Raoul, "Sir! you cannot but be aware of the gross affront you have put upon my friend." '

Raoul frowned.

'Sometimes – often indeed,' continued Porthos, with a twinkle in his eye, 'my friend has not been affronted at all, but has, really, insulted the other fellow. Do you observe how tricky I am?' And Porthos gave vent to a huge guffaw.

'Confound it!' said Raoul to himself, whilst Porthos's roar of laughter rang in his ears; 'I am infernally unlucky. De Guiche treats me with a coolness akin to indifference; d'Artagnan laughs at me; and, as to Porthos, he suggests pacific measures, and is absolutely lamb-like in his demeanour. No one seems willing to arrange the matter in *my* way. I thought to find in Porthos a man who would act as my second, and, behold, he talks of nothing but "courtesy" and "arrangement".'

Porthos, having recovered himself, continued: 'So, you see, in one short sentence, I put the adversary in the wrong.'

'Perhaps,' said Raoul, with a preoccupied manner.

'Perhaps! nonsense, *certainly!* I put him altogether in the wrong. Now, please observe with what extreme courtesy I bring about a happy result. I advance, in my most distinguished manner, and, grasping the hand of our adversary – '

'The devil!' interrupted Raoul.

' "Sir," I say to him,' continued Porthos, imperturbably, ' "now that you are convinced that you have insulted my friend, I have no fear but that you will be anxious to make what reparation it is in your power to afford him, that is, an exchange of courtesies. In short, monsieur, I have the honour to give you the length of my friend's sword." '

'What?' cried Raoul, springing to his feet.

'Wait a moment; "the length of my friend's sword. I have a spare horse, outside. My friend is at such-and-such a place, where he awaits your distinguished presence with the utmost impatience. We can call on the way, and take with us a friend of yours;" and the affair is arranged.'

'And, then,' said Raoul, pale with rage, 'I suppose you reconcile the two adversaries on the ground.'

'I beg your pardon,' said Porthos. 'Reconcile! What for?'

'Why, didn't you say the affair was arranged?'

'Undoubtedly, since I have my friend in readiness on the ground.'

'But what the devil did you send him there for?'

'To give him an opportunity of stretching his limbs; whereas his adversary, on the contrary, reaches the ground with limbs stiff from riding. They confront one another; my friend kills his man, and there is an end of the matter.'

'Oh, you are sure that he kills him?' said Raoul.

'*Pardieu!*' said Porthos; 'do you suppose that I have anything to do with duffers who allow themselves to be run through? I have a hundred and one friends, at the head of whom is your father. There are Aramis and d'Artagnan also; and all three are pretty much alive, I believe.'

'Oh, my dear, dear baron!' exclaimed Raoul, embracing Porthos in an ecstasy of delight.

'You approve of my method, then?' said the giant.

'I so far approve of it that I shall adopt it today, at once, this very instant. You are a man after my own heart.'

'Good; well, here I am. You want to fight?'

'Most assuredly.'

'It is only natural; who's your man?'

'Monsieur de Saint-Aignan.'

'I know him; a delightful fellow. I remember that he was deuced civil to me on the occasion when I had the honour to dine with the king. I shall now, certainly, return his courtesy, even if it were not my invariable custom to acknowledge politeness. And so he has offended you?'

'Mortally.'

'Good; then I can use the expression *mortally*?'

'You may make it stronger, if you can.'

'Capital! that is very convenient.'

'Then we may consider the affair *arranged*, may we not?' said Raoul, with a smile.

'Certainly; where will you wait for him?'

'Stop a bit; this is a rather delicate business, and, I fear, cannot be dealt with in an off-hand manner. You see, Monsieur de Saint-Aignan is a personal friend of the king's.'

'So I have heard.'

'And, if I should kill him – '

'*If* you should kill him? Oh, it's a dead certainty that you'll do that. There is no difficulty in arranging these affairs nowadays. You should have lived in my time; it was very different then.'

'My dear friend, you don't quite understand me. I mean that, Monsieur de Saint-Aignan being a friend of the king, the affair becomes more difficult to arrange, because there is always the possibility of his majesty getting wind of it beforehand.'

'Not the least fear of that. Why, you know my method – "Sir, you have insulted my friend, and – "'

'Yes, I know all that.'

'And then, "Sir, I have a horse outside at your service." Oh! it shall bring him along before he has had time to say a word to anybody.'

'But suppose he objects to being brought along.'

'*Pardieu!* I should like to see him object. It would be the first time my method was ever known to fail. Why, damme, I'll carry him off bodily, if necessary.'

And, suiting the action to the word, Porthos picked up Raoul, and carried him round the room under his arm.

'Very well,' said the young man, as Porthos set him down; 'it therefore only remains to state to Monsieur de Saint-Aignan the nature of my grievance against him.'

'But he knows that already, doesn't he?'

'Yes, yes, dear Monsieur Du Vallon, but nowadays it is the custom to state clearly to one's adversary the ground of quarrel.'

'Well, then, tell me what it is.'

'It is that – '

'Oh, botheration! this rigmarole worries me to death. In my time there was none of this palaver. Men fought for pure love of fighting, and I know of no better reason.'

'You are right, my friend.'

'Well, go on; I am waiting for *your* reasons.'

'I have a great deal to say. In the first place, it is necessary to particularise – '

'Oh, oh! the devil! to blazes with your new-fangled customs.'

'It is necessary, I repeat, to particularise, and, as this affair is beset with so many difficulties, the utmost caution must be used. In the first place, you will oblige me by informing Monsieur de Saint-Aignan that he has offended me by changing his lodgings.'

'By changing his lodgings,' repeated Porthos, commencing to tick-off on his fingers the several grounds of offence. 'Well, go on.'

'Next,' said Raoul, 'by having a trap-door made in his new apartment.'

'I see,' said Porthos; 'Ecod! that's a serious matter indeed. I don't wonder at your being enraged with him. It was like his damned impudence to have trap-doors made in his room without asking your permission. Trap-doors, indeed; it is monstrous! Why, I haven't such a thing myself, except in my dungeons at Bracieux.'

'And, finally,' continued Raoul, 'you will be good enough to say that I am aggrieved that he is in possession of a certain portrait. Monsieur de Saint-Aignan will know very well to which one I refer.'

'Yes, a portrait. Very well, I have it all now. A change of lodging, a trap-door and a portrait. But, my friend, one of these grievances would, by itself, be sufficient to set by the ears all the gentlemen of France and Spain – and that's not saying a little.'

'In that case you will be fully armed.'

'I will take a second horse with me. Say where we shall find you, and, whilst you are waiting, amuse yourself by making a few passes and practising methods of defence. You will find it a capital way of giving elasticity to your limbs.'

'Thanks; I will take your advice, and will wait for you in the Bois de Vincennes, close to the Minimes.'53

'You could not have suggested a better spot. And now, where shall I find Monsieur de Saint-Aignan?'

'At the Palais-Royal.'

Porthos rang a big hand-bell, and a servant appeared.

'My court suit,' commanded Porthos, 'my own horse, and a led one.' The servant bowed, and withdrew. 'By the way, does your father know anything about this business?' asked Porthos.

'No; but I am going to write to him.'

'Nor d'Artagnan?'

'No, he is so extremely cautious that he might dissuade me.'

'He is an excellent adviser, all the same,' said Porthos, whose modest loyalty was almost shocked at the idea of anyone presuming to think of himself whilst the world contained a d'Artagnan.

'Dear Monsieur Du Vallon,' replied Raoul, 'I entreat you not to question me any further. I have said all that I have to say. Now I want to take prompt and decisive action, such as you know so well how to arrange. That is why I sought you out.'

'You can depend upon my doing my best for you,' replied Porthos.

'And bear in mind, my dear friend, that no one but ourselves must know anything of this meeting.'

'Everyone will know,' said Porthos, 'when the dead body is found in the wood. I promise to do everything for you, except to conceal the corpse. There it will be, for all the world to see. That is inevitable. No, damme, I never bury 'em. That smacks too strongly of the assassin. Every risk must take its own chance, as they say in Normandy.'

'And now, my dear and brave old friend, get to work.'

'Depend on me,' said the giant, as he finished the bottle, whilst his servant spread out on a table an elegant laced suit.

As to Raoul, he left the house filled with a sense of secret satisfaction.

'Oh, perfidious and treacherous king,' he said to himself, 'I cannot reach *you*, for the person of the king is sacred; but your accomplice, the creature who panders to your desires, shall pay for your offence. I will kill him in your name, and afterwards – well, afterwards we will think about Louise.'

## CHAPTER 16

## *The new lodging, the trap-door and the portrait*

PORTHOS, CHARGED, to his intense satisfaction, with this cartel,[54] which made him feel quite young again, cut short, by at least half an hour, the time which he usually took to array himself for special occasions. As a man of the world, he had opened his proceedings by sending a servant to ascertain whether Monsieur de Saint-Aignan was at home. He was informed that the comte, with the rest of the court, had had the honour of accompanying the king to Saint-Germain, but that the comte himself had, that instant, returned. Having received this information, Porthos hurried off to the Palais-Royal, and arrived there just as Saint-Aignan was taking off his boots. The excursion to Saint-Germain had been a great success. The king, who was becoming more and more enamoured every instant, had been in an exceptionally good humour, and had made things pleasant for everyone by many acts of kindness and condescension.

Monsieur de Saint-Aignan was, it may be remembered, a poet, and he believed that he had proved, upon many memorable occasions, his incontestable right to the title. An indefatigable stringer-together of rhymes, he had, during the whole of the excursion, overwhelmed with all sorts of verse first the king, and afterwards La Vallière. He had even goaded the king to the perpetration of a distich, whilst La Vallière, in common with all women who are in love, had composed two sonnets. It will be seen, therefore, that Apollo[55] had no reason to complain of being neglected.

Now that he had come back to Paris, assured beforehand that his verses would have the run of the court, Saint-Aignan occupied himself sedulously with the composition of original verse, and, like a doting father about to send forth his children into the world, he was terribly anxious as to the kind of reception the public would give to the offspring of his brain. To calm his spirit, therefore, Monsieur de Saint-Aignan repeated to himself the following elegant and original lines, which he had previously recited, as an impromptu, to the king, and which he had promised to give to his majesty in writing:

> Iris, thine eyes do not impart
> The tender secrets of thy heart,
> But, dancing with malicious glee,
> They play the very deuce with me.

Beautiful and touching as this verse undoubtedly was, still Saint-Aignan, having reduced it to writing, could not repress the feeling that, somehow or other, it did not altogether do him justice. Thereupon, scratching his perplexed brow with the end of his pen, he began slowly to reread it to himself.

> 'Iris, thine eyes do not impart . . . '

'Well, dash it all,' said he, 'nobody can find fault with *that*; indeed, there is a little spice of Ronsard or Malherbe[56] about it that rather tickles me. Now for the second line.

> ' The tender secrets of thy heart . . . '

'Well, that's not so bad either, but, all the same, it has been truly said that the first line of a verse is always the easiest to write. Still, "tender secrets, etc." is distinctly poetical. We will let it pass.

> ' But, dancing with malicious glee . . . '

'Neat, you know, but not strictly accurate, because La Vallière is a somewhat tearful young woman. Still, there is such a thing as poetic licence, and as the line is evidently intended to be complimentary – yes, a child could see that – we will let it pass too.

> 'They play the very deuce with me.'

'There's a bold climax to have arrived at! A trifle too forcible, perhaps, considering the tender sentiment expressed in the preceding lines. But then, the charm of contrast! Life itself would be worth nothing without contrasts. Yes, decidedly it shall stand, and if jealous poetasters like to fall foul of my composition, let them do their worst. It would be awkward, though, if they spread about the idea that I am an indifferent poet, because if it should reach the ears of the king, he might be inclined to think so himself.'

Communing thus within himself, the comte proceeded to divest him of the rest of his riding costume, and had just pulled off his coat and waistcoat, when a servant announced the arrival of Monsieur le Baron Du Vallon de Bracieux de Pierrefonds.

'Gracious!' said Saint-Aignan, 'what a mouthful! I don't know him. Who the deuce is he?'

'He is,' answered the servant, 'a gentleman who had the honour of dining at the king's table when his majesty was staying at Fontainebleau.'

'With the king at Fontainebleau!' cried Saint-Aignan. 'Show him in at once.'

The servant hastened to obey this order, and Porthos entered the room.

Monsieur de Saint-Aignan, who had the retentive memory of a courtier, recognised him, at a glance, as the country magnate of wonderful reputation whom the king had received with so much favour at Fontainebleau, in spite of the significant smiles of many who were present. He advanced to meet him, therefore, with every show of courtesy, which seemed only natural to Porthos, who himself, when charged with a hostile message, was accustomed to use every form of exaggerated politeness.

Saint-Aignan ordered the servant who had shown him in to place a chair for Porthos; and the latter, who saw nothing unusual in these signs of politeness, sat down in it, and coughed.

After the interchange of some ordinary and commonplace remarks, the comte, as the receiver of the visit, enquired of Porthos to what happy circumstance he was indebted for the honour of it.

'Monsieur le comte,' said Porthos, 'that is exactly what I am about, in one moment, to explain to you; but, first, I am really sorry, but – '

'What is the matter?' asked Saint-Aignan.

'Why, I am afraid I have broken your chair.'

'Oh, not at all, not at all,' said Saint-Aignan, airily.

'I think it is a fact, all the same,' said Porthos, 'that I have broken it; and, what is more, if I continue to sit in it, I shall presently assume an undignified position which would ill accord with the gravity of the message which I have been entrusted to convey to you.'

Porthos rose accordingly, and it was quite time that he did so, for the chair had already given way several inches; Saint-Aignan looked round for a more solid article upon which to seat his guest.

'Modern furniture,' said Porthos, as Saint-Aignan tested the different chairs in the room – 'modern furniture is absurdly un-trustworthy. In my young days, when I was accustomed to sit down far more energetically than I do now, I cannot remember a single instance of having broken a chair – I don't, of course, include any tavern furniture which I may have broken hitting out with my fists.'

Monsieur de Saint-Aignan smiled sympathetically at this little pleasantry.

'But,' continued Porthos, gingerly disposing his huge bulk upon a substantial-looking sofa, which, although it groaned beneath his weight, still held together – 'but, unhappily, this is not the subject upon which I have called to see you.'

'Why unhappily? Can it be that you are the bearer of news of ill omen, baron?'

'Of ill omen to a gentleman? Certainly not, comte,' replied Porthos, majestically. 'My mission is simply to inform you that you have grossly insulted one of my friends.'

'I, sir!' cried Saint-Aignan; 'I insulted one of your friends! Which of them, in heaven's name?'

'Monsieur Raoul de Bragelonne.'

'I have insulted Monsieur de Bragelonne! It is absolutely impossible for me to have done so, for Monsieur de Bragelonne, whom I know so slightly that I might almost say that I don't know him at all, is, at the present time, in England, and I have not even seen him for a very long time. How, then, is it possible for me to have insulted him?'

'Monsieur de Bragelonne is, at the present time, in Paris, monsieur le comte,' replied Porthos, imperturbably; 'and, as to your having insulted him, it is certainly the case, because he has told me so himself. Yes, monsieur le comte, you have grossly, nay, mortally, insulted him, as I have the honour to repeat to you.'

'But I repeat that it is impossible; I declare to you, on my honour, that it is absolutely impossible.'

'Moreover,' added Porthos, 'you can scarcely be unaware of the circumstance, since Monsieur de Bragelonne has written to you to prepare you for my visit.'

'I give you my word that I have received no letter from him.'

'Well, that is extraordinary,' said Porthos. 'Raoul told me distinctly – '

'One moment, and I will convince you that I have heard nothing from him;' and he rang the bell. 'Basque,' he said to the servant who appeared, 'what letters or notes have arrived for me during my absence?'

'Three, monsieur le comte. A note from Monsieur de Fiesque, one from Madame de la Ferté and a letter from Monsieur de las Fuentes.'

'Is that all?'

'Everything, monsieur le comte.'

'Don't be afraid to speak the truth before monsieur le baron. I will take care that you get into no trouble through it.'

'Well, monsieur, I had forgotten a note from Mlle de Val – '

'That will do,' interrupted Porthos, discreetly; 'I am quite satisfied, and I believe your word, comte.'

Saint-Aignan dismissed the servant and went to the door to close it after him, but as he did so, he saw, protruding from the keyhole in the door of the next room, the identical paper which de Bragelonne had inserted before leaving.

'What have we here?' said he.

'Ah! what, indeed?' cried Porthos, who was sitting with his back to the door and turned round at Saint-Aignan's exclamation.

'A note stuck in the keyhole!' cried the latter.

'That will probably be the one in question, monsieur le comte. You had better read it.'

Saint-Aignan opened the paper. 'It *is* a note from Monsieur de Bragelonne,' said he.

'There,' said Porthos, 'you see I was right. Oh! when I say a thing – '

'And brought here by Monsieur de Bragelonne himself,' muttered Saint-Aignan. 'Oh! this is monstrous! How the devil could he have got in?' He rang the bell again, and Basque reappeared. 'Who has been in here since I have been absent with the king?'

'No one, monsieur.'

'That is absurd; someone *must* have been here.'

'But, comte, no one could possibly have got in, since I always carry the keys in my pocket.'

'Anyhow, I found this note in the keyhole. Someone must have put it there. It could not have got in by itself.'

Basque made a movement with his arms, to indicate that he could not explain the phenomenal appearance of the note.

'Probably Monsieur de Bragelonne put it in the keyhole himself,' said Porthos.

'But the keys have never been out of my possession,' persisted Basque.

Saint-Aignan crumpled up the paper after reading it.

'There is something mysterious under all this,' he murmured reflectively, and Porthos, for a few moments, left him to his reflections. Then he recurred to his mission.

'With your permission, we will now return to business,' he said to Saint-Aignan when the servant had left the room.

'I think that this note, which has so strangely come to hand, sufficiently explains it. Monsieur de Bragelonne informs me that a friend of his – '

'Yes, I am a friend of his, therefore it is *my* visit that he apprises you of.'

'For the purpose of bringing me a challenge?'

'Exactly.'

'And he complains that I have insulted him?'

'*Grossly! Mortally!*' roared Porthos, determined to carry out his instructions to the letter.

'May I ask in what way? For, really, this proceeding on the part of Monsieur de Bragelonne is so mysterious that I am altogether at a loss to understand it.'

'Sir,' replied Porthos, 'my friend *must* be right, and, as to his line of action, if there is anything mysterious in it, no one is to blame for it but yourself.'

Porthos pronounced these words with an assurance which, to a person unfamiliar with his peculiar methods, must have revealed an infinity of resource.

'So be it,' said Saint-Aignan; 'let us try to unveil the mystery, then.'

Porthos made a deprecating gesture. 'I think you will find it well not to enter too fully into details, monsieur, and I have excellent reasons for saying so.'

'I understand you perfectly. Let us touch only lightly on the subject, then. Pray go on, monsieur, I am all impatience.'

'In the first place, monsieur,' said Porthos, 'you have changed your apartments.'

'That is perfectly true,' said Saint-Aignan.

'You admit it, then?' said Porthos, with an air of marked satisfaction.

'Admit it? Of course I admit it. Why, in the name of all that's mysterious, should I not admit it?'

'You have admitted it; good,' said Porthos, and he held up one finger.

'Yes; and now tell me how my change of residence can possibly affect Monsieur de Bragelonne, for I declare that I am quite unable to guess what you are driving at.'

Porthos stopped him. 'Sir,' said he, gravely, 'this is but the first charge which Monsieur de Bragelonne brings against you. If he formulates his grievances, it is because he feels himself affronted.'

Saint-Aignan stamped his foot impatiently.

'Monsieur,' said he, 'this business looks like developing into a nasty quarrel.'

'Such an expression as *nasty*,' replied Porthos, with much dignity, 'is quite inadmissible when speaking of a gentleman of Monsieur de

Bragelonne's standing. But have you nothing to add on the subject of your change of lodging?'

'No; what next?'

'Ah! what next? But first, monsieur, we already have this charge, this grave offence, to deal with; and, as yet, you have offered no explanation, or, rather, no satisfactory one. How is this, monsieur? you actually change your apartments, thereby grossly affronting Monsieur de Bragelonne, and yet you offer no apology or excuse for your conduct? Very well.'

'What!' shouted Saint-Aignan, goaded to the verge of distraction at the absurdity of the situation. 'What! Is it necessary that I should consult Monsieur de Bragelonne as to changing my lodgings!'

'It is more; it is *absolutely imperative!*' bellowed Porthos, jumping up and staring his man straight in the face. 'And even this,' he continued, 'is a mere nothing as compared with the second grievance which Monsieur de Bragelonne has against you. The trap-door, sir! What about the trap-door?'

'The trap-door!' stammered Saint-Aignan, helplessly.

'Yes, sir, explain that if you can,' said Porthos, wagging his head.

Saint-Aignan bent his own. 'I have been betrayed,' he muttered; 'everything now is known.'

'Of course,' said Porthos, who knew nothing at all; 'everything is known.'

'You see me overwhelmed,' said Saint-Aignan, 'to such a degree that I am almost bereft of my wits.'

'Guilty conscience, no doubt,' growled Porthos. 'You are in a damned nasty hole, let me tell you; and when the matter is widely known, and the public form an opinion – '

'Oh, but,' interposed Saint-Aignan, quickly, 'such an affair as this must be jealously kept secret – even from one's confessor.'

'We will take steps,' said Porthos, 'to prevent it from travelling very far.'

'But,' said Saint-Aignan, 'Monsieur de Bragelonne, having made this discovery, must surely recognise the fact that he, as well as everybody else concerned, is in great peril.'

'Monsieur de Bragelonne runs no risk, Monsieur; neither does he fear any danger, as, please heaven, you will very soon find out.'

'Oh, this fellow is as mad as a hatter,' said Saint-Aignan to himself. 'What the deuce is he getting at?' Then he added aloud, 'Come, monsieur, this matter must be hushed up.'

'*You forget the portrait!*' roared Porthos, in a voice so terrible that it froze the other's blood.

As the portrait was that of La Vallière, and as no further misconception could exist, Saint-Aignan's eyes were suddenly opened.

'Ah!' he exclaimed, 'I quite forgot that he was engaged to her.'

Porthos, in total ignorance as to Saint-Aignan's meaning, frowned darkly, and assumed a haughty bearing.

'I don't care a damn,' said he, 'whether he was engaged or not; it is no business of mine, nor of yours either. Indeed, I think you have been guilty of great indiscretion in alluding to the subject at all. It will do your cause no good, I assure you.'

'Sir, you are the embodiment of all that is delicate and loyal. I now understand the whole matter perfectly.'

'So much the better,' said Porthos.

'And,' continued Saint-Aignan, 'you have shown the most delicate ingenuity in your manner of enlightening me. I thank you, monsieur, I thank you. And, now that I know everything, permit me to explain – ' Porthos intimated, by a gesture, that the matter had gone too far to admit of explanation, but Saint-Aignan, nevertheless, went on: 'I am distressed, beyond measure, at all that has happened, but what would you have done in my place? Tell me, between ourselves, how you would have acted?'

'What I should have done in your place,' said Porthos, 'doesn't affect the question at all. Let us keep to the matter in hand. There are three grievances with which you have to deal. You thoroughly understand that, I suppose?'

'As to the first, my change of abode. I put it to you, as a man of honour and common sense, when so august a personage expressed a desire that I should move, could I possibly disobey?'

Porthos opened his mouth, but, without giving him time to speak, Saint-Aignan continued: 'I see that you are touched by my frankness. I feel that you think I am right.'

Porthos made no reply.

'Now, with regard to this unfortunate trap-door,' continued Saint-Aignan, laying his hand on the arm of Porthos, 'which has been the cause and the means of so much that is regrettable, and which was constructed for – well, you know for what purpose. Do you think it likely that, of my own accord, I should have had it constructed in such a place, and for such a purpose? Oh no, I am sure you cannot think so. I know you must understand that I was influenced by a will more powerful than my own. You must perceive the infatuation – I do not speak of love – which was at work throughout. I am, indeed, fortunate in having to deal with a man so full of sensibility; otherwise, what an amount of suffering and scandal would she have to encounter, poor child! and he, also, whose name must not be mentioned.'

Porthos, overwhelmed and bewildered by the eloquence and gestures of Saint-Aignan, made every effort to grasp the meaning of this torrent of words, of which he understood not one, and could only sit upright and rigid in his seat, and gasp for breath.

Saint-Aignan, who had worked himself up to a high pitch of excitement, continued his oration with a fresh inflection of voice and still more animated gestures.

'And as to the portrait,' he cried, 'which I understand to be the chief grievance, am I to blame in that respect? Who desired to have the portrait? Was it I? Who is in love with the girl? Am I? Who painted the portrait? Did I? No! a thousand times no! I know that Monsieur de Bragelonne is in despair, and I know that he is the victim of a cruel misfortune. But I suffer as well, and nothing can be done. To offer resistance would be but to invite ridicule. If he persists he will be ruined. You will say that to despair shows weakness; but, at the same time, you are a sensible man, and understand me. I see by your serious, thoughtful, almost embarrassed manner, that you are thoroughly alive to the gravity of the situation. But to return to Monsieur de Bragelonne: thank him, as I would thank him myself, for having chosen to represent him a man of your calibre. Believe me, that, for my own part, I shall for ever feel indebted to the man who has so cleverly and ingeniously arranged this misunderstanding, and, although this secret is now known to four, instead of to three people, and it is a secret which would make the fortune of the most ambitious of mankind, I consider it a privilege to share it with you, monsieur. I rejoice that it is so from the bottom of my heart. From this moment I am altogether at your disposal. Only let me know what I can do for you, what favour I can ask, nay demand, for you. You have only to speak, sir;' and, according to the impulsive habits of the time, Saint-Aignan threw his arms round Porthos, and took him to his heart.

Porthos submitted to this demonstration of affection with the utmost resignation.

'Speak,' repeated Saint-Aignan; 'tell me what I can do for you.'

'Sir,' said Porthos, 'I have a horse below. Oblige me by mounting him. He has excellent manners, and will play you no tricks.'

'Mount a horse! Why, whatever for?' asked Saint-Aignan, astonished at the nature of the request.

'In order to accompany me to the place where Monsieur de Bragelonne is waiting for us.'

'Ah! he wishes to see me personally. Well, it is only natural that he should desire to hear some details of so delicate a business. But, unfortunately, I cannot go with you at this moment. The king is expecting me.'

'The king must wait, that's all,' said Porthos.

'Where is Monsieur de Bragelonne waiting for us?'

'At the Abbey of the Minimes, at Vincennes.'

'Well, I presume it is only to laugh over the affair?'

'I hardly think it likely. I, myself, see nothing to laugh at;' and Porthos called up the most severe expression that his face was capable of assuming.

'But the Minimes! Is not that a favourite place for hostile meetings? What, in heaven's name, should I go to the Minimes for?'

Porthos drew his sword. 'This is the length of my friend's weapon,' he said quietly.

'*Corbleu!* This man is mad!' cried Saint-Aignan.

Porthos flushed up to the ears. 'Sir,' said he, 'if I had not the honour to be under your roof, and acting in the interests of Monsieur de Bragelonne, I would throw you out of the window. However, it is only a ceremony postponed, and the pleasure will be none the less for being put off. Perhaps you will now come with me to the Minimes, monsieur?'

'But – '

'If you don't come voluntarily, I shall carry you, that's all.'

'Basque!' shouted Saint-Aignan.

Basque appeared. 'The king is asking for monsieur le comte,' said he.

'That makes a difference,' said Porthos: 'the king's service before everything. We can wait till the evening, monsieur;' and, saluting Saint-Aignan with his usual courtesy, Porthos took his leave, well satisfied at having arranged another affair.

Saint-Aignan watched him depart. Then, putting on again his coat and waistcoat, he hurried away, completing his toilette as he went, and muttering: 'The Minimes indeed! We shall see what view the king takes of this business; for the challenge is evidently aimed at him.'

## CHAPTER 17

## *Rival politicians*

THE KING, after this excursion, wherein so much homage was paid to Apollo, and in which each had offered tribute to the Muses, in the words of the poets of the time – the king, on his return to Paris, found Monsieur Fouquet awaiting him.

Close behind the king came Monsieur Colbert, who had waylaid his majesty in the corridor, and who now followed him like a dark and watchful shadow. Monsieur Colbert, with his square-shaped head and his untidy though rich dress, reminded one somewhat of a Flemish gentleman after a more than usually prolonged interview with a beer-jug.

Monsieur Fouquet, at the sight of his enemy, preserved his outward calmness of demeanour, and was careful not to pay Colbert the compliment even of allowing the contempt he felt for him to become visible.

Colbert, however, was at no pains to conceal the insolent satisfaction he felt at the turn which affairs had taken. In his opinion, Monsieur Fouquet had played his cards so badly as virtually to have lost, although the game was not yet over. He belonged to that school of politicians who admire the exercise of cunning, and have an eye for nothing beyond the ultimate success of their schemes. Colbert was not only a jealous and envious man, but one who had the true interests of the king at heart, because he was so strictly honest and conscientious in dealing with accounts that he could afford to pretend to himself that, in doing his best to bring about Monsieur Fouquet's ruin and downfall, he was acting solely for the welfare of the state and the preservation of the royal dignity.

None of these details escaped Monsieur Fouquet. Beneath the bushy eyebrows of his enemy, and in spite of the incessant movement of his eyelids, Fouquet could read his heart, and found it to be filled with hatred of himself and triumph at his approaching disgrace. Careful, however, whilst reading the thoughts of his enemy, to remain, himself, impenetrable, he composed his features and wore that charmingly sympathetic smile which was peculiarly his own, and which heightened not a little the easy grace of his manner as he approached the king.

'Sire,' he said, 'I gather, from the pleased expression of your majesty's face, that your excursion to Saint-Germain has been a success.'

'It was most charming, monsieur. You were wrong not to accept our invitation to make one of the party.'

'I was hard at work, sire,' replied Fouquet, who did not acknowledge Colbert's presence by so much as a turn of the head in his direction.

'Ah, the country!' cried the king; 'I should like to live there always in the fresh air and under the trees.'

'I trust that your majesty is not already tired of your throne,' said Fouquet.

'No; but a throne of green turf has a great attraction for me.'

'Truly, when your majesty so expresses yourself, you place a crown upon my desires, for it is anent the attractions of the country that I have a request to prefer.'

'On whose behalf, pray?'

'On behalf of the nymphs of Vaux, sire. Your majesty once deigned to make me a promise.'

'Which I recollect perfectly well,' said Louis XIV.

'The fête at Vaux – the famous fête, is it not, sire?' said Colbert, endeavouring to show his importance by joining in the conversation.

Fouquet treated the remark with contemptuous silence.

'Your majesty knows,' he said, 'that I am preparing my estate at Vaux for the reception of the most amiable of princes, the most powerful of kings.'

'I have promised,' said Louis; 'you have a king's word for it.'

'For my part,' said Fouquet, 'I can but assure your majesty that my sole ambition is to obey your slightest wish.'

'Have you many wonderful things to show us, monsieur?' And Louis XIV looked at Colbert.

'I am afraid I can hardly promise many wonders,' answered Fouquet, modestly; 'but I hope, nevertheless, to provide your majesty with some little amusement and temporary respite from the cares of state.'

'No, no, Monsieur Fouquet; I insist upon *wonders*. Oh! we know you to be a magician, and so powerful that you can find gold even when there is none to be had in the world. Why, people say you can make it.'

Fouquet perceived that this sally had a twofold signification, and that the king had shot at him an arrow from Colbert's bow, as well as one from his own.

'Oh!' said he, with a laugh, 'people know quite well from what mine I get my gold; they know it too well, perhaps. Only let me assure your majesty that the gold destined to pay for the fête at Vaux will cause neither blood nor tears to flow. It may entail a good deal of hard work, but one can always pay for that.'

This speech seemed to place Louis at a non-plus. He looked at Colbert, who was about to make some reply when an eagle's glance – a loyal, nay, almost royal, look – arrested the words on his lips.

The king, however, quickly recovered himself, and, turning to Fouquet: 'Then you give me a definite invitation?'

'Yes, if it please your majesty.'

'For what day?'

'For any day that will suit your majesty.'

'You speak as one who has the power of an enchanter. I am sure I could not say as much, Monsieur Fouquet.'

'Your majesty will do, at your own pleasure, all that a king can and ought to do. The King of France has at his command servants able to do anything in his service or for the gratification of his desires.'

Colbert tried to gather from Monsieur Fouquet's look whether he now regarded him with less hostile feelings. But Fouquet did not even condescend to glance in his direction. For him there was no Colbert. Such a person had no existence.

'Very good,' said the king. 'Will Sunday week suit you?'

'The time which your majesty deigns to grant will materially help the work which my architects must undertake for the entertainment of the king and his friends.'

'And, speaking of my friends,' said the king, 'whom of them do you propose to invite?'

'The king is paramount, sire. The king will make out his own list of invitations and issue his commands. Those whom the king may deign to invite will be received as my guests – my honoured guests.'

'Thanks,' said the king, in high appreciation of Fouquet's last speech; and, after a few words as to certain details, Fouquet took his departure.

He felt certain that Colbert would remain with the king, and that he himself would form the subject of their conversation. He felt, also, that neither would spare him. The gratification of giving a last and terrible blow to his enemy seemed, however, almost sufficient to compensate for all the suffering that might be in store for him. No sooner had he reached the door, therefore, than he returned, and, addressing the king, said: 'Pardon, sire! I crave pardon!'

'For what?' said the king.

'For a grave fault, sire, which I committed without being aware of it.'

'*You* have committed a fault? Well, Monsieur Fouquet, you are certainly pardoned beforehand. But against whom or what have you offended?'

'Against every law of propriety, sire. I have forgotten to inform your majesty of a recent occurrence of some little importance.'

'What is it?'

Colbert trembled; he feared that he was about to be denounced, and his conduct unmasked. A single word from Fouquet, a single proof formally tendered, and, such was the chivalrous nature of Louis XIV, that, in an instant, Colbert's favour would be a thing of the past. Colbert trembled, therefore, lest a bold stroke should be played which would bring down his entire scaffolding; and, indeed, the opportunity was such a grand one that a skilful player like Aramis would never have missed it.

'Sire,' said Fouquet, 'your majesty's forgiveness renders it easy for me to make my confession. This morning I sold one of my appointments.'

'Sold one of your appointments!' cried the king. 'Which of them have you sold?'

Colbert turned livid.

'That which conferred on me, sire, an imposing robe and an air of dignity – the post of Procureur-Général.'

The king uttered an involuntary exclamation, and looked at Colbert, who leant for support against the mantelpiece, and felt that he was about to faint.

'And to whom did you sell this appointment, Monsieur Fouquet?' asked the king.

'To a Councillor of the Parlement, sire, named Vanel.'

'Vanel?'

'Yes, a friend of Monsieur Colbert,' added Fouquet, letting his words drop slowly from his lips with inimitable unconcern, and with an expression of blissful unconsciousness which actor, poet or painter would despair of portraying with gesture, language or brush. Then, having finished what he had to say, and having crushed Colbert beneath the weight of his superiority, Monsieur Fouquet once more bowed to the king and took his leave, feeling himself half revenged by the stupefaction of the prince and the humiliation of the favourite.

'Is it possible?' said the king, when Fouquet had gone. 'Can he really have sold this appointment?'

'Yes, sire,' answered Colbert, with meaning.

'He must be mad!' said the king.

Colbert, this time, answered nothing. He had divined the king's thought. This thought avenged him also. Jealousy was now added to his hatred, and disgrace as well as ruin threatened his enemy.

Colbert had little uneasiness as to the future, for he felt that Louis XIV would be in accord with him in his hostility to Fouquet, and that the first false step made by the latter would only serve to hasten the calamity which, sooner or later, was bound to overtake him.

Fouquet had thrown aside his weapons, and hatred and jealousy had picked them up.

Colbert was invited by the king to the fête at Vaux. He bowed like a man quite sure of his own strength and accepted with the air of conferring a favour. The king was in the act of writing the name of Saint-Aignan upon his invitation-list, when an attendant announced 'the Comte de Saint-Aignan'; and, upon the arrival of the royal Mercury,[57] Colbert discreetly retired.

## CHAPTER 18

## *Rival lovers*

IT WAS BARELY two hours since Saint-Aignan had left Louis XIV, but, in the first ardour of his love, when Louis was unable to see La Vallière, he felt constrained to talk about her, and the subject being one upon which Saint-Aignan was the only person to whom he could speak without restraint, Saint-Aignan had become indispensable to him.

'Ah! is it you, comte?' he cried, as Saint-Aignan entered the room, doubly delighted to see him instead of Colbert, whose morose face had always a depressing effect on him. 'So much the better. I am glad to see you. You will join us in our little excursion party, I suppose?'

'Excursion party, sire?' asked Saint-Aignan. 'To what does your majesty allude?'

'To the fête which Monsieur Fouquet gives in our honour at Vaux, a few days hence. Ah! Saint-Aignan, you will witness a fête which will eclipse all our entertainments at Fontainebleau.'

'At Vaux? Monsieur Fouquet entertains your majesty at Vaux! Is that all?'

'Is that all!' echoed the king. 'It is really funny to see you turning up your nose in that way. If you don't know, my supercilious gentleman, let me tell you that when Monsieur Fouquet receives me at Vaux on Sunday week, people will be cutting one another's throats to get invited; and I repeat, Saint-Aignan, that you shall receive an invitation.'

'Very well, sire; although I fancy that, before the date in question, I shall have taken a longer and less agreeable journey.'

'What journey?'

'That across the Styx,[58] sire.'

'Nonsense!' said the king, laughing.

'I am quite serious, sire. I have received an invitation so pressing in its nature that I cannot see my way to refusing it.'

'I don't understand you. I see that you are in a poetical vein; but pray don't confuse Apollo with Phoebus.'[59]

'If your majesty will condescend to hear me, I will not keep you in suspense any longer.'

'Speak, then.'

'Does your majesty know the Baron Du Vallon?'

'Yes, indeed; a faithful servant of the king, my father, and a boon companion. He is the man who dined with us at Fontainebleau, is he not?'

'Exactly; but your majesty may not be aware that, in addition to these agreeable qualities, he is a noted swashbuckler – a regular fire-eater.'

'And does Monsieur Du Vallon desire to kill you?'

'He desires to get me killed, which is much the same thing.'

'The devil he does!'

'Do not laugh, sire. I am telling you no more than the exact truth.'

'And you say that he wants to have you killed?'

'At the present moment, that seems to be his sole object in life.'

'Don't be uneasy; I will protect you if he is in the wrong.'

'Ah! but there is an *if*.'

'No doubt; but answer as if you were referring to someone else's case instead of to your own. Is he right or wrong?'

'Your majesty shall judge of that.'

'What have you done to offend him?'

'Him, personally, nothing at all; but it seems that I have offended one of his friends.'

'That is the same thing; and is his friend one of the famous "four"?'[60]

'No; but he is the son of one of them.'

'Well, what have you done to him? Let us hear all about it.'

'Oh! I have helped someone to take his mistress from him.'

'And you admit it?'

'I have no choice but to admit it, since it is true.'

'In that case, you are in the wrong.'

'Is that your majesty's judgment?'

'Decidedly it is; and, if he kills you, it will serve you right.'

'And that is your majesty's deliberate conclusion?'

'Have you any reason to find fault with it?'

'It is a very expeditious way of settling the matter, at all events.'

'My uncle Henri IV[61] used to say, "Let justice be strict, and promptly administered." '

'Then, perhaps, the king will be good enough to sign my adversary's pardon. He is, at this moment, awaiting me at the Minimes, for the purpose of running me through the body.'

'Tell me his name, and give me a parchment.'

'Sire, a parchment lies on your majesty's table, and as for his name – '

'Well, what is it?'

'The Vicomte de Bragelonne, sire.'

'The Vicomte de Bragelonne!' exclaimed the king, whose laughter was instantly checked as he perceived the gravity of the situation. 'De Bragelonne,' he said again, as he wiped his forehead, upon which a perspiration had broken out.

'No other, sire,' said Saint-Aignan.

'De Bragelonne, who was affianced to – ?'

'The same, sire.'

'But I thought he was in London!'

'He was; but I can assure your majesty that he is not there now.'

'Is he in Paris, then?'

'He is, at the present moment, at the Minimes, waiting for me, as I have had the honour to inform your majesty.'

'And he knows everything?'

'And other things besides. Perhaps your majesty would like to see the letter which he has addressed to me?'

And Saint-Aignan produced from his pocket the letter we know of.

'When your majesty has read the letter, I shall have the honour to explain how it reached my hands.'

The king was much agitated while reading the letter. 'Well?' he said, after its perusal.

'Well, your majesty knows a certain chased lock which secures a certain ebony door, which separates a certain apartment from a certain still more private room that is furnished in blue and white?'

'Certainly – Louise's boudoir.'

'Well, sire, it was in the keyhole of that lock that I found the note. Who could have put it there? It must have been either Monsieur de Bragelonne or the devil; but as the note itself smells of amber, and not of sulphur, I conclude that it was Monsieur de Bragelonne, and not the other.'

Louis bent his head, and became immersed in thought, and, perhaps, at that moment, he felt something like remorse at heart.

'Ah,' said he, presently, 'the secret is discovered!'

'Sire, I shall do my best to bury the secret in the breast of the man who has obtained possession of it,' said Saint-Aignan, in a tone which was quite Spanish in its bravado, and was moving towards the door when a gesture of the king stopped him.

'Where are you going?'

'To the place where I am expected, sire.'

'To do what?'

'To fight Monsieur de Bragelonne, I suppose.'

'To fight?' cried the king. 'One moment, if you please, monsieur.'

Saint-Aignan shook his head after the manner of a spoilt child whom someone tries to prevent from falling down a well, or from playing with a knife.

'At all events, sire – ' he said.

'In the first place,' said the king, 'I am only, as yet, half enlightened.'

'I will endeavour to make clear any point which requires explanation. Your majesty has but to question me.'

'Who told you that Monsieur de Bragelonne got into the room in question?'

'The note which I found in the keyhole, as I have had the honour to tell your majesty.'

'But how do you know that it was de Bragelonne who put it there?'

'Who else would have dared to undertake such a commission?'

'That is true,' said the king; 'but how did he get into your rooms?'

'Ah, that is where the difficulty comes in, especially when it is borne in mind that the doors were locked, and that my servant had the keys in his pocket.'

'Someone must have bribed him.'

'Impossible, sire.'

'Why impossible?'

'Because, upon discovery being made, he would be at once suspected of having betrayed his trust; and no one who had bribed him would be likely to give the poor devil away, because his help might be required a second time.'

'That is true, also,' said the king. 'Well, now, I can conceive only one other way in which it could have been done.'

'Let me hear, sire, if your majesty's conjecture agrees with what is in my own mind.'

'I think that he could have got in only by making use of the secret staircase.'

'Alas! sire, I fear that is the only too probable explanation.'

'And it is no less probable that someone has sold the secret of the trap-door.'

'Either sold or given away.'

'Why do you draw that distinction?'

'Because there are certain persons who are beyond all suspicion of mercenary considerations. Such persons might *give*; they would never *sell*.'

'Explain yourself.'

'Oh, I feel that your majesty is too acute not to understand me, and will, I am sure, spare me the pain of mentioning a name.'

'Perhaps you are right,' said the king. 'I presume that you allude to Madame, who was probably alarmed at your change of apartments.'

'Madame – who has keys to the apartments of the maids of honour, and who alone had the power to discover what no one else, save your majesty's self, could find out.'

'And you think that my sister has allied herself with de Bragelonne, and has made him acquainted with these details?'

'Perhaps she has done even more than that.'

'More! Pray finish what you have to say.'

'Perhaps she even brought him to my rooms herself. Would your majesty be surprised if it were so?'

The king uttered an inarticulate exclamation.

'Listen, sire. Your majesty is aware that Madame is much addicted to the use of perfumes?'

'Yes; it is a habit which she contracted from my mother.'

'And she especially affects vervain?'

'Yes; it is her favourite perfume.'

'Well, my rooms are redolent of it.'

The king once more became wrapped in thought.

'But,' he continued, after a few moments' silence, 'why should Madame take de Bragelonne's part against me?'

By asking this question, which Saint-Aignan could easily have answered with the words 'woman's jealousy', the king sought to sound his friend with a view to finding out whether he knew anything of the attentions which he, Louis, had been paying to his sister-in-law. But

Saint-Aignan was too knowing a bird to be caught; moreover, he always fought shy of family secrets, and he was too well acquainted with the classics not to remember the unfortunate Ovid,[62] and the many tears he was condemned to shed in expiation of the crime of having been a witness of something, one does not know what, which took place in the Palace of Augustus. He, therefore, endeavoured to avoid giving any direct answer to the king's question. Unfortunately for him, however, he had shown so much sagacity in detecting the signs of Madame's presence in his apartments that the king would not be denied, but held him to the point.

'Why,' he repeated, with dogged determination – 'why should Madame take de Bragelonne's part against me?'

'Why?' repeated Saint-Aignan, hesitatingly. 'Has your majesty forgotten that the Comte de Guiche and the Vicomte de Bragelonne are close and intimate friends?'

'I fail to see the connection of ideas,' replied the king.

'Forgive me, sire,' said Saint-Aignan, 'but is not Monsieur de Guiche a particular friend of Madame?'

'That is so,' replied the king; 'the reason is not far to seek. The blow comes from that direction.'

'And does not your majesty think that the hit should be countered?'

'Yes, but not in the way it would be done in the Bois de Vincennes,' replied the king.

'I trust your majesty will not forget,' said Saint-Aignan, 'that I am a gentleman, and that I have been challenged.'

'The affair does not concern you at all.'

'Nevertheless, it is I who have been expected at the Minimes for more than an hour, sire, and I shall be dishonoured if I do not go.'

'The first duty of a gentleman is to obey his king.'

'Sire – '

'I order you to remain.'

'But, sire – '

'You will be good enough to obey.'

'Sire, it must be as your majesty pleases.'

'Besides, I must have this business cleared up. I want to know who has insulted me by so audaciously entering a room which should be sacred to myself. It is no part of your duty to call to account those who have acted with such insolence, for it is not *your* honour that has been attacked, but *my own*.'

'I trust that your majesty will not visit your displeasure too heavily upon Monsieur de Bragelonne, for, though he may have acted imprudently, he has never wavered in his loyalty.'

'Enough! I know how to act justly, even in the heat of passion. Above all, take care that not a word of this reaches Madame.'

'But what of Monsieur de Bragelonne, sire? He will be going in search of me, and – '

'Rest contented. I shall see him, or have him spoken to before the evening has passed.'

'Once more, sire, I entreat you to be lenient.'

'I have been lenient long enough, comte,' said Louis XIV, with an ominous frown, 'and it is high time to show certain persons that I intend to be master in my own house.'

The king had hardly uttered these words, indicating that old grievances[63] mingled with his present sense of injury, when an usher appeared at the door of the cabinet.

'What is it now?' asked the king, sharply; 'and what do you mean by coming here without being called?'

'Sire,' said the usher, 'your majesty has commanded me, once for all, to allow the Comte de la Fère to pass,[64] whenever he should desire audience of your majesty.'

'Well?'

'The Comte de la Fère is in attendance.'

At these words, the king and Saint-Aignan exchanged looks as full of apprehension as of surprise. Louis hesitated a moment; then, immediately afterwards, having formed his resolution: 'Go,' he said to Saint-Aignan, 'and find Louise. Let her know of the plot which has been hatched against us. Warn her that Madame will recommence her persecutions and that she has introduced into the affair people who would have done far better had they remained neutral.'

'Sire – '

'If Louise is upset, do your best to reassure her, and tell her that the king's love is an impenetrable shield for her protection. If, as I suspect, she already knows all, or if she has been subjected to attack from any quarter, tell her distinctly, Saint-Aignan,' added the king, trembling with rage, 'make her understand that, this time, in place of defending, I will avenge her, and that so terribly, that none henceforth will dare to raise their eyes towards her.'

'Is that all, sire?'

'That is all. Go as quickly as you can, and be loyal, you who live in the midst of this hell upon earth, without having, like me, the hope of paradise.'

Saint-Aignan exhausted himself in protestations of devotion. He kissed the king's hand, and left the royal presence beaming with satisfaction.

## CHAPTER 19

## King and nobles

THE KING took pains to compose his features for his coming interview with Monsieur de la Fère. He foresaw that this visit was no chance one, and that important issues were likely to be involved in it. He was anxious, therefore, not to allow his distinguished visitor to perceive, from his demeanour, that anything had occurred to ruffle his temper.

When the young king felt that he had regained his composure, he gave orders for the comte to be admitted. A few minutes later, Athos, attired in court dress, and wearing the decorations which he alone had the right to wear at the Court of France, presented himself with an air of such unusual gravity that the king saw at a glance that his instincts had not misled him.

Louis advanced a step to meet the comte, and, with a smile, extended his hand, over which Athos bowed with every mark of respect.

'Comte,' said the king, speaking with a rapid utterance, 'you so rarely pay me a visit, nowadays, that it is quite a pleasure to see you.'

Athos bowed as he replied, 'I should be glad always to be near your majesty.'

The tone in which he uttered this reply conveyed unmistakably that his meaning was that he would like always to be at the king's elbow, so as to be able to advise him against committing indiscretions.

The king thoroughly understood this, and at once decided to make every use of the advantage which complete self-possession and high rank would give him.

'I see that you have something to say to me,' he said.

'If it were not so, I should not have ventured to intrude myself upon your majesty.'

'Speak quickly; I am only too anxious to satisfy you,' replied the king, as he took a seat.

'I feel persuaded,' said Athos, not without emotion, 'that your majesty will give me every satisfaction.'

'Ah!' said the king, somewhat loftily, 'you have something to complain of, then.'

'It would be a complaint,' said Athos, 'but that your majesty – But, if you will permit me, sire, I will repeat the conversation from the beginning.'

'I am listening.'

'Your majesty may remember that, at the time of the Duke of Buckingham's departure,[65] I was honoured with an interview with the king.'

'I remember the circumstance, but the subject of the interview has escaped my recollection.'

'I shall have the honour to recall it to your majesty's recollection,' said Athos. 'It had reference to a marriage which Monsieur de Bragelonne was desirous of contracting with Mademoiselle de la Vallière.'

'Now the murder's out,' thought the king. 'I remember,' he said aloud.

'At that time,' continued Athos, 'the king condescended to express himself in such gracious terms to Monsieur de Bragelonne and myself that not a word of what he said has escaped my memory.'

'Go on,' said the king.

'And the king, of whom I asked the hand of Mademoiselle de la Vallière for Monsieur de Bragelonne, met my request with a refusal.'

'Quite true,' said Louis, dryly.

'On the ground,' added Athos, quickly, 'of the lady's lack of social position.'

Louis could scarcely restrain himself.

'That she was of comparatively obscure origin.'

The king became still more impatient.

'That she had no fortune, and but little beauty,' continued Athos, remorselessly.

This last thrust found its way to the heart of the royal lover, and, for the moment, overcame him. He threw himself back in his chair, and remarked: 'You have an excellent memory, monsieur.'

'I have sometimes found it useful, when I have had the distinguished honour of being received by your majesty,' replied the comte, imperturbably.

'Let it be admitted that I so expressed myself.'

'And I thanked your majesty, since your words implied that you took an interest in Monsieur de Bragelonne which could not fail to be highly gratifying to us both.'

'You may also remember,' said the king, weighing each word, 'that you yourself were much averse to this marriage.'

'It is true, sire.'

'And that the request was preferred against your better judgement?'

'Yes, your majesty.'

'And I also remember, for my memory is almost as good as your own – I remember, I say, that you made use of this expression, "I do not believe in Mademoiselle de la Vallière's affection for Monsieur de Bragelonne." '

Athos felt the hit, but he did not flinch.

'Sire,' he said, 'I have already begged your majesty's forgiveness, but there are certain points in that conversation which its result alone can render intelligible.'

'Let us have the final result, then.'

'It was this. Your majesty said that the marriage should be postponed in the interests of Monsieur de Bragelonne.'

The king did not reply.

'At the present time, Monsieur de Bragelonne is in such a perturbed state of mind that he can no longer defer asking your majesty for an explanation.'

The king turned pale; Athos looked at him attentively.

'And what,' said the king, in a hesitating voice, 'does Monsieur de Bragelonne actually require?'

'Simply what I asked of your majesty at our last interview – the king's consent to this marriage.'

The king did not answer.

'The obstacles in the way of the marriage no longer exist,' continued Athos. 'Mademoiselle de la Vallière, although possessed of neither fortune, high birth nor beauty, is, nevertheless, the one woman in the world for Monsieur de Bragelonne, since he loves her.'

The king made a movement of impatience with his hands.

'The king hesitates?' asked Athos, without the slightest diminution either of determination or politeness.

'I do not hesitate; *I refuse*,' replied the king.

Athos took himself in hand.

'I have had the honour,' he said, in his mildest manner, 'to point out to your majesty that no obstacle now stands in the way of Monsieur de Bragelonne's affections, and that he is not the least likely to change his mind.'

'There is my will,' said the king; 'is *that* no obstacle?'

'It is the most serious one of all,' replied Athos.

'I imagined that it would scarcely be ignored,' observed the king, sarcastically.

'And now, is it permitted humbly to ask the king his reason for this refusal?'

'The reason! a question to *me*!' exclaimed the king.

'Nay! a demand, sire.'

The king leant with both hands upon the table.

'You forget yourself,' he said. 'Let me remind you that, at court, it is not the custom to question the king.'

'That is true, sire; still, if it is forbidden to question, no one can be prohibited from forming what conjecture he chooses.'

'Conjecture! explain yourself, pray.'

'Conjecture, on the part of a subject, mostly implies doubt as to the perfect frankness of the king.'

'What do you mean?'

'And causes the subject to lose confidence,' pursued Athos, inexorably.

'I repeat that you forget yourself, monsieur,' said the king, unable any longer to restrain his wrath.

'Sire, I am compelled to seek elsewhere what I thought to find in your majesty. In place of obtaining an answer from the king, I am driven to make one for myself.'

The king rose from his seat. 'Monsieur,' said he, 'I have given you all the time that I have at my disposal.'

This was, of course, tantamount to a dismissal.

'Sire, I have not yet had time to say to the king what I came with the express purpose of saying, and I see your majesty so rarely that I feel I ought not to neglect the present opportunity.'

'You were speaking just now of conjecture; you are now passing from conjecture to offence.'

'Is it possible that I can offend your majesty? Never! I have all my life been under the impression that kings were above ordinary mortals, not only in rank and power, but in nobility of mind and in moral courage. Nothing shall ever make me believe that my sovereign, who gave me his word, did so with mental reservation.'

'I don't understand what you mean by mental reservation.'

'Allow me to explain,' said Athos, frigidly. 'In refusing the hand of Mademoiselle de la Vallière to Monsieur de Bragelonne, your majesty had in view another end besides the interests and future happiness of the Vicomte.'

'Monsieur, you insult me!'

'If you delayed the marriage solely to afford yourself an opportunity for sending Mademoiselle de la Vallière's betrothed out of the way – '

'How dare you, sir!' gasped the king, boiling over with indignation.

'It is what I hear said on all sides. Everywhere your majesty's infatuation with Mademoiselle de la Vallière is a topic of conversation.'

The king tore his gloves, which, in suppressed rage, he had been biting for some time.

'Let them beware,' he cried, 'who presume to meddle in my affairs! I have decided upon a certain course and I will break down every obstacle.'

'What obstacles?' said Athos.

The king stopped short, like a runaway horse suddenly checked by the curb.

'I love Mademoiselle de la Vallière!' he declared, with passionate emphasis, and not without dignity.

'But,' interrupted Athos, 'that does not prevent your allowing her to be married to Monsieur de Bragelonne. It is a sacrifice worthy of a king, and deserved by Monsieur de Bragelonne, who has served your majesty faithfully, and is certainly entitled to be looked upon as a brave and honourable man. The king, by thus making a sacrifice of his own affections, would prove, at the same time, his generosity, his gratitude, and would show a wise policy.'

'Mademoiselle de la Vallière,' said the king, in a hollow voice, 'does not love Monsieur de Bragelonne.'

'Is your majesty convinced of that?' asked Athos, with a scrutinising look.

'I know it,' said the king.

'But for a short time only, then; for, had you known it at the time when I first mentioned the subject, your majesty would surely have taken the trouble to tell me so.'

'I have known it but a very short time,' said Louis.

Athos was silent for a moment. 'I cannot understand, then,' said he, presently, 'with what object your majesty sent away Monsieur de Bragelonne to London. This act very naturally came as a surprise to all to whom the king's honour is dear at heart.'

'Who talks about the king's honour, Monsieur de la Fère?'

'The honour of the king, sire, comprises that of his entire nobility. When the king wrongs one of his gentlemen, that is to say, when the king takes from him the smallest shred of his honour, it is from the king himself that it has been taken.'

'Monsieur de la Fère!'

'Sire, you sent the Vicomte de Bragelonne to London before you became the lover of Mademoiselle de la Vallière, and since that time you have made love to her.'

The king, furiously incensed, now that he felt that he was being proved to be in the wrong, endeavoured to dismiss Athos with an imperious gesture.

'Sire, I will say everything that I have to say,' continued the comte, 'and I will not go away until I have been satisfied by your majesty, or by myself – satisfied, if you prove to me that you are right, satisfied if I prove to you that you are wrong. Oh! you must hear me, sire. I am an old man, and conservative of all that is truly great and powerful in your kingdom. I am a gentleman who has shed his blood for your father, and for yourself, without ever having asked any favours in return. I have never wronged anyone in the world, and kings have been under obligations[66] to me. Oh! you will listen to me. I am here to demand an account of the honour of one of your servants whom you have wronged by your duplicity, and betrayed by your indifference to the sufferings of others. I know that these words enrage your majesty; but, on the other hand, we, your servants, are slain by your actions. I know that you are considering with what punishment you will visit my temerity, and I, on my own part, know what punishment I shall pray God to inflict upon you, when I shall recount to Him your perjury, and the wrong my son has suffered at your hands.'

The king, with hand thrust into the breast of his coat and flashing eyes, strode hurriedly up and down the apartment.

'Why, sir,' he cried suddenly, 'were I, indeed, your king, you would already be punished; as it is, I am but a man with a right to love, upon this earth, those who regard me with affection, a happiness rarely granted me.'

'You have no more claim to such a right as a man than you have as a king; had you wished to behave loyally, you would have spoken candidly to Monsieur de Bragelonne, instead of sending him into exile.'

'I am absolutely drifting into a discussion with you,' interrupted Louis XIV, with that majesty and dignity of look and voice which none could assume like himself.

'I am still in hopes that you will favour me with a reply,' said the comte.

'You will have my reply soon enough, monsieur.'

'You already know my opinion,' replied Monsieur de la Fère.

'You forget that you are addressing a king. This is nothing less than an outrage.'

'You forget that you are blasting the lives of two men, sire. That is a mortal sin.'

'Leave the room at once, monsieur.'

'Not until I have finished, son of Louis XIII. You are making a sorry beginning of your reign, for you begin with seduction and disloyalty. I, and mine, are now absolved from all that allegiance to or respect for you which I made my son swear in the vaults of St Denis's.[67] You have become our enemy, sire, and, henceforth, we acknowledge no master but God Himself. Take warning!'

'You dare to threaten?'

'Oh no,' said Athos, sadly. 'I have no more sense of bravado than of fear in my heart. God, of whom I have spoken to you, sire, hears what I say; He knows that, for the integrity and honour of the crown you wear, I am even now ready to shed every drop of blood that twenty years of civil and foreign wars have left in my veins. I threaten the king as little as I do the man; but I tell you that you lose two servants, in that you have killed the faith in the father's heart, and the love which was in the son's. The one no longer believes in the word of the king, and the other believes no more in the loyalty of man, or in the purity of woman. You have destroyed the respect of the one, and the obedience of the other. Farewell!'

So saying, Athos broke his sword across his knee, gently laid down the two fragments on the floor, and, bowing to the king, who choked with rage and mortification, strode out of the cabinet. It was some minutes before Louis was able to master his agitation; then, suddenly rising, he rang the bell violently.

'Send for Monsieur d'Artagnan,' he said to the astonished ushers.

### CHAPTER 20

## After the storm

OUR READERS ARE, no doubt, wondering how it was that Athos, of whom we have lost sight for so long, happened so opportunely to appear upon the scene, as related in the last chapter. Our object, in writing this history, being to string together the chain of events in as logical a sequence as possible, we are in a position to explain the matter, and will, at once, proceed to do so.

Porthos, zealous in his duty as 'arranger of affairs', had, on leaving the Palais-Royal, hastened to rejoin Raoul at the Minimes, where he related to him every detail of his interview with Saint-Aignan. He added that he did not suppose that the delay occasioned by the king's summons would be anything more than trivial, and that no doubt Saint-Aignan, on being released by the king, would lose no time in making his appearance. But Raoul, more suspicious than his old friend, concluded, from Porthos's story, that, if Saint-Aignan had an interview with the king, he would tell his majesty the whole story, and that, if he did so, the king would certainly forbid him to go to the Minimes.

He had, therefore, thought it best to leave Porthos on the ground, in the improbable case that Saint-Aignan might arrive, but, at the same time, he enjoined him not to wait there more than an hour, or, at the outside, an hour and a half. To this arrangement, however, Porthos refused to agree, but, on the contrary, took up his station at the Minimes as if he intended to take root there, extracting a promise from Raoul that, upon leaving his father, he would go straight to his own lodging, and remain there, so that Porthos's servant might know where to look for him, supposing that Saint-Aignan should, after all, make his appearance at the rendezvous.

De Bragelonne, accordingly, had left Vincennes, and ridden straight to see Athos, who had arrived in Paris two days previously.

The comte, whom d'Artagnan had already apprised by letter of what was taking place, greeted his son affectionately and motioned him to a seat.

'I know,' said he, 'that you come to me as a man comes to a friend when he is in danger or difficulty; tell me, then, what is it that brings you here?'

The young man bowed, and began his story, and although at some of its details he could scarcely repress his emotion, he managed to get through it.

Athos was already acquainted with its purport, since, as we have said, d'Artagnan had written to him; but carefully maintaining that composure and self-possession which were habitual to him, he replied: 'Raoul, I do not believe everything that people say, and I refuse to believe that things are as you fear, although I must admit that the matter has been mentioned to me by persons who do not, as a rule, speak at random; but, upon my word and conscience, I think it absolutely impossible that the king can have been guilty of an outrage like this upon a gentleman. I will answer for the king, and will go at once, and bring you back a proof that my view is the correct one.'

Raoul, wavering between what his own eyes had shown him, and the unbounded confidence he had in a man who never condescended to lie, bowed, and contented himself with saying: 'Go, then, sir. I will await your return.'

Then he sat down, and buried his face in his hands, whilst Athos set out upon that visit to the king, with the details of which our readers are already acquainted.

Raoul remained in this despondent attitude until he was aroused by the sounds which announced the comte's return.

Athos entered the room, serious and pale of countenance. He handed his hat to a servant, dismissed him, and sat down by the side of his son.

'Well, sir,' said the young man, sadly, as he raised his head, 'are you convinced now?'

'I am, Raoul; the king is in love with Mademoiselle de la Vallière.'

'What! do you mean to say that he admits it?'

'Absolutely.'

'And she?'

'I did not see her.'

'But the king, I presume, spoke of her. What did he say?'

'Simply, that he loved her.'

'There! then you see how it is!' groaned Raoul, with a gesture of despair.

'Raoul,' continued the comte, 'I said to the king everything that you could possibly have said for yourself, and I trust that what I told him was expressed in becoming, if unmistakable, language.'

'And what did you tell him, sir, may I ask?'

'I told him that all was over between him and ourselves, and that you were no longer to be regarded as one of his servants; I told him that, for my own part, I should hold myself aloof. There is only one thing now that remains for me to ascertain.'

'And that is?'

'I wish to know if you have decided upon your own line of action.'

'In what respect, sir?'

'Why, in respect of your misplaced affection, and as to how you propose to avenge yourself. I fear you have not yet considered that question sufficiently, if at all.'

'Oh, as to my love, someday, perhaps, I shall succeed in rooting it out from my heart. I hope to do so – at all events, with heaven's aid, and the help of your wise counsel. As to vengeance, I have only dreamt of it under the influence of a malignant spirit, for I could never wreak my vengeance upon the real culprit. No, I have given up all thought of vengeance.'

'Then, I presume, you no longer think of picking a quarrel with Monsieur de Saint-Aignan?'

'No; I have already sent Monsieur de Saint-Aignan a challenge. If he accepts it, well and good, I shall be there; if not, I shall let the matter drop.'

'And La Vallière?'

'Why, sir, you cannot seriously suppose that I should dream of taking vengeance against a woman,' replied Raoul, with a smile so sad that it moistened the eyes of Athos, who had himself so often bent beneath the weight of his own grief and the sorrows of others. He held out a sympathetic hand to Raoul, who grasped it eagerly.

'And so you really think, sir, that, as the matter stands, there is no chance of my obtaining any redress?'

Athos shook his head. 'Poor fellow!' he said softly.

'You think that I still cherish a hope,' said Raoul, 'and you pity me. Ah! it is terrible, indeed, to have to think with contempt of one whom I have loved so fondly. If only I had some real ground for complaint against her, I should be happier, and might, in time, forgive her.'

Athos looked mournfully at his son. The words which he had just uttered found an echo in his own heart.

At that moment a servant announced Monsieur d'Artagnan. The name fell with a different signification upon the ears of Athos and Raoul.

The musketeer thus announced entered the room with an incipient smile upon his lips. Raoul stood still, whilst Athos advanced to meet his friend with an expression of countenance which did not escape de Bragelonne. D'Artagnan's reply to Athos was a slight contraction of the eyelid. Then he walked up to Raoul, and took his hand.

'Well,' he said, speaking for the first time, and addressing Athos, 'so you are doing your best to console the poor boy?'

'And it is like you,' said Athos, 'to come here to aid me in the difficult task;' and, so saying, he pressed d'Artagnan's hand, and Raoul fancied that something was conveyed in that touch quite apart from the words that accompanied it.

'Yes,' replied the musketeer, stroking his moustaches with his disengaged hand – 'yes, I thought I would look in.'

'And you are welcome, chevalier; not alone for the consolation which you bring, but for your own sake,' said Raoul, with the ghost of a smile, sadder than any tears that d'Artagnan had ever seen shed.

'Well, that's right,' said d'Artagnan.

'You are just in time,' continued Raoul, 'to hear the details of an interview which the comte has had with the king. You will permit him to relate them, will you not?' and the young man's eyes sought to penetrate to the bottom of the musketeer's heart.

'His interview with the king?' said d'Artagnan, in a tone of such genuine surprise that no one could have doubted that he was really astonished. 'Have you seen the king, Athos?'

Athos smiled. 'Yes,' he said, 'I have seen him.'

'But, did you really not know that the comte had seen him?' asked Raoul, only half convinced.

'Yes, indeed, that is so.'

'I am relieved to hear you say so,' said Raoul.

'Relieved! Why?' asked Athos.

'Nay,' said Raoul, 'I ask your forgiveness; but knowing, as I do, the love you bear me, I feared lest you might have been led into expressing yourself to his majesty in somewhat over-vigorous language; and that the king – '

'And that the king,' said d'Artagnan. 'Finish what you have to say, Raoul.'

'Forgive me, in your turn, Monsieur d'Artagnan,' said Raoul, 'but I admit that I feared that you had come less in the character of Monsieur d'Artagnan, than as captain of musketeers.'

'Nonsense, my good fellow,' cried d'Artagnan, with a laugh which an acute observer might have found somewhat forced; 'you must be crazy.'

'So much the better,' said Raoul.

'Yes, crazy; and now will you allow me to give you a piece of advice?'

'Say on,' replied Raoul; 'coming from you, the advice is sure to be valuable.'

'Very good; then I advise you, after your journey from London, after your visit to Monsieur de Guiche, after your visit to Madame, after your visit to Porthos, after your jaunt to Vincennes – I advise you, I say, after all this fatigue, to go to bed and get twelve hours' sleep. When you wake up, jump upon one of my horses and gallop him till he can't raise a trot;' and, drawing Raoul towards him, he embraced him as if he were, in truth, his own son.

Athos followed his example; but it might have been noticed that the kiss was more tender, and the pressure of the arms less powerful, in the case of the father than in that of the friend.

Raoul looked at the two men with the closest attention, but, neither from the smiling countenance of the musketeer, nor from the calm and self-possessed manner of the comte, was he able to form any idea as to their real feelings or intentions.

'Where are you going, Raoul?' asked the latter, as his son prepared to leave the room.

'To my own rooms,' answered Raoul, in his sad, mild voice.

'It is there, then, that you are to be found, should it be necessary to speak to you?'

'Yes; but do you anticipate that there will be something to acquaint me with?'

'How can I tell?' said Athos.

'Oh yes! there are, no doubt, fresh consolations in store for you,' said d'Artagnan, as he gently pushed Raoul towards the door.

Raoul, quite reassured by the perfect serenity of his two companions, left the room, feeling that he had now nothing but his own individual grief to trouble him.

'Thank heaven,' he said to himself, 'I have nothing but my own sorrow to brood over.' And, wrapping himself up in his cloak, so as to conceal from passers-by the dejection of his countenance, he made his way to his own apartments in accordance with his promise to Porthos.

The two friends looked after him with compassionate glances, and uttered the same words simultaneously, but with different emphasis.

'Poor Raoul!' said Athos, with a sigh.

'Poor Raoul!' repeated d'Artagnan, with a shrug of the shoulders.

CHAPTER 21

# Heu, miser!

'POOR RAOUL!' Athos had said. D'Artagnan had repeated, 'Poor Raoul!' To have excited the compassion of two strong-minded men like these, Raoul must indeed have been an object for commiseration.

Accordingly, when he found himself alone, and face to face with his own sorrow, away from his intrepid friend and his indulgent father; when he recalled the king's avowal of love for Louise de la Vallière, he felt that his heart would break – as we have all felt at the destruction of our first illusion, at the betrayal of our first love.

'Alas! it is over,' he muttered. 'I have nothing now to live for; nothing to look forward to; nothing to hope for. De Guiche, d'Artagnan and my own father have all told me so. Everything in this world is but a dream. The promise of happiness, which I have pursued for the last ten years, is but an idle chimera. This union of hearts – a dream; this life of love and happiness – still but a dream. But it would be the height of folly to proclaim my sorrow publicly, before friends as well as enemies, thus causing my friends pain and giving my enemies the opportunity of laughing at my grief. My misfortunes would soon be common property, and the subject of public comment, and ridicule.' And, in spite of his former protestations, Raoul could not restrain the utterance of a few words of deep menace.

'Nevertheless,' he continued, 'if I were named de Wardes, and if I had the strength of mind and the vigorous intellect of d'Artagnan, I could, at least, wear a smiling face before the world and could lead women to believe that this false-hearted girl, to whom I had given my love, had left me with but one regret – that of having been deceived by her assumption of candour and virtue. If sycophants should seek to amuse the king at my expense, I could lie in wait for and chastise some of them. Men would applaud my show of spirit, whilst with the third enemy whom I made to bite the dust, would come the adoration of the women. Yes; that must be my course of action, and it is one to which even the Comte de la Fère himself cannot demur. Did he not go through, earlier in life, what I am going through now? In his case, did not dissipation take the place of love? Nay! has he not told me so himself? Why, then, should I hesitate to deaden my grief in the pursuit of pleasure? He has suffered as much as I am suffering now – possibly more. The experience of one man is the experience of all mankind – more or less protracted, more or less painful. The voice of humanity at large is but one long cry of suffering.

'But how do the sufferings of others affect our own individual sorrows? Does the contemplation of an open wound in the breast of another relieve the pain of that which is in our own? Can the flow of another's blood stay the draining away of ours?

'Does universal suffering diminish individual pain? No; each must suffer for himself; each must do battle with his own grief; each must shed his own tears.

'Besides, what has life, hitherto, been for me? A cold and sterile plain on which I have continually fought for others, but never for myself. At one time, for a king; at another, for a woman. The king has betrayed me; the woman has treated me with disdain. Shall I not make all women do penance for the crime of one? And to accomplish this, what is necessary? Simply to be young, handsome, strong, brave and rich. Already some of these attributes are mine; in time I shall possess them all. Again, honour. What is honour? Everyone defines it after his own fashion. My father tells me that honour consists in the observance of the consideration which we owe to others, and especially of the respect which is due to ourselves. But de Guiche,

Manicamp[68] and, more particularly, Saint-Aignan, say that honour means pandering to the passions and pleasures of a king. It is easy enough to gain such honour as that, and, I dare say, in the long run, it pays one to achieve it. With honour like that I could retain my position at court, become a gentleman of the chamber, and take the command of a regiment whenever it is offered to me. With honour like that I might attain the dignity of a dukedom or a peerage.

'The stain which has been imprinted on me by that woman, the sorrow with which she has torn my heart – the heart of Raoul, the companion of her childhood – casts no stigma upon Monsieur de Bragelonne, the gallant officer who, at the first opportunity, will not fail to cover himself with glory, and who will become a hundred times of more importance than Mademoiselle de la Vallière, the king's mistress; for the king will never marry her, and the more publicly he proclaims her his mistress, the heavier will become the coronet of shame which she wears on her head in place of a crown; and in proportion as she is despised by others, as I myself despise her, so shall I become an object for adulation and a winner of renown. Alas! we have grown up together, she and I, and, hand in hand, we have travelled along the pleasant and flowery path of youth. Now we have arrived at crossways and here we separate, each to follow a path which leads us, with every step we take, wider and wider apart from each other, and I am left, despairing and alone, to follow my own pathway to its bitter end.'

Raoul was lost in these sad reflections when, mechanically, he placed his foot upon the doorstep of his home. He had arrived there without being conscious of the streets through which he had passed, nor did he know by what means he had arrived at all. He pushed open the door, walked in and ascended the staircase.

As in most of the houses of that period, both staircase and landing-places were very dark. Raoul, who lived on the first floor, stopped there and rang the bell, and Olivain, who appeared at once, relieved his master of his sword and cloak. Raoul opened a door which led from the antechamber to a sitting-room, appropriately furnished for a bachelor of his rank. Raoul was fond of flowers, and Olivain, there-fore, had taken care that there should be no lack of them in the apartments. In this room hung a portrait of La Vallière, which she herself had executed and given to Raoul. It hung immediately above a large easy-chair upholstered in dark-coloured damask, and was the first object which caught the eye of Raoul as he entered the room. Upon the present occasion, from force of habit, Raoul walked towards the picture, and kneeling upon the chair beneath it, looked at it with fixed, but sad attention. His arms were folded over his chest, his head was slightly thrown back, as, with half-closed eyes and a bitter smile upon his lips, he contemplated the portrait of Louise de la Vallière. As he gazed, all the suffering that he had recently endured recalled itself to his mind with terrible insistence, and he groaned aloud. As if in answer to his lament, a deep sigh issued from that part of the room to which he had his back. Turning round quickly, he perceived, in a corner of the room, the veiled form of a woman which had previously been concealed by the opened door. He was advancing towards this woman, who appeared thus unannounced in his presence, for the purpose of ascertaining what she wanted, when, suddenly, she let fall her veil, revealing a white and tear-stained face, and Raoul fell back as though in the presence of a ghost.

'*Louise!*' he gasped, in a hollow voice, and fell to trembling in every limb.

### CHAPTER 22

## *Pelion upon Ossa*

MADEMOISELLE DE LA VALLIÈRE, for it was indeed she, took a step forward.

'Yes, it is Louise,' she murmured.

During the interval, short as it was, Raoul had recovered his self-possession.

'You, mademoiselle!' he said; 'you here.'

'Yes, Raoul,' replied the girl; 'I have been waiting for you.'

'Forgive me; when I entered the room, I was not aware – '

'No; I begged Olivain not to tell you.'

She stopped short, and Raoul not being in a hurry to continue the conversation, there was a pause, during which nought was heard save the beating of their hearts, which, if they did not beat in unison, at least throbbed with equal violence.

Louise was the first to break the silence, which she did with an effort.

'I had to speak to you,' she said; 'it was necessary for me to see you, and alone. I have not shrunk from taking this step, which must remain a secret; for you alone, Monsieur de Bragelonne, can understand my motive in venturing upon it.'

'And that,' stammered Raoul, much agitated again, 'in spite of the good opinion you have of me. Well, I must confess – '

'Will you grant me the boon of sitting down, and listening to what I have to say?' interrupted Louise, in a gentle voice.

De Bragelonne looked at her for a moment; then, shaking his head sadly, he sat down in, or rather fell into, a chair.

'Speak,' he said.

She cast a furtive glance around her, which conveyed a more eloquent appeal for secrecy than could have been expressed in words.

Raoul rose, and opening the door, called out to his servant: 'Olivain, I am not at home to anyone;' then, turning towards La Vallière, he said, 'that, I think, is what you meant?'

It would be impossible to describe the effect which these words had upon Louise. They seemed to say to her, 'You see, I have not yet ceased to understand you.' She passed her handkerchief over her eyes to wipe away the tears she was unable to restrain; then, quickly recovering herself: 'Raoul,' said she, 'do not turn away from me your frank and honest eyes; you are not the kind of man to despise a woman because she has given away her heart, although her conduct may make him unhappy or wound his self-esteem.'

Raoul made no reply.

'Alas!' continued La Vallière, 'it is but too true. My cause is an unfortunate one, and I know not how to begin what I have to say. I think the best way will be to make a plain statement of what has happened to me. As I shall speak truthfully, I shall assuredly find my way through the obscurity, the doubt, and the obstacles which I shall have to encounter in order to solace my over-burdened heart, which lies broken at your feet.'

Raoul still kept silence; and La Vallière looked at him as if she would say, 'For pity's sake, give a word of encouragement.' But Raoul remained dumb, and she was obliged to continue.

'But just now,' she said, 'Saint-Aignan visited me on the part of the king,' and she dropped her eyes; whilst on his part, Raoul turned aside his own so that he might see nothing.

'Monsieur de Saint-Aignan came to me on the part of the king,' she repeated, 'and told me that you knew all;' and she tried to look in the face of him upon whom she inflicted this fresh wound, in addition to the many he had already received; but Raoul would not allow her to meet his eyes. 'He told me that you were very justly incensed against me.'

This time Raoul looked at her, and a contemptuous smile curled his lip.

'Oh!' she continued, 'I entreat you not to say that you have any feeling against me besides that of anger. Wait, Raoul, until I have told you everything; hear me to the end.'

By sheer force of will Raoul retained his self-possession, and the curl of his lip disappeared.

'First of all,' said La Vallière, with clasped hands and bowed head, 'let me ask pardon of you, who are the noblest and most generous of men. If I have allowed you to remain in ignorance of my feelings, I have, at least, never wilfully deceived you. Oh, I entreat you, Raoul, on my knees I beg you, to vouchsafe me a word, though it be one of reproach. Better that you should reproach me with your lips than harbour unjust suspicion of me in your heart.'

'I appreciate the admirable distinction which you draw, mademoiselle,' replied Raoul, at length. 'It seems, then, that to allow a man to be in ignorance that he is being deceived is perfectly loyal, although actually to deceive him is highly reprehensible; and of the latter course of conduct you are quite incapable.'

'Monsieur, for a long time I honestly believed that I loved you beyond anything else in the world, and, in that belief, I told you that I loved you. I certainly loved you when we were at Blois. Then the king came, but still I believed in my affection for you. I could have sworn upon the altar that I loved you. Then came a day when I was undeceived.'

'Upon that day, mademoiselle, seeing that my love for you had always remained unshaken, your love of candour should have compelled you to make me acquainted with your change of sentiments.'

'On that day, Raoul, when, looking into my own heart, I became conscious that you had ceased to be everything in the world to me; on that day, when a future opened out to me in which you had no part – on that day Raoul, alas! you were far from me.'

'But you knew where I was, mademoiselle; surely you could have written to me.'

'Raoul, I lacked the courage to do so. I knew so well how much you loved me that I trembled at the bare idea of the suffering which such a letter would cause you; and that is so true, Raoul, that now, as, with broken heart, I kneel before you, sorrowfully, tearfully, I feel that my only excuse lies in my present, if tardy, frankness, and my only grief is the sorrow which I read in your eyes.'

Raoul tried to smile.

'No,' continued Louise, in a voice of deep conviction – 'no, do not wrong me by attempting to disguise your present state of mind. You loved me; you were sure of your love for me; you did not deceive yourself, nor try to palter with your own heart; whilst, as for me – ' And, pale as death, and throwing up her arms, La Vallière sank down upon the floor.

'Whilst, as for you,' said Raoul, 'you told me that you loved me, when, in your heart, you loved another.'

'Alas, yes!' cried the poor girl, 'it is true; I loved another; but that other – My God! let me give the only excuse I have to offer, Raoul; that other I love more than my life – to me he is before God Himself. Forgive my fault, Raoul, or punish me for my treason. I have come here, not to defend my conduct, but to say to you, "You know what it is to love? Well, then, I love; I love to the extent of sacrificing both body and soul for him who has my affections. Should he cease to love me, I should die of grief, unless God, in pity for me, put an end to my affliction." Raoul, I have come here to submit myself to your will; even to die, should you desire my death. Kill me, Raoul, if in your heart you think that I deserve to die.'

'Gently, mademoiselle; the woman who thus courts death, does so from the feeling that she has nothing but her life to offer to the man she has wronged.'

'You are right,' she replied.

Raoul sighed deeply. 'You love without being able to forget!' he exclaimed.

'I love without wishing to forget – without a desire to love any, save one.'

'Well,' said Raoul, 'you have now said, it would seem, all that you had to say, and I have learnt all that I desired to know. It is now *my* turn to ask pardon of *you*. It is I who have been a stumbling-block in your path; it is I who have been wrong, and who, in deceiving myself, aided you in your own self-deception.'

'Oh!' said La Vallière, 'I do not ask for so much as that, Raoul.'

'It has been all my own fault,' continued Raoul. 'More worldly-wise than you, it was my place to have enlightened you as to the pitfalls of life. I ought not to have built upon an uncertainty, and should have known how to compel your heart to speak, instead of remaining satisfied with the utterances of your lips. I repeat, mademoiselle, that it is *I* who should ask pardon of *you*.'

'It is impossible!' cried Louise; 'you are but mocking me!'

'How impossible?'

'Yes, it is impossible that any man could be good and generous to such a degree as that.'

'Be careful,' said Raoul, with a bitter smile, 'or presently you will be saying that I do not love you at all.'

'Oh yes, you have a brother's love for me. Let me, at least, hope for as much as that.'

'A brother's love! Undeceive yourself, Louise. I love with a lover's, with a husband's love. I love you with as tender a love as man can feel for woman.'

'Raoul, Raoul!'

'A brother's love! Oh, Louise, I love you to the extent of shedding my blood for you drop by drop; for you I would sacrifice my future life hour by hour.'

'Raoul, Raoul! have pity on me!'

'I love you so much, Louise, that my heart is dead within me; I have lost my faith in everything; life is now to me a blank – a void. I have nothing now to live for.'

'Raoul, Raoul! spare me. Oh, if I had only known – '

'It is too late, Louise; you love, and you are happy; through your tears I see the joy which lurks behind them. Your sense of loyalty causes you to shed them, but they cannot hide the joy that sings in your heart. Louise, Louise, you have made me the most unhappy of men. Now leave me, I implore you. Adieu, adieu!'

'Say, at least, that you forgive me!'

'Have I not said more? Have I not told you that I love you still?'

La Vallière hid her face with her hands.

'And to tell you that – do you understand me, Louise? – to tell you that, at such a moment as this, is to pass upon myself the sentence of death. Adieu!'

La Vallière held out to him both her hands.

'We should meet again no more in this world,' he said.

Raoul stifled, with his hand, the cry which was rising to her lips. She kissed fervently the hand which he pressed upon her mouth, and, with a bitter sigh, fell back unconscious.

'Olivain,' said Raoul, 'be good enough to carry this young lady to her carriage. You will find it waiting at the door. As Olivain raised her in his arms, Raoul pressed forward as though to imprint a last kiss upon her lips, but, resisting the impulse, he only murmured to himself, 'No; she no longer belongs to me. God forbid that I should have no more sense of honour than the King of France;' and he turned back into the room, whilst his servant carried the fainting girl to her carriage.

CHAPTER 23

## Raoul's conjectures

As soon as Raoul had departed, and the two friends found themselves alone together, Athos resumed the serious look which the arrival of d'Artagnan had caused him to assume.

'Well, my dear fellow,' said he, 'what news have you brought me?'

'I?' asked d'Artagnan, with a look of assumed surprise.

'*You*, certainly. You would not have *dropped in* in this friendly manner without some good reason for doing so,' said Athos, with a significant smile.

'Oh, the devil!' said d'Artagnan.

'Come, old friend, let me put you at your ease. The king is furious, is he not?'

'Well,' said d'Artagnan, with a drawl, 'between ourselves, I should hardly describe his state of mind as being one of ecstatic delight.'

'And he has sent you to arrest me?'

'My dear fellow, with your usual perspicacity, you have solved the problem at the first attempt.'

'I quite expected it. Let us be off at once.'

'Well, upon my word, you seem to be in the devil's own hurry to be locked up.'

'I don't wish to hinder you in the performance of your duty – that's all.'

'Oh, there's plenty of time,' said d'Artagnan, cheerfully. 'Besides, don't you want to know what passed between the king and myself?'

'If you don't mind telling me, I shall be more than pleased to listen;' and Athos indicated, with a gesture, a large armchair, in which d'Artagnan at once assumed an attitude of complete repose and apparent enjoyment.

'All right,' he said, 'and I think it is worth listening to. Well, the king sent for me immediately upon your leaving; indeed, one of the musketeers told me, when I arrived, that you had but that moment disappeared down the staircase. Well, I was admitted to the king's presence. He was not *red* in the face. Oh dear no, he was *purple* – he was *black*. Of course, I was absolutely in the dark as to what had happened; but I noticed that upon the floor lay a broken sword.

' "Captain d'Artagnan!" he roared, as soon as he saw me.

' "Sire," I replied.

' "Monsieur de la Fère has just left me. He is a very insolent person!"

' "Insolent person?" I repeated, in a tone of voice which effectively stopped him.

' "Captain d'Artagnan," the king hissed between his clenched teeth, "you will be good enough to listen, and to obey my commands."

' "That is my duty, sire," said I.

' "I have desired to spare this gentleman, of whom I have still some kindly recollections, the indignity of being arrested in my presence."

' "Quite so," I said calmly.

' "You will, therefore, take a carriage – "

'At this I made a gesture.

' "Oh!" said the king, "if you dislike the duty of arresting him yourself, I will not force it upon you. You had better send the captain of the guards here."

' "There is no need to do that, sire," I replied, "seeing that *I* am on duty."

' "I should be sorry to place you in an invidious position," he said – and I must say very civilly – "for you have always served me faithfully, Monsieur d'Artagnan."

' "Have no compunction, sire," I said. "I am on duty, and that is enough."

' "But I thought," he said, "that the comte was your intimate friend?"

' "If he were my father, sire, I should arrest him all the same, if it were my duty to do so," I replied.

'The king looked at me steadily, but detecting no lack of determination in my face, he seemed satisfied.

' "Then you will arrest the Comte de la Fère?" he asked.

' "Most certainly I will, sire, if you command me to."

' "Very well, then," he said, "I order you to arrest him."

'I bowed. "Where is the comte, sire?" I asked.

' "You will go and look for him."

' "And am I to arrest him wherever I may find him?"

' "Yes; but I should prefer that you arrest him at his own house. If he should have left Paris for his own estates, follow him, and arrest him on the way."

'I bowed, but did not move.

' "Well," said the king, "what are you waiting for?"

' "For the signed warrant for the arrest, sire."

'This seemed to annoy the king. It involved a fresh exercise of arbitrary power. He took up a pen slowly and reluctantly, and wrote as follows: "Order to the Chevalier d'Artagnan, captain of my musketeers, to arrest the Comte de la Fère, wherever he shall be found." Then he turned towards me. I did not move a muscle. It is probable that he attributed my callous demeanour to bravado, for he signed the paper quickly, handed it to me, and said, "Go!" I obeyed, my dear Athos, and here I am.'

Athos pressed his friend's hand. 'Let us go,' he said.

'Oh!' said d'Artagnan, 'have you no little affairs to settle or arrange before leaving the house?'

'None at all.'

'None? Why, how is that?'

'Well, you know, d'Artagnan, that the simplest outfit has always been sufficient for me. I am ready, at a moment's notice, to go to the end of the world at the command of the king, or to quit this world for the next when God so wills it. A man so prepared has little to get ready. What does he require? simply a portmanteau or a coffin. I am ready now, as I have always been. Take me away, then.'

'But de Bragelonne?'

'I have brought him up in the same principles as govern my own conduct. You observed that he saw through the motive of your visit as soon as ever you made your appearance. His suspicions are, for the moment, allayed, but rest assured that he is too well prepared for what has happened to be unduly alarmed at it. Let us go.'

'Well, then, let us go,' acquiesced d'Artagnan, quietly.

'As I have broken my sword,' said the comte, 'and left it in two pieces at the king's feet, I cannot go through the formality of handing it to you.'

'Of course you can't,' replied d'Artagnan. 'But what the devil do you suppose I want with your sword?'

'Shall I walk in front of you, or behind you?'

'We will walk arm in arm,' said d'Artagnan; and thus, having descended the staircase, they reached the landing below.

Grimaud,[69] who met them in the antechamber, regarded the pair with an expression of uneasiness. He knew the world too well to doubt that something out of the common was in the wind.

'Ah! is it you, my good Grimaud?' said Athos; 'we are just going to –'

'Take a drive in my coach,' interrupted d'Artagnan, with a friendly nod of recognition.

Grimaud thanked d'Artagnan with a grimace, which he, no doubt, intended for a smile, and escorted them to the door. Athos got into the carriage first, and d'Artagnan quickly followed, without, however, giving any directions to the coachman. Their departure, being thus quiet and undemonstrative, caused no sensation in the neighbourhood, if, indeed, it attracted any attention at all. When the carriage had reached the quays, Athos remarked: 'I see that you are taking me to the Bastille.'

'I?' said d'Artagnan; 'I am taking you wherever you like to go – nowhere else.'

'I don't understand you,' said the comte, in astonishment.

'Confound it!' said d'Artagnan; 'can't you understand that I undertook this business with the sole object of enabling you to do exactly as you please? You surely don't suppose that I would have had any hand in an infernal job like this, had I not seen my way to being of service to you. No, I would have left it to the captain of the guards.'

'And so – ?' said Athos.

'And so, I repeat, we shall go wherever you direct.'

'Dear old fellow,' said Athos, seizing his friend's hand, 'how like you all this is.'

'Why, bless me!' said d'Artagnan, 'the whole thing is simplicity itself. The coachman will drive you to the Barrière du Cours-la-Reine, where you will find a horse, which I have ordered to be kept in readiness for you; with this horse you will be able to do three stages at a stretch, and I shall take good care not to let the king know that you have left Paris until it is too late to overtake you. In the meantime, you will have got to Havre, and from thence to England, where you can make yourself at home in the pretty little house which General Monk[70] was kind enough to present me with, to say nothing of the hospitality that King Charles will not fail to show you. Now then, what do you think of my little programme?'

'Better take me to the Bastille,' said Athos, smiling.

'How obstinate you are!' said d'Artagnan; 'just give yourself the trouble to reflect for one moment, will you?'

'Reflect? upon what?'

'That you are no longer twenty years of age. Believe me, old friend, I know what I am talking about. Imprisonment means death to men of our years. No, no, I am not going to see you put under lock and key, if I can prevent it. The very thought of it makes me ill.'

'My dear d'Artagnan, I am thankful to say that I have been created as strong in body as in will, and I am confident that I shall retain my powers of endurance to the very end.'

'But that is not strength, my dear fellow; it is simply obstinacy.'

'Not so, d'Artagnan; it is the highest form of reason. I do not suppose, for a moment, that you would hesitate to ruin yourself for the purpose of serving me, and I should do exactly what you propose if the question of escape entered into my plans. I should accept from you what I hope and feel you would accept from me, but I know you too well to think it necessary to touch upon that point any further.'

'If I had my way,' said d'Artagnan, 'I would send the king on a pretty chase after you.'

'Still, he is the king, after all, dear friend.'

'Oh! I don't care a button about that; and, all the same, I should say to him straight out, "Sire, imprison, exile, kill everyone in France or in Europe, order me to arrest or poniard anyone in the world, even were it monsieur your brother, but do not touch either of the four musketeers. If one of them be harmed, I will not answer for the consequences."'

'My dear friend,' said Athos, 'let me impress upon you this one thing; I wish to be arrested, it is the very thing that I am particularly anxious should happen.'

D'Artagnan's only answer was a shrug of the shoulders.

'I assure you,' continued Athos, 'that if you were to let me escape, I should return and give myself up. I wish to prove to this young king, who is dazzled with the splendour of his position, that he can be looked upon as a ruler amongst men only by showing himself to be wiser and more generous than others. He may punish, imprison, even torture me. He simply abuses his power; and I wish him to learn the meaning of remorse before it pleases heaven to visit him with chastisement.'

'My friend,' said d'Artagnan, 'when once you have made up your mind, I know that it is useless to attempt to argue with you. Tell me, do you *really* wish to go to the Bastille?'

'I *do* wish it.'

'Let us go, then,' said d'Artagnan; and he gave the necessary direction to the coachman. Then, throwing himself back in the carrriage, he gnawed his moustaches savagely, an action which signified to Athos that he had either taken a resolution or was forming one in his mind.

The carriage continued its way with neither accelerated nor diminished pace.

Athos again took his friend's hand. 'You are not vexed with me, d'Artagnan?' said he.

'I? Oh, bless me, no!' answered d'Artagnan. 'What you are doing from heroism, I might be pig-headed enough to do myself.'

'But you think that heaven will avenge me, do you not, d'Artagnan?'

'At all events, I know a few people on earth who will throw no obstacle in heaven's way,' answered the captain, dryly.

CHAPTER 24

## Where three guests are mightily astonished to find themselves together at the same supper-table

THE COACH, in due time, arrived at the outer gate of the Bastille. A sentry barred the way but at a word from d'Artagnan the vehicle was allowed to enter.

As they proceeded along the covered way which led to the governor's residence, d'Artagnan, whose sharp eyes nothing escaped, suddenly exclaimed: 'Halloa! what the deuce is going on there?'

'What can you see?' asked Athos, quietly.

'Look for yourself.'

'In the courtyard?'

'Yes; be quick!'

'Well, I see a carriage.'

'What do you make of it?'

'Probably some poor devil in a similar position to my own.'

'A prisoner! that would be too funny.'

'I don't understand you.'

'Look again, and see who is getting out of the carriage.'

At that moment they were stopped by a second sentry, with whom d'Artagnan had to go through certain formalities. Whilst this was being done, Athos had time to observe the person whom d'Artagnan had pointed out, and who was at no great distance away from them. The person in question got out of the carriage at the door of the governor's house.

'Well,' said d'Artagnan, 'do you see him?'

'Yes, a man in a grey coat.'

'What do you make of him?'

'Nothing at all; I simply see a man, dressed in grey, who is getting out of a carriage.'

'Athos, I'll bet you what you like I know who it is.'

'Who is it, then?'

'Aramis.'

'Aramis arrested! – impossible!'

'I did not say that he was under arrest. On the contrary, he seems to be alone.'

'What can he be doing here?'

'Oh, he knows Baisemeaux, the governor,' replied d'Artagnan, with a meaning look. 'By heaven! we have arrived opportunely.'

'For what?'

'For observation.'

'I rather regret this meeting, for Aramis will, no doubt, be annoyed both at seeing us and being seen by us.'

'Very likely.'

'Unfortunately, in the Bastille, one is not a free agent, and cannot draw back to avoid an undesirable meeting.'

'Athos, I have an idea in my head as to how Aramis is to be spared the annoyance which you foresee.'

'How is it to be done?'

'I will tell you how – or, rather, I will keep the matter entirely in my hands. I shall not ask you to tell any lies. I know it would be useless to do so.'

'What, then?'

'Oh, I shall tell lies for the pair of us. Lying comes quite naturally to a Gascon.'

Athos smiled, and the carriage presently drew up, in its turn, before the governor's door.

'Is it agreed?' asked d'Artagnan, in a low tone.

Athos made a gesture of consent, and they mounted the steps side by side. If the ease with which the Bastille was entered should seem remarkable, it must be remembered that, on their arrival there, d'Artagnan had announced that he was in charge of a state prisoner, and, once inside the outer gate, it was merely necessary for him to state that he had business with the governor to be allowed to pass without further questioning. Our friends soon found themselves in the governor's dining-room, where the first object that caught d'Artagnan's eye was the form of Aramis, who, seated by the side of Baisemeaux, was apparently awaiting the arrival of supper, the appetising smell of which already pervaded the apartment. If the surprise shown by d'Artagnan was affected, that of Aramis was certainly genuine, for he started and was evidently much embarrassed at the unexpected appearance of the two friends.

Athos and d'Artagnan, for their part, greeted the others in the most natural manner possible, whilst Monsieur Baisemeaux, who seemed absolutely bewildered, fussed about, hardly knowing whether he stood upon his head or his heels. Aramis, however, was soon at his ease, and was the first to speak. 'By what happy chance – ?' he began; when d'Artagnan cut him short with, 'That is the very question I was about to put to you.'

'Perhaps we are all prisoners!' said Aramis, with affected jocularity.

'Well,' said d'Artagnan, 'there is certainly a prison-like smell about the place; but Monsieur Baisemeaux, as he will tell you, was good enough to invite me to supper a few days ago.'

'I?' exclaimed Baisemeaux, with open mouth.

'Certainly you did,' said d'Artagnan. 'You surely must remember it, although, from your manner, one would think that Athos and I had dropped from the clouds.'

Baisemeaux, who turned all sorts of colours at once, looked in amazement at d'Artagnan, who returned his gaze with an uncompromising stare; then he managed to stammer out: 'Yes, of course – oh, certainly – charmed to see you, I'm sure – but, upon my word – dear, dear! what an atrocious thing it is to have a treacherous memory!'

'It would seem that I am in the wrong, nevertheless,' said d'Artagnan, with an offended air.

'Wrong! In what way?'

'In having remembered the invitation – at least, so it appears.'

'Ah, my dear captain, there is no need for ceremony between us. I have absolutely the worst head in the kingdom. Once take me away from my dovecote and my pigeons, and I am of no more use than a six-weeks' recruit.'

'Well, you remember now?' asked d'Artagnan, pointedly.

'Yes, yes; I seem to remember now,' replied the governor, with a little hesitation.

'It was at the Palais-Royal. You were telling me about some business you had transacted with Monsieur Louvières and Monsieur Tremblay.'

'Ah, yes; I remember perfectly well.'

'And you were saying how kind Monsieur d'Herblay had been to you.'

'Ah! you remember that?' cried Aramis, looking the unfortunate governor full in the eyes; 'I thought I understood you to say that you had no memory.'

Baisemeaux quickly interrupted the musketeer.

'Ah, yes!' he cried, 'you are quite right. I remember it as if it were taking place at the present moment. I ask a thousand pardons for my forgetfulness; but remember, dear Monsieur d'Artagnan, that, at all times, invited or not, everything here is at your disposal. Both you and your friend Monsieur d'Herblay are always welcome, and you, also, monsieur,' he added, bowing courteously to Athos.

'I feel sure of that,' said d'Artagnan; 'otherwise I should not have come. Having nothing to do at the Palais-Royal this evening, I thought I would drop in and take pot-luck with you, and, on my way hither, I met my friend the comte.'

Athos bowed.

'He had just left the king, and was bringing me a command which demanded immediate attention, but we were so close by here that I could not resist the temptation of shaking hands with you, and of introducing to you the comte, of whom you spoke in such handsome terms that same evening at the Palais-Royal.'

'Very good! excellent! the Comte de la Fère, is it not?'

'Exactly.'

'The comte is more than welcome.'

'And he will stay to supper, whilst I, unhappily for me, must run away to carry out my instructions. I feel quite envious of you all!' he added, with a portentous sigh of regret such as Porthos might have given vent to.

'Must you *really* leave us?' cried Baisemeaux and Aramis together, scarcely able to conceal their satisfaction at the prospect of getting rid of him; and the tone in which they spoke was quite appreciated by d'Artagnan.

'But I leave behind me an excellent representative,' he said, touching Athos lightly upon the shoulder.

Athos himself was somewhat astonished at this unexpected turn of events, and could not altogether conceal the surprise he felt; but this was noticed by Aramis alone, Monsieur Baisemeaux being too dull-witted to observe it.

'You are determined upon going, then?' said the governor.

'Yes; but I shall be back again in an hour or two.'

'Oh, in that case, we will wait supper for you,' said Baisemeaux.

'On no account,' replied d'Artagnan. 'I shall feel vexed if you do.'

'But you will come back, in any case?' asked Athos, with a shade of suspicion in his voice.

'Most certainly,' answered d'Artagnan, squeezing his friend's hand to emphasise his words. Then he added, in a low voice, 'Wait for me,

Athos, and be as cheerful as possible; but, for heaven's sake, don't touch upon business matters.' And, with a further pressure of the hand, he sought to impress upon Athos the necessity for the greatest circumspection.

Baisemeaux escorted d'Artagnan to the door, whilst Aramis, with a great display of civility, devoted himself to Athos, in the hope of making him talk; but the latter, who, when he thought it necessary, could talk as fluently as anyone, on the present occasion could not be induced to utter a syllable beyond the merest commonplaces.

Ten minutes afterwards the three gentlemen sat down to an excellent supper, consisting of a profusion of expensive dishes and wines, provided at the king's expense, the cost of which Monsieur Colbert might easily have reduced by two-thirds without depriving anyone at the Bastille of sufficient nutriment. Baisemeaux was the only one of the three who did justice to this repast, for although Aramis refused nothing, he merely played with his food; whilst Athos, after taking some soup, and tasting two or three of the *hors-d'oeuvres*, could not be induced to eat anything at all. The conversation was such as might be expected between three men, who, in tastes, as in temperament, had so little in common.

Aramis exhausted himself in speculation as to why Athos remained in d'Artagnan's absence, and as to what could have been the latter's motive in going away and leaving Athos behind.

Athos racked his brain in the endeavour to fathom the depths of the mind of Aramis – that man of subterfuge and intrigue – and to find out the particular project which he had then in hand. Next he tried to concentrate his attention upon his own position, and sought in vain for an explanation of d'Artagnan's recent line of action.

But we must now leave these three personages to their own devices, whilst we follow the footsteps of d'Artagnan, who, hurrying back to the carriage which had brought him to the Bastille, whispered in the coachman's ear: 'Drive to the palace, as hard as your horses can lay legs to the ground!'

## CHAPTER 25

### *What befell at the Louvre during the supper at the Bastille*

As HAS BEEN SHOWN in one of our previous chapters, Saint-Aignan had accomplished his mission to La Vallière, but, notwithstanding his eloquence, he had failed to convince her that the king was all-powerful to protect her, and that, with him on her side, she had nothing to fear. In fact, at the first intimation that the wonderful secret had been discovered, Louise had uttered such loud lamentations, and given herself up to such an abandonment of grief, that the king would hardly have been gratified had he been a witness of the scene. The ambassador, who was as much offended as his master would have been, returned to the king to report the result of his mission. Here, then, we shall find him, in a highly perturbed condition, closeted with the king, who was, if possible, more agitated than himself.

'But,' said the king, when Saint-Aignan had finished his report, 'what is she going to do? Shall I see her before supper? Will she come here, or shall I have to go to her?'

'I think, sire, that, if your majesty wishes to see her, you will not only have to make the first step, but you will have to go all the way.'

'She does not care for me,' muttered the king. 'That fellow de Bragelonne still has possession of her heart.'

'Oh, sire, that is not possible! Mademoiselle de la Vallière loves you, I am convinced, with the utmost devotion. But Monsieur de Bragelonne comes, as you know, of a stern race, who are prone to pose as Roman heroes.'

The king smiled feebly, as he recognised the truth of this; for had not Athos only just left his presence?

'As for Mademoiselle de la Vallière,' continued Saint-Aignan, 'she has been brought up under the wing of the old dowager duchess,[71] strictly and in seclusion. The two lovers have no doubt deliberately sworn fidelity to each other beneath the moon and stars, and to break such vows is, nowadays, looked upon as the very deuce and all!'

Saint-Aignan thought, by this speech, to make the king laugh; but, on the contrary, Louis, after smiling faintly, became more serious than ever. He already began to feel what the Comte de la Fère had prophesied to d'Artagnan he would suffer – remorse. He reflected that these two young persons loved one another, and had interchanged vows of fidelity; that one of them remained faithful, and that the other was too conscientious not to feel horrified at her own perjury. And, in addition to remorse, the king felt the sting of jealousy in his heart.

He did not say a word, and, instead of going to see his mother or the queen for a little cheerful society and to make the ladies laugh, as he himself used to say, he threw himself into the huge armchair in which his august father Louis XIII passed so many weary days and years in the company of Baradas and Cinq-Mars.[72]

Saint-Aignan, perceiving the king was not in a humour to be amused, as a last resource uttered the name of Louise, which at once had the effect of rousing Louis from his fit of abstraction.

'What is your majesty going to do this evening?' he asked. 'Shall Mademoiselle de la Vallière be informed that it is your intention to visit her?'

'It seems that she expects me already,' replied the king.

'Will your majesty walk?'

'One must go out to do that. No, Saint-Aignan, we will stay at home and dream. When Mademoiselle de la Vallière has finished her lamentations and stifled her remorse, perhaps she will condescend to let us hear from her.'

'Ah, sire, is it possible that you can thus misunderstand that devoted heart?'

A prey to vexation and jealousy, Louis, with flushed face, rose from his chair; Saint-Aignan was beginning to feel the position to be somewhat trying, when the curtain before the door was suddenly raised.

The king turned round quickly. His first idea was that La Vallière had written to him, but, instead of a messenger from her, it was the captain of the musketeers, standing 'at attention', who confronted him.

'Ah! it is Monsieur d'Artagnan,' he said. 'Well?'

The king and d'Artagnan both looked towards Saint-Aignan, who, taking the hint, bowed and withdrew.

'Is it done?' asked the king of d'Artagnan as soon as they were alone.

'Yes, sire,' replied the latter, gravely.

The king did not know what to say next, although his pride

forbade him to remain silent. When a king has taken a resolution, even an unjust one, he feels compelled to prove to all who may be present at the time, and especially to himself, that he was right in taking it. An almost infallible way of doing this is to dwell upon the gravity of the culprit's offence. Louis, brought up by Mazarin and Anne of Austria, understood kingcraft better than any contemporary prince, and he endeavoured to show this on the present occasion. After a moment's silence, during which all that we have just said flashed through his mind, he said carelessly: 'Well, what did the comte say?'

'He said nothing, sire.'

'But he could not have undergone arrest without saying a word?'

'He merely said that he expected to be arrested.'

The king raised his head haughtily. 'I presume, however,' said he, 'that the Comte de la Fère does not continue in his rebellious attitude?'

'It depends, sire, upon what you call rebellious,' replied the musketeer. 'Is a man rebellious who not only allows himself to be shut up in the Bastille, but who actually resists those who are unwilling to take him there?'

'Who are unwilling to take him there?' thundered the king. 'What am I to understand by that, monsieur? Are you mad?'

'I think not, sire.'

'You speak of persons who are unwilling to arrest Monsieur de la Fère?'

'Yes, sire.'

'And what persons are they?'

'Apparently, those whom your majesty has commanded to arrest him.'

'But it is *you* to whom I have given the order,' cried the king.

'Yes, to me, sire.'

'And you tell me that, in spite of my command, you had no intention of arresting the man who has insulted me!'

'Your majesty has understood me perfectly. I even went so far as to propose to the comte that he should escape on a horse, which I had ordered to be kept in waiting for him at the Barrière du Cours-la-Reine.'

'And what was your object in doing this?'

'Simply, sire, that the Comte de la Fère might reach Havre and, from thence, escape to England.'

'You would have been guilty of treason, then, monsieur?' cried the king, with wildly flashing eyes.

'Exactly,' replied d'Artagnan, unmoved.

There was no reply to be made to such utterances as these, and the king was thunderstruck at the rebellious spirit which d'Artagnan made no attempt to disguise.

'You have, I suppose, a reason to offer, Monsieur d'Artagnan, for this extraordinary line of conduct?'

'I always have a reason for everything I do, sire.'

'You cannot, at any rate, plead your friendship for the comte, which would be the only excuse that could possibly be of any avail to you, because, you must remember, that I gave you a free hand in the matter. Did I not give you the choice of arresting, or of not arresting, the Comte de la Fère?'

'Yes, sire, but – '

'But what?'

'You said, at the same time, that if I did not arrest him, you would order the captain of your guards to do so.'

'Did I not act handsomely towards you when I allowed you that choice?'

'Towards me, yes, sire; but not towards my friend.'

'No?'

'Certainly not, sire, because either alternative meant arrest for him.'

'And is this your loyalty to your sovereign, monsieur? A loyalty which stops to reason and to choose? You are no true soldier, monsieur.'

'It would interest me to learn what your majesty is pleased to consider me, then?'

'You are a *frondeur*.'

'But since the Fronde exists no longer, sire – '

'If what you tell me is true.'

'What I say is always true, sire.'

'Let us hear why you have come here.'

'I come here to say to the king – sire, Monsieur de la Fère is in the Bastille.'

'Through no fault of yours, it would appear.'

'That is perfectly true, sire; but he is there, nevertheless, and, being there, it is important that your majesty should know it.'

'What! Monsieur d'Artagnan, do you defy your king?'

'Sire – '

'Monsieur d'Artagnan, I give you fair warning that my patience is becoming exhausted. You are abusing it.'

'Not at all, sire.'

'Not at all? What do you mean?'

'I have come here to get myself arrested also.'

'To be arrested – you?'

'Certainly, sire. My friend will be horribly bored all by himself, so I have come to ask your majesty's permission to keep him company. If your majesty will trouble yourself to give the order, I will arrest myself. I will answer for it that there will be no need for the services of the captain of the guards.'

The king sprang to the table, and snatched up a pen for the purpose of writing the order for d'Artagnan's imprisonment. 'I give you notice, monsieur, that you will be imprisoned for life!' he cried, in a voice of dire menace.

'I expected nothing less,' replied the musketeer, 'for, after the perpetration of this noble deed, you will never dare to look me in the face again.'

The king dashed down his pen upon the table.

'Go!' he cried.

'With your permission, not so, sire; I came here to speak to the king temperately, but your majesty has been pleased to lose your temper. This is to be regretted, but, nevertheless, it will not prevent me from saying what I have come to say.'

'Your resignation, monsieur! your resignation!' demanded the king.

'Sire, you know how much the idea of resignation affects me, since, at Blois, on the occasion when your majesty refused to King Charles[73] the million which my friend the Comte de la Fère had given him, I, there and then, tendered my resignation.'

'Very well, then, tender it again, and at once.'

'No, sire, because my resignation in no way affects the point at issue. Your majesty has already taken up a pen with a view to consigning me to the Bastille. Why, so suddenly, change your mind?'

'D'Artagnan! pig-headed Gascon! are you king, or am I?'

'You, sire, unfortunately.'

'Unfortunately? What do you mean?'

'Oh, sire, because if I were king – '

'You would approve of Monsieur d'Artagnan's rebellious attitude, I suppose?'

'Certainly.'

'Really?' said the king, shrugging his shoulders.

'Yes,' continued d'Artagnan, 'and I should say to my captain of musketeers, looking at him with the eyes of a human being, and not with those of a wild beast – I should say to him, Monsieur d'Artagnan, I had forgotten that I was a king in that I have stooped from my throne to insult a gentlemen.'

'Monsieur,' said the king, 'do you imagine that you can excuse your friend by excelling him in insolence?'

'Oh! I will go much further than he would go, sire. I will say to you what that pure and high-minded gentleman would never cast in your teeth. I will say to you, sire, you have blasted the life of his son, whom he did but defend, and you have blighted his own existence. He appealed to you in the name of honour, of religion and of morality, and you have humiliated, discarded and imprisoned him. But I, who am made of sterner stuff than he, I say to you, take your choice, sire, between friends and sycophants; between soldiers and flunkeys; between men and dolls. Will you have men who serve you honestly and faithfully, or creatures who grovel on the earth before you? Do you prefer those who love you, or those who only fear you? If you prefer servility, duplicity and cowardice, only say so, sire, and we will go away – we, who are the sole remnant, nay, the sole examples, of a pre-existent chivalry – we, who are tried servants and who have equalled and, perhaps, surpassed in courage and fidelity those whose names will never be forgotten. Choose, sire, and make no delay. Look to it that you retain the few high-minded gentlemen who are left to you; of mere courtiers you will always have enough. Send me, then, to join my friend in the Bastille, for, if you have turned a deaf ear to the Comte de la Fère, than whom none could be more gently eloquent in the cause of honour – if you refuse to listen to the plain speaking of d'Artagnan, you are not a good king, and, tomorrow, may be a poor one. Bad kings are hated by their subjects; poor kings are dethroned. This is what I had to say to your majesty, and it is to be regretted that you have driven me to say it.'

The king, livid with anger and mortification, shifted uneasily in his chair. Had a thunderbolt fallen at his feet, he could not have been more astonished. D'Artagnan's plain speaking, as he called it, had pierced his heart like the blade of a sword.

D'Artagnan, having said all that he had to say, drew his sword and, respectfully approaching Louis XIV, laid it upon the table. But the king, with a furious gesture, pushed it away from him and it fell to the floor at d'Artagnan's feet. Master of himself as was d'Artagnan, he, in his turn, now grew pale and trembled with indignation.

'A king,' he said, 'may degrade a soldier, he may exile him, or sentence him to death, but he has no right to insult him by treating his sword with dishonour. Sire, no King of France has ever rejected contemptuously the sword of a man like me. This dishonoured sword, sire, shall now be sheathed in no other scabbard than in my heart or in your own. It shall be sheathed in mine, sire, and you may thank heaven and my forbearance that I have not determined otherwise.'

Then, taking up the sword, he cried, 'My blood be upon your head, sire;' and, with a quick movement, he rested the hilt upon the floor and directed the point at his own breast.

With a movement still more rapid than d'Artagnan's, the king sprang towards him, caught him round the neck with his right arm, whilst, with his left, he seized the sword by the middle, and silently restored it to its sheath. D'Artagnan, pale, and still trembling, allowed the king to do this without making any effort either to prevent or assist him.

Then Louis, with a softened aspect, took up a pen, wrote a few lines, signed them and held out the paper to d'Artagnan.

'What is this document, sire?' asked the captain.

'An order to Monsieur d'Artagnan to set the Comte de la Fère at liberty immediately.'

D'Artagnan seized the king's hand, and kissed it. Then, having folded up the order, he placed it in his belt and left the room. Neither he nor the king uttered a single syllable.

'Oh! human heart,' murmured Louis, when left to himself, 'compass by which kings steer their course, when shall I learn to read your depths as the leaves of a book? I am not a bad king, neither am I a poor one; but I am only a child still.'

CHAPTER 26

## Political rivals again

D'ARTAGNAN had promised Monsieur de Baisemeaux that he would rejoin his party at the supper-table, and he kept his word. They had just finished their meal, and were tasting some of the choice wines and liqueurs with which the governor's cellars had the reputation of being well stocked, when the captain's spurs were heard ringing on the pavement of the corridor, and the captain himself appeared in the doorway.

Athos and Aramis had played a close game, without either of them obtaining an advantage. During supper they had discussed the Bastille, the last visit to Fontainebleau and Monsieur Fouquet's forthcoming fête at Vaux; but no one, save Baisemeaux, had ventured to introduce into the conversation anything bearing upon private affairs. Upon the arrival of d'Artagnan, it was at once seen that he was considerably agitated, and Baisemeaux hastened to give him a chair. D'Artagnan raised a glass of wine to his lips and set the glass down empty. Athos and Aramis were quick to notice the peculiarity of d'Artagnan's manner, but Baisemeaux was conscious only that he had for a guest the captain of the kng's musketeers, and spared no pains to do him honour.

Although, as we have just said, Aramis at once perceived d'Artagnan's agitation, he was altogether at a loss to account for it, and Athos alone believed that he had penetrated the secret. To him, the return of d'Artagnan, and the obvious agitation of that usually impassive individual, signified, 'I have been to ask something of the king, which he has refused me;' and he felt convinced that the matter admitted of no other explanation.

Athos rose from the table with a smile, and made a sign to d'Artagnan, as if to remind him that they had other business in hand besides supping together. D'Artagnan understood him, and replied with another sign; whilst Aramis and Baisemeaux interrogated one another with their eyes. Athos, who felt that some sort of explanation was due to these two, then said: 'The truth is, my friends, that you, Aramis, have been taking supper with a state criminal, and that you, Monsieur de Baisemeaux, have been entertaining one of your own prisoners.'

Baisemeaux uttered an exclamation of astonishment, not unmingled with satisfaction, for he took a just pride in his fortress, and, apart from any mercenary considerations, the more prisoners he had under his charge the more contented he felt, and the higher they were in rank, the more self-important he became.

Aramis assumed a sympathetic look appropriate to the occasion.

'My dear Athos,' he said, 'pray forgive me, but I feared that this might be the case when I saw you come in. Some scrape that Raoul has got into about La Vallière, is it not?'

'Alas!' sighed Baisemeaux.

'And you,' continued Aramis, 'like the single-minded gentleman that you are, forgetting that courtiers exist, went and had it out with the king?'

'You have guessed rightly, my friend.'

'With the result?' said Baisemeaux, alarmed to find that he had been entertaining a man who had incurred the king's serious displeasure, 'with the result, comte?'

'With the result, my dear governor,' said Athos, 'that my friend, Monsieur d'Artagnan, is about to hand over to you the order for my imprisonment, which I see he carries in his belt.'

Baisemeaux mechanically held out his hand. D'Artagnan, accordingly, drew forth two papers, one of which he handed to the governor.

Baisemeaux received, unfolded it, and proceeded to read its intents in a half-audible voice, glancing, from time to time, at Athos, over the top of the paper.

' "Order to detain in my fortress of the Bastille – " Good! "In my fortress of the Bastille, monsieur le comte de la Fère," this is indeed a sad honour which is thrust upon me.'

'You will have a very patient prisoner, at all events,' said Athos, in his calm and gentle voice.

'And a prisoner who won't stay here a month, my dear governor,' remarked Aramis, whilst Baisemeaux made an entry, in his official registry, of the royal command.

'Not a day or, rather, not a night,' said d'Artagnan, producing the second order of the king; 'for now, Monsieur de Baisemeaux, you can make a note in your book of this further order, which gives the comte immediate liberty.'

'Ah!' said Aramis, 'you have anticipated me in obtaining his release, d'Artagnan,' and he pressed, in a significant manner, the captain's hand, and, at the same time, that of Athos.

'What!' exclaimed the latter, in surprise, 'has the king restored me my liberty?'

'Read, my dear fellow,' said d'Artagnan.

Athos took the paper and read it. 'It is true,' said he.

'Are you sorry?' asked d'Artagnan.

'Oh no; on the contrary, I wish the king no harm, and the greatest harm that one can wish a king is that he may commit an act of injustice. But you have been through a terrible ordeal, have you not, my friend?'

'Not at all,' replied the musketeer, cheerfully, 'the king simply did everything I wanted him to do.'

Aramis looked at d'Artagnan and saw that he lied; but Baisemeaux saw nothing in d'Artagnan but a wonderful man who could make the king do anything he wished.

'Has the king exiled Athos?' asked Aramis.

'No; the king has, as yet, given no intimation of his intentions as to the future. At the same time, I think that to get out of the way is the best thing the comte can do; unless, indeed, he desires to thank his majesty for his clemency.'

'Not I,' said Athos, with a smile.

'Well, then, I think that the best thing for the comte to do is to retire to his own estates; but, if any other place of residence would suit you better, I will do my best to obtain it for you. Only speak, my dear Athos, and tell me what you would like.'

'Thank you; no,' said Athos. 'I desire nothing better than to seek retirement, for a while, under the shade of my great trees on the banks of the Loire. If God is the supreme physician and healer of the broken-hearted, the contemplation of nature is a sovereign remedy. And now,' he continued, turning to Baisemeaux, 'I presume I am free to take my departure.'

'Yes, comte, I think and hope so, unless,' said the governor, turning over and over the two papers in his hands, 'Monsieur d'Artagnan is armed with a third order.'

'No, my dear Monsieur de Baisemeaux, I think we may safely act upon the one last handed to you.'

'Ah, comte,' said Baisemeaux, addressing Athos, 'you do not know what you are losing. I should have classed you with the thirty-livres prisoners,[74] such as generals. What am I saying? thirty livres? no, fifty livres, like princes, and you would have fared every day as you have supped this evening.'

'Thank you for your kind intentions,' said Athos, 'but I am not ambitious of any such distinction. And now,' he added, turning to d'Artagnan, 'let us go, my dear friend; can I hope to have your companionship?'

'As far as the city gate only,' replied d'Artagnan, 'and then I must say to you, as I said to the king, "I am on duty." '

'And you, my dear Aramis, will you not come with me? La Fère is on the way to Vannes.'

'I, my friend,' answered the bishop, 'I have an appointment to keep in Paris this evening, in which the very gravest interests are involved.'

'Then, my dear friend, it only remains for me to take my leave of you and to set out. My dear Monsieur Baisemeaux, many thanks for the goodwill you have shown me, and for this specimen of hospitality at the Bastille.' With these words, the comte embraced Aramis, shook hands with Baisemeaux and, accompanied by d'Artagnan, left the prison.

Whilst these events were taking place at the Palais-Royal and at the Bastille, let us see what happened at the residences of Athos and of de Bragelonne.

Grimaud, as we know, had accompanied his master to Paris, and had opened the door for him when he went out; he had seen him get into a carriage, and had seen d'Artagnan gnaw his moustaches. He had studied the expression of each, and had known them too long not to be aware that, behind the mask of impassibility, serious events were taking shape.

As soon as Athos had gone, Grimaud sat down to think. He recalled the strange manner in which Athos had taken leave of him, and the embarrassment, which he alone could detect, of that master whose wishes and ideas were generally so clearly and unhesitatingly expressed. Although Athos had taken with him nothing but what he stood up in, Grimaud had a presentiment that he would be absent more than an hour, perhaps more than a day; indeed, the very manner in which his master had pronounced the word 'Adieu' was sufficient to convince him that it would be long before he saw him again.

With his heart full of affection for Athos, Grimaud turned all this over in his mind, and a vague feeling of impending misfortune took possession of him, together with that dread of solitude which is never absent from the minds of those who love. All his reflections served only to make the poor fellow grow more and more sad and uneasy.

Without any definite object in view, Grimaud wandered about the place as though looking for some traces of Athos, like a faithful dog rendered uneasy by the absence of his master, except that, in Grimaud's case, a feeling of apprehension, which he could not shake off, was added to the restlessness which was instinctive. Having found nothing to guide him, and having neither seen nor discovered anything in confirmation of his fears, Grimaud was at his wits' end to conjecture what could possibly be the matter.

Not much consolation, however, was to be derived from any effort of imagination; indeed, the more Grimaud racked his brain, the more anxious did he become, for, as is usual in such cases, he could not divest his mind of the feeling that whatever had happened must be of a disagreeable nature. The pigeon which stays at home[75] is always in terror for the fate of the pigeon on the wing.

Grimaud thus passed from a state of uneasiness into one of absolute fright as he went over in his mind all that had taken place. There was d'Artagnan's letter to Athos, the receipt of which had apparently caused the latter considerable vexation; then, Raoul's visit to Athos, at the end of which Athos had called for his decorations and court suit; after that, the interview with the king, and the return from it of Athos, with a face full of gloom and despondency; then, again, the explanation which ensued between father and son, which had ended in a tender embrace between the two, and the sorrowful departure of Raoul to his own apartments; and, finally, the arrival of d'Artagnan, gnawing at his moustaches, who had carried off with him, in his carriage, the Comte de la Fère.

These various scenes composed a drama in five acts, which so keen a man of the world as Grimaud had no difficulty in understanding. Before all things, Grimaud was a practical man, and his first act was to search his master's pockets, in one of which he found d'Artagnan's letter, which ran as follows:

> DEAR FRIEND – Raoul has been here to make enquiries of me as to Mademoiselle de la Vallière's conduct during his absence in London. I am a poor captain of musketeers, whose fate it is, daily, to have dinned into his ears the irresponsible chatter of the barracks and the street corner. Had I told Raoul half of what I have been compelled to listen to, I believe it would have killed him; besides, being in the service of the king, it would ill become me to talk about his affairs. You will know how to act. The matter concerns you more than it does me, and perhaps more than Raoul himself.
>
> D'ARTAGNAN

Grimaud tore a few hairs out of his head. Had his locks been of more luxuriant growth, no doubt he would have pulled out a handful.

'There,' said he, 'is the explanation of the matter. This young woman has been playing tricks, and has deceived my young master, who, no doubt, has been told of her conduct. Then, what is rumoured about her and the king must be true. Monsieur le comte has been to the king, and spoken plainly to him. The king has sent Monsieur d'Artagnan to arrange the matter; and, good heavens!' continued Grimaud, 'I remember now that the comte returned without his sword.'

The recollection of this circumstance caused the perspiration to break out upon the worthy man's forehead; he wasted no more time in thought, but, clapping his hat on his head, made the best of his way to Raoul's lodging.

After the departure of Louise, Raoul had modified his grief, if not his love, and, forced now to look ahead upon the road along which his heedless impetuosity had started him, he saw, at a glance, that his father, having shown his resentment of the king's conduct, had thereby incurred the royal displeasure, the consequences of which were likely to be serious. Indeed, remembering the mysterious signs made by Athos upon d'Artagnan's unlooked-for arrival, the result of the conflict between king and subject was plainly revealed to him.

D'Artagnan, being on duty, and, so to speak, chained to his post, would not have paid Athos a visit for the mere pleasure of seeing him. No, he had come to tell him something – probably to give him warning of impending trouble. Raoul was shocked to think how selfishly he had acted in forgetting his father and thinking only of his own love affairs and in giving way to despair when he might, perhaps, have taken active measures to repel any attack with which Athos might be threatened.

At this reflection he sprang up, girded on his sword, and hurried back to his father's residence.

On his way, he ran up against Grimaud, who, equally eager to learn the truth, was, as we know, hastening at top speed in the opposite direction. The two men embraced instinctively, both from the same premises having arrived at similar conclusions.

'Grimaud!' cried Raoul.

'Monsieur Raoul!' cried Grimaud.

'Is all well with the comte?'

'You have not seen him?'

'No; where is he?'

'I am looking for him.'

'And Monsieur d'Artagnan?'

'They went out together.'

'When?'

'Ten minutes after you left.'

'In the coach?'

'Yes.'

'Where have they gone?'

'I don't know.'

'Did my father take any money with him?'

'No.'

'Did he take a sword?'

'No.'

'Grimaud!'

'Monsieur Raoul!'

'I have an idea that Monsieur d'Artagnan came to – '

'To arrest the comte; is that what you mean?'

'Yes, Grimaud.'

'I could have sworn it.'

'Which way did they drive?'

'Along the quays.'

'The Bastille!'

'Ah! by the Lord, yes.'

'Quick, let us run!'

'Yes, let us run.'

'But where to?' said Raoul, suddenly.

'We will, in the first place, go to Monsieur d'Artagnan's; perhaps we may gain some information there.'

'No; if they will tell me nothing at my father's house, they will tell me nowhere else. Let us go – but, good gracious! what an idiot I am! I had clean forgotten Monsieur Du Vallon.'

'Monsieur Porthos?'

'Yes, of course; and he is still waiting for me at the Minimes at Vincennes.'

'Fortunately, it is close to the Bastille!'

'Yes.'

'Well, sir, I will go and get the horses saddled.'

'Yes, friend; pray do so.'

CHAPTER 27

*In which Porthos is convinced without understanding*

THE WORTHY PORTHOS, faithful to all the traditions of ancient chivalry, had decided to wait for Monsieur de Saint-Aignan until sundown. As, however, Saint-Aignan did not come, as Raoul had omitted to send any message to his second and as the time of this enforced inactivity seemed unutterably long and tedious, Porthos had sent one of the gatekeepers to fetch him a few bottles of wine and a joint of meat, and, from time to time, regaled himself with a draught of the one or a few mouthfuls of the other. He had just finished these supplies when Raoul, accompanied by Grimaud, arrived at full gallop.

When Porthos perceived two horsemen approaching in such a manner, he did not doubt for a moment that they were Saint-Aignan and his second, and getting up from the grass upon which he had been reclining and stretching his limbs, he said to himself, 'See what it is to have contracted good habits. The fellow has turned up after all. Now, if I had gone away, he would have found no one here, and might have taken advantage of it.' Then, with hand on hip, he assumed an imposing attitude, making the very utmost of his gigantic stature. But in place of Saint-Aignan it was Raoul who, in a state of great distress, approached him, crying: 'Oh! my dear friend, pray forgive me, but a great misfortune has happened.'

'Raoul!' exclaimed Porthos, in astonishment.

'Yes; and you will pardon me, will you not?' continued Raoul, embracing his friend.

'What have I to forgive you for?'

'For having forgotten you for so long; but I declare to you that I am out of my senses.'

'Oh, nonsense!'

'But if you only knew what has happened!'

'Well, what is it? Have you killed him, then?'

'Whom?'

'Why, Saint-Aignan, of course.'

'Oh! it is worse than that. The matter is that the Comte de la Fère has been arrested!'

Porthos started, with a heave of his huge shoulders which would have brought down a wall.

'Arrested!' he cried – 'by whom?'

'By d'Artagnan.'

'Impossible,' said Porthos.

'It is true, nevertheless,' said Raoul.

Porthos turned for confirmation to Grimaud, who made an affirmative gesture.

'Where has he been taken to?'

'The Bastille.'

'How do you know that?'

'On our way here, we questioned some people who had seen the carriage pass, and others who had seen it enter the gates of the Bastille.'

'Oh! indeed,' muttered Porthos, advancing a couple of steps.

'What have you decided upon?' asked Raoul.

'I? Nothing. Only I don't intend Athos to remain in the Bastille.'

'But do you know that it is by the king's order that this arrest has been made?' asked Raoul, as he approached a step nearer to the worthy Porthos.

The latter looked at the young man as if to say, 'What does that matter to me?' and the mute language was so eloquent that Raoul asked no more questions, but mounted his horse, whilst Porthos, with Grimaud's assistance, mounted his own.

'Suppose we arrange our plans,' said Raoul.

'The very thing,' said Porthos. 'Let us arrange our plan of procedure.'

Raoul sighed deeply.

'What's the matter?' cried Porthos. 'Don't you feel well?'

'No; I feel how powerless we are. We three cannot take the Bastille by storm, I suppose?'

'Well,' replied Porthos, 'if we had d'Artagnan with us, I would not say that we could not.'

Raoul could not but admire the supreme and simple confidence of the man. He was, indeed, one of those heroes who, three or four at a time, had attacked armies and stormed castles. Men who had defied death itself, and who, remnants of a former generation, were yet stronger than the strongest of the young men of the present time.

'Monsieur,' he said to Porthos, 'you give me an idea. It is absolutely necessary to see d'Artagnan.'

'Undoubtedly; where shall we find him?'

'He would probably go straight home, after taking my father to the Bastille.'

'Better enquire at the Bastille first,' put in Grimaud, who spoke little, but always to the point.

Acting upon this suggestion, they reached the fortress without delay, and by a fortunate chance, Grimaud caught sight of the carriage they were in search of as it turned in under the great gate of the drawbridge. It was d'Artagnan returning from his interview with the king.

In vain did Raoul endeavour to press his horse alongside the carriage in order to see who was inside it. The horses had already stopped on the other side of the great gate, which immediately closed again, whilst one of the soldiers on guard struck Raoul's horse upon the nose with his musket.

Raoul turned round, glad enough to have, at least, discovered the whereabouts of the carriage which had contained his father.

'Now we have him,' said Grimaud.

'Yes, by waiting a little, we shall be sure to catch him when he comes out; shall we not, my friend?'

'Unless d'Artagnan is a prisoner also,' replied Porthos; 'in which case, the game's up.'

Even that might be possible, and Raoul made no reply. He told Grimaud, however, to take the horses out of sight into the little Rue Jean-Beausire, in order not to excite suspicion, whilst he himself watched for the out-coming of d'Artagnan or the carriage. This was the best thing he could have done, for, in less than twenty minutes, the gate reopened and the carriage reappeared. A flash of light prevented Raoul from seeing the occupants of the carriage distinctly, but Grimaud declared that it contained two persons, of whom one was his master. Porthos looked first at Raoul, and then at Grimaud, in an endeavour to guess what they thought about the position.

'It is certain,' said Grimaud, 'that the comte is in the coach, and that he has either been set at liberty or is being conveyed to another prison.'

'We shall be able to judge as to that by the direction the carriage takes,' said Porthos.

'If he has been set at liberty,' said Grimaud, 'they will take him to his own residence.'

'That is true,' replied Porthos.

'The carriage is not taking that road,' said Raoul; and, as a matter of fact, the horses were just disappearing in the Faubourg Saint-Antoine.

'Come on!' cried Porthos; 'we'll stop the carriage, and tell Athos to make his escape.'

'Rank rebellion!' murmured Raoul.

Porthos gave him a second look, as full of meaning as the first.

Raoul's sole reply was to shake up his horse.

A few moments after, the three horsemen had overtaken the coach, and were almost alongside of it. D'Artagnan, whose senses were always on the alert, heard the gallop of the horses, and, at the same moment, Raoul shouted to Porthos to ride past the carriage and see who was inside it with Athos. Porthos did as he was told, but was able to see nothing in consequence of the blinds being drawn down.

Anger and impatience got the better of Raoul. He had himself perceived how closely his father was concealed from observation and quickly decided to proceed to extremities. On the other hand, d'Artagnan, peeping through the blinds, had recognised both Raoul and Porthos, and had informed the comte of their presence upon the scene. He was curious to see what they would do under the circumstances.

He had not long to wait, for Raoul, pistol in hand, charged the carriage-horse nearest him and ordered the coachman to stop, while Porthos, the next instant, seized him and dragged him from his box. Grimaud tore open the carriage door, and Raoul, with open arms, shouted out his father's name.

'Ah, Raoul, is it you, my dear boy?' cried Athos.

'Not badly done, upon my word!' said d'Artagnan, with an

approving burst of laughter. And they both embraced the young man and Porthos, who had come to their rescue.

'My gallant Porthos, my excellent friend, who is always to be depended upon!' cried Athos.

'He is still only twenty years old,' said d'Artagnan.

'Well done, old fellow!'

'Oh, bother!' said Porthos, rather shamefacedly; 'we thought you were under arrest.'

'Whilst, all the time, I was merely taking a drive with d'Artagnan,' replied Athos.

'Anyhow, we have followed you from the Bastille,' remarked Raoul, half reproachfully.

'We have been to supper there with the excellent governor. You remember Baisemeaux, Porthos?'

'I should think so; quite well.'

'We met Aramis there.'

'At the Bastille?'

'He was one of the guests at supper. He sent a thousand civil messages to you.'

'Very good of him, I'm sure,' said Porthos.

'Where is monsieur le comte bound for?' asked Grimaud, whom Athos had already recognised and rewarded with a smile.

'We are going home to Blois,' replied Athos.

'Like this; straight away?'

'Just so.'

'What! without any luggage, monsieur?'

'Oh, Raoul would have found instructions either to send my baggage after me, or to bring it to me himself, that is, if he intends returning home.'

'If there is nothing to detain him in Paris,' said d'Artagnan, with a look that cut like a sword-blade for it reopened the young man's wounds, 'he will do well to follow you, Athos.'

'There is nothing to detain me in Paris,' said Raoul.

'Let us be off, then,' said Athos, quickly.

'And Monsieur d'Artagnan?'

'Oh, I shall go with you as far as the *barrière*, and then ride back with Porthos.'

'All right,' said the latter.

'Come, my boy,' said the comte, drawing Raoul within the carriage and embracing him again. 'And, Grimaud,' he continued, 'you will return quietly to Paris with your own horse and Monsieur Du Vallon's. Raoul and I will continue the journey on horseback, and leave the carriage for these two gentlemen to ride back to Paris in. When you reach home, you will pack up my letters and all my belongings and send them after us.'

'But,' observed Raoul, in an endeavour to get at the real reason for this sudden departure, 'when you return to Paris, there will be nothing there for you to use. That will, surely, be very inconvenient.'

'I think, Raoul, that it will be a long time before I see Paris again. Our last visit has not been so pleasant as to make me anxious to repeat it.'

Raoul hung his head, and was silent.

Athos got out of the carriage, and mounted the horse which Porthos had been riding, the change of plan apparently meeting with the latter's unqualified approval. Porthos and d'Artagnan promised to visit Athos at Blois at an early date, and d'Artagnan, giving Raoul a final shake of the hand, said: 'My dear lad, I will write to you.'

This was much for d'Artagnan to promise, for he was not addicted to writing letters; and Raoul, appreciating all that it conveyed, was touched, and warmly pressed his friend's hand. Then, with many expressions of friendship and goodwill, the others wished the two travellers Godspeed.

D'Artagnan joined Porthos in the carriage.

'Well, old fellow,' he said, 'what a day we've had!'

'Oh! the devil,' said Porthos, 'haven't we, indeed?'

'You must be pretty well knocked up?'

'Not overmuch,' replied Porthos; 'but I shall go to bed early tonight, so as to be ready for tomorrow morning.'

'What have you in hand for the morning?'

'I have to finish what I have begun.'

'Upon my word, you quite startle me. You look as savage as a bear. What the devil is there for you to finish?'

'Why, can't you understand that, as Raoul has not fought, of course I must do so?'

'Whom are you going to fight – the king?'

'The king!' said Porthos. 'What an absurd idea!'

'Yes, the king! you great baby, the king!'

'I assure you that it is only Monsieur de Saint-Aignan.'

'Yes; but let me tell you this – in fighting Saint-Aignan, you draw your sword against the king.'

'Good gracious!' exclaimed Porthos, staring in astonishment; 'are you sure of what you say?'

'Absolutely.'

'What is to be done, then?'

'We will try to eat a good supper, Porthos. An excellent table is always provided for the captain of the musketeers. You will meet Saint-Aignan there, and you will drink his health.'

'I?' said Porthos, aghast.

'You don't mean to say that you will refuse to drink to the king's health?'

'But, confound it all, I am not speaking of the king, but of Saint-Aignan.'

'But don't I tell you that it is the same thing?'

'Oh! well, of course, if you say so,' said Porthos, meekly.

'But you understand, don't you?'

'Not a bit,' said Porthos; 'but it is all the same.'

'Yes, it is all the same,' replied d'Artagnan. 'And now, let us go to supper, old friend.'

## CHAPTER 28

### Monsieur de Baisemeaux's 'society'

OUR READERS will not have forgotten that, on quitting the Bastille, d'Artagnan and the Comte de La Fère left Aramis and Baisemeaux in close conclave together.

Baisemeaux did not perceive that the conversation was in any way affected by the departure of his two other guests. He had a thorough belief in the properties of the excellent wine which was to be found in the cellars of the Bastille, and which he thought was strong enough to loosen the tongue of any man breathing, but he little knew Aramis, who was never more uncommunicative than under such conditions as the present. But Aramis gauged Baisemeaux to a nicety, and reckoned upon making him develop his views. Therefore, the conversation without appearing to languish, did so in reality, for Baisemeaux sustained it almost entirely by himself and confined it exclusively to the imprisonment of Athos and his prompt restoration to liberty.

Baisemeaux, moreover, had not failed to notice that both of the orders which he had received from d'Artagnan were in the king's own handwriting, and he knew, from that circumstance, that the occasion was no common one. All this interested and puzzled Baisemeaux in no small degree, whereas everything was perfectly clear to the acute Aramis, and he, who seldom allowed anything to interfere with his usual habits, had not yet explained to the governor why he had taken the trouble to pay him this visit.

Accordingly, he interrupted Baisemeaux in the middle of one of his beautifully-rounded periods.

'Tell me,' he said, 'dear Monsieur de Baisemeaux, have you, at the Bastille, no other form of entertainment beyond those at which I have recently had the honour of assisting?'

This question was sprung so suddenly on the governor that, like a weathercock impelled against the wind, he came to a complete standstill.

'Forms of entertainment,' he stammered presently – 'oh! yes, monseigneur, I have them continually.'

'I am glad to hear it; what sort of diversions do you indulge in?'

'Oh! all sorts, monseigneur.'

'You receive a good many visits, I suppose.'

'Well, no. Visitors are somewhat rare at the Bastille.'

'Rare, are they? you surprise me.'

'I may say, very rare.'

'Even society visitors?'

'What do you mean by "society visitors"? – the prisoners?'

'No, no! your prisoners, indeed! I know that it is *you*, on the contrary, who have to visit *them*. No, by your "society", dear Monsieur Baisemeaux, I mean the society to which you, yourself, belong.'

Baisemeaux stared hard at Aramis; then, as if the conjecture he had entertained for an instant was impossible, 'Oh!' he said, 'I see very little society nowadays. In fact I must admit to you, dear Monsieur d'Herblay, that the atmosphere of the Bastille is not attractive to the general run of people in society. Ladies, especially, suffer a certain trepidation, which I have the greatest difficulty in allaying in order to give them courage enough to come near me. In fact, they are affected, poor things, by the sight of the dungeons, and by the reflection that they are inhabited by unfortunate prisoners who – '

The longer and harder Baisemeaux fixed his eyes upon those of Aramis, the more and more did he become confused in his manner and falter in his speech, so that presently his tongue became paralysed, and refused to utter another syllable.

'You do not understand me,' said Aramis, when poor Baisemeaux had collapsed altogether, 'you do not understand me. I am not alluding to society in general, but to one *society* in particular, to that society, in short, to which you are affiliated.'

Baisemeaux nearly dropped the glass of wine which he was in the act of carrying to his lips.

'Affiliated,' he stammered, 'affiliated!'

'Certainly, *affiliated*,' repeated Aramis, with the utmost composure; 'are you not a member of a secret society, dear Monsieur de Baisemeaux?'

'Secret?'

'Well, secret or mysterious; we will not cavil about the exact term.'

'Oh, Monsieur d'Herblay! – '

'Don't attempt to deny it.'

'But believe me – '

'I believe no more than I know.'

'I swear to you – '

'Listen to me, dear Monsieur de Baisemeaux. I say yes; you say no! Now one of us speaks the truth, and, of necessity, the other says what is not the truth.'

'Well?'

'Well, then, we must come to an understanding.'

'Let us see,' said Baisemeaux, 'let us see.'

'Now, drink your wine,' my good Monsieur de Baisemeaux. What! the devil! you look frightened to death.'

'Oh! dear no; not the least in the world.'

'Well, then drink.' Baisemeaux drank, but his liquor went the wrong way.

'Now,' continued Aramis, 'if you do not belong to this society, secret, mysterious or whatever you like to call it – the name is quite immaterial – if, I say, you do not belong to any such society as the one I am attempting to describe, you will not understand a word of what I am going to say to you.'

'Oh! you may rest assured that I shall not understand a syllable.'

'Ah! well.'

'Try; let us see.'

'That is what I am about to do. If, on the contrary, you *are* a member of this society, you will at once answer yes or no.'

'Put your question,' faltered Baisemeaux trembling.

'For, you will agree with me, dear Monsieur de Baisemeaux, that one cannot be a member of such a society, and enjoy the privileges which are attendant upon such membership, without being compelled to conform to the rules and regulations of the society.'

'Yes,' stammered Baisemeaux, 'that would be clear enough, if – '

'Well,' continued Aramis, 'there is, in the society of which I speak, and with which it appears you have no connection – '

'Excuse me,' interrupted Baisemeaux, 'I should not like to say so absolutely.'

'There is,' pursued Aramis, 'an undertaking to which all governors and captains of fortresses who are affiliated to the order are obliged to subscribe.'

Baisemeaux turned pale.

'And this,' Aramis went on, 'is the undertaking in question.'

Baisemeaux rose, a prey to indescribable agitation. Then, as if reading from a book, Aramis began to quote the following paragraph: ' "The said captain or governor of a fortress shall, when it shall seem to be necessary, or at the request of a prisoner, admit to the fortress a confessor affiliated to the order." ' Aramis stopped, and Baisemeaux, so pale and abject had he become, was a pitiable sight.

'I think that is the exact wording of the rule; is it not?' asked Aramis calmly.

'Monseigneur!' began Baisemeaux.

'Ah! you are beginning to understand a little, I see?'

'Monseigneur, I beg of you not to take advantage of my weakness of mind. I feel that, as compared with you, I am but a poor creature, if you are determined to wring from me the little secrets of my administration.'

'Oh! don't be alarmed, dear Monsieur de Baisemeaux, the little secrets of your administration are nothing to me; it is your conscience that I desire to awake.'

'Well, my conscience, then, dear Monsieur d'Herblay; but pray have some consideration for my position, which is no ordinary one.'

'It is, indeed, no ordinary one,' continued the inflexible Aramis, 'if you are a member of the society, but, if you are not bound by any undertaking, it is a perfectly simple one, and you are responsible to no one but the king.'

'Well, well! I obey the king alone. Whom would you have a French gentleman obey, if not the king?'

Aramis did not give way an inch, but, in his suave manner, continued. 'It is very gratifying to a French gentleman and dignitary of the church to hear a man of your distinction express himself so loyally, and, having listened to you, to believe no more than you do yourself.'

'Did you doubt me, monseigneur?'

'I? Oh! no.'

'Anyhow, you doubt me no longer?'

'I no longer doubt that such a man as you faithfully serves the masters to whom, of his own free will, he has become bound,' said Aramis seriously.

'Masters?' cried Baisemeaux.

'I said "masters",' replied Aramis.

'Monsieur d'Herblay, you are joking, are you not?'

'Oh! I quite understand that it is somewhat more trying to have to obey several masters, than one only; but you must remember, dear Monsieur de Baisemeaux, that you have no one but yourself to thank for the embarrassment in which you now find yourself.'

'No, certainly,' replied the unfortunate governor, becoming more embarrassed than ever, 'but what are you about? – you are not going away?'

'Certainly, I am.'

'But this is very strange behaviour, monseigneur!'

'Strange! in what respect?'

'Have you sworn to put me on the rack?'

'No; I should be distressed to do anything of the kind.'

'Remain here, then.'

'I cannot do so.'

'And why?'

'Because I have nothing further to do here, and I have business to attend to elsewhere.'

'Business, at so late an hour?'

'Yes, and now listen to me, dear Monsieur de Baisemeaux; they told me, where I come from, "The said governor or captain, shall, whenever it is necessary, or at the request of a prisoner, admit to his fortress a confessor affiliated to the order." Accordingly, I have come here, and since you understand nothing that I say, I must go back to tell those who sent me that they are mistaken and had better send me somewhere else.'

'What! then you are . . . ?' cried Baisemeaux, staring at Aramis with a terrified expression.

'The confessor affiliated to the order,' returned Aramis in an unchanged voice.

But, gently as the words were spoken, they fell like a clap of thunder upon the ears of the poor governor. He became livid, whilst the eyes of Aramis seemed like two blades of fire which penetrated to the bottom of his heart.

'The confessor!' he murmured. 'Monseigneur the confessor of the order!'

'Yes, but, as you are not affiliated, I cannot discuss the matter with you.'

'Monseigneur!'

'And I quite understand that, not being affiliated, you naturally decline to be bound by any rules of the order.'

'Monseigneur, I do not say that I am wholly unconnected with the order.'

'Ah!'

'I do not say that I refuse obedience.'

'It looks very much like it, however, Monsieur de Baisemeaux, judging from what has just taken place.'

'Oh! no indeed, monseigneur, I was merely anxious to be quite sure.'

'To be quite sure of what?' said Aramis in a tone of infinite contempt.

'Of nothing at all, monseigneur,' and Baisemeaux lowered his voice and hung his head before Aramis. 'I am at all times, and places,' he said, 'at the disposal of my masters, but – '

'Very good; I much prefer you in that frame of mind, monsieur.'

Aramis resumed his seat at the table, and held out his glass to Baisemeaux, whose hand, however, shook so that he was unable to pour out the wine.

'You were saying *but*,' resumed Aramis referring to Baisemeaux's last speech.

'But,' said the unfortunate man, 'not having been apprised beforehand, I was far from expecting – '

'Does not the gospel say, "Watch, for no man knoweth the hour."[76] Do not the injunctions of the order say, "Watch, for what *I* will, that always should *you* will also"? And under what pretext have you not expected the confessor, Monsieur de Baisemeaux?'

'Because, at the present moment, no prisoner is ill in the Bastille, monseigneur.'

Aramis shrugged his shoulders.

'How do you know that?' he asked.

'Well, it seemed to me – '

'Monsieur de Baisemeaux,' said Aramis, turning round in his chair, 'here is your servant who wishes to speak with you,' and, as he said this, Baisemeaux's valet appeared at the door.

'What is it?' asked Baisemeaux sharply.

'Your honour,' said the valet, 'I bring you the report of the house-physician.'

Aramis looked at Baisemeaux with a keen and confident eye.

'Well, let the messenger come in,' he said.

The messenger came forward, bowed, and handed the report.

Baisemeaux cast his eyes over it, and, looking up with a surprised air, said, 'I see that No 12 in the Bertaudière is ill.'

'Then, why did you say that all the prisoners were well, dear Monsieur de Baisemeaux?' asked Aramis carelessly, taking a draught of wine, but not removing his eyes off Baisemeaux. The governor, having dismissed the servant with a nod, ventured to say, though he trembled still, 'I think that the text of the paragraph is, "at the request of a prisoner".'

'Yes, that is so,' replied Aramis, 'but had you not better see what is the matter now?'

At that moment a sergeant put his head in at the half-open door.

'What! again?' cried Baisemeaux irritably, 'am I not to be allowed ten minutes' peace?'

'Your honour,' said the sergeant, 'the prisoner who is unwell in No. 12 Bertaudière asks permission to see a confessor.'

Baisemeaux nearly had a fit; but Aramis studiously refrained from helping by word or look.

'What answer am I to give?' asked Baisemeaux.

'Answer whatever you like,' replied Aramis with tightened lips, 'it is your business entirely; I am not governor of the Bastille, am I?'

'Let the prisoner be informed,' said Baisemeaux hastily, 'that his request shall be acceded to.'

The sergeant left the room.

'Oh! Monseigneur, monseigneur,' murmured Baisemeaux, 'how could I have suspected – how could I have foreseen this?'

'Who told you to suspect? Who spoke to you about prevision? The order suspects, knows and foresees; is not that enough?'

'What do you order me to do?' said Baisemeaux.

'I? nothing, I am only a poor priest, a simple confessor. Do you order me to go to the sick man?'

'Oh, monseigneur, I do not order, I entreat you to do so.'

'Very well; then show me the way.'

CHAPTER 29

## *The prisoner*

SINCE THE STRANGE TRANSFORMATION of Aramis into a confessor of the order, Baisemeaux had been a different man.

Hitherto, Aramis had been, to the worthy governor, a prelate to whom he was indebted; but this sudden revelation of Aramis in his new character had upset all the governor's previous ideas, and he now felt his own inferiority and recognised Aramis as his chief.

He hastened to light a lantern, summoned one of the turnkeys, and turning deferentially to Aramis, said, 'I am at monseigneur's orders.'

Aramis made a movement with his head signifying 'It is well,' and, with a wave of his hand, signed to Baisemeaux to lead the way. Baisemeaux accordingly went on in front, and Aramis followed him.

It was a fine starlight night. The footsteps of the three men echoed along the paved terraces and the jingling of the keys which hung at the turnkey's waist was audible in the topmost towers and seemed to remind the prisoners of the hopelessness of escape. The change which was so apparent in Baisemeaux might have been said to make itself felt even by the prisoners themselves. The turnkey even, the same man who, on the occasion of Aramis's first visit,[77] had shown himself so inquisitive and dictatorial, was now not only dumb but even impassive. He walked with bowed head and seemed afraid even to make use of his ears.

In this order they reached the tower of the Bertaudière, to the second floor of which they climbed silently, and with almost painful slowness, for Baisemeaux, notwithstanding his protestations, showed little alacrity in obeying the commands of his chief. Having, at length, reached the door of which they were in search, the turnkey quickly opened it, and Baisemeaux was on the point of entering the prisoner's place of confinement when Aramis stopped him by saying, 'It is not stated in the rules that the governor is to listen to the prisoner's confession.' Baisemeaux bowed, and made way for Aramis, who, taking the lantern from the turnkey's hands, entered by himself, signing to the others as he did so to shut the door after him. For an instant he stood still, listening for the departure of his two companions, then, having assured himself that they had left the tower, he placed the lantern upon a table and looked about him. Upon a bed of green serge, exactly like all the rest of the beds in the Bastille, except that it looked a trifle newer, and behind half-closed curtains, lay a young man into whose presence we have already once before introduced Aramis.

According to the rules of the prison, the captive was in darkness, for, at the hour of curfew, he had been obliged to put out his candle; indeed, considerable favour had been shown him in allowing him to burn it even up to that time. Near the bed stood a great leathern armchair, with twisted legs, upon which the prisoner had placed some articles of clothing remarkable for their newness of appearance. A small table, upon which were neither books nor writing materials, stood disregarded near the solitary window, whilst several dishes of food, hardly touched, showed that the prisoner's appetite was anything but vigorous.

The young man lay stretched upon the bed, his face half hidden in his arms. He made no movement at the entrance of his visitor and seemed to be either asleep or waiting to be addressed. With the aid of the lantern, Aramis lit the candle, softly pushed the armchair to one side and approached the bed with mingled interest and respect. The young man raised his head, 'What do you want?' he asked.

'Have you not asked for a confessor?'

'Yes.'

'Because you are ill?'

'Yes.'

'Are you very ill?'

The young man looked keenly at Aramis, and replied simply, 'I thank you.'

After a moment's silence he said, 'Have I not seen you before?' Aramis bowed an affirmative. Without doubt, the examination which the prisoner had just made of the cold, crafty and imperious countenance before him had done little to reassure him, for he added, 'I am better now.'

'Yes?' said Aramis interrogatively.

'Well, being better, it seems to me that I have no longer need for a confessor, at all events for the present.'

'Nor even of the hair-cloth shirt alluded to in the note which was concealed in your loaf of bread?' The young man showed signs of agitation, but, without giving him time to reply, Aramis continued, 'Nor even of the priest who was to make an important revelation to you?'

'If that is the case,' said the young man falling back upon his pillow, 'it is different; I am all attention.' Looking at him more attentively, Aramis was struck with the air of simple majesty which sat so easily upon him, and which can never be acquired unless God has implanted it in the blood or heart.

'Take a seat, monsieur,' said the prisoner.

Aramis bowed and obeyed.

'How do you like the Bastille?' he asked.

'Very well.'

'You do not suffer?'

'No.'

'And you desire nothing?'

'Nothing.'

'Not even liberty.'

'What do you mean by liberty, monsieur?' asked the prisoner, with the accent of a man who was bracing himself up for a conflict.

'By liberty, I mean flowers, fresh air, light, the stars, the satisfaction of being able to go, at will, whithersoever the vigorous young limbs of twenty years desire to take you.'

The young man smiled; it would have been difficult to say whether with resignation or disdain.

'Observe,' said he, 'I have here, in this Japanese vase, two lovely roses, gathered yesterday, in the bud, from the governor's garden. They have come into full bloom this morning, and, under my eyes, have opened their damask chalices; with the unfolding of each petal, they breathe forth the treasure of their perfume, so that my chamber is sweet with it. Look at them, they are the most beautiful of roses, and roses are the most beautiful of flowers. Why then should I wish for other flowers, seeing that I am already possessed of the loveliest of all?'

Aramis looked at the young man with surprise.

'If flowers mean liberty,' continued the young man with a sad smile, 'then I have liberty, since I have flowers.'

'But the air!' cried Aramis, 'the fresh air! so necessary to life.'

'Well, monsieur, take the trouble to walk to the window; it is open. Between heaven and earth, the wind hurls its storms of ice, or of fire, its warm vapours or soft breezes. The air kisses my cheek when, mounted upon this chair, with my arm passed round yonder iron bar for support, I fancy myself sailing through space.'

The face of Aramis clouded over as the young man went on.

'And light?' he continued, 'have I not the light of the sun, a friend who comes to see me every day without needing the governor's permission and unaccompanied by a gaoler? He comes in at the window, bringing with him a long square of light which, starting from the window itself, reaches to, and illuminates the hangings of the bed even to the fringes. This luminous square grows larger and larger from ten in the morning until midday, and decreases between the hours of one and three, but slowly, as if, although in haste to come, it were reluctant to depart. When the last ray of sunlight disappears, I have enjoyed four whole hours of its presence. Is not that sufficient pleasure? I am told that there are unhappy beings who toil in the quarries and the mines and who never see the light of the sun at all.'

Aramis wiped the perspiration from his forehead.

'And the stars,' continued the young man, 'how delightful it is to look at them! They all resemble each other, differing only in size and brilliancy. I consider myself favoured; for, if you had not lighted that candle, you would have been able to see the star which I was looking at before you arrived, and which is dear to my eyes.'

Aramis bent his head. He felt overwhelmed by the flood of that bitter philosophy which is the religion of captivity.

'So much, then, for the flowers, the air, the sunlight and the stars,' continued the young man with the same composure. 'Now comes the question of exercise. Do I not, every day, in fine weather, walk in the governor's garden, or about my room, if it is wet; in the cool, when it is hot, and in the warmth, when it is cold; and have I not a stove to keep me warm during the winter months? Ah! believe me, monsieur,' added the prisoner, not without a slight touch of bitterness, 'men have done everything for me that a man has a right to hope or wish for.'

'Men, perhaps,' said Aramis raising his head, 'but it seems to me that you have forgotten God.'

'As a matter of fact, I have,' replied the prisoner without the least show of emotion; 'but why do you talk to me in this strain? What is the good of talking to prisoners about God?'

Aramis looked attentively at this strange young man who had the resignation of the martyr and the smile of the atheist.

'Is not God in everything?' he said in a tone of mild reproach.

'Say at the end of everything,' answered the prisoner unmoved.

'Well, well!' said Aramis; 'but suppose we return to our starting-point.'

'I desire nothing better,' said the young man.

'I am your confessor.'

'Yes.'

'Well then, as my penitent, you must tell me the truth.'

'I ask for nothing better than the opportunity of telling it.'

'No prisoner is placed in confinement unless he has committed a crime. What crime have *you* been guilty of?'

'You asked me that question on the occasion when I first saw you.'

'And, as before, you evade the question.'

'And why do you suppose that I shall answer today?'

'Because, today, I come in the character of your father confessor.'

'Then, if you wish me to tell you what crime I have committed, you must, first of all, explain to me what crime is. Now, as I am not aware that I have anything to reproach myself with, I maintain that I am not criminal.'

'A man is held to be criminal, sometimes, by the great ones of the earth, not because he has committed a crime himself but because he knows of one which has been committed.'

The prisoner now listened with the utmost attention.

'Yes,' he said after a moment's silence, 'I understand; and you are right, monsieur. It is quite possible that, in the way you indicate, I may be criminal in the eyes of some people.'

'Ah! then you know something?' said Aramis, who thought that he detected, if not a defect, still, a joint in the harness.

'No, I know nothing,' replied the young man, 'but I think sometimes, and I say to myself at such times . . . '

'What do you say to yourself?'

'That, if I think any longer, I shall either go mad, or make a shrewd guess at a great many things.'

'Well, and then?' asked Aramis impatiently.

'Then, I leave off thinking.'

'You leave off?'

'Yes; my head is not clear, and my ideas become sad. I feel tired of everything, and I wish – '

'What?'

'I hardly know; I feel that I don't want to encourage a longing for what I don't possess, seeing that I am really contented with what I have.'

'Do you fear death,' asked Aramis, who was becoming slightly uneasy.

'Yes,' answered the young man with a smile which seemed to chill Aramis, so that he shivered.

'Since you fear death,' he cried, 'you must know more than you admit.'

'But you, yourself,' asked the prisoner, 'at whose instigation I asked to be allowed to see a confessor, you, who, when I have made the request, come to me promising to make a host of revelations – how is it that you say nothing and that I do all the talking? Since it seems that we both wear masks, for heaven's sake, let us either continue to wear them or discard them at the same moment.'

Aramis could not help feeling the force and justice of this reasoning.

'I have no ordinary man to deal with,' he thought; then, without preparing the prisoner for the change in his tactics, he said aloud, 'Are you ambitious?'

'What is ambition?' asked the young man.

'It is a feeling,' replied Aramis, 'under the influence of which a man wishes for more than he has.'

'I have said that I am contented, monsieur, but it is possible that I deceive myself. I may be ambitious without being aware of it. I wish you would speak out what is in your mind.'

'The ambitious man,' said Aramis, 'covets something that is beyond the reach of persons in his own rank of life.'

'I covet nothing that is beyond *my* rank,' replied the young man with an assurance which caused the Bishop of Vannes to tremble once more.

He was silent; but the eager look, the puckered brow, and the expectant attitude of the prisoner, plainly told Aramis that something very different from silence was expected of him. He made haste, therefore, to break it.

'You lied to me, the first time I saw you,' he said abruptly.

'*Lied?*' cried the young man, springing up on his bed, in such a tone of voice, and with such a flash in his eyes, as made Aramis recoil in spite of himself.

'I should say,' said Aramis bowing, 'that you concealed from me what you remembered of your childhood.'

'A man's secrets belong to himself, monsieur, and not to the first person who wishes to learn them.'

'That is true,' said Aramis bowing more profoundly than before, 'but, today, am I the first comer? I entreat you to answer the question, *monseigneur*.'[78]

This title caused the prisoner a slight feeling of uneasiness, though he did not seem to be astonished that it should be applied to him.

'I do not know you, monsieur,' he said.

'Oh! if I dared,' said Aramis, 'I would kiss your hand.'

The young man made a slight movement as if he would give his hand to Aramis, but the momentary light which had shone in his eyes died out, and he remained cold and impassive.

'Kiss the hand of a prisoner!' he said. 'To what end?'

'Why have you said that you are contented here?' asked Aramis. 'Why have you said that you aspire to nothing? Why, in short, by speaking thus, do you prevent me from being frank with you?'

The light flashed into the young man's eyes for the third time, but died out, as before, without any result.

'You mistrust me?' said Aramis.

'Why should I?'

'Oh! for a very simple reason; if you know what you ought to know, you ought to mistrust everybody.'

'Then do not be astonished that I am distrustful, since you suspect me of knowing that which I don't know.'

Aramis felt the warmest admiration for this energetic resistance.

'Oh! you drive me to despair, monseigneur,' he cried bringing down his fist upon the armchair.

'And, as to me, I do not understand you, monsieur.'

'Well, try to understand me.'

The prisoner looked steadily at Aramis.

'It seems to me, sometimes,' continued the latter, 'that I have before me the man I am seeking – and then – '

'And then – this man suddenly disappears, does he not?' said the prisoner, smiling. 'Well, so much the better.'

Aramis arose.

'Assuredly,' he said, 'I have nothing to say to a man who distrusts me to the extent that you do.'

'And I,' said the prisoner in the same tone, 'have nothing to say to a man who will not understand that a prisoner should distrust everyone.'

'Even his old friends?' said Aramis, 'Oh! Monseigneur, that is carrying prudence a little *too* far.'

'Old friends! are you, then, an old friend of mine?'

'Let us see,' said Aramis, 'do you not remember having seen, long ago, in the village where you passed the years of your early childhood – '

'Can you tell me the name of the village?'

'Noisy-le-Sec,' answered Aramis confidently.

'Go on,' said the young man whose face betrayed nothing.

'Hold hard, monseigneur,' said Aramis, 'if you are really determined to continue this game, let us pause for a moment. I came here to tell you a great many things, it is true, but I must first feel assured that you desire to hear them. Before divulging the important information of which I am possessed, I should like you, at least, to meet me halfway, and to show a little sympathy, even if you feel little confidence in me; but, on the contrary, you envelop yourself in a cloud of assumed ignorance which paralyses me – Oh! not for the reason you think; for however ignorant you may be, or feign to be, you are, nevertheless yourself, monseigneur, and nothing, *nothing*, pray understand that, can ever make you anyone else.'

'I promise,' said the prisoner, 'to listen patiently to what you have to tell me; only, it seems to me that I have a perfect right to ask the question which I have already put; who are you?'

'You may remember, some fifteen to eighteen years ago, a gentleman coming to see you, accompanied by a lady who usually dressed in black and who wore flame coloured-ribbons in her hair.'

'Yes,' said the young man, 'I once asked that gentleman's name and was told that he was called the Abbé d'Herblay. I was rather surprised to see an abbé with such a martial appearance, but was answered that there was nothing astonishing in that, inasmuch as he was one of the musketeers of King Louis XIII.'

'Well, then,' said Aramis, 'that musketeer, then an abbé, but now Bishop of Vannes, was no less a person than myself – your confessor of today.'

'I know it; I had already recognised you.'

'Well, monseigneur, if you know that, I must tell you something that you don't know, which is that, if the presence here, this evening, of that musketeer, abbé, bishop and confessor, were known to the king, tomorrow he who has risked everything to pay you this visit would be made acquainted with the axe of the executioner in the depths of a dungeon far more dismal and obscure than your own place of confinement.'

On hearing these words, so emphatically spoken, the young man raised himself up on his bed and looked with more and more concentration into the eyes of Aramis. The result of this examination was the establishment of the prisoner's confidence.

'Yes,' he said softly, 'I remember perfectly. The lady you speak of came once with you and twice with another lady – ' He stopped short.

'With the lady who visited you every month, was it not, monseigneur?'

'Yes.'

'Do you know who this lady was?'

A light seemed ready to flash from the prisoner's eyes. 'I know that she was one of the ladies of the court,' he said.

'You have a distinct recollection of her?'

'Oh! my memory is hardly at all confused,' said the young prisoner. 'I once saw the lady with a man of, apparently, about forty-five years of age; I saw her once with you and with the lady who dressed in black and wore flame-coloured ribbons, and I have seen her twice since with the same person. These four with my tutor, old Perronnette, my gaoler, and the governor, are the only persons to whom I have ever spoken, indeed almost the only persons I have ever seen in all my life.'

'But you were in prison then?'

'If I am in prison here, I was comparatively free there, although my liberty was certainly much restricted. A house which I never went out of, a large garden enclosed by walls over which I could not climb – such was my place of residence. You know all about it, because you have been there and seen for yourself. For the rest, thoroughly habituated to life within these limits, I had no desire to stray beyond them. So, you see, monsieur, being absolutely unacquainted with the outside world, I know of nothing to wish for, and you will be obliged to explain to me everything in connection with what you may relate.'

'I shall be charmed to do so, monseigneur,' said Aramis bowing, 'besides it is only my duty.'

'Well then, be good enough to give me some information respecting my "guardian".'

'A gentleman, monseigneur, a conscientious and thorough gentleman, capable, at one and the same time, of instructing your mind and looking after your physical welfare. Have you ever had reason to complain of him?'

'Oh! no, monsieur, quite the contrary indeed, but this *gentleman* has, nevertheless, many times told me that my father and mother were dead; now did he lie when he said that or did he speak the truth?'

'He was compelled to obey the orders which were given to him.'

'Then he lied?'

'In a measure only; your father *is* dead.'

'And my mother.'

'She is dead to you.'

'But, so far as others are concerned, she lives?'

'Yes.'

'Whilst I,' said the young man, with a searching glance at Aramis, 'am condemned to live in the obscurity of a prison?'

'Alas! I fear so.'

'And that,' continued the young man, 'because my restoration to society would involve the disclosure of a weighty secret.'

'A weighty secret indeed, yes.'

'To be able to imprison a little child, such as I was, my enemy must be very powerful.'

'He is.'

'More powerful that my mother, I presume?'

'Why do you think so.'

'Because otherwise my mother would have protected me.'

Aramis hesitated before answering, 'More powerful than your mother, yes, monseigneur.'

'For my nurse and my guardian to have been taken away, and for me to have been separated from them, either they or I must have been a source of great danger to my enemy?'

'Yes, and a danger from which your enemy freed himself by causing the disappearance of both nurse and guardian.'

'Disappearance!' repeated the prisoner with surprise. 'In what manner did they disappear?'

'In the surest way possible,' replied Aramis; 'they died.'

The young man turned slightly pale and passed a trembling hand over his face.

'Did they die by poison?' he asked.

'By poison.'

'My enemy must either be atrociously cruel or have been in a terrible strait to have taken the lives of two innocent creatures who had never wronged any human being.'

'Necessity rules with a strong hand in your family, monseigneur, as does the necessity which has compelled me, to my great regret, to tell you that your nurse and your guardian were both murdered.'

'Oh! you tell me nothing new,' said the prisoner, with a contraction of the brow.

'How is that?'

'I have suspected it.'

'Why?'

'I am going to tell you.'

Here, the young man, supporting himself on his two elbows, brought his face closer to that of Aramis, with such a look of dignity and even of defiance that the bishop felt the electricity of enthusiasm flash, in burning sparks, from his withered heart to his hardened brain.

'Speak, monseigneur,' he said, 'I have already told you that I jeopardise my life by seeking this interview, but, however small may be its value, I beg you to accept it as a ransom for your own.'

'Well,' continued the young man, 'that was why I suspected that my nurse and my guardian had been murdered.'

'You used to call him your father.'

'Yes, I called him father, knowing full well that I was no son of his.'

'Why did you believe that?'

'Because his manner was too respectful for that of a father, in the same way that yours is too deferential for that of a friend.'

'I, at least,' said Aramis, 'have made no attempt at disguise.'

The young man, with an inclination of his head, continued, 'There can be no doubt that it was not intended that I should be shut up for ever, and what led me to think so, more than anything else, was the pains that were taken with my education. The gentleman in whose care I had been placed taught me all that he knew himself; mathematics, a little geometry, astronomy, fencing and riding. Every morning I fenced in one of the lower rooms, which we used for the purpose, and took riding lessons in the grounds in which the house stood. Well, one morning (it was in the summertime and the weather was very hot), I was asleep in the room I have spoken of. Up to that time, nothing, save the respect with which I was treated, had occurred to arouse my suspicions. I lived, as children, birds and plants live, in the fresh air and the sunshine, and I had just attained my fifteenth birthday.

'That would be eight years ago,' said Aramis.

'Yes, I suppose so; but I have ceased to take any note of time.'

'Excuse the interruption, but what did your instructor tell you in order to encourage you in these exercises?'

'He said that a man not born to fortune must carve out a fortune for himself; and added that, being poor, obscure and an orphan, I had nothing to rely on but my own exertions. He told me that no one had taken, or ever would take, any interest in me.

'Well, then, I was asleep in the fencing-room, being tired after my lesson. My tutor was in his own room, which was just overhead, and I was awakened by hearing him give vent to an exclamation of annoyance, and, immediately afterwards I heard him call out "Perronnette! Perronnette!" – that was the name of my nurse.'

'Yes, yes, I know; go on, monseigneur.'

'It seemed that she was in the garden, and my tutor ran down the staircase as quickly as he could. I got up, curious to know what was the matter. He opened the door which led from the vestibule into the garden, all the time calling out, "Perronnette, Perronnette!" The windows of my room looked out upon the courtyard, but both they and the shutters were closed. However, I managed, through a crevice in the shutter, to see my tutor running towards a large well which was situated almost directly beneath the windows of his study. He bent over the brink, looked down the well and renewed his shouts and gestures of discomposure. From my point of observation, I could distinctly see and hear everything that was taking place.

'Pray go on, monseigneur,' said Aramis.

'Dame Perronnette came running along in answer to his cries. He took her by the arm and dragged her to the brink of the well, over which they both bent and looked down. "Look, look!" cried my tutor, "what a misfortune!"

' "Calm yourself, for heaven's sake," said Perronnette, "whatever is the matter?"

' "That letter," cried my tutor, "can't you see the letter?" and he pointed with his finger to the bottom of the well.

' "What letter?" asked the nurse.

' "The letter which you see down there; it is the last one received from the queen."

'Upon hearing this, I trembled. My tutor, who passed as my father, and was always preaching to me modesty and humility, was, then, in correspondence with the queen!'

' "The queen's last letter?" cried Dame Perronnette, who did not, however, seem to be very much astonished except at seeing the letter in so strange a place, "how did it get into the well?"

' "By an accident! Perronnette, a most remarkable accident! As I opened the door of my room, where the letter was lying on a table close to the window, a gust of wind rushed in. I saw the paper blown off the table and recognised it as being the queen's letter. I ran to the window and saw it hover in the air for an instant, and then disappear down the well."

' "Very well," said Perronnette, "since the letter is at the bottom of the well, it is just the same as if it were burnt, and the queen, you know, always burns her own letters every time she comes – " ' Here the young man interrupted his own narrative by repeating 'every time she comes'. 'So,' he said, addressing Aramis, 'this lady who came to see me every month was the queen?'

Aramis made an affirmative gesture and the prisoner went on with his story.

' "Yes, no doubt," said the old man, "but this letter was full of instructions, and how on earth are we to carry them out?"

' "Write at once to the queen, tell her exactly what has happened, and she will write you another letter in the place of this one."

' "I am afraid the queen would not believe our story," said the good man shaking his head; "she might think that we wanted to retain this letter, instead of returning it to her as we have all former ones, in order to provide ourselves with a weapon. She distrusts Monsieur Mazarin so thoroughly – and this fiendish Italian is quite capable of having us poisoned at the first breath of suspicion!" '

Aramis smiled almost imperceptibly.

' "You know, Perronnette, how terribly touchy they are upon every point where Philippe is concerned." Philippe was the name they gave me,' explained the prisoner.

' "Well," said Dame Perronnette, "it is of no use to waste time in talking; someone must go down the well, that's all."

' "Yes, and so give someone the opportunity of reading the letter whilst he is down there."

' "We will find someone in the village who cannot read; so you may make your mind easy."

' "Yes; but don't you see that whoever went down the well would know that he would not be asked to risk his life in recovering a paper that was not of the utmost importance? Nevertheless, you have given me an idea, Perronnette; someone will go down the well, and that someone will be myself."

' "But against this proposal Dame Perronnette protested most vehemently, crying and making such a fuss that at last the old gentleman promised to go in search of a ladder long enough to reach to the bottom of the well, whilst it was agreed that she should go to the neighbouring farm and endeavour to get a plucky boy who could be told that a jewel, wrapped in paper, had been accidentally dropped down the well, and, "as the action of the water," observed my tutor, "would naturally cause the wrapper to unfold, the boy will not be astonished at finding nothing but an open sheet of paper."

' "Perhaps, by this time, the writing has already been rendered illegible," ' suggested Perronnette.

' "That is of little consequence, provided we recover the letter. If we return it to the queen, she will know that we have not betrayed her; and if we don't excite suspicion on the part of Mazarin, we have nothing to fear from him."

'Having come to this arrangement they separated. I pushed back the shutter, and, seeing that my tutor was preparing to return to the house, I threw myself upon my cushions with a whirling brain, consequent upon what I had seen and overheard.

'My tutor looked in at the half-opened door, a few seconds later, but, seeing me apparently asleep, softly closed it and withdrew. Hardly had he shut the door before I raised myself up, and listening attentively, heard the sound of his retreating footsteps. Then I returned to my shutter and saw the tutor and Dame Perronnette go out, leaving me alone in the house. They had securely shut the gate when, without troubling myself to go down the vestibule, I jumped out of the window and ran to the well. Then, as my tutor had done, I bent over the brink and looked down.

'Something which looked white and luminous could be seen lying beneath the green water of the well. This brilliant appearance fascinated and attracted me; my eyes became fixed upon it and I panted for breath. The well seemed to draw me into it, with its gaping mouth and ice-cold breath. I fancied I could see characters of fire traced upon the paper which the queen had touched. Then, without knowing what I was doing, and stirred by one of those unaccountable impulses which drive people to leap down precipices, I wound an end of the rope round the foot of the windlass, and lowered the bucket to within three feet of the water, taking care not to injure the precious paper which was beginning to change its colour from white to green – a proof that it was sinking; then, using a piece of damp cloth as a protection for my hands, I slid down the rope into the well.

'When I found myself hanging over that dark pool of water, and saw the disc of sky above my head growing smaller and smaller, I felt chilled to the bone and a ghastly sickness took possession of me, but I summoned up sufficient strength of mind to overcome my fright. Having reached the surface of the water, I at once dropped into it, holding on to the rope with one hand and seizing with the other the precious paper which the resistance of the water tore in half as I lifted it. I stowed away the two halves in my jacket, and, with the aid of my feet, which I pressed against the sides of the well, I contrived to swarm up the rope and finally to reach the top, deluging the margin, as I scrambled over it, with the water that streamed from my clothes. Once safely out of the well, I ran into the sunshine with the idea of concealing myself in a little shrubbery at the bottom of the garden.

'As I reached my hiding-place, I heard the little alarm bell which rang when the gate was opened and knew that my tutor had returned. I was only just in time.

'I reckoned that it would take him at least ten minutes to reach me even if, guessing where I had taken refuge, he came direct to my hiding-place, and twenty minutes if he had to hunt for me. This gave me ample time for reading the letter, the two halves of which I made haste to fix in proper position. I observed that the writing was already becoming indistinct. I managed, however, to read the contents of the letter.'

'And what did you read, monseigneur?' asked Aramis, greatly interested.

'Enough to show me, monsieur, that my tutor was a gentleman of rank, and that Perronnette, although not a titled lady, was vastly the superior of an ordinary servant; in short that I, myself, must be a person of consideration, seeing that the queen, Anne of Austria, and the prime minister, Mazarin, showed so much anxiety on my behalf.'

Here the young man, who appeared to be much affected, ceased his narrative.

'And what happened afterwards?' asked Aramis.

'The workman whom my tutor had brought back with him could, of course, find nothing in the well, but my tutor noticed the water which dripped from its brink, and the sun had not dried my clothes sufficiently to prevent Perronnette from noticing that they were very damp; and, finally, I was seized with violent fever consequent upon my ducking, and the chill and excitement which I had undergone. I became light-headed, and, in my delirium, blurted out all that had taken place, whilst, guided by my ravings, the tutor found the queen's letter concealed in my jacket.'

'Ah!' said Aramis, 'I understand everything now.'

'I can but conjecture what happened subsequently; but I think there can be no doubt that the unfortunate lady and gentleman, fearing to keep silence as to what had taken place, wrote a full account of it to the queen, and sent back to her the torn letter.'

'After which,' said Aramis, 'you were arrested, and sent to the Bastille.'

'As you see.'

'And then, your two attendants disappeared.'

'Alas!'

'We will not speak any more of the dead,' said Aramis, 'but confine ourselves to the living, and see what is to be done with them. You have told me that you are resigned to your fate?'

'Yes, and I repeat it.'

'You do not sigh for liberty?'

'I have told you so.'

'And you are without either ambition, regret, or thought for the future?'

The young man did not answer.

'Why are you silent?' asked Aramis.

'I think I have talked enough,' replied the prisoner, 'and that it is now your turn to speak. I am tired.'

'I will proceed to obey you, monseigneur,' said Aramis, and the grave expression which he assumed made it apparent that he was now about to undertake the most important part of his mission.

'One question before I begin,' he said. 'In the house where you lived, there was not such a thing as a looking-glass, or mirror, was there?'

'I don't understand the meaning of the words; what do they mean?' asked the young man. 'I have never heard them before.'

'Well, a looking-glass or mirror is an article which reflects objects; standing in front of one, you can see your own features or figure as clearly as you can see mine at the present moment with your naked eye.'

'No, there was certainly nothing of the sort in the house,' replied the young man.

'And I observe,' said Aramis, looking about him, 'that there is nothing of the kind here. The same precautions are taken here, as were used at the house?'

'For what purpose?'

'That you shall learn presently. And now, pardon me, you have told me that you were taught mathematics, astronomy, fencing and riding, but you have not once mentioned history.'

'Sometimes my tutor would tell me of the achievements of the good king St Louis, of François I[79] and of Henri IV.'

'Is that all?'

'Yes, or nearly so.'

'Ah! just so; I see that it was all part of the same scheme. As you were deprived of mirrors, which reflect the present, so you are kept in ignorance of history, which reflects the past. During your imprisonment, books have been withheld from you, so that you are unaware of many facts with the aid of which you could reconstruct the demolished edifice of your recollections and aspirations.'

'That is true,' said the young man.

'Listen then, and I will tell you, in a few words, what has taken place in France during the last twenty-three or twenty-four years, that is to say, since the probable date of your birth, in short, since the moment when your existence became a matter of grave importance.'

'Pray, go on,' said the young man with increasing interest.

'Do you know who was the son of King Henri IV?'

'At least I know who succeeded him.'

'How do you know?'

'I learnt it from the date of a coin, 1610, which represented Henri IV, and from another, dated 1612, which represented King Louis, and I judged, since there was between them only the short interval of two years, that Louis XIII succeeded Henri IV.'

'Then you know,' said Aramis, 'that the last reigning monarch was Louis XIII?'

'Yes, I know that,' said the young man with a slight flush of colour.

'Well, he was a prince whose mind was full of noble thoughts, and who cherished grand projects, which, however, were always thwarted by the disturbances of the times and by the conflicts in which his minister, Richelieu, was continually engaged with the nobility of France.

'Personally (I am speaking of King Louis XIII), he was a man infirm of purpose, and his lamented death took place while he was still young.'

'I know that, also.'

'He had, for a long time, been very anxious upon the subject of an heir. This is always a source of anxiety to princes who desire to leave behind them something more than a recollection of themselves, and would like to feel that their ideas have a chance of being carried out and their work continued.'

'Did King Louis die childless?' asked the prisoner with a smile.

'No, but the happiness of having an heir was, for a long time, denied him, and he had almost made up his mind that he should die without leaving one. This idea preyed upon his mind and he sank into a despondent condition, until, one day, his wife, Anne of Austria – '

The prisoner gave a start.

'Were you aware that the wife of Louis XIII was called Anne of Austria?' asked Aramis.

'Please go on,' said the young man, without answering the question.

'When, suddenly,' continued Aramis, 'Anne of Austria announced that she was likely to become a mother. There was great rejoicing at this intelligence, and a happy result was devoutly prayed for. On the 5th September 1638, the queen presented the king with a son.'

Here Aramis looked at his companion and fancied that he saw him turn pale.

'You are about to hear,' said Aramis, 'a story which is known to a very few at the present time; for the secret is supposed to have died with those who are dead, or to be hidden under seal of the confessional.'

'Are you going to entrust me with this secret?' asked the young man.

'Oh!' said Aramis in a tone which it was impossible to mistake, 'I don't know that I ought to risk telling it to a prisoner who has no desire to get out of the Bastille.'

'I hear, monsieur.'

'The queen, then, gave birth to a son. But, whilst the court was celebrating the occasion with all sorts of rejoicings, whilst the king, having shown the new-born infant to the nobles who were present and to the people, was sitting at supper in the highest spirits and good humour, the queen, left alone in her bedroom, was again attacked with the pains of labour and gave birth to a second son.'

'Oh!' said the prisoner, drawing a more subtle inference than he wished to make apparent, 'I thought that Monsieur was only born – '[80]

Aramis held up his finger.

'Wait till I have finished,' he said.

The prisoner sighed with impatience, but waited silently.

'Yes,' said Aramis, 'the queen gave birth to a second son, and that son, Dame Perronnette received in her arms.'

'Perronnette!' exclaimed the young man.

'A message was immediately sent to the king as he sat at table, and he was told in a whisper what had happened. He at once left the table, but, this time, with no expression of pleasure on his face but rather one of terror. This birth of a twin son completely effaced the happiness to which the birth of the first child had given rise, seeing that (and now I am going to tell you something of which, I feel sure, you are in ignorance), it is the eldest son who is heir to the throne.'

'I know it.'

'And that both doctors and lawyers maintain that there is a doubt whether the child who happens to be the first-born of twins is in reality the elder by the laws of heaven and of nature.'

The prisoner uttered a choked exclamation, and became whiter than the counterpane which covered him.

'You will now understand that the king, who had welcomed with such joy the birth of an heir to his throne, was more than a little disconcerted upon learning that now there were two, inasmuch as there was a possibility that the last-born might, in due time, dispute the claim of the child who had come into the world two hours previously, and who had already been proclaimed and recognised as the king's legal successor. Thus the second son, backed by party interest or caprice, might sow the seeds of discord, or even occasion civil war, so destroying the dynasty which he should have supported.'

'Oh! I quite understand that,' murmured the young man.

'Very well,' said Aramis, 'then you will understand how it is that one of the sons of Anne of Austria has been so shamefully separated from his brother and kept in seclusion and obscurity, and has disappeared so entirely that no one in the whole of France, with the exception of his mother, knows that he exists.

'Yes, his mother, who has forsaken him,' groaned the prisoner in accents of despair.

'Except, also,' continued Aramis, 'the lady of the black dress, and flame-coloured ribbons, and except one other.'

'That is to say, yourself? You who have come to tell me all this, and to awaken within me curiosity, hatred, ambition and, possibly, a desire to take vengeance for my wrongs: except you, monsieur, who, if you be the man I am expecting, the man whom the letter prepared me to meet, the man, in fine, who is sent to me by heaven, should bring with you – '

'What?' asked Aramis.

'A portrait of Louis XIV, who at the present moment occupies the throne of France.'

'Here is the portrait,' replied the bishop handing to the prisoner a beautifully executed miniature representing, with life-like fidelity, the proud and handsome features of the king.

The prisoner eagerly seized the portrait which he seemed to devour with his eyes.

'And now, monseigneur,' said Aramis, 'here is a mirror.' He paused, in order to give the prisoner time to collect his ideas.

'So high, so high!' murmured the young man, and he looked attentively at the portrait, which he compared with the reflection of his own face in the mirror. 'The king, monsieur,' he said sadly, 'is he who is on the throne, who is not in prison, but who, on the contrary, causes others to be put there. Royalty means power, and there is no need to point out to you how powerless *I* am.'

'Monseigneur,' replied Aramis with even more profound respect than he had, hitherto, shown, 'the king, take good heed of what I say, the king, if it be your desire, will be he who, leaving his prison, shall finally establish himself upon the throne where his friends mean to place him.'

'Do not tempt me, monsieur,' said the prisoner bitterly.

'Do not, monseigneur, give way to weakness,' persisted Aramis warmly. 'I have brought full proofs of your birth, examine them carefully, satisfy yourself that you are, indeed, a king's son, and, then, let us act.'

'No, no! it is impossible.'

'Unless,' continued the bishop, with a touch of irony, 'it is the destiny of your race that all brothers who are excluded from the throne are to be princes devoid of courage and honour, like your uncle, Monsieur Gaston d'Orléans, who conspired, ten times, against his brother, King Louis XIII.'

'My uncle, Gaston d'Orléans, conspired against his brother? cried the prince, astonished, 'Did he conspire to dethrone him?'

'Certainly, monsieur, for nothing else.'

'What is this you tell me?'

'The truth.'

'And he found friends, devoted ones?'

'As devoted as I am to you, monseigneur.'

'And what was the result of it all? He failed?'

'He failed, it is true; but it was entirely through his own fault; and in order to purchase not his life – for the life of the king's brother is sacred – but his liberty, he did not scruple to sacrifice the lives of all his friends, one after another. Therefore is his name reviled in history, and execrated by a hundred of the noblest families in the kingdom.'

'I understand, monsieur,' said the prince, 'and was it through weakness, or by treachery, that my uncle caused his friends to lose their lives?'

'Through weakness, which, in the case of princes, is always treachery.'

'May not failure be sometimes attributable to ignorance or incapacity? Do you imagine it to be possible that a poor captive, like myself, brought up, not only far from the court, but even from the world, do you believe it possible, I say, for such a one to be of assistance to any friends who might try to serve him?'

And, as Aramis was about to answer, the young man suddenly broke out with an impetuosity which betrayed the blood of his race, 'We speak of *friends*! but, by what chance can I have friends, I who am unknown, and who have neither liberty, money, nor interest at my back?'

'Have I not had the honour to offer myself to your royal highness?'

'Oh! it must be either in mockery or cruelty that you speak to me thus, monsieur. Do not encourage me to dream of anything beyond the walls of the prison which confines me, if not contented, at least submissive, in my captivity and obscurity.'

'Monseigneur! Monseigneur! if you repeat those discouraging words; if, after having the proof of your birth, you persist in showing this want of spirit and strength of mind, I will accept dismissal; I will go away and renounce for ever the service of a master to whom I came, eager to place my life and ability at his disposal.'

'Nay! but before saying all this, would it not have been better, had you reflected that you have, once and for all time, broken my heart?'

'That was what I desired to do, monseigneur.'

'Let me ask you, monsieur, whether a prison is a proper place in which to speak to me of grandeur, of power, and even of royalty itself? Can I believe in splendour whilst we remain here in the obscurity of night? You boast about glory, and here we sit, our words stifled beneath the wretched curtains of a prison mattress! You endeavour to make me understand what it is to have absolute power, and all the time, I can hear, in the corridor, the footsteps of my gaoler, a sound which is more terrifying to you than it is to me. If you wish to inspire me with a little more belief in what you say, take me out of the Bastille, let me get some fresh air into my lungs, put spurs on my heels and a sword into my hand, and then we may be able to come to an understanding.'

'I will give you all that, and more besides, if you will only say the word, monseigneur.'

'Listen, then, monsieur,' broke in the prince. 'I know that guards are stationed in every gallery, that there are bolts to every door, and that there are soldiers and cannons at every barrier. Can you overpower the guards and spike the guns? Can you withdraw the bolts and break through the barriers?'

'Monseigneur, by what means did you receive the note which you read and which apprised you of my visit?'

'It might not be difficult to bribe a gaoler where a note only is concerned.'

'Monseigneur, it is as easy to bribe ten gaolers, as it is to bribe one.'

'Well, I can conceive it possible to get a wretched captive outside the Bastille, and, perhaps, hide him so that he could not be recaptured by the king's agents, and even to keep the poor wretch alive in some secret retreat.'

'Monsieur!' remonstrated Aramis with a smile.

'I admit that I should consider him who could accomplish even this to be a man more than mortal; but you tell me that I am a prince, a king's brother! How do you propose to restore me to the rank and the position of which my brother and my mother have deprived me? Again, it seems that my life would be spent amidst hatred and scenes of conflict. How can you ensure me victory, and render me invulnerable to my enemies? Ah! Monsieur, think of it all! Hide me, tomorrow in some dark cavern at the foot of a mountain; let me taste the delights of freedom and of hearing the sounds of river and plain; let me see the blue sky, and the lowering clouds, and I will ask for nothing more. Do not, indeed, promise me more, for more it cannot be in your power to give, and it would be cruel to deceive me, since you say you are my friend.'

Aramis listened in silence.

'Monseigneur, I admire the sound common sense and the strength of reasoning of which your words show you to be possessed. I am fortunate in ascertaining my sovereign's attitude of mind.'

'Once again! Oh! for pity's sake,' cried the prince, pressing his throbbing temples with his cold hands, 'do not amuse yourself at my expense! It is not necessary that I should be a king in order to become the happiest of mankind.'

'But I, monseigneur, want you to become a king for the benefit of humanity.'

'Ah!' said the prince, whom the last word had inspired with renewed distrust, 'what has humanity to reproach my brother with?'

'I forgot to say, monseigneur, that, if you will deign to be guided by me, and if you will consent to become the most powerful prince on earth, you will forward the interests of all who are devoted to the success of our cause, and these friends are numerous.'

'Numerous?'

'And more powerful even than numerous, monseigneur.'

'Will you explain yourself?'

'It is impossible for me to do so now, but I swear before heaven that I will explain everything on the day that sees you seated on the throne of France.'

'And my brother?'

'You shall pronounce his fate. Have you any feeling of pity towards him?'

'Towards him, who would leave me to perish in a dungeon? No, I have no pity for him.'

'I am glad to hear it.'

'He might have come to me in this prison, have taken me by the hand, and said to me, "My brother, God created us to love one another, and not to be at enmity. I come to you. Barbarous prejudice has sentenced you to die in obscurity, far from the world and all its delights. I wish you to take your seat by my side. I wish you to wear our father's sword. Will you take advantage of this reconciliation to my detriment, or use my father's sword against me?" – "Oh! no," I would have replied, "I look upon you as my deliverer, and will always recognise you as my master. You give me more than it has pleased heaven to grant me, for you bestow upon me my liberty and give me the privilege of loving and being loved in this world."'

'And you would have kept your word, monseigneur?'

'Oh! on my life'

'Whilst now?'

'Whilst now I feel that I have to punish the guilty – '

'In what manner, monseigneur?'

'What do you say to this remarkable resemblance which I bear to my brother?'

'I say that, in that resemblance, there is an indication of the designs of providence which the king has no right to disregard. I say that your mother has been guilty of a crime in making a wicked distinction between those whom nature has made so much alike, and I am of the opinion that punishment should be inflicted for the purpose of restoring equilibrium.'

'Which means?'

'That, if you take your place upon your brother's throne, your brother should take his place in your prison.'

'Alas! a man must suffer much hardship in prison, especially when he has drunk so deeply of the cup of pleasure.'

'Your royal highness will, of course, be at liberty to act as may seem good to you; for instance, to pardon after having punished.'

'Good; and, now, shall I tell you something, monsieur?'

'Speak, my prince.'

'It is that I will not listen to another word from you until I am out of the Bastille.'

'I was going to observe to your royal highness that I shall only have the honour to seeing you upon one more occasion.'

'When will that be?'

'The day when my prince goes forth from these dark walls.'

'How will you give me notice of it?'

'By coming to fetch you.'

'By coming *yourself*?'

'My prince does not leave this chamber except with me. If you are compelled to leave it in my absence, remember that it will not be with my knowledge or approval.'

'Therefore, I am not to breathe a word on this subject to anyone but yourself?'

'To no one but myself.'

Aramis bowed low, and the prince extended his hand. 'Monsieur,' he said, in a tone that came from his heart, 'if you have come here with the view of effecting my destruction, if you are only an instrument in the hands of my enemies, if our interview, in which you have sounded the depths of my heart, results in something more disastrous to me than captivity, that is to say, death, accept my thanks, for you will be the means of putting an end to my sufferings, and peace will succeed the agonising torments of which, for the last eight years, I have been the victim.'

'Wait, monseigneur, before condemning me,' said Aramis.

'I have said that I will both thank and forgive you. If, on the contrary, you have come to restore me to the rank and position in the world which is mine in the sight of heaven; if, through your instrumentality, I am destined to live in the memory of man, and to be an honour to my race by means of noble actions or by benefits bestowed upon my people, if, by the help of your sustaining hand, I rise from the depths of despair, to the height of honour and fortune, for you, whom I bless and thank, shall be the half of my power and glory! Even this will be inadequate to prove my gratitude. My debt to you will never be repaid, since I cannot share with you all the happiness you will have procured for me.'

'Monseigneur,' said Aramis, moved by this speech,' the nobleness of your sentiments fills me with pride and admiration. It is not for you to thank me. Any thanks that I may deserve should come from the people, whom you will make happy, and from your descendants, whom you will render illustrious. Yes, I shall have given you more than life, I shall have made you immortal.'

The prince again gave his hand to Aramis, who kissed it respectfully.

'Oh!' exclaimed the prince with a becoming embarrassment.

'It is the first act of homage rendered to our future king,' said Aramis. 'When we meet again, I shall say, "Good-day, sire." '

'Till then,' said the prince placing his thin white hand upon his heart, 'till then, no more dreams, no more shocks to my system, a repetition of this scene would be my death. Oh! Monsieur, how small is my prison, how low the window, how narrow the doors! Is it possible that so much pride, splendour and happiness can enter through them to abide with me?'

'Your royal highness,' said Aramis, 'makes me proud indeed, since it is to me that you attribute the possibility of the event,' and he immediately tapped at the door. It was at once opened by the gaoler, with whom was Baisemeaux, who had been tempted, in spite of himself, to listen at the door, so greatly had he been wrought upon by his feelings of curiosity and uneasiness, and it was fortunate that neither the prince nor Aramis had once raised their voices during the interview.

'A remarkable confession!' said the governor with a poor attempt at jocularity, 'who would have thought that a man who has passed all his life in seclusion, and who is in a dying condition, could have found time and opportunity to commit such a number of sins as to take all this time in confessing?'

Aramis did not reply. He was anxious to get out of the Bastille, where the weight of his secret seemed to double the thickness of the walls.

When they reached the governor's residence, Aramis said, 'Now let us speak of business, Monsieur de Baisemeaux; you have to ask me for a receipt for one hundred and fifty thousand livres.'[81]

'And to hand over the first third of that amount,' added the unfortunate governor, with a sigh, as he moved slowly towards his iron safe.

'Here is the receipt,' said Aramis.

'And here is the money,' said Baisemeaux with a sigh still deeper than the last.

'My instructions are simply to give you a receipt for fifty thousand livres; nothing was said about taking the money. Adieu, sir governor.'

And he took his departure, leaving Baisemeaux almost choking with mingled surprise and delight at this munificent present from the Confessor Extraordinary to the Bastille.

## CHAPTER 30

*How Mouston presumed to wax fat without his master's permission, and what inconveniences the latter suffered in consequence of this inconsiderate behaviour*

AFTER THE DEPARTURE of Athos for Blois, Porthos and d'Artagnan rarely met, d'Artagnan's time being fully occupied with the king's affairs, and Porthos being extremely busy in buying all sorts of furniture, by the help of which he hoped to make his several residences conspicuous for that air of refinement and luxury which he had observed to prevail in the court surroundings.

One morning, however, d'Artagnan, having a few hours at his disposal, bethought him of Porthos, of whom he had heard nothing for upwards of a fortnight, and, strolling round to his residence, caught him in the act of getting out of bed.

The worthy baron wore a troubled, not to say a melancholy look. He was sitting upon the edge of his bed, and with dangling legs, was contemplating, in evident perplexity, a number of miscellaneous garments with which the floor of his bedroom was strewn.

Sad and preoccupied as La Fontaine's hare,[82] he did not notice d'Artagnan's entrance, screened, as it was for the moment, by the ample proportions of Monsieur Mouston, which, generous enough at any time to shelter a man from observation, seemed, on the present occasion, exaggerated by the skirts of a scarlet coat which he was holding up by the sleeves for his master's inspection. D'Artagnan stopped upon the threshold to contemplate, for a moment, the perplexed Porthos; and, seeing that the numerous garments which strewed the floor were the evident cause of his friend's disturbance, he thought it time he came to his assistance, and accordingly, announced his presence by a cough.

'Ah!' cried Porthos, his face lighting up with pleasure, 'here is d'Artagnan; now, at last, I shall get an idea.'

At these words, Mouston, becoming aware that he stood in d'Artagnan's light, stepped to one side, welcoming, as he did so, his master's friend with an affable smile. Porthos jumped up with an energy which made his huge knees crack, and, in two strides, was across the room, and taking d'Artagnan to his heart, with an affection which his prolonged absence seemed to have enhanced.

'You are always welcome, my dear fellow,' he cried, 'but today, you are, if possible, more welcome than ever.'

'Is anything the matter?' asked d'Artagnan. 'I fancy you seem low spirited.'

Porthos answered by a look expressive of sadness.

'Well, tell me all about it, old fellow, unless it is a secret.'

'My dear friend, you know very well that, from you, I have no secrets. This is what troubles me.'

'Wait a bit, Porthos, until I disentangle myself from all this velvet and satin litter.'

'Oh! never mind them; walk over the damned things; they're only cast off rubbish.'

'Rubbish, Porthos? What! cloth at twenty livres the ell, magnificent satin, and regal velvet!'

'You think, then, that they are – '

'Splendid, Porthos, splendid! I'll wager that no one else in the whole of France has such a supply, and if you never buy any more clothes, and live for a hundred years, which would not astonish me at all, you could put on a new coat on the day of your death, without ever troubling a tailor from this day to that.'

Porthos shook his head.

'My dear Porthos, this unnatural melancholy quite alarms me. Cheer up! and get out of the dumps as quickly as you can.'

'Yes, old fellow, I will do so, if it is possible.'

'Have you received any disquieting news from Bracieux?'

'No, they have cut down the trees, with the result of a third more timber than was estimated.'

'Has the water at Pierrefonds been unproductive?'

'No, they have fished the ponds, and still left fish enough to stock all the water in the neighbourhood.'

'Has Le Vallon, itself, been destroyed by earthquake?'

'No, my friend; on the contrary, a thunderbolt struck the ground a hundred yards from the château, and has disclosed a spring at the very spot where water was much needed.'

'Well then, whatever *is* it?'

'Well, the fact is that I have just received an invitation for the fête at Vaux,' answered Porthos with an expression of face which suggested some dire calamity.

'And you grumble at that? Really, Porthos, you are too absurd! Why, the king has caused heartburnings innumerable at court by declining to give invitations! And so you are really going to Vaux? Only think of it!'

'Yes, indeed I am.'

'You will witness a magnificent spectacle.'

'Alas! I have my doubts about it.'

'All the splendour of France will be on view there.'

'Ah!' groaned Porthos, and clutched wildly at his hair.

'Good heavens! man; what ails you? are you ill?'

'I am as strong as a bullock. It isn't that.'

'What *is* it then?'

'Well, the fact is I have no clothes.'

D'Artagnan was dumfounded.

'No clothes, Porthos, no clothes! when I see at least fifty suits on the floor!'

'Fifty, yes, and not one that fits me.'

'What! not one that fits you? Are you not measured for your clothes, then?'

'Yes,' it was Mouston who spoke, 'but unfortunately I have put on a good deal of flesh lately.'

'What! you have been growing stouter?'

'Until,' said Mouston – 'would you believe it monsieur? – I have grown stouter, absolutely stouter than the baron himself.'

'*Parbleu!* I think it is tolerably obvious.'

'Do you hear that, idiot!' cried Porthos, 'it is obvious.'

'But, all the same,' said d'Artagnan, 'I don't see why your clothes should not fit you, because Mouston has grown fatter.'

'I will explain, my dear fellow,' said Porthos. 'You may remember telling me the story of the Roman general, Antony, who always had seven boars on the spit at the same time, each cooked up to a different point, so that one of them might always be ready at whatever hour he chose to dine. Very well, then, seeing that, at any moment, I am liable to be sent for to court, and have to remain there a week, I resolved always to have seven suits ready for the occasion.'

'Very forcibly reasoned Porthos. But, in order to gratify a whim like that, a man must have an income as large as your own; and, without reckoning the time taken up in being measured so often, remember how fashions vary.'

'Quite so,' said Porthos, 'and here I flatter myself is just where my ingenuity comes in.'

'I should like to hear that – not that I doubt your genius.'

'You remember that Mouston was quite slim once upon a time?'

'Certainly; that was when he was called Mousqueton.'

'And you remember the period when he began to grow fat?'

'Well no, not precisely – forgive me, my dear Mouston.'

'Oh! not at all, monsieur,' said Mouston politely. 'Monsieur was in Paris at the time, and we were at Pierrefonds.'

'Well, my dear Porthos, there came a time when Mouston began to grow stouter; that is what you were saying I think?'

'Yes, my friend, and it is gratifying to me to remember that time.'

'I can easily believe it,' said d'Artagnan.

'Because, you see, it saved me an immense amount of trouble.'

'Well, no, I don't quite follow you there; but, no doubt, when you explain – '

'Well, look here, my friend. First of all, as you say, being measured runs away with a great deal of time, even when one goes through the operation only once a fortnight. Then, one may be travelling, and when one wants to keep seven suits always in hand – in short, my dear fellow, I positively loathe going to a tailor to be measured. What, the devil! one is a gentleman, or one is not, I suppose? It is humiliating, degrading, damn it, it is disgusting and repugnant to the feelings of a gentleman! Fancy allowing a mouldy rascal to maul one about, and measure one inch by inch, and find you too hollow here and too prominent there! – faugh! it's not to be thought of. When you escape from the hands of one of these scurvy knaves, you resemble a fortification whose strong and weak points have been scrutinised by a spy.'

'In truth, dear Porthos, you have some original ideas.'

'Oh! but when you are an engineer you know – '

'And have fortified Belle-Isle – just so, old fellow.'

'I had an idea, undoubtedly, which might have proved valuable, had it not been for this idiot Mouston.'

Mouston glanced at d'Artagnan as if he would say, 'Now I'm going to catch it; but, I ask you, was I to blame?'

'I congratulated myself, then, upon his increasing rotundity, I even helped, as far as I could, to fatten the beast, by feeding him upon all sorts of nourishing things, in the hope that he would soon equal me in circumference, so that I could send him to be measured in my place.'

'Oh! wonderful,' cried d'Artagnan, 'I understand now. Of course, you would be spared no end of degradation, and would save much time.'

'You may judge, then, of my satisfaction when, at the end of a year and a half, after a course of training, during which I gave him the most carefully selected and fattening kinds of food – I took the trouble to feed the villain myself – '

'I am sure, monsieur, I did all in my power to assist you,' said Mouston modestly.

'I admit it,' said Porthos. 'Well, judge of my delight when one morning I noticed that it was only with great difficulty, as great as I experienced myself, that Mouston was able to squeeze through the little secret door that those infernal architects had made in the chamber formerly occupied by the late Madame Du Vallon at Pierrefonds. And, whilst on the subject, let me ask you, my dear d'Artagnan, who are supposed to know everything, why the rascally architects, who ought, by reason of their calling, to be able to judge measurements with the naked eye, why, I say, do they persist in planning doorways through which none but thin people can pass?'

'Oh! those doors,' responded d'Artagnan, 'were intended for the use of gallants, who have, usually, slim figures.'

'Madame Du Vallon had no gallants,' said Porthos loftily.

'Quite so,' said d'Artagnan, 'but, no doubt, the architects contemplated the possibility of your marrying again.'

'Ah! yes, that is possible. And,' continued Porthos, 'now that I am satisfied on this point, let us return to the subject of the fattening of Mouston. But observe how the two subjects bear one upon the other. I have often noticed that ideas run side by side. Now remark this phenomenon, d'Artagnan; speaking of Mouston, who is fat, we come, in the most natural manner, to Madame Du Vallon – '

'Who was thin.'

'Hum! curious, isn't it?'

'My dear fellow, a learned friend of mine, Monsieur Costar,[83] has made precisely the same observation, only he made use of a Greek word which I cannot recollect.'

'Then my observation is not original?' cried Porthos in astonishment. 'I thought I had invented it.'

'My friend, the idea dates from before the time of Aristotle, that is to say nearly two thousand years ago.'

'It is none the less true for all that,' said Porthos highly gratified to find himself in agreement with the sages of antiquity.

'Marvellously! but suppose we return to Mouston. I seem to see him fattening under my very eyes.'

Mouston bowed gracefully.

'Well, Mouston fattened so beautifully that he fulfilled my fondest hopes, and grew, eventually, to my own girth. I had ample proof of this, for I caught the rascal wearing one of my waistcoats, which he had converted into a coat – a waistcoat the embroidery upon which cost a hundred pistoles.'

'I was only trying it on, monsieur,' said Mouston.

'From that moment, I determined to put Mouston in communication with my tailors, and send him to be measured instead of me.'

'An excellent idea,' said d'Artagnan, 'only Mouston is a foot and a half shorter than you are.'

'Just so. Accordingly they measure him down to the ground, which brings the bottom of the coat a few inches below my knee.'

'What a fellow you are, to be sure, Porthos. Such an idea could occur to no one but yourself.'

'Yes, I think I deserve to be complimented upon it. Well, it was just at this time, that is to say about two years and a half since, that I set out for Belle-Isle, leaving instructions to Mouston to be measured for a new coat every month, taking care that each garment was cut and decorated in the newest fashion.'

'And did Mouston fail to carry out your instructions? Oh! come; that was too careless of you, Mouston.'

'On the contrary, monsieur, on the contrary!'

'Oh! no, he did not fail to have the clothes made; but he forgot to tell me that he was increasing in bulk every day.'

'But I did not know it, monsieur. The tailor never told me that I was growing stouter.'

'And so, the booby,' continued Porthos, 'in two years, has increased eighteen inches in circumference, and my twelve last coats are all, from a foot to a foot and a half, too large for me.'

'But others; those which were ordered when you were both of the same size.'

'They are no longer in fashion, my dear fellow, and, if I were to put one of them on, people would think that I had just come from Siam, or some other outlandish place, and that I hadn't been at court for two years.'

'I understand your dilemma. How many new coats have you? thirty-six? and you can't wear one of them? Well, you must have a thirty-seventh, and the other thirty-six will do for Mouston.'

'Ah! thank you, thank you!' said Mouston, highly gratified; 'but, indeed, monsieur is always too generous to me.'

'Do you suppose that that idea has not already occurred to me, or do you think that I am deterred from adopting it by any consideration of expense? Just consider; the fête takes place in two days' time. I received my invitation yesterday and at once summoned Mouston to bring me my wardrobe, post haste. Thus, only this morning, do I realise the damnable predicament I am placed in. No decent tailor would undertake to supply me with a suitable coat in the time.'

'That is to say, a coat covered all over with gold, I suppose?'

'I should think so, indeed – all over!'

'All right, we will arrange it. You have not to start for three days from now. The invitations are for Wednesday and today is Sunday.'

'That is so; but Aramis has recommended me to be there at least twenty-four hours before the time named.'

'Aramis? What has he to do with it?'

'Oh! it was Aramis who brought me the invitation.'

'In that case, it would be through Monsieur Fouquet that you received it.'

'Not at all! The invitation comes from the king himself. Look, here is the letter; read the wording of it, "Monsieur le Baron Du Vallon is informed that the king has condescended to place his name on the list of invitations." There it is; a blind man could read it!'

'Yes, but you go there with Monsieur Fouquet.'

'And when I think,' roared Porthos, with a violent stamp of the foot, 'when I realise the awful fact that I have no clothes to go in, it makes me furious! – damme, I should like to choke somebody or smash something!'

'Do neither one nor the other, dear Porthos, but leave it for me to arrange. Just come with me to a tailor, and bring one of your thirty-six suits with you.'

'It will be of no use, my dear fellow; I have already tried every tailor in Paris.'

'Including Monsieur Percerin?'

'Who is Monsieur Percerin?'

'The king's own tailor, that's all.'

'Ah! yes, yes, of course I know that,' said Porthos, who did not wish to appear ignorant, but who, as a matter of fact, now heard the name of the king's tailor for the first time. 'Monsieur Percerin, the king's tailor; but I thought he would be too busy to attend to me.'

'He probably would be; but don't be alarmed, Porthos; I can make him do what no one else in the world can. Only, on this occasion, you must consent to be measured.'

'That,' said Porthos with a sigh, 'will be a nuisance, but "needs must when the devil drives".'

'Well, you are only asked to do what others do; what even the king himself does.'

'You don't mean to say that they have the damned impudence to want to measure the king? and that he submits to it?'

'The king, my dear fellow, has the most artistic ideas where dress is concerned; and so have you, whatever you may say to the contrary.'

'Come on, then,' said Porthos, 'let us be off at once. As the king allows himself to be measured, I think I may safely do so too.'

## CHAPTER 31

## *Introducing Messire Jean Percerin*

MESSIRE JEAN PERCERIN, the king's tailor, occupied a tolerably large house in the Rue Saint-Honoré, near the Rue de l'Arbre-Sec. He was a man possessed of a fine taste in elegant stuffs, velvets and embroidery, and had succeeded his father as tailor to the king. This hereditary succession dated back to the time of Charles IX,[84] when it was the custom to wear dress of the most extravagant and fantastic order.

The Percerin of that time was a Huguenot like Ambroise Paré,[85] whose life had been spared at the intercession of the Queen of Navarre, 'la belle Margot'[86] (as it was the fashion of the time to write and speak of her), and the clemency shown him was due to the circumstance that none but he could make those marvellously fitting riding-habits which it delighted the queen to wear, disguising, as they did, certain physical malformations which she spared no pains to conceal.

Percerin, out of gratitude, invented some wonderful black jackets, for which he took care not to overcharge Queen Catherine,[87] who ended by receiving into her favour this Huguenot, whom, up to that time, she had regarded in anything but a tolerant spirit. But Percerin was a shrewd and far-seeing man, who had heard it said that the smiles of Queen Catherine boded no good to a Huguenot, and, as he remarked that she smiled on him more frequently than she had been accustomed to do, he took the bull by the horns, and, together with his whole family, embraced the Catholic faith. He thus, at the same time, rendered himself unassailable on the point of religion, and secured the proud position of chief tailor to the crown of France, an eminence which, under the rule of the showy Henry III, might be compared to the highest peaks of the Cordilleras. Percerin had always been a clever man, and, as he wished his professional reputation to survive him, he skilfully contrived to leave the world as soon as his powers of invention began to fail him.

He left a son and a daughter, both of whom were worthy to take his place and maintain his reputation, the son being an incomparable cutter and the daughter equally skilful in the art of embroidery and of ornamentation.

The marriage of Henry IV and Marie de Medici,[88] the high approval accorded to his designs for the court mourning on the death of the late king, and, last but not least, a few words of praise which fell from the lips of Monsieur de Bassompierre,[89] the leader of fashion of the period, made the fortune of this second-generation Percerin.

The Signor Concino Concini and his wife Galigaï,[90] who subsequently made their mark at the French court, tried hard to bring into vogue the Italian fashion in dress, and, indeed, introduced some Florentine tailors, but Percerin, thus put upon his mettle, promptly knocked these interlopers out of time with some wonderful inspirations in brocades and embroidery, and Concini himself was one of the first to forsake his deluded fellow-countrymen, and transfer his patronage to the Frenchman. He ever afterwards refused to employ any other tailor, and it was remarked that on the day when Vitry blew out his brains on the Pont du Louvre, he was wearing a doublet of Percerin's production.

It was this very doublet from the workshop of Monsieur Percerin that the Parisians subsequently chopped into mincemeat, together with the human body which it clothed.

Notwithstanding the favour which Concino Concini had shown Percerin, King Louis XIII showed no ill-will towards him, and generously retained him in his service. At the time when Louis the Just set this great example of equity, Percerin had brought up two sons, one of whom set his foot upon the first rung of the ladder of fame by inventing for Cardinal Richelieu[91] the wonderful Spanish costume in which he danced a saraband at the marriage of Anne of Austria; he also made the dresses for the tragedy of *Mirame*,[92] and stitched upon the mantle of Buckingham those famous pearls which were fated afterwards to be scattered upon the pavements of the Louvre.

Celebrity is soon gained for one who is responsible for the dresses of such personages as Monsieur de Cinq-Mars, the Duke of Buckingham, Mademoiselle Ninon, Monsieur de Beaufort[93] and Marion de Lorme.[94] In short Percerin III had already reached the top of the ladder when his father died.

This same Percerin III, old, celebrated and rich, as he was, still continued to make clothes for the reigning monarch Louis XIV, and having been blessed with no son, to his great sorrow, because he was

now the last of the Percerins, having, we say, no son of his own, had
taken great pains in the training of several very promising pupils. He
kept his carriage, owned an estate, had the tallest menservants in
Paris and, by special permission of Louis XIV, was a master of
hounds. He worked for Messieurs de Lyonne and Letellier,[95] but
almost, as it were, with an air of patronage, but, being a keen
politician and well posted up in state secrets, he could never succeed
in making a garment of any kind to fit Monsieur Colbert. Great
minds are inspired by perceptions which are instinctive, and act
instinctively without knowing why. The great Percerin was inspired
when he cut a skirt for the queen, or a coat for the king; he would
conceive a mantle for Monsieur, or the clock of a stocking for
Madame, but, in spite of his supreme genius, he could never make
anything to fit Monsieur Colbert. 'That man,' he would often say, 'is
altogether beyond me; it is quite impossible for me to contrive
anything to suit him.' On the other hand, it is hardly necessary to say
that Percerin had no difficulty in dressing Monsieur Fouquet, and
the minister held him in high esteem. At this time, Monsieur
Percerin was nearly eighty years of age, but tolerably vigorous
nevertheless, and he looked so dry and sapless that the courtiers used
to say that he would someday snap in two like a dried stick. So great
were his fame and fortune that Monsieur did not hesitate to take his
arm when discussing questions of dress with him; and those at court
who, as a rule, were never too anxious to settle their bills, were afraid
to let their accounts with him get into arrears because, although
Percerin would execute a first order upon credit, he would not
undertake a second one until the first account was paid.

One can easily understand that a tailor of Percerin's importance
not only did not run after customers, but made it quite a favour to
receive an order from a new one. He positively refused to work for
the untitled citizen, and looked askance even at men who had but
recently been ennobled; a rumour was in circulation that Cardinal
Mazarin, in return for a magnificent set of cardinal's robes with
which he had been presented by Percerin, had slipped into his pocket
letters of nobility.

It was, then, to the house of this paragon of tailors that d'Artagnan
conducted the disconsolate Porthos. On the way thither, the latter
remarked to his friend, 'Be careful, my dear d'Artagnan, pray, be
careful not to compromise my dignity in the eyes of this arrogant
tailor who will I have no doubt be disposed to be impertinent; for I
give you warning that, if he treats me with the slightest disrespect, I
shall give him a thrashing.'

'Introduced by me, my friend,' replied d'Artagnan, 'you have nothing to fear, even were you – what you are not.'

'Ah! the fact is – '

'What now? Have you any grudge against Percerin, Porthos?'

'I think I once sent Mouston to a fellow of that name.'

'Well, what followed?'

'The scoundrel actually refused to accept my order.'

'Oh! some misunderstanding, no doubt, which must be set right at once; perhaps Mouston was mistaken.'

'Possibly.'

'He must have confused one name with another.'

'Very likely, he is such a fool that he can never remember a name properly.'

'I take all responsibility upon myself.'

'Very well.'

'Now stop the carriage, Porthos; here we are.'

'Here?'

'Yes.'

'How can that be? We are at the Halles, and you told me that the tailor lived at the corner of the Rue de l'Arbre-Sec.'

'Quite true; but just look.'

'Well, I am looking as hard as I can, and I see that we have arrived at the Halles. What the devil else is there to see?'

'I suppose you don't want our horses to climb upon the roof of the coach in front of us?'

'No.'

'Nor that coach to get on the top of the one in front of it?'

'Of course not.'

'Nor that the second coach should drive over the roofs of the thirty or forty others which have arrived here before us?'

'Ah! I see you are right; but what a devil of a lot of people! What are they all up to?'

'They are simply waiting for their turn.'

'Have the comedians of the Hôtel de Bourgogne[96] shifted their quarters?'

'No. These people are waiting for their turn to see Monsieur Percerin.'

'Then I suppose we must do the same.'

'No, we will be more enterprising and less ceremonious than they are.'

'What shall we do, then?'

'We will get out of the carriage, and make our way through the crowd of pages and footmen, then we will enter the tailor's house. I will answer for it that we get in, especially if you go first.'

'Come on, then,' said Porthos, and, accordingly the two friends, having got out of the carriage, made the best of their way in the direction of the tailor's house.

There was considerable crowding and confusion, evidently due to the circumstance that Monsieur Percerin's door was shut, whilst a servant, standing in front of it, explained to the illustrious customers of the illustrious tailor that, for the present, Monsieur Percerin could receive no one.

A rumour was spread abroad that this servant had whispered confidentially to the footman of one of his master's customers that Monsieur Percerin was shut up in his private room, and would be accessible to no one, until he had thought out the details of the cut and ornamentation of five suits of clothes which he had been commanded to make for the king. Some, who were satisfied with this explanation, turned away to pass it on to those in the rear, whilst others, more pertinacious, insisted that the door should be opened to them; amongst the latter being those *cordons bleus*[97] who were to take part in a ballet which they declared would be completely spoiled unless their costumes were made under the personal supervision of the great Percerin himself.

D'Artagnan pushing Porthos in front of him who, with his immense weight, easily bored through the crowd, reached one of the counters behind which Percerin's workmen were doing their best to reply to the questions with which they were assailed.

It should have been stated that an endeavour was made, at the door, to repulse Porthos as well as the rest, but that, upon d'Artagnan stepping forward and speaking the words, 'On the king's business,' the two friends were admitted without further question.

These poor devils of workmen had a difficult task to answer all the questions of the clamorous customers, but they did their best to grapple with the difficulty, often stopping in the middle of a stitch to turn a phrase, and occasionally escaping the abuse of an enraged client by diving beneath the counter and disappearing from view altogether. The long array of dissatisfied and indignant noblemen made a very interesting picture.

Our captain of musketeers, sure and quick of observation, took it all in at a glance; and soon, running his eye over the crowd, it was arrested by the sight of a man opposite to him. This individual was seated on a stool and his head only appeared above the counter, which hid the rest of his person.

He was a man of about forty years of age with a melancholy expression on his pale countenance, and with soft and lustrous eyes.

Supporting his chin upon his hand, he regarded d'Artagnan and the rest with calm curiosity, but upon perceiving, and, no doubt, recognising our captain, he pulled his hat over his eyes.

It may have been this movement which drew d'Artagnan's attention to him, in which case, the effect of pulling down his hat was very different from what he intended it to be. For the rest, he was quite plainly attired, and his hair was so simply cut and arranged that, at first sight, a casual observer would have taken him for one of Percerin's workmen, squatting behind a counter and stitching away for dear life. But on closer inspection it would have been seen that he raised his head to look about him too often to admit of his paying proper attention to the work in hand.

D'Artagnan was not deceived, however, and saw, in a moment, that, if this man was working, he was not, at any rate, stitching clothes.

'Halloa!' he said, addressing the man, 'so you have turned tailor's apprentice, Monsieur Molière?'[98]

'Hush, Monsieur d'Artagnan, be quiet for heaven's sake, or you will cause me to be recognised.'

'Well, what harm would there be in that?'

'No harm at all, but – '

'Neither would there be any good. Is that what you mean?'

'Alas! no, for I was engaged in observing some very interesting faces.'

'Go on, go on, Monsieur Molière, I understand the interest you take in such an occupation. I will not interrupt you any further.'

'Many thanks.'

'But only upon one condition, which is that you tell me where Monsieur Percerin really is.'

'I will tell you that with pleasure, he is in his own room, but – '

'But one may not go in?'

'He is not to be approached.'

'By no one?'

'By no one. He brought me here so that I might make my observations at my ease; and then he went away.'

'And you, dear Monsieur Molière, will go and tell him that I am here, will you not?'

'I?' cried Molière with the snarl of a dog from whom one tries to take a hard-earned bone, 'why should I be disturbed? It is not fair, Monsieur d'Artagnan, to expect this of me.'

'If you don't go, at once, and tell Monsieur Percerin that I am here,' said d'Artagnan very deliberately, 'I warn you, my dear Monsieur Molière, that I will refuse to introduce my friend to you.'

'Do you allude to that gentleman?' asked Molière with a glance at Porthos.

'Yes.'

Molière, hereupon, took a good look at Porthos, and satisfied, apparently, that he would be worth making a study of, he at once rose and went into the adjoining room.

## CHAPTER 32

### *The patterns*

DURING THIS TIME the crowd slowly melted away, each item of it, upon departing, being careful to hurl at the heads of the unfortunate workmen some expression indicating wrath and dissatisfaction. After an interval of about ten minutes Molière reappeared, making a sign to d'Artagnan to follow him. The latter at once sprang to his feet and, dragging Porthos after him, threaded a labyrinth of passages, finally running Monsieur Percerin to earth in his private sanctum. The old man, with upturned sleeves, was busily occupied with a piece of gold-flowered brocade, which he was twisting and folding in all directions with a view to displaying its richness and beauty to the best effect.

Upon seeing d'Artagnan, he left his work, somewhat grudgingly, and advanced to meet him, civilly enough, but still not disguising altogether his resentment at being disturbed.

'The captain of the musketeers,' he said, 'will, I am sure, excuse me, for I am terribly busy.'

'Oh! yes, with the king's clothes. I know all about it, dear Monsieur Percerin; indeed they say that you are making him three costumes.'

'Five, my dear sir, five!'

'I don't care a hang whether you are making five or fifty, but I know that nobody in the world can turn them out in such perfection as yourself.'

'Yes, everyone knows that. No doubt, when the costumes are finished, they will be the most beautiful in the world, but, in order to become so, they must be made, and, my dear captain, I am terribly pressed for time.'

'Oh! rubbish, you have two days in which to complete them, Monsieur Percerin, and I am sure that is more time than an artist of your calibre can require,' said d'Artagnan without a blush.

Percerin drew himself up with the air of a man unaccustomed to brook contradiction even in the smallest affairs of life, but d'Artagnan calmly ignored this assumption of indignation on the part of the illustrious tailor.

'My dear Monsieur Percerin,' he continued, 'the object of my visit is to introduce a new customer to you.'

'Indeed, sir,' replied Percerin with a not over-gracious bow.

''Tis the Baron Du Vallon de Bracieux de Pierrefonds.'

The bow which courtesy compelled Percerin now to make was by no means of a sort to find favour in the eyes of our terrible Porthos, who, since his entrance into the room, had looked at the tailor askance.

'One of my most intimate friends,' said d'Artagnan.

'I shall be happy to receive monsieur's commands,' said Percerin, 'but it must be at a future date.'

'At a future date! May I ask when?'

'When I have time.'

'You have already told my servant that,' blurted out Porthos, beginning to lose command of his temper.

'Possibly,' said Percerin, 'I am almost always pressed for time.'

'My friend,' said Porthos sententiously. 'One can always find time if one has the will to find it.'

Percerin became crimson, which is always a dangerous symptom in the case of men whom old age has rendered bloodless.

'Sir,' he gasped, 'you are always at liberty to bestow your custom elsewhere.'

'Come, come, Percerin,' said d'Artagnan, 'I fear you are not in the best of tempers today; but I will tell you, in a single sentence, something which will make you amenable to reason. Monsieur is not only a friend of mine, but a friend of Monsieur Fouquet.'

'Oh! indeed,' said the tailor, 'that puts another complexion on the matter.' Then, turning to Porthos, 'Monsieur,' asked he, 'is in the service of the minister?'

'I am in my own service,' roared the infuriated Porthos, and at the moment the curtain was raised to admit another party to the conversation.

Molière took in the situation at a glance.

D'Artagnan roared with laughter.

Porthos cursed and swore with indignation.

'My dear Percerin,' said d'Artagnan, 'you will make a costume for the baron at my request, will you not?'

'I don't say that I will refuse *you*, captain.'

'And, moreover, you will make it at once?'

'Utterly impossible for a week, at least.'

'You may just as well decline to make it altogether, because my friend proposes to wear it at the fête at Vaux.'

'I can only repeat that it is impossible,' replied the pig-headed old man.

'No, no, dear Monsieur Percerin, especially if I beg the favour of you,' said a gentle voice at the door, the sound of which made d'Artagnan prick up his ears. It was the voice of Aramis.

'Monsieur d'Herblay!' exclaimed the tailor.

'Aramis!' murmured d'Artagnan.

'Oh! our bishop!' said Porthos.

'Good-day, d'Artagnan, good-day Porthos, good-day my dear friends,' said Aramis. 'Come, come, dear Monsieur Percerin, make my friend's costume, and I will answer for it that Monsieur Fouquet will be much gratified.' And he accompanied the words with a gesture which implied, 'Say yes, and let them go.'

It seemed that Aramis had really more influence with Monsieur Percerin than had d'Artagnan himself, for the tailor made a sign of assent to Aramis and turned to Porthos.

'Go, and get measured on the other side,' he said rudely.

Porthos absolutely snorted with indignation.

D'Artagnan saw the impending tempest, and, turning to Molière, said in a low tone of voice, 'My dear sir, the man before you considers himself degraded if anyone presumes to measure the flesh and bones which God has given him. Observe this type of man, Master Aristophanes, and you will be repaid for your trouble.'

Molière required no second invitation, but, addressing Porthos, said, 'Monsieur, if you will do me the honour to come with me, I will undertake that you shall be measured for your costume without being touched by the tailor.'

'Oh!' said Porthos, 'how will you manage that, my friend?'

'I mean that no tape measure, or anything of the kind, shall be applied to your august person. The process to which I refer is one which has been quite recently invented, and is intended to obviate the necessity of gentlemen of rank being defiled by personal contact with the hands of the vulgar. Many gentlemen are too sensitive to endure such indignity, and you, monsieur, I take it, are one of them.'

'I am,' said Porthos, drawing himself up to his full height, and swelling with self-importance.

'Well, then, so far everything fits in delightfully, and you, monsieur, shall have the benefit of our invention.'

'But how the devil can it be done?' said Porthos in ecstasy.

'Monsieur,' said Molière with a bow, 'if you will take the trouble to follow me, you shall see.'

During this scene Aramis looked on in some little bewilderment. Perhaps he thought, having regard to d'Artagnan's evident enjoyment of it, that he would leave with Porthos, so as not to lose the end of the little comedy which had begun so amusingly. But sharp as Aramis was, this time he was mistaken, for Porthos and Molière went off together whilst d'Artagnan stayed on with Percerin. Why? Simply from curiosity, and for the purpose of enjoying for a short time longer the society of his good friend Aramis. Molière and Porthos having disappeared, d'Artagnan approached the Bishop of Vannes, a proceeding which appeared to disconcert the latter considerably.

'A costume for you, also, I suppose, my dear friend?'

Aramis smiled as he answered 'No.'

'But you are going to Vaux, nevertheless?'

'Yes, I shall be there, but not in a new costume. You forget, my dear d'Artagnan, that a poor Bishop of Vannes is not wealthy enough to afford a new coat for every fête that takes place.'

'Bah!' said the musketeer laughing, 'And what about the poems, do we write no more nowadays?'

'Oh! D'Artagnan,' said Aramis, 'I have long ceased even to think of such vanities.'

'Really?' said d'Artagnan still unconvinced.

As for Percerin, he had returned to the consideration of his brocades.

'Does it strike you,' said Aramis smiling, 'that we are somewhat in this old gentleman's way, my dear d'Artagnan?'

'Ah, ah!' said the latter to himself, 'this is as much as to say that you look upon my presence here as being somewhat of an infliction, my dear friend.' Then he added aloud, 'Oh! well, if you think so, let us be off; for my part, my business here is finished, and if you are free too, Aramis – '

'No, for my part, I want – '

'Oh! you have something private to say to Percerin? My dear fellow, why did you not say so before?'

'Something private, certainly, but nothing that I want to conceal from you, d'Artagnan. Pray believe that I have never anything to hide from an intimate friend like you.'

'Oh! not at all; I will be off,' said d'Artagnan, but in a tone of voice that betrayed his curiosity, for the annoyance of Aramis, well dissembled as it was, had not for a moment escaped his notice, and he knew that in that impenetrable brain, even the most trivial matters worked to an end, an unknown end, but one which, from his knowledge of his friend's character, the musketeer judged could hardly fail to be important.

Aramis, on his side, saw that d'Artagnan was suspicious, and accordingly pressed him to stay.

'Stay, my dear fellow, by all means,' he said, 'this is how it is.' Then, turning to the tailor,

'My dear Percerin,' he began, but suddenly breaking off, remarked, 'I am even very pleased you are here, d'Artagnan.'

'Really?' said the wily Gascon again, but he was no more taken in than he had been at first.

Percerin had never given the slightest attention to anything that had been said, being apparently absorbed in the contemplation of his brocades, but he was rudely recalled to consciousness by Aramis, who coolly snatched the stuffs out of his hands.

'My dear Percerin,' said he, 'I have close at hand Monsieur Le Brun,[99] who is one of the painters patronised by Monsieur Fouquet.'

'Oh! very good,' thought d'Artagnan, 'but why Le Brun?'

Aramis glanced at d'Artagnan, who appeared to be busy examining an engraving by Marco Antonio.[100]

'And you wish to have made for him a costume similar to those worn by the Epicureans?' said Percerin. And so saying the worthy tailor, in an absent-minded manner, endeavoured to recapture his piece of brocade.

'The dress of an Epicurean?' said d'Artagnan interrogatively.

'It would seem to be decreed,' said Aramis with one of his most captivating smiles, 'that our friend d'Artagnan is to learn all our secrets this evening.'

'Yes, my friend, yes. You have surely heard of Monsieur Fouquet's band of Epicureans; have you not?'

'Certainly; is it not a kind of society of poets of which La Fontaine, Loret, Pélisson, Molière, and the deuce knows who besides, are members? I think their headquarters are at Saint-Mandé.'

'You are quite right. Well, we put our poets into uniform, and enlist them for the service of the king.'

'Ah! very good, I think I understand exactly. A little surprise which Monsieur Fouquet is preparing for the king. Oh! don't be alarmed; if that is the secret of Monsieur Le Brun, it is perfectly safe with me.'

'You are always charming, dear d'Artagnan. But no, as it happens, Monsieur Le Brun is not on in this scene. The secret which concerns him is of far greater importance than the other.'

'Then, if it is so important as that, I should prefer to remain in ignorance of it,' said d'Artagnan, and he made a pretence of taking his leave.

'Come in, Monsieur Le Brun, come in,' said Aramis opening a side door with one hand, and restraining d'Artagnan with the other.

'Faith! I don't understand a word of it all,' said Percerin. Aramis forced the situation as they say on the stage. 'My dear Monsieur Percerin,' said he, 'you are making five costumes for the king, are you not? one in brocade, one in hunting cloth, one in velvet, one in satin, and one in Florentine stuff.'

'Well, yes,' admitted the astonished tailor, 'but how on earth do you know it, monseigneur?'

'It is the simplest thing in the world, my dear Percerin, there will be a hunt, a banquet, a concert, a promenade and a reception, and etiquette requires that these different dresses should be worn.'

'You know everything, monseigneur!'

'And one or two things besides,' said d'Artagnan under his breath.

'But,' cried the tailor triumphantly, 'what you do *not* know, monseigneur – prince of the church though you be – what nobody knows, except the king, Mademoiselle de la Vallière and myself, is the colour of the stuffs and the style of ornamentation, the cut and the general effect of the dresses.'

'Quite so,' said Aramis, 'and all that is exactly what I have come to ask you to tell me, dear Monsieur Percerin.'

'Ah, bah!' cried the tailor thoroughly frightened, although Aramis had conveyed his modest request in the mildest and most mellifluous of tones.

The impudence of the request appeared, in Monsieur Percerin's eyes, to be so enormous that, after softly chuckling to himself, he laughed aloud, finally absolutely going into shrieks of hysterical laughter. D'Artagnan roared also, not because he found the situation so excruciatingly comical after all, but because he did not wish to allow Aramis time to get cool. The latter let them both have their laugh out; then, when finally they had become calmer, 'At first sight,' said he, 'my request sounded altogether preposterous, did it not? D'Artagnan, however, who is the quintessence of wisdom, will tell you that I could not possibly have acted otherwise than as I did.'

'We shall see,' said the alert musketeer, whose fine instinct told him that only skirmishing had taken place up to then, but that now the battle was to begin indeed.

'Yes, we shall see,' echoed Percerin incredulously.

'Why,' continued Aramis, 'do you suppose that Monsieur Fouquet is holding this fête in honour of the king? Is it not to afford him gratification?'

'Certainly,' said Percerin, and d'Artagnan assented with a nod.

'By some happily conceived idea? By a succession of surprises like that of which we were speaking just now? – the enrolment of our Epicureans?'

'Admirable!'

'Well, then, here is the surprise, my good friend. Monsieur Le Brun here is an admirable artist, and paints with marvellous skill and accuracy.'

'Yes,' said Percerin, 'I have seen some of Monsieur Le Brun's work, I have observed that his dresses have been portrayed with wonderful fidelity and attention to detail. That is why I at once consented to make him a costume of whatever design he should choose.'

'Dear Monsieur Percerin, we will take your word for it, and will return to the subject later on. For the moment, however, Monsieur Le Brun is not in want of any dress that you can make for him, but of the dresses you are making for the king.'

Percerin gave a jump backwards, which that calm and appreciative observer D'Artagnan did not think exaggerated, so alarming were the possibilities to which the astounding request of Aramis might give rise.

'The king's dresses! To give to anyone on the face of the earth the king's dresses! Oh! Monseigneur, pray forgive me for saying so, but, this time your grace must really have taken leave of your senses,' cried the unfortunate tailor, at his wits' end.

'I must, then, appeal to you for help, d'Artagnan,' said Aramis more cool and smiling than ever. 'Help me to persuade this gentleman, for *you*, at least, understand the position, don't you?'

'No, I'll be hanged if I do,' replied his friend.

'What! my dear fellow, don't you understand that Monsieur Fouquet desires to afford the king the surprise of finding his portrait already painted upon his arrival at Vaux, and that the portrait, which will be a striking likeness, must be dressed in the costume which the king will be wearing on the day when he first sees it?'

'Ah! yes, yes,' cried the musketeer almost convinced, so plausible seemed the story, 'yes, my dear Aramis, you are right. It is a capital idea, and I will wager that it is one of your own conception?'

'Either my own or Monsieur Fouquet's,' answered the bishop carelessly, 'but what have *you* to say to the proposal Monsieur Percerin? Let us hear your opinion.

'I say that – '

'That you are at liberty to refuse, beyond doubt; I know that very well, and I certainly do not count on compelling you to comply, my dear sir; I will go further, and say that I appreciate all the delicacy you feel in falling in with this idea of Monsieur Fouquet. You would not like to be thought sycophantic even to gratify royalty. Well, that shows a noble and independent spirit, Monsieur Percerin.'

The tailor spluttered inarticulately.

'It would, really, be a very graceful compliment to pay the young prince,' continued Aramis. 'But Monsieur Fouquet said to me, "If Percerin refuses, tell him that it will make no difference in the opinion I hold of him, and that I shall always esteem him. Only – " '

'Only – ' repeated Percerin uneasily.

' "Only," ' continued Aramis, ' "I shall be obliged to say to the king" (you understand, dear Monsieur Percerin, that it is Monsieur Fouquet who is speaking), "I shall be obliged to say to the king, 'Sire, it was my intention to beg your majesty's acceptance of your portrait, but, through a feeling of delicacy, exaggerated perhaps, although commendable, Monsieur Percerin opposed the idea.'"'

'Opposed!' cried the tailor terrified at the responsibility with which he saw himself about to be saddled. 'I oppose the wish and the inclination of Monsieur Fouquet when his object is to give pleasure to the king! Oh! what a hateful expression to make use of, monseigneur! I to oppose! I thank God that it is not I who uttered it! I call you to witness, captain, that I have opposed nothing.'

D'Artagnan made a sign indicating that he declined to have anything to do with the matter, for he saw that beneath it lay some plot or intrigue the nature of which he could not guess. He would have given his ears to have been able to fathom it, but thought it prudent, for the present, to steer clear of the whole business.

Percerin, however, pursued by the idea that the king would be told that he had set his face against something which would give his majesty pleasure, had already offered Le Brun a seat, and was taking from a wardrobe four magnificent costumes (the fifth being still in the hands of the workpeople), which he was displaying on as many lay figures,[101] which, brought into France in the time of Concini, had fallen into the hands of Percerin after the discomforture of the Italian tailors who had been ruined by competition in business.

The painter at once began to draw and then to colour the dresses, but Aramis, who was closely watching the work, suddenly stopped him.

'I think you have not quite caught the right effect, my dear Monsieur Le Brun, and that you have not quite hit off on the canvas the perfect likeness which is absolutely necessary. I think you require more time in order to reproduce faithfully all the delicate tints.'

'That is quite true,' said Percerin, 'but we have not the time at our disposal and, as to that, I think you will agree, monsieur, that I can do nothing.'

'Then the thing will be a failure,' said Aramis with a resigned air, 'and all because the colouring is defective.'

Nevertheless, Le Brun continued to copy the stuffs and ornamentation with the greatest fidelity, whilst Aramis looked on with ill-concealed impatience.

'What the devil does it all mean?' d'Artagnan kept asking himself meanwhile.

'Decidedly this will never do,' said Aramis presently. 'Monsieur Le Brun, shut up your paint-box and roll up your canvas.'

'But, monseigneur,' cried the vexed painter, 'the light here is execrable.'

'An idea, Monsieur Le Brun, an idea! assuming that we had a sample of the stuffs, more time and a better light?'

'Oh! in that case,' cried Le Brun, 'I would answer for the result.'

'Good!' thought d'Artagnan, 'this seems to be the crux of the difficulty. What they want is evidently a pattern of each piece of stuff used for the dresses. I wonder whether old Percerin will let them have it.'

Percerin beaten back into his last trench, and duped, moreover, by the pretended geniality of Aramis, cut off five patterns and gave them to the Bishop of Vannes.

'That is better; don't you think so?' asked Aramis of d'Artagnan.

'My opinion, my dear Aramis,' replied d'Artagnan, 'is that you are always the same.'

'And, consequently, always your good friend,' said the bishop with one of his charming smiles.

'Yes, yes,' said d'Artagnan aloud; then added in a low tone, 'If I am your dupe, you infernal Jesuit, at least, I will not be your accomplice, and, in order not to become your accomplice, it is quite time for me to get out of this place. Adieu, Aramis,' he added aloud, 'adieu, I am going to find Porthos.

'Then wait for me,' said Aramis, pocketing his samples, 'for I have finished my business here and shall not be sorry to say a parting word to our old comrade.'

Le Brun packed up his traps, Percerin returned the dresses to the wardrobe, Aramis felt his pocket to make sure that it still contained the precious patterns, and Monsieur Percerin was, once more, left in undisturbed possession of his sanctuary.

## CHAPTER 33

## *What very likely gave Molière his first idea for* Le Bourgeois Gentilhomme[102]

D'Artagnan found Porthos in an adjoining room, but no longer an irate Porthos or a disappointed Porthos but a Porthos expansive, radiant with smiles and chatting with Molière, who was looking at him in undisguised admiration as at a creature whom it would be impossible to excel, and who probably could never be equalled.

Aramis walked straight up to Porthos, and held out to him a delicate white hand which was instantly engulfed in the enormous paw of his old comrade.

Aramis never went through this friendly ceremony without a certain amount of apprehension, but, on the present occasion, Porthos kindly refrained from inflicting an unbearable amount of anguish, and the Bishop of Vannes was enabled to return to Molière's side in a tolerably sound and uncrumpled condition.

'Well, monsieur,' said he, 'will you come with me to Saint-Mandé?'

'I will go wherever you please, monseigneur,' replied Molière.

'To Saint-Mandé?' cried Porthos, astonished to see the haughty Bishop of Vannes on terms of familiarity with a tailor's apprentice. 'Hang it, Aramis, surely you are not going to take that fellow to Saint-Mandé!'

'Yes,' said Aramis with a smile, 'there is no time to be lost.'

'Besides, my dear Porthos,' said d'Artagnan, 'Monsieur Molière is not exactly what you take him for.'

'How is that?' asked Porthos.

'Why, he happens to be one of Monsieur Percerin's principal clerks, and is expected at Saint-Mandé to try on the Epicureans the costumes which Monsieur Fouquet has ordered for them.'

'Yes, that is so, monsieur,' assented Molière.

'Let us go then, my dear Monsieur Molière,' said Aramis, 'provided always that you have quite finished your business with Monsieur Du Vallon.'

'Oh! yes, we have nothing more to do,' said Porthos.

'And are you satisfied?' asked d'Artagnan.

'Perfectly satisfied,' replied Porthos.

Molière took his leave of Porthos with effusive politeness, and pressed the hand which d'Artagnan furtively held out to him.

'Take care that you are punctual, sir,' said Porthos in his grandest manner.

'Monsieur le baron, you shall have your costume tomorrow,' replied Molière meekly, and, so saying, he took his departure with Aramis.

Then d'Artagnan took Porthos by the arm and asked what the tailor had done to him to put him in such good humour.

'What has he done, my friend,' shouted Porthos enthusiastically, 'What has he done?'

'Yes, that is what I want to know.'

'My dear fellow, he has done what no tailor has ever done before! He has taken my measure without laying a finger on me!'

'No, really? tell me how he managed it, my friend.'

'Well, in the first place, they brought in a row of lay figures all of different sizes – the Lord alone knows where they get 'em from – in the hope one of them might be of my own proportions, but bless you, the biggest of 'em – a drum-major of the Swiss Guards – was two inches below my height, and a half a foot less round the body!'

'You don't say so!'

'It is as I have had the honour to tell you, my dear d'Artagnan,' answered Porthos. 'But oh! what a great man, or rather a great tailor, is this Monsieur Molière! he was not a bit disconcerted.'

'What did he do next?'

'Oh! the simplest thing in the world. Upon my word, it seems incredible that people can have been such asses as never to have thought of it before. What a world of pain and humiliation I might have been spared!'

'To say nothing of the costumes, old fellow.'

'Yes, only fancy! *Thirty costumes!*'

'Tell me then, my dear Porthos, what method did Monsieur Molière adopt?'

'Molière? is that really his name? I shall make a point of recollecting it.'

'Yes, or Poquelin if you like it better.'

'No, I prefer Molière. When I want to remember his name, I shall think of Volière[103] as I have one at Pierrefonds – '

'Excellent! but what of his method?'

'Well, it was this: instead of punching and mauling me about – as all these rascals do – to make me bend in my back, or double up my limbs, which are disgusting and degrading practices – '

Here d'Artagnan nodded in approval

' "Monsieur," said he to me,' continued Porthos, ' "a gentleman of your rank should measure himself; be so good as to stand in front of this looking-glass." I did so at once, but I admit, without understanding at this time what this excellent Monsieur Volière was after.'

'Molière.'

'Ah! Molière, Molière, of course. Well, as the dread of being measured still haunted me, I said to the fellow, "Be very careful, not to play any pranks with me; I give you warning that I am very touchy." But he, in a courteous tone – for we must give him credit for being a well-mannered fellow, my friend – but he, in a most polite way, said, "Monsieur, in order to ensure a good fit, your dress must be made according to your figure. Now your figure being exactly reflected in the mirror, we will take the measurements of the reflected figure instead of the figure itself." '

'Good,' said d'Artagnan, 'you saw yourself in the mirror; but how the deuce did they find one big enough to reflect the whole of you at once?'

'My dear fellow, this mirror is the one used by the king himself.'

'Yes, but the king is a foot and half shorter than you are.'

'Well, I can't exactly explain it, perhaps it was a way of flattering the king, but, anyhow, the mirror was too large even for me. It is true however, that its height was caused by three plates of Venetian glass, superimposed, as it were, one on the other, while its breadth was formed by the juxtaposition of three other sheets of glass of com-mensurate proportions.'

'My dear Porthos, what admirable language you have at command! Where the deuce did you pick it up?'

'At Belle-Isle. I heard Aramis talking to the architect.'

'That was very clever of you, but suppose we return to the mirror.'

'Well, this admirable Monsieur Volière – '

'Molière.'

'Yes, Molière, of course. You shall see, my dear friend, how carefully I will remember the name in future. Well, this worthy Molière began to trace lines upon the mirror with a piece of Spanish chalk, following the slope and conformation of my arms and shoulders, and, all the time, expatiating upon the soundness of this maxim, which I think is an admirable one. "A dress must not be allowed to encumber its wearer." '

'A capital rule,' said d'Artagnan, 'and it is a pity that it is not more generally carried out.'

'That is what I found so much more astonishing when he expatiated on it.'

'Ah? he <u>expatiated</u> on it, did he? let us hear, my dear Porthos, what he had to say.'

' "It is possible," he said, "for a gentleman to find himself in an awkward position, and have his shoulder encumbered with a garment which he may be unwilling to take off." '

'That is very true,' said d'Artagnan.

' "And that," continued Monsieur Voliére – '

'Molière.'

'Quite so, Molière. "And that," continued Monsieur Molière, "he may wish to draw his sword, being, at the time, encumbered with his doublet. Now, in such a case, monsieur, what should you do?"

' "Why, pull it off, of course," I replied.'

' "Oh, no," he said.'

' "How is that?" I asked.'

' "I say that a dress should be so well made as to be no impediment even to the drawing of a sword. Throw yourself on guard, monsieur," he continued. I fell into the required attitude, and with such hearty goodwill that two panes of glass were shaken out of the window. "That is of no consequence at all, monsieur," said he, "be good enough to remain in that position." I raised my left arm in the air, the forearm gracefully bent, the ruffle hanging, and the wrist curved, whilst the right arm, half extended, covered the belt with the wrist.'

'Yes, yes,' said d'Artagnan, 'I know; the true academic guard.'

'That's it, dear friend. In the meantime Volière – '

'Molière.'

'Stop a moment; I think, after all, I prefer to call him – what did you say was his other name?'

'Poquelin.'

'Well, I would rather call him Poquelin.'

'But how will you remember that name any better than the other?'

'Why, look here, his name is Poquelin, isn't it?'

'Yes.'

'Very well, then, I shall call to mind Madame Coquenard.'[104]

'Very good.'

'I shall change *Coque* into *Poque*, *nard* into *lin*, and, in place of *Coquenard*, I shall have *Poquelin*.'

'That is really most ingenious!' said the astonished d'Artagnan. 'Do go on, old fellow, I could listen to you all night.'

'This Coquelin sketched my arm on the mirror.'

'Excuse me, *Poquelin*.'

'What did I say, then?'

'You said *Coquelin*.'

'Ah! I believe I did. Well, as I was saying, this Poquelin made a sketch of my arm upon the glass; but he took his time about it, and, from time to time, looked at me long and earnestly – the fact being that I was looking very handsome. "Does this tire you?" he enquired presently. "A little," I answered, relieving for a moment the strain upon my limbs, "but still I can hold out for another hour." "No, no," he said, "I cannot allow it; we have some very willing fellows here who will think it no trouble to support your arms, as formerly the arms of the prophets were supported whilst they supplicated the Lord!" "Very well," said I. "You won't consider it degrading?" he asked. "My friend," I replied, "it strikes me that there is a vast difference between being supported and being measured." '

'A very proper distinction to draw,' here interrupted d'Artagnan.

'Then,' continued Porthos, 'he made a signal, and a couple of the workmen came forward, one of whom held up my left arm, whilst the other supported my right. "Another man!" cried Poquelin, and a third fellow, accordingly, made his appearance, and was ordered to support my waist.'

'So that you felt no fatigue at all?' asked d'Artagnan.

'Absolutely none,' replied Porthos, 'and Poquenard drew me on the glass.'

'Poquelin, you mean.'

'Yes, I should have said Poquelin; but hold hard a minute, I think I should prefer to call him Volière, after all.'

'Very well, we will settle it so.'

'And, all the time, Volière was drawing me on the glass.'

'Devilish clever of him, too,' said d'Artagnan.

'I think very highly of his method; it is respectful, and keeps everyone in his proper place.'

'And so that was the end of it?'

'Yes, and not a single person touched me.'

'Except the three fellows who held you up?'

'Ah! yes, of course; but I think I have already pointed out the difference between being supported and being measured.'

'That is true,' replied d'Artagnan who, immediately afterwards added to himself, 'Unless I am greatly mistaken, I have dropped a good windfall into the hands of that rascally Molière, and we shall shortly see the scene drawn to the life in one of his comedies.'

Porthos smiled.

'What are you laughing at?' asked d'Artagnan.

'Must I tell you? Well, then, I am chuckling at my own good luck.'

'That is quite excusable; I don't know a happier man than yourself. But what particular piece of good fortune has now fallen to your share?'

'Oh! my dear fellow, congratulate me.'

'With all my heart.'

'There can be no doubt that I am the first man who has ever been measured in this new manner!'

'Are you quite sure of that?'

'Almost quite certain. Certain signs of intelligence which were exchanged by Volière and his assistants have proved the fact to me almost indisputably.'

'Well, my dear fellow, that does not surprise me so far as Molière is concerned.'

'You mean Volière.'

'Oh! no, no, what an idea! You may call him Volière if you like, but, for my part, I shall continue to speak of him as Molière. Well, then, as I was saying, what you have told me causes me no surprise so far as Molière is concerned, because he is a deuced clever fellow, and it was you who first inspired him with his ingenious idea.'

'It will be of great service to him later on, I feel quite sure of that.'

'Be of great service to him! I should think it will indeed, for Molière is, of all living tailors, the man who best takes the measure of our barons, and Counts, and marquises.'

On this observation, the truth or depth of which we will not here stop to discuss, Porthos and d'Artagnan quitted the abode of the worthy Monsieur Percerin and went in search of their carriage. And here we will leave them, with the reader's permission, and see how Aramis and Molière were faring at Saint-Mandé.

CHAPTER 34

## *The beehive, the bees and the honey*

THE BISHOP OF VANNES, terribly put out at having met d'Artagnan at Monsieur Percerin's house, was in no very good temper when he returned to Saint-Mandé. Molière, on the other hand, delighted at having made a satisfactory sketch of Porthos, and at knowing where to find the original whenever he wanted to turn the sketch into a finished picture, arrived there in the best of humours.

The whole of the first storey of the left wing of the house was given up to the most celebrated Epicureans in Paris, and these, very much at home, were all hard at work, each in his own compartment like bees in their cells, making the honey which was to sweeten the royal cake that Monsieur Fouquet was having prepared for the delectation of his majesty Louis XIV at the forthcoming fête at Vaux.

Pélisson, his head resting on his hand, was sketching the outline of the prologue to *Les Fâcheux*,[105] a comedy in three acts which was to be produced by Poquelin de Molière, as d'Artagnan called him, or Coquelin de Volière as he was called by Porthos.

Loret, with true journalistic ingenuousness – and everyone knows how artless all journalists have been since the printing of the first newspaper, was writing a description of the fêtes at Vaux long before they had taken place.

La Fontaine, flitting from one to the other, like a wandering, distraught, unhappy and intolerable ghost, mumbled over the shoulder of each innumerable poetic absurdities and succeeded in worrying Pélisson to such an extent that the latter, raising his head, said with a touch of asperity, 'At least, La Fontaine, I think you might find me a rhyme since you say that you are so familiar with the gardens of Parnassus.'

'What rhyme do you want?' asked the *fabler*, as Madame de Sévigné called him – 'I want a rhyme to *lumière*.'[106]

'Ornière,' replied La Fontaine, promptly.

'But, my good fellow, how can one speak of *wheel-ruts* when one is extolling the delights of Vaux?' asked Loret.

'Moreover, the words do not rhyme,' said Pélisson.

'What! don't rhyme?' cried La Fontaine in surprise.

'Of course they don't; you have an atrocious habit my dear fellow – one which will effectually prevent you from being classed as a poet of the first rank – your rhyming is slovenly.'

'Oh! oh! and what do you say, Pélisson?'

'I agree with Loret. Remember that a rhyme is never good if a better one can be found.'

'Then, in future, I shall confine myself to prose,' said La Fontaine, who had taken Pélisson's remark seriously. 'Alas! I have often suspected that I am but a feeble poet, and now I am sure of it.'

'Don't talk like that, my dear fellow, you are taking an exaggerated view of the matter; besides, there is much that is excellent in your fables.'

'And to show that I am in earnest,' continued La Fontaine, pursuing his own train of thought, 'I will go and burn a hundred verses that I have just composed.'

'Where are the verses?'

'In my head.'

'Well, if they are in your head you cannot burn them.'

'That is true,' said La Fontaine, 'still, if, I do not burn them – '

'Well, what will happen then?'

'Why, they will remain in my brain and I shall never forget them.'

'The devil!' said Loret, 'that would be dangerous. They might drive you out of your mind.'

'Oh! I dear, oh! dear!' said poor La Fontaine, 'what *am* I to do?'

'I can tell you,' said Molière, who came in at the moment.

'What, then?'

'Why, write them first, and burn them afterwards.'

'Simplicity itself; but I should never have thought of it. What a clever rascal this Molière is,' said La Fontaine, and added, striking his forehead, 'Ah! you will never be but an ass, Jean La Fontaine.'

'What is that you say, my friend?' cried Molière who had caught La Fontaine's aside.

'I say that I shall never be but an ass, my dear brother-scribbler,' replied La Fontaine with a deep sigh and tearful eyes. 'Yes, my friend,' he continued with increasing sadness, 'it seems that my rhymes are slovenly.'

'That is not so.'

'Ah! I am but a sorry fellow.'

'Who has said so?'

'*Parbleu!* it was Pélisson. Did you not, Pélisson?'

But Pélisson, once more in the throes of composition, took good care to ignore the question.

'But, if Pélisson has said that you are but a sorry fellow,' cried Molière, 'Pélisson has grossly insulted you.'

'Do you think so?'

'Yes, and let me tell you that, being a gentleman, you cannot allow such an affront to pass unpunished.'

'Alas!' sighed La Fontaine.

'Did you ever fight?'

'Once, with a lieutenant of light horse.'

'What was your grievance against him?'

'It seems that he made love to my wife.'

'Ah, ah!' said Molière turning slightly pale, but, as at La Fontaine's avowal, the others had turned round, Molière kept his lips framed into the half-mocking smile which had been on the point of disappearing, and continued to make La Fontaine talk. 'And what,' he asked him, 'was the result of the duel?'

'The result was that my adversary, having first disarmed me, apologised, and promised never to set foot in the house again.'

'And you were satisfied with that?'

'Not at all, on the contrary! I picked up my sword. "Pardon me, sir," I said to him, "I have not fought you because you have made love to my wife, but because I was told that I ought to challenge you. Now, as I never had any peace until you came to the house, I beg that you will do me the favour to continue your visits as heretofore, otherwise, *morbleu!* we shall have to fight it out." With the result,' continued La Fontaine, 'that he was obliged to go on making love to my wife, and I have been happy ever since.'

Everyone shouted with laughter, with the exception of Molière, who drew his hand across his eyes, perhaps to wipe away a tear, perhaps to stifle a sigh. Alas! we know that, although Molière was a moralist, he was no philosopher.[107]

'It is all the same,' he said returning to the original subject of discussion, 'Pélisson has insulted you.'

'Ah! so he has; I had quite forgotten it.'

'And I am going to call him out on your behalf.'

'By all means, if you think it imperative.'

'I *do* think it imperative, and I am going to do it.'

'But wait a moment,' said La Fontaine, 'I want to ask your opinion.'

'Upon what? – this affront?'

'No, but I want you to tell me whether *lumière* does not really rhyme with *ornière*.'

'I should make them rhyme, and I have made a hundred thousand such verses in my time.'

'A hundred thousand!' cried La Fontaine. 'Four times the number of verses in *La Pucelle*[108] which Monsieur Chapelain is meditating. Is it also upon this theme that you have written a hundred thousand, my friend?'

'Listen to me, you everlasting wool-gatherer!' said Molière.

'It is certain,' continued La Fontaine, 'that *légume*,[109] for example, rhymes with *posthume*.'

'In the plural especially.'

'Yes, especially in the plural because then it rhymes not with three letters but with four as *lumière* does with *ornière*. Put *lumières* and *ornières* in the plural, my dear Pélisson,' said La Fontaine slapping him on the shoulder, 'and they rhyme to perfection.'

'What?' said Pélisson, whose affront La Fontaine had again forgotten.

'Why Molière says so; and Molière knows what he's talking about. He declares that he himself has written a hundred thousand verses.'

'Listen to him,' said Molière laughing, 'he has started now.'

'It is the same with *rivage*, which rhymes perfectly with *herbage*; I'll eat my hat if it doesn't.'

'But – ' began Molière.

'I tell you this,' interrupted La Fontaine, 'because you are writing a comedy for Sceaux, are you not?'

'Yes, *Les Fâcheux*.'

'Exactly so, *Les Fâcheux*. I remember perfectly now. Well, I have been thinking that a prologue would be an additional attraction to your comedy.'

'Undoubtedly, it would suit it admirably.'

'Ah! you are of my opinion, then?'

'So much so, that I asked you to write the prologue for me.'

'What, do you mean to say that you have asked *me* to write it?'

'Yes, *you*, and, moreover, on your refusing to undertake it, I begged you to hand the work over to Pélisson, who is engaged upon it at this very moment.'

'So that is what Pélisson is doing! Upon my word, my dear Molière, you are certainly right in your judgement at times.'

'When, for example?'

'When you say that my wits go wool-gathering. It is a most abominable failing, and I must cure myself of it, and, in the meantime, I will write your prologue.'

'But how can you, when Pélisson already has it in hand?'

'That is true; unutterable blockhead that I am! Loret was quite right when he said I was but a poor creature.'

'But it wasn't Loret who said so, my friend.'

'Oh! well I don't care who said it. Anyhow your comedy is called *Les Fâcheux*. Now then, the question is, can you make *heureux* rhyme with *fâcheux?*

'Oh! yes, at a pinch.'

'And the same with *capricieux*.'

'No, no, hardly, I think.'

'You think it would be too risky? but why?'

'Because the terminations differ.'

'I was thinking,' said La Fontaine, leaving Molière and turning to Loret, 'I was thinking – '

'Well, what were you thinking? said Loret peevishly, and pausing in the middle of a phrase. 'Let us hear; look sharp.'

'Let me see, it *is* you who are writing the prologue to *Les Fâcheux*, isn't it?'

'Oh? confound it, no, it is Pélisson.'

'Ah, it is Pélisson!' cried La Fontaine trotting over to him. 'I was thinking,' he continued, 'that the nymph of Vaux – '

'Ah! good!' cried Loret. 'The nymph of Vaux. Excellent! Thank you, La Fontaine. That gives me an idea for my concluding couplet.

> And saw the gracious nymph of Vaux
> A guerdon for their toil bestow.

'Bravo! that is capital!' cried Pélisson. 'I say, if you could only rhyme like that, La Fontaine, old fellow.'

'But it strikes me that I *do* rhyme like that. Did you not hear Loret say that he was indebted to me for the couplet?'

'Oh! well, if you can rhyme like that, I wish you would give me an idea for the commencement of my prologue.'

'Well, I should begin something like this; *Oh! nymph who* – well, then I should use a verb in the second person singular, of the present tense, of the indicative mood, and then I should go on to say something like *cool retreat.*'

'But the verb, man, the verb?' demanded Pélisson.

'*To lay thy homage at the great king's feet,*' continued La Fontaine.

'But the *verb?*' persisted Pélisson, 'this verb in the second person singular of the present indicative?'

'Oh! well, *comest.*'

> Oh! nymph who comest from thy cool retreat
> To lay thy homage at the great king's feet.

'Hum; I don't think very much of that,' said Pélisson.

'My dear fellow,' said La Fontaine, 'you are so dreadfully fastidious!'

'I think it is rather weak myself, my dear La Fontaine,' said Molière; 'fancy making the nymph *lay* homage – as if it were an egg.'

'Ah! well, then you see after all that you were quite right in calling me a fraud.'

'I never said anything of the kind.'

'Well, then, as Loret said.'

'It was not Loret either; it was Pélisson.'

'Well, Pélisson was right a hundred times over. But what worries me more than anything else, my dear Molière, is that I don't believe we shall ever get our Epicurean dresses.'

'You reckoned upon having yours for the fête?'

'Yes, for the fête, and for after the fête. My housekeeper has already hinted that my own clothes are a bit rusty.'

'Your housekeeper is quite right. I think they are rather beyond the *rusty* stage.'

'Yes, but that is easily accounted for; you see, I left my coat upon the floor in my room, and the cat – '

'Well, what did the cat do?'

'Why she kittened on it and, I am afraid, stained it a little.'

Molière shouted with laughter, Loret and Pélisson following his example.

At this moment the Bishop of Vannes entered the room carrying a roll of plans and parchments. It was as if the angel of death had frozen at its source the mirth of these light-hearted mortals, as if that pallid face had frightened away the graces to whom Xenocrates[110] sacrificed, so instantaneously did silence reign in the room, whilst each, with solemn countenance, resumed his pen.

Aramis distributed amongst them sundry notes of invitation, and thanked them in the name of Monsieur Fouquet. Monsieur Fouquet, he said, being kept in his study by business, could not pay them a visit, but begged that they would send him some specimens of their day's work as some compensation for the fatigue created by his labour of the night.

On hearing this, all set to work with the greatest assiduity, La Fontaine himself seizing pen and paper and scribbling away for dear life; Pélisson made a fair copy of his prologue; Molière contributed fifty new verses with which his visit to Monsieur Percerin had inspired him; Loret his article descriptive of the fête, as yet to take place; and Aramis, loaded with spoils like the king of the bees – a big black drone, adorned with purple and gold – returned to his own apartments with silent footstep and thoughtful brow. But before leaving he said, 'Do not forget, gentlemen, that we all set out from here tomorrow evening.'

'In that case, I must leave word at home,' said Molière.

'Ah! yes, poor Molière,' grinned Loret, '*he loves* his home.'

'*He loves*, yes,' said Molière with his sad smile; 'but *he loves* does not always imply *he is loved*.'

'For my part,' said La Fontaine, 'they love me at Château-Thierry, I am quite sure of that.'

Aramis, who had been gone but a few moments, here re-entered the room.

'Will anyone come with me?' he asked. 'After an interview with Monsieur Fouquet, which will not occupy more than a quarter of an hour, I am off to Paris, and can give anyone a lift in my carriage.'

'Thanks, I shall be very glad,' said Molière, 'time is of consequence to me.'

'I shall stay here to dine,' said Loret. 'Monsieur de Gourville has promised me some crayfish. Find a rhyme for that La Fontaine.'

Aramis went out laughing as he alone could laugh, and Molière followed him. They had reached the bottom of the stairs, when La Fontaine shouted after them through the half-opened door.

> He promised that the gay crayfish
> Should grace the poet's supper-dish.

The laughter with which the Epicureans greeted this poetic effort reached the ears of Monsieur Fouquet as Aramis opened the door of his room, in order to say a few parting words, Molière, meanwhile, having undertaken to order the carriage to be got ready.

'How they are laughing up there!' said Fouquet with a sigh.

'And do you not laugh, monseigneur?'

'I have forgotten how to laugh, Monsieur d'Herblay.'

'The fête is drawing near.'

'Money is disappearing.'

'Have I not already said that that is my affair?'

'But you have promised me millions.'

'They shall be forthcoming the day after the king's arrival at Vaux.'

Fouquet looked narrowly at Aramis and passed his icy hand across his moist forehead. Aramis understood that Fouquet either suspected him, or doubted his ability to procure so much money. How was it possible for Fouquet to believe that a poor bishop, ex-abbé and musketeer could find it?

'Why do you doubt me?' said Aramis.

Fouquet smiled sadly, and shook his head.

'Oh! man of little faith!' added Aramis.

'My dear Monsieur d'Herblay,' replied Fouquet, 'if I fall – '

'Well, if you fall.'

'If I fall, I shall fall from such a height that I shall be broken beyond repair.'

Then shaking his head, as if to dispel his gloomy thoughts, 'Where do you come from, my dear friend?' he asked.

'From Paris – from Percerin's shop.'

'You had private business to transact with him, I presume, for I don't suppose you take much interest in our poet's dresses?'

'No; I went there to arrange a surprise.'

'Indeed?'

'Yes, a surprise which you are to give the king.'

'Will it cost much money?'

'Oh! a hundred pistoles which you will give Le Brun.'

'A picture! not a bad idea; and what is to be the subject of it?'

'I will tell you presently, and then, notwithstanding what you have said, I had a look at our poet's dresses.'

'What did you think of them? I hope they will be handsome.'

'They are magnificent. There will be few noblemen with any so good. They will show the difference that exists between the courtiers of riches and those of friendship.'

'Always epigrammatic and lavish, dear bishop.'

'I have learned to be so in your school.'

Fouquet pressed his hand. 'And where are you going now?' he asked.

'I start for Paris as soon as you have given me a letter.'

'To whom?'

'A letter to Monsieur de Lyonne.'

'And what do you want with Lyonne?'

'I want him to sign a *lettre de cachet*.'[111]

'A *lettre de cachet!* Are you going to put someone in the Bastille?'

'No, on the contrary, I am going to get someone out.'

'And who may that be?'

'A poor devil of a young man, quite a boy still, who has been shut up there for ten years for having written a couple of Latin verses against the Jesuits.'

'Two Latin verses! and for these he has been imprisoned for ten years, poor devil?'

'Yes.'

'And he has committed no other offence?'

'Beyond those two verses, he is as innocent as you or I.'

'I may take your word for it?'

'My word of honour.'

'What is his name?'

'Seldon.'

'It is really too bad that, knowing of this, you have not told me of it before.'

'It was only yesterday that his mother approached me on the subject, monseigneur.'

'Is the woman poor?'

'In the greatest distress, monseigneur.'

'Heaven,' said Fouquet, 'sometimes permits such acts of injustice that one can readily understand the refusal of the victims to believe in the existence of a deity. Now then, Monsieur d'Herblay.' And, taking a pen, Fouquet rapidly wrote a few lines to his colleague Lyonne.

Aramis took the letter and turned to leave the room.

'Wait,' said Fouquet.

He opened a drawer and took out ten drafts on the treasury, each of which was for a thousand livres.

'There,' he said, 'liberate the son, and give this to the mother; but do not let her know – '

'What, monseigneur?'

'That she is ten thousand livres richer than I; she would think me a poor minister. Now go, and may God bless those who remember the poor.'

'I echo that sentiment,' said Aramis, and, kissing Fouquet's hand, he went out quickly, armed with the letter for Lyonne and the money for Seldon's mother. Molière who was getting tired of waiting was thankful that, at last, there was a prospect of starting on their journey.

## CHAPTER 35

## *Another supper at the Bastille*

THE GREAT CLOCK of the Bastille struck the hour of seven in the evening, the great clock which, as in the case of all the accessories of the state prison – the very use of which is a torture – reminded the prisoners of the doom contained in each hour of their punishment. The great clock of the Bastille, adorned with figures, as were most of the clocks of the period, represented St Peter bound in prison.

It was the prisoners' supper time. The doors, grating on their huge hinges, opened to admit the trays and baskets laden with food, the quality of which, we have Monsieur Baisemeaux's own authority for stating, was regulated by the social position of the prisoner.

We know already the theory held by Monsieur Baisemeaux, sovereign dispenser of gastronomic delicacies, chief cook of the royal fortress, whose well-filled baskets were carried up the steep stair-cases taking to the unhappy prisoners such consolation as was to be found in the honestly filled bottles which they contained.

The governor of the Bastille also had supper at this hour. He had a guest this evening, and the spit turned more heavily than usual. Roast partridges flanked by quails and flanking a larded leveret, boiled fowls and ham cooked in white wine, *cordons* of Guipuzcoa and *bisque d'ècrevisses*: these delicacies, in addition to the various soups and *hors-d'oeuvres*, formed the supper menu of his worship the governor.

Baisemeaux rubbed his hands with satisfaction as he took his place at the table opposite to the Bishop of Vannes, who, clad in grey, booted and with a sword at his side, incessantly complained of hunger and showed the utmost impatience to attack the supper.

Monsieur Baisemeaux was not accustomed to being treated on terms of equality by so illustrious a personage as Monseigneur de Vannes, but this evening Aramis relaxed and treated him with condescending familiarity. He sank the prelate in the musketeer, and even touched upon subjects which could scarcely be described as strictly clerical, and to this phase of the conversation Monsieur Baisemeaux, like most commonly bred people, addressed himself with the greatest gusto.

'Monsieur,' said he, 'for, upon my word, I hardly like to say monseigneur this evening – '

'Quite right,' said Aramis, 'call me monsieur by all means; besides tonight I am a musketeer.'

'Do you know, sir, whom you remind me of this evening?'

'I can't guess,' said Aramis filling his glass, 'but I trust that it is of a boon companion.'

'You remind me of two, monsieur – François, shut that window; monseigneur will feel a draught.'

'And let him leave the room,' said Aramis, 'we've got everything we want, and we can get on very well without attendance. I much prefer it when I am supping with only one friend.'

Baisemeaux bowed respectfully.

'I like,' continued Aramis, 'to wait on myself.'

'François, you may leave the room,' cried Baisemeaux.

'I was saying, monsieur, that you remind me of two persons; one of them was illustrious; I allude to the late cardinal, the great Cardinal Richelieu, who was booted like yourself. Am I right?'

'Upon my word, I think so,' said Aramis. 'And who is the other?'

'The other is a certain musketeer, handsome, brave, intrepid and fortunate, who changed from abbé to musketeer, and from musketeer to abbé.'

Aramis condescended to smile.

'From abbé,' continued Baisemeaux, waxing bolder under the smile, 'from abbé he rose to be bishop, and from bishop – '

'I think we will stop there, if you please,' said Aramis.

'I declare that you are already a cardinal in my eyes.'

'Let us change the conversation, dear Monsieur Baisemeaux, but although I am as you say *booted* like a cavalier, I have no desire, even upon an occasion like this, to be in conflict with the church.'

'But you have evil intentions, nevertheless, monsieur.'

'Yes, evil in the sense that all things mundane are evil.'

'But you frequent all sorts of strange places, in disguise.'

'Quite so, in disguise.'

'And you wear a sword.'

'Yes, but only when I am compelled to wear one; and now, will you do me the favour to call in François?'

'You would like some other sort of wine?'

'It is not for wine, but the room is frightfully hot and the window is closed.'

'I had the windows shut at supper time so as not to be disturbed by the noise made by the arrival of the couriers.'

'Ah! yes; you can hear them when the window is open?'

'Only too well; and it is an annoyance. You understand.'

'Meanwhile, I am suffocating. François!'

François promptly made his appearance.

'Open the window, for heaven's sake, François. You will permit it, dear Monsieur Baisemeaux?'

'Monseigneur is at home here,' replied the governor, and the window was opened.

'I am thinking,' said Baisemeaux, 'that you will miss Monsieur de La Fère very much now that he has returned to his household gods at Blois. He is one of your very old friends, is he not?'

'You know that as well as I do, Baisemeaux, since you were in the musketeers with both of us.'

'Bah! With my friends, I count neither bottles nor years.'

'And you are quite right. But I do more than merely feel affection for Monsieur de La Fère. I revere him.'

'Ah! well, you may think it strange, but, for my part,' said the governor, 'I prefer Monsieur d'Artagnan. Now there's a man if you like! Bless me! I believe he could drink for ever and a day. There is no difficulty in telling what a straightforward fellow like that is thinking about.'

'Baisemeaux, old fellow, let's get drunk together tonight as we used to do in the days that are no more; and, if I have one regret at the bottom of my heart, I promise that it shall be as apparent to you as a diamond at the bottom of your glass.'

'Bravo!' cried Baisemeaux, and, pouring out a bumper, he swallowed it, trembling with joy at the thought that he was sinning in such distinguished company.

Whilst thus employed in fuddling himself, he failed to notice how anxiously Aramis was listening to every sound in the great courtyard outside.

A courier arrived just as François placed the fifth bottle on the table, and although a great noise was created by his arrival Baisemeaux heard nothing of it.

'The devil fly away with him!' cried Aramis all at once.

'With whom?' asked Baisemeaux, 'I hope nothing is wrong with the wine nor with him who invites you to drink it?'

'No, it's only one confounded solitary horse in the courtyard which is making clatter enough for an entire squadron of cavalry.'

'Oh! one of those infernal couriers,' replied the governor, as he tossed off another bumper. 'You're quite right; to hell with him! and so quickly that we shall never hear the beggar speak again. Hurrah! hurrah! What, the devil! who's afraid?'

'You are forgetting me, Baisemeaux! my glass is empty,' said Aramis holding it out.

''Pon honour, you charm me – François, more wine!' François entered. 'Wine! you villain, more wine!' roared Baisemeaux, 'and of the best!'

'Yes, your honour, but – there is a courier – '

'Oh! tell him to go to the devil; that's what I say.'

'Yes, your honour, but still – '

'Tell him to leave his confounded dispatch at the office. We'll see about it tomorrow. There will be plenty of time tomorrow; besides which there will be daylight,' replied Baisemeaux, singing the last few words in a kind of unmusical cadenza.

'Ah! your honour, your honour,' remonstrated the shocked François, in spite of himself.

'Take care,' said Aramis, 'pray take care.'

'What of, dear Monsieur d'Herblay?' asked Baisemeaux by this time more than half drunk.

'A letter for the governor of a fortress, which is sent by a courier, is not unlikely to be an order.'

'Such letters nearly always are.'

'And these orders are issued by ministers?'

'Yes, undoubtedly, but – '

'And do not these ministers countersign orders which are signed by the king?'

'Perhaps you are right. Nevertheless, it is most annoying, when you are sitting at a well-supplied table, and enjoying a confidential talk with a friend – Ah! pardon me, I am forgetting that you are my guest, and that I am speaking to a future cardinal.'

'Never mind that, dear Baisemeaux, let us return to our soldier – to François.'

'And what has François done?'

'He has protested.'

'Then, he was wrong.'

'He has, nevertheless, protested you understand, and he would not have taken such a liberty, had not something out of the common been in the air. It seems quite possible that it was not François who was wrong in protesting but that you were wrong for giving no heed to him.'

'What! I am in the wrong rather than François? That seems to be a rather strong pill for me to swallow.'

'Let us call it a slight error of judgment. Pardon me, but I thought it right to make an observation which, in my opinion, is of importance.'

'Oh! perhaps you are right,' stammered Baisemeaux. 'An order from the king is sacred! But, as to orders which arrive when one is having supper, may the devil – '

'If you had said so much as that to the great cardinal, eh! my dear Baisemeaux, and the order happened to have been one of importance – ?'

'I act thus, rather than put a bishop to inconvenience. Should I not be justified if I pleaded that?'

'Do not forget, Baisemeaux, that I have been a soldier, and accustomed to see discipline enforced, and orders obeyed.'

'You wish, then – ?'

'I wish you to do your duty, my friend, at all events before this soldier.'

'That is common sense, anyhow' said Baisemeaux; whilst François, standing at attention, waited for orders. Baisemeaux pulled himself together. 'Let the king's order be brought to me,' he commanded. Then, addressing Aramis, he added in a lower tone of voice, 'Do you know what it is ? I warrant it is something about as interesting as this: "Keep fire away from your powder magazine," or, "Keep an eye on so-and-so; he is an expert gaol-breaker." Ah! if you only knew, monseigneur, how often I have been suddenly awakened from the soundest and most refreshing sleep by the arrival, post haste, of an orderly to say to me, or rather to give me a piece of paper bearing the words, "Monsieur Baisemeaux, what news?" It is very obvious that those who waste their time in writing such trumpery orders have never passed a night in the Bastille, or they would know the thickness of my walls, the vigilence of my officers, and the number of times we go the rounds. But what can one do, monseigneur? It is their business to harass me with vexatious messages when I want to be quiet, and to annoy me when I am happy,' added Baisemeaux with a bow to Aramis. 'Well; let them do their duty.'

'And do you do yours,' said the bishop, whose steady look conveyed a command in spite of the smile by which it was accompanied.

François re-entered the room and Baisemeaux received from his hands the minister's order. He leisurely unsealed and read it, whilst Aramis, pretending to drink, watched him through the bottom of his glass.

'There!' said Baisemeaux, when he had finished reading, 'what did I tell you?'

'What is it?' asked the bishop.

'An order of release. Isn't that a fine thing to disturb us for?'

'It's a fine thing, at any rate, for the prisoner concerned, my dear governor.'

'And at eight o'clock at night!'

'That is a kindness.'

'Oh! yes; kindness is all very well in its way, but, in this case, it is for a fellow who is in a state of extreme discomfort and not for me who am in a state of extreme content and don't want to be annoyed,' grumbled Baisemeaux.

'Will you lose anything through the prisoner's release? Is he one of those who pay on a high scale of charges?'

'Oh! yes, very much so, a dirty five-franc rat!'

'May I be allowed to see the order?' asked Monsieur d'Herblay.

'Oh! certainly; read it by all means.'

'It is marked *urgent*; did you notice that?'

'Yes, capital, is it not? A man has been here ten years, and it is *urgent* that he be set at liberty tonight, when it is already eight o'clock,' and Baisemeaux, with a shrug of the shoulders, threw down the order and reseated himself at the table.

'They are always playing games like this,' he said with his mouth full. 'They arrest a man one fine day; they keep him for ten years, and write to you, "keep a sharp eye on this fellow" or "take care that this man is strictly guarded", and then, when one has become accustomed to look upon him as a dangerous customer, comes an order to set him at liberty, and the order is marked *urgent*. Upon my word, monseigneur, it is enough to make a man shrug his shoulders.'

'Well, it can't be helped' said Aramis. 'You receive an order, and you have to carry it out.'

'Good! good! carry it out indeed – oh! patience! I hope you don't suppose that I am altogether a slave?'

'Good heavens! my very dear Monsieur Baisemeaux, whoever suggested such an idea? Your independence of spirit is too well known.'

'Thank God for that!'

'But your kindness of heart is well known also.'

'Oh! don't speak of it.'

'And your ready obedience to your superiors. Once a soldier, you see Baisemeaux, always a soldier.'

'And I shall strictly obey orders in the present instance; at daybreak tomorrow the prisoner shall be liberated.'

'Tomorrow?'

'The very first thing.'

'But why not tonight seeing that the *lettre de cachet* is marked *urgent* both inside and out?'

'Because this evening we are at supper, and *our* business is *urgent* also.'

'Dear Baisemeaux, booted though I be, I cannot forget that I am a priest, and charity, in my mind, takes precedence over hunger and thirst. This unhappy prisoner has suffered long enough, since you tell me that he has been under your charge for ten years. Shorten his suffering. A happy moment is in store for him; let him enjoy it as quickly as possible. God will repay you in Paradise with years of felicity.'

'You desire it?'

'I implore you.'

'What! in the middle of supper?'

'Yes, this action is worth ten Benedicites.'

'Well, it shall be as you please; only, our supper will get cold.'

'Oh! that is of no consequence.'

Baisemeaux, leaning back to ring for François, by a very natural movement turned towards the door. The order of release lay on the table, and Aramis took advantage of the moment when Baisemeaux was not looking to change it for another paper, folded in the same manner, which he took from his pocket.

'François,' said the governor, 'let the major and the gaolers of the *Bertaudière* be sent for immediately.'

CHAPTER 36

## *The General of the Order*

A SHORT INTERVAL of silence reigned between the two companions, during which Aramis never took his eyes off the governor. The latter seemed only half determined thus to disturb himself at supper, and it was evident that he sought a pretext, good or bad, for postponing the business, at all events until after dessert. This pretext, he appeared, all at once, to have discovered.

'Eh! but,' he cried, 'it is impossible!'

'What do you mean by *impossible*?' said Aramis. 'I should like you to point out the impossibility, if you will.'

'It is impossible to liberate the prisoner at such an hour. He is quite unfamiliar with Paris, and where is he to go to?'

'He will go where he can; that is his affair.'

'But you might as well set a blind man free.'

'Well, my carriage is here; I will take him wherever he wants to go.'

'You have an answer ready for everything. François, let the major have instructions to open the cell of Monsieur Seldon, No. 3, *Bertaudière*.'

'Seldon?' said Aramis, with an innocent air. 'You said Seldon, did you not?'

'Certainly I said Seldon; it is the name of the prisoner who is to be released.'

'Oh! you mean to say Marchiali,' said Aramis.

'Marchiali? No, no, Seldon.'

'I think you are in error, Monsieur Baisemeaux.'

'I read the order.'

'So did I.'

'And I saw "Seldon" in letters as big as that,' and Baisemeaux held up a finger.

'And I read "Marchiali" in letters as big as this,' and Aramis held up two fingers.

'Well, the matter is easily settled,' said Baisemeaux, feeling sure that he was right, 'here is the order; look for yourself.'

'I read "Marchiali",' said Aramis, spreading out the paper. 'Look.'

Baisemeaux looked, and his arms fell to his sides.

'Yes, yes,' he faltered, overwhelmed, 'yes, Marchiali. It is certainly written here "Marchiali"; it is quite true.'

'Ah!'

'But Marchiali is the man of whom we have talked so much, and of whom I was enjoined to take such particular care.'

'The order says "Marchiali",' said Aramis inflexibly.

'I must admit it, monseigneur, but I don't understand it at all.'

'You can believe your own eyes, nevertheless.'

'Good Gracious! only to think that it should really be Marchiali!'

'And in good handwriting, too.'

'It is marvellous. I can still see the order and the name of Seldon, Irishman. I see it as plainly as I see you. Yes, and I can even call to mind that, underneath the name, there was a blot of ink.'

'No, there is no ink; there is no blot.'

'Oh! but there *was* most certainly. Why, I rubbed off some sand that covered the blot.'

'Well, however that may be, and whatever you may have seen, the order is signed for the liberation of Marchiali, blot, or no blot.'

'The order is signed for the liberation of Marchiali,' repeated Baisemeaux mechanically, as he made an effort to recover his wits.

'And you are going to liberate him accordingly. If the tenderness of your heart prompts you to set free Seldon as well, I assure you I shall not offer the faintest objection.' Aramis emphasised these words with a smile, the irony of which went far towards sobering Baisemeaux and giving him a little courage.

'Monseigneur,' he said 'this Marchiali is the very same prisoner whom, the other day, a priest, a confessor of *our order*, came to visit with such authority and secrecy.'

'I know nothing about that, sir,' replied the bishop.

'And yet it is not so very long ago, dear Monsieur d'Herblay,'

'True; but *with us* it is as well that the man of today should know nothing whatever of the actions of the man of yesterday.'

'In any case,' said Baisemeaux, 'the visit of the Jesuit confessor must have been a source of great comfort to this man.'

Aramis made no reply, but, reseating himself at the table, commenced a fresh attack upon the neglected supper. As for Baisemeaux, having no longer any appetite, he produced the order again and subjected it to renewed and close examination.

Under ordinary circumstances, this proceeding would have made the ears of the impatient Aramis tingle with resentment, but the Bishop of Vannes did not become enraged at so little, especially as he told himself that it would be dangerous to lose his temper.

'Are you going to liberate Marchiali?' he asked. 'By the by, this is an excellent glass of sherry, my dear governor.'

'Monseigneur,' replied Baisemeaux, 'I shall liberate the prisoner Marchiali when I have seen the courier who brought the order, and when, by questioning him, I have satisfied myself – '

'But all orders are sealed, and the purport of them, of course, unknown to the courier who brings them. Of what avail then would it be to question the courier in the present instance?'

'Then, monseigneur, I shall send the order back to the ministry, and Monsieur de Lyonne can either confirm or withdraw it.'

'What will be the good of that?' said Aramis, coldly.

'What good?'

'Yes, I ask what useful purpose will it serve?'

'It will ensure me against deceiving myself, monseigneur, against being wanting in that respect which a subaltern owes to his superiors, and against infringing the rules of the service in which I am employed.'

'Very good; you speak so eloquently that I quite admire you. It is quite true; a subaltern owes his superiors respect; he is culpable if he deceives himself, and he will be punished if he infringes the rules and regulations of the service.'

Baisemeaux looked at the bishop in astonishment.

'And therefore,' continued Aramis, 'you are seeking advice in order that your conscience may be at rest?'

'Yes, monseigneur.'

'And, if a superior gives you an order, you will obey it?'

'Without doubt, monseigneur.'

'You are well acquainted with the king's signature, Monsieur Baisemeaux?'

'Yes, monseigneur.'

'Is it not on the order of release?'

'It is, certainly; but then it might be – '

'Might be forged, you were going to say.'

'That is obvious, monseigneur.'

'You are right. And the signature of Monsieur de Lyonne?'

'It is also upon the order: but, if the king's signature could be forged, so also, or even more readily, could Monsieur de Lyonne's be counterfeited.'

'Your logic is irrefutable, Monsieur Baisemeaux, and your argument irresistible; but what is it that leads you to doubt the genuineness of these particular signatures?'

'It is this, the absence of counter-signatures. The king's signature is not vouched for, and Monsieur de Lyonne is not here to tell me that either signature is genuine.'

'Very well, Monsieur de Baisemeaux,' said Aramis, with the piercing glance of an eagle, 'so frankly do I sympathise with you in your doubts, and approve of your proposed method of setting them at rest, that I will take a pen if you will be good enough to give me one.'

Baisemeaux handed him a pen.

'And, as I shall sign what I am about to write in your presence, you cannot very well contest the authenticity of my signature, however sceptical you may be inclined to be.'

Baisemeaux turned pale under this icy assurance. It seemed to him that the bishop's voice, up to that time so gay and pleasant, had suddenly become funereal and ominous, that the wax-lights had changed into the tapers of a mortuary chapel and that the glasses of wine had turned into chalices of blood.

Aramis took the pen and began to write, the terrified Baisemeaux looking over his shoulder. 'AMDG'[112] wrote the bishop and he drew a cross under the four letters, which stand for *Ad Majorem Dei Gloriam*. Then he continued:

It is our pleasure that the order brought to Monsieur de

Baisemeaux de Montlezun, governor for the king of the Royal Fortress of the Bastille, shall be deemed good and valid and shall be executed forthwith.

[signed] D'HERBLAY
by the grace of God, General of the Order

Baisemeaux was so profoundly astonished that his features became rigid, his eyes stared and he stood, with open mouth, without being able to articulate a word. No sound was to be heard in the large chamber but the buzzing of a moth as it fluttered round the candles. Aramis, without even deigning to look at the man whom he had reduced to so pitiable a condition, drew from his pocket a small case containing black wax; he sealed his letter, impressed it with a seal which hung at his breast, beneath his doublet, and, this proceeding being terminated, he handed the letter to Baisemeaux, without a word. The latter received it with trembling hands and cast a dull and dazed look upon the seal. Then suddenly a light seemed to dawn upon him and he fell into a chair as though struck by lightning.'

'Come, come,' said Aramis after a long silence, during which the governor of the Bastille gradually recovered his wits, 'don't try to make me believe that the presence of the general of the order is as terrible as that of the Deity, to look upon whom is to die. Take courage! get up; give me your hand and obey.'

Baisemeaux reassured, if not satisfied, obeyed; he kissed the bishop's hand and stood up. 'Immediately?' he murmured.

'Oh! you need not be in a violent hurry, my host; sit down again, and let us do justice to this excellent dessert.'

'Monseigneur,' said Baisemeaux, 'I feel that I shall never recover from this shock. To think that I should have laughed and joked with you! to think that I have presumed to treat you on terms of equality!'

'Tut, tut, old comrade,' replied the bishop, who felt how severe was the tension and how dangerous it might be to snap the cord, 'say no more about it. Let each of us lead his own life in his own way; to you, my friendship and protection; to me, your obedience. These two conditions realised, all will be well.'

Baisemeaux reflected; he saw, at a glance, the consequences of releasing a prisoner under a forged order, but the guarantee of protection which the general of his order offered him, seemed, when placed in the opposite scale, heavy enough to outweigh them. Aramis read his thoughts.

'My dear Baisemeaux,' said he, 'don't be a simpleton. What necessity is there for you to think, whilst I take the trouble to think for you?' and, at a fresh gesture which he made, Baisemeaux bowed again.

'What do you command me to do?' said he.

'What is the ordinary routine for releasing a prisoner?'

'I have the regulations.'

'Very well, follow them.'

'I go with my major to the prisoner's cell, and, if he is a person of importance, I bring him out myself.'

'But this Marchiali is not a person of importance?' said Aramis carelessly.

'I don't know,' said the governor in a tone which implied, 'It is for you to tell me that.'

'Then, if you know nothing about him, I am right; just treat Marchiali as if he were an ordinary prisoner.'

'Very well; that will be in accordance with the regulation which directs that the gaoler, or some other subordinate officer, is to bring the prisoner before the governor in his office.'

'Well, that is a very wise regulation. What next?'

'The prisoner then has restored to him any articles of value which he may have had upon him at the time of his arrest, as well as his clothes and papers, provided that the ministry has not ordered that they be disposed of in some other manner.'

'What were the orders as regards this Marchiali?'

'There were no orders in his case, since, when he was brought here, he had neither jewellery, nor papers; indeed, he had scarcely any clothes.'

'Well, see how this simplifies matters! Really, Baisemeaux, you make mountains out of molehills. Just remain where you are and have the prisoner brought in.'

Baisemeaux obeyed. He called his lieutenant, and gave him an order, which the latter passed on, quite as a matter of course, to the next official concerned.

A quarter of an hour afterwards a door in the courtyard was heard to shut; this was the door of the dungeon which had just rendered up its prey to the free air.

Aramis blew out all the candles in the room with the exception of one which flickered to such an extent that it was impossible to see, by its light, any object distinctly. Footsteps were heard approaching.

'Go, and meet your men,' said Aramis to Baisemeaux.

The governor obeyed, and, having dismissed the major and the gaolers, returned to the room bringing with him a prisoner. Aramis had placed himself in the shadow, where he could see without being seen.

Baisemeaux, in a voice which faltered slightly, intimated to the young man that an order for his release had been received.

The prisoner received the intelligence in silence, and without showing the slightest agitation.

'You will swear – this is required by the regulations,' added the governor, ' – that you will divulge nothing that you may have seen or heard in the Bastille.'

The prisoner, seeing a crucifix, raised his hand and took the required oath.

'And now, sir, you are free. Where do you think of going to?'

The prisoner looked round the room as though missing something he had expected to see.

Then Aramis showed himself. 'I am here,' he said, 'to place my services at your disposal.'

The young man coloured slightly, and then, without hesitation, placed his arm within that of Aramis.

'God have you in His holy keeping,' he said in a voice, the firmness of which made the governor feel uneasy, whilst the form of the benediction surprised him more than a little.

Aramis shook hands with Baisemeaux, saying, as he did so, 'Does my order cause you uneasiness? Are you not afraid that it will be found here if they come to search the place?'

'I wish to keep it, monseigneur,' said Baisemeaux; 'if it were found here, it would certainly indicate my ruin, but, in such a case, I should have you to fall back upon as a last and powerful resource.'

'Being your accomplice, you would say?' replied Aramis shrugging his shoulders. 'Adieu, Baisemeaux!'

A carriage and pair were in attendance, the horses making the harness rattle with their impatience. Baisemeaux escorted the bishop to the bottom of the steps. Aramis signed to his companion to get into the carriage, and then followed him, his sole direction to the coachman being, 'Drive on.'

The carriage rattled over the pavement of the courtyard, an officer bearing a torch preceding it and giving orders to the various guards that it was to be allowed to pass unchallenged.

During the time which it took to open all the barriers, Aramis scarcely breathed, and his heart might have been heard beating against his ribs, whilst the prisoner, ensconced in a corner of the carriage, gave no more sign of being alive than did his companion.

At length a jolt, harder than the others, informed them that they had cleared the last water-kennel;[113] and the last gate – that of the Rue Saint-Antoine – was closed behind the carriage. No more walls either to right or left; but everywhere sky, life and liberty. The horses, held in hand until the middle of the *faubourg* was reached, then broke into a trot. Little by little, whether because they warmed to their work or because their driver bustled them, the pace improved, until, by the time Bucy was reached, the carriage seemed to fly, so high-mettled were the splendid animals attached to it. The first stage ended at Villeneuve-Saint-Georges where a change of horses awaited them, four instead of two, and this team took them on at a rattling pace in the direction of Melun, making a temporary halt in the midst of the forest at Sènart. The order to stop there had no doubt been given by Aramis in advance, for it was not necessary for him to give a single direction.

'What is the matter?' asked the prisoner, as if awakening from a long dream.

'It means, monseigneur,' said Aramis, 'that, before we go any farther, your royal highness and I must have a little conversation together.'

'I will wait for a fitting opportunity, monsieur,' replied the young prince.

'There could not be a better than the present one, monseigneur; here we are in the midst of a wood, and with no one to listen to what we say.'

'Except the postillion.'

'The postillion for this stage is deaf and dumb, monseigneur.'

'Well, I am at your disposal, Monsieur d'Herblay.'

'Will it please you to remain in the carriage?'

'Yes, we shall be quite comfortable, seated here; besides, I like this carriage, it has given me my liberty.'

'A moment, monseigneur, there is still one other precaution to take.'

'What is it?'

'We are here upon the high road, along which carriages and people on horseback may, at any time, be expected to pass. Such people seeing us at a standstill, might think that we had had a breakdown, and it would be wise to avoid the chance of any offers of assistance which might be made to us.'

'Tell the postillion to pull the carriage into a side road.'

'That is precisely what I should have suggested, monseigneur.'

Aramis touched the postillion, and made a sign. The latter, dismounting, took the leaders by the bridles and led them across the mossy herbage into a winding lane, at the bottom of which, on this moonless night, the shadows formed a curtain as black as ink. This done, the man stretched himself out upon a grassy slope, close to his horses, which cropped, to right and left of them, the young shoots of the oak trees.

'I am all attention,' said the young prince to Aramis, 'but what are you doing?'

'I am relieving myself of my pistols which I no longer require, monseigneur.'

## CHAPTER 37

### *The tempter*

'MY PRINCE,' said Aramis, seating himself in the carriage, and turning towards his companion, 'however insignificant may be my individuality, however moderate my ability and however low may be my place in the ranks of intelligent humanity, I have never hitherto talked with a man without being able to penetrate through that living mask which reflects the working of the brain. But this evening, sitting here in the dark, and having to contend against the reserve in which you are pleased to wrap yourself, I can read nothing from the expression of your face, and something tells me that I would have considerable difficulty in extracting from you the candid expression of your thoughts. I implore you, then, not for love of me – for subjects should weigh nothing in the balance held by princes – but for your own sake, to take note of, and remember every syllable that falls from my lips, every inflection even of my voice, for, in our present most grave and difficult position, every one of them will have a meaning and a value to which too great importance cannot be attached.'

'I hear you,' said the young prince with great deliberation, 'but I am neither particularly anxious to learn, nor afraid to listen to what you have to tell me,' and he buried himself still deeper amongst the thick cushions of the carriage as if he would hide from his companion not only the sight of himself but the very impression of his presence.

The darkness was intense, falling thick and impenetrable from the tops of the interlacing trees. The carriage, enveloped in the vast pall, could not have received a particle of light even had it been possible for a ray to have penetrated the dense mist in which the wood was hidden.

'Monseigneur,' Aramis continued, 'you are acquainted with the history of the government which rules France today. The king came forth from a childhood of captivity similar to your own, his position as obscure and circumscribed as yours; only, in place of having undergone, as you have, slavery in a prison, obscurity in solitude and straitened circumstances in confinement, it has been his lot to suffer all these hardships, humiliations and difficulties in broad daylight under the pitiless sun of royalty, upon a pinnacle, bathed in light, where every speck appears a formidable blemish and every glory a blot. The king has suffered, and, in the recollection of his suffering, will be keen to avenge himself. He will be a bad king. I do not mean that he will cause blood to be shed as did Louis XI or Charles IX,[114] for he has no mortal injuries to avenge, but he will devour the money and the substance of his people, because his own interests have suffered in a pecuniary sense. I have no compunction, therefore, in discussing openly the merits and demerits of this prince, knowing that my conscience will absolve me, even should I be constrained to pronounce judgment against him.'

Aramis paused, but it was not to listen whether silence still reigned in the forest; it was to seek fresh inspiration and to give his companion time to digest what he had already said to him.

'Everything done by God is well done,' continued the Bishop of Vannes, 'and so thoroughly am I persuaded of this, that I have long congratulated myself upon having been chosen as the repository of the secret which I have put you in the way of discovering. For the accomplishment of a great work, a just and all-wise providence requires an instrument at once persevering, possessing penetration and convinced of the justice of his cause. I am that instrument. I have acumen, perseverance and the necessary conviction. Moreover, I govern a mysterious people who have taken God's own motto for theirs, *Patiens quia aeternus*!'[115]

The prince made an involuntary movement.

'I notice, monseigneur, that you raise your head, as if you hear with amazement of the people whom I govern. You did not suspect that you were dealing with a king. Oh! Monseigneur, I am king of a people much humbled and disinherited: humbled, because their sole strength now lies in crawling; and disinherited, because never, almost never, in this world, have they reaped the harvest they have sown or gathered the fruit they have cultivated. They work for an abstraction. They heap together all their atoms of power for the formation of a man, and for this man, with the sweat of their toil, they create what the genius of the man shall, in his turn, convert into a nimbus glorified with the rays of all the crowns in Christendom. You know now what manner of man you have by your side, monseigneur, and he is here to tell you that he has taken you out of the abyss for a great purpose, and that, in furtherance of that design, he desires to place you above all the powers of the earth – even above himself.'

The prince laid his hand lightly upon the bishop's arm. 'You tell me,' he said, 'of this religious order of which you are chief, and, judging from what you say, it seems to me that, when you desire to throw down the man you have placed on a pinnacle, there is nothing can prevent his overthrow; you hold him in the hollow of your hand.'

'You are the son of King Louis XIII, and the brother of King Louis XIV, and you are the natural and legitimate heir to the throne of France. By keeping you near him, as he has kept Monsieur your younger brother, the king secured to himself the right of legitimate sovereignty. God, and the doctors alone can dispute his title, but doctors prefer a king who actually reigns to one who does not. God has decreed that you should be persecuted, but this persecution today places the crown upon your head. You had a right to reign, since your right has been disputed; you had a right to be proclaimed, seeing that you were kept in concealment; you are of the blood-royal, for they dare not spill your blood as they have shed that of your servants. Now see what providence, of whose workings you have so often complained, has done for you. You have been given the features, shape, age and voice of your brother, and all the causes of your persecution now become the causes of your restoration. Tomorrow, the day after tomorrow, at the earliest possible moment, royal phantom, living shade of Louis XIV, you will sit upon his throne, from which God, confiding the execution of His will to the arm of man, shall have hurled him, never to return.'

'I understand' said the prince, 'that no attempt will be made to shed my brother's blood.'

'His fate will be altogether in your hands.'

'And this secret which they have used to my detriment – '

'You will use against him. What did he do to hide it? He hid you, because, a living image of himself, you would inevitably confound the plot of Mazarin and Anne of Austria. You will have the same interest in concealing him; the parts will be reversed, but the likeness between prisoner and king will remain unaltered.'

'To return to what I was saying; who will guard him?'

'Who guarded you?'

'You know this secret, and have made use of it to my advantage. Who knows it besides yourself?'

'The queen, and Madame de Chevreuse.'

'What will they do?'

'Nothing at all. What *can* they do? They cannot recognise you, so long as you act with ordinary prudence.'

'That is true; but still there are grave difficulties.'

'Name them, prince.'

'My brother is married. I cannot take over his wife.'

'Spain shall consent to a divorce; it is in the interest of your new policy and of human morality; it embraces everything that is really noble and useful in this world.'

'Then, there is the imprisoned king; he will talk.'

'To whom can he talk? To the walls?'

'By *walls* you mean the men in whom you place confidence?'

'If need be, yes, your royal highness. And besides – '

'Besides?'

'I wish to impress upon you that the designs of God are not to be frustrated, and that each one is worked out, beforehand, to a result, like a mathematical calculation. The king, imprisoned, will not be to you the source of embarrassment that you were to the king, enthroned. He is proud and impatient by nature, but he has become demoralised by the homage and the exercise of sovereign power to which he has grown accustomed. God, who has decreed that the result of the mathematical calculation – of which I have had the honour to speak to you – should be your accession to the throne, and the undoing of him who has injured you, has also decreed that, before long, his sufferings shall cease altogether, and has, therefore, given him strength for a short conflict only. Imprisoned, as you were, as a private individual, left alone with your thoughts and deprived of every comfort, you still had the physical power and the strength of mind to enable you to endure all this misery; but your brother, captive, forgotten and under the most vexatious restraint, will not be able to endure it, and God will take him to Himself in his own good time – that is to say *soon*.'

At this point of the bishop's gloomy analysis, a night-bird, from the depths of the forest, uttered that long and wailing note to which no creature can listen without trembling.

'I shall send the dethroned king into exile,' said Philippe, shuddering; 'it will be more humane.'

'That is a matter entirely for the king's decision,' replied Aramis.

'And now, have I put the problem clearly before you? and is the solution of it such as your royal highness desired or foresaw?'

'Yes, monsieur, indeed you seem to have forgotten nothing – except, perhaps, two things.'

'What is the first?'

'Let us discuss it at once, and with the same frankness with which we have, hitherto, spoken. Let us consider the causes which can bring about the frustration of the hopes we have nourished; let us consider the risks which we run.'

'They would be tremendous, infinite and almost insurmountable, did not circumstances conspire to render them of no account. There are absolutely no risks for you and me, if your royal highness's courage and discretion equal in perfection the likeness to the king which nature has given you. I repeat that there is no danger; there are only *obstacles*, a word which occurs in every language, but which, had I the power, I would order to be expunged as useless and absurd.'

'Yes, indeed, monsieur, there is a very serious obstacle – an insurmountable danger which you appear to overlook.'

'Ah!' said Aramis.

'There is conscience, which cries aloud, and there is remorse which tears the heart.'

'True,' said the bishop; 'you remind me that faint-heartedness has to be reckoned with. Oh! you are quite right; that is, of course, a tremendous obstacle. The horse that is afraid to face the ditch boldly, jumps into the middle of it, and likely as not, is killed. The man who fights with trembling sword leaves loopholes through which his adversary deals him death. Yes, yes, you are right, monseigneur.'

'Have you a brother?' the young man asked Aramis.

'I am alone in the world,'[116] replied the latter in a voice as toneless and hard as the report of a pistol.

'But, surely, you love someone in the world?' urged Philippe.

'Not a soul – unless, indeed, it be yourself.'

The young man sank into so profound a silence, that the beating of his own heart sounded noisily in the ears of Aramis.

'Monseigneur,' he continued, 'I have not yet said all that I have to say to your royal highness; I have not yet offered to my prince all the salutary and useful advice that I have in store. It is, no doubt, unwise to dazzle with a brilliant light the eyes of the man who loves the shade, nor to deafen with the cannon's roar the ears of him who would fain seek the quietude of country life. Monseigneur, I have your happiness at heart; and do you, who prize so dearly the blue sky, the green fields and the fresh air, gather and treasure up the words I am about to utter. I know a country full of delights, an unexplored paradise, a corner of the world where, alone, unfettered and unknown, in the woods, in the midst of flowers and babbling streams, you may quickly forget all the suffering which human frailty has imposed on you. Oh! listen to what I say, my prince, for this is, indeed, no jest. I have a soul which can read the depths of your own. I will not take you, all unprepared, and cast you into the crucible of my own desires, caprice or ambition. All or nothing. You are chilled, unnerved and almost exhausted with the excess of emotion which an hour's liberty has caused you, and that is, for me, a certain indication that you cannot, for any length of time, endure the novelty of absolute and unchallenged freedom.

'Suppose you were to try a less ambitious life – a life more suited to your powers of endurance. God is my witness that I have no desire save that your welfare and happiness should result from any course which we may decide upon taking.'

'Speak, speak!' cried the prince, and he displayed a degree of vivacity which gave Aramis food for reflection.

'I know,' continued the bishop, 'in Bas-Poitou, a district of which scarcely anyone in France knows the existence. It covers twenty leagues of country – immense, is it not? Twenty leagues, monseigneur, of water, reed and rush, the whole studded with beautifully wooded islands. This huge marsh, clothed with reeds as with a thick mantle, slumbers silently and peacefully beneath the smiling heavens. A few fishermen, with their families, live lazily upon it, in large house-rafts of poplar or alder, the flooring of which is composed of reeds, whilst rushes, woven together, form the roof. These barks, or floating houses, are blown hither and thither at the caprice of the wind. If, by chance, they touch a bank, the shock of the contact is so slight that it rarely wakes the sleeping fisherman, who, if he goes ashore, only lands for the purpose of snaring or shooting some of the landrail, lapwing, wild duck, plover, teal or snipe with which the marshes abound. Silvery shad, enormous eels, voracious pike and perch, both grey and red, are taken by hundreds in his nets, so that he can choose the best of them and throw back the rest into the water. Never has the inhabitant of a town, never has a soldier, never, indeed, has anybody penetrated into this country, with its mild and delightful climate. Certain parts of the land produce vines which bear the most beautiful grapes, both black and white, and every week a boat is sent to fetch from the oven, which is common to all, the newly-baked bread, the appetising odour of which can be scented from afar. You would live there in all the pristine simplicity of the golden age. Happy with your dogs, your fishing lines, your guns and your pretty housecraft, you would live upon the spoils of the chase in the plenitude of security. Thus would you pass your life until, in the fulness of time, you would have fulfilled the destiny which heaven had appointed for you. There are a thousand pistoles in this bag, monseigneur, which is more than enough to purchase the whole district of which I have been speaking; more than enough to support you for as many years as you have days to live; and more than enough to make you the richest, most independent and happiest man in the whole country. Accept, as I offer it frankly and with all my heart. Then, you shall take a couple of these carriage horses, and, with my deaf and dumb servant to act as guide, you shall make the best of your way to the place I have been telling you about, taking care to travel only by night and to rest during the day. I shall thus have the satisfaction of knowing that I have rendered my prince the service which he has demanded at my hands, and I shall feel, moreover, that I have been the means of making a fellow-creature happy – a far more desirable achievement than making him powerful, seeing that it is so much more difficult of accomplishment.

'And now, what do you say, monseigneur? Here is the money, and, pray, do not hesitate to take it. You risk nothing at Poitou beyond the chance of catching a fever of which the natives would gladly cure you for a small sum out of your money bag. If you play the other part – I need not describe it – you run the risk of being assassinated on the throne or strangled in a prison. Upon my soul, I declare that, having weighed one position against the other, I should be puzzled, myself, to tell which to accept.'

'Monsieur,' replied the young prince, 'before I come to a decision, I should like to get out and walk about a little; perhaps God will direct me as to what I ought to do. You shall have my answer in ten minutes.'

'By all means, monseigneur,' said Aramis, bowing respectfully, so solemn and august was the voice which had just addressed him.

CHAPTER 38

## Crown and tiara

ARAMIS was the first to get out of the carriage, the door of which he held open for the prince, whom he watched as he tremulously set foot upon the ground, and with uncertain, almost staggering, steps, took a few paces backwards and forwards. It was painfully evident that this poor prisoner was quite unaccustomed to freedom of action.

It was the 15th of August, and getting on towards eleven o'clock at night. Heavy banks of clouds, which foretold a coming storm, obscured the sky, effectually shutting out all light and rendering it impossible to distinguish surrounding objects, even the openings of the various avenues of the wood being only just discernible through the general obscurity. But the scent which rose from the grass; the fresher and more pungent odours which the oaks exhaled; the sweet and balmy atmosphere which now, for the first time after so many years, surrounded him, the delightful sense of being at perfect liberty in the open country; all these things so appealed to the prince that, whatever may have been the reserve of his character – natural or assumed – he could no longer resist their influence, and gave vent to his emotion in a huge sigh of content. Then, little by little, he raised his heavy head and drank in great draughts of the sweet air which played about his upturned face, folding his arms across his chest, as if to repress, as far as possible, any outward manifestation of enjoyment. The sky above his head, the sound of flowing water, the movement of living creatures about him – was not this reality? And Aramis knew perfectly well that nothing, save such thoughts as these, could, for the present, occupy his companion's mind. The enchanting pictures of country life, free from all trouble, anxiety and restraint; that eternity of happy days to come, to which the youthful mind ever looks forward, should prove a tempting bait wherewith to take captive an unfortunate prisoner grown wan through confinement and sickly through inhaling the tainted air of the Bastille. Such was the prospect, it will be remembered, which was shown to him by Aramis, when he offered him the thousand pistoles which he had brought with him and the enchanted paradise which the envious deserts of Bas-Poitou hid from the eyes of the world. Such were the reflections of Aramis as he followed, with indescribable anxiety, the movements of Philippe, whom he saw gradually sink into a condition of profound meditation. The young prince, indeed, absorbed in thought, was no longer conscious of his immediate surroundings, but was engaged in praying for guidance at this momentous epoch of his career. This was, indeed, a trying moment for the Bishop of Vannes, who had never before found himself in such a state of perplexity. He, whose tact and strength of mind had, hitherto, enabled him to override and make light of obstacles which would have proved unsurmountable to less gifted men, was he to be baffled in the vast scheme which he had conceived through failing to make allowance for the effect which sudden freedom might have upon a man who had been shut up for years in solitary confinement? He waited in an extremity of agitation whilst Philippe did battle with his conflicting emotions, and the ten minutes for consideration for which the young man had stipulated were soon exhausted. Suddenly Philippe lowered his head, and his thoughts sank once more to the level of the earth. His look hardened, his brow contracted and his mouth assumed an expression of fierce determination. His look once more became resolute, but, this time, it reflected worldly ambition and resembled the look of Satan upon the mountain as he tempted with earthly splendour the Saviour of mankind. The look of Aramis softened as Philippe came forward and seized his hand. Then, said Philippe, 'We will go where the crown of France is to be found.'

'Is this your decision, my prince?' said Aramis.

'It is my decision.'

'Your irrevocable decision?'

Philippe did not deign to answer, but he looked at the bishop as if enquiring whether, having once made up his mind, a man would be likely to change it.

'Such looks are the flashes of fire which indicate the character of men,' said Aramis as he bowed over Philippe's hand. 'You will be a great man, monseigneur, I will stake my reputation on it.'

'We will now resume our conversation,' said the prince. 'There were two points upon which I required to be satisfied. The first was with regard to the dangers and difficulties which are likely to confront us. Well, that question has been disposed of. The other is as to the conditions you think of imposing upon me. It is now your turn to speak, Monsieur d'Herblay.'

'The conditions, monseigneur?'

'Yes; I presume you will not allow a trifle like that to stop me; and I trust you do not take me for a simpleton who thinks that you are acting altogether from disinterested motives. Have the goodness, then, to state openly and candidly what you have in view.'

'This is it, then, monseigneur; when once you are king – '

'When will that be?'

'Tomorrow evening – or rather some time tomorrow night.'

'I shall be glad if you will be a little more explicit.'

'I must first ask your royal highness a question.'

'By all means.'

'I sent to your highness, by a person in my confidence, a quantity of closely written and carefully considered notes which furnish your highness with full particulars as regards the persons who will form your court, and with whom you will be brought into daily contact.'

'I have read them all.'

'Carefully?'

'I know them by heart.'

'And you understood them? Forgive the question, but, in the present position, it is necessary that I should ask it. Of course, in a week's time, when you will be in full possession of liberty and power, it would be ridiculous to make such an enquiry.'

'Question me, then; and I will be the scholar repeating to his master the lesson he has learned by heart.'

'In the first place, then, as regards your family, monseigneur.'

'My mother, Anne of Austria? Oh! I know all about her troubles, and the complaint she suffers from.'

'And your second brother?' said Aramis, with a bow.

'You have added to your written notes a series of portraits so accurately drawn and painted that I have fitted them, without any difficulty, to the persons whose characters you have described. My brother is a dark, and rather handsome man, with a pale face; he does not love his wife, Henrietta, for whom I, Louis XIV, once had a fancy, and with whom I still carry on a flirtation, notwithstanding the grief she caused me when she dismissed Mademoiselle La Vallière from her service.'

'You must be very careful with that young lady,' said Aramis, 'because her attachment to the king is serious and genuine, and it is difficult to deceive the eyes of a woman who is really in love.'

'She is fair and has blue eyes, the tenderness of which will assure me of her identity. She walks with a slight limp, and every day writes a letter which I shall send a reply by Monsieur Saint-Aignan.'

'Do you know *him*?'

'As if he was before my eyes, and I know, moreover, the verses which he composed for me and those which I wrote in return.'

'Very good. Now we come to the ministers. Do you know them?'

'There is Colbert, whose face is plain, gloomy, but intelligent; his hair grows low down on his forehead; his head is large, and heavy-looking, and he is the mortal foe of Monsieur Fouquet.'

'Ah! we need not take the trouble to discuss *him*.'

'No, because, necessarily, I shall have to send him into exile.'

Aramis was lost in admiration. He contented himself, however, with repeating, 'You will be a very great man, monseigneur.'

'You see,' said the prince, 'that I have learnt my lesson thoroughly, and with God's aid, and your own, I can scarcely go wrong.'

'You have still a very sharp pair of eyes to deal with, monseigneur.'

'Ah! you mean Monsieur d'Artagnan, the captain of musketeers; he is your friend, I think.'

'I can truly describe him as "my friend", monseigneur.'

'It was he who escorted La Vallière to Chaillot; and delivered Monk, shut up in an iron box, to Charles II; it is he who has served my mother so well and faithfully, and to whom the crown of France is so much indebted as really to owe everything to him. Will you want me to send him into exile, too?'

'Never, monseigneur. D'Artagnan is a man to whom, at the proper time, I shall divulge everything. But be on your guard with him, monseigneur, for if he ferrets out the plot before it is revealed to him by me, you or I will either be taken or killed. D'Artagnan is a man of action.'

'I will not forget your warning. Now, as regards Monsieur Fouquet, what do you wish me to do with him?'

'Another moment, I beg of you, monseigneur, and forgive me if, in questioning you in this manner, I appear to be wanting in respect.'

'It is your duty, nay, your right to question me.'

'Before speaking of Monsieur Fouquet, I must not forget to mention another of my friends.'

'Monsieur Du Vallon; the Hercules of France? Well, his fortune seems to be already assured.'

'No, it is not of him that I would speak.'

'Then, it is the Comte de la Fère?'

'Yes, and of his son, who is, indeed, the son of all four of us.' – 'Ah! the poor fellow who is dying of love for La Vallière, of whom my brother deprived him so disloyally. Be easy on that head; I shall find a way to give her back to him. But tell me one thing, Monsieur d'Herblay; do people who are in love forget their injuries? Does a man ever forgive the woman who has deceived him? Is it a French characteristic? Is it one of the laws which govern the human heart?'

'A man who is as deeply in love as is Raoul de Bragelonne, generally, in the long run, forgets the crimes of the woman he adores; but I cannot say whether this will be so in Raoul's case.'

'I will bear it in mind. Is that all you have to say to me about your friend?'

'That is all.'

'Well, then, now as to Monsieur Fouquet. What is to be done with him?'

'By all means, let him retain his position of minister.'

'So be it; but he is now prime minister, is he not?'

'Not exactly.'

'But a prime minister of state will, surely, be necessary to an inexperienced and embarrassed king such as I shall be.'

'Your majesty will want a friend.'

'I have but one, and that is yourself.'

'You will have others later on, but none more devoted or more zealous in your interests.'

'You shall be my prime minister.'

'Not at once, monseigneur. That would cause too much suspicion and surprise.'

'Monsieur de Richelieu who was prime minister to my grandmother Marie de Medici, was simply Bishop of Luçon, as you are Bishop of Vannes.'

'I see that your royal highness has profited by reading my notes, and your wonderful discernment fills me with admiration.'

'And I am well aware that Monsieur de Richelieu, under the queen's patronage, quickly became cardinal.'

'It would be better for me to be created cardinal before becoming your majesty's prime minister.'

'You shall be cardinal before two months have passed, Monsieur d'Herblay, but that is a very small matter. You will fill me with regret if you confine yourself to so modest a request as that.'

'There is, indeed, something more to which I aspire, monseigneur.'

'Let me hear what it is.'

'Monsieur Fouquet cannot always remain at the head of affairs. He will soon be old. Thanks to the youthfulness which still remains to him, he is fond, when his duties will admit of it, of taking his pleasure; but he will lose this capacity for enjoyment with the first trouble or illness with which he may be afflicted. We will spare him trouble because he is a generous and noble-hearted man, but it is out of our power to prevent his falling ill. That is quite clear. When you have paid all Monsieur Fouquet's debts, and placed the finances of the state upon a sound basis, Monsieur Fouquet can still remain at the head of his little court of poets and painters, and we shall have the satisfaction of knowing that we have made him rich. Then, when I shall have become prime minister to your royal highness, I can turn my attention to your interests, and to my own.'

The young man looked at Aramis, curiously.

'Monsieur de Richelieu, of whom we were speaking,' continued the latter, 'committed the great mistake of confining himself to France alone. He allowed two kings, Louis XIII and himself, to occupy the same throne, whereas they might much more conveniently have had a throne each.'

'Two thrones?' exclaimed the young man in surprise.

'Yes,' said Aramis quietly, a cardinal who is prime minister, and is backed by the approval and powerful aid of the most Christian king of France, a cardinal to whom his master lends his treasures, his army and his counsel: such a man would be doubly in the wrong if he applied such powerful resources to France alone.

'Besides,' continued Aramis, looking Philippe straight in the eyes, 'you will not be such a king as was your father, in ill health, hesitating and tired of everything. You will be a king who will make use of his brains and of his sword. You will be able to govern by yourself, and I should but be in your way. The possibility of our friendship being, I will not say weakened, but in any way affected by mental reservation is not to be contemplated. I will give you the throne of France; you shall give me the throne of St Peter. When your loyal, firm and mailed hand shall have for its fellow the hand of such a Pope as I shall be, neither Charles V,[117] who possessed two-thirds of the world, nor Charlemagne,[118] who owned the whole of it, will be able to raise their heads higher that your waistband. I have formed no alliances; I have no prejudices; I will not involve you in the persecution of heretics; I will not embroil you in family quarrels; I will say, "The universe belongs to us two; to me the souls; to you the bodies," and, as in the course of nature I shall be the first to die, you will succeed to everything. What do you say to my scheme, monseigneur?'

'I say that I understand you thoroughly, and that you have made me both proud and happy; Monsieur d'Herblay you shall be cardinal, and my prime minister. Then you shall tell me what it is necessary for me to do in order to have you elected Pope, and I will do it. Ask of me any guarantee you like.'

'It would be useless. I shall never act unless something to your advantage will result from my action. I shall never mount the ladder without taking care that you have secured a safe footing upon the rung above me. I shall keep at a sufficient distance to avoid exciting your jealousy and sufficiently near to watch over your interests and retain your friendship. Most of the world's contracts are broken because the interests involved are one-sided. This, however, will never be the case with us, and guarantees are quite unnecessary.'

'And my brother – he will disappear?'

'Quite simply. He will be removed from his bed by means of a plank which yields to the pressure of a finger. He will go to sleep a crowned king, and will wake up a captive. From that moment you, alone, will rule, and you will have no interest more important than that of keeping me near you.'

'It is true. Here is my hand, Monsieur d'Herblay.'

'Allow me to kneel to you, sire, with every mark of respect. We will embrace upon the day when each shall have attained the object of his ambition. For you the crown; for me the tiara.'

'Embrace me today, as well; and, for my sake, be more than great, more than skilful and more than sublime in genius. Be good to me; be to me as a father.'

Aramis was almost overcome upon hearing the prince express himself in this manner, and felt in his heart what he had never before experienced. This feeling, however, he quickly managed to suppress.

'His father,' thought he, 'yes, his *holy father!*'

They then resumed their places in the coach which drove away at a rapid pace in the direction of Vaux-le-Vicomte.

CHAPTER 39

## The Château of Vaux-le-Vicomte

THE CHÂTEAU OF VAUX-LE-VICOMTE, which was situated about a league from Melun, was built by Fouquet in 1635.[119] There was, at the time, but little money in France, and of this Mazarin had taken the greater part, whilst Fouquet had expended the rest. However, as the defects of certain men are fertile and their vices useful, Fouquet, in squandering millions upon the erection of this palace, had brought together, in the process, three men of note: Levau, the architect, Le Nôtre, who laid out the gardens, and Le Brun, who decorated the interior.[120]

If there was a defect with which the château could be reproached, it was to be found in the extravagance and pretentiousness of its style, and, to this day, people speak of the number of acres covered by its roof, the very repairing of which would cost a fortune – as fortunes are reckoned nowadays.

Vaux-le-Vicomte, when its principal entrance-gates, supported by caryatides,[121] had been passed, presented to the view its main frontage, which looked upon a vast *cour d'honneur*, surrounded by deep moats, round which ran a magnificent stone balustrade.

Nothing more noble-looking could be conceived than the central façade of the building, raised upon a flight of steps – like a king upon his throne – and standing in a quadrangle provided at each corner with a handsome pavilion, of which the majestic Ionic columns rose to the very summit of the edifice.

The friezes ornamented with arabesques, and the pediments with which the pillars were crowned, gave to the structure an appearance of richness and grace, whilst the domes which surmounted the whole conferred a sense of scope and majesty. This palace, built by a subject, reminded one of those royal residences which Wolsey[122] believed it to be incumbent upon him to present to his master in order to allay the fits of jealousy to which he was prone.

But if magnificence and beauty greater than usual were to be found in any particular part of the palace, if anything could surpass the splendour of the interior arrangements, the richness of the gilding or the profusion of paintings and statues, it was to be sought in the park and the gardens of Vaux. The wonderful fountains which, in 1635, were looked upon as marvels, are still so regarded, and the cascades excited the admiration of kings and princes. We will not attempt to describe the famous grotto, which has been the theme of so much versification, and where dwelt the celebrated Nymph of Vaux whom Pélisson made converse with La Fontaine, lest we should recall the criticisms of Boileau:

> *Ce ne sont que festons, ce ne sont qu'astragales . . .*
> *Et je me sauve à peine au travers du jardin.*

> The house is all festoons and fillets, pillars and
> pilasters; . . . even the gardens are artificial, I can find
> scarce a trace of nature there.

We will follow the example of Despréaux[123] and enter the park, which has only existed eight years, but in which stand lofty trees, their foliage already gilded by the first rays of the rising sun.

Le Nôtre, with the view of pleasing his Maecenas[124] by bringing the park to a state of perfection as rapidly as possible, had despoiled all the nurseries, for miles round, of such trees as had had their growth accelerated by artificial means. Every tree in the neighbourhood of promising appearance had been taken up by the roots and transplanted to the park. Fouquet might well purchase trees for the adornment of his park, seeing that he had already bought three entire villages, as they stood, in order to enlarge it. Monsieur de Scudéry[125] said of this palace that, in order to provide for it a sufficient supply of water, Monsieur Fouquet had converted a river into a thousand fountains and reunited the waters of a thousand fountains in the formation of torrents. Monsieur de Scudéry, in his *Clélie*, said many other things about this palace, the attractions of which he describes with great minuteness, but we would rather send any of our readers, who may feel sufficient curiosity on the subject, to Vaux itself, than refer them to *Clélie* for information, for there are as many leagues between Paris and Vaux, as there are volumes of the work in question.

This splendid mansion had now been prepared for the reception of the greatest monarch on earth.

Monsieur Fouquet's friends had brought with them some actors with their theatrical scenery, others, a crowd of sculptors and painters, whilst others, again, arrived with newly mended pens eager to perpetrate the numerous *impromptus* which the occasion demanded.

The cascades, which the presiding nymphs seemed unable to control, poured forth torrents of water brighter than crystal and drenched the bronze Tritons and Nereids with spray that sparkled like fire in the rays of the sun.

An army of attendants hurried hither and thither about the courtyards and corridors, whilst Fouquet, who had only arrived that morning, calmly surveyed the scene and gave his final orders after the officers appointed for the purpose had completed their inspection.

It was, as we have said, the 15th of August. The sun's scorching beams fell upon the shoulders of the bronze and marble deities, warmed the water in the conch-shells and ripened the magnificent peaches in the fruit-gardens, those same peaches of which the king spoke regretfully fifty years after, when at Marly, there being a scarcity of the fruit in the gardens which had cost twice as much money as had been spent on the gardens at Vaux, he remarked to someone, 'You are too young to have tasted Monsieur Fouquet's peaches.'

Alas! for human gratitude; alas! for vaunted fame; alas! for all earthly glory. This was the man who prided himself upon being quick to recognise merit in any shape; who had absorbed the inheritance of Nicolas Fouquet; who had appropriated his Le Nôtre and Le Brun, and condemned him to lifelong confinement in a state prison; this was the man, we say, who now only deigned to remember his fallen enemy for the excellence of the peaches which grew on his walls.

What use to have thrown his thirty million into the waters of his fountains, the casting furnaces of his statuaries, the portfolios of his poets, the paint-boxes of his limners? Fouquet, for all his sacrifices, had failed lamentably and conspicuously to preserve his memory green amongst posterity.

Yet a ripening peach half concealed by the green leaves amid which it had grown, a paltry globe which a field-mouse could have nibbled up in five minutes, sufficed to recall to the king's memory the unhappy shade of the last of the great finance ministers of France.

Satisfied that Aramis had seen to the proper disposition about the palace of his numerous guests, and had made due provision for their comfort, Fouquet no longer troubled himself with details, but surveyed the arrangements in their entirety. Gourville showed him where the fireworks would be exhibited and Molière took him to inspect the theatre. At length, having been the rounds of the chapel, the reception-rooms and all the galleries, Fouquet, thoroughly tired out, was descending the staircase when he caught sight of Aramis, who was beckoning to him. He made haste to join his friend, who brought him to a halt in front of a large painting to which Le Brun, bathed in sweat, besmeared with paint and pale from fatigue and inspiration, was in the act of putting a few finishing touches. This was the portrait of the king, dressed in the court-suit which Percerin had allowed the Bishop of Vannes to see upon the occasion described in a previous chapter. Fouquet placed himself in front of this portrait, which seemed to live, so perfect were the effects of its flesh-tints and warmth of colouring. He looked at it with admiration, and recognised the immense amount of work which must have been bestowed upon it: then, at a loss to find a fitting recompense for this Herculean labour, he threw his arm round the artist's neck and embraced him. It is true that, by thus coming into close contact with the painter, he ruined a suit of clothes worth a thousand pistoles; but no matter, Le Brun was overjoyed and Fouquet was content. If this was a moment of triumph for the artist, it was one of bitterness for

Percerin, who had followed in the wake of Monsieur Fouquet, and who now recognised in Le Brun's portrait the costume which he had made for the king – a work of art, he said, the equal of which could not be found, except, perhaps, in the wardrobe of Monsieur Fouquet himself. His lamentations were cut short by a signal which was made from the roof of the mansion, from which the sentinels of Vaux had descried the procession of the king and the queens approaching, across the open plain from the direction of Melun, through which place the king had passed attended by a long train of carriages and horsemen.

'In an hour,' said Aramis to Fouquet.

'In an hour,' repeated the latter, with a sigh.

'And the people are asking of what good are these royal fêtes!' continued the Bishop of Vannes, with his false laugh.

'Alas! I, myself, who am not "the people", am asking that question also.'

'I will answer it in twenty-four hours, monseigneur; now, you must wear a smiling face, for this is a day of rejoicing.'

'Well, believe me if you can, d'Herblay,' continued the minister in a confidential tone, pointing with his finger to the royal procession which was now visible in the distance, 'there is, I am afraid, no love lost between us, but I don't know how it is that since I see him approaching my doors – '

'Well, what?'

'Since he is coming here as my guest, he seems to be more sacred to me; I seem to recognise him as my lawful sovereign; he seems almost dear to me.'

'*Dear?* Oh! yes,' said Aramis, playing upon the word as, later on, did the Abbé Terray[126] with Louis XV.

'Don't joke, d'Herblay. I really feel that, if he would let me, I could love that young man.'

'It is not to me that you should say so, but to Monsieur Colbert.'

'To Monsieur Colbert?' cried Fouquet, 'and why to him?'

'Because when he becomes minister, he might give you a pension from the king's privy purse.'

Having fired this shot, Aramis bowed, and turned away.

'Where are you going?' asked Fouquet, who had suddenly become thoughtful.

'I am going to change my clothes, monseigneur.'

'Which room do you occupy, d'Herblay?'

'The blue room, on the second floor.'

'The one which is immediately over the king's?'

'Exactly.'

'But you will be under great restraint there! You won't be able to move for fear of disturbing his majesty.'

'At night, monseigneur, I either sleep or read in bed.'

'But your attendants?'

'I shall only have my reader with me. And now, adieu, monseigneur: don't over-fatigue yourself. Remember that you must keep in good trim to receive the king.'

'I shall see you presently, I suppose, and your friend Monsieur Du Vallon too?'

'Yes; his room is close to my own. He is dressing at the present moment.'

Fouquet, with a bow and a smile, then moved away, with the air of a commander-in-chief about to visit his outposts upon receiving intelligence of the enemy's approach.

## CHAPTER 40

## *The wine of Melun*

THE KING had really entered Melun merely with the intention of passing through the town. He was eager for amusement; only twice during the journey had he been able to catch sight of La Vallière, and, foreseeing that he would not be able to speak to her until the evening, after the reception and its attendant ceremonies, he was anxious to push on to Vaux with as little delay as possible. But he had reckoned without his captain of musketeers and Monsieur Colbert.

Like Calypso, who was inconsolable at the departure of Ulysses,[127] our Gascon's mind was terribly exercised at not being able to guess why Aramis had wanted Percerin to show him the king's new costumes.

'It is certain,' he said to himself, 'that my friend, the Bishop of Vannes, would not have been so persistent unless he had some object in view,' and again he cudgelled his brains to no purpose.

D'Artagnan, so much in his element amidst all the intrigues of the court, d'Artagnan, who understood Fouquet's position better than Fouquet did himself, had conceived the wildest suspicions upon the announcement of this fête, the cost of which would ruin a rich man, whilst, to a man already ruined, the very idea of such an undertaking seemed to be absolute madness. Then, again, there was the presence of Aramis who had returned from Belle-Isle, and been appointed, by Monsieur Fouquet, director in chief of all the arrangements. How was the extraordinary interest he showed in the minister's affairs to be accounted for? And, again, why had he visited Baisemeaux at the Bastille? All this mystery had haunted d'Artagnan incessantly during the last few weeks, and his inability to explain it had almost driven him crazy.

'It is only,' said he, 'by attacking him sword in hand, that it is possible to get the better of a man like Aramis. So long as Aramis was simply a soldier, one stood some chance against him, but, now that he wears a stole[128] in addition to a breast-plate, a man has no chance at all. But what the deuce is he after?' and, once more, was d'Artagnan wrapped in a brown study.

'After all, if his only object is the overthrow of Monsieur Colbert, what does it matter? and what else can he have in view?' and d'Artagnan scratched his forehead, that generous soil from which so many brilliant ideas had, from time to time, been turned up by the plough-share of his nails. It occurred to him to tackle Monsieur Colbert on the subject; but friendship, and the oath of long ago,[129] so bound him to Aramis that he at once dismissed the idea, the more readily because, in his heart, he hated the financier.

Then, again, he might unbosom himself to the king; but the king would understand nothing of his suspicions, which, after all, rested on no solid basis. Finally, he resolved to address himself to Aramis direct, the very first time he saw him.

'I will ask him point-blank, without any warning; I will place my hand upon his heart, and he will tell me – what will he tell me? Well, he will tell me something at all events, for I am convinced that there is a great deal to be divulged.'

Having thus calmed his mind, d'Artagnan busied himself with his preparations for the journey, and paid the utmost attention to the military division of the king's household, which was as yet inconsiderable, taking care that what there was of it should be efficiently officered, and properly disciplined. The result was that the king reached Melun at the head of his musketeers, his Swiss Guards and a picket of the French Guards – quite a little army.

Monsieur Colbert looked upon these warriors with the greatest satisfaction, and, indeed, expressed a wish that they had been a third more in number.

'Why?' asked the king.

'To do greater honour to Monsieur Fouquet,' replied Colbert.

'To ruin him more quickly,' thought d'Artagnan.

The army appeared before Melun, and the chief authorities presented the keys of the town to the king, inviting him to enter the Hôtel-de-Ville in order to drink the wine of honour.

The king, who had reckoned upon passing straight through the town and reaching Vaux without any stoppage, got red in the face with anger.

'Who is the fool who is responsible for this nonsense?' he muttered between his teeth, whilst the chief magistrate waded through a long and dutiful address.

'Not I,' replied d'Artagnan, 'but I think Monsieur Colbert arranged it.'

'What is Monsieur d'Artagnan pleased to say?' enquired Colbert, who caught the sound of his own name.

'I was pleased to ask whether it was not you who arranged for the king to halt here and taste the wine of Brie?'

'Yes, monsieur, it was I.'

'Then, it was you whom the king called by a certain name.'

'What name was that, sir?'

'I hardly remember, for the moment. Let me see – idiot? no, that was not it. I think *stupid fool* was the name. His majesty applied to the genius who conceived the idea of delaying his journey for the purpose of drinking the wine of Melun.'

Having fired this volley, d'Artagnan placidly patted the neck of his horse, whilst Colbert's great head swelled up to the size of a bushel-basket. D'Artagnan, seeing how ugly his rage made him look, did not stop halfway. The magistrate still droned on with his address and the king was becoming redder and more furious every instant.

'Look at the king,' continued the musketeer coolly, 'he'll have a fit in another minute. What the devil put this idea into your head, Monsieur Colbert? 'Tis a damned unlucky one.'

'Sir,' answered the financier, stiffly. 'I was inspired by my zeal for the service of the king.'

'Bah!' cried d'Artagnan.

'Why, sir! Melun is a place of some importance, and, moreover, a town which pays up well; it would be extremely impolitic to put a slight upon its inhabitants.'

'There now!' said d'Artagnan, 'I, who am no financier, should have given you credit for quite another motive.'

'What motive would you have attributed to me, monsieur.'

'That of annoying Fouquet, who is awaiting our arrival in a fever of impatience.' This was a home thrust which knocked Colbert off his perch and caused him to retire with his tail between his legs.

Fortunately the address had, by this time, come to an end; the king tasted some wine which was handed to him, and the cavalcade resumed its progress through the city. The king bit his lips, for night was coming on apace and all hope of a walk with La Vallière had to be abandoned.

Thanks to the elaborate instructions which had been given, it would take at least four hours before the whole of the king's household could be disposed of at Vaux, and the king, who was boiling over with impatience, hurried on, with the queens, as fast as he could so as to arrive before nightfall; but as soon as the procession had made a fresh start new difficulties arose.

'Is not the king going to sleep at Melun?' asked Colbert of d'Artagnan in a low voice.

It was anything but a happy inspiration which prompted Monsieur Colbert to ask this question of the chief of the musketeers. The latter guessed that the king would not be contented to stay where he was, but he did not wish him to reach Vaux unless suitably attended and he was anxious that His majesty should be accompanied by a full escort. On the other hand he could not but see that the prospect of further delay would be extremely irritating to that impatient character. How then was he to reconcile the two difficulties? D'Artagnan finally decided to repeat Colbert's question to the king.

'Sire,' said he, therefore, 'Monsieur Colbert desires to know whether it is your majesty's pleasure to sleep at Melun tonight?'

'Sleep at Melun! What for?' exclaimed Louis XIV. 'Sleep at Melun! Who the devil would dream of such a thing, when Monsieur Fouquet is expecting us this evening?'

'It was,' replied Colbert quickly, 'the fear of causing delay to your majesty who, according to the laws of etiquette, cannot enter any place, with the exception of one of the royal residences, until the quarters for the soldiers have been marked out by the quartermaster and the garrison properly disposed of.'

D'Artagnan, biting his moustaches, listened with all his ears, and the queens listened attentively also. They were tired and wanted to rest, and were especially anxious that no opportunity should be afforded the king of walking, in the evening, with Monsieur de Saint-Aignan and the ladies of the court; for, if etiquette confined the princesses to their own apartments, there was nothing to prevent the ladies, their duties having been performed, from amusing themselves in any way that seemed good to them.

It was plain that these conflicting interests, accumulating in vapours, must produce clouds, and that these clouds must be indications of a coming tempest. The king, having no moustaches to bite, gnawed the handle of his whip in his perplexity. D'Artagnan was looking as amiable, and Colbert as ill-tempered, as possible.

Whom was there for his majesty to fasten his teeth into?

'We will consult the queen,' said Louis XIV, bowing to the ladies.

This attention touched the heart of Maria-Theresa, whose instincts were kind and generous, and, who, left to her own free will, replied, 'I desire to do whatever your majesty wishes.'

'How long will it take to reach Vaux?' asked Anne of Austria, speaking slowly and holding her hand to her breast, which was the seat of her suffering.

'An hour for your majesty's carriages,' replied d'Artagnan who, catching the king's eye, hastened to add, 'and a quarter of an hour for his majesty.'

'We could arrive there by daylight,' said the king.

'But the billeting of the military escort,' objected Colbert gently, 'will cause the king to lose any time that he may previously have gained by travelling quickly.'

'Double-dyed ass!' thought d'Artagnan, 'it is well for you that I have no interest in destroying your credit, for I could demolish it in ten minutes. Were I in the king's place,' he added aloud, 'and were paying a visit to Monsieur Fouquet, I should leave my escort behind me, and go simply as a friend. I should merely take with me my captain of musketeers; it would be paying my host a very high compliment.'

The king's eyes shone with delight.

'That is excellent advice, Mesdames,' said he, 'we will go as friend to friend. You, gentlemen, who are in charge of the carriages will come on at an easy pace; but we who are on horseback will ride forward in advance.' He rode off followed by all who were mounted, with the exception of Colbert, who hid his ugly head behind his horse's neck.

'I shall be compensated,' said d'Artagnan, as he galloped along, 'by having a little talk with Aramis in the course of the evening. And, then, Monsieur Fouquet is a man of honour. *Mordieu!* I have said so, and who shall doubt my word?'

Thus it came to pass that, towards seven o'clock in the evening, without sound of trumpet or advanced guard, without outriders or musketeers, the king presented himself at the gates of Vaux, where Monsieur Fouquet, who had been warned of his approach, had awaited him for the last half hour, with uncovered head, in the midst of his household and his friends.

CHAPTER 41

## *Nectar and ambrosia*

MONSIEUR FOUQUET held the king's stirrup. The monarch, dismounting from his horse, bowed graciously and, more graciously still, held out his hand to Fouquet, who, in spite of a faint resistance on the part of the king, carried it respectfully to his lips. His majesty decided to await the arrival of the carriages in the outer court-yard. Nor had he to wait long, for the roads had been so cleared and levelled, by Fouquet's orders, that it would have been difficult to find, between Melun and Vaux, a stone as big as an egg. The carriages, therefore, travelling smoothly, as if on a carpet, conveyed the ladies without any jolting or fatigue, and arrived at their destination at about eight o'clock. They were received by Madame Fouquet, and at the precise moment of their arrival a light, brilliant as the day, shot out from each tree, vase and marble statue, and this enchantment lasted until their majesties had entered the palace.

All these wonders which the chronicler has collected and preserved in his account of the proceedings, at the risk of being considered a teller of fables, these magical effects which abolished night and improved upon nature, in short, this combination of everything that was beautiful and luxurious, did Monsieur Fouquet, in sober earnest, lay at the feet of his sovereign, in this place of enchantment, of which no monarch in Europe could flatter himself that he possessed the equal.

We will pass over the grand banquet, at which their majesties met again, the concerts and the fairy-like spectacles which were provided, and content ourselves with mentioning that the king's face, which at first was all brightness and animation, quickly clouded over and showed unmistakable symptoms of discontent. He was comparing his own residences with Fouquet's, and remembering that such poor attempts at luxury as they contained, although intended for his use, were in no sense his own personal property. The great vases of the Louvre, the old furniture and plate of Henri II, of François I and Louis XI were only historical monuments, mere works of art, which came to him, as a matter of course, in his capacity of reigning sovereign.

With Fouquet, the value of his possessions lay as much in the workmanship which had been bestowed on them as in the articles themselves. Fouquet ate from a service of gold plate which had been specially cast and engraved for himself; he had wines of which the King of France did not even know the names, and he drank them out of goblets, each of which was worth more than the whole royal cellar.

What can be said of the apartments, the hangings, the pictures, the servants and officers of all sorts? Who shall describe the wise ordering of the household, where common sense reigned rather than etiquette, and ceremonial was made subservient to comfort, and where, by order of the host, the pleasure and gratification of the guests took precedence over everything?

The swarm of people who noiselessly performed the duties allotted to them; the vast number of the guests – which yet was smaller than that of the servants deputed to wait on them – the immense quantity of gold and silver plate, the floods of light, the masses of rare flowers for which the hot-houses had been ransacked and which were of unrivalled beauty; the perfect harmony which prevailed; all these things, which were but a prelude to what was to follow, filled everyone with admiration, and the visitors continually showed their surprise and delight, not by gesture or exclamation, but in that silent enjoyment which is manifested by the courtier who is no longer under the influence of a master's retaining hand.

The king, whose eyes swelled with surprise, dared not look at the queen, and Anne of Austria, haughtier than any other living being, did her best to show her host that she was quite indifferent to all the pains that were being taken for her gratification. The young queen, on the other hand, who was naturally kind-hearted and a trifle inquisitive, appreciated everything that was done for her, made an excellent dinner and enquired the names of several of the fruits on the table.

Fouquet replied that he did not know their names, although the fruits were of his own growing, and he often, personally, attended to their cultivation, being indeed, an expert in all that related to the rearing of exotics. The king noticed and appreciated the delicacy of his conduct, but felt, none the less, the humiliation of his position. He thought that the queen was a little too unreserved and Anne of Austria a trifle too stately. For his own part, he did his best to maintain a happy mean between an excess of dignity and an extreme of condescension. But Fouquet had foreseen it all, as, indeed, he foresaw everything.

The king had stated expressly that, during his stay with Monsieur Fouquet, he did not wish to dine by himself, according to the rules of strict etiquette, but that he should prefer to join the general dinner table; Fouquet had, however, contrived that Louis, although seated in the midst of his other guests, should still be served apart from the rest of them. He took care, moreover, that the dinner, which was wonderful if only on account of the multiplicity of the dishes which composed it, should include everything that the king liked best, so that Louis, who had the reputation of being first trencherman in the kingdom, had no excuse for saying that he was starved. Fouquet did better even than that, for, although, at the king's express desire, he took his seat at the table, no sooner did the soup make its appearance than he rose, and personally waited on his majesty, whilst Madame Fouquet attended to the wants of the queen mother. The disdain of Juno and the surliness of Jupiter[130] were not proof against these acts of extreme courtesy, and, accordingly, the queen ate a biscuit dipped in San-Lucar wine, whilst the king devoured everything that was offered him, frequently assuring the gratified Monsieur Fouquet that it would be impossible for anyone to provide a better dinner. Hereupon the remainder of the guests fell upon the food with such gusto and determination as to remind one of a flight of locusts devastating a countryside, and destroying, to the last blade, every green thing that appeared above the surface of the soil. All this, however, did not prevent the king from becoming as gloomy after dinner as he had been good-tempered and affable during its progress, and his dissatisfaction was in no way decreased by the marked deference with which Monsieur Fouquet was treated by the courtiers.

D'Artagnan, who ate a great deal and drank hard without showing it, kept a vigilant eye upon his surroundings and made a number of observations which proved useful to him.

When dinner was over, the king expressed a wish to walk in the park, which was brilliantly illuminated. The moon, too, as if she had placed herself at the orders of the Lord of Vaux, shed her silvery light upon the trees and lakes. The evening air was mild and the paths and avenues were so well gravelled as to make walking a pleasure. The fête was a complete success, for the king having come across La Vallière in one of the winding paths of the wood, was able to press her hand and say, 'I love you,' without being overheard by anyone except d'Artagnan who followed and Monsieur Fouquet who led the way.

This night of enchantments wore on, and the king asked to be shown to his room. This was the signal for a general movement. The queens retired to their respective apartments to the sound of soft music. The king, on going up to bed, found the staircase lined by his musketeers, whom Fouquet had brought from Melun and invited to supper.

D'Artagnan cast from him all his mistrust; he was tired, had made an excellent dinner and was determined thoroughly to enjoy a fête given upon a scale of such princely magnificence.

'Monsieur Fouquet,' he said, 'is the man for me.'

With much ceremony, the king was conducted to the Chamber of Morpheus,[131] of which we will now attempt to give our readers a slight description.

It was the largest and most beautiful apartment in the palace. Le Brun had decorated the dome with paintings depicting the dreams, both pleasant and painful, which Morpheus presents to the sleeping senses of kings no less than of ordinary mortals. Every bright vision which is conjured up in dreams had the painter made use of for the embellishment of his frescoes, one part of which soothed whilst the other terrified the senses, and cups of poison, daggers in murderous hands and phantoms in hideous masks appeared as companion pictures to the more attractive paintings.

The king shivered as he entered this magnificent room, and Fouquet anxiously enquired it he were ill.

'No, I am only tired,' said Louis, who looked very pale.

'Will your majesty have your attendants sent to you at once?'

'No, I have several persons to speak to first,' replied the king. 'Let Monsieur Colbert be sent for,' and Fouquet bowed, and left the room.

CHAPTER 42

## *A Roland for an Oliver*[132]

D'ARTAGNAN was not the man to let the grass grow under his feet, and, upon learning that Aramis was at Vaux, he at once went in search of him.

Now, the king being safe inside the palace, Aramis had shut himself up in his room for the purpose, no doubt, of maturing some fresh scheme for his majesty's entertainment. Having caused his name to be announced, d'Artagnan found the Bishop of Vannes, in the company of Porthos and two or three modern Epicureans, seated in the chamber which, from the colour of its hangings, was known as the blue room.

Aramis arose to welcome his friend, offering him the most comfortable chair in the room, and, as it was quickly apparent that he had something of a private nature to say to the bishop, the Epicureans discreetly withdrew. Porthos, alone, did not move; but he had dined well, and was sound asleep in the chair, so that his presence was no restraint upon the conversation of the others. He slept on placidly, whilst his friends talked to the harmonious bass of his snoring. D'Artagnan felt that it devolved upon him to open the conversation, and, recognising that the subject upon which he had to speak was a somewhat difficult one, he plunged into it at once.

'Well, here we are at Vaux,' he began.

'Yes, d'Artagnan, here we are; how do you like the place?'

'Very much, and I also like Monsieur Fouquet immensely.'

'Yes; is he not charming?'

'No one could be more so.'

'I am told that the king was rather cool to him at first, but that afterwards his manner thawed a little.'

'Did you not notice it yourself, then, that you say "I am told"?'

'No; I was engaged with the gentlemen who have just left the room in making arrangements for the theatrical performances and the tournament to be held tomorrow.'

'Ah! is that so? Then, I suppose you have been appointed master of the ceremonies?'

'Well, you know that I have always been rather addicted to any form of amusement that gives scope to the imagination. I have always had a touch of poetry in my composition.'

'Yes! I remember you used to write verses, and very charming ones, too.'

'For my part, I have forgotten them; but I like to hear the verses of other men, especially when they bear the names of Molière, Pélisson, La Fontaine, etc.'

'Do you know the idea that occurred to me at dinner-time?'

'No; please enlighten me. I should never guess it; you are so full of ideas.'

'Well, then, it occurred to me that Louis XIV is not the real King of France.'

'No?' said Aramis, with an involuntary start, 'who is then?'

'Monsieur Fouquet.'

Aramis gave a sigh of relief, and smiled. 'Why, you are like all the rest – jealous!' he said. 'I will wager it was Monsieur Colbert who put that idea into your head!' and, here, d'Artagnan, to avert suspicion, related the little episode of Colbert and the wine of Melun.

'He is a low-bred ruffian, that Colbert!' said Aramis.

'He is that,' asserted d'Artagnan.

'And only to think,' continued the bishop, 'that he will be minister in four months' time.'

'Bah!' said d'Artagnan.

'And that you will give him unquestioning service, as you did Richelieu and Mazarin.'

'And as you do Fouquet,' said d'Artagnan.

'With this difference, my friend, that Fouquet is not Colbert.'

'That is true,' said d'Artagnan, affecting a gentle melancholy.

'But,' he added after a short pause, 'Why do you say that Colbert will be minister in four months?'

'Because Monsieur Fouquet will, then, be minister no longer.'

'Do you mean that he will be ruined?'

'Absolutely.'

'Why, then, does he give these fêtes?' said the musketeer, in so natural a tone of benevolent interest that Aramis was for the moment taken in by it. 'Why did you not dissuade him from giving them?'

This was going a little too far, and Aramis was on his guard again in a moment. 'It is done,' he said, 'with the object of making interest with the king.'

'What! by ruining himself?'

'For the king, yes.'

'That seems to be a strange view to take.'

'It is necessity, my friend.'

'I really can't see that, my dear Aramis.'

'No? but have you not remarked the growing antagonism of Monsieur Colbert, and how he is urging the king to get rid of Monsieur Fouquet?'

'Yes, of course; that must be obvious to everybody.'

'And you are not aware that a cabal has been formed against Monsieur Fouquet?'

'Yes, I know that amongst other things.'

'Well, then, ask yourself what sort of a figure the king would cut were he to ally himself with a party whose object is to ruin the man who has spent his last penny in doing honour to his majesty.'

'That is true, certainly,' said d'Artagnan slowly, and but half convinced, whilst he was anxious to approach the subject from another point of attack.

'There are follies *and* follies,' he continued, 'and I must say I do not like those which you are committing.'

'Which do you mean?'

'I grant you that the banquet, the ball, the concert, the tournament, the cascades, the fireworks, the presents and the illuminations are all very well, but surely you might have stopped there! Was it necessary to put the entire household into new liveries and costumes, for example?'

'I agree with you there, and I pointed it out to Monsieur Fouquet myself. He replied that were he rich enough, he would have prepared, for the king's reception, a château absolutely new from weathercock to basement, new both inside and out, and that, when the king had left, he would have set fire to the whole, so that it might never be used by anyone else.'

'A purely Spanish idea!'

'I told him so, and he added, "I shall consider him an enemy who counsels me to spare expense." '

'It is madness, I tell you, and so is that portrait.'

'What portrait?' said Aramis.

'The portrait of the king, and the *surprise*, too.'

'What surprise?'

'The surprise in connection with which you procured those patterns from Monsieur Percerin.' D'Artagnan stopped short.

He had shot his arrow, and could now only watch its flight.

'It is a graceful compliment to pay the king,' said Aramis.

D'Artagnan walked up to his friend and, taking him by both hands, looked him straight in the eyes. 'Aramis,' he said, 'do you still care for me a little?'

'What a question to ask!'

'Good! do me a favour then, and tell me for what purpose you procured those patterns of the king's costumes from Percerin.'

'Come with me, and ask poor Le Brun, who has been at work on them for the last two days and nights.'

'Aramis, you may tell that tale to everyone else; but, to me – '

'Really, d'Artagnan, you astonish me!'

'Just tell me the truth, like a good fellow. You would not like anything unpleasant to happen to me, would you?'

'My dear fellow, you become more and more incomprehensible; what the devil have you got into your head?'

'You used to believe in the correctness of my instincts. Do you still believe in it? Well, my instincts tell me that some hidden project is on foot.'

'A project which I am concealing?'

'Well, of course I do not actually *know*, but I could swear to it, nevertheless.'

'D'Artagnan,' said Aramis, 'you cause me great pain. If any project existed which I felt it my duty to conceal from you, I should hold my tongue. If, on the contrary, there were one which I considered you ought to know of, I should have revealed it to you before now.'

'No, Aramis, no; certain projects are only to be revealed at a favourable opportunity.'

'Well, then, my friend,' said the bishop, laughing, 'all I can say is that the favourable opportunity has not yet arrived.'

D'Artagnan shook his head with a mournful smile.

'Oh! friendship, friendship!' he cried, 'you are, indeed, but an empty name. Here, for instance, is a man who would allow himself to be cut in pieces for my sake.'

'And that is a fact,' said Aramis proudly.

'And yet this man, who would shed his blood for me, will not open the smallest corner of his heart to me. Friendship! I repeat that like everything that glitters in this world, you are but a delusion and a snare.'

'Do not speak like that of our friendship,' replied the bishop, 'It cannot be of such friendship as *that*, that you are speaking.'

'Look at us, Aramis, here are three out of the four of us. You are deceiving me; I am suspicious of you; and Porthos is sound asleep. A nice trio of friends, isn't it? A pretty relic of old times!'

'I have only one thing to tell you, d'Artagnan, and I swear it on the gospel. You are as dear to me as ever. If ever I doubt you, it is on the part of others, and not because of anything which concerns you and me alone. Of every undertaking in which I may be successful, a fourth share will always be yours. Make me the same promise.'

'That is a very generous sentiment, Aramis.'

'Possibly.'

'If you are merely conspiring against Monsieur Colbert, tell me so at once, for I am possessed of an instrument with which I can draw the tooth at any moment.'

Aramis could not conceal the smile of disdain which flitted across his handsome face. 'And, if I *were* conspiring against Colbert, where would be the harm?'

'It would be too small a business for you to handle. Besides, it was not for the purpose of overthrowing Colbert that you obtained those patterns from Percerin. Oh! Aramis, we are not enemies – we are brothers. Tell me what enterprise you have undertaken, and on the word of d'Artagnan, if I cannot help you, I swear that I will remain neutral.'

'I am undertaking no enterprise,' said Aramis.

'Aramis, a voice within me speaks, a voice which has never yet deceived me, and it says: *It is the king your enterprise is against.*'

'The king!' exclaimed the bishop with a show of indignation.

'The expression of your face carries no conviction with it; and I repeat that it is *the king*.'

'And you will help me?' asked Aramis, laughing ironically.

'Aramis, I will do more than help you, I will do more than remain neutral; I will save you.'

'You are mad, d'Artagnan.'

'I am the saner of the two.'

'You suspect that I want to assassinate the king?'

'Who hinted at such a thing?' said the musketeer.

'Well, let us understand each other. I fail to see what one could do to a legitimate sovereign like our own, unless one were to assassinate him.'

D'Artagnan made no answer.

'Besides, you have your guards and musketeers here,' continued the bishop.

'True,' said d'Artagnan.

'You are not in Monsieur Fouquet's house; you are at home.'

'True,' said d'Artagnan again.

'Also you have on the spot Monsieur Colbert, who advises the king, to Monsieur Fouquet's detriment, everything that perhaps you, yourself, would advise, did I not happen to be concerned in the matter.'

'Aramis, Aramis! for mercy's sake, trust me as a friend!'

'It is, as a friend, that I am telling you the exact truth. If I have conceived the idea of laying a finger on the son of Anne of Austria, the true king of this realm of France; if it be not my intention to prostrate myself at the foot of his throne; if, so far as I can conjecture, tomorrow, here at Vaux, be not the most glorious day that my king has ever known, may I be struck by lightning on the spot!'

Aramis, as he uttered these words, had his face turned towards the alcove in his room, and d'Artagnan, who had his back to it, had no reason to suspect that anyone was lying concealed there. The emphasis and studied deliberation with which Aramis had spoken, together with the solemnity of his oath, completely disarmed the musketeer, who seized both of the bishop's hands and pressed them warmly. The latter who had listened to his friend's reproaches without changing colour, now reddened to the roots of his hair upon hearing himself praised. He felt that to be able to hood- wink d'Artagnan was a credit to him; but d'Artagnan, trustful and confiding, was now before him, and he blushed with shame.

'Are you going?' he asked, as he embraced the musketeer in order to hide his confusion.

'Yes, I am on duty. I have to give the watchword for the night.'

'Where do you sleep?'

'In the king's antechamber, I suppose. But what is to be done with Porthos?'

'I wish you would take him away with you; his snores are deafening.'

'Oh! he is not sleeping here, then?' said d'Artagnan.

'Oh! no; he has a room to himself, but I don't know where it is situated.'

'Very good,' said the musketeer, whose last suspicions were removed by the knowledge that Aramis and Porthos would be separated for the night, and he shook the latter by the shoulder. 'What's the matter?' asked Porthos with a yawn. 'Halloa! D'Artagnan, old fellow – what the deuce – ? Oh! true; I remember now; I am at the fête at Vaux.'

'And you have your handsome new costume with you?'

'Oh! yes; devilish civil of old Coquelin de Volière to get it ready, wasn't it?'

'Pray don't make such a noise,' expostulated Aramis, 'if you tread so heavily, you will break in the flooring.'

'That is true,' said the musketeer; 'this room is directly over the dome.'

'And it is not intended to be used as a fencing-room,' added the bishop. 'The ceiling of the king's bedroom is decorated with frescoes depicting the pleasures to be derived from sleep, and don't forget that the floor of my room is immediately above it. Well, good-night, my friends. For my part, I shall be asleep in ten minutes,' and Aramis, laughing softly to himself, conducted them to the door. As soon as they were outside, he quickly shot the bolts and stopped up all the crevices in the windows; then, he called: 'Monseigneur! Monseigneur!' and Philippe came out of his hiding place through a sliding-door which was behind the bed.

'How terribly suspicious Monsieur d'Artagnan is,' he remarked.

'Ah! then, you recognised d'Artagnan?'

'Even before you mentioned his name.'

'He is your captain of musketeers.'

'He seems to be very devoted to *me*,' replied Philippe with a stress upon the personal pronoun.

'He is as faithful as a dog, although he bites occasionally. If d'Artagnan does not find you out before *the other* disappears, you may rely upon him till the end of time, for, in that case, not having seen anything, he will preserve his fidelity. If he sees too late, he is a Gascon and will never admit that he has been deceived.'

'I thought so. Well, what are we to do next?'

'You will place yourself at our point of observation, and watch the ceremonial that is observed when the king goes to bed.'

'Very good, where shall I stand?'

'You can sit down in the folding chair. I am going to slide back a part of the flooring, and you can look through the opening thus made, which corresponds with the false windows let into the dome of the king's Chamber. Now, tell me what you can see.'

'I see the king,' said Philippe, and he started as if in the presence of an enemy.

'What is he doing?'

'He seems to be inviting someone to take a seat.'

'Ah! Monsieur Fouquet, no doubt.'

'No, it is not Fouquet; wait a bit – '

'Look at my notes, and my portraits, monseigneur.'

'The man whom the king wishes to sit down in his presence is Monsieur Colbert.'

'Colbert sit down in the king's presence! Impossible!'

'Well, see for yourself.'

Aramis looked through the opening in the floor.

'Yes,' he said, 'it is Colbert sure enough. Ah! Monseigneur, what are we about to listen to? What will be the result of this intimacy?'

'It bodes no good for Monsieur Fouquet, I am afraid' – and the prince was right.

We have seen that Louis XIV had sent for Colbert, and that Colbert had arrived. To accord him a private conversation, like this, was one of the highest favours that the king had ever granted; but it is true that, so far as Louis was aware, there were no witnesses to the interview.

'Take a seat, Colbert,' he said, but Colbert, overjoyed – for he had expected nothing less than dismissal – declined the signal mark of favour.

'Does he accept?' said Aramis.

'No, he remains standing.'

'Let us listen to what takes place.'

And the future king and the future pope listened anxiously to what was said by the two unsuspecting mortals in the room beneath their feet.

'Colbert,' said the king, 'you annoyed me very much today.'

'Sire, I know it.'

'Good; I like your answer. You knew it, but had the courage to do it, nevertheless.'

'If I risked incurring your majesty's displeasure, it was because I had your best interests at heart.'

'How is that? Had you reason to fear something on my account?'

'I had, sire, if it were only an attack of indigestion; for such banquets as that provided today are only placed before kings in the hope that they may be suffocated under the weight of good living.'

Having delivered himself of this coarse pleasantry, Colbert paused to watch its effect upon the king. Louis XIV, although the vainest and most fastidious of men, was pleased upon this occasion to overlook the vulgarity.

'Monsieur Fouquet,' he said, 'certainly gave us a most excellent dinner. Now, tell me, Colbert, where does he get the money from to defray the enormous expense of this entertainment. Do you know?'

'Yes, sire, I know.'

'Is your information well authenticated!'

'I can easily prove it – almost to a farthing.'

'I know that you are usually very accurate.'

'It is the first qualification of which a minister of finance should be possessed.'

'Nevertheless, they do not all possess it.'

'I thank your majesty for the implied compliment.'

'Monsieur Fouquet must be rich – enormously rich, and I suppose everybody knows it.'

'Everyone, sire, the living and the dead, also.'

'What do you mean by that, Monsieur Colbert?'

'To the living, Monsieur Fouquet's wealth is obvious, and they marvel at and applaud what he is able to effect by means of it; but the dead, who know more than we do, know in what manner that wealth was obtained, and they condemn the means by which he acquired it.'

'You imply that those means were not altogether legitimate?'

'Men, whose positions give them the opportunity of handling large sums of money, can, if they choose, make their appointments extremely lucrative.'

'You have something to tell me of a still more confidential nature? If so, don't be afraid to speak: we are quite alone.'

'I fear nothing when I have the approval of my own conscience, and your majesty's protection,' said Colbert with a bow.

'Then, were the dead to speak – ?'

'They do speak sometimes, sire: will your majesty read this?'

'Ah!' said Aramis, in the ear of the prince who had not lost a word of this dialogue, 'since you are here, monseigneur, to learn how to play the part of king, listen to a piece of infamy which is truly royal in its dimensions. You are about to witness one of those scenes which God or rather the devil alone could conceive and execute. Listen attentively, monseigneur, you may learn something that may be of use to you in the future.'

The prince redoubled his attention and saw Louis XIV take from Monsieur Colbert a letter which the latter held out to him.

'This is in the handwriting of the late cardinal!' exclaimed the king.

'Your majesty has an excellent memory,' replied Colbert bowing, 'and it is of great advantage to a king, who has a lifetime of work before him, to be able to recognise handwriting at a glance.'

The king read Mazarin's letter, the contents of which it is unnecessary to state here, since, in the relation of the quarrel between Madame de Cheveuse and Aramis, the reader has already been made acquainted with them.

'I do not understand this very clearly,' said the king, greatly interested nevertheless.

'Your majesty has not been accustomed to investigate matters involving accounts.'

'I see that it relates to money given to Monsieur Fouquet.'

'Yes, thirteen million – a nice little sum.'

'Quite so; and these thirteen million are required to make the accounts balance. But I do not understand the why and wherefore of this deficit.'

'That I cannot explain; but the fact that there is a deficit of thirteen million cannot be disputed.'

'You say that that is absolutely the case?'

'I do not say so; it is the registry that declares it.'

'And this letter of Monsieur Mazarin shows that such a sum was employed, and gives the name of the person to whom it was entrusted?'

'As your majesty will see for yourself.'

'Yes; it seems that Monsieur Fouquet has still thirteen million to account for. This is what the accounts show.'

'Yes, sire.'

'Well, and then?'

'Well, and then, sire, as Monsieur Fouquet has not restored, or accounted for the thirteen million, it stands to reason that he must have kept them for himself, and with such a sum as that he could go to four times the expense, and a fraction over, that was incurred by your majesty at Fontainebleau where, as you may be pleased to remember, we spent only three million altogether.'

For a clumsy man, this was a really very skilfully planted blow, recalling, as it did, to the king's mind the fête which had been given by him, and which had been, in every respect, inferior to the entertainment now provided by Monsieur Fouquet. Fouquet was now receiving at Vaux the treatment to which he had subjected Colbert at Fontainbleau, and the latter intended to pay him back with interest. Having brought the king into the state of mind necessary for the furtherance of the end he had in view, as was indicated by the gloom which had overtaken Louis, Colbert felt that his mission was practically fulfilled. He, nevertheless, waited for the king to speak with as much anxiety as did Philippe and Aramis from their point of vantage overhead.

'Do you know what will be the result of all this, Monsieur Colbert?' said the king after some moments' reflection.

'No, sire, I cannot tell,' replied Colbert.

'Well, then, if the appropriation of the thirteen million can be proved – '

'It is proved already, sire.'

'I mean if it were *legally* proved, Monsieur Colbert.'

'That, I think, could be done tomorrow, if your majesty – '

' – were not Monsieur Fouquet's guest, you would say,' said the king, not without dignity.

'The king is at home everywhere, sire, and more especially in houses which have been paid for with his money.'

'I really think,' said Philippe, 'that, having regard to the use to which this dome can be put, the architect should have so constructed it that it could be made to collapse upon the heads of black-hearted scoundrels like this fellow Colbert.'

'I think so too,' said Aramis; 'and Colbert is standing very close to the king at the present moment.'

'True; and such an incident would open the succession.'

'Of which your younger brother would reap all the benefit. But never mind, let us keep quiet, and listen.'

'There will not be much more to listen to,' said the young prince.

'How is that?'

'Because, if I were in the king's place, I should not utter another word.'

'What would you do, then, monseigneur?'

'I should give myself until tomorrow for reflection.'

Louis XIV at length raised his head, and, seeing that Colbert still awaited his next remark, instantly changed the conversation by saying, 'Monsieur Colbert, it is getting late; I shall go to bed.'

'Ah!' said Colbert, 'I shall have – '

'I shall have made up my mind by tomorrow morning,' interrupted the king.

'Very good, sire,' replied Colbert in a state of vexation, which, however, he took care to disguise in the king's presence.

The king made a gesture in token of dismissal, and Colbert backed out of the apartment.

Louis called for his attendants who made their appearance with commendable promptitude.

Then, seeing that Philippe was about to quit his post of observation, Aramis signed to him to remain where he was. 'What has just taken place,' he said, 'is a mere matter of detail and tomorrow will have no concern for us whatever; but the ceremony observed in putting the king to bed is very important. Pray take particular notice, sire, of the manner in which you will be expected to go to bed. Look. look!'

## CHAPTER 43

### *Colbert*

HISTORY WILL TELL US, or rather history has told us, of the events of the next day and of the magnificent fêtes wherewith the minister entertained his royal master. Two well-known writers have given an account – in allegory – of the contention between the Cascade and the Fountain[133] as to which was the more worthy of admiration. All kinds of amusements were provided in addition to the promenade, the banquet and the comedy, and Porthos was much surprised at recognising his friend Monsieur Coquelin de Volière in one of the characters in the *farce* of *Les Fârcheux*, for so it pleased Monsieur de Bracieux de Pierrefonds to style Molière's production. That this was not the view taken of the comedy by La Fontaine may be gathered from the following lines which the poet wrote to his friend Monsieur Maucrou:[134]

This comedy I do declare
A masterpiece by Moliére,
A writer whose enchanting style
Does mirth compel, and gladsome smile.
No poet shall take rank above him;
So human he, I can but love him.

Porthos was, however, to a certain extent of the same opinion as La Fontaine, for he had been heard to exclaim, '*Pardieu!* this fellow Molière is the man for me!' It should be stated, however, that his admiration was excited solely by the cut and style of the author's dress, since of Molière, as a writer of plays, he had a very mean opinion.

Preoccupied with his conversation with Colbert of the previous evening, and feeling the effects of the moral poison with which that individual had done his best to inoculate him, the king, during the whole of that brilliant day, and notwithstanding the wonders from *The Thousand and One Nights* which seemed to be for ever springing up from beneath his feet, was cold, reserved and silent. Nothing seemed capable of putting him in good humour; and it was evident that a deep-seated resentment, which like the tiny stream in which a river has its source increases in volume until it becomes a mighty torrent, had taken possession of him. It was not until close upon midnight that he seemed to recover his serenity, the probability being that, by that time, he had determined upon a definite course of action.

Aramis, who followed him step by step, in his thoughts as well as in his walk, perceived that the climax which he was expecting would not be long delayed.

Colbert, again, seemed almost to be acting in concert with the Bishop of Vannes, and, indeed, every stab with which he wounded the king's feelings might well have been inspired by Aramis himself.

During the whole of the day, the king, evidently anxious to obtain relief from thoughts which disturbed his peace of mind, sought the society of La Vallière, whilst he avoided as much as possible that of Messieurs Fouquet and Colbert.

In the evening, His majesty expressed a wish to play cards before taking his walk in the park, and, accordingly, cards were at once introduced.

The king, having won, and pocketed, a thousand pistoles, at length rose from the table saying, 'Now, gentlemen, we will take a stroll in the park.' He found the ladies of the court already there.

The king, as we have said, was the winner of a thousand pistoles, but Monsieur Fouquet had contrived to be the loser of ten thousand, so that the rest of the players had won, between them, no less than a hundred and ninety thousand livres,[135] a circumstance which afforded them unmitigated satisfaction and delight.

This satisfaction, however, was by no means reflected in the countenance of the king, upon which, in spite of his winnings, a shadow of discontent appeared to linger. At the corner of the avenues, and apparently by appointment, he met Colbert and immediately signed to him to attend him in his walk.

La Vallière, also, had perceived the discontented and threatening aspect of the king, none of whose thoughts were impenetrable to her love, and she had, at once comprehended that his gloomy look boded no good to someone, and she placed herself in the path of his vengeance like an angel of mercy.

Sad, agitated and greatly distressed at having been so long separated from her lover, and disturbed by the sight of the king's emotion, she presented herself before Louis in a state of confusion which he, in his then condition of mind, interpreted unfavourably.

Then, finding themselves alone, or as good as alone, for Colbert took care to keep at a discreet distance, the king approached La Vallière and, taking her by the hand, said, 'Mademoiselle, may I presume to ask if anything ails you? you appear to breathe with difficulty, and your eyes are full of tears.'

'Oh! sire, if that is the case, and if I look sad, believe me it is only because I perceive that something troubles your majesty and makes you sad.'

'Sad? indeed, mademoiselle, you are mistaken. It is not sadness that I feel; it is humiliation.'

'Humiliation? Oh! what a word for your majesty to use.'

'I contend, mademoiselle, that, wherever I may be, no one else has the right to be master, whereas, observe how I, the King of France, am eclipsed on every hand by the king of this domain. And oh!' continued Louis, clenching his fist, 'and oh! when I think that this king – '

'Yes, sire?' interrogated Louise alarmed.

'– that this king is a treacherous servant enriched and rendered arrogant by the money which he has stolen from me! However, I will take care to change this insolent minister's fête into such a scene of confusion and of despair as will live in the recollection of the Nymph of Vaux, of whom the poets talk, for many a long day.'

'Oh! your majesty – '

'Well, mademoiselle, are you going to defend Monsieur Fouquet?' interrupted Louis impatiently.

'No, sire, but I would venture to ask whether you are quite sure that you have been correctly informed. Your majesty has had more than one experience of the value to be placed upon court accusations.'

The king made a sign to Colbert to join them.

'Speak, sir,' he said, 'for it seems to me that Mademoiselle La Vallière considers that the king's word needs corroboration. Tell mademoiselle what Monsieur Fouquet has done? And you, mademoiselle, be good enough to pay attention; the story will not take long to tell.'

Why did Louis XIV insist upon this? For a very simple reason. He was far from easy in his own mind and only half convinced; he could not divest himself of the idea that some secret and crooked intrigue lay behind the story of the thirteen million, and he was anxious that La Vallière, who would be horrified at the very suspicion of dishonesty, should signify – if only by a word – her approval of the resolution he had taken but which he still hesitated to put into execution.

'Speak, sir,' said La Vallière to Colbert, as he advanced towards her, 'speak, since it is the king's will that I should listen to you. Tell me of what crime has Monsieur Fouquet been guilty?'

'Of a not very serious one, mademoiselle,' replied that sombre personage, 'merely of an abuse of confidence – '

'Tell her all about it, Colbert, and when you have spoken, leave us; also, let Monsieur d'Artagnan be informed that I have some orders to give him.'

'Monsieur d'Artagnan, sire!' cried La Vallière. 'I entreat you to tell me why you send for him.'

'*Pardieu!* to arrest this arrogant Titan[136] who, faithful to his traditions, threatens to storm my heaven.'

'To arrest Monsieur Fouquet, do you say?'

'Yes, mademoiselle; does it astonish you?'

'In his own house?'

'Why not? If he is guilty at all, he is as guilty in his own house as he would be anywhere else.'

'Monsieur Fouquet, who at this very moment is ruining himself in order to do honour to his sovereign?'

'I really believe, mademoiselle, that you are inclined to side with the traitor.'

Colbert did his best to suppress a chuckle, but the king heard him, and turned round sharply.

'Sire,' said La Vallière, 'it is not Monsieur Fouquet whom I defend; it is yourself.'

'Myself! – you defend me?'

'Sire, in ordering Monsieur Fouquet to be arrested, you would do yourself dishonour.'

'Dishonour!' said the king, turning pale with anger. 'Upon my word, mademoiselle, you express yourself with strange assurance.'

'If I am unduly emphatic, sire,' replied La Vallière, 'it is only in your majesty's own interest, and, were it necessary, I would lay down my life for you with the same enthusiasm.'

Seeing that Colbert seemed inclined to demur to the way in which matters were shaping themselves, La Vallière, usually so timid and retiring, turned upon him like a tigress, and, with a flash from her eye, effectually silenced him.

'Sir,' said she, 'so long as the king acts justly, even though his action should entail suffering upon me or upon my friends, I am silent; but should he act unjustly, even to serve me or those I love, I should not hesitate to offer my humble remonstrance.'

'But you seem to forget, mademoiselle,' Colbert ventured to say, 'that I, as well as you, love the king.'

'Yes, yes! we both love him, but in different ways,' replied La Vallière, in accents which went to the young king's heart, 'I love him so passionately that all the world knows it; so purely that the king himself has no doubt of my affection. He is my king and my master; I am his humble servant. Whoever touches his honour, touches my life; and I repeat that they dishonour the king who would prevail upon him to arrest Monsieur Fouquet in his own house.'

Colbert hung his head, for he felt that the king was no longer on his side, but he, nevertheless, murmured, 'Mademoiselle, I have only one word to say.'

'Do not say it, sir, for I will not listen to you. Besides, what could you say? That Monsieur Fouquet has committed a crime? I am aware of it; the king has said so, and when his majesty makes an assertion, I do not require the confirmation of the statement from the lips of anyone else. But Monsieur Fouquet – no matter what he may be – so far as the king is concerned, is sacred, because his majesty is his guest. If his house were a den of infamy, if Vaux were a place of resort for coiners or thieves, it is sacred and inviolable, since Monsieur Fouquet's wife lives here, and it is an asylum which even executioners would be afraid to enter by force!'

La Vallière was silent, and the king could not but admire her, so much was he impressed by her ardour and the rectitude of the cause she had espoused, whilst Colbert, overwhelmed by the odds against him, surrendered at discretion. At last the king, with a strange sense of relief, shook his head and held out his hand to La Vallière.

'Mademoiselle,' he said gently, 'why do you take up arms against me? Do you know what this fellow will do, if I give him breathing time?'

'Can you not lay your hand upon him at any moment?'

'But what if he escapes and absconds?' cried Colbert.

'It would be,' said La Vallière, 'to the king's eternal glory, were he to allow Monsieur Fouquet to escape. The more guilty he may have been, so much the more will it be to the king's honour to let him go free, instead of subjecting him to the shame of being arrested in his own house.'

The king sank upon his knees, and kissed her hand.

'I am done for,' thought Colbert, 'but no, no, no!' he added to himself, as his face brightened, 'by the Lord! no. I'm not half beaten yet;' and as the king, hidden from sight by intervening shrubbery, took La Vallière to his heart, Colbert, searching in his pocket-book, produced from it a paper folded in the shape of a letter, rather yellow perhaps, but no doubt valuable for all that, judging from the grin of satisfaction with which he regarded it. Then he turned once more, with a look of intense hatred towards the pretty group formed by the girl and her lover as they stood half concealed amongst the trees; suddenly, however, they were brought into prominence by the light flashed upon them from approaching torches.

Louis saw the light reflected from La Vallière's white dress. 'Run away, Louise,' said he, 'someone is coming,' and the girl quickly disappeared amongst the trees, whilst, in order to hasten her footsteps, Colbert called after her, 'Mademoiselle, mademoiselle! they are coming!'

'Mademoiselle has dropped something,' he added immediately afterwards to the king.

'What is it?' asked Louis.

'A paper; it looks like a letter; it is something white anyhow. Look, there it is, sire.'

The king hastily picked up the letter, crushing it in his hand, and, at the same moment the torches arrived, rendering surrounding objects as bright as day.

## CHAPTER 44

### *Jealousy*

THIS ARRIVAL, together with the general enthusiasm which prevailed, was sufficient to prevent Louis XIV from immediately carrying out the resolution which he had formed in regard to Monsieur Fouquet, more especially as it had already been considerably shaken by the attitude assumed by Louise de la Vallière. He even felt almost grateful to Fouquet for having afforded La Vallière an opportunity of showing the generosity of her nature, which had so powerful an influence over his own.

The moment, it seemed, had now arrived for the crowning display of all, and no sooner had Fouquet and the king turned their faces in the direction of the château, than, with a deafening roar, a vast volume of flame burst from the dome of Vaux, lighting up and rendering distinct the remotest corners of the surrounding grounds.

An exhibition of fireworks then took place. Colbert, at twenty paces from the king, who formed the centre of an admiring and adulating crowd, sought, by maintaining a gloomy expression, to recall to the king's recollection Monsieur Fouquet's alleged crime, which the splendour of the spectacle seemed in danger of making him forget. The king, indeed, was on the point of giving Monsieur Fouquet a hand-shake of congratulation, when the action reminded him of the crumpled letter which he was still holding, and which he believed was from La Vallière and intended for himself. By the light of the fireworks which seemed each moment to increase in brilliancy – so that loud cries of astonishment and delight were raised in all the neighbouring villages – the king read the letter, and, as he read, a deathly pallor overspread his countenance; but the expression of his features only faintly portrayed the fury which was in his heart, or else everyone who observed him would have trembled indeed.

From the moment when the truth was revealed to him, jealousy and rage took possession of Louis to the utter extinction of every gentler sentiment, and even of the rights of hospitality; indeed, in the bitterness of his heart, he could scarcely restrain himself from uttering a cry of alarm and summoning his guards to attend him.

This letter, which, it is needless to tell the reader, had been dropped at the king's feet by Colbert, was that with which the grey-haired Toby[137] had disappeared at Fontainbleau, after the attack which was made by Fouquet upon the heart of La Vallière.

Fouquet observed the king's pallor, but was at a loss to account for it; Colbert saw the king's rage, and looked forward to the bursting of the storm with the liveliest satisfaction.

The voice of Fouquet aroused the young prince from his angry reflections.

'What is the matter, sire?' he enquired with every show of affectionate concern.

Louis, controlling himself with an effort, replied, 'Nothing.'

'I feared that your majesty was suffering.'

'I am suffering; I have already said so, sir; but it is nothing,' and, without waiting for the end of the fireworks, the king turned towards the house. Fouquet followed the king, the crowd followed Fouquet, and the rest of the fireworks were left to fizzle out by themselves.

The minister made another attempt to find out what was the cause of this sudden discomposure, but could obtain no answer from the king. He could only conjecture that Louis had had a little tiff with La Vallière, and was, in a fit of ill-temper, visiting the sins of his mistress upon those about him. There was consolation in this idea, and he wished the king good-night with a smile intended to be friendly and sympathetic.

The king's troubles, however, did not end here, for he had, upon this occasion, to submit to being put to bed with greater ceremony than usual. The morrow was the day fixed for his leaving Vaux, and he was obliged to give his hosts what equivalent he could in return for the twelve million which they had spent upon entertaining him. The most civil thing that Louis could bring himself to say to Monsieur Fouquet, upon taking leave of him, was, 'Monsieur Fouquet, you shall hear from me; have the goodness to cause Monsieur d'Artagnan to be informed that I desire to see him at once.' The blood of that arch-dissembler, Louis XIII, boiled in his veins, and he was quite as ready to have Fouquet's throat cut as his predecessor had been to cause the assassination of Maréchal d'Ancre.[138] He managed, however, to disguise his sinister intention with one of those royal smiles which sometimes indicate that a *coup d'etat* is to be expected.

Fouquet took the king's hand, and although Louis shuddered all over at the contact, he allowed him to touch it with his lips. Five minutes afterwards d'Artagnan, to whom the royal command had been transmitted, entered the chamber of Louis XIV.

Meanwhile Philippe and Aramis, from their place of observation in the room above, looked on and listened to every word.

Upon seeing his captain of musketeers, the king rose hastily from his seat, and advanced to meet him. 'Take care,' he cried, 'that no one else is admitted.'

'Very good, sire,' replied the soldier, who saw at a glance the ravages which passion had made on the king's countenance. Having given the necessary order at the door, he turned towards Louis. 'Has anything fresh happened to your majesty?' he asked.

To this question the king responded only by another.

'How many men have you here?' he enquired.

'For what purpose, sire?'

'*How many men have you here?*' repeated the king, stamping his foot with impatience.

'I have the musketeers.'

'Any more besides?'

'I have twenty Guards, and thirteen Swiss.'

'How many men will you want to – ?'

'To do what, sire?' asked the musketeer placidly.

'To arrest Monsieur Fouquet,' snapped the king.

D'Artagnan recoiled a pace or two.

'To arrest Monsieur Fouquet!' he exclaimed in astonishment.

'Perhaps you will tell me that it is impossible?' said the king viciously.

'I *never* say that a thing is impossible,' replied d'Artagnan, wounded to the quick.

'Well then, do it.'

D'Artagnan was at the door in half a dozen strides; then, halting, 'Pardon me, sire,' he said.

'What is it?' said the king.

'I should like to have a written order for this arrest.'

'For what purpose? and since when has the king's verbal command ceased to be sufficient for you?'

'Because any command of the king, issued under the influence of passion, is likely to undergo alteration when his anger has had time to cool.'

'Don't beat about the bush, monsieur. You have some other thought which you are concealing.'

'Oh! I have always a great many thoughts, which, unfortunately, some people have not,' replied d'Artagnan, impertinently.

The king, even in the height of his resentment, recoiled before this bold speech, as a horse is brought back on his haunches by the strong hand of his rider.

'What is your thought?' he demanded.

'This is it, sire. You are going, in a fit of anger, to order the arrest of a man whilst you are still a guest under his roof. When you have had time to reflect, you will be sorry for what you have done. Therefore, I wish to be able to show you your own signature. This may not mend matters, but it will, at least, show that the king is wrong to get in a passion.'

'Get in a passion!' shouted the infuriated king, 'did the king my father, and my grandfather, before him, never get in a rage?'

'The king your father and your grandfather never lost their temper except they were in their own palaces.'

'The king is master wherever he may be.'

'The deceptive phrase of a courtier and worthy of Monsieur Colbert himself; but it is not the truth. The king is only master in another man's house when he has driven out of it the rightful owner.'

Louis bit his lips with vexation.

'This is how the matter stands,' continued d'Artagnan. 'Here is a man who is ruining himself merely to afford you pleasure, and you want to place him under arrest! By heaven! sire, if my name were Fouquet, and were I subjected to any such treatment, I would swallow half a dozen sky-rockets, set fire to them and blow myself up with everyone around me. But no matter, it is your wish, and I go to obey your command.'

'Yes, go,' said the king, 'but are you sure you have men enough?'

'Do you imagine, sire, that I am going to take a battalion with me? To arrest Monsieur Fouquet is so easy a business that a child could do it. It is like taking a glass of bitters – one makes a wry face, and swallows it – that is all.'

'But if he resists – '

'Is it likely that he will resist, when a harsh step like this will at once elevate him to the rank of martyr? Why, I will bet that, if he has a million left – which I very much doubt – he would gladly give it to ensure such a result. I go, at once, to carry out your orders, sire.'

'Stay,' said the king, 'I do not wish him to be publicly arrested.'

'That makes it difficult, sire.'

'In what way?'

'Because nothing would be easier than to go to Monsieur Fouquet when he is surrounded by an enthusiastic crowd of admirers, and say to him, "Monsieur Fouquet, I arrest you in the king's name." But to hunt and dodge him about until he is penned up in a corner so that escape is impossible; to spirit him away from his companions, and keep him a prisoner for you, without a single word of remonstrance from him being overheard by a soul, that is a matter of such extreme difficulty that I confess I hardly see my way to doing it.'

'You had better say at once that it is impossible,' said Louis, ironically, 'it would save a great deal of time. Ah! my God! to think that I am surrounded by people whose sole idea seems to be that of throwing obstacles in my path!'

'I do nothing of the kind,' said d'Artagnan. 'Are your majesty's instructions final?'

'Keep your eye upon Monsieur Fouquet until tomorrow; by that time I shall have finally decided how to act.'

'It shall be done, sire.'

'And come back, at my hour for rising in the morning, for fresh instructions. I would, now, be alone.'

'Do you not even wish to see Monsieur Colbert, sire?' said d'Artagnan, firing a parting shot as he reached the door.

The king started. Absorbed as he had been in his scheme of vengeance, he had temporarily forgotten this *fons et origo*[139] of all the trouble. 'I wish to see no one,' he said, 'leave me.'

When d'Artagnan had taken his departure, the king, having fastened the door with his own hands, commenced to pace furiously up and down the room, like a wounded bull who drags about with him the streamers and the darts which infuriate him. At length, he gave vent to his feelings in words.

'Ah! the miserable scoundrel!' he cried, 'not only has he robbed me, but he has made use of the stolen money to corrupt my secretaries, friends, generals and artists, and has even dared to attempt to take my mistress from me! That is why the treacherous little devil stood up for him so warmly. Out of gratitude, no doubt; yet, who knows? it may even have been out of love for him!' And he gave himself up for an instant to torturing doubts.

'He is a satyr!' he thought, with that feeling of intense dislike which very young men have for those of maturer age who dare to fall in love; a faun who, in his love affairs, never meets with a rebuff; a man who scatters gold and diamonds, and keeps a staff of artists to paint portraits of his mistresses arrayed as goddesses. He defiles everything that belongs to me with his odious touch. He is ruining me and will ultimately kill me! This man is too much for me; he is my mortal enemy! But he shall come down with a crash! I hate him, I hate him; oh! how I hate him!'

As he uttered these words, he struck violent blows upon the arms of his chair, from which he suddenly rose like a man attacked by epilepsy.

'But tomorrow, tomorrow,' he continued, 'when morning dawns, I shall have no other rival but the sun himself; this man shall fall from such a height, that others, seeing the condition to which I will reduce him, shall be forced to acknowledge my immeasurable superiority!'

Then, unable, any longer, to control himself, the king overturned, with a blow of his fist, a small table which stood at his bedside, and, boiling over with spite and rage, threw himself, fully dressed as he was, upon the bed and gnawed the covering in impotent fury.

The bed groaned beneath his weight, and then, but for the sound of a few sighs which from time to time escaped him, all was silence in the Chamber of Morpheus.

## CHAPTER 45

## *High treason*

THE UNCONTROLLABLE RAGE into which the reading of Fouquet's letter to La Vallière had thrown the king simmered down, by degrees, to a state of exhaustion. Youth, full of health and vigour, and finding it necessary constantly to restore the energy it has expended, is never subjected to that chronic sleeplessness which recalls to the minds of those who suffer from it the fable of the fortunate vulture which found an inexhaustible feast in the ever-renewed liver of the unhappy Prometheus.[140]

The man of middle age whose strength is matured and the old man whose powers are on the wane both find that their troubles are ever with them, whilst the young man overtaken by unlooked-for misfortune exhausts himself in unavailing lamentations and struggles and is thus the more easily overcome by the enemy with whom he is in conflict; but, once overcome, his suffering ceases.

Louis was soon beaten, and, in a quarter of an hour, had ceased to clench his fists and to fulminate against the objects of his hatred; he stopped his ravings against Fouquet and La Vallière; he dropped from fury to despair, and from despair to prostration. After twisting and turning about for some minutes, his arms fell nerveless to his sides; his head dropped upon his pillow and, whilst his limbs, from time to time, twisted spasmodically, his dolorous sighs became less frequent and in a short time ceased altogether.

The god Morpheus, who reigned supreme in this chamber which had been named after him, and to whom Louis turned his inflamed and swollen eyes, showered upon him the poppies with which his hands were filled, and the king, gently closing his eyes, fell asleep.

Then it seemed to him, as often happens in that first sleep which lightly lifts the body from the couch and the soul above the earth, it seemed to him, we say, that the painting of the god Morpheus upon the ceiling looked down upon him with strangely human eyes; that something bright and shining moved in the dome above him; and that the disquieting dreams which troubled him all at once gave place to the face of a man who, with finger on lip, was observing him in contemplative meditation. And, stranger still, this man bore so striking a resemblance to the king himself, that Louis took the vision for a reflection of his own face in a mirror, and noticed, moreover, that it bore a saddened look as if influenced by a feeling of profound pity. Presently, it seemed to him that the dome receded and was escaping from his vision, and that Le Brun's paintings which adorned it were gradually becoming less distinct as their distance from him increased. The bed, too, began to move, with a sensation of falling, like that caused by a ship as she dips to the waves. No doubt, the king was dreaming, and, in his dream, the golden crown which held together the curtains receded from him as did the dome from which it was suspended; so that the winged figure which held the crown in her hands seemed to be calling in vain to the king as he sank out of sight. Still the bed continued to sink, and Louis, with eyes wide open, thought himself the victim of a strange hallucination. At length the light of the room disappeared altogether, to be succeeded by gloom and a cold, inexplicable something which pervaded the air. No longer were pictures, gilding or velvet curtains to be seen, but instead of them, dull grey walls the tint of which grew darker and darker every instant. The bed still descended until, at the end of a minute – which seemed to the king an hour – it reached a stratum of black and ice-cold air and then it stopped.

The king could now only see the light of his room as one sees the daylight from the bottom of a well.

'What a horrid dream!' he thought. 'It is time to awaken from it. Now then, wake up!'

Everyone has experienced the sensation; there is no one who, under the influence of nightmare – by the help of that light which is still alive in the brain whilst all the senses are deadened in sleep –

there is no one who has not said to himself, 'This is nothing but a dream, after all.'

That is what Louis XIV told himself, but as he said, 'Wake up!' he became aware that not only was he already awake but that his eyes were wide open; and, this being the case, he made use of them to look about him.

To right and left of him stood a masked and armed figure wrapped in a great cloak. One of these men carried a small lamp, the rays of which illuminated the gloomiest picture that ever king was called upon to look at.

Louis told himself that this was all a part of his dream, to terminate which he had only to move an arm or say something aloud. He sprang from the bed and found himself standing upon cold, damp ground. Then, addressing the man who held the lamp, 'What is this, monsieur?' he said, 'what is the meaning of this pleasantry?'

'It is no pleasantry,' replied the man in a deep voice.

'Do you belong to Monsieur Fouquet?' asked the bewildered king.

'No matter to whom we belong,' answered the phantom, 'we are your masters – and let that suffice.'

Louis, more indignant than alarmed, turned to the second figure.

'If this is part of a comedy,' he said, 'you will find, Monsieur Fouquet, that I fail to appreciate it and that I desire that it may end at once.'

The man whom the king now addressed was of great stature, and enormous girth. He held himself stiff and motionless as a block of marble.

'Well,' said the king, stamping his foot with anger, 'do you not intend to answer?'

'We do not answer you, my little man,' roared the giant in a stentorian voice, 'because we have no answer to give you, unless, indeed, it be that you, as chief of the malcontents, ought to have been included in Monsieur Molière's comedy of Les Fâcheux.'

'But what do you want with me?' asked Louis, drawing himself up and folding his arms.

'That you will learn later on,' said the man with the lamp.

'In the meanwhile, perhaps you will tell me where I am?'

'Look for yourself.'

Louis looked about him, but, by the light of the lamp which the man held up, he could distinguish nothing beyond damp walls which were marked, here and there, with the slimy traces of snails.

'Oh! a dungeon, I suppose,' he said.

'No; merely an underground passage.'

'Which leads to – '

'Have the goodness to follow us, and you will see.'

'I will not stir an inch!' cried the king.

'If you show the slightest signs of mutiny, my young friend, I shall simply roll you up in this cloak, and carry you under my arm,' said the big man. 'Of course, should you be suffocated during the process, that will be so much the worse for you;' and, with these words, the speaker stretched out towards the king a threatening hand which Milo of Crotona[141] might have envied when he conceived the unfortunate idea of splitting his last oak.

The king, who had the greatest dread of violence, saw clearly that these two men, in whose power he found himself, were not the sort of fellows to stick at trifles, but would certainly carry out whatever object they had in view. Shaking his head, therefore, he replied, 'It would seem that I have fallen into the hands of two assassins. Lead on!'

Neither of the men made any reply, but he who carried the lamp walked on in front; the king followed him, and the other man brought up the rear.

In this order they traversed a long and tortuous passage, out of which led as many staircases as are to be found in the mysterious and sombre palaces described in the romances of Mrs Radcliffe.[142] Their walk, during which the king frequently heard the sound of water overhead, ended, at last, in a long corridor closed by an iron door. The man with the lamp opened this door with one of a large bunch of keys which hung at his waist and which had been heard jingling as he walked.

When the door was opened, and the fresh air freely admitted, the king smelt the sweet odours which trees give out after the heat of a summer's day. It caused him to pause for a moment, whereupon he was roughly pushed out of the underground passage by the gigantic fellow behind him.

'What! again?' said the king, turning round upon the man who had had the temerity to lay a hand on his sovereign, 'Is it thus you treat the King of France?'

'You had better forget that title,' said the lamp-bearer in a tone which admitted of no more reply than did the famous decrees of Minos.[143]

'You deserve to be broken on the wheel for what you have just said,' added the giant, as he extinguished the lamp which his companion handed to him; 'but the king is very forbearing.'

At this threat, Louis made a movement as if he would have attempted to escape, but the huge hand of the giant came down upon his shoulder and rendered any further effort in that direction impossible.

'But will you not tell me where we are going?' said the king.

'Have the goodness to come with me,' replied the leader of the two men, and, with a certain air of respect, he led his prisoner towards a coach which was in waiting.

The vehicle was completely hidden by the trees and two horses with <u>hobbled</u> legs were tied up with halters to the branches of a neighbouring oak.

The same man opened the door, let down the steps and invited the king to get in.

Louis, accordingly, took a seat within the vehicle, the door of which was immediately shut and locked upon him and the man who had him in custody, whilst the giant, having removed the hobbles from their legs, harnessed the horses to the carriage and mounted the box, of which he was the sole occupant.

The carriage at once set out at a smart pace along the road to Paris, halting for a few minutes in the forest of Sénart, where a fresh pair of horses was found tied to trees, as had been the two animals originally attached to the carriage.

The man on the box quickly shifted the harness, and drove on rapidly in the direction of Paris, reaching that city towards three o'clock in the morning. The carriage rolled along the Faubourg Saint-Antoine and, calling out to the sentinel on duty, 'By order of the king!' the coachman turned his horses sharply into the purlieus of the Bastille and then into the Cour du Gouvernement, finally pulling up at the steps which led to the main entrance to the fortress.

'Let the governor be called immediately!' shouted the coachman to the sergeant of the guard, in a voice of thunder.

With the exception of this voice, which might have been heard at the far end of the Faubourg Saint-Antoine, not a sound was audible, deep silence being maintained by the occupants of the carriage, whilst those in the château were probably all fast asleep. In ten minutes, Monsieur Baisemeaux appeared, in his dressing-gown, on the threshold of the great gate.

'What is it, now?' he cried, 'and whom have you got there?'

The man who had carried the lantern opened the carriage-door and said two words to the coachman, who, jumping down from his box, seized a musket which had been lying at his feet and applied its muzzle to the prisoner's breast.

'Shoot him if he attempts to open his mouth!' said the man who got out of the carriage in a voice audible to all.

'Right!' answered the other laconically.

Having given this order, the first man ran up the steps, at the top of which the governor awaited him.

'Monsieur d'Herblay!' exclaimed the latter.

'Hush!' said Aramis, 'let us go inside.'

'Good heavens! whatever brings you here at this hour?'

'A slight mistake,' replied Aramis quietly. 'It seems that you were right after all, the other day.'

'What about, pray?' asked the governor.

'Why, as to that order of release, my friend.'

'Pray explain yourself, monsieur – I mean, monseigneur,' spluttered Baisemeaux, choking with astonishment and fright.

'It is very simple; you recollect, dear Monsieur Baisemeaux, an order of release being sent to you?'

'Yes, for Marchiali.'

'For Marchiali, as we both thought at the time.'

'Certainly; nevertheless, if you remember, I had a doubt about it, and should not have given him up so readily but that you compelled me.'

'What an expression to use, dear Monsieur Baisemeaux! You mean that I *strongly advised* you, do you not?'

'Strongly advised! Well then you *strongly advised* me to give him up to you, and you took him away in your own carriage.'

'Well, dear Monsieur Baisemeaux, that was a mistake. The ministry have recognised it, and, consequently, I am here with the king's order for the release of that poor devil of a Scotchman, Seldon.[144] You remember about him?'

'Seldon? Are you sure you are right, this time?'

'Read for yourself,' said Aramis handing him the order.

'But,' said Baisemeaux, 'this is the very same order which was sent to me in the first instance.'

'Really?'

'Yes, it is the very same order that I assured you I had received the other evening. Here is even the blot of ink which I spoke of, and by which I now identify it.'

'I don't know anything about that. All I know is that I bring it to you *now*.'

'But, what about the other?'

'What other?'

'Marchiali.'

'I have brought him back to you.'

'But that is not sufficient. I must have a fresh order for his reimprisonment.'

'Nonsense, my dear Baisemeaux, you talk like a child. What have you done with the order for his release?'

Baisemeaux went to his iron chest, from which he produced it.

Aramis took the order from him; coolly tore it into four pieces, and held them in the flame of the lamp until they were consumed.

'What on earth are you doing?' cried Baisemeaux, half paralysed with fear.

'Just consider the situation, my dear governor,' said Aramis imperturbably, 'and you will find it very simple. You have no longer any order giving you authority to release Marchiali.'

'My God! no; I am a ruined man!'

'Not at all, since here is Marchiali himself. From the moment that I restore him to you, the position is precisely the same as if he had never been let out at all.'

'Ah!' gasped the bewildered governor.

'Of course it is; and I presume you will put him under lock and key again, immediately.'

'You may depend upon my doing that.'

'And you will hand over to me this man Seldon, whom the new order sets at liberty. You will then have acted in absolute conformity with the instructions which you have received. Do you not see that?'

'I – I.'

'Yes, I see, you understand perfectly. That is well.'

Baisemeaux, in his agitation, clasped his hands together. 'But why, after taking Marchiali away, do you bring him back again?' he asked.

'From a faithful friend and devoted servant like yourself,' said Aramis, 'I have no secrets.' And he placed his mouth to the governor's ear.

'You know,' he said, in a low tone of voice, 'what a strong resemblance there is between this unfortunate fellow and – ?'

'And the king, yes.'

'Now, what do you suppose was the first thing that Marchiali did upon regaining his liberty?'

'How is it possible for me to guess?'

'He declared himself to be the King of France.'

'Oh! the villain!' cried Baisemeaux.

'He even went so far as to copy the dress worn by the king, and to maintain that he was really Louis XIV.'

'Gracious heaven!'

'Now you see why I bring him back to you. He is mad, and proclaims his madness to all the world.'

'What is to be done, then?'

'Simply to take care that he is not allowed to hold communication with anyone. You see, when all this reached the ears of the king, who had released him out of pity for his misfortunes, and his majesty learnt the base return that Marchiali had made him for his clemency, he was naturally deeply incensed against him. So much so, indeed, that now – and pay particular attention to this, my dear Baisemeaux, for it concerns you very closely – that, now, sentence of death has been passed upon those through whose negligence Marchiali may be allowed to communicate with anyone, save with me, or with the king himself. You understand, Baisemeaux, sentence of death!'

'Yes, yes, I understand.'

'Very well, then, you had better go now and take the poor devil back to his cell, unless you want him up here.'

'What should I want him up here for?'

'Oh! well, I thought it would be as well to enter his name in the prison books as soon as possible.'

'Yes, certainly; that should be done at once.'

'Well, have him up, then.'

Baisemeaux ordered drums to be beaten and a bell to be rung which was a signal for everyone about the prison to retire, so as to avoid meeting any prisoner whom it was considered expedient to receive secretly. Then, when all was in readiness, the governor went to fetch the prisoner, at whose breast Porthos, faithful to his trust, still pointed his loaded musket.

'Ah! here you are, you miserable rascal!' cried Baisemeaux upon seeing the king. 'Well, that is good! excellent, indeed!'

And, immediately, making the king get out of the carriage, he led him, accompanied by Porthos, still wearing his mask, and by Aramis, who had resumed his, to the *Bertaudière* and opened the door of the prison-room where for six long years[145] Philippe had bewailed his fate.

Pale and haggard, the king entered the chamber without uttering a single word.

Baisemeaux closed the door upon him and, having double locked it, returned to Aramis.

'There is no doubt,' he said in a low tone of voice, 'that he is uncommonly like the king; but hardly so like him as you represented.

'So that you would not have been deceived, had it been attempted to substitute another person for him?'

'What a question!'

'You are a very valuable man, my dear Baisemeaux. Now, suppose you go and set Seldon at liberty.'

'Yes, yes; I declare I had almost forgotten him. I will give the order at once.'

'Bah! tomorrow will be time enough.'

'Tomorrow? no, no, at once; God forbid that I should delay his release for a second.'

'Go, then, and perform your duty, and I will go about my own business. But it is quite understood, is it not?'

'What is quite understood?'

'That no one is to have access to the prisoner without an order from the king, which will be brought by me in person.'

'It is, certainly, quite understood. Adieu, monseigneur.'

Aramis rejoined his companion. 'Now then, Porthos, old fellow,' he said, 'let us be off to Vaux as fast as the horses can lay legs to the ground!'

'A man,' said Porthos, 'feels an immense amount of satisfaction in knowing that he has faithfully served his king, and that, in serving him, he has served his country. I feel quite light, so to speak, and the horses will have no weight to drag. Come along;' and the carriage, relieved of the prisoner, who, indeed, had been no light weight to Aramis, cleared the drawbridge of the Bastille, which was immediately raised again behind it.

CHAPTER 46

## A night in the Bastille

SUFFERING, IN THIS LIFE, is proportioned to the strength of the sufferer. We do not mean by this that heaven always grants to man strength commensurate with the suffering which it calls upon him to endure, because such an assertion would be anything but accurate, seeing that God permits death, sometimes the only refuge of souls too sorely tried and harassed in the flesh. No; suffering is in proportion to strength, in the sense that, *caeteris paribus*,[146] the weak feel it more keenly than the strong.

Now what are the elements of which human strength is composed? Are they not mainly exercise, habit and experience? This is an axiom – a proposition which, being self-evident, we shall not trouble ourselves to demonstrate.

When the young king, crushed and stupefied, found himself in a cell at the Bastille, he had a kind of hazy idea that death, like sleep, must have its dreams; it seemed to him that his bed at Vaux must have broken through the flooring of his room, thus causing his death, and that, in pursuance of his dream, the king, being dead, dreamt of these horrors – impossible in real life – which are known as dethronement, and consequent imprisonment and insult.

To be present, as a materialised phantom, at the scene of his own suffering in the body, to hover therein an incomprehensible and mysterious atmosphere, between resemblance and reality, to be able to see and to hear everything and still be unable to abridge or alleviate the agony of which he was the witness, was not this, the king asked himself, only the more terrible in that it might possibly last for ever.

'Is this what is meant by eternity, by hell?' Louis XIV murmured to himself as the door of his cell was closed on him by Baisemeaux. He would not even look around him, but leaning against the wall he abandoned himself to the idea that he was dead, and closed his eyes in terror lest he should see things still more horrifying than those which had already been revealed to him.

'How did I meet with my death?' was the next question which occurred to him. 'Could the bed have been let down through the floor by artificial means? Hardly, for I met with no bodily injury, and I felt no shock. They could more easily have poisoned my food, or stifled me with the fumes of wax, as they did my ancestress Jeanne d'Albret.'[147]

All at once the cold air of the chamber fell like a cloak upon Louis's shoulders chilling him to the bone. 'I saw,' he said, 'my father lying dead upon his bed in his robes of state. His calm, pale face, his nerveless hands, his stiffened limbs, gave no indication that his brain could be influenced by dreams. And how terrible were the dreams with which the dead man might have been troubled! dreams of those whom he himself had had condemned to death! No; that king still remained a king; as he was upon his throne of state, so was he upon his funeral couch. He had lost nothing of his majesty; and God, who did not punish him, of a surety will not punish me, who have committed no crime.'

A strange noise presently attracted the young man's attention. He looked in the direction from whence it came, and saw upon the mantelpiece, underneath a roughly-painted crucifix which adorned the wall, an enormous rat engaged in nibbling a dry crust of bread, but keeping, all the time, a vigilant eye upon the new occupant of the apartment. The king, who was both frightened and disgusted at this spectacle, raised a loud cry as he retreated towards the door, and this cry was all that was needed to recall him to himself. He now knew that he was living and in his right mind.

'A prisoner!' he cried, 'I, the king, am actually imprisoned!' and he looked about for a bell.

'There are no bells in the Bastille,' he said, 'and it is the Bastille in which I am confined. The question is who has caused my imprisonment. Of course, Monsieur Fouquet is at the bottom of the conspiracy, and I was inveigled into going to Vaux to my own destruction. But Monsieur Fouquet cannot have planned and carried out all this villainy by himself. His agent – that voice – I recognise it as being the voice of Monsieur d'Herblay. Then, Colbert was right. But what was Fouquet's motive? Did he think that he could reign in my place? Impossible! still, who knows?'

Such were the king's gloomy reflections.

'My brother, the Duc d'Orléans,' he went on, 'is, perhaps, treating me as my uncle never ceased, during his lifetime, trying to treat my father. But the queen, my mother, and La Vallière, oh! La Vallière! she will be handed over to the tender mercies of Madame, and they will shut her up as they have imprisoned me. We are separated eternally!' and, at the mere idea of separation, the unhappy lover bemoaned himself with sobs and sighs and bitter tears.

'However, there is a governor here,' he presently said, 'I will call for him, and demand an explanation.'

He called aloud, but no voice replied to his own. He seized the chair and battered the heavy oaken door with it. He made a terrible din and awoke many mournful echoes in the depths of the staircase; but of a human voice, there was not a sound. This was, to the king, but another proof of his own unimportance in the Bastille.

Presently, when his first fit of fury had subsided a little, having observed a barred window through which passed a stream of light, lozenge-shaped, and which he knew must betoken the break of day, Louis shouted, not loudly at first, but afterwards furiously, but all to no purpose; no answer came to him. He called out again and again, twenty times, but with no better result. Then his blood boiled, and rushed to his head. Accustomed to command, this neglect and inattention astonished him, and his rage increased, little by little, until he was in a state of frenzy.

His chair being too heavy to be conveniently used as a battering-ram, he broke it up and with one of its legs commenced a renewed assault upon the door. He struck so quickly and with such goodwill that the perspiration soon streamed from his forehead, and, at length, as the result of the loud and continued noise, some half-smothered cries arose in various directions.

These sounds had a strange effect upon the king, and he stopped hammering in order to listen, for they were the voices of prisoners, once his victims, now his companions in misfortune.

These voices penetrated like vapour through the thick ceilings and the dense walls, and accused the author of this uproar, as, no doubt, the prisoners in lower tones, and with sighs and tears, cursed the author of their captivity. After having deprived so many people of their liberty, the king had now come to rob them of their sleep.

This reflection maddened him and redoubled his strength or rather his determination to have the matter explained and brought to an end, and the chair-leg was again brought into play in another attack upon the door of the cell.

At the end of about an hour, Louis heard a sound in the corridor, and presently a vigorous thump upon the outer side of the door caused him to discontinue his own exertions.

'Now then! have you gone mad?' cried a rough voice, 'what the devil ails you this morning?'

'This morning!' the king repeated to himself in surprise, and then said, aloud and politely, 'Pray, sir, am I addressing the governor of the Bastille?'

'Look here, young fellow,' replied the voice, 'you seem to be a bit lightheaded this morning, but that is no reason why you should kick up this infernal racket; hold your noise and be damned to you!'

'But are you the governor?' asked the king again.

A door clanged, and the gaoler walked away without deigning any reply to the question.

When there seemed to be no doubt that the man had really gone away, the rage of the king knew no bounds. With the activity of a tiger he sprang from the table at the bars with which his window was secured and shook them furiously. Then he dashed his fist through a pane of glass, and, as the shattered fragments tinkled harmoniously upon the flagstones beneath, roared out order upon order for the immediate attendance of the governor of the Bastille. This fit of fury lasted for upwards of an hour, at the end of which Louis was in a burning fever.

With his hair in disorder and matted upon his forehead, his clothes torn and marked with whitewash from the walls, and with his linen in rags, the king only ceased his exertions when utterly exhausted; then, and then only, did he understand the pitiless thickness of the walls and the strength of the cement which could be penetrated only by time, aided by the energy of despair.

He pressed his forehead against the door and strove to calm the beating of his heart which threatened to burst with each additional throb. 'The time must come,' he said, 'when they will bring the prisoners' food, and I will then speak and demand an answer.' He tried to recollect the hour at which the prisoners in the Bastille were given their first meal, but could not remember that he had ever known it. He was struck with remorse, as with a dagger, when he reflected that although he had lived for twenty-five years in regal splendour, he had never once bestowed a thought on the sufferings of the many unhappy beings who had been unjustly deprived of their liberty, and he blushed for very shame, feeling that God, in permitting him to undergo this terrible humiliation, had but visited upon him some of the torture which he had inflicted upon others.

Nothing could be more efficacious for reawakening, in a mind thus tormented, a sentiment of religion, but Louis dared not kneel in prayer to God to put an end to this terrible ordeal. 'God is just,' he said, 'and it would be cowardly to ask of Him that which I have so often refused to others in my present position.'

At this point, his reflections were interrupted by a voice, on the other side of the door, similar to the one he had heard previously, but this time it was accompanied by the grating of a key in the lock and of bolts being withdrawn from their staples.

The king sprang forward to meet the person who was about to enter, but as quickly drew back, assuming a calm and dignified demeanour, more suited to his dignity as a sovereign, and he placed himself with his back to the light so as to render his agitation as little apparent as possible. The new arrival turned out to be merely a turnkey with some food in a basket. The king looked at him uneasily, whilst waiting for him to speak.

'Ah!' said the man, 'so you've smashed your chair have you? That is just what I said you had done. You must have suddenly gone crazy!'

'My good man,' said the king, 'be careful what you say. It may be a very serious matter for you.'

The man placed his basket upon the table, and stared at the king in surprise. 'What?' he said.

'Send the governor to me,' said Louis majestically.

'Now, look here, young man,' said the gaoler, 'you have always hitherto been very well conducted, but people sometimes break out and become very troublesome; well, we're not going to stand any nonsense from you. You have broken your chair and made a disturbance, an offence which is punishable by confinement in a dungeon; but, if you will promise me to behave yourself in future, I won't say anything about it to the governor, this time.'

'I wish to see the governor,' said the king repressing a frown.

'He will only put you in one of the dungeons, and I advise you not to get yourself sent there!'

'I *order* it; do you not hear?'

'Oh! come,' said the man, 'you look very wild about the eyes. I shall take away your knife,' and, taking it from the table, he left the room, shutting the door after him and leaving the king, who was speechless with indignation, worse off and more solitary than before.

It was in vain that the king recommenced his attack upon the door; in vain that he hurled plates and dishes through the window, no one took the least notice of him.

Within the space of two short hours, he, who had been a king, a gentleman and an intelligent being, had become, to all intents and purposes, a madman, tearing at the door with his fingernails and endeavouring to prize up the flooring of his cell, whilst so loud and terrifying were his cries that the old Bastille seemed to tremble to its very foundations with the consciousness of having rebelled against its master.

No one, however, thought it worth while to disturb the governor on this account. The turnkeys and the sentinels had, as a matter of course, reported the occurrence to him, but there seemed to be no reason for taking any special steps. After all, madmen were common enough in the fortress, and the walls were far stronger than the madmen.

Monsieur Baisemeaux, thoroughly impressed with the importance of what Aramis had said to him, and secure in being possessed of the king's order, only asked one thing, viz.: that Marchiali might be mad enough to hang himself from his bedpost or from the grating of his window. In short, the prisoner *did not pay*, and, to use an everyday expression, was more plague than profit. This confusion between Seldon and Marchiali, then the liberation and subsequent re-imprisonment of the latter, as well as the strange circumstance of the personal resemblance, seemed, at last, to have culminated in a very desirable result, with which, as Baisemeaux had not failed to remark, Monsieur d'Herblay himself seemed perfectly satisfied.

'And then, really,' said Baisemeaux to his lieutenant, 'an ordinary prisoner is quite unhappy enough in the fact that he *is* a prisoner to make it but a charity to wish that death may speedily put an end to his sufferings. With still more reason then may such a wish be entertained when a prisoner goes mad, and bites, and kicks, and creates a disturbance in the Bastille; it would even be a praiseworthy action to put the poor fellow quietly out of his misery,' and, so saying, the worthy governor sat down to his noonday breakfast.

CHAPTER 47

## The shadow of Monsieur Fouquet

D'ARTAGNAN was so upset by the conversation which had just taken place between the king and himself that he could but wonder if he were really in his right senses; if all this had really happened at Vaux; if he, d'Artagnan, were really captain of musketeers; and if Monsieur Fouquet were really the owner of the château where the king was staying as a guest.

These questions which he put to himself were not the vapourings of a brain excited by drink, although everything had been provided at Vaux upon a most lavish scale, and the excellence of Monsieur Fouquet's wines had been duly appreciated. D'Artagnan was always calm and self-possessed and the mere touch of his sword blade was, at any moment, sufficient to render him as cool as the steel itself.

'Well,' he said, as he left the royal apartment, 'I now seem to be involved in the destinies of the king and his minister; it will be written that Monsieur d'Artagnan, a cadet of Gascony, placed his hand upon the shoulder of Monsieur Nicolas Fouquet, minister of finance of France. My descendants, if I have any, will make capital out of this arrest, as the Messieurs de Luynes[148] did in the case of poor Maréchal d'Ancre. It only remains for me to carry out the commands of the king in accordance with my instructions – a task of no little difficulty. Anyone could say to Monsieur Fouquet: 'Your sword, monsieur,' but it is not everyone who could keep ward and watch over him without anyone else suspecting the actual state of affairs. How am I to manage so that, unknown to all, the minister will fall from the height of favour to the lowest depths of disgrace, and exchange the sceptre of Ahasuerus for the gallows of Haman,[149] or to take a French example, of Enguerrand de Marigny?'

As he reflected thus, d'Artagnan's brow became overcast with care, for the musketeer had serious scruples about delivering up to death – seeing how bitterly the king hated Fouquet – a man who had won the goodwill of everyone else, and he found it difficult to reconcile his conscience to the performance of so repugnant a duty.

'It seems to me,' said d'Artagnan to himself, 'that, unless I am a mean-spirited rascal, I should make Monsieur Fouquet acquainted with the king's intentions regarding him. Yet, on the other hand, were I to warn him, I should be guilty of abusing my master's confidence, and should be a traitor, a crime for which military law makes ample provision, as I have good reason to know; for, during the late wars, I have seen at least twenty poor devils strung up by the neck for doing, in a small way, precisely what I feel tempted to do on a much larger scale. No, I think that a man of my intelligence and resource ought to find a better way than that of getting out of the difficulty. The question is, have I brains enough to contrive it? Upon my word, I think it doubtful, for during the last forty years I have made so many calls upon my wits that if what remains of them be worth a pistole I may consider myself lucky,' and d'Artagnan, in his perplexity, buried his face in his hands, and tugged viciously at his moustaches.

'What can be the reason,' he continued presently, 'of Monsieur Fouquet's disgrace? There seem to be three reasons for it: in the first place, Monsieur Colbert doesn't like him; then, he tried to make love to La Vallière; and, again, the king is fond both of mademoiselle and of Colbert. I am afraid he is ruined and done for; but shall I be the man to put my foot upon his neck whilst he is a victim to the intrigues of a pack of women and simpletons? No, *damn me* if I do! Of course, should he prove to be a source of danger to the king, I shall know how to act; but, whilst he is merely the victim of persecution, I will content myself with looking on, and I defy the king, or any other man, to make me change my determination. Were Athos here, he would act in the same manner. Therefore, in stead of rudely apprehending Monsieur Fouquet wherever he is to be found, I shall make a point of treating him with the utmost courtesy. This will lead to a discussion of the matter, of course; but I do not think that the verdict will be against me.'

Hitching up his cross-belt with a movement peculiar to himself, d'Artagnan went straight off to Monsieur Fouquet, who, having just taken leave of some ladies, was promising himself a good night's rest after the fatigues and triumphs of the day.

The air was still heavy with the smell of the fireworks, the wax lights were at their last flicker, flowers that had become detached from garlands strewed the floor together with stray grapes which had been dropped by the dancers and courtiers about the room.

Surrounded by a circle of friends with whom he was exchanging compliments stood Monsieur Fouquet, with eyes half-closed from fatigue. He longed for repose, and to rest upon his hardly-earned laurels. It might have been said that he bent his head beneath the weight of the debts which he had recently contracted for the purpose of making his fête as brilliant and successful as possible. Monsieur Fouquet had just retired to his chamber, still smiling, but feeling more than half dead. He was quite incapable of giving further attention to anything and his bed possessed for him an irresistible attraction. The god Morpheus, who ruled over the dome decorated by Le Brun, had extended his drowsy influence over the adjoining chambers and showered down his most sleep-compelling poppies upon the master of the house.

Fouquet had surrendered himself into the hands of his personal attendant when d'Artagnan suddenly made his appearance upon the threshold of the apartment.

D'Artagnan had never allowed himself to become common at court, and, although seen at all sorts of times and places, he always produced an effect whenever and wherever he made his appearance. It is natural to some people to resemble, in this respect, thunder and lightning. Everyone knows what they are, but, nevertheless, they are always received with a certain amount of surprise, and they always leave behind them the impression that their last appearance has been more remarkable than any that have preceded it.

'Why! here is Monsieur d'Artagnan!' exclaimed Fouquet, who had already got his right arm out of the sleeve of his coat.

'At your service,' replied the musketeer.

'Come in, my dear Monsieur d'Artagnan.'

'Thank you.'

'Have you come to favour me with one of your clever criticisms of the fête?'

'No, indeed.'

'Have you been put to any inconvenience?'

'To none at all.'

'Perhaps you are not comfortably lodged?'

'Oh! as to that, nothing could be better.'

'Well, I am glad of it; and I thank you for expressing yourself in such handsome terms.'

It was easy to perceive that these words meant, 'My dear Monsieur d'Artagnan, since it seems that you have nothing particular to say, for heaven's sake go to bed, and leave me to do the same.'

D'Artagnan, however, declined to take the hint.

'Are you going to bed already?' he asked.

'Yes; unless you have anything to say to me.'

'Nothing, indeed, nothing whatever. You sleep in this room, then?'

'As you see.'

'Monsieur, you have given the king a magnificent fête.'

'You really think so?'

'It was superb.'

'And the king was pleased with it?'

'Delighted.'

'And have you come, on his majesty's part, to tell me so?'

'He would not have chosen so unworthy a messenger, monseigneur.'

'You are too modest, Monsieur d'Artagnan.'

'Is this the bed you sleep in?'

'Yes; but why do you ask such a question? Is not your own bed comfortable?'

'May I be perfectly frank with you?'

'Certainly.'

'Well, then, it is not.'

Fouquet felt uneasy. 'Monsieur d'Artagnan,' he said, 'allow me to place my own room at your disposal.'

'And deprive you of it, monseigneur? Never!'

'What is to be done, then?'

'Allow me to share it with you.'

Fouquet looked hard and steadily at the musketeer.

'Ah!' he said, 'you have just left the king?'

'Yes, monseigneur.'

'And the king desired you to remain in my room?'

'Monseigneur – '

'Very well, Monsieur d'Artagnan, very well. You are master here, and must do as you please.'

'I assure you, monseigneur, that I have no wish to take advantage – '

Here Monsieur Fouquet turned to his attendant and said, 'You may leave us.' The valet retired.

'You have something to say to me, Monsieur d'Artagnan.'

'I?' said d'Artagnan.

'It is of no good to mince matters,' said Fouquet. 'A man of your stamp does not come to talk to a man like myself, at this hour of the night, unless he has something important to communicate.'

'Pray do not ask me any questions.'

'On the contrary, I must know what you want with me.'

'Nothing beyond the pleasure of your society.'

'Let us take a stroll in the garden, then, or in the park.'

'No,' replied the musketeer, promptly and decidedly, 'no.'

'Why not?'

'The air, out of doors, is very keen – '

'Come, why not say frankly that you have come to arrest me?'

'Never!' said the musketeer.

'But you intend to keep guard over me?'

'In all honour, monseigneur, yes.'

'Ah! I see; I am arrested in my own house!'

'Do not say that, monseigneur.'

'On the contrary, I will call it out aloud.'

'If you do that, monseigneur, I shall be under the painful necessity of enforcing your silence.'

'You would use violence towards me, in my own house? Ah! that would be well, indeed!'

'We don't seem to understand one another at all. See, there is a chessboard. Let us play a game at chess, monseigneur.'

'Monsieur d'Artagnan, I am in disgrace, then?'

'Not at all; but – '

'But you do not intend to let me go out of your sight?'

'I don't understand a word of what you are saying, monseigneur; but, if you wish me to retire, tell me so.'

'Dear Monsieur d'Artagnan, your ways are really most exasperating. Just now, I was half dead with sleep, but you have thoroughly awakened me.'

'I shall never forgive myself for it; and if you would reconcile me with myself – '

'Well?'

'Well, go to bed at once, and pay no attention to me. I shall be delighted.'

'But you will still have me under your eye?'

'Then I shall go away.'

'I don't understand you.'

'Good-night, monseigneur,' and d'Artagnan made a pretence of leaving the room.

Monsieur Fouquet stopped him. 'I shall not go to bed,' he said; 'and, since you will not treat me as a man and say frankly what your motive is in coming here, I must force your hand.'

'Bah!' cried d'Artagnan, pretending to laugh.

'I shall order my carriage and leave immediately for Paris.'

'In that case, monseigneur, it will be different.'

'You will arrest me, then?'

'No, but I shall go with you.'

'Enough! enough! I see that it is not for nothing that you have gained a reputation for intelligence and resource, but, in this case, I will not put you to the test. Let us come to the point. Will you do me a service? Tell me why I am arrested and what I have done.'

'I know nothing as to what you have done; moreover, I do not arrest you – tonight.'

'Tonight!' cried Fouquet, turning pale, 'but what about tomorrow?'

'Oh! tomorrow has not come yet, monseigneur, and it is impossible to tell what a day may bring forth.'

'Quick, quick, captain: let me speak to Monsieur d'Herblay.'

'I am sorry, but that is impossible, monseigneur; I have strict orders to allow you to hold no communication with anybody.'

'But with Monsieur d'Herblay; with your own friend!'

'Monseigneur, does my friend Monsieur d'Herblay happen to be the only person with whom it is my duty to prevent you from holding communication?'

Fouquet coloured up, and assuming an air of resignation, said, 'Monsieur, you are right. You teach me a lesson which I should not have provoked. A fallen man ceases to have a right to anything, even at the hands of those whose fortunes he has helped to build; far less has he a right to expect anything from those to whom it has not been his good fortune to be of service.'

'Monseigneur!'

'It is true, Monsieur d'Artagnan, your relations with me have always been such as were consistent with the character of a man destined, one day, to arrest me. You have never asked a favour at my hands.'

'Monseigneur,' replied the Gascon, deeply touched, 'permit me to ask one now. Give me your word of honour, as a gentleman, that you will not leave this room.'

'What would be the good of that, my dear Monsieur d'Artagnan, since you are here to prevent me from leaving it. Do you imagine that I am anxious to come into personal conflict with the best swordsman in the kingdom?'

'It is not that, monseigneur; but I propose to go in search of Monsieur d'Herblay for you, and shall, consequently, have to leave you by yourself.'

Fouquet uttered an exclamation of pleasure and surprise.

'You are going to find Monsieur d'Herblay! and to leave me alone!' he cried, clasping his hands together.

'Monsieur d'Herblay is lodged in the blue room, is he not?'

'Yes, my friend, yes.'

'Your friend, monseigneur; I thank you for conferring that title upon me today, even if you have never done so before.'

'Ah! you have saved me!'

'It will take me about ten minutes to go to the blue room and back again, will it not?'

'About that time.'

'And to wake Aramis, who is a sound sleeper, it will take five minutes more, so that I shall be gone fifteen minutes in all. Now, monseigneur, give me your word that you will make no attempt to escape, and that I shall find you here on my return.'

'I give it,' said Fouquet. He shook hands with the musketeer in grateful recognition of the service he was about to render him, and d'Artagnan disappeared.

As soon as d'Artagnan had gone and the door had closed behind him, Fouquet seized his keys and opened several secret drawers. He sought in vain for some documents which had probably been left behind at Saint-Mandé, and seemed much disturbed at not being able to find them.

He, next, hurriedly made into a heap a number of letters, contracts and other papers and burnt them upon the marble hearth-stone, without taking the trouble to remove the pots of flowers with which the fireplace was decorated.

Having thus destroyed his papers, Fouquet, like a man who has just escaped from some great peril, and whose braced-up nerves give way when the danger is past, sank exhausted into an armchair, and here d'Artagnan found him upon his return.

The worthy musketeer did not for a moment imagine that Fouquet, having pledged his word, would dream of breaking it; but he thought that the minister would be glad of an opportunity for getting rid of any papers which might increase the danger of his already sufficiently perilous position. When, therefore, he smelt the odour of the burnt paper he made a movement of the head which signified his satisfaction.

Fouquet raised his head upon the entrance of d'Artagnan, none of whose movements escaped his observation. Then, the eyes of the two men met, and each felt that he thoroughly understood the other, though never a word had passed between them.

Fouquet was the first to break the silence.

'Well,' he said, 'and what news of Monsieur d'Herblay?'

'Faith! Monseigneur,' replied d'Artagnan, 'I think that Monsieur d'Herblay must be addicted to nocturnal rambles, and to composing verses by moonlight with one of your poets, for he is not in his own quarters.'

'What! not there?' cried Fouquet from whom all hope seemed now to have fled, for, although he could not have told in what way the Bishop of Vannes was likely to be of service to him, he knew perfectly well that no one else had it in his power to help him.

'Well, if he *is* in his room,' said d'Artagnan, 'he has his own reasons for not answering.'

'But, perhaps, you did not call loud enough for him to hear you, monsieur.'

'You do not suppose, monseigneur, that, having already exceeded my orders, which was not to lose sight of you for an instant, I should be idiot enough to arouse the entire household, so that everybody might see me in the corridor of the Bishop of Vannes and give Monsieur Colbert the opportunity of declaring that I was giving you time to burn your papers?'

'My papers?'

'Certainly; at least that is what I should have done had I been in your place. If I see a loop-hole, I am not above taking advantage of it.'

'Well, I *have* taken advantage of it; and I thank you for giving me the chance.'

'And you have been quite right. *Morbleu!* we all have secrets with which nobody else has any concern. But, to return to Aramis, monseigneur.'

'Ah! well, I was saying that perhaps he failed to hear you because you did not call loudly enough.'

'Monseigneur, however softly Aramis may be called, he always hears, if it is to his interest to hear. I repeat, then, that Aramis is not there, or that, in not acknowledging my signal, he is actuated by motives with which I am unacquainted, and of which, perhaps, you yourself are ignorant, however much monseigneur the Bishop of Vannes may be your liegeman.'

Fouquet sighed, took a few turns up and down the room, and finally, in a state of dejection, sat down upon the side of his handsomely furnished bed.

D'Artagnan looked at him with pitying eyes.

'I have seen, in the course of my life,' said the musketeer, 'a number of persons arrested. Monsieur de Cinq-Mars and Monsieur de Chalais. I was very young at the time. Then I witnessed the arrest of Monsieur de Condé, with the princes, and was present when Monsieur de Retz and Monsieur Broussel[150] were taken. Now, monseigneur, it may seem a strange thing to say, but, of the whole of them, you most resemble, at the present moment, the unfortunate Broussel. It would not take much to make you do as he did, namely, put your table-napkin into your portfolio and wipe your mouth with your papers. *Mordieu!* Monsieur Fouquet, a man like you should not give way to despair in this manner! Suppose any of your friends were to see you!'

'Monsieur d'Artagnan,' said Fouquet, with the ghost of a smile, 'you do not, I fear, understand me at all. It is precisely because my friends do *not* see me, that I am as you see me now. I cannot bear to live alone; I am nothing if left by myself. My whole life has been spent in gathering around me friends whom I could look to for comfort and support. In prosperity, all their happy voices, made happy by me, joined together in expressions of gratitude and kindly feeling. In disfavour, these humble voices attuned themselves to the murmurings of my heart. I have never known isolation. The phantom poverty, I have, indeed, sometimes imagined as waiting for me in rags at the end of my career! But poverty is only a spectre of which many of my friends have, for years, made sport, and have poetised and made much of in so delightful a manner as to make me love them. Poverty! oh! I am ready to accept, to recognise it, and to take it to my heart as a disinherited sister; for it means neither solitude, exile nor prison! Can I ever be poor whilst I have such friends as Pélisson, La Fontaine and Molière, and such a mistress as – But, solitude! think what it means to me, a man of action and pleasure; a man who exists only in the existence of others! Oh! if you only knew how utterly alone I feel at this moment! and how you appear to me a being who separates me from all I love, the very incarnation of solitude, annihilation and death!'

'But I have already said, Monsieur Fouquet,' protested d'Artagnan, greatly moved, 'that you exaggerate things. The king likes you.'

'No,' said Fouquet, shaking his head, 'no.'

'Monsieur Colbert hates you.'

'Monsieur Colbert? Of what importance is he?'

'He will ruin you.'

'I defy him to do that, for I am ruined already.'

Upon hearing this strange avowal, d'Artagnan threw a look round the room of such significance that, although he said not a word, Fouquet understood him at once, and added, 'Of what use is an exhibition of wealth like this to a penniless owner? Do you know what effect such possessions have upon rich people? It is simply to make the possessors disgusted with and intolerant of anything less costly. You speak of the wonders of Vaux. Well, what of them? What is the good of them? If I am a ruined man, how can I fill the urns of my naiads with water, supply my salamanders with fire, and fill the lungs of my tritons with air? To be rich enough to do this, Monsieur d'Artagnan, is to be too rich.'

D'Artagnan shook his head.

'Oh! I know quite well what you are thinking,' continued Fouquet quickly, 'were you the owner of Vaux, you would sell it, and buy, with the proceeds, an estate in the country, comprising woods, fields and orchards, which would be productive enough to support its owner. With forty million, you might – '

'Ten million,' interrupted d'Artagnan.

'Not *one* million, my dear captain. No one, in France, is rich enough to give two million for Vaux, and keep up the place in its present style. No one could do it; no one would know how.'

'Well, hang it all!' said d'Artagnan, 'when all's said and done, a million does not imply actual destitution.'

'But it is hard on it, nevertheless, my dear monsieur.'

'How do you make that out?'

'Oh! you would never understand; but be assured that under no circumstances would I *sell* Vaux. I don't mind making you a present of it, if you care to accept it,' said Fouquet, accompanying his words with a movement of the shoulders impossible to describe.

'You would make a much better bargain by giving it to the king.'

'There is no necessity for me to do that because the king could help himself to it, if he coveted the place; and, for that very reason, I would rather see it destroyed altogether. Look here, Monsieur d'Artagnan, if the king were not a guest under my roof, I would set alight a number of chests full of fireworks which are in reserve in the dome and burn the whole place down to the ground.'

'Bah!' said the musketeer contemptuously, 'what would be the good of that? Why, even then, you could not destroy the gardens, and they are worth all the rest of the place put together.'

'And yet,' continued Fouquet, after a pause, 'what have I been saying? Burn down Vaux! destroy my palace! Still, Vaux is not really mine. It is true that the man who paid for all these treasures has a right to enjoy them, but they really belong to the man who created them, Vaux belongs to Le Brun, to Le Nôtre, to Pélisson, to Levau and to La Fontaine. It belongs to Molière, the author and producer of *Les Fâcheux*. Vaux, in short, belongs to posterity. You see, then, Monsieur d'Artagnan, that my own house no more belongs to me.'

'A very pretty sentiment indeed,' said d'Artagnan, 'and one in which I recognise Monsieur Fouquet. It dispels altogether the vision of the snivelling Broussel. If you are ruined, monseigneur, you must look the thing squarely in the face; you, yourself, also belong to posterity, and you must be careful to act with becoming dignity, and not to undervalue yourself. Just look at me, who have for the moment the semblance of authority over you, because it has been my duty to arrest you. Fate, which allots to every player on this world's stage the part he has to play, has cast me in a far more unenviable one than your own. I am one of those who prefer the part of a king to that of a peasant, and who think it more agreeable to wear good clothes and express oneself in refined language, than to go about in worn-out shoes or have one's back tickled with a rope's end. In short, you have had the unlimited control of money, have been in a position to command and to enjoy life; whilst I have never been free from a tether and am always at the beck and call of a master. Well, monseigneur, however unimportant I may be as compared with yourself, I assure you that the recollection of what I have gone through acts as a stimulus and prevents me from prematurely bowing my old head. I shall be a good old trooper to the very last, and when the end comes, I shall die in harness. You will not find yourself in any the worse plight if you follow my example. A crisis, like the present one, happens to a man but once in his lifetime, and when it comes, it behoves him to rise to the occasion and meet it manfully. There is a Latin proverb, the words of which I forget, but the meaning of which I remember, for I have often thought of them. It says, "the end crowns the work".'[151]

Fouquet left his seat, put his arm round d'Artagnan's neck and pressed him to his heart, whilst with the hand which was at liberty he gave him a hearty grip.

'An excellent sermon,' he said, after a pause.

'A soldier's sermon, monseigneur.'

'You must take an interest in me to give me such sound advice.'

'Perhaps I do.'

Fouquet became thoughtful; then, after a short interval, he said, 'Where can Monsieur d'Herblay be?'

'Ah! I wonder,' said d'Artagnan.

'I suppose I must not ask you to make another endeavour to find him?'

'You may ask, Monsieur Fouquet, but I cannot do it. It would be highly imprudent. People would know it; and Aramis, who is not mixed up in this business, would be compromised, and involved in your disgrace.'

'Then, I will wait until tomorrow.'

'That will be the wisest thing to do.'

'What shall we do in the morning?'

'I have no idea, monseigneur.'

'Will you do me a favour, Monsieur d'Artagnan?'

'Very willingly.'

'Assuming that I remain here, and that you keep guard over me, you will then be carrying out your instructions, will you not?'

'Certainly.'

'Well then, stay here, and be to me as a shadow. You are a shadow that I prefer to any other.'

D'Artagnan bowed his acknowledgments.

'But forget that you are Monsieur d'Artagnan, captain of musketeers; forget that I am Monsieur Fouquet, minister of finance, and let us talk of my affairs.'

'The deuce! that is a ticklish subject to dwell upon.'

'Really?'

'It is, indeed. However, for your sake, Monsieur Fouquet, I will strive to perform an impossibility.'

'Many thanks. Tell me what the king said to you.'

'Nothing.'

'Is that the way you answer me? Tell me, then, what you think of my present position.'

'Nothing.'

'Nevertheless, unless you bear me some ill-will – '

'Your position is a difficult one.'

'Why so?'

'Because you are in your own house.'

'You said you would be frank. But are you, seeing you refuse to give me the slightest atom of information!'

'Shall I say, then, that I should not have had for anyone else the consideration that I have shown you?'

'Ah! there I am quite with you.'

'Listen, then, monseigneur, and learn how I should probably have acted in the case of anyone but yourself. I should have presented myself at your door when your friends had left you. If they had not gone away, I should have waited, as one waits for rabbits to come out of a bolt-hole, and should have captured them one after the other and placed them under lock and key without making the slightest noise. Then I should have stretched myself out in your corridor, able to place my hand upon you at any moment, and so have held you in safe keeping for my master's breakfast. In this way, all scandal, resistance and noise would have been avoided; but, on the other hand, Monsieur Fouquet would have received no warning, his feelings would not have been considered, nor would he have had the advantage of those acts of courtesy which well-bred people show each other upon trying occasions, like the present. What would you have said to treatment of that kind?'

'It makes me shudder to think of it.'

'I don't wonder at it. It would have been devilish unpleasant for you had I appeared without any warning and demanded your sword.'

'Oh! indeed, sir, I should have died of shame and anger.'

'I have done nothing to call for any extravagant expression of gratitude.'

'That, allow me to say, is an opinion which I shall never share with you.'

'Well, then, since you approve of what I have done, and have recovered from the shock, which I did my best to render as gentle as possible, we can now take time to preen our wings a little. You are worried and have, no doubt, many important things to think about. I strongly recommend you, therefore, to go to sleep, or pretend to do so, either in or on your bed. I will sleep in this armchair, and when I am once asleep, you might fire off cannon in my ear without awakening me.'

Fouquet smiled.

'Unless,' continued the musketeer, 'a door should open, and then, no matter how discreetly and noiselessly a person may attempt either to enter or leave the room, I am wide awake instantly. My ear becomes preternaturally sensitive and I start up at the faintest sound. You can move about *inside* the room at your pleasure; you can write, blot out, tear up or burn at your discretion; but do not attempt to turn the key in the lock, or to turn the handle of the door, or you will cause me to wake with a start and play the devil with my nerves.'

'Upon my word, Monsieur d'Artagnan, you are the most considerate and courteous person of my acquaintance; you make me regret not having known you before.'

D'Artagnan sighed, as if he would say, 'Alas! I am afraid that, as it is, you have made my acquaintance only too soon.'

Then he threw himself into his armchair, whilst Fouquet lay upon his bed and, supporting himself on his elbow, surveyed his position and endeavoured to arrange his plans for the future.

In this manner, the two men, leaving the candles to burn themselves out, awaited the coming day, and the deeper the sighs of Fouquet the louder became the snores of d'Artagnan. No visitor, not even Aramis, disturbed their repose; not a sound was audible throughout that vast mansion.

Out of doors, the watchmen going their rounds and the patrols of musketeers made the gravel-paths crunch beneath their footsteps, only, however, to add to the peace and tranquillity of those who slumbered. The sighing of the wind and the eternal plashing of the fountains still continued, undisturbed by the petty cares and incidents which make up the sum of human life.

## CHAPTER 48

## *In the morning*

HAD THE EVENTS here chronicled taken place in classical times, the historians of the period, skilled in the arts of ancient rhetoric, would inevitably have laid stress upon the antithesis presented by the dreadful destiny of the king, imprisoned in the Bastille, tearing at the bolts and bars in his despair, in contrast with the picture of Philippe, calmly sleeping beneath the royal canopy. Not that we mean to say such rhetoric must, of necessity, be meretricious, or that the profusion with which it scatters its embellishments over the pages of history is always ill-judged. Only on this present occasion, we shall please ourselves – and our readers too, we trust – by carefully refraining from any labouring of the antithesis in question. We shall pass lightly therefore over the picture which would have formed such a notable pendant to that which we have already presented.

The young prince descended from Aramis's room in the same manner that the king had descended from his bedchamber. The dome sank slowly beneath the pressure of Monsieur d'Herblay and Philippe found himself standing beside the royal bed, which, after depositing the king in the vault beneath, had been raised to its former position. Left to himself in the midst of all this magnificence, which reminded him of the vast power suddenly thrust upon him and the difficult part he was called upon to support, Philippe began to feel, for the first time, his soul expanding under the influence of those proud emotions which to a king are as the breath of life. But, as he looked at the bed, still disordered from having been recently occupied by his brother, he turned pale. Having fulfilled its part in the plot, the bed, a mute accomplice, had returned to its appointed place, but it returned bearing traces of the crime; it spoke to its fellow-conspirator with that brutal frankness with which accomplices usually express themselves to each other. Moreover, it spoke the truth. Bending over the bed in order to observe more closely, Philippe noticed the handkerchief, still damp, with which Louis XIV had wiped the cold sweat from his forehead. It gave Philippe a shock like that which Cain may have felt at the sight of Abel's blood.

'At last I am face to face with my destiny,' mused Philippe, his cheeks livid, his eyes injected with blood. 'Will it prove more terrible than even my captivity? Obliged at every moment to bend my thoughts in unwonted channels, must I still be tormented by the promptings of my conscience? . . . Yes, the king has slept in this bed; this impression in the pillow was caused by the king's head; his bitter tears have moistened this handkerchief, and I hesitate to occupy the bed – to touch this handkerchief embroidered with the royal arms and cipher! . . . Away with these scruples! I will follow the example of Monsieur d'Herblay, whose actions are even more vigorous than his thoughts – who works with his own hand and who holds that it is but ordinary prudence to deceive or to injure one's enemies and quite in accordance with the rules of honourable conduct. This bed – this handkerchief – would have been my own had not my mother criminally allowed Louis XIV to usurp my rights. Philippe, son of France, resume what by right belongs to you! – Philippe, sole legitimate heir of Louis XIII, waste no pity upon the usurper, who, even at this moment, feels no remorse for all he has made you suffer!' Therewith, in spite of his natural shrinking, Philippe jumped into the bed, still warm from contact with its late occupant. As his head touched the pillow, he saw above him the crown of France sustained, as we have already said, by an angel with golden wings.

It may easily be imagined that this royal intruder found his position anything but conducive to repose. He trembled violently. His position may be likened to that of a tiger, terrified by a midnight hurricane, who has crept through the rushes fringing some unknown ravine to the temporarily vacated lair of a lion. Attracted by the scent, he discovers the bed of dry grass, sees the crushed and mangled fragments of bones; he glares into the darkness of the cavern, shakes the water from his tawny limbs, his coat all matted with mud and slime; then sinks wearily upon his haunches, drooping his formidable muzzle upon his huge paws, his eyes heavy with sleep, yet none the less ready for instant battle. From time to time a vivid flash, lighting up the darkness of the cavern, or the crashing of timber beneath the fierce blast of the tempest, cause him a vague feeling of apprehension which arouses him from the lethargy induced by weariness and hunger.

All of which goes to show that, even if one might be fired with the eccentric ambition of sleeping in a lion's den, one could not reasonably expect to pass a comfortable night there.

Philippe lay awake, listening to every sound, his heart beating, his mind filled with vague terrors; at length, by a powerful effort of will, he regained a degree of confidence and determined to abide the issue and to wait until some decisive circumstance should give him an opportunity of judging whether his fears were well grounded. He hoped that, confronted by a real danger, he would be able to discover the direction in which lay safety – just as the steersman is enabled by the lightning to navigate his bark clear of the dangers which threaten it in a tempest at sea.

His apprehensions were not immediately realised. Silence, which is so unnerving to those who are in suspense – so galling to those whose ambitions allow them no rest – profound silence oppressed the heart of Philippe, future King of France, lying there with the gilded crown above his head.

With the first glimmer of dawn, a shadow, rather than a being of flesh and blood, glided into the room. Philippe had been expecting its approach and therefore exhibited no surprise.

'Well, Monsieur d'Herblay?' said he.

'Well, sire, all is done.'

'Did he resist?'

'Vociferously, at first.'

'And afterwards.'

'He seemed to fall into a stupor, and at last he was removed in perfect silence.'

'Had the governor of the Bastille any suspicions?'

'None whatever.'

'Ah! of course, we resemble each other perfectly in appearance; but the prisoner will not fail to make his case known – even I succeeded in doing that – and I had a far more powerful adversary to contend against than he will have. Have you thought of this?'

'I have provided for every possible contingency. In a few days –

sooner, if necessary – we will transfer our captive from the Bastille and send him out of the country to a place of exile so remote – '

'People have been known to return from exile, Monsieur d'Herblay.'

' – so remote, I was saying, that it shall be beyond the power of man to return from it.'

Again the eyes of Aramis met those of the young king with a glance of sinister meaning. In order to change the subject, Philippe asked, 'Where is Monsieur Du Vallon?'

'He will be presented to you during the course of the day; you will congratulate him on his success in coping with the serious danger caused by the appearance of the usurper.'

'How is he to be rewarded? Confer a dukedom upon him, I suppose?'

'Yes! make a duke of him,' replied Aramis, with an enigmatical smile.

'Why do you smile, Monsieur d'Herblay?'

'I smiled because I admired your majesty's far-seeing caution.'

'What do you mean?'

'No doubt your majesty fears that poor Porthos might become an awkward witness, and therefore you think of silencing him.'

'By making him a duke!'

'Certainly. The joy would kill him, and then the secret would die with him.'

'Good God! what an idea!'

'And I should have to deplore the loss of a faithful friend,' said Aramis, imperturbably.

In the reaction which followed the anxiety they had suffered during the past few days – in their relief and joy at the successful result of their plot, they were conversing thus upon trivial matters when all at once a sound was heard which made Aramis prick up his ears.

'What is it?' asked Philippe.

'Day has come, sire.'

'Well?'

'Well, before you retired to bed last night, no doubt you decided to do something or see somebody at daybreak this morning?'

'I told my captain of musketeers I should expect him,' replied the young man, quickly.

'In that case, he will certainly be here, for he is the very soul of punctuality.'

'I hear a footstep in the vestibule.'

'It is he.'

'Well then, let us open the attack,' said the young man, with decision.

'Take care,' cried Aramis; 'to open the attack with d'Artagnan would be the height of folly. D'Artagnan has seen and heard nothing – d'Artagnan is very far from suspecting our plot; but if he should be the first to visit you this morning, he will probably get an inkling that something is going forward which requires his attention. Before allowing d'Artagnan to enter, we ought to air the room a little – allow plenty of people to pass in and out in order to confuse the scent, for d'Artagnan is the keenest sleuth-hound in the kingdom.'

'But how am I to avoid seeing him, since I gave instructions for him to be present?' asked the prince, eager to pit himself against such a redoubtable adversary.

'I will attend to that,' replied the bishop, 'and I will start by striking a blow which will make our man reel.'

'In the matter of striking, he seems to have forestalled you,' said the prince, as at that moment, a knock was heard at the door.

Aramis had not been mistaken; it was no other than d'Artagnan who thus announced his arrival. We have seen how he had spent the night in philosophising with Monsieur Fouquet; but the musketeer had not enjoyed himself – he was tired of even pretending to be asleep; and as soon as dawn began to illumine the gilded cornices in the minister's apartment, d'Artagnan rose from his chair, adjusted his sword, passed his sleeve over his coat and brushed his hat, like a guardsman suddenly called upon to undergo inspection before his superior officer.

'Are you going?' Fouquet had asked.

'Yes, monseigneur; what are you going to do?'

'I shall stay here?'

'Do you mean it?'

'Upon my honour.'

'Very good. Besides, I am only going out to get that answer – you know what I mean.'

'That *sentence*, you mean to say.'

'Stay. I am a trifle superstitious, and I noticed when I got up this morning that my sword-hilt did not get entangled with my lace, and that my shoulder-belt slipped on easily. It is an infallible sign.'

'Do you mean that it is a good omen?'

'Yes, you may lay odds on it. Every time my confounded belt stuck, it was always a sign that I was in for a wigging from Monsieur de Tréville or that I should fail to get some money out of Mazarin.

Every time my sword-knot got twisted in the baldric it meant that I might expect to be let in for some unthankful task such as I have had to put up with all my life. Whenever the sword worked loose in the sheath, it meant a duel in which I should spit my opponent. If it caught me a blow on the shins I knew I should be wounded slightly; but if it jumped right out of the scabbard I could reckon I was fairly in for it. That signified being dropped on the field of battle and two or three months' messing about with surgeons and bandages.'

'Ah! I didn't know your sword was such a clever prophet,' said Fouquet, bravely forcing a smile for he would not seem to give way to the anxiety which oppressed him. 'Have you then inherited *Tizona* or *Colada*, the enchanted swords of the Cid of Spain? Is your blade a magic brand, a faëry falchion?'

'Why, you see, my sword is almost a part of me. I have heard of some men who are warned by a twinge in the leg or by a pulsation in the temple in the same way that my sword gives me warning. Well, it told me of nothing this morning. Stay, though – why! it just slipped of its own accord underneath the belt. Do you know what that indicates?'

'No.'

'Well, it is an indication that I shall have to arrest somebody today.'

'Ah! but you said that your sword predicted nothing unpleasant for today,' said Fouquet astonished rather than annoyed to find the musketeer so outspoken. 'Then I must take it you will not be displeased to arrest me.'

'Arrest you! – *you*!'

'Of course – is not the augury – ?'

'It does not concern you, since you are already under arrest; consequently it is not you whom I shall have to arrest. That is the reason why I feel so pleased, and why I say that I am going to spend a pleasant day.'

And with these words spoken in a tone of hearty goodwill, the captain took leave of Monsieur Fouquet in order to wait upon the king. He was just passing through the doorway, when Fouquet said to him.

'Grant me one more token of your kindness.'

'What can I do, monseigneur?'

'Allow me to speak to Monsieur d'Herblay.'

'I will go and see if I can bring him back with me.'

D'Artagnan had spoken better than he knew. It was decreed that the day should pass in such a manner as to realise the predictions he had made that morning.

As we have said, he went and knocked at the king's door. The door was immediately opened. The captain might have thought that the king would have come to open it himself – a supposition by no means improbable considering the excitement in which the musketeer had left Louis XIV the previous night. But instead of seeing the king, whom he had prepared to greet respectfully, he perceived the long, impassive face belonging to Aramis. His astonishment was so extreme that he barely succeeded in smothering the startled exclamation which rose to his lips. He stared incredulously.

'Aramis!' he exclaimed.

'Ah! is that you, my dear d'Artagnan? Good-morning,' said the bishop coolly.

'You here?' stammered the musketeer.

'His majesty begs you will let it be known that he is now asleep, after having passed a restless night.'

'Ah!' exclaimed d'Artagnan. He was quite at a loss to comprehend how the Bishop of Vannes, who was very far from being a favourite of the king the night before, had contrived, in the short space of six hours, to become the most colossal mushroom of fortune that had ever sprung up by a king's bedside. For indeed, to be in a position to transmit a king's desires at the door of a monarch's bedroom to those obediently waiting in the corridor – to give commands in his name within a couple of paces of the king himself – indicated that his influence was greater than even that of Richelieu with Louis XIII. D'Artagnan's expressive eye, his mouth half-opened, his bristling moustache, expressed all these objections in the clearest possible language, although the haughty favourite remained absolutely unmoved.

'Moreover,' continued the bishop, 'you will have the goodness, captain, to permit only those to enter who have special privileges. His majesty wishes to sleep this morning.'

'But, my lord bishop, his majesty ordered me to wait upon him this morning,' objected d'Artagnan, prepared to dispute the orders he had received, and ready to give vent to the suspicions which the king's silence had awakened in his breast.

'Come again later,' said a voice from the interior of the room, in a tone which made d'Artagnan start although he had no doubt that it was the king's.

Bewildered and dumbfounded by the crushing smile of Aramis as the king pronounced these words, the musketeer could only bow.

'And, by way of reply to the question you intended to put to his majesty,' said the bishop, 'take this order, my dear d'Artagnan, and make yourself acquainted with the contents immediately. The order concerns Monsieur Fouquet.'

D'Artagnan took the document handed to him – 'An order to release the prisoner?' he thought. 'Ah!' He began to think he could see daylight in the mystery, for this order would explain the presence of Aramis in the king's bedroom. The fact of his having obtained this clemency towards Monsieur Fouquet would seem to argue that he had made considerable progress in the royal favour and, if such were the case, it would go some way towards explaining the almost incredible assurance with which Monsieur d'Herblay issued orders in the king's name. D'Artagnan, when once he had a clue, soon became acquainted with the whole case. He bowed, and made to retire. 'Stay,' said the bishop, 'I will accompany you.'

'Where to?'

'To see Monsieur Fouquet. I should like to congratulate him on the good news.'

'Ah! Aramis what a surprise you gave me just now!' exclaimed d'Artagnan.

'But now you understand, of course?'

'Understand? Why to be sure!' replied d'Artagnan. To himself he added – 'Devil take me if I have the slightest idea what it all means! No matter, I have an order in writing.' Then aloud – 'Come then, monseigneur.' And d'Artagnan conducted Aramis into the presence of Fouquet.

CHAPTER 49

## The king's friend

FOUQUET had been waiting anxiously. He had already dismissed several servants and some friends who had called upon him earlier than he was generally accustomed to receive visitors. To none of them had Fouquet said a word about the danger which was hanging over his head, contenting himself with asking them for information as to the whereabouts of Aramis. When he caught sight of d'Artagnan returning, with Aramis immediately behind, his spirits rose; he was as much overjoyed as he had been depressed before. The sight of Aramis seemed to the minister a sufficient compensation for the misfortune of his arrest. The prelate was in a taciturn humour; and as for d'Artagnan he was stupefied by the succession of incredible incidents he had witnessed.

'Ah! captain, I see you have brought Monsieur d'Herblay,' said Fouquet, briskly.

'Yes, monseigneur and, what is better, I have brought the order for your release.'

'I am free!'

'Yes! by the king's command.'

Fouquet at once resumed his wonted composure. He threw a questioning glance towards Aramis.

'Yes,' continued d'Artagnan, 'you have to thank the Bishop of Vannes for it is he who has worked this change in the king's mind.'

'Oh!' said Fouquet, grateful for the service done him yet mortified by the necessity of accepting such service.

'But you, who are able to protect Monsieur Fouquet,' said d'Artagnan, addressing Aramis, 'can't you also do something for me?'

'Whatever you please, my friend,' replied the bishop, in a tone of quiet assurance.

'I only ask one thing: tell me how it is you have suddenly become a favourite of the king, you who have scarcely spoken to him twice in your life?'

'I have no secrets from an old friend such as you are,' said Aramis, suavely.

'Ah! thank you! then pray tell me – I am dying of curiosity.'

'Well, you imagine I have hardly seen the king more than twice, but the fact is, I have spoken to him a hundred times. Only we kept the matter secret, that is all.'

Well aware that he had still further whetted d'Artagnan's curiosity, which he had no intention of allaying, Aramis turned towards Monsieur Fouquet, who was as much astonished as the musketeer. 'Monseigneur,' he continued, 'the king bids me tell you that he is better disposed towards you than ever, and that he is deeply sensible of your kindness and generosity in organising this magnificent fête.' And he bowed ceremoniously to Fouquet, who, dumbfounded at the marvellous vigour of the bishop's diplomacy, remained, not only speechless, but quite incapable of thought or action.

D'Artagnan had an idea that these two men had something to say to one another, and was about to obey the tactful impulse which, in such circumstances, causes the one who feels that his presence might be inconvenient to the others, to efface himself; but his lively curiosity, already piqued by the prevailing air of mystery, counselled him to linger. Aramis turned towards him, and said, with a pleasant smile,

'You haven't forgotten, I suppose, my dear d'Artagnan, the king's order with regard to those whom he does not wish to see on rising?' The hint was too obvious to be ignored, and the musketeer, having bowed to Monsieur Fouquet, saluted Aramis with ironical deference and took his departure. Fouquet, who had scarcely been able to conceal his impatience, sprang to the door and fastened it; then, turning to the bishop, he said, 'I think, my dear d'Herblay, it is time you gave me an explanation of what has taken place, for deuce take me! if I have the faintest idea what it all means.'

'You shall have a full explanation,' said Aramis, seating himself and handing a chair to Fouquet. 'Where shall we begin?'

'Before you tell me anything else, let me know why the king has given me my liberty.'

'You ought rather to ask why he had you arrested.'

'Since I have been under arrest, I have had time to think it over, and I have come to the conclusion that jealousy had something to do with it. This fête of mine upset Monsieur Colbert, and Colbert has brought forward some cause of complaint against me; I shouldn't wonder if it were Belle-Isle.'

'No; that business is all over and done with.'

'What is it, then?'

'You remember those vouchers for thirteen million which Mazarin managed to get hold of, and which you ought to have retained?'

'Yes, yes; well?'

'Well, it has been declared that you appropriated the money.'

'Great God in heaven!'

'And that is not the whole of it. You remember that letter you wrote to La Vallière?'

'Unfortunately, I can't help remembering.'

'You are accused of bribery and high treason.'

'Then why has the king pardoned me?'

'We will let that question remain open for a moment. First of all, I wish you to be quite clear with regard to the facts. Keep this well in your mind: the king knows you to be guilty of misappropriation of the public funds.'

'Oh! good Lord.'

'Yes – I am well aware that you have done nothing of the sort; but, at any rate, the king has not seen the vouchers, and he cannot believe otherwise than that the crime is proved against you.'

'Pardon me, I don't see – '

'I will explain presently. The king, moreover, having been shown the letter you wrote to La Vallière offering her your interest, cannot entertain the slightest doubt with regard to your intentions towards her; is that clear?'

'Perfectly. But let me hear the rest.'

'I am coming to it. In consequence of these crimes you have rendered the king your mortal enemy, beyond any possible hope of forgiveness.'

'I am bound to agree with you, but am I then so all-powerful that he dares not attack me, notwithstanding all the weapons with which my weakness and misfortune have furnished him, and the bitter hatred he bears me?'

'I think, then, you agree with me that the king is incensed against you beyond hope of reconciliation,' said Aramis, calmly.

'Nay, but he has – '

'Can you really believe he has pardoned you?' said the bishop, glancing keenly at his companion.

'I can say nothing as to the feeling which prompted the action, but I must believe in the reality of the action itself.' Aramis gently shrugged his shoulders. 'Why else,' continued Fouquet, 'did Louis charge you with the message you delivered to me?'

'He gave me no message to deliver to you.'

'What!' exclaimed the minister, taken back. 'Is this order, then, also worthless?'

'By no means,' replied Aramis, with a singular inflection, which Fouquet, notwithstanding his perturbation, found awe-inspiring.

'Ha! you are concealing something from me,' cried the minister.

Aramis stroked his chin with his slender fingers

'Does the king mean to banish me?'

'You seem to imagine we are playing hide and seek. Do you expect me to tell you when you are *warm*, as children say?'

'Well, tell me then.'

'Guess.'

'You frighten me.'

'Pooh! then it is evident you have not guessed.'

'What *was* it the king said to you? In the name of friendship, do not keep me in suspense!'

'The king said nothing to me.'

'Can't you see I am bursting with impatience, d'Herblay? Tell me at once, am I still minister of finance?'

'If you care to remain minister.'

'By what means have you acquired the extraordinary influence you seem to have over the king? You make him act just as you wish.'

'You are quite right.'

'It seems incredible!'

'It certainly has that appearance.'

'D'Herblay, for friendship's sake, for my sake, I conjure you, by all you hold dear, tell me, I entreat you. How came you to exercise such control over Louis XIV? He has always regarded you coolly, that I know.'

'However, the king has the utmost confidence in me *now*,' declared Aramis emphatically.

'There is some secret between you?'

'Yes, there is a secret.'

'Of such a nature as entirely to change the king's whole policy?'

'You are a man of admirable discernment, monseigneur: you have guessed it exactly. I have indeed discovered a secret of a nature to change the entire policy of the King of France.'

'Ah!' said Fouquet, refraining, with a gentleman's instinctive delicacy, from forcing a friend's confidence by questioning him.

'You shall judge for yourself and tell me if I am mistaken as to the importance of this secret.'

'Since you are so good as to take me into your confidence, I am listening. Only pray observe, my dear friend, that I have in no way invited it. Keep your own secret if you wish.'

Aramis paused a moment to arrange the matter orderly in his mind – 'Do you remember,' he resumed, 'the occasion of the birth of Louis XIV?'

'As though it had happened yesterday.'

'Did you ever hear of any particular circumstances in connection with his birth?'

'No – unless you mean that it was stated that the king was not indisputably the son of Louis XIII.'

'That is a matter of no consequence to us or to the kingdom. The law of France declares a child to be the child of the man whom the law recognises as its father.'

'True; but it is a weighty question when it has to do with the purity of a race.'

'Oh! a question of secondary importance. Then you heard of nothing in particular?'

'Nothing.'

'Well, there comes in my secret. I must tell you that the queen, instead of giving birth to one son only, was delivered of twins.'

Fouquet looked up, 'And the other died, I suppose?' said he.

'You shall hear. These two boys should have been their mother's pride and the hope of France; but the king's cowardice and super-stition led him to dread the consequences which might arise from the fact of there being two heirs of equal rights; he feared a conflict – perhaps Civil War – and he suppressed one of the twin princes.'

' "Suppressed", did you say?'

'Stay a moment. The two children grew up; one of them – whose minister you are – mounted the throne; the other grew up in obscurity, cut off from the world.'

'And that one – ?'

'That one is my friend.'

'Great heavens! What is this you are telling me, Monsieur d'Herblay? And what is this poor prince doing?'

'Ask me rather, what has he *done*?'

'Yes, what?'

'He passed his boyhood in a remote part of the country, and afterwards was shut up in a fortress which is called the Bastille.'

'Can it be possible!' cried Fouquet, his hands clasped in a very ecstasy of surprise and amazement.

'One of them was the spoiled child of Fortune. Whilst the other was the most miserable wretch alive.'

'And does his mother know all this?'

'Anne of Austria knows everything.'

'And the king?'

'Ah! the king – he knows nothing about it.'

'I am glad to hear that!' said Fouquet. This remark appeared to impress the bishop strangely. He regarded his companion anxiously. 'Pardon me, I have interrupted you,' said Fouquet.

'I was saying then, that this poor young prince was the most unhappy of mortals; but God, who cares for all His creatures, interposed in order to alleviate his lot.'

'Ah! in what way?'

'You shall see. The reigning king – you understand why I say "the reigning king"?'

'No – why?'

'Because both of them, in virtue of their birth, are equally entitled to reign. You are of my opinion?'

'I agree with you.'

'Positively?'

'Positively. Twins are one person in two bodies.'

'I am glad that so distinguished a jurist as yourself should have pronounced this opinion. We have established, then, that the rights of both were equal, have we not?'

'Incontestably. Good God! what a marvellous story!'

'Wait a little – you have not yet heard all. God in His wisdom has seen fit to raise up a protector of the oppressed – an avenger, perhaps. It happened that the reigning king, the usurper – you quite agree with me, do you not, that the selfish enjoyment of the whole heritage, when one is only entitled to half of it, can only be called usurpation?'

'It is the right word.'

'Then I will continue. God willed it that the usurper should be served by a minister who is not only a man of rare talents, but also a generous and noble-hearted gentleman.'

'Ah! very good, I understand you,' cried Fouquet. 'You are counting upon my help to repair the wrong done to the poor brother of Louis XIV? You were right – I will assist you to the utmost. Thanks, d'Herblay, thanks!'

'No, it is not that at all. You do not allow me to finish,' said Aramis, impassively.

'I will say no more.'

'I was saying,' continued Aramis, 'that the reigning king, having conceived a violent aversion to his minister, Monsieur Fouquet, threatens him with ruin and loss of liberty – possibly with death. But heaven – still watching over the interests of that unhappy prince, sacrificed from motives of policy – heaven has permitted that Monsieur Fouquet, in his turn, should find a devoted friend who was cognisant of this state secret, and who had the courage to bring it to light, after having had the self-control to keep the secret locked up for twenty years in his own breast.'

'You need say no more,' cried Fouquet, unable to refrain from expressing the eager generosity of his mind, 'I understand you perfectly. You went to the king as soon as you heard of my arrest; you interceded for me; he refused to listen to you; then you threatened to expose this secret, and Louis XIV, terrified, was forced by his fear of your disclosures to concede that which he had refused to your generous intercession. I understand; you have the king in your power – I understand!'

'You misunderstand entirely,' said Aramis, 'and here you have been again interrupting me, my friend. And, moreover, you will permit me to remark that your reasoning is unsound, and you are forgetting something which it is of importance to remember.'

'What do you mean?'

'You know the circumstances I laid stress upon at the beginning of this conversation?'

'You mean the king's unconquerable aversion towards me; but surely, in face of such a threat, he cannot continue – '

'Ah! that is where your reasoning is at fault. What! can you really imagine that, if I had made such a revelation to the king, I should still be alive at the present moment?'

'But it was only ten minutes ago that you were speaking to the king.'

'True: he would scarcely have had time to put me to death; but he would have had quite time enough to have me gagged and thrown into a dungeon. Come now, a little more precision in your reasoning, *mordieu!*' And, by the mere use of this barrack-room expletive – a momentary forgetfulness on the part of a man who never forgot himself – the singular exaltation of the present mood of the Bishop of Vannes, always so calm and impenetrable, was made startlingly apparent to Fouquet. 'And then,' continued Aramis, after pausing in order to recover his usual calmness, 'should I be the man I am – should I be a true friend – were I to expose you, you whom the king already hates, to bear the brunt of the young king's resentment, increased a thousandfold by such a revelation? To have robbed him is nothing, to have made overtures to his mistress – that is a mere trifle; but to hold at your mercy both his crown and his honour – why! he would strangle you with his own hands rather than suffer it!'

'Then you have told him nothing of your secret?'

'I would sooner have tried to avoid death by swallowing as much poison as Mithridates[152] drank in twenty years!'

'What did you do, then?'

'Ah! now we come to the interesting part. You still give me your attention, do you not?'

'I should think I do, indeed! Speak!'

Aramis rose and made a circuit of the room, assured himself that no third person was within earshot, and then returned and stood beside the armchair in which Fouquet was seated, awaiting the bishop's revelations with the most anxious interest

'I forgot to mention,' resumed Aramis, 'one remarkable circumstance with regard to these twins: it is this. The resemblance between them is so great that God alone could distinguish one from the other were they summoned before His tribunal. Certainly their own mother could not.'

'Is it possible?' exclaimed Fouquet.

'The same noble cast of countenance, the same height and carriage – even the same voice!'

'But as regards their minds, are they equal in intelligence?'

'Oh! in that respect, monseigneur, they are dissimilar. The prisoner of the Bastille is incontestably superior to his brother; and were this poor victim to be raised to the throne, France would have had no master more distinguished for genius and loftiness of character since first she began to be a nation.'

Oppressed by the weight of this terrible secret, Fouquet covered his face with his hands. Aramis bent over him, and in low, earnest tones, continued to act the part of tempter.

'They are unlike in yet another respect, monseigneur,' he said, 'for of these twin sons of Louis XIII there is one who is unacquainted with Monsieur Colbert.' Fouquet raised his head quickly; his face drawn and pale. The blow had struck home, if not to his heart, at least to his understanding

'I see your drift,' he murmured: 'it is a conspiracy you ask me to engage in.'

'I do not deny it.'

'One of those attempts which alter the fate of nations, as you said when we began this conversation.'

'And also the fate of ministers; yes, monseigneur!'

'In short, you are proposing to substitute the son of Louis XIII who is now a prisoner, for that other son of Louis XIII who is asleep in the Chamber of Morpheus?'

Aramis gave a sinister smile – the reflection of the sinister thought which was in his mind – 'You have said it,' he replied.

'But,' rejoined Fouquet, after a moment of tense silence, 'you cannot have reflected that this conspiracy which you are contemplating is of a nature to throw the whole kingdom in confusion; that to dethrone a king and to set up another in his place would be like tearing up a tree whose roots are of infinite extension, and planting another in the same spot. The earth around could never be trimmed so exactly that the new king might be safeguarded against the final blast of the tempest which had torn up his predecessor, or even against the oscillations caused by his own weight.'

Aramis was still smiling.

'Think!' continued Fouquet, his quick imagination warming up as he considered all the aspects of the case with that breadth of view which foresees every consequence, 'think! it will be necessary to summon meetings of the nobility, the clergy and the people; to depose the reigning prince; to disturb the tomb of Louis XIII with the terrible scandal; to attack the honour and even the life of Anne of Austria – a woman; and also the peace of mind of another woman, Maria Theresa; then, when all that is done – if it ever *is* done – '

'I fail to understand you,' said Aramis, coldly. 'In all that you have just said, there is not a single word which has any useful bearing upon the matter.'

'What!' cried the minister, in surprise, 'you have not thought of ways and means – a practical man like you! You have contented yourself with the childish delight of contemplating a pleasant illusion, and you neglect all the opportunities of putting it into execution – in a word, you neglect reality to chase a bubble – can it be possible?'

'My dear friend,' said Aramis, in a slightly contemptuous tone of familiarity, 'how does God act when He wills that one king should be raised up in place of another?'

'Ah!' cried Fouquet, 'He gives a command to His agent, who seizes upon the condemned, removes him, and seats his triumphant successor upon the vacant throne. But do not forget that His agent is Death. Good heavens! Monsieur d'Herblay, can the idea have entered your mind – ?'

'There is no question of death, monseigneur. Really, you overshoot the mark; who has said a word about putting Louis XIV to death? Who speaks about imitating the workings of fate in all their details? No; I meant only to say that God accomplishes these changes without confusion, without scandal, almost without exertion; and that men inspired by God succeed in all that they undertake with the same completeness of method.'

'What are you saying?'

'I mean to say, my friend,' rejoined Aramis, with the same inflection he had previously adopted; 'I mean to say that I defy you to show that there has been any confusion or scandal caused by the substitution of the prisoner in the place of the king.'

'Eh!' cried Fouquet, his face suddenly gone whiter than the handkerchief with which he wiped his brow. 'You say – ?'

'Go to the king's bedroom,' continued Aramis, quietly, 'and even now that the mystery has been explained to you, I defy you to notice that it is the prisoner of the Bastille who is lying in his brother's bed.'

'But the king?' stammered Fouquet, horror-stricken at the news.

'Which king?' asked Aramis with his most suave accent. 'The one who hates you, or the other?'

'The king – who was king yesterday – ?'

'The king of yesterday? Have no fear; he has been taken to the Bastille to take the place which his victim occupied too long.'

'Great God! And who took him there?'

'I myself.'

'*You?*'

'Yes, quite simply. I carried him off last night, and whilst he was descending into obscurity, the other was gaining the sunshine. I think there has been no unseemly scuffle. Sheet lightning, my friend, wakes nobody.'

Fouquet gave vent to a strange cry, as though he had been struck by an invisible hand. 'You did that?' he whispered.

'Yes, and rather cleverly, too. Don't you agree with me?'

'*You* have dethroned the king? *You* have cast the king into the Bastille?'

'That is the fact.'

'And the deed was done *here*, at Vaux?'

'Here, at Vaux, in the Chamber of Morpheus. Would it not seem as if it had been constructed expressly for the purpose?'

'And you say it took place last night?'

'Between midnight and one o'clock.'

Fouquet made a sudden movement as though he were about to throw himself upon Aramis, but he checked himself. 'At Vaux! In my own house!' he said, in a strangled voice.

'Why! of course; and it is still your house, since Monsieur Colbert will no longer have the power to deprive you of it.'

'Good heavens! That such a crime should be committed under my roof!'

'Crime!' repeated Aramis, thunder-struck.

'An abominable crime!' cried Fouquet, with growing excitement; 'a crime more dastardly than assassination! A crime which brands my name with lasting infamy, and will render it a byword for dishonour for generations yet unborn!'

'Monsieur Fouquet, you are raving!' replied Aramis, in a voice which had lost its previous assurance. 'You speak too loudly; hush! – take care!'

'I will shout! – the whole world shall hear me!'

'Again I say, take care!'

Fouquet turned sharply round and looked steadily in the prelate's face. 'You have dishonoured me,' he said, 'by this act of treason – this foul crime – committed upon my guest, who had placed himself in my hands. Would that I had died before such vile treachery could be practised upon a guest of mine!'

'The treachery belongs to him who, even while under your roof, was plotting your disgrace and ruin; never forget that.'

'He was my guest – he was my king!'

Aramis rose. His eyes were bloodshot, his mouth drawn into a convulsive grin. His whole form seemed suddenly aged. 'Am I speaking to a madman?' he said, hoarsely.

'You are speaking to an honest man.'

'*Fool!*'

'One who will prevent you from completing your crime.'

'Fool!'

'A man who would die – who would kill you – rather than permit you to complete his dishonour.'

And Fouquet made a spring towards his sword, which d'Artagnan had replaced at the head of the bed. He drew the shining blade from its sheath, his hand shaking with excitement. Aramis's brow lowered, he thrust his hand into his breast as though in search of a weapon. His movement did not escape Fouquet; with noble magnanimity he flung his sword clattering along the floor; then approaching Aramis he laid his unarmed hand upon his shoulder. 'Monsieur d'Herblay,' said he, 'gladly would I die here in order not to outlive my shame. I entreat you, if you still have any regard for me, to kill me!'

Aramis maintained a stony silence. 'You do not answer me,' continued Fouquet. Aramis slowly raised his head; a gleam of hope appeared in his eyes. 'Reflect, monseigneur,' he began. 'Think what we have to expect. This act of justice achieved, the king still lives, and his imprisonment means that your life is saved.'

'Yes,' replied Fouquet, 'I do believe that you acted in what you thought to be my interests, but I cannot accept the service at your hands. Still, I would not have you ruined; you must leave this place at once.'

The light died out of Aramis's eyes; he felt in his heart the bitterness of death. 'The duties of hospitality are sacred,' continued Fouquet, with noble dignity; 'your safety shall be no further imperilled than the safety of him whose ruin you have attempted.'

'But *your* ruin is certain – certain,' said Aramis with prophetic emphasis. 'Mark my words!'

'So be it, Monsieur d'Herblay; but that consideration shall not stop me. You must leave Vaux – get clear of France; I give you four hours to put yourself beyond the king's reach.'

'Four hours?' repeated Aramis, with bitter irony.

'Upon my word of honour! You shall not be pursued until four hours have elapsed. You have four clear hours to distance those whom the king may send after you.'

'Four hours!' repeated Aramis, in a voice that was almost a groan.

'It is longer than you will need to reach the sea in order to cross to Belle-Isle, which I offer you as an asylum.'

'Ah!' murmured Aramis.

'Belle-Isle is mine only that it may be placed at your service, just as Vaux is mine to place at the king's disposal. Away, d'Herblay, away! So long as I live, not a hair of your head shall be injured.'

'I thank you,' said Aramis, bitterly.

'Go, then; and promise me that you will travel as swiftly to ensure your safety as I shall, in order to save my honour.'

Aramis withdrew his hand from his bosom. It was red with his own blood; he had torn the flesh with his nails, as though to chastise the body which had harboured so many projects, more vain, more foolish and fleeting than the life of man itself. Fouquet was struck with horror and pity; he opened his arms to Aramis. 'I had no weapon,' muttered the latter, harshly. Then, without noticing Fouquet's outstretched hand, he turned, and made two steps towards the door. His last word was a blasphemy! his last gesture with his hand, which sprinkled some drops of blood upon Fouquet's face, was a curse! Both men left the room and plunged down the secret staircase which led to the enclosed courtyard.

'Shall I go alone?' thought Aramis. 'Shall I warn the prince? Hell and furies! What use to warn the prince? Take him with me – drag after me a perpetual accusation? What then? War? Civil war – swift and relentless? Ah! impossible! We have no resources. What will become of him without me? Oh! he will do as I do – he will fall in the dust. Who knows? Well, let destiny take its course! He was condemned to misery; let him remain miserable! God! – hell and damnation! O! thou dark and mocking power called the Genius of Mankind, thou art more fitful, more uncertain than the wind in the mountains. Chance thou hast been named, but thou art nothing; thou art a part of all men's destiny, thou canst even move mountains. yet suddenly thy force leaves thee in the presence of the Cross, made of dead wood, but behind which stands another power, invisible like thyself – whom mayhap thou hast denied, and who wreaks His vengeance upon thee by hurling thee to nameless ruin! Ruin! I am ruined! What is to be done? Go to Belle-Isle! Yes, and leave Porthos here to talk – to tell everything to anyone who questions him! Porthos too may be involved – may have to suffer for my deeds. By hell! it shall not be! Porthos shall not suffer – Porthos, who trusted me – though the whole world be ruined. He is part of myself, his misfortunes are my own. Porthos shall go with me, Porthos shall follow my destiny. I am a broken man, but he will not reproach me.'

And Aramis, apprehensive of meeting anyone to whom his haste might appear suspicious, gained Porthos's room without having been seen by a soul. Porthos, who had only just returned from Paris, was already sleeping the sleep of the just. His huge bulk was as little affected by fatigue as his head was occupied with thought. Aramis entered quietly as a shadow, and laid his hand upon the giant's shoulder. 'Come, Porthos,' he cried, 'wake instantly.'

Porthos rose obediently, opening his eyes even before he had shaken sleep from his brain.

'We must be off,' cried Aramis.

'Ah!' said Porthos.

'We must ride, ride – faster than we have ever ridden before.'

'Ah!' said Porthos, once more.

'Come, dress yourself, old friend,' and he assisted the giant to dress, then hastily stuffed his valuables into his pockets. Whilst he was engaged in this operation, a slight noise made him pause, he looked round and saw d'Artagnan standing in the doorway watching him. Aramis started.

'What the devil are you up to that you are in such a bustle?' asked the musketeer.

'Hush!' breathed Porthos, mysteriously.

'We are just starting on a mission,' said the bishop.

'You are very lucky!' said the musketeer.

'Pooh!' said Porthos, 'I feel a trifle tired; I would sooner have slept; but the king's service, you know – !'

'Have you seen Monsieur Fouquet?' asked Aramis of d'Artagnan.

'Yes, only this very moment, in his carriage.'

'What did he say to you?'

'He said, "Adieu." '

'Was that all?'

'What else should he have to say to me? Am I of any consequence since all you people are in the royal favour?'

'Listen,' said Aramis, as he embraced the musketeer, 'your good times are returning; you will have no reason to be jealous of anyone.'

'Nonsense!'

'I predict that an event will happen this very day which will raise your position considerably.'

'Really?'

'You know that I know how matters are going.'

'Oh! yes!'

'Come, Porthos, are you ready? We must be off.'

'I am with you, Aramis.'

'Don't forget to embrace d'Artagnan.'

'Not likely!'

'Are the horses saddled?'

'Plenty of them here. Would you like to have mine?' said d'Artagnan.

'No; Porthos keeps his own stable. Adieu, d'Artagnan!'

The fugitives mounted their horses under the eyes of the captain of musketeers, who held the stirrup for Porthos. His glance followed the two friends until they had disappeared from view.

'In any other circumstances,' thought the Gascon, 'I should have said those two were escaping; but, nowadays, politics are so different from what they used to be that the new name for escaping is "going on a mission". Well, it's no affair of mine; let me attend to my own business.'

And with this philosophical reflection he returned home to his quarters.

## CHAPTER 50

## *How orders were obeyed at the Bastille*

FOUQUET had jumped into his carriage and was being driven towards Paris at top speed. His mind was agitated during the whole of the journey with the horror inspired by the plot which had just been revealed to him. 'Great heavens!' he thought, 'what must these extraordinary men have been in their youth – these men who, in their old age, have vigour still to conceive and execute unflinchingly schemes of such tremendous magnitude!'

At one moment he would almost persuade himself that all that Aramis had related to him was a dream; or again, the idea seized him that the whole story was a fable purposely designed to entrap him, and he felt a presentiment that, on arriving at the Bastille, he, Fouquet, would find himself confronted with a warrant for his arrest which would send him to rejoin the king who had been dethroned. While this idea was strong in his mind, he wrote and sealed several orders as he was being whirled along, and dispatched them at the first halt, while the horses were being changed. These orders were addressed to d'Artagnan and to all the other officers of the guards whose fidelity to the king was unquestionable. 'Whether I am a prisoner or not,' said Fouquet to himself, 'I owe it to my honour to take every possible precaution to ensure the defeat of this conspiracy. These letters will not be delivered until after I return, if I am allowed to return, and, consequently, the seals will be unbroken and I can recall them. On the other hand, if I am delayed, it will mean that some misfortune has happened to me; and then these orders will ensure assistance both for the king and for myself.'

Before he arrived at the Bastille, all his arrangements were completed. The minister of finance had covered the fourteen miles within the hour. His access to the Bastille was barred by obstacles which Aramis had never in any of his visits had to encounter. In vain did Fouquet announce his name, equally in vain was he recognised by the sentinels; he could not obtain admittance. By dint of entreaties, commands and even threats, he prevailed upon a sentry to speak to one of the subalterns, who, in his turn, passed the word to the major. As for the governor, nobody even ventured to think of disturbing him. Fouquet, seated in his carriage, which had been halted at the gates of the fortress, was fretting with impatience while he awaited the return of the subaltern, who at last came back, sulkily enough. 'Well,' said Fouquet, irritably, 'what does the major say?'

'Well, sir,' growled the soldier insolently, 'the major burst out laughing in my face. He says that Monsieur Fouquet is at Vaux, and even if he were in Paris, Monsieur Fouquet would not rise at such an hour as this.'

'By the Lord! you are a pretty set of rascals,' cried the minister, springing out of the carriage, and, before the subaltern had time completely to close the gate, Fouquet slipped through the opening, and ran towards the guardhouse, heedless of the angry challenge of the soldier, who shouted for assistance. Fouquet gained ground, quite regardless of the disturbance he had caused; but the man, having by this time nearly caught up with him, roared to the next sentry who was stationed at the second gateway. 'Hi! there, look out, sentry!' The man crossed his pike to bar the minister's passage, but the latter, strong and active, and inflamed with anger as he was, wrested the pike from the hands of the soldier, and belaboured him lustily over the shoulders with it. The subaltern, approaching too closely, also received his share of the blows; both bellowed with rage, and hearing the cries, the whole body of the advance-guard turned out and hurried to the spot. Among the later arrivals there happened to be a man who recognised Fouquet. 'Monseigneur! – Ah! Monseigneur!' he cried. 'Hold hard, you fellows!' And he succeeded in checking the guards, who were preparing to avenge their comrades. Fouquet ordered the gate to be opened, but the men refused to open without the countersign. Fouquet then commanded them to apprise the governor; but the latter, hearing the row at the gate, had already learned the cause of it; he ran forward at the head of a picket of twenty men, followed by the major, quite under the persuasion that the Bastille was being taken by assault.

Baisemeaux at once recognised Fouquet, and lowered the sword which he had been brandishing as he ran up. 'Ah! Monseigneur,' he stammered, 'pray accept my apologies – !'

'Monsieur,' cried the minister, hot and out of breath, 'permit me to compliment you on the extremely efficient guard you keep.'

Baisemeaux turned pale, for he believed that Fouquet spoke ironically and he expected the sarcasm to be followed by a formidable explosion of anger. But Fouquet had regained his breath, and with a gesture he bade the subaltern and the sentry to approach. They came forward rubbing their shoulders. 'Here are twenty pistoles for the sentry,' said he, 'and fifty for the officer. Accept my compliments, gentlemen, I will mention to the king your devotion to your duty. Now, Baisemeaux, a word with you in private.' There was a murmur of general satisfaction, and he followed the governor to his residence. Baisemeaux still appeared crestfallen, and trembled with apprehension. The early visit which Aramis had paid him recurred to his mind, and he foresaw that it would lead to consequences highly unpleasant for an official in his position. His apprehension was by no means lessened when Fouquet, looking at him with the eye of a master, said curtly, 'Have you seen Monsieur d'Herblay this morning?'

'Yes, monseigneur.'

'Well, sir, and are you not horror-stricken at the crime of which you have been made the accomplice?'

'Halloa, that sounds black!' thought Baisemeaux. Then he replied aloud, 'Crime? – what crime, monseigneur?'

'A crime for which you are liable to be drawn and quartered, sir – keep that well in your mind! But this is not the moment for recrimination. Take me to the prisoner instantly.'

'What prisoner?' asked Baisemeaux, in great perturbation.

'Ah! you pretend ignorance – very well! By heavens! you are right to do so, for were you to admit your complicity, there would be short shrift for you! However, I am very willing to act as though I believed your assumption of ignorance, if you think it will save your neck.'

'Monseigneur, I beg you – '

'Enough said. Lead me to the prisoner.'

'Do you refer to Marchiali?'

'Who is Marchiali?'

'The prisoner whom Monsieur d'Herblay brought here this morning.'

'So he is called Marchiali?' said Fouquet whose conviction of Baisemeaux's guilt began to waver in face of his innocent assurance.

'Yes, monseigneur, that is the name under which he was entered in the register.'

Fouquet fixed a penetrating glance upon the governor, as though to read the thought lurking at the bottom of his heart. With that faculty which he possessed, in common with all men accustomed to the exercise of authority, of reading the hearts of men, he could see in the present case nothing but absolute sincerity. Besides, the mere observation of Baisemeaux's unintelligent features was sufficient to convince him that Aramis would never have taken such a man into his confidence. 'Is he the same prisoner whom Monsieur d'Herblay took away with him the day before yesterday?' he asked.

'Yes, monseigneur.'

'And brought back this morning?' added Fouquet, sharply, for he at once gathered the whole of Aramis's plan of action.

'Yes, monseigneur; that is the fact.'

'And you call him Marchiali?'

'Marchiali. If monseigneur has come here with the intention of removing him, so much the better; I had intended writing again on the subject.'

'What has he been doing then?'

'He has been harassing me extremely ever since he returned this morning; he gives way to such violent explosions of fury that one would think he would pull down the Bastille bodily.'

'The fact is I *have* come with the intention of ridding you of him,' said Fouquet.

'Ah! I am glad to hear it.'

'Lead me to his cell.'

'Monseigneur will, of course, give me the warrant – '

'What warrant?'

'An order signed by the king.'

'Wait a moment. I will write you one.'

'That will not be sufficient, monseigneur; I must have an order with the king's signature.'

Fouquet began to manifest some irritation. 'Since you are so scrupulous,' said he, 'with regard to allowing prisoners to leave, no doubt you can show me the warrant which authorised this man's leaving.'

Baisemeaux produced the warrant to release Seldon. 'Well,' cried Fouquet, this is for Seldon, not for Marchiali.'

'But Marchiali has not been released, monseigneur; he is here.'

'But you tell me that Monsieur d'Herblay took him away and brought him back.'

'That is not what I said.'

'It is certainly what you said – why! I remember the very words.'

'Then it was a slip of the tongue.'

'Monsieur de Baisemeaux, I warn you, take care!'

'I have nothing to fear, monseigneur; I have acted according to regulations.'

'Have you the effrontery to tell me that?'

'I would swear to it before the Pope. Monsieur d'Herblay brought me a warrant to release Seldon, and Seldon has been released.'

'I tell you that it was Marchiali who left the Bastille.'

'I must ask you to prove that statement, monseigneur.'

'Will you let me see him?'

'Your lordship, who holds a hand in governing this kingdom, knows very well that none are permitted to visit the prisoners without a special order.'

'However, Monsieur d'Herblay was allowed to.'

'That is what I have asked you to prove, monseigneur.'

'Monsieur de Baisemeaux, once more I say, take heed of what you are telling me.'

'I have all the documents.'

'Monsieur d'Herblay is disgraced.'

'Disgraced! – Monsieur d'Herblay! – Impossible!'

'It is plain that he has influenced you.'

'I am influenced only by the king's service, monseigneur; I am doing my duty; give me an order from the king, and you shall enter.'

'Stay a moment, governor. I give you my word that if you allow me to visit the prisoner I will give you an order from the king that very moment.'

'Give it me now, monseigneur?'

'And I may add that, should you refuse, I will have you arrested on the spot, with all your officers.'

'Before committing such an act of violence, monseigneur, I am sure you will reflect,' said Baisemeaux, his face very pale, 'that we should only obey an order from the king; and it would be quite as easy for you to procure an order for Marchiali's liberation as to get one to do such an injury to me – an innocent man.'

'True, true!' cried Fouquet furiously, 'you are right. Well, Monsieur Baisemeaux,' he added, in slow, emphatic tones, drawing the badgered governor towards him by the lapel of his coat, 'do you know why I am so anxious to speak to the prisoner?'

'No, monseigneur; and I beg you will be so kind as to notice the terror you are causing me; I am trembling so much that I feel ready to swoon.'

'You will swoon outright in a moment, Monsieur Baisemeaux,

when I return at the head of ten thousand men and thirty pieces of artillery – '

'Great heavens! Monseigneur, surely you are not in your senses!'

' – When I raise the whole populace of Paris[153] against you and your cursed towers – when I have forced your barricades, and have ordered you to be hanged from the battlements of yonder tower!'

'Monseigneur, monseigneur! – for pity's sake – !'

'I give you ten minutes to decide,' added Fouquet quietly. 'I will sit here in this chair and wait. If in ten minutes' time you still persist, I leave you; you may think me as crazy as you please, but you will see!'

Baisemeaux shuffled his feet like a man in the last extremity of despair, but made no reply.

Fouquet's brow grew black; his eye flashed ominously; his jaw set firmly; and seizing a pen, he wrote:

> Order to the provost of the guilds to call out the train-bands and to march upon the Bastille.
>
> IN THE KING'S NAME

Baisemeaux ventured to shrug his shoulders nervously. Fouquet wrote:

> Order to his highness the Duc de Bouillon and to his highness the Prince de Condé to assume command of the household troops and the Swiss Guards and to march upon the Bastille.
>
> IN THE KING'S NAME.

Baisemeaux appeared to be reflecting. Fouquet wrote again:

> Order to every soldier, gentleman and commoner to seize and to apprehend the bodies, wherever they may be found, of the Chevalier d'Herblay, the Bishop of Vannes, and his accomplices, to wit:
> 1 Monsieur de Baisemeaux, governor of the Bastille, suspected of the crimes of high treason and rebellion – '

'Stop, stop, monseigneur!' cried Baisemeaux, almost snivelling; 'I understand absolutely nothing of all this; but such a train of grievous misfortunes, even were they brought upon us by an act of madness, might happen within the next two hours that the king, who will judge of my conduct, will perhaps consider that I was wrong not to waive the countersign in face of such dire calamities. Come with me to the *donjon*, monseigneur; you shall see Marchiali.'

Fouquet darted out of the room, followed by Baisemeaux, who was wiping the cold sweat from his forehead.

'Phew! what a devil of a morning! – what a humiliation!' he muttered.

'Walk faster!' cried Fouquet.

Baisemeaux made a sign to one of the turnkeys to go in advance; he was in bodily fear of his companion. Fouquet noticed it, and said roughly – 'Enough of this childishness. Let that man stay where he is; take the keys yourself, and show me the way. Nobody must know what is going to take place – do you hear?'

'H'm,' muttered Baisemeaux, hesitatingly.

'Again!' cried Fouquet. 'Ah! then, say "No" decidedly, and I will leave the Bastille and carry those dispatches myself.'

Baisemeaux dropped his head, then took the keys and, accompanied by the minister, mounted the staircase of the turret. The higher they advanced upon the winding stairs, the more distinct became a certain stifled murmur, and at last frightful cries mingled with terrible imprecations could be heard.

'What is that?' asked Fouquet.

'That is your Marchiali,' replied the governor; 'that is the way they all yell when they go mad.' And he accompanied the remark with a glance which conveyed the injurious allusions he was so impolite as to hint with regard to Fouquet's own demeanour.

Fouquet shuddered; for in a cry more terrible than any they had yet heard, he had recognised the king's voice. Upon the landing he paused and took the bunch of keys from Baisemeaux's hand. The latter believed the other madman was about to crack his skull with one of the keys.

'Ah!' cried Baisemeaux, 'Monsieur d'Herblay did not warn me of this.'

'Give me the keys, will you?' cried Fouquet, and he snatched them away from Baisemeaux. 'Which is the one which belongs to the door I am going to open?'

'This is the key.'

A hideous yell, followed by a terrible crash upon the door, raised the echoes in the corridor.

'You may go!' said Fouquet to Baisemeaux, in a threatening tone.

'Faith! I wish nothing better,' muttered the latter. 'One of them will be eaten, I am certain.'

'Be off!' said Fouquet. 'If you dare to set foot on this staircase until I call you, you shall go and take the place of the most wretched prisoner in the Bastille.'

'This will be the death of me, I am sure it will,' moaned Baisemeaux as he made off with a tottering step.

The prisoner's cries became more and more terrifying. Fouquet waited to make sure that Baisemeaux had reached the bottom of the staircase before he inserted the key in the first lock.

Then it was that he could hear clearly the words of the king, who was crying, in a strangled voice – 'Help! help! – I am the king!'

The key of the second door was not the same which had served to open the first. Fouquet was obliged to try the keys one by one. Meanwhile the king, beside himself, mad with rage and terror, yelled at the top of his voice – 'Fouquet is the scoundrel who has brought me here! Help against Fouquet! I am the king! Help! help!'

These vociferations struck the minister of finance to the heart. They were followed by loud blows upon the door with the remains of the chair which the king was using as a battering-ram. At last Fouquet found the right key. The king was almost exhausted; he could no longer articulate; he bellowed – 'Death to Fouquet! – Death to Fouquet the traitor!'

At that moment the door opened.

## CHAPTER 51

## *A king's gratitude*

THE TWO MEN, finding no obstacle between them, were about to dart towards each other but, with a flash of mutual recognition, they stopped short suddenly, each uttering a cry of horror.

'Have you come to murder me?' cried the king.

'The king! – in such a state as this!' exclaimed the minister. For indeed, nothing could be more terrifying than the appearance of the young prince at the moment when Fouquet had surprised him. His clothes were in shreds; his shirt, open and torn, was stained with blood and sweat from his lacerated chest and arms. Haggard, pale, with foam upon his lips, his hair in wild disorder, Louis XIV presented the most perfect picture it was possible to conceive of despair, hunger and fear, united in a single figure. Fouquet was shocked, yet moved with pity at the same time. With tears in his eyes and with open arms he moved towards the King. Louis brandished the club of which he had made such formidable use.

'Sire,' said Fouquet, his voice shaking, 'do you fail to recognise the most faithful of your friends?'

'*You*, a friend!' cried Louis, harshly. He ground his teeth in savage hatred, and prepared to wreak summary vengeance.

'Nay, a devoted servant,' added Fouquet, throwing himself upon his knees. Louis dropped his weapon, and Fouquet approached and clasped the king's knees in an access of tender solicitude. 'My king! my poor child!' said he, 'how you must have suffered!'

Louis, recalled to himself by this change in the position of affairs, glanced at the disordered state of his attire and, filled with shame at the sorry figure he made and at his own wild outburst and even more deeply mortified at receiving protection, he recoiled sharply. Fouquet could not guess what was passing in the king's mind; it did not strike him that Louis would never be able to forgive him for having witnessed his complete loss of self-control.

'Come, sire,' said the minister, 'you are free.'

'Free?' repeated Louis. 'So then you restore your king to liberty after having dared to lay violent hands upon him?'

'You cannot believe it!' cried Fouquet, with indignation. 'Surely you cannot think I could be guilty of such a crime!' And rapidly – vehemently – he burst out with a disclosure of the whole intrigue so far as he knew the details of it. During the recital, Louis was a prey to extreme anguish of mind; and when Fouquet had finished speaking, the king was painfully struck with the magnitude of the peril he had escaped, even more than with the importance of the secret relative to his twin brother.

'Monsieur,' he said suddenly to Fouquet, 'all this you have told me about a double birth is a lie; it is impossible you can have been deceived by such a story.'

'Sire!'

'I say it is impossible to suspect my mother's honour – my mother's virtue. Can it be that my Prime Minister has not yet delivered up the criminals to justice?'

'Think, sire, before you give way to anger,' replied Fouquet. 'Your brother's exalted birth – '

'I have but one brother, and he is Monsieur; you know him as well as I do. There is a conspiracy, I tell you, in which the first to be implicated is the governor of the Bastille.'

'Sire, I am certain the man has been imposed upon, like everybody else, by the extraordinary resemblance – '

'Resemblance? Nonsense!'

'But the likeness which Marchiali bears to your majesty must indeed be great, since all who have seen him have been deceived,' insisted Fouquet.

'Absurd!'

'Do not think it, sire; those who were prepared to confront the man with your mother, with your family and with your ministers and officers, must have placed strong reliance upon the resemblance.'

'Ah! and where are those people?'

'Sire, they are still at Vaux.'

'At Vaux! you allow them to remain there!'

'It seemed to me that it was of the most extreme urgency to effect your majesty's release. This duty I have accomplished; and now the king has but to command. I await your orders.'

Louis stopped for a moment and reflected.

'First of all, let a strong body of troops be mobilised in Paris,' said he, at length.

'Orders have already been given to that effect,' replied Fouquet.

'Have you given orders?' cried the king.

'With regard to the military, yes, sire. Within an hour your majesty will be at the head of ten thousand men.'

At this reply, the king grasped the hand of his minister with such hearty pressure that it became evident he had, until that moment, retained a feeling of mistrust towards Fouquet, in spite of the opportune intervention of the latter. 'And with these troops,' continued the king, 'we will march upon Vaux to attack these rebels, who, doubtless, have already fortified your château.'

'I should be much surprised if that were the case,' replied Fouquet.

'Why?'

'Because the principal conspirator – the soul of the enterprise – having been unmasked by me, the whole fabric of the plot, I take it, will fall to the ground.'

'You have unmasked the pretender, then?'

'No, I have not seen him.'

'To whom, then, do you refer?'

'The head of the enterprise is not that unfortunate prince, destined, as I perceive, to lifelong misery; he is but a tool in the hands of the arch-conspirator.'

'His name?'

'The Abbé d'Herblay, Bishop of Vannes.'

'A friend of yours, I think?'

'He was my friend, sire,' replied Fouquet, nobly.

'An unfortunate circumstance for you,' said the king, drily.

'Sire, I am not dishonoured by admitting such a friendship, because I knew nothing of the crime.'

'That remains to be proved.'

'If I am guilty, I submit myself to your majesty's displeasure.'

'Ah! Monsieur Fouquet, that is not what I meant to convey,'

replied the king, annoyed with himself for having thus allowed his rancour to appear. 'Well, I may tell you that, in spite of the mask behind which the scoundrel concealed his treasonable designs, I have always had a vague feeling of suspicion with regard to him. D'Herblay, as you say, was the chief contriver of the plot; but he had a henchman – a brawny ruffian who threatened me with his Herculean strength – what is his name?'

'That must be his friend, Baron Du Vallon, formerly a musketeer.'

'One of d'Artagnan's friends? and a friend of the Comte de la Fère? Ah!' cried the king, as the latter name recurred to his mind, 'we must not forget the relations which exist between the conspirators and Monsieur de Bragelonne.'

'Sire, sire, do not go too far! Monsieur de la Fère is the most honourable man in France. I beg you will rest satisfied with those whom I shall deliver up to you.'

'You mean that you will deliver up the guilty parties?'

'What does your majesty mean to do?' asked Fouquet.

'I intend,' replied the king, 'that we shall march upon Vaux with a large force, and destroy that nest of vipers – not one shall escape us.'

'Your majesty, then, is determined to put these men to death?'

'Without doubt.'

'Oh! sire!'

'Let us understand one another, Monsieur Fouquet,' said the king, haughtily. 'We are not living at a period when kings are obliged to have recourse to assassination as the sole means of attaining their ends. No, thank God! there is an institution in France called a Parliament, which executes justice in my name; and there are such things as scaffolds, upon which my sovereign decrees can be carried out!'

Fouquet changed colour. 'I shall take the liberty of observing to your majesty,' said he, 'that if these men are brought to public trial, it will cause a scandal which will jeopardise the dignity of the Crown. The exalted name of Anne of Austria must not be bandied from lip to lip by a vulgar crowd who smile at the mention of it.'

'Nevertheless, justice must be done.'

'Sire, it is not fitting that blood royal should be shed upon a scaffold!'

'Blood royal! you believe that?' cried Louis, stamping his foot on the floor furiously. 'I tell you all this is pure fable about a double birth; and in the invention of this fable lies Monsieur d'Herblay's greatest crime. This is the crime which I intend to chastise far more severely than their violence and insults.'

'You will punish them with death?'

'Yes, monsieur, with death.'

'Sire,' said the minister firmly, as he proudly raised his head, 'your majesty may, if you will, have Philippe of France, your own brother, beheaded, that is a matter which concerns yourself, and no doubt you will consult your mother, Anne of Austria, before taking any decided step. Whatever you may command will be for the best: I shall no longer interfere, even though I might consider such a course detrimental to the honour of your crown. But there is one boon I crave of your majesty – '

'Speak,' said the king, somewhat perturbed by the minister's last words. 'What is it you wish to ask?'

'Mercy for Monsieur d'Herblay and for Monsieur Du Vallon.'

'My assassins?'

'Nay, your majesty, only rebels.'

'Ah! I understand; you ask pardon for your friends.'

Fouquet was deeply wounded by this imputation.

'My friends you call them, sire!' he said.

'Yes, your friends; but the security of the state requires that those who are guilty should receive exemplary punishment.'

'I have not reminded your majesty that I have just restored you to liberty and perhaps saved your life.'

'Monsieur Fouquet!'

'Nor have I reminded you that, had Monsieur d'Herblay contemplated your assassination, he might easily have accomplished the regicide this morning in the Forest of Sénart, and all would have been over.' The king shuddered. 'A pistol-shot through the head,' continued Fouquet, 'and the features of Louis XIV rendered unrecognisable, who would ever have succeeded in bringing home the crime to Monsieur d'Herblay?' The king turned white as he realised the peril he had escaped. 'If Monsieur d'Herblay,' said Fouquet, 'had indeed been an assassin, he would have had no need to disclose the plan to me in order to ensure its success. Having got rid of the real king, he would have rendered the usurpation of Philippe impossible of detection. Even had the pretender been recognised by Anne of Austria, she would still have remembered that he was her own son. Monsieur d'Herblay may well have salved his conscience by the consideration that the usurper was a king of the blood of Louis XIII, whatever might be urged against his claim to the throne. Moreover, the conspirator could rest secure in the knowledge that his secret was inviolable. All this would have been effected by a single pistol-shot. Then grant me his pardon, your majesty, as you hope for salvation!'

So far from being softened towards Aramis by this evidence of his magnanimity, the king felt himself cruelly humiliated by it. Pride was his master-passion; and in his haughty arrogance he could not brook the thought that a subject had held a king's life in the hollow of his hand. Every consideration which Fouquet had urged, in the full belief that he was benefitting the cause of his friends, served only to augment the bitter rancour in the king's heart, and rendered him inflexible.

'Really, monsieur,' he burst out, impetuously, 'I don't know why you should ask pardon for these people! Of what use to ask for what you can obtain without asking?'

'Sire, I do not understand you.'

'Oh! it is quite simple. Where am I at present?'

'In the Bastille, sire.'

'Yes, in a cell. The gaolers think me mad, do they not?'

'I cannot deny it, sire.'

'And they only know me as Marchiali?'

'That is true.'

'Well, you have but to let matters rest as they are. Leave the madman in his cell in the Bastille, and Messieurs d' Herblay and Du Vallon will have no need of my pardon. Their new king will give them absolution.'

'Your majesty does me injustice,' replied Fouquet, coldly. 'Monsieur d'Herblay is not so inept, nor I so simple, as to have failed to take into account such obvious considerations. If, as you suggest, I had thought of transferring my allegiance, I should have had no occasion to come here to open the door of your cell; it would show a lack of common-sense. Your majesty's judgment is obscured by anger, or you would not thus insult, without reason, a devoted servant who has loyally hastened to your assistance.'

Louis perceived that he had gone too far; for he was gradually loosening the floodgates of the minister's pent-up wrath, whilst still the portals of the Bastille were closed upon him.

'I would not humiliate you intentionally – God forbid!' he replied. 'Only you asked me to grant their pardon, and I replied to you according to my conscience, which tells me that the traitors of whom we are speaking are unworthy of pity.' Fouquet made no reply. 'You have acted nobly, but my decision required courage as great as your generosity – nay, even greater – since I am entirely in your power, and if I refuse the conditions you have stated, it may be at the price of my liberty and even of my life.'

'Ah! Sire, I was wrong! – yes, I admit it – I seemed to be extorting a concession. I am sincerely sorry, and crave your majesty's forgiveness.'

'Say no more – say no more, my dear Monsieur Fouquet!' said the king, with a smile that restored the expression of serenity which the trouble he had undergone during the last few hours had banished from his features.

'And now you have forgiven *me*, sire, what is to be said about d'Herblay and Du Vallon?' persisted Fouquet.

'There is no forgiveness for either of them, so long as I live,' replied the king, inflexibly. 'Please not to speak of it again.'

'Your majesty's wishes shall be obeyed.'

'And I trust you bear me no ill-will?'

'Oh! no, sire; I anticipated your refusal.'

'Indeed!'

'Certainly; and I took measures accordingly.'

'What do you mean?' cried the king, in astonishment.

'Sire, Monsieur d'Herblay came to me, and, in disclosing the plot, threw himself upon my generosity. Monsieur d'Herblay left to me the happiness of saving my king and my country: how could I condemn Monsieur d'Herblay to death? I could not leave him exposed to your majesty's justifiable resentment – it would have been the same as if I had killed him with my own hands.'

'Well, what did you do?'

'Sire, I gave Monsieur d'Herblay the best horses in my stables, and they have four hours start of any whom your majesty may send in pursuit of them.'

'Very well; but the world is wide enough to give those I send in pursuit ample scope for making up the four hours start you have given to Monsieur d'Herblay,' said the king, speaking half to himself.

'In giving him four hours, sire, I know that I have secured his safety – he will not be caught, sire.'

'How is that?'

'He will not spare spur until he reaches Belle-Isle, where I have allowed him to take refuge, and he will never be less than four hours' journey in advance of your musketeers.'

'Well and good; but you must not forget that you made me a present of Belle-Isle.'

'But not for you to arrest my friends there.'

'Then you repent of your generosity and would retain Belle-Isle?'

'Only for this purpose, sire.'

'My musketeers shall capture it, and that will settle the matter.'

'It is not to be captured by your musketeers nor even by your whole army, sire,' replied Fouquet, coldly. 'Belle-Isle is impregnable.'

At this reply Louis could scarce conceal his fury; he darted a savage glance at the minister. Fouquet felt that he was lost; but he was not the man to shrink from the course which honour bade him pursue. He bore without flinching the king's malevolent glance; and the latter, smothering his spite, said, after a moment's pause – 'Shall we return to Vaux?'

'I am at your majesty's disposal,' replied Fouquet, with a profound obeisance; 'but I think you will find it necessary to obtain a change of clothes before appearing before your court.'

'We shall pass the Louvre, and I will attend to it there,' replied the king. 'Come, Monsieur Fouquet.'

And they quitted the prison, leaving Baisemeaux stupefied at the sight of Marchiali being again carried off and tearing at the scanty remainder of his hair in his perplexity. We will not conceal the fact, however, that Fouquet gave him a perfectly regular discharge for the prisoner, with the king's superscription: – 'Seen and approved: Louis' – a piece of midsummer madness which impelled poor Baisemeaux, incapable of putting together two ideas, to strike himself, in the extremity of his bewilderment, a violent blow on the jaw.

## CHAPTER 52

## *The usurper*

IN THE MEANTIME, at Vaux, Philippe had been playing his part right royally. He gave orders for a full reception at his *petit lever*[154] – an order which the persons and personages concerned had been expecting some little while. Philippe decided to give this reception, notwithstanding the continued absence of Monsieur d'Herblay, who, as our readers are aware, had other matters to attend to. Believing, however, that the bishop could not fail to put in an appearance soon, the prince, like all venturesome spirits, felt impatient to put his courage and his fortunes to the test of circumstances in which he would be unable to count upon the advice or assistance of his protector. Moreover, he was impelled to take this course by another consideration: he was about to meet Anne of Austria – the guilty mother was about to find herself in the presence of the son she had wronged; and Philippe was unwilling that the man, before whom he would need to display the greatest self-control, should be a witness of the weakness he might be unable to restrain at the first sight of his mother.

Philippe threw open both wings of the folding doors and several persons entered quietly. The prince had made no movement while he was being dressed by his attendants; for he had noticed, the evening before, that his brother was accustomed to act in this manner; and it was necessary to adopt the same habits in order to avoid raising suspicions. Therefore, when his visitors arrived, they found him fully dressed, and in hunting costume. His memory, and the notes with which Aramis had furnished him, allowed him to recognise among the first arrivals Anne of Austria, leaning upon the arm of Monsieur, and then Madame, accompanied by Monsieur de Saint-Aignan. Philippe smiled in token of welcome, yet could not repress a start as he recognised his mother. Her noble and striking countenance, upon which suffering had set its mark, pleaded powerfully in the heart of the prince on behalf of that famous royal lady who had sacrificed her child to the fetish of the security of the crown. His mother seemed to him beautiful; he knew that Louis XIV loved her, and he resolved to love her, promising himself that he would never prove a scourge for the punishment of her declining years. Philippe looked at his brother with feelings of affection – the brother who had usurped the rights of none, and had in no way overclouded his life – and determined that he would act towards him in a brotherly spirit, keeping him well supplied with money, since money was all that he needed to make him happy. The prince greeted Saint-Aignan kindly, and Saint-Aignan was all smiles and bows in consequence; then he extended a hand which trembled slightly to Henrietta, his sister-in-law, for her beauty made a powerful impression upon him. He could perceive, however, that her manner towards him was distant, for she had not forgotten her quarrel with Louis. Philippe was rather pleased than otherwise at her coldness, which promised to lighten the difficulty of their mutual relationship for the future – 'How much easier,' he thought, 'will it be for me to act as the brother of this woman than as her gallant, if she shows towards me a coolness which my brother could not feel towards her, but which duty imposes upon myself.' The only visit to which he now looked forward with apprehension was that of the queen; for he had already undergone one ordeal which had tried him severely, and he feared lest his self-control, great though it was, should break down under another such trial. Fortunately, the queen did not make her appearance.

Anne of Austria launched out into a discussion of the political aspect of Monsieur Fouquet's entertainment of the royal family. Her tone was obviously hostile to the minister, but she contrived to introduce into her discourse allusions flattering to the king's vanity, while making enquiries with maternal solicitude as to his health, like the skilful mistress of diplomatic artifice that she was. 'Well, my son,' she concluded, 'have you made up your mind with regard to Monsieur Fouquet?'

'Saint-Aignan,' said Philippe, 'be so good as to go and make enquiries about the queen.' At these words, the first which Philippe had pronounced audibly, the slight difference between the tone of his voice and that of Louis XIV became noticeable to his mother's ear; Anne of Austria looked at her son sharply.

Saint-Aignan having gone, Philippe continued.

'Madame, I regret to hear you speak ill of Monsieur Fouquet; you know him well, and you have, before now, spoken to me in his favour.'

'That is true; but I questioned you merely to ascertain your own opinion with regard to him.'

'Sire,' said Henrietta, 'for my part, I have always liked Monsieur Fouquet. He is a man of excellent discernment, and a thoroughly good fellow.'

'A minister who is never guilty of parsimony,' added Monsieur; 'he has never yet failed to cash my drafts upon him.'

'All you people think too much of your own interests,' said Anne; 'nobody consults the interests of the state, and it can scarcely be denied that Monsieur Fouquet is ruining the kingdom.'

'Come, mother,' rejoined Philippe in a low tone, 'can it be that you also are a supporter of Monsieur Colbert?'

'How can you say that?' cried Anne of Austria in some surprise.

'Because really,' replied Philippe, 'you have been speaking as I should have expected your old friend, Madame de Chevreuse, to have spoken.'

Anne of Austria changed colour, and bit her lip. Philippe had stirred up the sleeping lioness.

'Why have you mentioned Madame de Chevreuse?' she enquired. 'You are treating me rather strangely this morning.'

'Is it not a fact that Madame de Chevreuse is perpetually engaged in some plot or other to ruin somebody? It seems to me that she must have been visiting you lately.'

'Louis,' replied the old queen, 'you speak to me in such a manner that I can almost fancy I am listening to your father.'

'My father disliked Madame de Chevreuse, and not without good reason,' said the prince. 'For my part, I like her no better than he did; and if she should have the temerity to come, as she was formerly in the habit of doing, in order to sow dissension and foment quarrels under pretext of begging money, well – '

'Well?' said Anne of Austria, stiffly, by no means seeking to avoid a storm.

'Well,' replied the young man, firmly, 'in that case I will have Madame de Chevreuse put over the frontier, together with all the rest of these wretched mischief-makers.' Perhaps he had not calculated the consequences of his stern rebuke, or it may have been that he was impatient to judge the effect of his words; just as people who are suffering from a gnawing pain will sometimes seek to break the monotony of their sufferings by a sudden pressure upon the sore place in order to render the pain acute. However that may be, his words produced such an effect that Anne of Austria almost fainted; her eyes remained open, but fixed like those of a corpse; she feebly stretched out her arms towards her other son, who immediately embraced her without troubling to think whether or not the king might be annoyed.

'Sire,' faltered Anne, 'you are treating your mother very cruelly.'

'In what respect, madame?' said Philippe. 'I am only speaking of Madame de Chevreuse, and I cannot believe that my mother sets this woman before the security of the state and the safety of my person. I am in a position to tell you that Madame de Chevreuse has returned to France with the object of raising money, and that she applied to Monsieur Fouquet in the hope of selling him a certain secret.' Anne of Austria could not repress a startled exclamation. 'A secret,' continued the prince, 'concerning certain large sums of money which she had the impudence to assume that the minister had stolen – a manifest lie. Monsieur Fouquet indignantly refused to listen to her, preferring to rely upon the king's esteem rather than to have any dealings with dishonest schemers. Accordingly, Madame de Chevreuse made her bargain with Monsieur Colbert; but her greed is insatiable, and, not content with having extorted a hundred thousand crowns from that underling, she has played a far higher game in her shameless hunt after lucre. Am I not right, madame?'

'You are well informed, sire,' said the queen, her annoyance giving way to a feeling of uneasiness.

'Then,' pursued Philippe, 'I am fully justified in the loathing I feel towards this harpy who comes to my court to plot the dishonour of one and the ruin of others. If God has allowed certain crimes to be committed, yet has suffered them to be buried in oblivion, I do not admit that Madame de Chevreuse has the right to thwart the will of heaven by bringing them to light.'

The latter part of Philippe's discourse had so greatly discomposed the queen mother that her son was struck with pity. He took her hand and kissed it tenderly, but she could not know that the kiss, given in spite of some instinctive revulsion, signified a full pardon for the eight long years of agony[155] she had made him suffer. Philippe allowed a few moments to pass in silence whilst he recovered his equanimity, and then said, quite cheerfully: 'We will not leave here today; an idea has struck me.' He looked round towards the door, expecting every moment to see Aramis enter, for his absence began to weigh upon his spirits. The queen mother was about to take leave.

'Stay a moment, mother,' he said; 'I wish you to become reconciled to Monsieur Fouquet.'

'But I have no quarrel with him; I was only alarmed at his prodigality.'

'That shall be corrected, and we shall only find employment for the minister's good qualities in future.'

'For whom is your majesty looking?' asked Henrietta, seeing the king's glance constantly directed towards the door. She believed that he was expecting to see La Vallière or to receive a letter from her; and she could not resist the chance of dropping a little gall into the king's heart.

'Dear sister,' replied the young man, guessing her intention, thanks to his wonderful intuition, of which, in all probability, he would be enabled to avail himself from this day forward, 'dear sister, I am expecting a man of most distinguished character – a most able adviser – whom I shall have the honour of presenting to you, and of recommending to your good graces – Ah! come in, d'Artagnan.'

The captain of musketeers came forward. 'What are your majesty's wishes?' he asked.

'Tell me, where is your friend, the Bishop of Vannes?'

'Why, sire – '

'I am expecting him, but I have not seen him arrive. Let him be sent for.'

D'Artagnan remained for a moment in silent stupefaction; then, remembering that Aramis had departed secretly from Vaux on a mission for the king, he concluded that his majesty wished it to be kept secret.

'Sire,' he replied, 'does your majesty absolutely insist upon Monsieur d'Herblay being brought here?'

'Not *absolutely*. I don't need his presence altogether so much as that; still, if someone were to find him – '

'I have guessed it,' thought d'Artagnan.

'This Monsieur d'Herblay,' said Anne of Austria, 'is Bishop of Vannes, is he not?'

'Yes, madame.'

'And a friend of Monsieur Fouquet?'

'Yes, madame, and formerly a musketeer.' Anne of Austria coloured. 'One of those four brave men who, in days gone by, achieved such brilliant feats.'

The queen mother regretted having spoken, and, in order to avoid further discomfiture, she retired from the discussion. 'Whatever decision your majesty may make,' said she, 'will, I am sure, be excellent' – a remark with which all present testified their concurrence by an inclination of the head.

'You will find in him,' continued Philippe, 'the profound sagacity of a Richelieu, with none of the avarice of a Mazarin.'

'Is he to be minister of state, sire?' enquired Monsieur, with some trepidation.

'You shall hear all about it, my dear brother; but it is very strange that Monsieur d'Herblay has not been here yet.' He called to an attendant – 'Let Monsieur Fouquet be informed that I desire to speak to him – oh! don't go away – I wish you all to hear what I have to say to him.'

At this moment Saint-Aignan returned bearing satisfactory news of the queen, who had kept her bed simply as a matter of precaution to recruit her strength in order to be able to keep pace with the king in the fatiguing business of pleasure-making. Whilst Monsieur Fouquet and Aramis were being sought for everywhere, the new king continued worthily to play his role – indeed, so exactly similar were his voice, his gestures and his manner that everybody present, not only officers and servants but even his own family, remained absolutely unconscious of the deception. Philippe made mental comparisons of the faces which surrounded him with the notes and drawings with which Aramis had supplied him, and thereby was enabled to regulate his conduct so as to excite no suspicion. The usurper felt that henceforth he need have no anxiety; the game was in his own hands. With what strange facility had providence exalted the lowly in the seat of one of the mighty ones of the earth! Philippe was filled with wonder and awe as he contemplated the benefits which heaven had showered upon him, and he resolved to assist the workings of providence by every means at his disposal. Still, a shadow now and then seemed to steal across his mind, dimming the radiance of the glory with which he had been newly invested and whose glamour he had felt for so short a time. Aramis did not appear.

The conversation began to languish; Philippe, occupied with his own thoughts, forgot to give Henrietta and his brother the signal permitting them to withdraw. This caused them some surprise, and at length they grew impatient. Anne of Austria bent over towards her son and addressed a few words to him in Spanish. Philippe was completely ignorant of the language, and, confronted by this unexpected obstacle, he changed colour; but, as though the spirit of the imperturbable Aramis had clothed the prince with his own infallibility, instead of showing any signs of embarrassment, Philippe rose to his feet – 'Well, what do you say? you have not answered me,' said Anne of Austria.

'What noise is that?' asked Philippe, turning towards the door which led to the private staircase. A voice was heard crying – 'This way – this way! A few more steps, sire!'

'That is the voice of Monsieur Fouquet,' said d'Artagnan, who was standing beside the queen mother.

'Then Monsieur d'Herblay cannot be far away,' remarked Philippe. Next moment he saw something which he was very far from having expected to see so close to him. All eyes were directed towards the door by which Fouquet was about to enter; but the man who entered was not he. A terrible cry resounded in every part of the room – a cry of fear and wonder from the king and from all the courtiers. The royal apartment, at that moment, afforded a spectacle which has hardly a parallel in the experience of mankind – not even in the experience of men to whom destiny has assigned the most incredible adventures and the strangest chances.

The window-shutters, half-closed, allowed but a feeble light to filter into the room through the thick silken curtains. Upon entering the room, one was at first unable to see clearly; the courtiers recognised their neighbours rather by intuition than by sight. But, as always happens in these circumstances, the eyes gradually become accustomed to the gloom, so that at length every detail of the surroundings becomes clearly visible; and any fresh object which may present itself appears sharply outlined as though it were broad daylight.

So it was now, when Louis XIV appeared in the doorway with pale face and lowering brow. Behind him stood Fouquet, wearing an expression of gloom and severity. The queen mother, who was holding Philippe's hand, gave a scream as though she had seen a ghost. Monsieur, in his bewilderment, made an aimless movement, then turned his glance from the king whom he saw in front of him, to the one who was beside him. Madame moved forward a step, thinking that it was her brother-in-law's reflection in the mirror that she had seen; for indeed, that illusion was possible. The two princes, both white to the lips – for we shall not endeavour to depict the terrible state of mind into which Philippe had been plunged – stood trembling, each with a hand clenched convulsively, glaring at one another like serpents about to strike. Mute – bent forward – fetching their breath in gasps, they eyed one another as though about to close in a mortal encounter. This miraculous resemblance of features, expression and figure; everything, even to the similarity of their costumes – a similarity which was the result of chance, for Louis XIV had chosen at the Louvre a suit of violet velvet – this perfect likeness between the two princes had the effect of completely overwhelming the faculties of Anne of Austria. Nevertheless, she had not guessed the truth. There are certain calamities which one refuses to accept – one prefers to believe in the supernatural or even in the impossible.

Louis had not reckoned upon encountering any obstacles. He had expected to be recognised the moment he appeared. Accustomed to regard himself as the sun of his own particular firmament, he could not endure the thought that any other could rival him; he had felt convinced that his mere appearance would cause every lesser luminary to pale into insignificance. Consequently, at the aspect of Philippe, he was perhaps more terrified than anyone else present; and his silence and immobility were due to his urgent need of collecting his scattered forces – the ominous calm which precedes the tempest. But who shall describe the numbing shock which Fouquet received when confronted with that living portrait of his royal master? Fouquet felt that Aramis had been right; that the newcomer was of as pure race as the other, and that he himself was a visionary fool for having repudiated all participation in the *coup d'état* so adroitly effected by the General of the Jusuits – he called himself a misdirected enthusiast, unfit to meddle with matters political. Moreover, he was sacrificing the blood of Louis XIII to gratify a selfish ambition – for the right to retain his present position he was throwing away the chance of still higher honours. The full extent of his folly was revealed to him by the mere aspect of the usurper.

None present could judge of what passed through Fouquet's mind during the five minutes he was left to meditate upon the case of conscience – five minutes which seemed like five centuries, yet were scarcely long enough for the two kings and their family to recover breath after the terrible shock they had experienced. D'Artagnan, leaning against the wall opposite to Fouquet, his forehead resting on his clenched fist, was staring in amazement, and asking himself the meaning of this strange portent. He had been unable to explain why he suspected Aramis, but he knew that his suspicions were well grounded, and that in this meeting of the two princes lay the whole problem which had been agitating his mind for some days past with regard to the bishop's conduct. Vague, inchoate ideas passed through his brain, and the actors in this weird drama seemed to emerge, ill-defined, through the mists of a confused waking dream.

Louis XIV, more impatient and more accustomed to command than his brother, was the first to recover his self-possession. Suddenly he ran to the window and pushed open the shutters, tearing the curtain in his impetuous haste. A flood of daylight entered the room, causing Philippe to draw back into the alcove. Louis eagerly availed himself of this seeming retreat, and, addressing himself to the queen – 'Mother,' he cried, 'you, at least, will recognise your son, even though everybody else has forgotten the appearance of his king!'

Anne of Austria, unable to articulate a word, shuddered, and raised her hands appealingly to heaven.

'Mother,' said Philippe, without a tremor in his voice, 'do you not recognise your son?'

It was now the turn of Louis to draw back. As for Anne of Austria, struck to the heart with remorse, she fell back swooning in her chair. No one went to her assistance, for all present were petrified. The spectacle before his eyes, and the affront which the general silence conveyed, were unendurable to Louis; his head began to swim! he tottered as he leant against the door. 'Captain!' he cried, in an agonised tone, 'surely you know me? Look at us both, and see which of us two is the paler!'

His cry thrilled through d'Artagnan's heart and recalled him to the old habit of obedience. He shook off his stupor, and, no longer hesitating, strode across the room to where Philippe was standing. Laying a hand upon his shoulder, he said, 'Monsieur, you are my prisoner.'

Philippe remained motionless as if rooted to the spot, his eyes fixed sternly upon his brother's face. In sublime silence he seemed to be reproaching him for all the long years he had suffered and was again to suffer. Before this mute language of the soul the king was abashed; he lowered his eyes, then precipitately drew his brother and his sister-in-law away, entirely forgetting his mother lying bereft of strength within a few paces of the son whom she was about to abandon to his fate a second time. Philippe approached Anne of Austria and said to her gently, with a break of noble emotion in his voice, 'If I were not your son, I should curse you as the cause of my misery.'

D'Artagnan felt a shudder pass through the very marrow of his bones. He saluted the young prince respectfully, saying, 'Forgive me, monseigneur, I am but a soldier, and I am sworn to obey him who has just left the room.'

'Thank you, Monsieur d'Artagnan. But what has become of Monsieur d'Herblay?'

'Monsieur d'Herblay is in safety, monseigneur,' said a voice behind them, 'and no one, as long as I am alive and free, will be able to harm a hair of his head.'

'Monsieur Fouquet!' said the prince, smiling sadly.

'Forgive me, monseigneur,' said Fouquet, falling on his knees, 'but he who has just gone was my guest.'

'Ah! noble hearts and faithful friends!' said Philippe, half to himself. 'You make me regret the world I am leaving. I am ready to follow you, Monsieur d'Artagnan.'

Just as the captain of musketeers was about to depart with his charge, Colbert appeared, and after handing d'Artagnan an order from the king, again retired. D'Artagnan read the order and crumpled up the paper furiously.

'What is it?' enquired the prince.

'Read, monseigneur,' replied the musketeer. Philippe read these words hastily scrawled by the hand of Louis XIV. 'Monsieur d'Artagnan will conduct his prisoner to the Iles Sainte-Marguerite. He will take the precaution of covering the said prisoner's face with a mask of iron,[156] which the latter is forbidden to remove under pain of death.

'So be it,' said Philippe, resignedly. 'I am ready.'

'Aramis was right,' whispered Fouquet in d'Artagnan's ear; 'this man is every whit as much a king as his brother.'

'More!' replied the captain. 'He only needed you and me on his side!'

CHAPTER 53

### *Where Porthos quite thinks he is hunting down a dukedom*

PROFITING by the four hours' grace which Fouquet had accorded them, Aramis and Porthos maintained a pace which did honour to French horseflesh and French horsemanship. Porthos had no very definite notion as to the nature of the mission which called for such extraordinary haste; but seeing that Aramis pressed forward eagerly, he, Porthos, spurred his horse furiously. Thus they soon covered thirteen leagues; and it then became a matter of necessity to change horses and organise some sort of service of relays.

It was during one of these changes that Porthos ventured discreetly to question Aramis.

'Never mind just now,' replied the latter; 'all that you need to know is that our fortune depends upon our speed.'

As if he were still the penniless musketeer, without a change of clothes to his name, that he had been in 1626, Porthos pressed forward. The magic word *fortune* always retains some glamour in the ears of men. For those who have nothing, it signifies a competence; for those who have enough, it means superabundance.

'I shall be made a duke,' said Porthos aloud, though merely speaking to himself.

'Very possibly,' replied Aramis, with his enigmatical smile, as Porthos's horse passed ahead of him. Notwithstanding his impassive manner, Aramis's brain was on fire; his bodily exertion had not yet succeeded in calming the fever of his mind. Internally, the defeated prelate was consumed with furious rancour; mentally he was grinding his teeth and hurling savage imprecations against the man who had ruined his schemes. His countenance bore visible traces of the seething tumult within him. Upon the open highway, Aramis no longer felt the necessity of curbing his passion, nor did he refrain from cursing savagely every time his horse swerved upon the rough road. Pale, saturated with sweat, sometimes at fever heat, then cold as death, he punished his mounts unmercifully with spur and lash, until their flanks were in a lather of blood and sweat – so unmercifully, that even Porthos, who was by no means sensitive, groaned aloud.

Thus they rode for eight long hours and at length reached Orléans. It was four o'clock in the afternoon. Aramis bethought himself that there was no indication that pursuit was possible; for it would have been an unprecedented occurrence if a troop of horse, of sufficient strength to capture Porthos and himself, had found sufficient relays available to enable them to cover forty leagues in eight hours. And, even if pursuit were admitted – a circumstance by no means evident – the fugitives still had a good five hours' start of their pursuers. Aramis thought he might even venture safely to stay and rest awhile, but decided to press forward in order to avoid possible risk of mischance. Twenty leagues more, performed at the same pace, and nobody, not even d'Artagnan, would be able to overtake the king's enemies. Aramis therefore inflicted upon Porthos the inconvenience of getting into the saddle once more. They continued their flight until seven in the evening; one more stage and they would be at Blois; but now they were confronted with a formidable obstacle which greatly alarmed Aramis. No fresh horses were to be had. The prelate asked himself by what infernal machination his enemies had contrived to deprive him of the means of continuing his flight; for he refused to recognise the existence of chance and saw a cause for every effect, and he preferred to believe that the postmaster's refusal, at such an hour and in such a place, was due to an order from his superiors – an order given with the object of arresting the king-maker in full career. He was just about to give way to his anger and peremptorily demand either a horse or the reason for its refusal, when an idea suddenly occurred to him. He remembered that the Comte de la Fère resided in the neighbourhood.

'I am not travelling any great distance,' said he, 'I am not even going one whole stage. Give me a couple of horses to carry us as far as the seat of a nobleman of my acquaintance, who lives close by.'

'What nobleman?' asked the postmaster.

'The Comte de la Fère.'

'Ah! a most worthy gentleman,' replied the postmaster, doffing his hat respectfully. 'But, however great my desire to serve you and to please him, to my great regret I find myself unable to supply you with two horses; all the horses here have been ordered in advance by the Duc de Beaufort.'

'Ah!' exclaimed Aramis, disappointed.

'But,' continued the postmaster, 'if you care to make use of a little carriage which belongs to me, I will have an old, blind horse put in it – he has still four legs and he will pull you as far as the Comte de la Fère's château.'

'That is worth a louis,' said Aramis.

'Nay, monsieur, only a crown; that is what Monsieur Grimaud, the comte's steward, pays me whenever he borrows my carriage; and I should be sorry to incur the comte's reproach by imposing upon a friend of his.'

'It shall be as you please,' said Aramis, 'and especially as the Comte de la Fère pleases, whom I am very far from wishing to disoblige. Very well then, let us say a crown; only I am entitled to make you a present of a louis for your happy idea.'

'Certainly,' replied the man, delighted. And he hurried off to harness the old horse to his delapidated and creaking vehicle. During this colloquy, Porthos's face was a study. He imagined he had guessed the secret, and he was impatient to be off; firstly, because he was delighted with the idea of seeing Athos, and then again, because he looked forward to a good supper and a good bed. After he had put the horse in, the postmaster called a servant, to whom he gave instructions to drive the strangers to La Fère. Porthos climbed into the back of the carriage beside Aramis and whispered in his ear, 'I understand now.'

'Ah!' replied Aramis, 'and what do you understand, my dear friend?'

'We are going to make some important proposal to Athos from the king.'

'Pooh!' exclaimed Aramis.

'You need not tell me anything,' added the excellent Porthos, trying to adjust his weight so as to avoid the jolting; 'don't tell me anything, I shall guess.'

'That is right, my dear Porthos, guess away!'

It was nearly nine when they reached La Fère and a magnificent moonlight night. Porthos was charmed beyond expression by this admirable clearness; but Aramis was annoyed by it in an almost equal degree. He allowed his uneasiness to become apparent to Porthos, who said – 'Good! I have guessed it again: the mission is to be kept dark!' He said no more, for at that moment the driver turned round and remarked – 'Gentlemen, this is your destination.' Porthos and his companion got out of the carriage and found themselves before the door of the little château. Here we are about to meet Athos and Bragelonne once more, who had gone into retirement since the discovery of La Vallière's infidelity. There is undoubtedly a great deal of truth in the saying that great griefs carry within them the germs of consolation. In truth, the painful wound which Raoul had received had served to draw together father and son; and heaven

knows that the words of consolation were sweet which flowed from
the elegant tongue and generous heart of Athos. The wound was by
no means healed; still, by his conversation and by the force of
sympathy which had bent his more mature mind to enter into the
feelings of the younger man, Athos had brought Raoul to understand
that disillusionment is the common lot, and that everyone who has
loved has at some time experienced it. Raoul indeed listened, and
even agreed with his father. Nevertheless these sayings never struck
him with the force of conviction; for when a man's affections are
deeply engaged, there is nothing which can efface the remembrance
or replace in his heart the object of his worship. Raoul would reply to
his father – 'All that you say, sir, is true; I believe that no one has
suffered more in this way than yourself; but your mind is so fine and
sorrow has deepened your sympathies so much that you can deal
leniently with a soldier who complains of his first wound. A second
time, I should feel less pain; bear with me, therefore, and permit me
to bury myself in my grief until I attain self-forgetfulness by drowning my reason in it.'

'Raoul! Raoul!'

'Let me speak, sir. Never shall I grow accustomed to the idea that
Louise, the purest and sweetest of women, could so basely and
cruelly deceive a man who loved and trusted her as I did; never shall
I be able to realise that her candid features may wear an expression of
falseness or sensuality. Louise ruined! Louise dishonoured! Ah! Sir,
the thought would hurt me more, far more, than the remembrance
of her having thrown me over and left me to my wretchedness.'

Athos then employed heroic measures. He defended Louise
against Raoul, pleading for her love for another as her justification –
'A woman who had yielded to the king merely because he was the
king,' said he, 'would deserve to be called by a shameful name; but
Louise loves Louis. Remember that both are young; his hot blood
has made him forget his rank, and she has forgotten her vows. Love
excuses all things, Raoul. These two young people love one another
without restraint.' And, having dealt this stroke, Athos saw with a
profound sigh how Raoul flinched under the cruel wound, and would
hasten to hide his grief in the depths of the forest or in his own room,
whence, an hour later, he would return, pale and trembling, it is true,
but nevertheless subdued. With a smile upon his lips, he rejoined
Athos, kissing his hand, as a dog who has received chastisement
returns to caress a loved master in order to redeem his fault.

Thus passed the days which followed the scene in which Athos had
so violently shaken the king's ungovernable pride. In speaking to his

son he never alluded to that scene; he never gave him the details of the outspoken reproof he had administered, though perhaps had he done so the young man might have felt some consolation in hearing of his rival's humiliation. Athos did not wish that the jealousy of a lover should cause Raoul to forget the respect due to his king. And sometimes Bragelonne, giving rein to his anger, would speak bitterly and contemptuously of faith in the royal word, and of the fools who put their trust in the promises of princes; sometimes his mind, crossing the gulf of two centuries like a bird crossing the seas in its flight from one continent to another, would foresee a time when kings would appear no greater than other men.[157] Then Athos would say to him in his serene persuasive voice – 'You are right, Raoul; all that you have predicted will, one day, come to pass; monarchs will lose their divinity, just as those stars fade which have run their course. But, when that day comes, Raoul, we shall not be living; and ponder well what I am about to say. In this world everyone, kings as well as subjects, must live for the present; we should only live for the future so far as to render ourselves fit for immortal life.'

As usual, Athos and Raoul were conversing in this manner as they strolled backwards and forwards in the long avenue of lime trees in the park, when all at once they heard the sound of the bell which announced to the comte either the dinner-hour or the arrival of a visitor. Mechanically he turned and, accompanied by his son, walked towards the château, only to find himself, at the end of the avenue, in the presence of Aramis and Porthos.

## CHAPTER 54

## Last farewells

RAOUL gave a cry of joy and hastened to greet his valued friend Porthos. Aramis and Athos embraced one another less heartily; they were old, and the vivacity of youth had long been a stranger to them. Aramis's greeting was especially perfunctory; he felt that he had scarce time to talk – 'My friend,' said he, 'we are not with you for long.'

'Ah!' replied the comte.

'Long enough to tell you of my good fortune,' broke in Porthos.

'Ah!' cried Raoul.

Athos glanced searchingly at Aramis. He had been already struck by the bishop's unwonted air of distraction, which seemed little in accordance with the good news of which Porthos spoke.

'Well, and what is this good fortune? Come now, tell us,' said Raoul, with a smile.

'The king is going to create me duke,' replied the worthy Porthos in a mysterious whisper, bending over to reach the young man's ear. But Porthos's asides were always loud enough to be heard by everybody; his most subdued utterance was a sort of lion's roar. Athos, hearing him, gave vent to an exclamation which made Aramis start. The latter took Athos's arm, and with Porthos's permission, drew him aside to speak privately to him – 'My dear Athos,' said he, 'you see me overwhelmed with grief.'

'Ah! my dear friend! How sorry I am!' cried the comte.

'I will explain in two words. I have conspired against the king; the plot has failed, and doubtless, at this very moment, I am pursued.'

'Pursued! – A conspiracy! – Ah! my friend, what is this you tell me!'

'The sad truth. I am absolutely ruined.'

'But Porthos – this title of duke – what does all this mean?'

'That is what affords me the sharpest sting; that is where I am most sorely wounded. Believing success assured, I have involved Porthos in the conspiracy. He has entered into it, as you know he would do, with heart and soul, aiding me to the utmost of his ability, without knowing a word about the reason, and now he is so far compromised with me as to be ruined as utterly as I am myself.'

'Great God! how dreadful!' And Athos turned his head towards Porthos, who, noticing the glance, smiled amiably.

'I must make you understand the whole of the matter; listen,' continued Aramis. And he repeated the whole story which we have already told. During the recital, Athos was profoundly moved.

'It was a great idea,' said he, 'but it was also a most culpable one.'

'And I have my punishment, Athos.'

'And I shall not tell you all I think,' continued Athos.

'Nay, speak out.'

'It is a crime.'

'A capital crime – I know it. It is high treason!'

'Poor Porthos!'

'What could I do? I was certain of success, as I have told you.'

'Monsieur Fouquet is a man of honour.'

'And I – I am a fool, to have misjudged him,' said Aramis. 'Ah! – man's wisdom, what a poor thing it is! – Oh! the mills of God,[158] which grind the whole world with such seeming regularity, yet whose workings are altered by the grain of sand which falls, no one knows how, amidst the wheels?'

'Say rather, by a diamond, Aramis – Well, the evil is done. How are you going to act?'

'I must take Porthos with me. The king will never believe that the good fellow acted unknowingly, and that Porthos thought he was serving the king when he acted as he did. His head would pay for my crime. By heaven! it shall not be!'

'Where shall you take him?'

'In the first place, to Belle-Isle. The fortifications are impregnable. Thence I can escape by sea; I have a vessel which can take me either to England, where I have some influence, or – '

'You – in England?'

'Yes – or in Spain, where I have still greater influence.'

'By taking Porthos out of the country, you ruin him irretrievably, for the king will confiscate his estates.'

'I have foreseen everything. Once having reached Spain, I shall find a means of making my peace with Louis XIV and of restoring Porthos to favour.'

'I begin to see that you have some influence, Aramis!' said Athos, deprecating further confidences of the bishop's private business.

'Indeed I have, and it is entirely at the service of my friends.' And he accompanied the words with a warm pressure on Athos's hand.

'Thank you,' replied the comte.

'And since we are on this subject,' continued Aramis, 'you also have cause of dissatisfaction with the king – you and Raoul – you both have cause for discomfort. Follow my example then. Come with me to Belle-Isle. Afterwards, we will see – I declare to you, upon my honour, that war will be declared within a month between France and Spain over this matter of the son of Louis XIII, who is also an Infante,[159] and who is receiving barbarous treatment at the hands of the French king. But Louis XIV will be unwilling to go to war about such a cause as this; and I am in a position to promise you that I can make a deal, the result of which will be to exalt Porthos and myself and to bring you a duchy in France – since you are already a grandee of Spain.[160] Are you willing to join me?'

'Not I; I prefer to have something to reproach the king with; it is a trait of hereditary pride to consider my race superior to that of kings. Were I to fall in with your proposal, I should be beholden to the king; certainly I might gain worldly advantage, but only at the expense of my conscience.'

'Then I will ask of you only two things, Athos: your absolution – '

'Oh! it is yours, if you have really been animated by the desire of helping the cause of the weak against his oppressor.'

'That is sufficient for me,' replied Aramis, colouring painfully, though his emotion passed unnoticed in the gloom, 'And now,' he continued, 'give me your two fastest horses to enable us to reach the next post. I was refused at the last stage under pretext that they were retained by the Duc de Beaufort for a journey he is making in these parts.'

'My best horses are at your service, Aramis, and I commend Porthos to your care.'

'Oh! rest assured I shall watch over him. One word more; do you think I am acting rightly by him in doing as I intend?'

'In the circumstances, yes; for the king would not pardon him. Besides, whatever Fouquet may have said to the contrary, he will never abandon you, since he also is deeply compromised notwithstanding his heroic action.'

'You are right, and that is the reason why, instead of putting to sea at once – which would show fear and proclaim my guilt – I shall remain upon French soil. But, indeed, Belle-Isle will be whatever soil I choose – English, Spanish or Roman – it entirely depends upon what standard I may think proper to raise.'

'How can that be?'

'It is I who fortified Belle-Isle, and, while I hold it, none will be able to attack it with success. And then, as you have just remarked, there is Monsieur Fouquet to be reckoned with. Belle-Isle cannot be attacked without his signature.'

'That is true. Still, take care: the king is both strong and cunning.' Aramis smiled.

'I commend Porthos to you,' repeated the comte with a sort of cold persistence.

'Whatever happens to me, comte,' replied Aramis in the same tone, 'will be shared by our dear old friend Porthos.'

Athos inclined his head, and then, after pressing Aramis's hand, he turned and embraced Porthos with warmth.

'I was born under a lucky star, don't you think so?' muttered the latter, as he tranquilly enveloped himself in his cloak.

'Come, Porthos, my dear fellow,' said Aramis.

· Raoul had gone off to give orders for the horses to be saddled. The group was already separated.

Athos saw his two friends on the point of leaving, and something like a mist passed before his eyes, and weighed upon his spirits – 'Strange!' he thought. 'Whence comes this strong desire to embrace

Porthos once more?' While the thought was passing through his mind, Porthos turned and approached his old friend with open arms. This last embrace was as tender as in the days of their youth – in the days when their hearts beat high and life was glorious. Porthos then mounted his horse. Aramis also turned back to throw his arms once more round Athos's neck. The latter watched them as they rode off along the highway, their white cloaks standing out from the surrounding gloom. Like two phantoms, their figures appeared to grow larger and to rise from the ground. Nor did they disappear gradually in the mist, or become hidden by a slope in the road; they remained visible until they reached the end of the perspective, and then vanished as suddenly as if they had dissolved into vapour.

Sick at heart, Athos returned to the house, saying to Bragelonne – 'Raoul, something – I know not what – tells me that I have seen these two men for the last time.'

'I am not surprised that such a thought should come to you, sir,' replied the young man, 'for the same feeling has just come over me; I have a presentiment that I also shall never see Messieurs Du Vallon and d'Herblay again.'

'Oh!' said the comte; 'your presentiment is due to a very different cause; in your present state of mind everything wears a gloomy aspect. But you are a young man, and should it happen that you never see these old friends again, it will be because they have departed from this world, where you have still many years to live. But I – ' For all reply Raoul gently shook his head, resting his hand affectionately upon the comte's shoulder. The hearts of both were full to overflowing, and neither was able to say another word.

Suddenly a sound of voices and of horses approaching from the direction of Blois drew their attention to that quarter. Soon they saw a number of men on horseback bearing torches which they were waving merrily to light up the route; they pulled up their horses from time to time in order not to outdistance the cavaliers who followed them. The lights, the noise and the dust raised by a dozen richly caparisoned horses formed a strange contrast to the weird and melancholy disappearance of the two shades of Porthos and Aramis. Athos retired towards the house, but scarcely had he crossed the threshold when the entrance gates of the park were lit up with a blaze of light; all the torch-bearers had come to a halt; and a shout was heard – 'Way for the Duc de Beaufort!' Athos left the house and sprang forward to meet his visitor. The duke had already dismounted and was gazing about him – 'Here I am, monseigneur!' cried Athos.

'Ah! delighted to see you, my dear comte!' replied the prince, with that bluff cordiality which won him the goodwill of all. 'Not too late, I hope, for a friendly visit?'

'Come in, come in, prince!' cried the comte. And, with the Duc de Beaufort leaning upon the arm of Athos, they entered the house, followed by Raoul, who, with his accustomed modesty, walked amidst a group of the prince's officers, among whom he found several acquaintances.

## CHAPTER 55

### Monsieur de Beaufort

THE DUKE turned round just as Raoul, in order to leave his grace and Athos together, was closing the door, to retire with the officers into an adjoining room – 'Is that the youngster I have heard the prince speak so well of?' asked Beaufort.

'Yes, monseigneur, that is he,' replied Athos.

'A fine figure of a soldier! Let him stay, comte; he won't be in the way.'

'Remain with us, Raoul, since monseigneur permits it,' said Athos.

'I' faith, a tall and well set-up lad!' continued the duke. 'Would you let me have him, comte, if I were to ask you?'

'What do you wish me to understand by that, monseigneur?'

'Why, I have come here to bid you farewell.'

'You are going away, monseigneur?'

'Troth, yes. Haven't you heard about what I am going to become?'

'You will be the same as you have always been, monseigneur – a brave prince and a gallant gentleman.'

'Well, I'm going to become an African prince and a Bedouin nobleman. The king is sending me on an expedition against the Arabs.'

'What is this you are telling me, duke?'

'Sounds queer, doesn't it? A man such as I am, Parisian of the Parisians – I, who have been a sort of king of the Faubourgs – am I not called the Roi des Halles?[161] – about to exchange the Place Maubert for the minarets of Jijeli,[162] to become an adventurer after being a *frondeur*!'

'Well, monseigneur, if you had not told me this yourself – '

'You wouldn't have believed it, eh? Well, you may take my word for it, so let us say goodbye. Aha! my friend, you see what it is to be in favour again!'

' "In favour", you call it?'

'Certainly. You smile? Ah! my dear comte, do you know why I accepted? Can't you guess?'

'Because your grace loves glory above everything.'

'Oh! no; there is no glory to be got by shooting down a pack of savages. It won't be glory that I shall get over there – more probably something quite different. But I have always wished – you understand, my dear comte? – and I still wish, to add yet another phase to the queer experiences I have gone through during the last fifty years. For you must admit that it is not exactly the common lot to be born the son of a king; to make war upon crowned heads; to have been reckoned among the principal figures of the age; to have kept a leading position, to feel myself a chip off the old block – Henri IV, I mean; to have been High Admiral of France – and after all, to go and get myself killed at Jijeli, among all those Turks, Saracens and Moors.'

'Monseigneur, you dwell upon this subject very strangely,' said Athos, disquieted. 'How can one believe that a brilliant career like yours should end in such a pitiful fashion?'

'Do you really believe – good man and true that you are – do you really believe that if I undertake this expedition with such an absurd motive, I shall not do my utmost to put the thing through without making myself ridiculous? Shall I not get myself talked about? And to get talked about, what else is there left for me these times, when I have rivals of the capacity of Monsieur le Prince, Monsieur de Turenne[163] and many others – what else is there for me, Admiral of France, son of Henri IV, King of Paris, but to go and get myself killed? *Cordieu!* I tell you I will be talked about! I will go and get killed whatever you may say; and if not there, why then, it will be somewhere else!'

'Monseigneur, you are exaggerating,' replied Athos, 'and I have never noticed that trait in your character before – unless it be your exaggerated bravery.'

'What, a pest! Bravery, do you call it? To go and face scurvy, dysentery, locusts and poisoned arrows, as my ancestor St Louis did, that is bravery, if you like! By the way, do you happen to know if the rascals still use poisoned arrows! Besides, I think you know me pretty well after all these years; and you know, when I make up my mind to have a thing, I don't rest till I get it.'

'You made up your mind not to remain in Vincennes,[164] monseigneur.'

'Aye, aye, old friend; but *you* helped me there – and that reminds me: I keep looking about all over the place, and I don't see good old Monsieur Vaugrimand.[165] How is he?'

'Monsieur Vaugrimand is still your grace's very respectful servant,' replied Athos, smiling.

'I have brought a hundred pistoles for him by way of a legacy. I have made my will, comte.'

'Ah! Monseigneur, monseigneur!'

'But, you see, if Grimaud's name were to appear in the will – ' The duke burst out laughing, then, turning to Raoul, who, from the beginning of the conversation, had fallen into a fit of abstraction, he said, 'Young man, there used to be a certain vintage of Vouvray here, and I think – '

Raoul jumped up, and hastened off to give the necessary order. The Duc de Beaufort took hold of Athos's hand.

'What are you going to make of him?' he asked.

'Nothing, just at present, monseigneur.'

'Ah! yes, I know – h'm – since the king has taken up with – La Vallière, is it?'

'Yes, monseigneur.'

'So then, it is true, all that? I fancy I used to know her myself – that little girl, La Vallière. She is not much of a beauty, it seems to me – '

'No, your grace,' said Athos.

'Do you know whom she reminds me off?'

'Does she remind your grace of someone?'

'Yes, she reminds me of a tolerably amusing young woman, whose mother used to live in the Halles.'

'Oho!' exclaimed Athos, with a smile.

'Ah! the good old days!' added the duke, reflectively.

'And she had a son, had she not?'

'I fancy you are right,' replied the duke, in a tone of easy carelessness and total forgetfulness to which mere words cannot do justice. 'So then, poor Raoul – by the way, he *is* your son, I suppose?'

'He is my son, yes, monseigneur.'

'Well, the poor lad is out of favour with the king and sulks a bit, I suppose?'

'Nay, he shows great forbearance.'

'Are you going to let him waste his time here? It is not right. Come now, let me have him.'

'I wish to keep him beside me, monseigneur. He is all the world to me, and so long as he is willing to remain – '

'Very well, very well!' replied the duke. 'Still, I warrant I could soon have brought him round. I can see he is of the stuff of which Marshals of France are made – I have seen more than one made of very similar material.'

'It may be as you say, monseigneur; but it is the king who creates Marshals of France, and Raoul would never accept anything at the king's hands.'

The conversation was interrupted by the return of Raoul, followed by Grimaud, whose hands were still steady enough to carry the salver with a glass and a bottle of the duke's favourite wine. Catching sight of his old protégé, his grace gave an exclamation of pleasure. 'Grimaud! why, how goes it, old fellow?' he cried.

The servant was deeply gratified by the duke's kind enquiry, and bowed profoundly.

'Two old friends!' said the duke, laying both hands on honest Grimaud's shoulder, and shaking him with hearty vigour. Another bow from Grimaud, if possible deeper than the last, for he was gratified beyond measure. 'What's this I see, comte? Only one glass?'

'I do not drink with your grace unless your grace invites me,' said Athos, with noble humility.

'*Cordieu!* you did quite right to have only one glass brought; we will both drink out of it like brothers in arms. You drink first, comte.'

'Pray complete the honour you are doing me,' said Athos, gently pushing back the glass.

'You are truly a charming companion,' replied the Duc de Beaufort. He drank, and refilling the goblet with the amber wine, passed it to his host. 'But that's not all,' he continued: 'I am still thirsty, and I should like to drink to this fine young fellow who stands here. I bring good luck, vicomte,' said he to Raoul; 'wish for something while you are drinking out of my glass, and rot me! if your wish doesn't come true.'

He held the goblet to Raoul, who barely moistened his lips before he said, hastily, 'I have made my wish, monseigneur.' His eyes sparkled with a gloomy fire, and the blood rose to his cheeks. Athos, who was watching him, was alarmed, if only by his smile.

'And what is your wish?' rejoined the duke, throwing himself back in his armchair, and at the same time handing back the empty bottle to Grimaud, accompanied with a purse.

'Monseigneur, will you promise me to grant it?'

'To be sure I will; have I not said so!'

'I wish to accompany your grace to Jijeli.' Athos grew pale, and could not succeed in hiding his agitation.

The duke looked at his friend as though to help him to resist this unexpected blow. 'It is difficult, my dear vicomte, very difficult, that which you ask,' he said, rather in an undertone.

'Forgive me, monseigneur, I was taking advantage of your kindness,' replied Raoul, in an assured tone; 'but you yourself invited me to wish – '

'To wish to leave me,' said Athos.

'Oh, sir, can you believe such a thing?'

'Come, the little vicomte is right, *mordieu!*' cried the duke. 'What on earth should he do here? He will get the dry rot.' Raoul coloured, and the duke, warming up with his subject, continued, 'War is a jolly game, when all's said and done; one makes one's fortune, and only stands to lose one thing – life – well! what's the odds?'

'One may obtain forgetfulness,' cried Raoul, quickly. Seeing Athos rise and open the window, he repented his hasty words. No doubt the comte wished to hide his emotion. Raoul sprang towards him, but he had already mastered the feeling which had prompted him to turn away for he returned within the circle of light wearing his accustomed expression of serenity.

'Well,' cried the duke, 'how's it to be? Is he to go or stay? If he goes with me, comte, he shall be my aide-de-camp – he shall be as if he were my son.'

'Monseigneur!' cried Raoul, bending his knee in respectful gratitude.

'Monseigneur!' cried the comte, seizing the duke's hand, 'Raoul shall do as he pleases.'

'Nay, sir, it shall be as you please,' broke in the young man.

'Ods body!' shouted the prince, 'it shall not be as either of you please: it shall be as *I* please. I take him. That settles it. Let me tell you, young man, the navy offers a splendid career.'

Raoul smiled, this time so sadly that his father's heart was wrung, and Athos replied to it with a look of severity. Raoul understood; he recovered his calmness, and held himself so well in check that he spoke not another word.

Noticing the lateness of the hour, the duke rose, and said, in his quick, excitable way, 'I am pressed for time just now, but if anyone tells me I have been wasting time in chatting with a friend, I can reply that I have found an excellent recruit.'

'Pardon me, your grace,' interrupted Raoul, 'but pray do not tell the king that, for it is not the king whom I shall be serving.'

'Why then, my friend, whom will you serve? The times are passed when you might have said, "I belong to the Duc de Beaufort." No, no; nowadays we are all the king's men, great or small. Therefore, my dear vicomte, there is no help for it, if you serve on board my ships, you will be serving the king.'

Athos waited with a sort of joyful impatience to hear what reply Raoul, in his fixed hostility towards his rival, the king, would make to this awkward dilemma. The father hoped in his heart that the obstacle would prove insuperable. He felt almost grateful to the duke, whose levity of mind – or perhaps thoughtful generosity – had rendered his son's departure doubtful. But Raoul replied, with quiet firmness – 'I have already considered in my mind, your grace, the objection which you have just raised. I will serve on board your vessel, since you have done me the honour of offering me the chance; but I shall serve a higher master than the king – I shall serve God.'

'How so?' exclaimed Athos and the duke, both together.

'I purpose taking the vows and becoming a Knight of Malta,'[166] added Bragelonne, letting his words fall icily, one by one, like the drops which fall from the bare trees after a wintry tempest. Under this last blow, Athos staggered, and the prince himself was not unmoved. Grimaud groaned aloud, and let fall the bottle, which broke into a thousand pieces without anyone seeming to be aware of it. Beaufort looked at the young man steadily, and could read in his face, although his eyes were lowered, an expression of fixed resolution which nothing could shake. As for Athos, he knew his son's gentle, yet inflexible character; he had no hopes that he would deviate from the fatal path he had chosen.

The duke grasped Athos's hand.

'Comte,' said he, 'in two days' time I leave for Toulon. Will you come and see me in Paris and let me know your decision?'

'I shall have the honour of calling upon you in order to thank you for your great kindness, prince,' replied the comte.

'And bring the vicomte with you in any case, whether he goes with me or not,' added the duke; 'I have pledged my word, and I only ask your consent.'

Having applied this healing balm to the father's heart, the duke playfully pulled the ear of Grimaud, who was blinking his eyes rather more than seemed quite natural. He then rejoined his escort.

The horses, rested and refreshed by the coolness of the beautiful night, soon put a considerable distance between the château and their master. Athos and Bragelonne found themselves left face to face. The clock struck the hour of eleven. Father and son both maintained a painful silence – a silence more eloquent than tears. The nature of both men was of a fine temper which made it possible for them to repress all expression of an emotion which they had resolved to confine within their own hearts. Thus silently and almost without breathing they passed the hour between eleven and midnight. It was only when the clock struck that they realised how long their souls had been wandering amidst the immensity of their recollections of the past and of their fears for the future. Athos was the first to rise, saying – 'It grows late – Until tomorrow, Raoul!'

Raoul rose in his turn and embraced his father. Athos strained him to his breast, and said, in an altered voice, 'In two days, then, you are going to leave me – to leave me for ever, Raoul?'

'Sir,' replied the young man, 'I had designed to run my sword through my heart, but you would have considered it the act of a coward; I have renounced that idea, and therefore we must part.'

'You will have your wish, Raoul.'

'Let me finish, sir, I beg you. If I remain here, I shall die of a broken heart. I know that my days are numbered. Let me leave you soon, or you will see that I am coward enough to die under your eyes, in your house; my love is stronger than my will – I have no strength left to combat it – you may see that during the last month I have lived thirty years, and that I am approaching the end of my life.'

'Then,' said Athos, coldly, 'you are going away with the intention of getting yourself killed in Africa? Oh! confess it – do not lie to me.'

Every particle of colour left Raoul's face, and for some moments he remained silent – moments fraught with agony for his father. Then he said, suddenly – 'Sir, I have promised to devote myself to God. In exchange for the sacrifice that I am making of my youth and my liberty, I ask of Him but one thing, and that is, to preserve me to you, since you are the sole tie which attaches me to this world. God alone can give me the strength to keep in remembrance all I owe to you, and to keep me from forgetting that you should occupy a place in my heart before all others.'

Athos tenderly embraced his son, and said, 'You have spoken like a brave man; in two days, we shall be with the Duc de Beaufort in Paris; and afterwards, I am convinced that you will act in a manner becoming you. You are free, Raoul! Adieu.' And with a slow step he moved towards his bedroom.

Raoul went down into the park, where he passed the night pacing to and fro in the avenue of lime trees.

## CHAPTER 56

## *Preparations for departure*

ATHOS made no further attempt to shake his son's fixed resolution. He gave all his attention, during the two days which the duke had allowed them, to the necessary preparations for Raoul's departure. The principal part of the work fell to Grimaud, and the faithful servant immediately applied himself to it, as might have been foretold, with all his heart and understanding. When the whole equipment was ready, Athos instructed the good old man to go in advance to see everything was in order in Paris. Then, in order to avoid all risk of keeping the duke waiting, or at leastnot to delay Raoul should the duke require his presence, he also set out for Paris accompanied by his son upon the day following that of Monsieur de Beaufort's visit.

It may easily be understood with what emotions the poor young man returned to Paris where he would meet so many people whom he had known, and who had a sincere regard for him.

Every face recalled to him some circumstance connected with his unhappy love-affair. By the time he reached de Guiche's room he was more dead than alive. He was informed that Monsieur de Guiche was in attendance upon Monsieur.

Raoul made towards the Luxembourg, and having passed through the gateway and reached the palace, without ever suspecting that he was approaching a place where La Vallière had lived, his ears were assailed by music and the sound of joyous laughter, and he caught sight of so many dancing shadows that he would have remained there but a few moments and then have gone away never to return had his presence not been noticed by a kindly disposed woman, as he stood, pale and melancholy, in one of the doorways. He had passed through the first ante-chambers and had only stopped because he did not wish to mix with the crowd of happy beings whose voices he heard in the adjoining rooms. One of Monsieur's attendants, who recognised him, had asked if he desired to see Monsieur or Madame, but Raoul had scarcely replied, and had sunk upon a seat beside the velvet curtain in the doorway, his eyes fixed upon a clock which had stopped an hour before. The attendant had gone on, and another servant, still better acquainted with Raoul, had come to enquire if he wished Monsieur de Guiche to be informed of his arrival. Even this name failed to recall poor Raoul to himself. The servant, a persistent and persevering rogue, had gone on to relate how de Guiche had just invented a new sort of lottery which he was teaching the ladies. Raoul had stared at the man absent-mindedly without replying; the fellow had made him even more low-spirited than before. In a state of utter dejection Raoul remained forgotten in the antechamber, when all at once the swish of a skirt was heard as it brushed past the door of a saloon which opened out from the side of the corridor where he was seated. A pretty young lady appeared, followed by one of the officers of the household with whom she was laughingly expostulating and expressing herself with a good deal of freedom. The officer, with mock-gravity, answered her calmly but firmly in well-chosen phrases; evidently it was a little matter of courtship between lovers rather than a quarrel between courtiers; and it finished by the gentleman kissing the lady's hand. Suddenly perceiving Raoul, the lady stopped short in the middle of a remark, and, giving the officer a push, 'Run away, Malicorne,'[167] she said, 'I didn't know there was anybody here. If he has seen or heard us, I'll never forgive you!'

Malicorne fled; the girl slipped behind Raoul, and bending over him with her piquant, laughing face close to his shoulder, she said, in a low tone, 'You are a gentleman, monsieur, and no doubt – ' She interrupted herself with a startled exclamation. 'Raoul!' she cried, the colour rising to her cheeks.

'Mademoiselle de Montalais!' cried Raoul, pale as death. He rose to his feet staggeringly, and attempted to cross the slippery mosaic. The girl had understood the terrible grief to which he was a prey; still she felt that Raoul's flight betokened an accusation or, at least, a suspicion against herself. Always alert and self-possessed, she thought she ought not to let slip this opportunity of justifying herself; and therefore she stopped Raoul before he was halfway across the corridor, although he did not yield without a struggle. He replied to her in such a cold and constrained manner that if anyone had surprised them thus, all doubts as to Mademoiselle de Montalais's participation in the affair of the trap-door would have been entirely removed.

'Ah! Monsieur,' said Montalais, with a shade of contempt, 'your conduct, let me tell you, is scarcely that of a gentleman. Old friendship prompted me to speak to you; you compromise me by your manner, which amounts almost to incivility – you are wrong, monsieur – you do not know how to discriminate between your friends and your enemies. Adieu!'

Raoul had sworn never to speak of Louise – never again to see any who might have seen Louise – he was about to depart for another continent that he might never again meet with anything she had seen or touched. But, after the first shock to his pride, after having met Montalais, who had been La Vallière's inseparable companion, and the sight of whom recalled to his memory the little turret at Blois and the happy days of his boyhood, all his resolution vanished. 'Forgive me, mademoiselle,' he stammered; 'I am very far from wishing to appear discourteous.'

'You wish to speak to me?' said Montalais, with the bright smile that he had been accustomed to see on her face. 'Very well; but come away somewhere else; we are liable to be surprised here any moment.'

'Where?' he asked.

She looked undecidedly at the clock; then, after considering a moment, 'Come to my room,' she said, 'we can have an hour to ourselves,' and, followed by Raoul, she ran upstairs to her room lighter than a fairy. Once inside the room, she closed the door, and having handed to her attendant the mantle she had been carrying on her arm, she said to Raoul – 'Do you wish to see Monsieur de Guiche?'

'Yes, mademoiselle.'

'I will ask him to come up here in a moment, when I have had a talk to you.'

'Thank you.'

'Do you bear me any malice?'

Raoul looked at her a moment; then, lowering his eyes, he replied, 'Yes.'

'You think I had something to do with the plot which caused your quarrel?'

' "Quarrel!" ' said Raoul, bitterly. 'Oh! Mademoiselle, how could there have been a quarrel where there was no affection?'

'You are mistaken,' replied Montalais, 'Louise regarded you with great affection.'

Raoul started.

'Not love exactly, I know; but she had a strong liking for you, and you ought to have married her before you went to London.'

Raoul laughed harshly; his sinister mirth caused a shiver to run through Montalais. 'You tell me that, mademoiselle, as though it were the easiest thing in the world! Does anyone marry the woman he loves? You forget that the king had even then designed to make his mistress the woman of whom we are speaking.'

'Listen,' rejoined the girl, clasping Raoul's cold hands in her own, 'you alone were entirely to blame; a man of your age should not have left a woman of her age unguarded.'

'Then faith no longer exists in the world,' said Raoul.

'That is true, vicomte,' replied Montalais, imperturbably. 'Still I ought to tell you that if, instead of loving Louise coldly and philosophically, you had awakened her to the meaning of love – '

'No more of this, I beg you,' interrupted Raoul. 'I feel that you all belong to another century; I belong to a previous age. You know how to treat these matters lightly: you consider love a subject for mirth, but I – I loved Mademoiselle de – ' He could not utter the name. 'I loved her; that means, I trusted her. Well, no matter, I love her no longer.'

'Oh! Vicomte!' said Montalais, showing him his reflection in a mirror.

'I know what you would say, mademoiselle; I am greatly altered, am I not? Well, shall I tell you the reason? My face is the mirror of my heart, which has changed too.'

'You have found consolation then?' said Montalais sharply.

'Nay, I shall never find consolation.'

'You are incomprehensible, Monsieur de Bragelonne.'

'What care I? I understand myself only too well.'

'You have not attempted to speak to Louise?'

'Speak to her!' cried the young man, his eyes flashing. 'Really, I wonder you don't advise me to marry her! Perhaps the king would have no objection now.' And, full of anger, he rose to his feet.

'I perceive,' said Montalais, 'that you are not cured, and that Louise has one enemy the more.'

'An enemy the more?'

'Yes, those who are favourites of the king are not exactly loved at the Court of France.'

'Oh! so long as she has her lover to defend her, it should suffice. She has chosen one against whom no enemy can prevail.' Then, turning round suddenly, he added, with a little sting of irony which did not fail to penetrate – 'And then, mademoiselle, she has *you* for a friend.'

'*I?* – oh! no; I am not of those whom Mlle de la Vallière deigns to look at, but – '

This last word was significant, in the mouth of a woman like Montalais, of such dire misfortune for the woman whom he had so deeply loved that it made Raoul's heart ache. Montalais's further remarks were cut short by a noise behind the wainscot in the alcove, clearly audible to both speakers. Montalais pricked up her ears, and Raoul was already about to retire, when a woman entered without any sign of flurry, by the secret doorway, which she closed behind her.

'Madame!' exclaimed Raoul, recognising the king's sister-in-law.

'Idiot that I am!' murmured Montalais, springing up to hide Raoul, but too late. 'I have made a mistake of an hour!' However, she had time to forestall Madame, who was turning towards Raoul.

'Your royal highness,' began Montalais, 'has been kind enough to think of this lottery, and – '

The princess began to lose countenance. Raoul was about to take leave hastily, for although he scarcely understood the position of affairs, he could feel that his presence was inconvenient. Madame was thinking of some trivial phrase to enable her to recover her self-possession, when all at once a closet opposite to the alcove was opened and admitted de Guiche, his face wreathed in smiles. The surprise was painful. Still, it must be admitted, Raoul's face was still the palest, although the princess nearly fainted, and leant heavily against the foot of the bed. No one ventured to go to her assistance. For some minutes there was a dead silence, which Raoul was the first to break; he went to the comte, whose agitation was extreme, and, taking his hand, he said, 'My dear comte, you will explain to Madame that I am too unfortunate not to merit forgiveness; you will tell her that I also have loved, and have such a horror of the unfaithfulness of which I am the victim, that it renders me very severe towards any treason which I see committed around me. That is why, mademoiselle,' he continued, turning to Montalais with a smile, 'I shall never divulge the secret of my friend's visits to you. Obtain your forgiveness from Madame also, who is so kind and generous, Madame who has, at this moment, surprised your secret. Both of you are free – love one another, and be happy!'

For one moment the princess remained in utter despair; in spite of the delicacy displayed by Raoul, it hurt her cruelly to feel herself at the mercy of a possible indiscretion on his part. It was equally galling to have to accept the means of escape afforded by the misunderstanding his tact had prompted him to assume. In her nervous agitation she strove to hide the mortification she felt.

Raoul understood her feelings, and again came to her aid. Bending his knee before her, he said, in a low tone, 'Madame, in two days' time I shall be far away from Paris, and in a fortnight I shall be far away from France, where never again shall I set foot.'

'You are going away?' she murmured, relieved.

'With Monsieur de Beaufort.'

'To Africa!' cried de Guiche, in his turn. 'Oh! my dear friend, it is a fatal place!' And, forgetful of everything – forgetting that his forgetfulness was even more compromising to the princess than his presence – he exclaimed, 'you are unkind – you have not even spoken to me of it.' He embraced Raoul tenderly. Meanwhile, Montalais had seized the opportunity to lead Madame from the room, and had disappeared herself.

Raoul passed his hand over his forehead, and said with a smile half to himself, 'I have had a dream.' Then, to de Guiche, he said warmly, 'My very dear friend, I have nothing to hide from you; I shall die over yonder. Before a year is gone your secret will be buried with me.'

'Raoul, be a man!'

'Do you know my thought, de Guiche? It is this: I shall be more alive when I am dead and buried than I have been during the last month. I am a Christian, but if such suffering were to continue, I would not answer for my soul's health.' De Guiche made a motion of dissent. 'Enough about myself,' continued Bragelonne; 'but let me give you a piece of advice, my dear friend; what I am about to say is of far higher importance.'

'How is that?'

'Unquestionably, for you stand to lose far more than I, since you are beloved.'

'Oh!'

'It makes me happy to be able to speak to you freely! Well, what I have to say is, beware of Montalais.'

'But she is my very good friend!'

'She was a friend of – her whom you know of. But she ruined her by appealing to her ambition.'

'You are mistaken, I am sure.'

'And now that she has ruined her, she seeks to deprive her of the sole excuse she had for her conduct.'

'And that is?'

'Her love.'

'What do you mean?'

'I mean that there is a conspiracy formed against her who is the king's mistress, a plot hatched among Madame's household.'

'Can you really believe it?'

'I am certain of it.'

'By Montalais?'

'You may reckon her as the least dangerous of those whose enmity she has to fear.'

'Explain yourself better, my dear friend, and if I understand you – '

'In two words: Madame is jealous.'

'I know it – '

'Oh! do not be afraid, she loves you and you love her, de Guiche; do you know the full meaning of those words? They signify that you can hold up your head; that you can sleep in peace; that you may thank God every moment of your life! She loves you – that means, you can comprehend all, even the advice of a friend who wishes to preserve your happiness. She loves you, de Guiche, she loves you! You have not to endure those nights of agony – those endless nights of torment which fall to the lot of such as are destined to die. You will live long if you watch your happiness as a miser watches his gold. You are beloved! – Then permit me to tell you what you must do that you may always retain your happiness.'

De Guiche looked compassionately at the young man, half mad with despair, and felt almost ashamed of his own happiness. Raoul restrained his feverish excitement and forced himself to appear calm.

'They will make her suffer,' he continued, 'she whose name I cannot speak. Swear to me that you will not countenance it, nay more, that, if necessary, you will defend her, as I would have done myself.'

'I swear it!' replied de Guiche.

'And someday,' continued Raoul, 'when you have rendered her a great service – one day when she wishes to thank you, promise me that you will say to her, "I have done you this kindness because Bragelonne begged me to serve you – de Bragelonne whom you have so deeply injured." '

'I swear it,' murmured de Guiche, full of compassion.

'That is all – Adieu! Tomorrow or next day I leave for Toulon. If you can spare a few hours, devote them to me.'

'By all means – my time is yours.'

'I thank you.'

'And where are you going now?'

'I am going to rejoin the comte, my father, at Planchet's place, where we hope to meet Monsieur d'Artagnan. I should wish to embrace him before I leave. He is one of the best of men, and he loves me. Goodbye for the present; no doubt someone is expecting you; you can see me again when you please at the comte's lodgings.'

The two young men parted. If anyone had observed them, he would probably have pointed out Raoul as the happier of the two.

CHAPTER 57

*Planchet makes an inventory*

WHILST RAOUL was making his visit to the Luxembourg, Athos had gone to Planchet's to obtain news of d'Artagnan. On arriving in the Rue des Lombards, the comte found the establishment of the worthy grocer in great confusion; the shop was littered with goods, but it was not the litter caused by the briskness of business or the arrival of fresh consignments of merchandise. Planchet was not to be seen as usual enthroned upon a pile of sacks or barrels. No; a youth with a pen behind his ear was walking round with another youth armed with a notebook, in which he was inserting formidable columns of figures, whilst a third was busily counting packages and weighing groceries. They were taking an inventory of the stock. Athos, who knew nothing about business, felt somewhat daunted by the material obstacles in his way, as well as by the haughty, inaccessible air assumed by the young men as they performed their mysterious rites. He noticed several customers turned away, and began to ask himself if his visit, since he came to make no purchases, would not be considered still more inexcusable. Therefore his manner was deprecative as he ventured to ask the young men if Monsieur Planchet was to be seen. They replied, a trifle superciliously, that Monsieur Planchet was packing his trunks. These words made Athos prick up his ears.

'Packing up, is he?' he asked. 'Is Monsieur Planchet going away, then?'

'Yes, monsieur, almost immediately.'

'Then, gentlemen, perhaps you would be so good as to let him know that the Comte de la Fère wishes to speak to him a moment.'

On learning this name, one of the apprentices, no doubt accustomed to hearing it mentioned with respect, left his occupation to go and inform Planchet. It was at this moment that Raoul, after the painful scene with Montalais, arrived at the grocer's. Planchet, as soon as the message was delivered to him, left his job and hurried out to meet the comte.

'Ah! Monsieur le comte,' said he, 'this is indeed an honour! what good star brings you here?'

'My dear Planchet,' said Athos, pressing his son's hand, for he had noticed at first glance his air of more than usual melancholy, 'my dear Planchet, we have come to ask you – But what a dreadful muddle you are in! you are as dusty as a miller; where on earth have you been grubbing about?'

'Ah! the deuce! Take care, sir; don't come too near until I have had a good brushing.'

'Pooh! why not? It is only flour, I suppose?'

'No, no, it is not flour. This white you see on my sleeve is arsenic.'

'Arsenic!'

'Yes, it is intended for the rats.'

'Ah! of course, the rats play an important part in a business of this kind.'

'Oh! I was not thinking about this place, sir; I am having an inventory taken, as you may see.'

'Are you retiring from business?'

'Well, yes; I am passing the business over to one of my apprentices.'

'Ah! so you are a man of means?'

'Why, sir! I am sick of the city; I don't know if it is because I am getting old; I once heard Monsieur d'Artagnan remark that when a man grows old he thinks more and more about the scenes of his youth; at any rate, for some time past I have felt my mind running on country life and gardening; I was brought up as a boy on a farm.'

Planchet qualified the confession with a laugh a trifle more conceited than was strictly compatible with the humility of his words.

Athos nodded approvingly. 'You are buying land, I suppose?'

'I have already bought a little place, monsieur.'

'Ah! so much the better.'

'A little house at Fontainebleau, with about twenty acres of land.'

'Excellent, Planchet! I congratulate you.'

'But we cannot talk comfortably here. There! this cursed dust has set you coughing. *Corbleu!* I shouldn't like to poison the most worthy gentleman in the kingdom.'

Athos received without a smile the little pleasantry which Planchet had attempted by way of essaying the tone of a man of the world. 'Yes,' said he, 'let us have a bit of private talk – in your own room, if you like. You have a room here, I suppose?'

'Certainly, sir.'

'Upstairs, is it?' and Athos, seeing Planchet a trifle embarrassed, wished to relieve him by going first.

'Yes, but –' began Planchet, hesitatingly. Athos misunderstood the reason of his hesitation, putting it down to the grocer's diffidence with regard to the hospitality he was, at that moment, in a position to offer.

'Never mind, never mind!' said he, still going on, 'a merchant's room, in this quarter of the town, one doesn't expect to find a palace. Come along.'

Raoul preceded him, and entered the room. Two cries were heard at the same moment: one might perhaps have said three. The dominant cry was a woman's scream; the other was from Raoul – it was an exclamation of surprise. He had scarcely opened the door when he hurriedly reclosed it. The third cry was one of fright: it was Planchet who had uttered it. 'I am very sorry,' he added, 'Madame is dressing.'

No doubt Raoul had had ocular demonstration of the truth of what Planchet said, for he turned to retrace his steps.

'Madame – ?' said Athos. 'Ah! forgive me, Planchet, I didn't know you had upstairs – '

'It is Trüchen,' added Planchet, a trifle red in the face.

'It is whoever you please, my good Planchet, pardon our indiscretion.'

'No, no, gentlemen, pray go upstairs again.'

'We will do nothing of the sort,' replied Athos.

'Oh! now madame has had notice, she will have had time – '

'No, Planchet; goodbye.'

'But, gentlemen, you will not be so unkind as to leave my house without having sat down a little while!'

'If we had known there was a lady upstairs,' replied Athos with his customary self-possession, 'we should have asked permission to pay our respects.' This little piece of sarcasm disconcerted Planchet somewhat; to hide his confusion he pushed through the passage and opened the door himself, in order to allow the comte and his son to enter. Trüchen was now completely dressed, smartly, if a trifle vulgarly; she had expressionless German eyes attempting French vivacity. After bowing to each gentleman, she gave up the room and went downstairs into the shop. Not, though, before she had listened at the door to hear what the visitors would say about her to Planchet. Athos shrewdly suspected this, and turned the conversation into quite another channel. Planchet, however, was burning to explain the very point which Athos sought to avoid, and such was his persistency that the latter found himself obliged to listen to Planchet's idyllic story, related in language more chaste than that of Longus.[168] He told them enthusiastically that in Trüchen he had found the solace of his declining years, that she had brought good luck to his business, and was to him as Ruth was to Boaz.[169]

'Then the only thing you can desire is an heir to your property,' said Athos.

'If I had a son, he would inherit three hundred thousand livres,' replied Planchet, expanding his chest.

'You ought to have an heir, if only to leave him your little fortune.'

These last words served to restore Planchet to his proper position, just as the sergeant's voice used to check him when he was but a private in the Piedmont regiment in which he had been enlisted by Rochefort.[170] Athos gathered that the grocer intended to marry Trüchen; and would be the founder of a family whether he wished it or not – a suspicion which only appeared better grounded when he learned that the young man to whom Planchet was transferring his business was Trüchen's cousin. Athos seemed to remember the fellow as a fresh-coloured, curly-haired, sturdy young rascal. At any rate, he heard all that he cared to know about the prospects of the retiring grocer, and it seemed unlikely that Trüchen would consider her fine dresses sufficient compensation in themselves for the boredom she would suffer from living in the country in company with a grey-haired husband. All this, as we have said, Athos understood, but suddenly changing the conversation, 'What has become of d'Artagnan?' he asked, 'I didn't see him at the Louvre.'

'Oh! Comte, Monsieur d'Artagnan has disappeared.'

'Disappeared?' cried Athos in surprise.

'Oh, sir! we both know what that means.'

'I don't know for my part.'

'When Monsieur d'Artagnan disappears, it is always to attend to some mission or some other important business.'

'He would have spoken to you about it?'

'Never.'

'However, you knew about it when he went to England.'

'Ah! that was because of the speculation,'[171] said Planchet, thoughtlessly.

'The speculation?'

'I mean to say – ' stammered the grocer, confused.

'Well, well; I have nothing to do with your business nor that of d'Artagnan; it is only the interest we take in him that induced me to question you. Since the captain of the musketeers is not here, and since you can't give us any information as to where he is to be found, we will take leave of you. *Au revoir*, Planchet, *au revoir!* Come, Raoul!'

'Oh, sir, I only wish I were able to tell you – '

'By no means – I am not the man to reproach a servant for his discretion.'

The word *servant* fell unpleasantly on the wealthy Planchet's ear, but the respect with which he regarded the comte and his natural good-nature prevailed over his pride. 'There is no indiscretion in telling you that d'Artagnan was here a few days ago,' he said.

'Ah!'

'Yes, and he remained here several hours consulting a map.'

'You are right, my friend, say no more.'

'And in proof of what I say, here is the map,' said Planchet, indicating on the wall the map which the captain had consulted on his last visit to Planchet. It was a map of France upon which Athos's sharp eye noticed a route pricked out with pins, or rather, the holes indicated where the pins had been stuck. Following the route with his eye, Athos saw that d'Artagnan must have travelled southward to the Mediterranean towards Toulon. In the neighbourhood of Cannes, the line of punctures ceased. The Comte de la Fère racked his brains for some moments to guess the motive which had sent the musketeer to Cannes, and especially what motive he could have had to make an examination of the banks of the Var. Reflection furnished no clue. For once his accustomed perspicacity was at fault. Raoul was equally unable to guess.

'No matter!' said the young man to the comte, who had pointed out to him the route with his finger, 'one might almost say that there is a special providence which connects our destiny with that of Monsieur d'Artagnan. You see he is on the south coast in the neighbourhood of Cannes, and you, sir, have promised to accompany me as far as Toulon. Rest assured we shall come across him much more easily on our journey than upon this map.'

Then taking leave of Planchet, who was scolding the apprentices – even Trüchen's cousin, his successor – the gentleman went off to pay a visit to the Duc de Beaufort. As they left the shop, they saw the coach destined in future to carry the charming Mademoiselle Trüchen and the money-bags of Monsieur Planchet.

'Every man travels towards happiness by the road which he chooses,' said Raoul, thoughtfully.

'To Fontainebleau!' cried Planchet to his coachman.

CHAPTER 58

*Monsieur de Beaufort likewise makes an inventory*

To HAVE SPOKEN TO PLANCHET about d'Artagnan, to have seen Planchet leave Paris to bury himself in the country, seemed to Athos and his son like a last farewell to the capital and to their former life. For indeed what did these two men leave behind them – one of whom had exhausted all the glories of the last age, and the other all the misfortunes of the present? Evidently, neither of them had anything further to ask of their contemporaries. It only remained for them to pay a visit to the Duc de Beaufort in order to arrange the details of their departure.

The duke was magnificently lodged in Paris. He maintained one of those superb establishments which certain old men of a bygone generation remembered to have seen among men of great fortunes in the more spacious times of Henri III. Then, indeed, there were certain powerful noblemen who were richer than the king. Moreover, they were aware of it, and did not deprive themselves of the pleasure of humiliating his royal majesty now and then. This was the arrogant aristocracy which Richelieu had constrained to expend its blood, its treasure and its obedience in what from that time began to be styled the service of the king. From Louis XI – that terrible scourge to the nobility – down to the time of Richelieu, how many noble families had proudly raised their heads! How many, from the time of Richelieu to that of Louis XIV, had bowed their heads who would never again raise them! But Monsieur de Beaufort had blood in his veins such as is never shed upon a scaffold, unless, indeed, by a decree of the people.[172]

This prince had kept up the old style of living. How did he pay for his horses, his servants, his table? That was a question which nobody could answer, he himself least of all. Only, he had always the privilege which sons of kings then enjoyed, to whom nobody could refuse to become a creditor, whether this was due to respect, to devotion or to the comfortable belief that they would eventually be repaid.

Athos and Raoul found the prince's residence in disorder as they had found that of Planchet. The duke was also engaged in making an inventory; that is to say, he was distributing among his friends and his creditors every article of any value in the house. In debt to the amount of nearly two million – an enormous sum in those days – the duke had calculated that he could not leave for Africa without obtaining a considerable amount of money, and in order to procure this sum, he was distributing among his old creditors plate, arms, jewels and furniture, which were too magnificent to sell, and which would thus bring him in double. For how can a man to whom one owes ten thousand livres refuse to accept a present worth six thousand, its value, moreover, enhanced by the fact that it had belonged to a descendant of Henri IV? and how, after having carried away this present, can he refuse to lend another ten thousand to such a generous nobleman? This, then, is what took place. The prince no longer possessed a house to live in, for it would have been useless for an admiral, whose ship is his home. He no longer owned any weapons beyond what were needful, since he was about to find himself in the midst of his cannons; no more jewels, which the sea might have swallowed up; but he had the useful sum of three or four hundred thousand crowns in his coffers. And everywhere throughout the house people were moving about joyously, under the impression that they were plundering monseigneur. The prince possessed in a supreme degree the art of rendering happy those duns who had the most to complain of. Every man who was pressed for money, every empty purse could count upon a patient hearing and intelligent sympathy. To one he would say, 'I only wish I had as much as you have, and I would give it to you.' To another, 'I have only this silver ewer; still, it is worth at least five hundred livres; take it.' Thus it came about that the prince continually found himself able to renew his creditors – so true is it that courtesy is equivalent to coin of the realm. On this occasion he waived all ceremony; he gave away everything – you would have said the place was being sacked. The Oriental fable of the poor Arab who carries away from a looted palace an old cooking-pot, at the bottom of which he had hidden a bag of gold, and whom everybody allows to pass freely without an attempt to rob him – this fable had become a truth in the duke's mansion. Many tradesmen recouped themselves out of the prince's kitchens. Thus, a provision merchant who plundered the clothes-presses or the harness-room considered the trifles he picked up of little value, though saddlers or tailors would have valued them highly. Eager to carry home to their wives the preserves which monseigneur distributed, men could be seen joyfully staggering along under the weight of earthen jars and bottles gloriously sealed with the prince's arms. Monsieur de Beaufort finished by giving away his horses and the hay in the lofts. He made more than thirty people happy with his cooking utensils and three hundred with the contents of his cellar. Moreover, all these people went away convinced that Monsieur de Beaufort acted in this manner only in anticipation of a new fortune which he expected to find hidden under the Arab tents. They repeated to each other, while they were devastating the mansion, that the king was sending him to Jijeli in order to reconstruct his lost fortune; that the treasures of Africa were to be divided equally between the admiral and the King of France; that these treasures consisted of diamond mines, or mines of other fabulous stones, the silver mines in the Atlas not even obtaining the honour of being named. Besides the mines to be worked – this could not be undertaken, of course, until after the campaign – there was the booty to be captured by the army. Monsieur de Beaufort would reap the benefit of all the wealth accumulated by the infidel Corsairs who had ravaged Christendom since the Battle of Lepanto.[173] The number of millions was quite incalculable. Therefore why should one who was going in quest of such treasures take the trouble to keep the poor utensils of his past life? And, on the other hand, why should one spare the property of him who spared it so little himself?

Such then was the position of affairs, which Athos took in at a single glance. He found the Admiral of France slightly elevated, for he had just left table – a table of sixty covers – at which a number of toasts to the success of the expedition had been honoured, and where, after dessert, the remains of the banquet had been abandoned to the servants, and the empty plates and dishes to the collector of souvenirs. The prince was intoxicated by his ruin as well as by his popularity. He had drunk his old wine to the health of his future wine. As he caught sight of Athos with Raoul, he said, 'Halloa! here's my aide-de-camp. Come in, comte! Come in, vicomte!'

Athos sought a passage through the litter of plate and linen.

'Ah! yes, just step over it,' said the duke. He filled a glass with wine and offered it to Athos. The latter accepted, but Raoul hardly moistened his lips. 'Here's your commission,' said the prince to Raoul. 'I reckoned upon your coming, so I had it made out. You will go on in advance of the fleet as far as Antibes.'

'Yes, monseigneur.'

'Here's the order,' continued the duke, handing the parchment to Raoul. 'You have served at sea, I believe?'

'Yes, monseigneur, I have made several cruises with Monsieur le Prince.'

'Good. You must collect all these barges and lighters to form an escort and to transport provisions for the fleet. The army must be embarked in a fortnight at latest.'

'It shall be done, monseigneur.'

'This order empowers you to visit and search all the islands along the coast; you will recruit or impress as many men as you can find for me.'

'Yes, Monsieur le Duc.'

'And as you are energetic and a good worker, you are bound to spend a good deal of money.'

'I hope not, monseigneur.'

'Not at all – I hope you *will*. My steward has made out drafts of a thousand livres each payable in the coast towns. You will be supplied with a hundred of 'em. Now, be off with you, Vicomte.'

Athos interrupted the prince. 'Keep your money, monseigneur; among the Arabs war is waged with gold quite as much as with lead.'

'I intend to try the contrary,' rejoined the duke; 'besides, you know my ideas with regard to this expedition, plenty of noise and plenty of firing – and, if it comes to a pinch, I disappear in the smoke.' And, with this, the duke was about to burst into a laugh, only he perceived that neither Athos nor Raoul seemed to be amused.

'Ah!' said he, with the frank and cheerful egotism of his caste and of his period, 'you are not the sort of people one ought to see after dinner: there you are, stiff as ramrods and chilly as icicles, whilst you see me full of wine, fire and life. No, devil take me! Vicomte, I shan't see you unless I'm fasting; and as for you, comte, if you continue like this, I shan't see you at all.' He accompanied the words with a warm pressure of Athos's hand.

'Monseigneur,' replied the latter with a smile, 'because you are well supplied with funds, pray do not think it necessary to begin with a splash and a flourish. I predict that before a month is out you will be stiff and cold enough yourself when you look at your empty coffers, and then you will have the surprise of seeing Raoul by your side gay and lively and with piles of silver to offer you.'

'I believe you, my boy!' cried the duke, delighted. 'Comte, you mustn't go – you must stay with me.'

'No, monseigneur, I must go with Raoul: the duties you have entrusted to him are difficult and troublesome. He would scarcely be able to fulfil them satisfactorily alone. You must not forget, monseigneur, that the commission you have just given him is one of the highest importance.'

'Pooh!'

'And in the navy, too!'

'True: but when one gets hold of a young fellow of his stamp, doesn't he always do all that's required of him?'

'Monseigneur, I think I may say that nowhere will you find more zeal and intelligence or more genuine courage than you will find in Raoul; but if he should fail to make all preparations for your embarkation, it would be only what you deserve.'

'Ecod, sir! you are scolding me now!'

'Why, to victual a fleet – to organise a service of lighters – to recruit your sailors – why! it is a year's work for an admiral. Raoul is a cavalry officer, and you give him only a fortnight!'

'I tell you he will manage it.'

'I believe he will; but I shall help him.'

'I reckoned upon you, and I also reckon that when once you have reached Toulon, you will not permit him to go away alone.'

'Oh!' cried Athos, shaking his head.

'Wait and see!'

'Monseigneur, permit us to withdraw.'

'Go then, my dear fellow, and may you share my good luck!'

'Adieu, monseigneur, and may your good luck continue!'

'Upon my word, a good beginning to the enterprise!' said Athos to his son. 'No provisions, no reserves, either of men or ships; how can the thing be done in this way?'

'If they are all going there to do as I do, there will be no want of provisions,' murmured Raoul.

'Vicomte,' replied Athos, severely, 'do not be unjust as well as foolish in your selfishness, or in your grief, whichever you please to call it. If your only intention in going there is to get killed, you might have gone without the help of anyone: it was scarcely worth the trouble to recommend you to Monsieur de Beaufort. But since you are acting for the prince in command of the expedition – since you have accepted the responsibility of a post in the forces, it is no longer a question for yourself alone; you have to think of all those poor soldiers who, like yourself, have a heart and a body, who will be lamented by their country and who will have to suffer the misfortunes which humanity is heir to. You must know, Raoul, that an officer should regard his men as a priest regards his flock, and that he needs more charity than a priest.'

'Monsieur, I know it, and I have tried to practise it – I should still have done so, but – '

'You must remember also that you belong to a country proud of its military glory; go to your death if you will, but let it not be death without honour, or without profit for France. Do not let my words grieve you; I love you and therefore I wish to see you perfect.'

'I love your reproaches, sir,' said the young man gently; 'they are salutary, and they prove to me that there is one who still loves me.'

'And now let us go, Raoul; the weather is so fine, the sky so clear – the sky which you will find still more clear at Jijeli, and which will recall me to your memory yonder, as here it recalls me to thoughts of God.'

The two gentlemen then began to discuss the recklessness of the duke, and agreed that France would be but poorly served both with regard to the conception and to the carrying-out of the expedition; and, having summed up the whole political question in the single word foolishness, they set off, in obedience to their will rather than to their destiny. Thus the sacrifice was consummated.

## CHAPTER 59

### *The silver platter*

THE JOURNEY was a tolerably pleasant one. Athos and his son travelled across France by stages of fifteen leagues or so a day, sometimes more, according as Raoul's grief urged to more or less strenuous travelling. They reached Toulon at the end of a fortnight, and entirely lost traces of d'Artagnan at Antibes. It was to be assumed the captain of the musketeers was desirous of remaining *incognito* for Athos gathered from his enquiries that the cavalier whom he described had been seen to exchange his riding-horses for a well-closed carriage when he arrived at Avignon. Raoul was in despair at not meeting d'Artagnan; his affectionate nature felt the need of a parting grip of the hand from that staunch and trusty friend. Athos knew from experience that d'Artagnan became impenetrable when engaged in any matter of importance, either for himself or in the service of the king. He even feared that he might inconvenience his friend or thwart his plans by enquiring too closely into his movements. However, when Raoul had begun his work of classifying the fleet according to burthen, and of collecting lighters and forwarding them to Toulon, the comte learned from one of the fishermen that his boat was undergoing repairs after having been engaged by a gentleman who had been in a great hurry to embark.

Believing that the man was deceiving him with the object of retaining
his boat in order to earn more money by fishing when all his rivals'
vessels were engaged, Athos insisted upon a full explanation. The
fisherman told him that about a week previously a man had come to
hire his boat in order to take a trip by night to the Ile Saint-Honorat.
The price was agreed upon; but the gentleman had brought down the
body of a carriage which he insisted upon putting on board, in spite of
the great difficulties which such an operation presented. The fisherman had wished to cry off the agreement – he had even threatened,
but his threats had only served to procure him a sound drubbing,
which the gentleman administered cunningly, with science and a
stick. Howling and cursing, the man had applied to the syndic of the
fishermen at Antibes, where the fraternity form a little community
for mutual protection and settle their own disputes; but the gentleman had produced a certain paper, at sight of which the syndic had
bowed almost to the ground, and had ordered the fisherman to obey,
rating him soundly for his insubordination. He had accordingly given
way and had put off to sea with the load which had been the cause of
strife.

'But all this does not tell us,' said Athos, 'how your boat got
damaged.'

'Well, you see, your honour, it was like this. I sailed her over to
Saint-Honorat, as arranged with the gentleman; but then he changed
his mind, "for," says he, "you can't take a boat south'ard of the
abbey".'

'Why not?'

'Because, your honour, there's a reef in a line with the square
tower of the Benedictines called the Monk's Bank; the rocks are just
awash, and the channel is dangerous, but I've gone through them a
thousand times. Howsoever, the gentleman tells me I must land him
at Sainte-Marguerite.'

'Well?'

'Well, your honour,' continued the fisherman, in his broad
Provençal dialect, 'either a man's a sailor or he isn't; either he knows
the channels, or he's no better than a soldier. I stuck out, for I'd
made up my mind to go through that channel, or to know the reason
why not. The gentleman took me by the collar, and says he, quite
quiet, "I'm going to strangle you." My mate he gets hold of a hatchet,
and I do the like; for why? – we'd got to pay him for that little
business overnight. But the gentleman he out with his sword and he
lays about him so lively that neither me nor my mate can come anear
him. I was just getting ready to heave the hatchet at his head, which

I'm sure your honour will allow I'd a perfect right to do, for a sailor is master in his own boat, just as much as a landlubber is master in his own private house. Well then, I was just a-going to chop the gentleman in two, when, all at once, believe me or believe me not, your honour, that there carriage-body opens – how is more than I can tell you – and out pops a sort of evil spirit, with his head all covered with a black helmet and a horrible black mask, and he shakes his fist at us horrible for to see.'

'What was it?' asked Athos.

'It was the Devil, your honour! for the gentleman, says he, quite pleased – "Ah! thank you, monseigneur." '

'Strange!' muttered Athos, glancing at his son.

'What did you do?' asked the latter of the fisherman.

'Well, your honour, you see, of course, we two poor men was hardly a match for two gentlemen, anyhow – let alone standing up against the Devil – ah! no, that's a bit too much! My mate and I, we didn't stop to argue the point – we makes one jump into the sea, for we was within two or three hundred yards of the beach.'

'And what then?'

Then, your honour, as there was still a bit of a breeze from the sou'-west, the boat keeps slipping along and runs ashore at last on the beach of Sainte-Marguerite.'

'Oh! – but the two passengers?'

'You haven't got no call to be afeared for them! For why? – one of them was the Devil, and he'd look after his friend – and the proof of it is that when we swam off to the boat again, instead of finding those two on the beach dead corpses, why, we found nothing at all, not even the carriage.'

'Strange! strange!' repeated the comte. 'But what did you do afterwards?'

'Why, your honour, I complained to the governor of Sainte-Marguerite, but he only lays a finger alongside his nose, and says he – "If you come here telling me any such yarns, you shall have a thorough good leathering." '

'The governor said that?'

'Yes, your honour; but howsoever, my boat was stove in – stove in, says I? – she was smashed so bad that her bows remained fast on Sainte-Marguerite's point, and the carpenter, he says, "She can't be made good under a hundred and twenty livres," believe me or believe me not, your honours.'

'Very well,' said Raoul, 'you are exempted from serving. You may go.'

'If you like, we will go to Sainte-Marguerite,' said Athos to Bragelonne, when the fisherman had taken himself off.

'I agree with you, sir, for there seems to be something which requires clearing up; it did not appear to me that the man was telling the truth.'

'Nor to me either, Raoul. This story of a masked gentleman and a disappearing carriage gives me the impression of having been invented in order to conceal some deed of violence upon the open sea committed by these ruffians in revenge for his having insisted upon their carrying out the agreement.'

'That is a suspicion which struck me also; and probably the carriage contained valuables – it is hardly likely there would have been a man in it.'

'We must find out about it, Raoul. It seems certain that the gentleman resembles d'Artagnan; I recognised his touch. Heigho! we are no longer young and invincible as we were once. Who knows but this miserable boatman, armed with a hatchet or a marline-spike, has succeeded where the finest swordsmen in Europe have failed, to say nothing of all the bullets that have been fired at d'Artagnan during forty years!'

That same day they started for Sainte-Marguerite on board a lugger which had arrived under orders from Toulon. The impression which they received as they landed was a strangely pleasing one. The island was embowered in flowers and there were fruit trees in profusion, for the whole of the cultivated portion of it was set apart for the governor's garden. Orange, pomegranate and fig trees bent beneath the weight of their golden or purple fruits. All around this garden, in the uncultivated parts of the islet, coveys of red-legged partridges ran through the undergrowth of brambles and juniper-bushes, and at every step which the comte and Raoul took, a startled rabbit would forsake the thyme and ling and scuttle off to his burrow. Nevertheless, this island of the blessed was inhabited. Flat, with but a single cove where boats could land, the governor protected and shared the profits of the smugglers, whom he allowed to use the island as an intermediate depot on the understanding that they were not to disturb the game or rob the garden. Thanks to this wise arrangement, the governor had need of only eight men to guard the fortress in which twelve rusty cannon were mouldering. He was a sort of happy bucolic, cultivating his vineyards, harvesting his figs, oil and oranges, and ripening lemons and citrons within his sunny casemates. The fortress, encircled with a deep ditch, its sole protection, lifted up its three turrets like three heads, connected the one with the other by terraces overgrown with moss.

Athos and Raoul wandered for some time round the fence which enclosed the garden without finding anyone who might conduct them to the governor. At length they decided to enter the garden uninvited. It was now the hottest part of the day, when every creature seeks shelter among the grass or under a rock. The heavens stretch their fiery veils as if to stifle every sound and to enwrap the throbbing earth. Partridges take refuge beneath the whins, flies settle under the leaves – all are wrapped in sleep, and even the very sea lies slumbering beneath the torrid sky. Athos saw no living creature with the exception of a single soldier upon the terrace between the second and third towers, who was carrying upon his head what appeared to be a basket of provisions. The man returned almost immediately without the basket, and disappeared within the shadow of the turret. Athos guessed that he had been carrying dinner to someone, and that, having accomplished this duty, he had gone to his own dinner. All at once Athos heard a voice calling, and raising his head, he perceived something white between the bars of a window, like a hand waving, and something bright like a polished weapon glittered in the rays of the sun. Then, before they could decide what it was they had seen, their eyes were caught by a luminous streak, accompanied with a curious whistling noise in the air, which withdrew their attention from the *donjon* to the ground. They heard a thud in the ditch, and Raoul ran forward and picked up a silver platter which had imbedded itself in the dry sand. The hand which had thrown it made a sign to the two gentlemen, and immediately disappeared. Raoul carried the platter to where Athos was standing and both examined its dusty surface carefully. They discovered characters scratched with the point of a knife upon the under side, and read these words:

> I am a brother of the King of France, today a prisoner, tomorrow a madman. French gentlemen and Christians, pray to God for the soul and the reason of a son of your masters.

The dish fell from Athos's hand, whilst Raoul was endeavouring to penetrate the mysterious meaning of those pathetic words. At the same moment a cry was heard from the top of the keep. Quick as thought, Raoul ducked his head and forced his father to do likewise. A musket-barrel glittered over the crest of the wall. A jet of white smoke floated like a feather from the muzzle of the gun and a bullet flattened itself against a stone within six inches of the two gentlemen. A second musket appeared, and was levelled at them.

'*Cordieu!*' exclaimed Athos, 'do they murder people here? Come down, you cowardly rascals!'

'Come down,' shouted Raoul in a fury, shaking his fist at the castle.

One of the two assailants – the one who was just about to fire – replied to these cries by an exclamation of surprise, and as his companion showed a disposition to continue the attack, and had reloaded his musket, he who had cried out jerked the weapon upwards so that the shot was fired in the air. Athos and Raoul, seeing the men had left the embrasure, and supposing they would come down to them, remained quietly waiting. Before five minutes had elapsed, the drum sounded the alarm and the eight soldiers who formed the garrison ranged themselves on the other side of the ditch with shouldered muskets. At the head of these men was the officer whom the Vicomte de Bragelonne recognised as the man who had fired the first shot.

'Make ready! Present!' roared the officer.

'We are going to be shot down!' cried Raoul. 'Out sword and let us leap the ditch and at them! We can each of us kill at least one of these rascals when they have emptied their muskets.' Suiting the action to the word, Raoul sprang forward, followed by Athos; when a well-known voice behind them cried. 'Athos! Raoul!'

'D'Artagnan!' cried both gentlemen together.

'Ground arms, damn you!' yelled d'Artagnan to the soldiers. 'Ah! I felt sure I was right!'

The men obeyed the order, and lowered their muskets.

'What on earth does this mean?' asked Athos. 'What! are we going to be shot down without any warning?'

'I was just going to fire upon you myself,' replied d'Artagnan, 'and I should not have missed you, though the governor did. 'Slife, it's a fortunate thing I'm accustomed to take long aim, instead of firing the instant the sights come in line! It seemed to me that I knew you. Ah! my dear friends, what a lucky thing!' and d'Artagnan mopped his brow, for he had been running and, besides, his emotion was very real.

'What!' exclaimed Athos, 'you tell me it was the governor of the fortress himself who fired upon us?'

'The governor himself.'

'But why? How have we transgressed?'

'*Pardieu!* you picked up what the prisoner threw to you.'

'True, but – '

'That platter – the prisoner has written something on it, has he not?' – 'Yes.' – 'Ah! I was afraid of it – that's the very devil!' And d'Artagnan, with every sign of extreme perturbation seized the platter in order to read the inscription. When he had read it, his face grew pale beneath the tan – ' 'Tis the very devil!' he repeated. 'Hush! not a word – here comes the governor.'

'But what can he do to us? Is it our fault?' said Raoul.

'Then it is true?' said Athos, in a low tone.

'Quiet! quiet! – not a word, I tell you! If anyone thinks you have read it – if they suppose you have understood – I love you dearly my friends, I would willingly die for you, but – '

'But what?' said Athos and Raoul.

'But I couldn't save you from imprisonment for life, even if I could prevent your being shot. Silence, then – silence I say!'

The governor approached, having crossed the ditch by a gangplank – 'Well,' said he to d'Artagnan, 'what is it hinders us?'

'You are Spaniards – you don't understand a word of French,' whispered the captain quickly to his friends – 'Well, I was right,' he said, addressing the governor, 'these gentlemen are Spanish officers, whose acquaintance I made last year at Ypres – they don't know a word of French.'

'Ah!' exclaimed the governor, with a shade of suspicion in his tone, and taking the platter, he was about to read the inscription, when d'Artagnan, snatching it out of his hands, effaced the words with the point of his sword.

'What are you doing?' cried the governor, 'I shan't be able to read it.'

'It is a state secret,' replied d'Artagnan, curtly. 'You know the king's orders, and you are forbidden to penetrate the secret under pain of death; but, if you like, I'll let you read the inscription, and have you shot immediately afterwards.'

While d'Artagnan was giving this warning, half in earnest and half ironically, Athos and Raoul stood by in silence, cool and unconcerned.

'But,' said the governor, 'these gentlemen must understand at least a few words of French.'

'What if they do? Even if they understand what is said to them, they can't read it. Why, they don't even read Spanish! You know, I suppose, that a Spanish hidalgo is not expected to be able to read.'

The governor was obliged for the moment to rest satisfied with this explanation; still, he was of a persevering disposition – 'Invite these gentlemen into the castle,' he said.

'By all means,' replied d'Artagnan. 'I was going to propose it.' – The fact was, however, that the captain would have preferred any other arrangement – he would have wished his friends a hundred miles away. But he was obliged to make the best of it. He addressed an invitation in Spanish to the two gentlemen, which they accepted. They all turned in the direction of the gateway, and the incident being closed, the eight soldiers resumed their pleasant pastimes, momentarily interrupted by the remarkable adventure we have related.

CHAPTER 60

## *The captive and his goalers*

ONCE WITHIN THE FORTRESS, and whilst the governor had left them for a moment to give orders for the entertainment of his guests, Athos turned to d'Artagnan, saying – 'Come then, a word of explanation now that we are by ourselves.'

'It is simply this,' replied the musketeer. 'I have conducted a prisoner to the island, whom the king has forbidden anyone to see. You came here, and he threw something to you from his window; I was dining with the governor, and I saw the thing thrown and Raoul picking it up. I make up my mind quickly, and I jumped to the conclusion that you were trying to establish communication with the prisoner, so – '

'So you ordered us to be shot.'

'Faith!' I admit it; but if I was the first to seize a musket, fortunately I was the last to level one at you.'

'If you had killed me, d'Artagnan, I should have had the happiness of dying for the Royal House of France – and to die by your hand would be an honour, for you are its most gallant and loyal defender.'

'That's good! Athos, what on earth are you telling me about the royal House?' stammered d'Artagnan. 'What! is it possible, comte, that a man of your experience and discernment can attach credit to the ravings of an idiot?'

'I believe it.'

'We are all the more inclined to believe it since you have orders to kill all those who do,' said Raoul.

'Because any slander, provided only that it is sufficiently absurd, has an almost certain chance of being spread,' replied the captain of the musketeers.

'No, d'Artagnan,' replied Athos, quietly, 'it is because the king will not have this family secret leak out, for it would cover with infamy the executioners of this son of Louis XIII.'

'Come, come, no more of this nonsense, Athos, or I shall be inclined to rate your wits with those of the prisoner. Besides, can you explain to me how a son of Louis XIII should be in the Iles Sainte-Marguerite?'

'A son whom you conducted hither masked, in a fisherman's boat,' said Athos; 'why not?'

D'Artagnan was almost nonplussed – 'Oho!' he cried, after a pause, 'where did you learn that a fisherman's boat – '

' – brought you to Sainte-Marguerite with the prisoner shut up in a carriage – a prisoner whom you called "Monseigneur"? Oh! I have been told about things,' replied the comte.

D'Artagnan bit his moustaches – 'Supposing it were true, all that you have said, what is there to prove that he is a prince – a prince of the House of France?'

'Oh! you may ask Aramis that question,' said Athos, coolly.

'Aramis!' cried the musketeer, taken aback. 'Have you seen Aramis?'

'After his discomfiture at Vaux, yes – Aramis a fugitive, ruined; and Aramis told me enough to make me believe the words scratched by the unfortunate man upon the silver dish.'

D'Artagnan was completely overcome, and drooped his head – 'Thus does heaven mock the puny efforts of men!' he said. 'A fine secret indeed which at this moment is shared by twelve or fifteen persons! – A cursed chance this, Athos, which has brought you and me together in this matter, for now – '

'Well,' said Athos, with gentle severity, 'is your secret in danger because I know it? Have I not borne secrets equally heavy? – Consult your memory, my dear friend.'

'You have never shared one so dangerous,' replied d'Artagnan gloomily. 'I have a sort of a dark presentiment that all who have known this secret will die, and die miserably.'

'God's will be done, d'Artagnan! – But here comes your friend the governor.'

D'Artagnan and his friends immediately resumed their parts. The governor, a hard and morose man, showed himself polite, not to say obsequious, towards d'Artagnan. He contented himself with watching his guests closely while attending to their material comforts. Athos and Raoul noticed that he made many attempts to confuse them by sudden questions, and sought to catch them tripping when off their guard; but neither of the two gentlemen gave him an opportunity. If the governor did not believe what d'Artagnan had told him, at any rate he was unable to confirm his suspicions. After a while, they rose from the table in order to rest a little – 'What is the name of this man?' asked Athos of d'Artagnan in Spanish. 'I don't like the look of him.'

'De Saint-Mars,'[174] replied the captain.

'He is the prince's gaoler, I suppose?'

'Eh! How do I know? I may be kept at Sainte-Marguerite for ever.'

'You? – Oh! nonsense!'

'My dear friend, I am a good deal like a man who finds a treasure in the middle of a desert. He would be overjoyed to carry it away with him, but he cannot; he would fain leave it, but he dare not. The king will not recall me, fearing that another might not guard the prisoner so well; he will be sorry to be without me, feeling that no one else will serve him personally so well as myself. However, it will be as God pleases.'

'But,' observed Raoul, 'your being left in doubt proves that your position here is only temporary, and that you will return to Paris.'

'Ask these gentlemen,' interrupted Saint-Mars,' what was their object in coming to Sainte-Marguerite.'

'They came here because they had heard the Benedictine convent at Saint-Honorat was worth seeing; and they were told there was excellent shooting to be had in Sainte-Marguerite.'

'Quite at their disposal,' replied Saint-Mars, 'and yours also, captain.' D'Artagnan expressed his thanks. 'When do they intend leaving?'

'Tomorrow,' replied d'Artagnan. With this the governor went off to make his rounds, leaving the captain with the supposed Spaniards – 'Oh!' cried the musketeer, 'the life here and the society don't agree with me in the least. This man is under my orders, and he gets in my way, devil take him! – Come, suppose we go and have a shot at the rabbits. We shall have a pleasant walk at any rate, and we shan't find it tiring, for the island is only a couple of miles long and a mile broad – a perfect park. Come, let us amuse ourselves.'

'Wherever you please, d'Artagnan, not so much for the amusement as for the sake of talking freely.'

D'Artagnan spoke a few words to a soldier, who went out and returned shortly with guns for the party, then took himself off to attend to his duties – 'And now,' said the musketeer, 'suppose you give me an answer to that killjoy Saint-Mars's question: what is the reason of your being here among the Iles Lerins?'

'We came to bid you farewell.'

'Why, what does that mean? Is Raoul going away?'

'Yes.'

'I'll wager he is going with Monsieur de Beaufort.'

'You are right: you always guess correctly, my dear friend.'

'Oh, it's a habit of mind – '

Leaving the two old friends talking together, Raoul sat down upon a mossy rock with his gun over his knees. His heart was heavy, and he fell to contemplating the sea and sky, giving free rein to his sad thoughts until at length he was separated from the others by some considerable distance. D'Artagnan noticed his absence – 'He still takes it to heart, then,' he said to Athos.

'He is wounded to the death!'

'Oh! I think you exaggerate. Raoul is made of good stuff. Men of his stamp can bear more than would kill less stouthearted fellows; they have a sort of second cuirass over their hearts – the first may be pierced, but the second resists the blow.'

'No,' replied Athos, 'Raoul will die of it.'

'Nonsense!' cried d'Artagnan, but his tone had something less that its usual assurance. For a moment he found nothing to add, but at last he said – 'Why do you let him go?'

'Because he wishes it.'

'Then why don't you go with him?'

'Because I cannot bear to see him die.' D'Artagnan looked his friend steadily in the face – 'You know very well,' continued the comte, linking his arm in that of his companion, 'You know very well that in the course of my life there are few things of which I have been afraid. Yet I tell you that now I am afraid – I am haunted by a constant gnawing dread – I fear that a day may come when I shall hold in my arms the dead body of my boy.'

'Oh! Athos – my dear friend!' murmured d'Artagnan.

'He will die – I know it – something tells me that he is going to die – I cannot see him die.'

'Oh! come, Athos! What! you meet your old friend, your own d'Artagnan, whom you say is the bravest man you ever knew – this man without equal, as you used to say at one time – you come to him with your arms folded, and tell him you are afraid of seeing your son dead – you, who have looked upon death in every form and have experienced most misfortunes which can fall to the lot of mortals! Why should you fear it, Athos? A brave man should be prepared to dare all things, and to suffer every reverse which a man in this world is called upon to suffer.'

'Listen, dear friend: after having spent my life in buffeting with this world of which you speak, I have lost all my illusions and retained but two faiths – faith in immortality, the love and fear of

God; and faith in friendship and my duties as a father. I have an inward conviction that if God should decree that a friend or a child of mine should breathe his last in my presence – Oh! no, not even to you, d'Artagnan, would I tell my thought.'

'Tell me, Athos.'

'I am strong – strong enough to bear calamity – any calamity – except only the death of one I love. That alone is irreparable. To die is gain – the loss is his who sees his loved ones die. No – think what it means! – to know that nevermore on this earth shall I see him whose presence was my joy – to know that nowhere in all the world does there exist a d'Artagnan, nowhere a Raoul – oh! – I am old, d'Artagnan, old – and I have no longer the courage. I pray to God to spare me in my weakness; but should He strike me this crushing blow, I feel that I should curse Him. A Christian gentleman ought not to be driven to curse his God, d'Artagnan; he has gone far enough in having cursed his king!'

Much perturbed by this violent tempest of grief, d'Artagnan could only murmur his sympathy.

'D'Artagnan, my dear friend, you who love Raoul – see!' continued Athos, pointing towards his son. 'You see that his melancholy has not abated. Can you conceive anything more dreadful than to have to see the incessant agony he suffers and to be unable to alleviate it?'

'Let me speak to him, Athos; who knows?'

'Try by all means; but I feel the conviction that it will be useless.'

'I shall not attempt to console him, I shall try to be of use to him, for if she were to repent of her infidelity, it would not be the first time a woman had done it. I will go and speak to him.'

Athos shook his head, and continued his walk alone.

D'Artagnan made a short cut through the brambles, and, approaching Raoul, gave him his hand, saying – 'Well, you have something to say to me, I think.'

'I have a service to ask of you,' replied Bragelonne.

'What is it?'

'You will someday return to France?'

'I hope so, at least.'

'Do you think I ought to write to Mlle de la Vallière?'

'Decidedly not.'

'But I have so much to say to her!'

'Go and say it to her, then.'

'Never!'

'Why, what virtue do you attribute to a letter that your spoken word does not possess?'

'Perhaps you are right.'

'She loves the king,' said Artagnan, bluntly; 'she is an honest girl.' Raoul gave a start, for the captain had touched his wound with no light hand – 'And you – you whom she has rejected – she loves you perhaps better than the king, though in another fashion.'

'D'Artagnan, do you think she really loves the king?'

'She idolises him – she has no room left in her heart for any other feeling. You should not leave her quite – you should remain near her – you ought not to deprive her of your friendship.'

'Ah!' exclaimed Raoul, his heart yearning passionately, in spite of himself, for this painful consolation,

'Are you willing?'

'Nay, it would be cowardly.'

'So absurd a remark would lead one to form a paltry opinion of your wits, Raoul. There is nothing cowardly in yielding to forces beyond one's control. If your heart whispers that you must go back to her or die – why! go, Raoul – listen to your heart's promptings. Was she brave or cowardly, think you, in owning her preference for the king, notwithstanding her affection for you? – She acted as the bravest of women, Raoul. Follow her example – be true to yourself. Do you know one thing of which I am sure?'

'What is that?'

'If you are near her, you will find that by regarding her with the eyes of a jealous man, you will finish by ceasing to love her.'

'You convince me, my dear d'Artagnan.'

'To return and see her?'

'No, to go away and never see her again, for I wish to love her as long as I live.'

'Now, frankly, that is the very last conclusion I should have expected you to arrive at!'

'Stay a moment, dear friend, you will see her again, you will give her this letter and you will tell her, if you think proper, as from yourself, what is passing in my heart. Read the letter: I wrote it last night. I had a feeling that I should meet you next day.'

D'Artagnan took the letter and read:

MADEMOISELLE – I do not hold you culpable because you do not love me. The only wrong you did me was in allowing me to believe you loved me. It is a mistake which will cost me my life. You I forgive freely, but I can never forgive myself. It is said that those who are fortunate in their love are careless of the pain suffered by rejected lovers. It will not be so with you, for you did not love me, except in fear and trembling. I feel assured that if I had persisted in trying to change your friendship towards me into love, you would have yielded from dread of being the cause of my death or from that of lessening the regard I had for you. It is sweet to die knowing that my death will leave you free and happy. Then you will think of me more kindly when you no longer have occasion to fear my presence or my reproaches. You will love me because, however enthralling your new love may be, God has made me inferior in no respect to him you have chosen; and my devotion, my sacrifice, my sad end assure me of a certain superiority over him in your eyes. In the simple trustfulness of my heart I allowed the treasure which I held to escape me. Many have assured me that you loved me enough to have afforded the certainty that you would come to love me deeply. This thought removes all bitterness from my heart, and leads me to look upon myself as the sole cause of my unhappiness.

You will accept this last farewell, and you will bless me for having journeyed to that bourne where all unkindness is extinguished and where love endures for ever. Farewell, Louise. Were it necessary to shed my blood to purchase your happiness, my blood should be spent to the last drop.

RAOUL, VICOMTE DE BRAGELONNE

'Yes, the letter is very well,' said the captain, 'I have only one fault to find with it.'

'And that is – ?'

'The letter tells everything except the fact that you still love her madly.' Raoul made no reply. 'Why did you not say simply, "Mademoiselle, instead of cursing you, I love you and I die." '

'You are right,' said Raoul, with a sinister kind of joy; and, tearing up the letter which the other had just handed him back, he wrote these words upon a leaf of his tablets: *In order to have the happiness of telling you once more that I love you, I am coward enough to write to you, and as a punishment for my cowardice, I give up my life.* 'You will give her these tablets, captain, will you not?' he said.

'When am I to give them to her?'

'Upon the day you are able to put a date to these words,' replied Raoul, showing him the last phrase of the writing. And with that he left d'Artagnan abruptly and hastened to join his father, who was approaching with slow steps.

While they were returning to the castle, the waves began to rise, and with that suddenness and vehemence which is characteristic of a squall in the Mediterranean, the sea, hitherto so calm, was soon raging tempestuously. Over towards the mainland they perceived an object of uncertain form, tossed hither and thither by the billows. 'What is that?' said Athos. 'Some wrecked boat, perhaps.'

'No, it is not a boat,' replied d'Artagnan.

'Pardon me, I think you are wrong,' said Raoul, 'it looks like a boat trying to make the harbour.'

'If you mean that vessel yonder in the bay which is sensible enough to run for shelter, you are right; but Athos is pointing to that piece of wreckage on the beach – '

'Ah! yes, I see.'

'That is the carriage I threw into the sea after I landed with my prisoner.'

'Well,' said Athos, 'if you'll take my advice, you will burn that carriage, lest the fishermen at Antibes, who think they had to do with the Devil, should try to prove that your prisoner was only a man after all.'

'Your advice is good, Athos, and I will see to it that the thing is destroyed this very night – or rather, I will attend to it myself. But let us hurry, for it is coming on to rain, and the lightning is terrific.'

As they passed along the ramparts towards the gallery of which d'Artagnan had the key, they saw Monsieur de Saint-Mars going in the direction of the prisoner's room. Upon a sign from d'Artagnan they concealed themselves in an angle of the staircase. 'What is it?' asked Athos.

'You will see. Look yonder – the prisoner is returning from the Chapel.' And by the red flashes of lightning which lit up the bluish haze which, driven before the wind, had obscured the sky, they saw a man dressed in black and masked by a visor of burnished steel, which formed part of a helmet of the same material entirely covering his head. He was walking with a grave step a few paces behind the governor. The lurid gleams from the sky were reflected from the polished surface – reflections which danced strangely as he walked, as if they were angry glances from the eyes of the unfortunate man, darting curses. When he had reached the middle of the gallery, the prisoner stopped for a moment to contemplate the broad horizon, to respire the heavy, tempest-laden atmosphere and to feel the warm rain. He heaved a sigh which resembled a groan – 'Come, monsieur,' said Saint-Mars roughly, for he already began to feel uneasy at seeing his prisoner look so eagerly beyond the walls. 'Come away, monsieur!'

'Call him *monseigneur*,' cried Athos to Saint-Mars from where he was standing in a corner of the stairway, in a voice so solemn and impressive that the governor gave a start. It was characteristic of Athos to insist upon respect for fallen majesty. The prisoner turned his head.

'Who spoke?' asked Saint-Mars.

'It was I,' replied d'Artagnan, advancing promptly and showing himself. 'You know quite well that it was in your orders.'

'Call me neither monsieur nor monseigneur,' said the prisoner in his turn, in a voice that made Raoul shiver; 'call me THE ACCURSED!'

He passed on. The iron door screamed on its hinges as it closed behind him.

'There goes a man who is indeed unhappy!' said the musketeer to Raoul in a tone of deep pity, as he pointed to the room which the prince occupied.

## CHAPTER 61

## *Promises*

SCARCELY HAD D'ARTAGNAN re-entered his room accompanied by his friends before one of the soldiers appeared with a message to say that the governor was seeking him. It appeared that the lugger which Raoul had noticed at sea making strenuous efforts to reach the harbour, had brought to Sainte-Marguerite an important dispatch for the captain of the musketeers. D'Artagnan tore open the letter and at once recognised the king's handwriting. The message was in these terms:

> MONSIEUR D'ARTAGNAN – No doubt you have by this time executed my orders. Return to Paris immediately, and wait upon me at the Louvre.

'Hurrah! I am recalled!' cried the musketeer, much elated. 'Thank God, I am a gaoler no longer!' And he showed the letter to Athos.

'So then you are going to leave us,' said the latter, regretfully.

'Only for the moment, my dear friend, for Raoul can very well manage to see himself off with Monsieur de Beaufort; and I am sure he would prefer to let his father return home in my company rather than allow him to travel alone those two hundred leagues – is it not so Raoul?'

'Certainly,' replied the latter, but a shade of disappointment was noticeable in his tone.

'No, d'Artagnan,' broke in Athos, 'I must stay beside Raoul until the day his ship sails. So long as he remains in France we must not be separated.'

'As you will, Athos; but at any rate we can leave Sainte-Marguerite together; let us take advantage of the opportunity of this boat's arrival.'

'Very willingly; the sooner we get away from the sad spectacle we have just seen the better.'

Accordingly the three friends, after taking leave of the governor, left the islet and saw for the last time the walls of the fortress gleaming white under the final flashes of the fast vanishing thunderstorm.

That same night d'Artagnan took leave of his friends. He had previously seen the flames from the carriage which had been burnt on the beach at Sainte-Marguerite by the orders of Saint-Mars, acting upon a hint from the captain. After embracing Athos, d'Artagnan was about to mount his horse when a thought struck him.

'Forgive me if I tell you,' said he, 'that you look very much like a couple of deserters. It seems to me that Raoul will have need of your help, Athos, to support his authority. How would it be if I were to ask leave to go with you to Africa with a hundred picked men? The king would not refuse, and we could all go together.'

'Thanks, thanks, for your offer, Monsieur d'Artagnan,' replied Raoul, pressing the musketeer's hand warmly, 'we are more than grateful to you – I speak for my father as well as for myself. I am young, and fatigue of body and mind are salutary for me, and, I think, necessary; but the comte has need of rest; I commend him to your care. In watching over him, you will hold our two existences in your hand.'

'I must be starting; my horse is getting impatient,' said d'Artagnan changing the subject – with him the clearest possible indication that he was profoundly moved.

'By the way, comte, how many days has Raoul still to remain here?'

'Three days at the utmost.'

'And how long do you allow yourself for the return journey?'

'Oh! plenty of time,' replied Athos. 'I shall be in no hurry to increase the distance which separates us; in a short time he will be far enough away from me, even though I stay here. I shall return by half stages.'

'But why, my dear friend? It is dull work travelling slowly, and living in inns is hardly suitable for a man like you.'

'I travelled here on post-horses, but I intend to buy a couple of good horses to make the journey back. So I can scarcely do more than seven or eight leagues a day if I wish them to reach home in anything like condition.'

'Where is Grimaud?'

'He arrived yesterday morning with Raoul's baggage, and I have left him to sleep off his fatigue.'

'You mean he will never return.' The words escaped before d'Artagnan could check himself. 'Well, Athos, I will say goodbye till we meet again – and the faster you travel, the sooner that will be.' He mounted his horse, Raoul holding the stirrup, and amidst the farewells of his friends, his horse sprang forward.

This scene had taken place outside the house chosen by Athos, close to the gates of Antibes, where d'Artagnan had ordered the horses to be led round after he had had supper. It was here that the high road started, stretching out into the distance like a white band through the dusk of the evening, until its windings were lost in the gloom. The horses snuffed eagerly the strong air, impregnated with the salt reek of the marshes which fringed the sea. D'Artagnan shook his horse into a trot, and Athos turned sadly and went back with Raoul into the house. All at once they heard the sound of hooves returning. At first they believed it to be that peculiar reverberation caused by the bends and inequalities of the roads which so frequently deceived the ear; but next moment they saw that d'Artagnan had turned, and was coming back at a gallop. Both gave vent to a cry of joyful surprise, and the captain, flinging himself from his saddle like a young man, sprang forward with his arms outstretched and again embraced the two men whom he loved so well. For some moments he held them clasped without uttering a word, without allowing the sighs pent up in his breast to escape him. Then, mounting once more, he dashed his spurs into his horse's flanks and departed as swiftly as he had come.

A slow, reluctant sigh escaped from the comte's lips.

D'Artagnan, while making up for lost time, was repeating to himself, 'A bad omen! I could not give them a smile. It is a bad omen!'

Early next morning, Grimaud was up and about. The duties imposed upon Raoul by the duke had been successfully accomplished. The fleet of fishing-boats and lighters which he had taken so much trouble to collect was under way for Toulon, towing a train of tiny cockleshells, in which were the wives and relations of the smugglers and fishermen who were required to serve in the duke's ships.

The little time which remained for father and son to be together seemed to fly with ever increasing swiftness – just as those who are about to enter the kingdom of eternity can almost hear the rushing of Time's wings as they linger upon the brink.

Athos and Raoul returned to Toulon. The town was noisy with the sound of warlike preparations and with the neighing of horses. Martial strains from the brazen throats of trumpets and the crisp rattle of drums filled the air. The streets were blocked with soldiery, merchants and camp-followers. The Duc de Beaufort was everywhere, bustling about like a good captain to hasten forward the embarkation of the troops. He had a word of encouragement for even the most humble of his attendants; he growled at his officers, however considerable their rank. Artillery, baggage, stores – he insisted upon seeing to everything himself; he examined the accoutrements of every soldier and assured himself of the condition of every horse. One felt that, whatever levity, selfishness or boastfulness he might have exhibited while he led a life of ease in his own mansion, when brought face to face with the responsibility he had accepted, the careless gentleman became a soldier once more – the irresponsible nobleman a worthy leader of men. Nevertheless, it must be admitted that, however commendable the briskness of his preparations for departure, one could not but notice the reckless haste and total absence of all necessary precautions. Such a state of affairs is of only too frequent occurrence, but it renders the French soldier the finest in the world, since he is called upon to display greater individual resource than the fighting man of any other nation.

Everything being accomplished to the apparent satisfaction of the admiral, he paid his compliments to Raoul and gave him his final orders; the time for sailing was fixed for the following morning at daybreak. He then invited the comte and his son to dine with him, but they excused themselves on the plea of some necessary matters of service to be attended to, and managed to withdraw. On reaching the inn where they were lodged – a hostelry fronted with trees, situated in the principal square – they took a hurried meal; afterwards they went out and wandered amidst the hills which overlook the town – those vast bare crags which command a view of an infinite expanse of sea, the horizon seeming on a level with the hills themselves, so clear is the air and so great the distance. The night was fine as it always is in that perfect climate. The moon, rising behind the hills, spread out as it were a white cloth across the blue carpet of the sea. The vessels in the roads silently moved to take their appointed stations in order to embark the troops. The sea shone with a phosphorescent gleam beneath the keels of the vessels engaged in trans-shipping baggage and stores; every time their bows dipped into the watery gulf they stirred up pale gleams of fire, and from every oar dropped liquid diamonds. The voices of sailors, made happy by the admiral's bounty, could be heard singing their endless, monotonous songs – those shanties with their nonsensical words in which mariners delight. Now and again the grinding rattle of chains mingled with the dull noise of ammunition being shot into the holds. These sights and sounds oppress the heart with fears, even while they speak of life and hope, for all this activity impresses one with a sense of impending death. Athos and his son sat amidst the mossy crags on the slope of the headland. Overhead flitted hither and thither big bats in the giddy whirl of their nightly chase. Raoul's feet hung over the edge of the cliff into empty space, which induces vertigo and invites to self-destruction. When at length the moon, risen to its full height, was caressing with her gentle light the neighbouring heights; when the sea was illuminated across its whole breadth, and tiny red lights pierced holes in the black masses of the vessels' hulls, Athos, summoning all his resolution and collecting his thoughts, said to his son, 'All this that we see is God's handiwork, Raoul; He has fashioned us also, poor atoms in His vast universe. Like those lights yonder our vital spark shines for its little day, we sigh and murmur like the waves, we suffer like those ships, worn with their ceaseless toil in ploughing the waters in obedience to the winds which impel them, as the breath of God directs us, towards the appointed haven. All seek to preserve life, Raoul, and all living things have a beauty of their own.'

'Indeed, sir, it is a beautiful sight we have before us,' replied the young man.

'How good d'Artagnan is!' resumed Athos abruptly, 'and what rare good fortune it is to have had such a friend to lean upon for a whole lifetime! It is such a friend that you have needed, Raoul.'

'A friend?' cried the young man, 'have I suffered from the want of a friend?'

'Monsieur de Guiche is a charming companion,' rejoined the comte, coldly; 'but it seems to me that the men of the present day are more occupied with their own affairs and pleasures than formerly. You chose to live secluded; such a life has its attractions, but it has undermined your strength of character. We four, accustomed to harder living and careless of the refinements which you set such store by, were far better armed to resist misfortune.'

'I did not interrupt you, sir, to tell you I had a friend, and this friend was Monsieur de Guiche. However, he is good and generous, and he loves me. But I had it in mind to say that I have lived under the guardianship of another friendship, quite as devoted and quite as precious to me as that of which you speak – the friend to whom I allude is yourself, sir.'

'I have been no friend to you, Raoul.'

'How do you mean, sir?'

'Because I have led you to believe that there is but one point of view from which life can be regarded; because my reserve and severity have repressed in you the natural gaiety of youth, though God knows it was not my intention; because now I am forced to regret that I did not bring you up in a freer, more expansive atmosphere, so as to render you more fitted to take an active part in the world.'

'I know your reason for telling me this, sir. No, you are wrong; it is not you who have made me the man I am – it is this unhappy love affair which grew upon me from the first moment when it began as a mere boyish inclination; it is the natural constancy which is part of my character, though with other people only a habit. I believed that I should always be as I was – I believed that God had set me upon a straight path, bordered with flowers and fruit. I felt that I could count upon your strength and vigilance; and I believed myself also to be strong and vigilant. I had no warning; the ground was cut from beneath me suddenly, and I fell, and my fall has completely broken my courage. Were I to say that I am a broken man, I should be speaking the truth. Oh! no, sir; your influence over me has always been for my happiness and my good, and in you is my only hope for the future. No, I have nothing to regret, or to reproach you with in the life you planned for me; I bless you and I love you dearly.'

'My dear boy, your words do me good – they give me the assurance that you will think of me a little and act for my sake in the days which are coming.'

'It is for you alone that I shall act, sir.'

'Henceforth, Raoul, I will act differently with regard to you; I will be your friend instead of being only your father. When you come back, we will mix more with the world and its enjoyments instead of living the life of recluses; you will soon return, will you not?'

'Without doubt, sir, for an expedition of this kind cannot be of long duration.'

'Soon Raoul, very soon, we will change our mode of life; instead of living in a small way upon my revenues, I will realise and make over to you the capital of part of my estates. It will be sufficient to support your position in the world until I die, and I hope, before then, you will give me the consolation of knowing that our race will not become extinct.'

'I will do whatever you command me, sir,' replied Raoul, deeply moved.

'Because you are an aide-de-camp, Raoul, it does not follow that you ought to rush into hazardous enterprises. You have already proved your valour, and you are known to be cool under fire. Remember that Arab warfare is a war of ambuscades, surprises and assassinations.'

'So it is said, sir.'

'It is always inglorious to fall into a trap. To lose one's life in that manner always implies a certain amount of foolhardiness or lack of foresight. Often, indeed, a man who falls into an ambuscade is not even regretted, and those who die unregretted, Raoul, die uselessly. Moreover, the enemy rejoices, and it is not seemly that we Frenchmen and Christians should give those besotted infidels cause to laugh at our mistakes. You will not misunderstand me, Raoul? Heaven forbid that I should encourage you to be backward in an engagement!'

'I am naturally cautious, and I am always extremely lucky,' said Raoul, with a smile that sent a chill to the poor father's heart. 'You know,' the young man hastened to add, 'that I have taken part in twenty engagements, and have never received more than a scratch.'

'Then again, there is the climate to be feared,' said Athos; 'to die of fever is a poor sort of ending. St Louis used to pray to be killed by an arrow or the plague, rather than by fever.'

'Oh! with moderate living, sir, and a reasonable amount of exercise – '

'I have already got Monsieur de Beaufort to promise,' interrupted Athos, 'that he will send dispatches to France every fortnight. It will fall within your duties as his aide-de-camp to make arrangements for sending them off; I am sure you will not forget me.'

'No, sir,' said Raoul, in a strangled voice.

'Above all, Raoul, as we are both good Christians, we ought to be able to count upon the special protection of God and of our guardian angels. Promise me that if at any time a misfortune should happen to you, you will think of me first of all.'

'Yes, indeed – indeed I will!'

'And you will call me to you?'

'At once!'

'Do you ever see me in your dreams, Raoul?'

'Every night, sir. When I was quite a child, you used to visit me in my dreams, and I saw your kind and gentle face as you came and laid your hand on my brow – that is why I slept so peacefully – *then!*'

'Since we two love one another so dearly,' said the comte, 'a portion of our two souls will always be together though we are separated the one from the other. When you are sad, Raoul, I feel that my heart also will be plunged in sadness, and whenever you think of me with kindness, do not forget that a ray of your joy will reach me, though we may be severed by the breadth of the earth.'

'I cannot promise you that my heart will be joyous,' replied the young man; 'but be sure that never an hour will pass but I shall think of you – not a single hour, I swear it – unless, perchance, I have ceased to live.'

Athos could no longer restrain his emotion; he clasped his son tenderly in his arms and held him to his heart in a close embrace.

The moon began to pale in the twilight which precedes the dawn; soon a golden streak rose above the horizon announcing that day was near. Athos threw his own cloak over Raoul's shoulders, and together they returned towards the town – already in motion, like a vast ant-hill, with porters hurrying to and fro with loads upon their backs.

At the landward extremity of the headland which Athos and Raoul were just quitting, they saw a dark shade moving backwards and forwards uneasily, as though ashamed of being seen. It was Grimaud who, in his anxiety, had dogged his masters' footsteps and now awaited their approach.

'Ah! Grimaud, my good fellow,' cried Raoul, 'what is it? you have come to tell us it is time to be gone, have you not?'

'Alone?' queried Grimaud, addressing Athos in a tone of reproach which showed how greatly the old man had been unhinged by recent events.

'Ah! Grimaud, I understand you – you are right!' said the comte. 'No, Raoul shall not go alone – no, he shall not lack a friendly face to remind him, in a foreign land, of all he loved at home.'

'Can *I* go?' asked Grimaud.

'You will come with me? Yes, yes! and I thank you heartily,' cried Raoul, profoundly touched.

'Aye! Grimaud, my good Grimaud, it is an old man you are!' said Athos, with a sigh.

'All the better,' replied the old man, with a depth of feeling that was intuitive.

'But see, the ships are ready to sail,' said Raoul, 'and you have made no preparations.'

'Yes, I have,' replied Grimaud, showing the keys of his boxes on the same bunch as the keys of his young master's trunks.

But another objection occurred to Raoul. 'You cannot go with me and leave the comte alone – your master from whom you have never been separated.'

Grimaud turned his dim eyes towards Athos, as though to read in his face whether he could bear the absence of his old and faithful servant, knowing well that the comte would make the sacrifice for his son's sake. Athos said not a word. 'Monsieur le comte would sooner I went with you,' said Grimaud. Athos inclined his head in token of assent.

At that moment a rolling of drums was heard from the massed bands, and the clear, insistent notes of the bugles filled the air with their inspiring calls. The regiments began to march out of the town towards the ships. One after another, five regiments went past, each formed up in forty companies. The Royals, easily to be recognised by their white uniforms with blue facings, led the van. Their regimental colours, violet and orange quarterly, charged with golden fleurs-de-lis, were dominated by the king's standard, white, charged with a saltire fleur-de-lisé. Flanking the Royals marched the musketeers, forked gun-rest in hand and with shouldered muskets; in the centre were the pikemen with their lances, fourteen feet long, marching briskly towards the boats which were to transport them in detachments to the ships. Then followed the regiments of Picardy, Navarre and Normandy, and a large body of marines. It was evident that Monsieur de Beaufort had known how to select his troops. He himself was to be seen, surrounded by his staff, bringing up the rear; and it was a full hour before the rearguard could get down to the quay.

Raoul, accompanied by Athos, directed his steps leisurely towards the shore in order to be beside the prince when he stepped aboard. Grimaud, burning with the ardour of a young man, superintended the dispatch of Raoul's baggage to the admiral's ship. Athos linked his arm in his son's – the son whom he was about to lose, and absorbed in the most gloomy meditations, became deaf to the noise and clamour around him. Presently an officer appeared, charged with a message from the Duc de Beaufort, who had manifested a desire to see Raoul beside him.

'Be so good as to say to the prince, monsieur, that I shall be glad if he will permit me to remain with monsieur le comte for one hour longer.'

'No, no,' broke in Athos; 'an aide-de-camp ought not to desert his general thus. Tell the prince, monsieur, that the vicomte will be with him in a moment.'

The officer went off at a gallop.

'Whether we say goodbye here or over yonder,' added the comte, 'we must part in either case.' He carefully brushed the dust off his son's coat with his hand as they walked along, and passed his fingers over Raoul's long hair.

'By the way,' he said, 'you will want money, Raoul; Monsieur de Beaufort lives in extravagant style, and besides, you will wish, no doubt, to buy horses and arms over there, for both are excellent in that country. Then, as you are not in the service either of the king or the duke, but are acting entirely independently, you cannot count upon receiving pay or bounties from Monsieur de Beaufort. I should not like you to want for anything at Jijeli. Here are two hundred pistoles; spend them, Raoul, if you wish to please me.'

Raoul pressed his father's hand. At that moment they caught sight of the duke, mounted upon a magnificent white horse, which curvetted proudly in response to the applause from the fair on-lookers. The prince called Raoul to him, and gave the comte his hand. They had a long conversation, and Beaufort spoke in so kindly and considerate a way that the poor father was in some degree consoled. Still, it seemed to both father and son that their walk was becoming agony. It was a terrible moment for them when the soldiers and sailors, as they were about to leave the shore, exchanged their last kisses with their families and friends – that moment when, in spite of the clearness of the sky, the warmth of the sun, the perfumed air and the vigorous life circulating in their veins, they feel the full bitterness of parting in the despair of the moment and almost feel disposed to doubt the goodness of God. It was customary for the admiral and his suite to be the last to embark; the guns were ready, and waiting to announce with their formidable voice that the leader of the expedition had set foot aboard his ship. Athos, forgetting everything, even his own dignity as a man and a soldier, opened his arms and strained his son convulsively to his breast.

'Come on board with us,' said the duke, touched by his friend's grief, 'you will gain another half-hour.'

'Nay,' replied Athos, 'nay, our farewells are said. I could not go through the pain of parting a second time.'

'Then away with you on board, vicomte!' added the prince, wishing to cut short the sufferings of these two men, whose hearts were bursting. And tenderly and paternally, with the strength of another Porthos, he picked up Raoul in his arms and put him in the boat. Then, giving a sign to the boatmen, the oars dipped and the boat glided from the quay. As for himself, he sprang on to the decked end of the boat, and, heedless of ceremony, pushed her off with a vigorous foot.

'Farewell!' cried Raoul.

Athos replied only with a sign. Grimaud, who had seen to the baggage, was now about to embark in his turn; he kissed his master's hand with loving respect and then sprang down the steps of the pier into a two-oared dingy which had just been made fast to the stern of a barge served by twelve long sweeps. Athos sat down upon the mole, feeling stunned and helpless, his eye fixed upon the boat which was separating him from his son. Gradually the boats grew less and less, until the men on board them were scarcely to be distinguished one from another. Athos saw his son mount the ladder of the admiral's ship, he saw him on the quarterdeck, leaning his arms upon the rail in such a position that his father might still follow him with his eyes. In vain did the guns thunder, in vain did the crews burst into tumultuous cheering, responded to from the shore by frenzied acclamations – the noise could not distract the father's attention from the figure on the quarterdeck. Raoul remained visible to the last moment, but gradually the ships faded from Athos's sight, though he remained gazing long after their hulls had disappeared below the horizon. Towards noon, when the tops of their masts were alone visible above the shining line where sea met sky, Athos saw a faint thin wisp of shadow rise like a phantom and immediately vanish from sight; it was the smoke of a parting gun fired by Monsieur de Beaufort as a last goodbye to the coast of France.

The last ship having sunk beneath the horizon, Athos rose painfully and returned to his inn with a slow step.

CHAPTER 62

*Women's ways*

D'ARTAGNAN had not succeeded so well as he could have wished in hiding his feelings from his friends. Overcome by his presentiments of impending evil, the stoical and impassive soldier had given way to human weakness. He felt the need of violent exertion to restore tone to his nerves; and therefore, as soon as he had recovered an appearance of outward calm, he turned to his servant – a man of few words, but always sharply alert to obey promptly any order that his master gave him – and said, 'Rabaud,[175] we must travel thirty leagues a day, do you understand?'

'Very good, captain,' replied Rabaud.

And from that moment d'Artagnan, sitting his horse easily like a veritable centaur, occupied his mind no further about anything – that is to say, not consciously, for the fact was, he thought about everything. He asked himself why the king had recalled him; why the Iron Mask had thrown the silver dish at the feet of Raoul. With regard to the first question, he arrived at a negative result: he knew quite well that if the king sent for him, it was because he needed him; he knew, moreover, that Louis XIV must be burning with impatience to have a private interview with a man whom the knowledge of such an important secret put on a level with the most powerful statesmen in the kingdom. But to say exactly what was in the king's mind d'Artagnan found was beyond his powers. As for the motive of the unfortunate prince in disclosing his rank, the musketeer found no difficulty in discovering it. Imprisoned for ever within a mask of iron; exiled to a region where men seemed to be mere slaves of the elements; deprived even of the society of d'Artagnan, who had acted towards him with the most chivalrous courtesy and attention, Philippe had had nothing in this world but the miserable expectation of being left in solitude to brood over his unhappy lot; so that, goaded by desperation, he had succumbed to the temptation of making his case known, no doubt hoping by this means to find an avenger. The manner in which the musketeer had so narrowly escaped shooting his friends recurred incessantly to his mind; then he pondered the strange chance which had drawn Athos into sharing this state secret. Then again his mind would revert to Raoul's leave-taking and the melancholy forebodings which had assailed him, and he found that he could not shake off these gloomy thoughts by dint of hard riding as formerly he had been able to do. These considerations gave way to the recollection of his other old friends, Porthos and Aramis, outlawed and proscribed. In imagination he saw them in flight, hunted, both of them utterly ruined – these two men who had been the architects of their fortunes, which had now fallen about their ears like a house of cards. Knowing that the king was accustomed to summon his principal executive agent when he wished to wreak vengeance on his enemies, d'Artagnan trembled lest he should be required to execute some commission which would need a harder heart than he possessed. Now and again as his winded horse toiled slowly up some hill with heaving flanks and expanded nostrils, the captain, his mind more at liberty, thought of Aramis, that powerful and subtle intellect, whose genius for intrigue[176] had been rivalled by two men only, whom the Fronde and the Civil War had produced. Soldier, priest and diplomatist, a courtier and a gallant, yet at the same time avaricious and crafty, Aramis had never acquired the good things of life except as stepping-stones to more influential, if less straightforward positions. Large-minded, if not noble-hearted, he never did a bad action except to increase his reputation. At the height of his career, at the moment of grasping his object, he had made one false step and fallen into utter ruin. But Porthos – good and simple-minded Porthos! To see Porthos without means of subsistence – to see Mousqueton shorn of his gold lace and perhaps thrown into prison – to know Bracieux and Pierrefonds rased to the ground, their woods levelled – all these anticipations were so many sharp stabs for d'Artagnan, under which he winced like a horse stung by a gadfly. But never is a man of spirit a prey to *ennui*, while he is fatiguing his body by exercise; never is a man in sound health weary of life, if only his mind is occupied. Riding hard, and thinking deeply, d'Artagnan reached Paris as fresh as a daisy, and his muscles as supple as those of an athlete ready for the arena. The king had not expected him so soon and had just gone to hunt in the direction of Meudon. Instead of riding after the king as he would have done at one time, d'Artagnan unbooted, took a bath, and then waited quietly until his majesty should return, tired and dusty, from the chase. He occupied the five hours' interval in 'taking opinions', as the lawyers say, in order to arm himself against mischance. He learned that the king's manner during the last fortnight, had been gloomy; that the queenmother had been ill; that Monsieur, the king's brother, had manifested a tendency towards religion; that Madame had the vapours, and that Monsieur de Guiche had retired to one of his estates. Furthermore, he learned that Colbert was radiantly cheerful and that Monsieur Fouquet consulted a fresh physician every day, none of whom could effect a cure, for his principal complaint was not of a nature to be cured by physicians, unless, indeed, by political practitioners. The king, d'Artagnan was informed, showed extreme kindness towards Monsieur Fouquet, whom he scarcely allowed out of his sight; but the minister, pierced to the heart like some stately tree through which a worm has burrowed, had languished in spite of the royal smile which is the sun of such trees as grow at court. D'Artagnan learned that La Vallière had become indispensable to the king who, when engaged in hunting, would write to her, if she had not accompanied him, not merely once, but several times – no longer in verse, it is true, but in prose, which is worse – whole pages of it. Accordingly 'the most exalted of monarchs' – as he was styled in the fulsome language of the poets of the period – was to be seen dismounting 'with unparalleled ardour', in order to scribble flamboyant phrases, which Saint-Aignan, as perpetual aide-de-camp, conveyed to La Vallière at the imminent risk of killing his horses. In the meantime, the game enjoyed a holiday, and it was freely said that the art of venery ran great risk of becoming a dead art at the Court of France.

D'Artagnan thought of poor Raoul's words, and of the despairing letter addressed to a woman who spent her life in gaiety and bright hopefulness; and as the captain was something of a philosopher, he resolved to profit by the king's absence to obtain a moment's conversation with Mademoiselle de la Vallière. This was an easy matter, for while the king was hunting, Louise was walking with some other ladies in one of the galleries of the Palais-Royal, where as it happened the captain of the musketeers had to inspect some of the guards. D'Artagnan did not doubt that if he could lead the conversation towards Bragelonne, Louise would give him occasion to write a consoling letter to the poor exile! for in the forlorn state in which he had left Raoul, hope, or at least, some sort of consolation, meant life itself for two men whose welfare our captain had very near at heart. Accordingly he turned in the direction where he knew La Vallière was to be discovered. He found her the centre of a bevy of young ladies. In her apparent solitude, the king's favourite received the homage of a queen, or even more – the homage of which Madame had been so proud when, distinguished by the king's favour, she had attracted the attention of all the courtiers. D'Artagnan was no carpet-knight, still he was always certain of a distinguished reception from both ladies and gentlemen; he had all the true politeness of a gallant gentleman, and his formidable reputation had secured him as much friendship from the men as admiration from the women. Therefore, as he made his appearance in the gallery, the ladies of honour began to speak to him at once, and naturally began by questioning him. Where had he been? What had he been doing? Why had he not been seen lately caracoling on his beautiful horse to the admiration of the loungers on the king's balcony?

D'Artagnan replied that he had come from the land of oranges. This reply made the ladies laugh. At that time everybody travelled, although a journey of a hundred leagues then was a problem frequently solved by death.

'From the land of oranges?' cried Mademoiselle de Tonnay-

Charente. 'Do you mean Spain?'

'Aha!' said the musketeer, archly.

'Malta?' hazarded Montalais.

'I' faith! you are getting near it, ladies!'

'Then it is an island?' asked La Vallière.

'Mademoiselle,' said d'Artagnan, 'I won't mystify you any longer: I have some from where Monsieur de Beaufort has just embarked his expedition to Africa.'

'Did you see the army?' asked several of the more warlike spirits.

'As well as I see you,' replied d'Artagnan.

'And the fleet?'

'I saw everything there was to be seen.'

'Do we know anyone connected with the expedition?' asked Mlle de Tonnay-Charente, carelessly, but in a manner which called attention to her question, which she had put with a calculated aim.

'Why, yes; there is Monsieur de la Guillotière – there is Monsieur de Mouchy – there is Monsieur de Bragelonne.'

La Vallière turned pale.

'Monsieur de Bragelonne?' cried the treacherous Athenaïs. 'What! has he gone to the wars, too?' Montalais trod on her foot, but she did not choose to take the hint. 'Do you know what I think,' she continued, addressing d'Artagnan.

'No, mademoiselle, but I should like to hear.'

'Well, it's my belief that the men who are taking part in this expedition have all been jilted, and they are going over there to find black women who will treat them less cruelly than they have been treated by the white.'

Some of the ladies began to laugh; La Vallière lost her composure; Montalais's coughs would have called a dead man to attention.

'Mademoiselle,' broke in d'Artagnan, 'you are making a mistake if you suppose the ladies of Jijeli are black – they are not. I can scarcely say they are white, certainly – in fact they are yellow.'

'Yellow!' cried the ladies, disdainfully, in chorus.

'And a very excellent colour too! Combined with black eyes and ruby lips, I don't know a better.'

'So much the better for Monsieur de Bragelonne!' cried Mlle de Tonnay-Charente, returning to the attack. 'The poor fellow will be the better able to find consolation.'

A dead silence fell upon the group. D'Artagnan had leisure to reflect that women, gentle as doves though they may seem, are more cruel than tigers in their treatment of one another. Athenaïs was not satisfied with having made La Vallière turn pale; she wished to make her blush. Dropping disguise, Athenaïs resumed – 'Do you know, Louise, this is a sin which ought to weigh upon your conscience.'

'What sin are you speaking of,' faltered the poor girl, vainly looking round for support.

'Why,' said Athenaïs, 'this poor young man who was betrothed to you. He loved you, and you refused to marry him.'

'Any honest woman has the right to do as much,' said Montalais. The words were irreproachable in themselves, but the tone in which they were uttered was ambiguous. 'When one feels unable to make a man happy, it is best to refuse to marry him.'

Louise hardly knew whether to be thankful or otherwise to the girl who had defended her thus.

'Refuse to marry him? That is all very well,' said Athenaïs, 'but that is not the sin with which Louise has to reproach herself. The real wickedness lies in having sent poor Bragelonne off to the wars, where he runs a great chance of losing his life.'

Louise made a nervous gesture with her hand.

'And if he dies,' continued the girl, remorselessly, 'you will be the cause of his death. That is where the fault comes in.'

Louise, ready to faint, took the arm of the captain of the musketeers, whose face betrayed signs of unwonted feeling.

'You have something to say to me, Monsieur d'Artagnan,' said she, in a voice shaking with grief and resentment. 'What is it you have to say?'

D'Artagnan, with Louise on his arm, walked some few paces along the gallery, and when he was out of earshot of the rest he said, 'What I have to tell you, mademoiselle, is that which Mademoiselle de Tonnay-Charente has just been expressing, brutally, it is true, but completely.'

She uttered a faint cry, and, cut to the heart by this fresh wound, she released her hold of d'Artagnan's arm and staggered feebly towards the door; like a bird which, wounded to the death, seeks the shelter of a thicket under which to die. She disappeared by one door just as the king entered by another. Louis's first glance was directed towards the chair vacated by his mistress; not seeing La Vallière, he frowned. At that moment he caught sight of d'Artagnan bowing to him.

'Ah! Monsieur,' he said, 'you have indeed lost no time. I am pleased with you.'

This was the king's highest expression of satisfaction, and many a man would willingly have died to earn such praise from the royal lips. The maids of honour and the courtiers, who had made a respectful group around the king when he entered, drew aside as they perceived that he had something to say in private to his captain of musketeers. After again looking all round in search of La Vallière, whose absence he could not account for, Louis led the way out of the room. When quite beyond the hearing of inquisitive ears, he said, 'Well, Monsieur d'Artagnan, the prisoner – ?'

'Is in prison, sire.'

'Did he say anything on the road?'

'Nothing, sire.'

'What did he do?'

'On one occasion, when the fishermen, on board whose boat we were crossing to Sainte-Marguerite, turned mutinous and tried to kill me, the – the prisoner helped to defend me instead of trying to escape.'

The king changed colour. 'That will do,' he said.

D'Artagnan bowed. Louis began to pace backwards and forwards in the cabinet.

'You were at Antibes, were you not?' he said, all at once, 'when Monsieur de Beaufort arrived there?'

'No, sire, I was leaving when the duke arrived.

'Ah!' Again there was a pause. 'What did you see there?' asked the king, at length.

'A number of people,' replied d'Artagnan, coolly.

The king perceived that d'Artagnan was unwilling to speak.

'I sent for you, captain, because I want you to go and make arrangements for my stay at Nantes.'

'At Nantes?' cried d'Artagnan.

'At Nantes, in Brittany.'

'Yes, sire, in Brittany. Your majesty intends to make this long journey to Nantes?'

'The States-General[177] are about to assemble there,' replied the king. 'I have two demands to bring before them, and I must be there.'

'When shall I start?' asked the captain.

'Tonight – tomorrow – tomorrow evening, for you will need to rest a little.'

'I have rested, sire.'

'That is well. Then we will say sometime between now and tomorrow evening, at your own convenience.'

D'Artagnan bowed as though about to take his leave, but seeing the king hesitating, and apparently somewhat confused, he drew a step nearer to him, saying, 'Does the king intend the court to accompany him?'

'Certainly.'

'Then, no doubt the king will require his musketeers.' The captain's scrutinising glance made Louis lower his eyes.

'Take a single brigade,' replied the king.

'Very well. Has your majesty any further orders to give me?'

'No. Ah! yes, by the way – '

'Yes, sire?'

'At the Château of Nantes, which, I hear, is very ill-arranged, you will adopt the practice of posting a guard of musketeers at the doors of all the more important officials who accompany me.'

'The principal ones?'

'Yes.'

'As for example, at Monsieur de Lyonne's door?'

'Yes,'

'Monsieur Letellier's?'

'Yes.'

'Monsieur de Brienne's?'[178]

'Yes.'

'And Monsieur Fouquet's?'

'Certainly.'

'Very well, sire, I shall leave here tomorrow.'

'Just one word more, Monsieur d'Artagnan. You will come across the Duc de Gesvres[179] in Nantes, the captain of the Guards. Take the precaution of installing your musketeers before his Guards arrive. Those who get there first will have the precedence.'

'Yes, sire.'

'And if Monsieur de Gesvres should question you – '

'Pooh! Who is Monsieur de Gesvres that he should question me!' and, turning cavalierly upon his heel, the musketeer took his departure.

As he was descending the staircase, he said to himself, 'Nantes he says he is going to. Why hadn't he the spirit to say outright that he was going to Belle-Isle?'

As he reached the main gateway, one of Monsieur de Brienne's clerks caught him up. 'Monsieur d'Artagnan,' he cried, 'excuse me – '

'Well, what is it, Monsieur Ariste?'

'The king sent me to give you this draft.'

'Upon your treasury?' asked the musketeer.

'No, monsieur, upon that of Monsieur Fouquet.'

Somewhat taken by surprise, d'Artagnan examined the document, which bore the king's handwriting and was for two hundred pistoles. Having thanked the clerk politely, the captain resumed his way, thinking to himself – 'So they mean me to make this journey at

Monsieur Fouquet's expense! *Mordieu!* it is a touch of pure Louis XI. Why not have made it payable upon Colbert, who would have been delighted to have paid it!' And d'Artagnan, in accordance with his rule of never allowing a draft payable at sight to grow stale, made it his first business to call upon Monsieur Fouquet in order to draw his two hundred pistoles.

CHAPTER 63

## *What befell during supper at Monsieur Fouquet's*

UNQUESTIONABLY the minister had received notice of the contemplated transference of the court to Nantes, for he was giving a farewell dinner to his friends. The whole house was in a bustle with servants hurrying to and fro carrying dishes and with clerks making up their accounts; it was plain that all this activity denoted that a drastic change was about to take place, both in the counting house and in the kitchens.

Order in hand, d'Artagnan presented himself to the cashier, who told him that it was too late to draw the money that day as the accounts had been balanced. The captain made use of the magic formula – 'the king's service'. Somewhat disquieted by the musketeer's serious manner, the man of ink and quills admitted the validity of the argument, but added that the business regulations of the house ought also to be respected; and therefore he must ask the bearer to be so obliging as to call again next day. D'Artagnan asked to see Monsieur Fouquet. The clerk countered the attack by saying that the minister never interfered with such petty details, and emphasised his remark by shutting the door abruptly in d'Artagnan's face. The latter had expected this manoeuvre, and put his foot between the door and the jamb so that the lock did not catch, and the startled clerk found himself once more face to face with a man determined to draw the money, even if it cost him as much trouble as drawing a badger. This induced a sudden change in the cashier's tone, who said to d'Artagnan with scared politeness – 'If the gentleman wishes to speak with his excellency the minister, perhaps he would not mind walking as far as the antechambers; these are the offices, and monseigneur never comes here.'

'Oh! very well! I have no objection!' replied d'Artagnan.

'At the opposite side of the courtyard,' said the clerk, delighted to be rid of an implacable dun.

D'Artagnan crossed the courtyard and fell amongst a tribe of lacqueys – 'Monseigneur does not see visitors at this time,' was the answer he received from a fat and insolent rascal who was carrying a silver-gilt dish with three pheasants and a dozen quail. 'Tell him,' said the captain, stopping the fellow by grasping the dish, 'that I am Monsieur d'Artagnan, captain-lieutenant of his majesty's musketeers.'

The lacquey gave a grunt of startled surprise and vanished. D'Artagnan walked slowly in the same direction and arrived in the antechamber just in time to meet Monsieur Pélisson, who, a trifle pale, had hurried from the dining-room to learn what was the matter.

D'Artagnan smiled – 'Nothing unpleasant, Monsieur Pélisson – merely a small order I want cashing.'

'Ah!' exclaimed Fouquet's friend, with a sigh of relief. And, taking the captain by the hand, he drew him into the saloon, where the minister, surrounded by a number of his intimate friends, was seated in a cushioned armchair. There were assembled all the Epicureans who, a short time before, had done the honours of his mansion at Vaux and had helped to make Monsieur Fouquet's good taste and lavish generosity famous. Though careless and easy-going, they were for the most part sincerely attached to their patron, and in spite of the warnings they had received, had not fled at the approach of the storm which threatened his ruin; notwithstanding the ominous shaking of the earth they remained beside him, smiling and attentive, and as entirely devoted in his misfortune as they had been in the height of his prosperity. At the minister's right hand sat Madame de Bellière, and on his left Madame Fouquet. It was as though the man's two guardian angels, despising all conventional rules of propriety, had united to lend him their support in the moment of his urgent need. Madame de Bellière was pale and trembling, and showed herself full of respect towards the minister's wife, who, with one hand laid upon her husband's, was looking anxiously towards the door by which Pélisson was about to lead d'Artagnan into the saloon. The captain entered with a courteous salute, and was struck with admiration when his infallible glance had taken in the signification of the expression on every face. Rising from his chair, Fouquet said to the captain – 'Forgive me, Monsieur d'Artagnan, for not having come to receive you when you have come in the king's name.' And he gave a certain gloomy emphasis to the last words which caused a shiver of apprehension to run through the circle of friends gathered round him.

'Monseigneur,' said d'Artagnan, 'I have come to your house in the king's name, but merely to request payment of a draft for two hundred pistoles.'

An expression of relief was visible on every face, Fouquet's excepted, for his features still remained overcast – 'Ah! then you are also going to Nantes, monsieur?' he said.

'I scarcely know yet where I am going, monseigneur.'

'At any rate,' said Madame Fouquet, who had now recovered her composure, 'you are not so pressed for time, captain, that you cannot do us the honour of remaining with us this evening.'

'Madame, it is I who would esteem it a great honour, but I have so little time to spare, that, as you see, I have even allowed myself to interrupt you in order to get my note cashed.'

'You shall have the gold at once,' said Fouquet, making a sign to his steward, who immediately went out, taking the note which d'Artagnan handed to him.

'Oh!' cried the captain, 'I had no fears about that; the position of this house is sound.'

Fouquet smiled sadly.

'Are you in pain?' asked Madame de Bellière.

'Another attack?' asked Madame Fouquet.

'Thank you – it is nothing!' replied the minister.

'Another attack?' repeated d'Artagnan, in his turn. 'Are you ill, then, monseigneur?'

'I have a tertian fever[180] which came on after the fête at Vaux.'

'Ah! the night air in the grotto?'

'No, no; it is due to the excitement, that is all.'

'The excessive hospitality you displayed in entertaining the king,' said La Fontaine calmly, quite unconscious that he was uttering a blasphemy.

'One cannot display too great hospitality towards the king,' said Fouquet gently to the poet.'

'Monsieur La Fontaine meant to say "too great anxiety",' interrupted d'Artagnan with ready tact. 'The simple fact is, monseigneur, that the hospitality of Vaux beats all previous records.'

Madame Fouquet's face clearly expressed her thought that if Fouquet had behaved handsomely toward the king, the latter had by no means responded in the same fashion. D'Artagnan, however, was aware of the terrible secret which was the immediate cause of the king's conduct. He and Fouquet were the only two persons present who knew it, and he no more had the courage to condole with Fouquet than Fouquet had the right to accuse the king.

On receiving his two hundred pistoles, the captain was about to take leave, when Fouquet rose and taking a glass himself, filled another for d'Artagnan – 'Sir,' said he, 'to the health of the king, whatever happens!'

'And to your health, monseigneur, *whatever happens!*' said d'Artagnan, as he drained the glass. And having uttered these words of sinister augury, he bowed to the company, who rose to return the salute; then a moment afterwards they heard the clanking of his spurs as he descended the dark staircase.

'I thought for a moment it was myself he wanted instead of my money,' said Fouquet, trying to laugh.

'You!' cried his friends in chorus – 'Good heavens! why?'

'Oh!' cried the minister, 'do not deceive yourselves, my dear brothers in Epicurus – God forbid that I, the most miserable of sinners, should dream of comparing myself with the Saviour of mankind, but, as you know, He once sat down with his disciples to a meal which has been called the Last Supper, and which was a farewell dinner like that we are having at this moment.'

A cry of pained surprise and incredulity arose from all parts of the table – 'Shut the doors,' said Fouquet, and the servants left the room – 'My friends,' he continued, dropping his voice, 'what was my former position, and what is my position today? Consult your memories and you will be able to answer. A man such as I am inevitably sinks, merely if he does not continue to rise – what shall we say then when he is plainly seen to be sinking? I have neither money nor credit left – I have now only powerful enemies and powerless friends.'

'Quick!' cried Pélisson, rising, 'since you give us so frank an explanation, we must be equally frank. To begin with, how much money have we left?'

'Seven hundred thousand livres,' said the steward.

'Enough to keep us in bread,' murmured Madame Fouquet.

'Order relays of horses,' said Pélisson, 'and away!'

'Where am I to go?'

'To Switzerland – Savoy – anywhere, only make haste.'

'If monseigneur runs away,' said Madame de Bellière, 'it will be said that he is guilty and afraid to face the consequences.'

'More than that; it will be said that I have bolted with twenty million.'

'We will have accounts drawn up in your justification,' said La

Fontaine; 'but you must go at once!'

'I shall stay,' said Fouquet.

'You have Belle-Isle!' cried the Abbé Fouquet.

'And I can go there by way of Nantes without rousing suspicion,' replied the minister. 'Patience, patience – everything will come right.'

'But what a distance to travel before you reach Nantes!' said Madame Fouquet.

'Yes, but it cannot be helped,' replied Fouquet. 'The king summons me to attend the states-general. I know he intends to ruin me, but I cannot refuse to go without betraying my fears.'

'Well, I have discovered a means of arranging everything,' cried Pélisson. 'You are going to set out for Nantes' – Fouquet looked at him with an air of surprise – 'but in the company of your friends – by carriage as far as Orléans; thence to Nantes in your barge – always ready to defend yourself if attacked, to escape if threatened. In a word, you will take your money with you in any case, and you will be obeying the king even while you are making good your escape. Then you can reach the sea whenever you please and sail across to Belle-Isle, and from Belle-Isle you can go wherever you choose – like an eagle when he is driven from his eyrie.'

Pelisson's proposal met with general approval.

'Yes, that is what you must do,' said Madame Fouquet to her husband, and her words were echoed by all.

'Well, I will do as you suggest,' said Fouquet. 'I will make all preparations and within an hour I shall be away.'

'Go at once!'

'With seven hundred thousand livres to the good, you can build up a fresh fortune,' said the Abbé Fouquet. 'What is to prevent you from fitting out privateers at Belle-Isle?'

'And if necessary we can go and discover a new world,' added La Fontaine, intoxicated with his own enthusiastic projects.

At that moment a knock at the door interrupted the chorus of felicitations.

'A courier from the king!' announced the master of ceremonies. A profound silence fell upon the company. It seemed as though the message brought by the courier was a reply to all the plans formed a moment before. Everyone present looked at the master to see what he would do. The perspiration was rolling down Fouquet's face, and truly at that moment he was suffering from fever. He rose and passed into the cabinet to receive the message from his majesty. The silence throughout the whole house was such that his guests could distinctly hear Fouquet's reply to the messenger.

'Very well, monsieur' – in a voice which shook with weariness and emotion. A moment afterwards, Fouquet called Gourville, who crossed the gallery amidst a hush of general expectation. At length the minister reappeared among his guests, but his face was barely recognisable; pale before, he had now become livid. A living phantom, he staggered forward with arms outstretched, like a ghost come to salute his friends of former days. Everyone rose in consternation, uttering exclamations of surprise and commiseration, and running to Fouquet's support. The minister leant upon his wife's arm and pressed Madame de Bellière's icy hand.

'Good God! what has happened!' they all cried. Fouquet opened his right hand, clammy with perspiration, and displayed a paper, which Pélisson seized with terrified eagerness. He read the following lines written by the king himself:

> DEAR AND WELL-BELOVED MONSIEUR FOUQUET – Pay over to us out of what cash of ours you have in hand, a sum of seven hundred thousand livres, which we shall require before our departure today. And, as we are aware that you are indisposed, we pray God that He may restore your health and have you always in His holy keeping. LOUIS
> (This letter will serve as a receipt.)

A murmur of consternation circulated through the room.

'Well,' cried Pélisson at last, 'you have this letter – '

'I have this receipt, yes.'

'Then what do you intend to do?'

'Nothing, since I have the receipt.'

'But – '

'If I have the receipt, Pélisson, it means that the money is paid,' said the minister simply,

'You have paid it!' cried Madame Fouquet, in despair. 'Then we are indeed ruined!'

'Come, come, enough of this useless talk,' interrupted Pélisson. 'Now that he has your money, the next thing he will require is your life. To horse! to horse! Monseigneur!'

'And leave us here!' cried the two women, wild with grief.

'See, monseigneur, in saving yourself, you save us all. To horse!'

'But look! he can scarcely stand!'

'Oh! but he will pull himself together!' cried stout-hearted Pélisson.

'He is right,' murmured Fouquet.

'Monseigneur! Monseigneur!' shouted Gourville as he rushed up the stairs, four steps at a time.

'Well, what is it?'

'As you know, I followed the courier with the money.'

'Yes!'

'Well, when I got to the Palais-Royal, I saw – '

'Wait a moment and recover your breath, friend, you will choke!'

'What did you see?' cried the friends, on thorns with impatience.

'I saw the musketeers preparing to mount,' gasped Gourville.

'See! there is not a moment to lose,' cried someone.

Madame Fouquet rushed to the head of the stairs and cried out orders to bring horses. Madame de Bellière ran after her, and seizing her arm said – 'Madame, for heaven's sake, do not let your anxiety be noticed – do not show that you have anything to fear.' Pélisson ran out to see to the horses being put in the carriage.

Meanwhile Gourville was collecting in his hat all the money which the minister's weeping and terrified friends could contribute – a final offering, the pious dole which poverty made to misfortune. Monsieur Fouquet himself, carried rather than led, was taken to the carriage and the door closed upon him. Gourville mounted the box and gathered up the reins. Pélisson was supporting madame, who had fainted. Madame de Bellière had greater strength; she received her reward, for she had Fouquet's last kiss. Pélisson explained glibly to the servants that the sudden departure was due to an order from the king summoning the ministers to Nantes.

## CHAPTER 64

## *In Monsieur Colbert's travelling coach*

As Gourville had seen, the king's musketeers had mounted their horses and were ready to follow their captain. The latter, not wishing to be impeded in his movements, left his brigade under the command of his lieutenant, and started off alone to make the journey on post-horses, after having recommended his men to make all possible speed. However rapidly they might travel, they could not reach their destination before him.

As he passed along the Rue Croix-des-Petits-Champs, he had leisure to notice a thing which gave him food for reflection. He saw

Monsieur Colbert leaving his house in order to enter a carriage drawn up before the door. Inside the carriage d'Artagnan perceived certain feminine head-gear, and being naturally inquisitive, he wished to ascertain the names of the women whose faces were hidden beneath their hoods. To obtain a glimpse of them, d'Artagnan was obliged to have resource to stratagem, for they were sitting with their faces turned in the opposite direction. He rode his horse so close to the carriage that his big riding-boot came in contact with the apron, shaking the whole carriage and its occupants. The ladies were startled; one of them gave vent to a slight scream, by which d'Artagnan could judge that she was young; the other rapped out an oath with all the vigour and aplomb which a woman of the world can acquire in fifty years. They threw back their hoods; one of the ladies was Madame Vanel, and the other the Duchesse de Chevreuse. D'Artagnan's sight was keener than that of the two women, for although he recognised them, they failed to recognise him. They began to laugh at the fright they had had.

'Good!' said d'Artagnan to himself, 'the old duchess is not so exclusive as she used to be with regard to her acquaintances; here she is paying court to Monsieur Colbert's mistress! Poor Monsieur Fouquet. This bodes no good to him.' And he rode on.

Monsieur Colbert got into the carriage and the noble trio were driven off at a moderately slow pace towards the Bois de Vincennes. The duchess stopped the carriage to set down Madame Vanel at her husband's house, and then continued the drive with Colbert, with whom she chatted about men and matters. The dear lady had an inexhaustible fund of anecdote, and as her stories were always at somebody else's expense and to her own advantage, her companion was amused and at the same time impressed with a sense of her cleverness.

She informed Colbert – who, of course, was quite ignorant of it – how great a minister he was, and how Fouquet would soon become a negligeable quantity. She promised him the support, when he had acquired Fouquet's office, of the old nobility of the kingdom, and questioned him as to the amount of influence it would be proper to allow La Vallière to retain. She mixed flattery with censure in a manner which delighted and bewildered him. She showed him the inner workings of so many secrets that, for a moment, Colbert feared that he had to do with the Devil. She proved to him that it rested with her to make or mar the Colbert of today, as she had held in the hollow of her hand the Fouquet of yesterday; and as Colbert was simple enough to ask her point-blank the reason why she hated the minister so bitterly, she replied, 'Why do you hate him yourself?'

'Madame,' he answered, 'in politics, a difference in policy may lead to a split between those who hold opposite opinions. The system practised by Monsieur Fouquet has always appeared to me to be opposed to the true interests of the king.'

She interrupted him. 'Let us say no more about Monsieur Fouquet. The king's journey to Nantes will settle the matter for him. I regard Monsieur Fouquet as a man whose day is over, and you should regard him in that light also.' Colbert made no reply, and she continued, 'On his return from Nantes, the king, who is only seeking a pretext, will find that the conduct of the states has been unsatisfactory – that they have shown a grudging spirit. The states will reply that the taxes are too heavy and they have been ruined by the manner in which the taxes have been farmed. The king will make Monsieur Fouquet responsible, and then – '

'And then?' said Colbert.

'Why! he will be disgraced. Do you not agree with me?'

Colbert threw a glance at his companion, as much as to say, 'If he is no more than disgraced, it won't be *your* fault.'

Madame de Chevreuse hastened to add, 'It is necessary that your position should be marked out beforehand, Monsieur Colbert. Do you know of anybody who stands between you and the king when once Monsieur Fouquet has fallen?'

'I don't understand,' said Colbert.

'You will understand in a moment. How high does your ambition lead you to aspire?'

'Ambition? – I have none.'

'In that case, it was unnecessary to have brought about Monsieur Fouquet's downfall. Oh! come, it is idle to say that, Monsieur Colbert!'

'I have had the honour to tell you, madame – '

'Oh! yes, yes; the king's interests – I know all that; but now let us speak about your own interests.'

'My interest consists in attending to his majesty's business.'

'Well now, are you ruining Monsieur Fouquet, or are you not? Come, give me a direct answer.'

'Madame, I am ruining nobody.'

'Then I hardly understand why you went to the great expense of purchasing those letters of Monsieur Mazarin concerning Monsieur Fouquet. Nor do I quite see your idea in bringing these letters to his majesty's notice.'

Colbert was taken aback; he stared at the duchess and then said in a tone of constraint – 'And I understand still less, madame, how you, who received the money, can reproach me with having paid it.'

'Why, the fact is,' said the old duchess,' that even if one cannot have what one wants, one cannot help wishing for it all the same.'

'H'm,' growled Colbert, somewhat confounded by such uncompromising arguments.

'And that is exactly your position, is it not, Monsieur Colbert?'

'I admit that I am unable to counteract certain influences which govern the king.'

'Influences which fight for Monsieur Fouquet? What are they? Stay, perhaps I can help you.'

'Pray do so, madame.'

'La Vallière, for instance?'

'Oh! her influence is slight – no knowledge of business and very little energy. Monsieur Fouquet has paid court to her.'

'But in defending him, she would accuse herself, would she not?'

'Yes, I think so.'

'There is still another influence, is there not?'

'Yes, and a powerful one.'

'The queen mother, perhaps?'

'Her majesty the queen mother has a feeling for Monsieur Fouquet which is very prejudicial to her son's interests.'

'Do not believe it,' said the old woman, with a smile.

'Oh; but I have so often felt the consequences of it,' exclaimed Colbert, incredulously.

'Formerly, no doubt.'

'And even recently, madame – at Vaux. It is she who persuaded her son not to arrest Monsieur Fouquet.'

'My dear sir, one is not always in the same mood every day. What the queen may have wished recently, she would probably not wish today.'

'Why?' asked Colbert, surprised.

'Oh! the reasons are of no consequence.'

'On the contrary, madame, they are important; for could I be certain of not displeasing her majesty the queen mother, all my scruples would be removed.'

'Well, in all probability you have heard some talk about a certain secret.'

'A secret?'

'Call it what you please – but in short, the queen mother has conceived a horror of all who have in any way been mixed up in its discovery, and I fancy Monsieur Fouquet is one of them.'

'Then,' cried Colbert, 'one could count upon the queen mother's acquiescence?'

'I have only this moment left her majesty, who assures me of it.'

'Then so be it, madame.'

'Moreover, there are others: perhaps you know the man who was Monsieur Fouquet's intimate friend – a Monsieur d'Herblay – a bishop, I believe?'

'Bishop of Vannes.'

'Well, this Monsieur d'Herblay also knew the secret, and the queen mother is bitterly hostile to him.'

'Really?'

'So bitter is she, that, were he dead, she would demand his head in order to satisfy herself that he would speak no more.'

'Is that the queen's wish?'

'It is her command.'

'Then Monsieur d'Herblay will be hunted down, madame!'

'Oh! we know quite well where he is.'

Colbert looked at the duchess. 'Tell me, madame.'

'He is at Belle-Isle-en-Mer.'

'The residence of Monsieur Fouquet?'

'Certainly.'

'He will be taken!'

It was the duchess's turn to smile.

'Do not believe that so easily,' said she, 'and do not be so ready to promise.'

'Why not, madame?'

'Because Monsieur d'Herblay is not one of those men who can be caught just when you please.'

'Then he is a rebel?'

'Oh! we old people, Monsieur Colbert, have more or less passed our life in open rebellion, yet you see, so far from being caught ourselves, it is we who catch others.'

Colbert fixed upon the old duchess one of those lowering looks of his to which no words can do justice, and then, with an emphasis which was not wanting in dignity, he said: 'These are no longer the times when a subject can gain a duchy by making war upon the King of France. If Monsieur d'Herblay hatches treason, he will die upon the scaffold. It matters little to us whether or not that will please his enemies.'

This word *us*, coming strangely from Colbert's lips, made the duchess thoughtful. She caught herself reckoning seriously with this man. Colbert had gained the ascendancy in the conversation, and determined to keep it. 'You ask me, madame, to have this Monsieur d'Herblay arrested?' he said.

'I? Not at all; I ask nothing of you.'

'I thought I understood that, madame; but since I am mistaken, let it pass. The king has not yet said anything about it.' The duchess bit her nails. 'Besides,' continued Colbert, 'what a paltry capture this bishop would be! Scarcely the sort of game for a king to hunt! Oh! no, no, I shall not even trouble about him.'

The duchess could no longer conceal her hatred. 'Fit game for a woman, though – and the queen is a woman,' she cried. 'If she wishes to have Monsieur d'Herblay arrested, she has her reasons for it. Besides, is he not a friend of the man who is about to be disgraced?'

'Oh! that is a consideration which doesn't weigh. The man will not be persecuted so long as he is not an enemy of the king. Does that displease you?'

'I shall say nothing.'

'Ah! yes, you would like to see him in prison – in the Bastille, for example?'

'I consider a secret would be better concealed behind the walls of the Bastille than behind those of Belle-Isle.'

'I will consult the king, who will clear up this point.'

'And while you are discussing the matter, monsieur, the Bishop of Vannes will have fled. In his place I should do the same.'

'Fled! and whither should he flee? Europe is ours, in will, if not in actual fact.'

'He will always find somewhere to go, monsieur. It is evident that you do not know the man with whom you are dealing. You do not know Monsieur d'Herblay, and you have not known Aramis. He was one of those four musketeers who, under the late king, made Cardinal Richelieu tremble, and during the Regency caused so much anxiety to Monseigneur de Mazarin.'

'But, madame, what can he do – unless indeed he has a kingdom of his own?'

'He has one, monsieur.'

'Monsieur d'Herblay possesses a kingdom?'

'I repeat, sir, that if he has need of a kingdom, either he possesses or will possess one.'

'Well, then, since you are so greatly concerned to prevent his escape, I assure you, madame, that this rebel shall not escape us.'

'Belle-Isle is fortified, sir, and by Monsieur d'Herblay himself.'

'And even were Belle-Isle to be defended by him, the place is not impregnable. If the Bishop of Vannes has shut himself up in Belle-

Isle, we will lay siege to the place and capture it.'

'You may rest assured, monsieur, that the zeal you display in the interests of the queen mother will earn her majesty's lively gratitude and will bring you a magnificent reward; but what am I to say about your plans with regard to this man?'

'Why, once we have caught him, he will be shut up in a fortress, and his secret will never be disclosed.'

'That is all very well, Monsieur Colbert; and we may from this moment congratulate ourselves upon having formed a solid alliance, you and I; and henceforth I am very much at your service.'

'It is I, madame, who am at your service. This Chevalier d'Herblay is a spy in the Spanish service, is he not?'

'He is a great deal more than that.'

'A secret ambassador?'

'You must go still higher.'

'Stay – King Philip III[181] is a bigot. He is – he is the king's confessor?'

'Still higher.'

'*Mordieu!*' cried Colbert, forgetting himself so far as to swear in the presence of a lady, 'a friend of the queen mother, and the Duchess de Chevreuse to boot – Then he must be the General of the Jesuits?'

'I believe you have guessed it,' replied the duchess.

'Ah! then, this man will ruin us all, madame, unless we take care to ruin him first, and that speedily!'

'That was my opinion, monsieur, but I did not venture to tell you it.'

'And it is fortunate for us that he has attacked the throne instead of attacking us.'

'But mark this well, Monsieur Colbert: nothing is capable of discouraging Monsieur d'Herblay, and if this blow has failed he will make a fresh start. If he has let slip the opportunity of putting on the throne the man he designed, he will do as much sooner or later for some other man; and then it is very certain you will not be his prime minister.'

Colbert's brows lowered threateningly. 'I am convinced, madame, that a prison will settle this matter in a way which will be satisfactory to both of us,' he said.

The duchess smiled. 'If you only knew how many times he has escaped from prison!'

'Oh!' retorted Colbert, 'we will take steps to prevent his repeating that experience.'

'You cannot have paid attention to what I have just told you.

Remember that Aramis was one of the four invincibles of whom Richelieu stood in dread. And at that period the four musketeers lacked that which they now possess – money and experience.'

Colbert bit his lip. 'Then we will give up the idea of prison,' he said, speaking half to himself. 'We will find a retreat whence even a man who is invincible cannot escape.'

'Well spoken, my trusty ally!' replied the duchess. 'But it grows late; had we not better return?'

'The more willingly, madame, for the reason that I have my preparations to make before I leave with the king.'

'To Paris!' cried the duchess to her coachman. And the carriage returned to the Faubourg Saint-Antoine after the treaty had been concluded which delivered up to death Fouquet's last friend, the last defender of Belle-Isle, the former friend of Marie Michon and the recent enemy of the Duchess de Chevreuse.

CHAPTER 65

## *The two barges*

D'ARTAGNAN had left Paris; Fouquet also had gone – the latter with a headlong speed which only increased the solicitude of his friends. For the first few miles of the journey, or rather flight, they were constantly in dread that all whom they saw on the road behind Fouquet's carriage were in pursuit of him.

Indeed, it was not to be expected that Louis XIV, if he had intended Fouquet to be seized, should have allowed him to escape thus. The young lion was already a skilful hunter, and his hounds were sufficiently well trained for him to be able to depend upon them.

Gradually, however, their fears subsided. By the rapidity of his flight the minister placed so great a distance between himself and his persecutors that there seemed no reasonable expectation of their overtaking him. Besides, his friends had supplied him with an excellent justification. Was he not going to join the king at Nantes, and his very haste, was it not a testimony of his zeal? He arrived at Orléans, weary in body, but comforted in mind. There he found, thanks to the care of a courier who had preceded him, a handsome barge manned by eight rowers. These barges, something the shape of a gondola but a trifle clumsy and broad in the beam, had a small decked cabin as well as a sort of shelter at the stern formed by a tent. At that time there was a service of such boats on the Loire between Orléans and Nantes; and this passage, which would be considered tedious in these days, was then considered more pleasant and comfortable than the long journey by road, mounted on indifferent post-horses or driving in a badly-hung carriage. Fouquet stepped on board the barge, which immediately pushed off. The watermen, knowing that they had the honour of conveying the minister of finance, tugged at their oars right manfully, for the magic word *finances* seemed to promise them a liberal recompense, and they wished to show themselves deserving of it. The barge flew swiftly over the waters of the Loire. The weather was magnificent – one of those glorious sunrises which throw a purple mantle over the landscape whilst leaving to the stream all its limpid serenity. Aided by the current, the rowers made the boat leap forward like a bird on the wing, and soon Fouquet arrived at Beaugency without any untoward incident having occurred. Fouquet hoped to be the first to arrive at Nantes, and once arrived, he decided that he would see the Notables[182] in order to gain support among the principal members of the states-general; he would make himself necessary to them – a matter easy of accomplishment for a man of his talents – and thus would be enabled to postpone the catastrophe, even if he could not entirely avert it.

'Besides,' said Gourville to him, 'when we get to Nantes we shall be able to guess your enemies' intentions; we can have horses ready to take you to the trackless regions of Poitou, or a boat to reach the sea; and once at sea, Belle-Isle is a safe refuge. So far, you see, you have neither been watched nor pursued.'

He had scarcely spoken when they noticed in the distance, behind a bend in the river, the masts of a barge which was also travelling downstream. 'What is it?' asked Fouquet.

'That, monseigneur,' replied the captain of the barge, 'is what I should call a most extraordinary thing. That barge is coming along like a house a-fire.'

Gourville was startled, and climbed upon the cabin-deck in order to obtain a better view. Fouquet remained where he was, but he said to Gourville, restraining his uneasiness – 'See what it is, my dear fellow.'

The barge had just turned the bend. She came on so fast that behind her the water was lashed by the oars into a long streak of foam, shining in the light of early morning.

'Lord! what a pace!' the skipper kept repeating – 'what a pace! I should say those men must be well paid. I wouldn't have believed, if I hadn't seen it with my own eyes, that any oars ever made of wood could have beaten ours; but there! – that proves it.'

'So they ought!' cried one of the rowers. 'There are twelve of them, and we are only eight.'

'Twelve!' exclaimed Gourville, 'twelve rowers? Impossible!' The number of eight rowers in a barge had never been exceeded, even for the king. This honour had been paid to the minister of finance more on account of his haste than out of respect.

'What is the meaning of it?' asked Gourville, trying to distinguish the passengers under the tent, which was now visible; but the keenest eye would have been unable to recognise their features at that distance.

'They must be in a deuce of a hurry! For the king is not on board,' said the skipper. Fouquet started. 'How do you know it is not the king?' asked Gourville.

'Why, to begin with, she doesn't fly the white flag with fleurs-de-lis, which is always at the mast-head of the royal barge.'

'And then,' said Fouquet, 'it is impossible that it could be the king, Gourville, because only yesterday the king was in Paris.' Gourville replied to this objection by a look which signified, 'You also were in Paris yesterday.' 'And how do you know that they are in a hurry,' continued Fouquet, in order to gain time.

'Because, monseigneur,' replied the captain, 'those people must have left a long time after us, and yet you see they have caught us up, or very nearly.'

'Pooh!' exclaimed Gourville, 'how are you to know that they did not start from Beaugency, or even from Niort?'

'We have seen no barge of that size, unless it was at Orléans. She has come from Orléans, sir, and at top speed.'

Fouquet and Gourville exchanged glances. The captain noticed their uneasiness and, to mislead him, Gourville said, 'It is a friend of ours who has wagered he would catch us – let us make him lose his wager by not letting him overtake us.' The captain had opened his mouth to give the necessary order to his men, when Monsieur Fouquet said coldly, 'If it should be someone who wishes to join us, let him come.'

'We can do our best, monseigneur,' said the captain, with diffidence. 'Halloa there, you fellows, put a little spunk into it! Pull!'

'No,' said Fouquet, 'on the contrary, I tell you to stop the boat.'

'Monseigneur, this is folly!' whispered Gourville in his ear.

'Stop the boat!' repeated Fouquet. The eight oars stopped, and then, backing water, checked the boat's way and in a moment brought her to a dead stop. The twelve rowers in the boat behind did not at first notice this manoeuvre, and continued to propel their barge so vigorously that they soon brought it within musket-shot. Fouquet's sight was not good, and Gourville had the sun in his eyes; the skipper alone, with the clear sight which constant exposure to the elements usually gives, could distinctly see the passengers in the barge which was approaching. 'I see them,' he cried, 'there are two of them.'

'I can't see anybody,' said Gourville.

'You will be able to very soon; with a few more strokes they will be within twenty paces of us.'

But what the skipper had predicted was not realised. The barge followed the example of that of Monsieur Fouquet, and instead of rowing alongside in order to join the supposed friends, she stopped short in mid-stream.

'I don't understand what all this means,' said the skipper.

'Nor I,' said Gourville.

'Since you can clearly distinguish the men in yonder boat,' said Fouquet, 'try and give us a description of them, captain, before we get too far away.'

'I thought I saw two,' replied the waterman, 'but now I can only see one under the tent.'

'What is he like?'

'A dark man, with broad shoulders and a thick neck.' At that moment a tiny cloud, passing across the blue sky, darkened the sun. Gourville, who was still looking out, with his hand shading his eyes, could now see what he was looking for, and suddenly springing from the deck, he entered the cabin where Fouquet was awaiting him and said in a voice shaking with excitement, 'Colbert!'

'Colbert?' repeated Fouquet. 'That is very strange – oh! it is impossible!'

'But I tell you I recognised him, and he knew me so well that he has just retired into the aftercabin. Perhaps the king has sent him to bring you back.'

'In that case he would have come alongside instead of lying off. What can he be doing there?'

'No doubt he intends watching us, monseigneur.'

'I cannot bear uncertainty,' cried Fouquet, 'let us row up alongside of him.'

'Oh! Monseigneur, don't do that. The barge is full of armed men.'

'Then you think they would arrest me, Gourville. If that is their intention, why do they not come?'

'Monseigneur, it does not befit your dignity to go to meet even your ruin.'

'But to allow myself to be hunted like a malefactor.'

'There is nothing to show that they are after you, monseigneur – have a little patience.'

'What is to be done, then?'

'Do not stop here; you were only travelling so quickly to appear to be zealous in obeying the king's orders. Wait and see what happens.'

'You are right. Come!' cried Fouquet, 'since they insist upon keeping in the background, we will get forward.'

The captain gave the signal, and his men resumed their labours all the more vigorously from having enjoyed a rest. Scarcely had the barge gone a hundred yards before the other boat with the twelve rowers resumed its progress also. This state of affairs continued the whole of the day without any increase or lessening of the distance between the two vessels. Towards evening Fouquet determined to force his persecutor to reveal his intentions. He ordered the boat to be steered towards the bank, as though he were about to land. Colbert's barge turned sharply towards the bank also. By pure chance, it happened that at the very spot where Fouquet had made a feint of landing, a groom from the stables of the Château de Langeais was riding along the flowery banks with three led horses. No doubt the people in the barge with the twelve rowers believed that Fouquet was directing his course to reach the horses which had been brought there to assist his flight. for four or five men, armed with muskets, leapt out of the boat and ran along the bank, as though to cut off the horses. Satisfied with having drawn the enemy, Fouquet took it as demonstrated, and ordered the boat to proceed. Colbert's men at once regained their own boat, and the pursuit was renewed. Seeing this, Fouquet felt his danger so keenly that he said to Gourville in a prophetic tone – 'Well, my dear friend, what did I tell you at supper last night? Am I going to my ruin or not?'

'Oh! Monseigneur.'

'These two boats which are racing along as though they were disputing the championship of the Loire, do they not represent our two fortunes, that of Colbert and my own; and can you help thinking that one of the two will be wrecked at Nantes?'

'At any rate,' objected Gourville, 'the thing is still uncertain; you are going to appear before the States and show the sort of man you are; your eloquence and your business talent are the sword and buckler which will serve to defend you, if not to conquer. The Bretons do not know you yet, but when they do, you will have won your cause. Let Monsieur Colbert take care, for his barge is just as liable to be capsized as your own. They are both swift – he has the advantage of speed, it is true – but we shall see which is the first to be wrecked.'

Taking Gourville's hand, 'My dear friend,' said Fouquet, 'I am afraid it will be a case of first come first served. You see Colbert takes care not to pass me. A prudent man, Colbert!' He was right: the two boats held their course as far as Nantes, still watching each other. Gourville hoped that when the minister landed he would be able to seek a refuge at once and to have relays of horses got ready. But as he was about to land, the second barge pulled up to the quay, and Colbert approaching Fouquet saluted him with every mark of the most profound respect, so publicly expressed and so significant that they resulted in attracting quite a crowd of people to the quay. Fouquet retained his self-possession perfectly. He felt that there were certain duties which he owed to himself in his last moments of greatness. He resolved to fall from such a height that the shock would crush one at least of his enemies. If Colbert stood in the way, so much the worse for Colbert.

Accordingly the minister, turning to Colbert, greeted him with that arrogant droop of the eyelids peculiar to him, 'What! is it you, Monsieur Colbert?'

'To offer you my respects, monseigneur,' replied the latter.

'Were you in that barge yonder?' and he pointed to the famous twelve-oar.

'Yes, monseigneur.'

'With a dozen rowers? You are putting on style, Monsieur Colbert! I thought for a moment it must be either the queen mother or the king.'

'Monseigneur – ' began Colbert, reddening.

'An expensive trip for those who will have to pay for it, Monsieur Colbert,' said Fouquet. 'However, you have arrived. But you see,' he added, after a moment's pause, 'that I arrived before you, although I had but eight oars.' And he turned his back upon Colbert, leaving it to remain in doubt whether or not the manoeuvres of the second barge had been observed by the first. At any rate, he would not give Colbert the satisfaction of allowing him to see that he had been frightened.

Colbert was somewhat disconcerted, but still kept his ground. 'I should have arrived sooner, monseigneur,' he replied, 'but that I stopped every time your boat stopped.'

'And why?' cried Fouquet, stung by Colbert's impudence. 'Why, since your crew was superior to mine, did you not join me, or go on in advance?'

'I was withheld by a feeling of respect,' replied Colbert, bowing to the ground.

Fouquet stepped into a carriage which had been sent for him by the authorities of the town – for what reason, we cannot say – and was driven to the Maison de Nantes, escorted by a large crowd, for the people had been excited for some days past by the anticipation of the states-general which had been convened. No sooner had he taken up his quarters than Gourville went off to make arrangements for horses along the road to Poitiers and Vannes, and for a boat at Paimboeuf. He accomplished this service with so much secrecy and activity, and with so lavish an outlay, that never had Fouquet, at that moment suffering from an attack of fever, been more assured of safety – barring always the interference of that great disturber of human plans, chance.

That night a rumour was current in the town that the king was travelling in great haste by post-horses, and would arrive in ten or twelve hours. Whilst waiting to see the king, the people revelled in the spectacle of the musketeers, who had just entered the town with their captain d'Artagnan at their head, and had marched through to take up their quarters in the château. There they formed guards of honour and occupied all the stations.

Monsieur d'Artagnan with his native courtesy presented himself before the minister towards ten o'clock in order to offer him his respectful greetings; and although Fouquet was feverish and in pain, and bathed in perspiration, he was pleased to receive Monsieur d'Artagnan, who, on his side, was charmed with the honour, as will be seen by the conversation which they had together.

CHAPTER 66

*Friendly advice*

FOUQUET had retired to bed, like a man who clings to life and is anxious to economise the delicate tissue of existence, so liable to irreparable injury from the slings and arrows of mundane fortune.

D'Artagnan received an affable welcome as he appeared in the doorway. He returned the greeting, and made enquiries as to how

Fouquet had borne the journey.

'Tolerably well, thank you,' replied the latter.

'And how is the fever?'

'Still no better. I have an intolerable thirst, and I had scarcely arrived before I levied upon Nantes a contribution of cooling drinks.'

'The first thing to do is to get some sleep, monseigneur.'

'The deuce! I should be very glad to get some sleep, Monsieur d'Artagnan, but – '

'Why, who hinders you?'

'You, in the first place.'

'I? – Ah! Monseigneur – '

'Certainly. Do you tell me that here in Nantes, as in Paris, you have not come in the king's name?'

'For God's sake, monseigneur,' replied the captain, 'let the king rest a little! When I have occasion to wait upon you for the reason you suggest, I promise you I shall not leave you in suspense. You will see me lay a hand upon my sword, according to book, and the first words you will hear me pronounce, in the voice I reserve for grand occasions, will be – "Monseigneur, in the name of the king, I arrest you." '

Fouquet trembled in spite of himself, so natural and vigorous had been the accent of the keen-witted Gascon. The rehearsal of the arrest was almost as terrifying as the actual deed would have been.

'You promise to treat me thus frankly?' said the minister.

'Upon my honour! But, take my word for it, we haven't come to that yet.'

'Who has put that idea into your head, Monsieur d'Artagnan? For my part, I believe the exact contrary.'

'I have heard mention of nothing of the kind,' replied d'Artagnan. 'Pooh, pooh! absurd! – for, in spite of your fever, you are a pleasant companion, and the king cannot help a liking for you at the bottom of his heart.'

Fouquet made a grimace. 'But Monsieur Colbert?' he said. 'Is Monsieur Colbert as fond of me as you say?'

'I don't speak about Monsieur Colbert,' replied the captain. 'He is a man of exceptional tastes! Very possibly he dislikes you, but deuce take it! the squirrel has no need to be afraid of the adder, however willing the adder may be to sting.'

'Upon my word, you treat me in a most friendly manner,' replied Fouquet, 'and I declare I have never met a better hearted man or a man of sharper wit.'

'Very kind of you to say so,' said d'Artagnan. 'But why have you waited until today before paying me this compliment.'

'How blind we are!' murmured Fouquet.

'There now, your voice is getting hoarse,' said d'Artagnan. 'Drink, monseigneur, drink.' And he handed the minister a draught with the most cordial goodwill. Fouquet thanked him with a smile. 'Things like this only happen to me,' growled the musketeer. 'Here have I been living under your very nose for the last ten years, all the time you were shifting gold by the ton – you were clearing a cool four million a year – and you never even noticed me, and now you become aware of my existance just at the very moment – '

'When I am about to fall,' interrupted Fouquet. 'Is it true, Monsieur d'Artagnan?'

'I did not say that.'

'Still, you thought it. Well, if I fall, I do assure you that I shall never pass a day without cursing my folly in not having employed Monsieur d'Artagnan while he was available and in not having made his fortune!'

'You overwhelm me!' said the captain, 'for indeed, I have the greatest esteem for you.'

'Another man who does not think with Colbert,' cried the minister.

'How this Colbert sticks in your gorge! He is worse than your fever!'

'Ah! and with good reason,' replied Fouquet. 'Judge for yourself.' And he related the details of the journey by boat and of Colbert's artful persecution. 'Do you not agree with me that it is the best sign of my approaching ruin?'

D'Artagnan became serious – 'You are right,' he said. 'Yes, it smells bad, as Monsieur de Tréville used to say.' And he fixed upon Fouquet a look of intelligence and meaning.

'Don't you think, captain, that it wears a significant aspect? Has not the king sent me to Nantes in order to get me away from Paris, where I have so many partisans, and to have the opportunity of seizing Belle-Isle?'

'Where Monsieur d'Herblay is at present,' added d'Artagnan. Fouquet raised his head. 'Speaking for myself, monseigneur,' continued the captain, 'I assure you that the king has not spoken to me against you.'

'Really?'

'Certainly, the king ordered me to Nantes, and instructed me to say nothing to Monsieur de Gesvres.'

'Who is a friend of mine.'

'Yes – to Monsieur de Gesvres,' continued the musketeer, his eyes speaking a very different language from that of his lips. 'Then the king ordered me to take a brigade of musketeers – more than enough, it seems to me, for the country is tranquil.'

'A brigade?' exclaimed Fouquet, raising himself on his elbow.

'Yes, monseigneur – ninety-six men – the same number as were employed to effect the arrest of Messieurs de Chalais, de Cinq-Mars and Montmorency.'[183] At these words, spoken without apparent intention, Fouquet pricked up his ears. 'And what then?' he asked.

'Oh a few trifling orders, such as to guard the château – to guard every lodging – not to allow any of your friend Monsieur de Gesvres's men to mount guard.'

'And what orders concerning myself?' cried Fouquet.

'Concerning you, monseigneur, not a word.'

'Monsieur d'Artagnan, it may be a question of saving my life and my honour! You would not deceive me?'

'Deceive you? Why should I? – Is your safety in any way threatened? Certainly, an order has been issued respecting carriages and boats – '

'An order?'

'Yes, but it need not concern you. A simple police precaution.'

'What is it, captain, what is it?'

'It is to stop all horses or boats leaving Nantes without a permit signed by the king.'

'Good God! why – '

D'Artagnan burst out laughing. 'But it only comes into execution after the king's arrival at Nantes; therefore you see, monseigneur, that the order does not concern you in any way.' Fouquet grew thoughtful, and d'Artagnan feigned not to notice his preoccupation. 'Since I have disclosed to you the tenor of the orders which have been given me, it shows that I wish you well, and am trying to prove that none of them are directed against yourself.'

'No doubt,' said Fouquet, absently.

'I will repeat what I have said,' continued the captain, still regarding the minister with a look charged with meaning – 'A specially strict guard to be kept over the château, where, I understand, you are to be lodged. Do you know the château? – Ah! Monseigneur, it is a regular prison! – Total exclusion of Monsieur de Gesvres, who has the honour of being one of your friends – All the city gates and those leading to the river to be closed, except by special permit, but only after the king's arrival. You will observe, Monsieur Fouquet, that if I were speaking to an uneasy conscience, instead of to a man like you, one of the greatest in the kingdom, I should compromise myself eternally! A splendid opportunity for anyone who wished to make a dash for liberty! No police, no guards, no orders – the roads open and the river free – Monsieur d'Artagnan obliged to lend his horses if they were required of him! All this ought to reassure you, Monsieur Fouquet; for the king would not have allowed me to remain unfettered by restrictions if he had harboured any evil designs. Indeed, monsieur, you may demand from me whatever you have a mind to; I am quite at your service; and the only service I have to ask of you in exchange is to be so kind as to remember me to Porthos and Aramis should you have occasion to go to Belle-Isle, as you have a perfect right to do, without even changing your clothes – in your dressing-gown, as you are at this moment.'

With these words, still accompanied with the same significant glance, the musketeer made a low bow, and immediately left the room and the building. He had scarcely gained the street when Fouquet, wild with apprehension, seized the bell-rope and shouted at one and the same time – 'My horses! My barge!'

But there was no reply. The minister dressed himself in haste in the first garments which came to hand – 'Gour–ville! – Gourville!' he cried as he slipped his watch into his pocket. Gourville appeared, pale and breathless – 'We must be off!' cried Fouquet, the moment he caught sight of him.

'Too late!' gasped poor Gourville, overwhelmed with grief – 'Too late? Why?' – 'Listen!' A fanfare of trumpets and the rolling of drums could be heard in the courtyard of the château – 'What is it, Gourville?'

'The king's arrival, monseigneur.' – 'The king?' – 'Yes, the king, who has ridden double stages – who has been killing his horses to reach this place eight hours before he was expected.'

'Then we are lost!' muttered Fouquet. 'True-hearted d'Artagnan, thou hast warned me too late!'

It was indeed the king who had arrived; soon the guns on the ramparts fired a salute and were answered by the guns of the ships in the lower reaches of the river. Fouquet's brow grew black. He called his servants and had himself attired in court costume. He could see from his window the excited crowds and the movements of a large troop of horse which had followed the king – how, it is impossible to guess.

His majesty was escorted to the château in great state, and Fouquet saw him dismount beneath the portcullis and speak a few words in the ear of d'Artagnan, who had held his stirrup. When the king had passed under the archway, d'Artagnan turned in the direction of the house where Fouquet was lodged, but with such great deliberation, and with so many halts to speak to his musketeers who were lining the route, that one would have said that he was pausing to count the steps before delivering his message. Fouquet opened his window to speak to him in the courtyard – 'Ah!' cried d'Artagnan, as he perceived him, 'then you are still there, monseigneur.' The word *still* was sufficient to prove to Monsieur Fouquet how much information and salutary advice were to have been gathered from the captain's first visit. The minister sighed – 'Yes,' he replied, 'the king's arrival has upset my plans.'

'Ah! you are aware that the king has just arrived?'

'Yes, sir, I have seen him, and this time you come in his name – ?'

'Merely to enquire after you, monseigneur, and to beg you, if your health permits, to be so obliging as to repair to the château.'

'Without a moment's delay, Monsieur d'Artagnan.'

'Ecod!' said the captain of musketeers, 'now that the king is here, there is no more walking abroad for anybody – no more doing as one pleases – everything is ordered by countersign now, for me as well as for you.'

Fouquet heaved another sigh, then, as he was too weak to walk, he got into his carriage and was driven to the château, escorted by d'Artagnan, whose politeness was no less terrifying, this time, than it had previously been reassuring.

CHAPTER 67

## How King Louis XIV played his little part

As FOUQUET was leaving his carriage to enter the Château of Nantes, he was accosted by a man who, with every sign of the deepest respect, handed him a letter. D'Artagnan felt it his duty to prevent the man from speaking to the minister and thrust him aside, not however before the message had been delivered. Fouquet broke the seal and read it; an expression of vague terror, which d'Artagnan did not fail to notice, overspread his features. The minister slipped the paper into a portfolio which he carried under his arm, and passed on towards the king's apartments. As he mounted the staircase behind Monsieur Fouquet, d'Artagnan saw, through the small window which lit each landing in the round tower, the man who had brought the note, after looking cautiously about, make signs to certain individuals who, after they had repeated these signals, immediately disappeared down the adjacent streets,

Fouquet was obliged to wait a moment upon the terrace, which abutted on a short corridor, beyond which was the room where the king had established his cabinet. Here d'Artagnan, who had been following Fouquet respectfully, passed him and entered the royal closet.

'Well?' cried Louis XIV, catching sight of the captain and covering over the papers upon the table with a large green cloth.

'Your order has been executed, sire.'

'And Fouquet?'

'His Excellency is following me,' replied d'Artagnan.

'Let him be introduced in ten minutes' time,' said the king, dismissing d'Artagnan with a gesture. The latter withdrew, but scarcely had he reached the corridor, at the end of which Fouquet was awaiting him, than he was recalled by the sound of the king's bell.

'Did he seem surprised?' asked the king.

'Who, sire?'

'Fouquet,' replied the king, again omitting the courtesy title of *Monsieur*, a circumstance which confirmed the musketeer's suspicions.

'No, sire,' – 'Very well.' And for the second time Louis dismissed d'Artagnan.

Fouquet had not moved from the terrace where the captain had left him; he was reperusing the note, which was in these terms:

> There is some scheme on foot against you. Perhaps they will not dare to carry it out in the château; but in that case it will be postponed until you return to your lodgings. The house is surrounded by musketeers. Do not return. A white horse is in waiting for you behind the esplanade.

Fouquet recognised the handwriting as that of Gourville. Unwilling that, in case of misfortune to himself, his faithful friend should be compromised, the minister carefully tore up the paper into a thousand pieces and flung them over the balustrade to be scattered by the winds. D'Artagnan surprised him as he was watching the last shreds being blown away into space – 'Monsieur,' said he, 'the king is expecting you.'

Fouquet traversed without haste the little corridor where Messieurs Brienne and Rose[184] were busy writing, whilst the Duc de Saint-Aignan, seated upon a low chair in the same corridor, with his sword between his legs, was apparently waiting for some orders and yawning in an agony of impatience. It struck Fouquet as singular that these gentlemen, usually so attentive and even obsequious, scarcely troubled to move as he, the Prime Minister, passed. But what else could be expected from courtiers when their master called his minister plain *Fouquet*? He raised his head, determined to face unflinchingly whatever evil fortune might be in store for him, and entered the king's apartment after his presence had been announced by the sound of the bell. The king nodded to him without rising and then enquired after his health with interest.

'I am still suffering from my attack of fever,' replied Fouquet, 'but I am nevertheless quite at the king's disposal.'

'Very good. The states will assemble tomorrow; have you a speech ready?'

Fouquet looked at the king in astonishment – 'I have not prepared one,' he said, 'but I shall be able to speak extempore. I am too well acquainted with the details of the business to feel any embarrassment. I have a question to ask, if your majesty will permit me.'

'By all means.'

'Why has your majesty not done your Prime Minister the honour of giving him notice of this while in Paris?'

'You were ill, and I did not wish to fatigue you.'

'I have never found necessary work – or preparing an explanation – fatiguing, sire; and since the moment has come for me to ask an explanation of my king – '

'Oh! Monsieur Fouquet – an explanation? Upon what, pray?'

'With regard to your majesty's intentions towards me.' – The king coloured. 'I have been slandered,' pursued Fouquet, with some heat, 'and I rely upon the king's justice to institute an enquiry.'

'All this is very useless, Monsieur Fouquet; I know what I know.'

'Your majesty can only know what has been told you, and, for my part, I have said nothing, whilst others have spoken to you often and often'

'What do you wish to say?' cried the king, impatient to put an end to this embarrassing discussion.

'I will go straight to the point, sire. I accuse a man of having influenced your majesty against me.'

'No one has done that, monsieur.'

'That reply, sire, only proves to me that I am right.'

'Monsieur Fouquet, I do not like to hear accusations.'

'But when one has been accused?'

'We have already said more than enough on this matter.'

'Will your majesty not allow me to justify myself?'

'I tell you once more that I am not accusing you.'

Fouquet retired a step and made a half-bow – 'It is evident,' he thought, 'that the king has made his decision, for it is only those who are unable to retreat who show such unreasonable obstinacy. I should indeed be blind if I could not see the danger now – and stupid if I do not take steps to avoid it.' – Then aloud he added – 'Your majesty has sent for me about some business?'

'No, Monsieur Fouquet; merely to give you a piece of advice.'

'Which I shall listen to with respect, sire.'

'Rest yourself, Monsieur Fouquet; do not waste your strength; the states will be in session but a short time, and when once my secretaries have finished with it, I don't want to hear any more talk about business for a fortnight.'

'Has the king no instructions to give me with regard to this assembly?'

'No, Monsieur Fouquet.'

'Not to me, the minister of finance?'

'Pray rest yourself; that is all I have to say.'

Fouquet bit his lip. He was evidently turning over some disquieting thought in his mind. The king became infected with his uneasiness.

'Are you displeased at having to remain inactive?' he asked.

'Yes, sire, I am not accustomed to inactivity.'

'But you are ill, and you must take care of yourself.'

'Yet your majesty spoke just now of a speech to be prepared for tomorrow.'

The king made no reply, for he found Fouquet's words embarrassing. Fouquet felt that the king's hesitation boded him no good. He thought he could read a danger-signal in the king's eyes, and to have shown uneasiness would have hastened the catastrophe. 'If I let him see that I am afraid,' he thought, 'I am ruined.'

The king, on his side, was only uneasy lest Fouquet should take the alarm – 'Has he got wind of anything?' he asked himself.

'If he should begin in a tone of severity' – so ran Fouquet's thoughts – 'if he should show irritation – or feign anger as a pretext – how shall I get out of the difficulty? Better attempt to smooth matters. Gourville was right. – Sire,' he resumed, suddenly, 'since your majesty has so kindly testified a regard for my health so far as to permit me to remain idle, may I venture to hope that you will consent to my absence from tomorrow's Council? I will spend the rest of the day in bed, and perhaps the king would allow his physician to visit me to see if he can cure this cursed fever.'

'It shall be as you wish, Monsieur Fouquet, you have permission to be absent tomorrow, and you shall have my physician, and I trust he will be able to benefit you.'

'Thank you, sire,' said Fouquet with a bow. Then taking a bold move – 'Shall I not have the honour of conducting the king to my place at Belle-Isle?' he asked. He watched Louis's face to see the effect of this stroke.

The king again coloured.

'Do you know,' he said, forcing a smile, 'that you have just said, "my place at Belle-Isle"?'

'Yes, sire.'

'Well, have you forgotten,' continued the king, still in the same pleasant tone, 'that you made me a present of Belle-Isle?'

'That is true, sire; only as you have not yet taken it, you will go and take possession.'

'I shall be delighted.'

'Besides, it was your majesty's intention as much as my own, and I cannot express to you how proud and happy I shall be to see the whole of the household troops come from Paris in order to take possession of the place.'

The king stammered out that he had not brought his musketeers for that purpose alone.

'Oh! I know very well,' said Fouquet, quickly, 'that your majesty has but to go there alone and lift your walking-cane to bring to the ground all the fortification of Belle-Isle.'

'Deuce take it!' cried the king. 'I don't wish to see them fall – these splendid works which have cost so much money. No! let them remain intact against the Dutch and the English. You would hardly guess what it is I wish to see at Belle-Isle, Monsieur Fouquet; I want to see your pretty peasant girls and women, both of the country and of the coast, who dance so charmingly and look so betwitching in their scarlet petticoats! I have heard a great deal about your fair vassals, monsieur. Come now, I should like to have a look at them.'

'Whenever your majesty pleases.'

'Have you any means of conveyance? It shall be tomorrow if you like.'

The minister felt the thrust, which could scarcely be called a subtle one, and he replied quietly – 'No, sire, I was unaware of your majesty's wish, and still less did I think that you would decide to go there so soon; consequently, I have made no arrangements at all.'

'Still, you have a boat of your own, I think?'

'I have five, but they are all either in the port or at Paimboeuf, and it would take at least twenty-four hours to reach them or to have them brought here. Had I not better send a messenger?'

'Wait, wait! let the fever be cured first – wait until tomorrow.'

'Ah! true. Who knows but we may have a hundred other ideas tomorrow?' replied Fouquet, his suspicions now thoroughly confirmed, and very pale. The king started, and stretched out his hand towards the bell, but Fouquet forestalled him – 'Sire,' said he, 'I am feverish – I have a trembling fit on me. If I stay here a moment longer, I fear I shall faint. I beg your majesty's leave to go and hide myself under the bedclothes.'

'Indeed, I see you are shivering – it is painful to watch you. Go, Monsieur Fouquet, by all means. I will send and make enquiries after you.'

'Your majesty overwhelms me. In an hour's time I shall be much better.'

'I will send for someone to see you back to your house.'

'As you please, sire. I should be glad of the support of somebody's arm.'

'Monsieur d'Artagnan!' cried the king, as he rang the bell.

'Oh! Sire,' interrupted Fouquet, with a laugh which made Louis shiver, 'are you sending for a captain of musketeers to conduct me to my lodgings? A doubtful honour, sire! A simple lacquey and no more, I beg.'

'But why, Monsieur Fouquet? Monsieur d'Artagnan often renders me this service.'

'Yes; but when he attends upon you, sire, it is to take your orders, but for me – '

'Well?'

'If I were to return home attended by your captain of musketeers, it would be said everywhere that you were having me arrested.'

'Arrested?' cried the king, paler than Fouquet himself – 'Arrested; oh – '

'What will people not say?' continued Fouquet, still with the same laugh. 'Moreover, I will warrant there would be plenty of people ill-mannered enough to rejoice!' This jest disconcerted the monarch still further. Fouquet was clever enough or fortunate enough to make Louis XIV shrink from the avowal of the blow which he meditated. When d'Artagnan made his appearance he received the order to instruct a musketeer to attend the minister to his house – 'Unnecessary!' said the latter. 'Gourville, who is waiting below, would serve me just as well. Still, I am always pleased with Monsieur d'Artagnan's society. I shall be very glad for him to see Belle-Isle, he who is such a judge of fortifications.' D'Artagnan bowed, understanding nothing of what was happening. Fouquet again bowed to the king, and went out affecting the deliberate gait of a man who is merely taking a stroll. 'Once outside the château,' he muttered – 'I am saved! Ah! you, you may see Belle-Isle, treacherous king, but it will be when I am not there!' and he hastened away.

D'Artagnan had remained with the king. 'Captain,' said Louis, 'you will follow Monsieur Fouquet at a hundred paces.'

'Yes, sire.'

'He is returning to his lodgings. You will accompany him.'

'Yes, sire.'

'You will arrest him in my name, and you will lock him in a carriage.'

'In a carriage. Very good.'

'And take care that he speaks to no one, nor throws notes to any whom he may meet.'

'Ah! that will be difficult, sire.'

'Not at all.'

'Pardon me, sire; I cannot stifle Monsieur Fouquet, and if he asks to be allowed to breathe, I cannot fasten all the windows and blinds and prevent him. He can hardly be prevented shouting and throwing any number of notes through the windows.'

'All that has been foreseen, Monsieur d'Artagnan – a carriage with an iron lattice will obviate those two difficulties which you have raised.'

'A carriage with an iron lattice?' cried d'Artagnan. 'But such a thing cannot be got ready in half an hour! And I understand your majesty to command me to arrest Monsieur Fouquet at once.'

'The carriage in question has already been provided.'

'Ah! that alters the case,' said the captain. 'If the carriage is already provided, very well – we have only to get it under way.'

'It is waiting with horses already harnessed.'

'Ah!'

'And the coachman, with the outriders is waiting in the courtyard behind the castle.'

D'Artagnan bowed.

'It only remains for me to ask where the king wishes me to take Monsieur Fouquet.'

'To the Castle of Angers, first of all.'

'Very well.'

'And afterwards, we will see.'

'Yes, sire.'

'Monsieur d'Artagnan, one word more; you notice that I have not employed my guards to execute this arrest. Monsieur de Gesvres will be furious.'

'Your majesty does not employ your Guards,' said the captain, slightly crestfallen, 'because you do not care to trust Monsieur de Gesvres – that is the only reason.'

'That is to say, monsieur, that I repose full trust in you.'

'I know it well, sire; and there is no need to remind me of it.'

'I say it for this reason, captain; if it should happen from this moment, by any chance whatever, that Monsieur Fouquet should escape – such things have happened, Monsieur – '

'Oh! frequently, sire; such things happen with others – never with myself.'

'What do you mean?'

'I mean, sire, that for a moment, I had an idea of saving Monsieur Fouquet.'

The king frowned.

'When I had the right to save him,' continued the captain; 'having guessed your majesty's plans before you spoke a word to me about them, and because I had a regard for Monsieur Fouquet, I was free to testify my goodwill towards him.'

'Really, monsieur, your words scarcely reassure me that your services will be such as I have a right to expect from you!'

'If I had saved him then, I should have acted with a perfectly clear conscience. I will go further. I should have done a good action, for Monsieur Fouquet is not a bad man. However, he was not willing – he has let the chance of freedom escape him. So much the worse! Now, I have my orders, and they shall be obeyed. As for Monsieur Fouquet, you may consider him already arrested. Monsieur Fouquet is in the Castle of Angers.'

'Oh! you have not got him yet, captain!'

'That concerns me – every man to his trade, sire. Only, I beg you will again reflect. Do you seriously order me to arrest Monsieur Fouquet, sire?'

'Yes, a thousand times, yes!'

'Then please to put it in writing.'

'Here are your written instructions.'

D'Artagnan took and read the document, then bowed to the king and went out. As he passed along the terrace he caught sight of Gourville, beaming with joy, and going in the direction of Monsieur Fouquet's lodgings.

CHAPTER 68

## White horse and black horse

'THAT'S VERY ODD,' mused the captain, 'Gourville looking as pleased as possible and running about the streets when he must be pretty nearly sure that Monsieur Fouquet is in danger, when it is almost a certainty it was he who sent Monsieur Fouquet that warning letter just now – that letter which was torn up and scattered to the winds by the minister. There is Gourville rubbing his hands as if he had done something clever. Where has he been? Gourville is coming from the Rue aux Herbes. Where does the Rue aux Herbes lead to?' And d'Artagnan, casting his eye over the tops of the houses of Nantes dominated by the castle, followed the line traced by the streets, as though he was studying a map; only in place of a flat, lifeless sheet of paper, the living map rose in relief, filled with the movements, the sounds and the shadows of men and things. Beyond the outskirts of the city lay the broad, cultivated plains bordering the Loire, stretching away until they were lost in the horizon, a purple streak intersected with bright lines of water and patches of the dark green of the marshes. Immediately outside the gate of Nantes could be seen two white lines of roads which diverged at an angle like fingers of a gigantic hand. D'Artagnan's eye, which had taken in the whole panorama with a single glance as he passed along the terrace, was led by the line of the Rue aux Herbes to the spot where one of these roads took its rise beneath the gates of Nantes. A few steps more, and he would have reached the staircase which led from the terrace to the round tower in order to take the barred carriage and go towards Monsieur Fouquet's house. But as chance would have it, as he was about to set foot on the stairs, his attention was attracted by a moving point which was gaining ground along the road in the distance. 'What is that?' thought the musketeer. 'A horse galloping – a runaway, no doubt. Ecod! it is moving at a pretty good pace!' The tiny moving speck left the road and gained the open fields of clover. 'A white horse,' continued the captain, who could now observe the sharp contrast made by the colour of the animal against the dark background; 'and he has a rider – some youngster, I suppose, whose horse is thirsty and has run away with him by a short cut across country to the nearest ford.' These reflections flashed across d'Artagnan's mind at the same instant that the objects themselves were focused on his retina, and he had already forgotten them by the time he had descended the first few steps. A few scraps of paper were strewn about on the stairs, plainly to be seen against the dingy masonry. 'What's this?' said the captain to himself. 'Seems to be part of the letter which Monsieur Fouquet tore up. Poor man! he gave his secret to the winds – the winds reject it, and bring it back to the king. Decidedly, my poor Fouquet, you are the sport of adverse fortune! The odds are against you, and fortune frowns. Your star is eclipsed by that of Louis XIV – the serpent is more subtle than the squirrel.' D'Artagnan picked up one of these scraps of paper as he descended. 'It is Gourville's neat little handwriting! I was not mistaken.' He read the word 'horse'. 'Aha!' he cried, then picked up another piece, which, however, was blank. Upon a third scrap he found the word 'white'. '*White – horse*,' he repeated, like a boy learning to spell. 'By all that's holy!' he cried, struck by the coincidence, 'a white horse!' And, like a grain of powder whose volume expands a hundredfold when the match is applied, d'Artagnan, his mind seething with ideas and suspicions, ran up the stairs again and sprang upon the terrace. The white horse was still forging ahead in the direction of the Loire, where, out towards the sea and almost indistinguishable in the haze, appeared a tiny sail.

'Oho!' cried the musketeer, 'it is only a man who is trying to escape who would ride at that pace across ploughed fields – it is only a financier like Fouquet who would care to ride thus, in broad daylight, on a white horse! It is only the lord of Belle-Isle who would attempt to escape by sea when there are such dense forests to hide in. And there is only one d'Artagnan in the world who can catch Monsieur Fouquet, now that he has a thirty minutes' start and will be able to reach his boat within an hour.'

The musketeer dashed down the stairs and gave rapid orders for the closed carriage to be driven at once to a clump of trees situated just outside the town. He selected the likeliest horse he could find, sprang into the saddle and rode off at a gallop along the Rue aux Herbes, and then turned off, not by the road which Fouquet had taken, but by the road skirting the Loire. He was convinced that he would thus gain ten minutes in the total of the distance to be traversed; he would overtake the fugitive, who would not suspect pursuit in this direction, at the spot where the two lines intersected. In his headlong race, and with all the eagerness of a huntsman in the excitement of the chase, or as though he were charging the enemy at the head of a squadron, d'Artagnan found himself, much to his surprise, becoming savage and almost bloodthirsty, notwithstanding his goodwill towards Fouquet. For a long time he raced on without catching sight of the white horse. He was lashed into fury by the thought that, after all, he might have taken the wrong road. He supposed that Fouquet was hidden in a sunken road, or that he had stopped to exchange his white horse for one of those celebrated black chargers, swift as the wind, whose strength and courage d'Artagnan had so often admired enviously when at Saint-Mandé. At these moments, when the sharp wind brought the moisture to his eyes, when the saddle grew hot beneath him, when his horse, spurred to the quick, snorted with pain, and, lashing out with his hind hoofs, made a shower of sand and stones fly behind him, d'Artagnan, rising in his stirrups and seeing nothing upon the water, nothing beneath the trees, would burst into imprecations like a madman. He was taking leave of his senses. In his rage and disappointment mad ideas of means of escape through the air, the invention of later generations, came into his mind – he remembered Daedalus[185] and his artificial wings which had saved him from a Cretan prison. A hoarse sigh broke from his lips. Tortured by the fear of ridicule he kept repeating to himself – 'Great God! can it be that I – *I* have been fooled by Gourville? They will say I am growing old – they will say I have taken a bribe of a million to let Fouquet escape!' And he jammed his spurs into his horse's flank. He had covered a league in two minutes.

Suddenly, at the end of a stretch of pastureland, behind a hedge, he caught sight of a white object which showed itself for an instant, then disappeared, and finally became visible upon a section of higher ground. D'Artagnan experienced an access of joy: his mind instantly became tranquil. He mopped the sweat from his forehead and eased the pressure of his knees to admit of his horse breathing more freely; then he took it somewhat easier, for it was necessary to economise the strength of his partner in this desperate manhunt. He now had leisure to observe the lie of the ground and his position relative to Fouquet.

The minister's animal was pretty well pumped through being ridden over the heavy land. His rider felt the necessity of getting upon sounder ground and turned his horse's head in a line for the highway. D'Artagnan, on his side, had merely to pass the escarpment of a cliff bordering the track, which concealed him from his enemy, in order to cut him off when he reached the road. Then the real race would begin – then would the struggle come to a crisis.

D'Artagnan allowed his horse to recover its wind. He observed that the minister had slackened his pace to a trot – that is to say, he also was nursing his mount. But both were too anxious to get forward to continue long at this pace. As the white horse felt firm ground beneath his hoofs, he sprang forward like an arrow. D'Artagnan shook his bridle, and his black charger broke into a gallop. Both were now on the same road: the fourfold echoes of the horses' hoofs were intermingled, and Fouquet had not yet become aware that he was pursued. But as d'Artagnan passed the ridge where the cliff ended, the echo ceased, yet Fouquet could still hear what seemed to be an echo, but which was in reality the thunder of the hoofs of d'Artagnan's horse. Fouquet turned in his saddle. A hundred paces behind him he saw his enemy, bent low over his horse's neck and approaching like a whirlwind. There was no room for doubt – the shining baldrick and the red tunic revealed the musketeer. Fouquet shook up his white horse, which made a gallant effort and increased the distance between the adversaries by twenty feet. 'Oho!' thought d'Artagnan, rendered a trifle uneasy, 'that is no screw which Monsieur Fouquet is riding – careful, now!' – And with practised eye he examined attentively the shape and action of the famous white charger. Good quarters; tail well set on; plenty of bone; clean, flat legs and a shapely hoof. He spurred his own mount, but the distance between the two remained the same. D'Artagnan listened intently; not a sound could he hear – although he was riding against the wind – which gave any indication that the white horse was distressed. The black horse, on the contrary, began to show symptoms of 'bellows to mend' – 'I must get there if I burst the brute!' thought d'Artagnan. And he settled himself in the saddle and rode him with hand and heel. The gallant animal, by a game effort, reduced the other's lead by twenty yards and brought his rider within pistol-shot of Fouquet. 'Courage!' cried the musketeer; 'Courage! The white horse will be played out soon, perhaps, and even if the nag holds out, his rider may drop from fatigue.' But neither of these alternatives happened, and the leading horse gradually increased his advantage. D'Artagnan fairly yelled with rage, which caused Fouquet, whose horse still gamely struggled on, to look back over his shoulder. 'Grand horse! – and well ridden!' growled the musketeer, surprised into involuntary admiration. 'Hold hard! Damnation! – hold hard, Monsieur Fouquet, in the name of the king!' Fouquet made no reply. 'Do you hear me?' roared d'Artagnan. At that moment his horse stumbled. 'I am not stone deaf,' replied Fouquet sarcastically, catching short hold of his horse's head. D'Artagnan was no longer master of himself; he saw red. 'In the king's name,' he shouted once more, 'stop, or I fire.' – 'Fire away then,' replied Fouquet, still keeping his horse going. D'Artagnan seized one of his pistols and cocked it, hoping that the click of the lock would induce his enemy to alter his mind. 'You are armed too,' he cried; 'defend yourself.' The sound of the pistol did indeed cause Fouquet to turn. Looking d'Artagnan full in the face, he opened with his right hand the cloak which enveloped him, but his hand made no movement in the direction of his holsters. The adversaries were now separated by twenty paces. ' 'Sdeath!' cried d'Artagnan, 'I am not going to murder you! If you refuse to fire at me, surrender! What is imprisonment?' 'I will die sooner,' replied Fouquet, 'my sufferings would be less.' Wild with despair, d'Artagnan hurled his pistol to the ground – 'I will take you alive,' he muttered hoarsely. And by a prodigy of horsemanship, of which that incomparable cavalier was alone capable, he contrived to push his horse within ten paces of the other. Already his hand was stretched out to seize his prey. 'Kill me,' cried Fouquet, 'it will be more merciful.' 'No, alive! I will take you alive!' A second time the captain's horse stumbled; Fouquet once more gained a lead. It was an unheard-of spectacle, this race between two spent horses, only kept going by the superb horsemanship of their riders. Their furious gallop had degenerated into a canter, the canter had slackened to a trot. The pace had equally told upon the two exhausted men. D'Artagnan, at the end of his resources, laid hold of his other pistol and aimed at the white horse. 'Not at you!' he cried to Fouquet – 'at your horse!' He pulled the trigger. The shot struck home in the white horse's flank; he gave a furious plunge and then staggered. D'Artagnan's horse lurched and fell stone dead. 'My honour is lost, I am broken and good for nothing,' thought the musketeer. 'For pity's sake, Monsieur Fouquet,' he shouted, 'throw me one of your pistols and I will blow my brains out.' Fouquet's horse was still on its legs and covering ground. 'For mercy's sake!' cried d'Artagnan; 'what you refuse to do now, I shall do myself in an hour's time; but here, upon this road, I shall die honourably and save my repution. Do me this service, Monsieur Fouquet.'

Fouquet made no reply, and rode on. D'Artagnan began to chase his enemy on foot. Successively he divested himself of his hat, his doublet, which hindered his free movement, then the scabbard of his sword, which kept knocking against his legs. Finally the sword itself, which he held in his hand, became too heavy and he flung it after the scabbard. The white horse began wheezing, and d'Artagnan gained upon him. From a trot, the spent animal sank into a staggering gait, his head shaking with giddiness; his mouth flecked with bloody foam. D'Artagnan made a despairing effort, and hurling himself upon Fouquet, seized him by the leg and gasped out breathlessly – 'I arrest you – king's name – knock me on the head – shall have both done our duty.'

Fouquet threw his pistols away into the river – the pistols which d'Artagnan might have used upon himself, and flinging himself off his horse, 'I am your prisoner, sir,' he said, 'will you take my arm, for I think you are going to faint?'

'Thank you,' faltered d'Artagnan, who, in fact, felt the earth slipping from under his feet and the sky falling upon his head. He rolled over upon the ground, utterly spent. Fouquet descended the slope to the brink of the river, filled his hat with water, returned and bathed the musketeer's temples and moistened his lips with a few drops of the cool liquid. D'Artagnan picked himself up and looked around him with a wandering eye. He saw Fouquet kneeling with the wet hat in his hand, greeting him with a smile of genuine goodwill.

'You are not gone then?' he cried. 'Oh! monsieur, the man who is really a king for true nobility is not Louis, at the Louvre, nor Philippe at Sainte-Marguerite – it is you, the condemned outlaw!'

'If I am ruined today, it is by a single error, Monsieur d'Artagnan.'

'Good God! and what is that?'

'I should have had you for a friend. But how are we to get back to Nantes? We are very far away from the town.'

'That is true,' replied d'Artagnan, gloomy and pensive.

'The white horse will perhaps recover sufficiently. Ah! he was a superb animal! Mount him, Monsieur d'Artagnan – I will go on foot until you are rested a little.'

'Poor brute! wounded too!' said the musketeer.

'He will go, I tell you. I know his powers. Better still, we will both mount him.'

'We can try,' said the captain.

But the animal staggered beneath the double burden. He rallied, and paced on for several minutes, then gave a lurch and fell beside the black horse, whose carcass he had managed to reach.

'We must go on foot, since it is decreed – well, it will be a charming walk,' said Fouquet, passing his arm through that of d'Artagnan's.

'*Mordieu!*' cried the latter, his eye fixed, his brow contracted and his heart swelling – 'a day of shame!'

Slowly they trudged the four leagues which separated them from the wood where the carriage lay concealed with its escort. When Fouquet caught sight of this sinister contrivance, he said to d'Artagnan, who lowered his eyes, for he felt himself blushing for his royal master – 'This is an idea, captain, which would never have occurred to a gentleman: it is not your idea. What are these iron gratings for?'

'To prevent you from throwing letters out of the carriage.'

'The notion is ingenious!'

'But if you cannot write, you can speak,' said d'Artagnan.

'May I speak to you?'

'Why, of course – if you wish to.'

Fouquet thought a moment; then looking the captain straight in the face, he said – 'One word only: shall you remember it?'

'I shall remember.'

'Will you tell it to whom I please?'

'I will.'

'Saint-Mandé, is the word,' breathed Fouquet.

'Very good. For whom is it?'

'Either for Madame de Bellière or for Pélisson.'

'It shall be done.'

The carriage traversed the city of Nantes and took the road to Angers.

CHAPTER 69

## Where the squirrel falls and the serpent flies

IT WAS TWO O'CLOCK in the afternoon. The king, consumed with impatience, was pacing to and fro continually between his closet and the terrace, occasionally opening the door leading on to the corridor in order to see what his secretaries were doing. Colbert, seated in the same place which Saint-Aignan had so long occupied that morning, was conversing in a low tone with Monsieur de Brienne. The king opened the door suddenly, and addressing the two, he asked, 'What is it you are discussing?'

'We are speaking about the first sitting of the states-general,' replied Monsieur de Brienne, rising.

'Well and good,' said the king, and returned once more to his room. Five minutes later the sound of his bell summoned Rose, whose turn it was to be in attendance upon the king.

'Have you finished making out the copies?' asked Louis.

'Not yet, sire.'

'Then go and ascertain if Monsieur d'Artagnan has returned.'

'He has not returned yet, sire.'

'Strange!' muttered the king. 'Call Monsieur Colbert.'

Colbert entered; he had been anticipating this moment ever since the morning.

'Monsieur Colbert,' said the king, very sharply, 'I must know what has become of Monsieur d'Artagnan.'

Colbert replied calmly, 'Where would your majesty suggest he should be sought for?'

'What, monsieur, do you mean to say you don't know where I sent him?' cried Louis, irritably.

'Your majesty has not told me.'

'There are some things, sir, which one should guess; and you, above all others, ought to guess.'

'No doubt I have my own ideas, sire; but I should not presume to be positive.' Colbert had scarcely uttered these words, when the dialogue between the monarch and his man of affairs was rudely interrupted by a voice far more energetic than that of the king.

'D'Artagnan!' exclaimed the king, with evident relief.

D'Artagnan entered. He was pale and in furious ill-temper. 'Sire, did your majesty give any orders to my musketeers?' he began.

'What orders?' asked the king.

'With regard to Monsieur Fouquet's house.'

'None,' replied Louis.

'Ha!' cried d'Artagnan, gnawing his moustache. 'I was not mistaken then; it was this gentleman.' And he nodded towards Colbert.

'What were the orders? Let me hear,' said the king.

'Orders to rummage the whole house – to beat Monsieur Fouquet's servants and officials – to force the drawers – to put a peaceable house to the sack! what the devil! 'tis the behaviour of a savage!'

'Sir!' cried Colbert, who had become very pale.

'Sir,' interrupted d'Artagnan, 'the king alone – the king alone, you understand, has the right to give orders to my musketeers. As for you, I forbid you to order them – and I tell you this in the presence of his majesty. Gentlemen who wear swords are not clerks – you must be taught to distinguish between gentlemen and quill-drivers!'

'D'Artagnan! D'Artagnan!' murmured the king in a tone of deprecation.

'It is shameful!' continued the musketeer; 'my soldiers are dishonoured. I command neither a horde of pillagers nor a parcel of treasury-clerks, mordieu!'

'What is all this about? Let me hear,' said the king, in a tone of authority.

'It is this, sire. This – gentleman, unable to guess your majesty's orders, and therefore unaware that I was engaged in arresting Monsieur Fouquet – this gentleman, I say, who has had an iron cage built for the man who yesterday was his master, has sent Monsieur Roncherat to Monsieur Fouquet's rooms, and for the sake of getting hold of the minister's papers, they have carried away all the furniture. My musketeers have been surrounding the house since the morning. These are the orders I complain of. How dare he presume to give such orders to my men? Why has he been allowed to make my musketeers his accomplices by forcing them to assist in this barbarous pillage? Devil take it! we serve the king, we soldiers, but certainly not Monsieur Colbert!'

'Monsieur d'Artagnan,' said the king, severely, 'take care! It is not in my presence that such explanations should be made, and least of all in that tone.'

'I have only acted as seemed best for the king's interests,' said Colbert, in an agitated voice. 'It is hard that I should be treated in this manner by one of his majesty's officers, and that without the chance of obtaining redress, because of the respect I owe to the king.'

'The respect you owe to the king!' shouted d'Artagnan, his eyes flashing fire. 'Let me tell you, sir, that it consists in making his authority respected and his person beloved. Every agent of an absolute monarch represents his authority, and when the people curse the hand which chastises them, it is the monarch himself who is culpable in God's sight. Do you understand? Must a soldier, hardened by forty years' experience of wounds and bloodshed, read you this lesson, sir? Is all the mercy to be on my side and the ferocity on yours? You have caused the innocent to be arrested, bound and cast into prison!'

'The accomplices of Monsieur Fouquet, perhaps,' said Colbert.

'Who told you that Monsieur Fouquet has any accomplices – or even that he is guilty himself? That is for the king alone to decide; his justice is capable of discovering the guilty. When the king says – "Arrest such and such people," his orders will be obeyed. Do not speak to me of your respect for the king, and be careful of your words if they seem to imply any threat, for the king will not permit those who serve him well to be menaced by those who do him

disservice – and if I served, which God forbid! a master so ungrate-
ful, I myself would teach you to treat me with due respect.'
D'Artagnan drew himself up proudly, with flashing eye, his hand
upon his sword and his lip trembling, affecting even more anger
than he actually felt.

Humiliated, and ready to burst with spleen, Colbert bowed to the
king, as though asking permission to withdraw. Louis, put in a
dilemma between his pride on the one hand, and his curiosity on the
other, knew not which side to take. D'Artagnan saw his hesitation.
To have remained longer would have been a tactical blunder. It was
necessary to obtain a triumph over Colbert, and that could only be
done by forcing the king to extremities so that his majesty should
have no option but to choose between the antagonists. Thereupon
d'Artagnan made his bow to the king as Colbert had done, but Louis,
who was anxious before all things to hear an exact and detailed
account of the arrest of the minister of finance, who, for a moment,
had caused the king to tremble – Louis, we say, understood that
d'Artagnan's anger would oblige him to wait half an hour at least for
the details he was burning to hear. Therefore, forgetting Colbert,
who had no such interesting news to impart, Louis called back his
captain of the musketeers. 'Come, monsieur,' he said, 'let us hear the
result of your commission – you can go and rest afterwards.'

D'Artagnan, who had just reached the doorway, stopped on
hearing the king's voice and retraced his steps. Colbert was forced
to give way. His face grew purple, his black eyes glared savagely
beneath his shaggy eyebrows; he yielded his place, and then having
again bowed to the king, he drew himself up as he passed before
d'Artagnan, and hastily left the room with gall and wormwood in his
heart. D'Artagnan, left with the king, instantly resumed his wonted
composure. 'Sire,' said he, 'you are still a youthful monarch. It is by
the morning sky that one judges whether or not the day will be fine.
What augury, sire, will the people whom God has confided to your
charge, what augury will they draw of your reign if you permit
arbitrary and violent ministers to act between yourself and them? –
But to speak of myself, sire. Let us drop a discussion which may
appear idle to you, or even impertinent. Let us speak of myself. I
have arrested Monsieur Fouquet.'

'And you have taken plenty of time in doing it,' exclaimed Louis
sharply.

D'Artagnan looked at the king a moment. 'I perceive that I have
expressed myself badly,' he said. 'Did I announce to your majesty
that I had arrested Monsieur Fouquet?'

'Yes; well?'

'Well, I should have said to your majesty that Monsieur Fouquet arrested me. I will restate the fact, then; I have been arrested by Monsieur Fouquet.'

The king's astonishment was expressed in his face. With his quick glance, d'Artagnan could appreciate what was passing in the mind of his master. He allowed him no time to frame a question. He related, with a wealth of picturesque detail, of which perhaps he alone, at that period, possessed the art, the story of Fouquet's escape, of the pursuit, the desperate race and, finally, the matchless generosity of the Minster, who, with numberless opportunities of escape or of killing his pursuer, had preferred to suffer imprisonment or worse, rather than to humiliate the man who was sent to deprive him of his liberty. In proportion as the tale advanced, the king's excitement increased; he listened with breathless interest to the musketeer's words – 'All this leads me to the conclusion, sire, that one who acts in this manner is a gallant man, and cannot be an enemy to the king. That, I repeat to your majesty, is the opinion I have formed. I know that the king will tell me – "reasons of state", and I bow to this decision – in my eyes it is worthy of all respect. Still, I am a soldier; I have received my orders and the orders are carried out – much against my will, I confess – but none the less thoroughly. I say no more.'

'Where is Monsieur Fouquet at the present moment?' asked Louis after a moment's silence.

'Monsieur Fouquet, sire, is inside the iron cage which Monsieur Colbert had made for him and rolling along the road towards Angers behind four strong horses.'

'Why did you leave him on the road?'

'Because your majesty gave me no orders to accompany him to Angers. The proof – the best proof I could have – is that the king was expecting me just now. And besides, I had another reason.'

'What was it?'

'So long as I was there, poor Monsieur Fouquet would have made no effort to escape.'

'Well?' cried the king, greatly taken aback.

'Your majesty must well understand that my dearest wish is to see Monsieur Fouquet at liberty. I left him under the charge of one of my subalterns – the biggest blunderhead I could find among all my musketeers – in order to give the prisoner a chance of escaping.'

'Are you mad, d'Artagnan?' cried the king, exasperated. 'Does one say such insane things, even if one has the temerity to think them?'

'Ah! Sire, you cannot surely expect me to regard Monsieur Fouquet as an enemy after all that he has done for me and for you? No, sire; never give me the duty of guarding him if you are anxious for him to remain in durance, for however strongly his cage may have been built, the matter would finish by the bird flying away.'

'I am surprised,' said the king in a tone of resentment, 'that you did not follow the fortunes of the man whom Fouquet attempted to seat on my throne. You would have received from him all that you desire – affection and gratitude. In my service, monsieur, you find only a master.'

'If Monsieur Fouquet had not gone to seek you in the Bastille, sire,' replied d'Artagnan, letting his words fall with impressive clearness, 'there is but one man who would have gone, and that man is myself. You know it right well, sire.'

The king checked himself. He had nothing to reply to these words, so frankly spoken and so true. In listening to his captain of musketeers, Louis recalled the d'Artagnan of former days who, at the Palais-Royal, had remained behind the curtain of the king's bed when the populace of Paris, led by the cardinal de Retz, had come to assure themselves of the king's presence; the d'Artagnan beside the carriage door, to whom he had waved his hand as he was repairing to Notre-Dame, on his return to Paris; the soldier who had quitted him at Blois; the lieutenant whom he had recalled to his presence when Mazarin's death had put the reins of government in his hands; the man whom he had always found brave, loyal and devoted. Louis went to the door and summoned Colbert. Colbert had not quitted the corridor where the the secretaries were at work; he at once responded to the king's call.

'Colbert, you have ordered a domiciliary visit to Monsieur Fouquet?'

'Yes, sire.'

'And what is the result?'

'Monsieur Roncherat, who was sent with your majesty's musketeers, has brought me these papers, sire.'

'I will look at them. Now, Monsieur Colbert, give me your hand.'

'My hand, sire?'

'Yes, I wish to place it in that of d'Artagnan. The fact is, d'Artagnan,' he went on, turning with a smile towards the soldier, who at the sight of the man of quills, had resumed his scornful bearing, 'you do not know this man. Make his acquaintance. In inferior positions he is but an indifferent servant, but he will be a great man when I have raised him to the highest rank.'

'Sire!' murmured Colbert, divided between joy and apprehension.

'I understand why,' said d'Artagnan aside to the king; 'he was jealous.'

'Exactly, and jealousy has tied his wings.'

'And now he will become a winged serpent,' growled the Musketeer, who still retained some feeling of resentment against his adversary of an hour ago. But Colbert's expression as he approached the captain had undergone a complete alteration; he wore a look of such good-natured frankness, his eyes took such an expression of rare intelligence, that d'Artagnan, who was a judge of faces, was struck by it, and felt his convictions shaken.

Colbert clasped his hand warmly. 'What his majesty has just said, Monsieur d'Artagnan, proves how well he understands men. The implacable opposition I have today displayed – against abuses, not against individuals – only proves how desirous I am of assuring for my king a glorious reign and for my country an unexampled prosperity. I am full of ideas, Monsieur d'Artagnan; you will be able to see them develop in the sunshine of public peace; and if, unfortunately, I lack the gift of winning the friendship of men of distinction, at any rate I shall know how to obtain their esteem. For their admiration I would give my life.'

This sudden change, this exaltation of his sentiments, together with his majesty's mutely expressed satisfaction, afforded the musketeer matter for deep reflection. He bowed with much civility to Colbert, who had not taken his eyes off him. Seeing the two men reconciled, the king dismissed them, and they went out together. Once outside the room, the newly-appointed minister, laying a hand upon d'Artagnan's arm, said to him, 'Can it be possible, monsieur, that a man of your discernment should not at first glance have recognised me for the man I am?'

'Monsieur Colbert,' replied the musketeer, 'when one has the sun in one's eyes, one fails to notice any common fire, however brightly it may burn. As you know, when a man is invested with authority he shines. Since you are now in that position, why do you continue to persecute one who has fallen into disgrace, and fallen from such a height?'

'Oh! Monsieur d'Artagnan, you mistake – I persecute no one. I wished to administer the finances, and to administer them alone, in the first place because I am ambitious, and then because I have entire confidence in my own ability. As minister of finance, all the revenues of the kingdom will pass through my hands, and the thought is gratifying to me because I know the money is in capable hands, and that not a sou will stick to my fingers if I were to live for another thirty years. With this money under my control, I will build granaries and public works, cities and harbours – I will create a Navy and equip fleets which shall spread the name of France among the farthest nations of the earth; I will institute libraries and found colleges; I will make France the richest and most enlightened country in the world. These are the reasons for my animosity towards Monsieur Fouquet, who prevented me from putting my ideas into execution. And afterwards, when my position is assured and when France is great and powerful, I, in my turn, will cry "Mercy!" '

' "Mercy", did you say? Then ask his liberty of the king. If the king crushes him today, it is on your account.'

Colbert looked at the musketeer mildly. 'You are well aware that is not the case, monsieur,' he said. 'The king has private causes of quarrel against Monsieur Fouquet; it is not for me to teach you that.'

'Time will take the sharp edge off the king's resentment. He will forget.'

'The king never forgets. Monsieur d'Artagnan. Stay, his majesty is calling and is about to give an order. I have not influenced him, have I? Well, listen.'

They heard Louis call one of his secretaries. Then, 'Monsieur d'Artagnan?' said he.

'I am here, your majesty.'

'Let Monsieur de Saint-Aignan take twenty of your musketeers in order to guard Monsieur Fouquet.'

D'Artagnan and Colbert exchanged glances.

'And they will conduct the prisoner from Angers to Paris, and lodge him in the Bastille.'

'You are right,' said the captain to the minister.

'Saint-Aignan,' continued the king, 'you will have anyone shot who may attempt to speak to the prisoner on the road.'

'But myself, sire?'

'You, sir, will only speak to him in the presence of the musketeers.'

The duke bowed, and retired to attend to the carrying-out of the order. D'Artagnan was about to retire also, but the king stopped him.

'Monsieur d'Artagnan,' said he, 'you will set out immediately for Belle-Isle-en-Mer, and you will take possession of the island and the rest of the fief.'

'Very well, sire. Am I to go alone?'

'You will take a sufficient body of troops to enable you to avoid a check should the place hold out.'

An incredulous murmur, flattering to the king's vanity, arose from the group of courtiers.

'That is pretty nearly certain,' said d'Artagnan.

'I saw the place some years ago,' continued the king, 'and I don't care to see it again now. You have my instructions. Go, monsieur, and do not return without the keys of the fortress.'

Colbert approached d'Artagnan. 'An undertaking which will be worth a marshal's baton to you if carried out successfully,' he said.

'Why do you say, "if carried out successfully"?'

'Because it is a difficult undertaking.'

'Indeed! in what way?'

'You have friends in Belle-Isle, Monsieur d'Artagnan, and it is not easy for men of your character to climb into a position over the bodies of their friends.'

D'Artagnan hung down his head, and Colbert returned beside the king. Fifteen minutes later the captain received orders in writing to destroy the fortress of Belle-Isle in case of resistance, together with power of life and death over all the inhabitants or *refugees*, with an injunction not to allow a single one to escape. 'Colbert was quite right,' thought d'Artagnan, 'my marshal's baton seems likely to cost my two friends their lives. Only they appear to forget that my friends are no more stupid than the wild birds that do not wait until the fowler stretches out his hand before taking flight. They shall see the fowler's hand so clearly that they won't remain in any doubt. Poor Porthos! poor Aramis! No, my fortune shall never cost a feather of your wings.'

Having arrived at this conclusion, d'Artagnan went off to muster the royal forces. He ordered the troops to embark at Paimboeuf, and set sail without the loss of a moment.

## CHAPTER 70

## Belle-Isle-en-Mer

AT THE EXTREMITY of the mole, along the raised walk beside which the tide races so furiously, two men were walking arm in arm, conversing freely in animated tones. Not a human being could hear their words, for they were carried away as they passed their lips by violent gusts of wind mingled with stinging spindrift. The sun had just set redly beneath the ocean, which glowed with the dull fire of a red-hot crucible. From time to time one of the two men turned towards the east and threw a look of anxious enquiry across the sea. The other, studying his companion's face, seemed to be trying to guess the meaning of his anxiety. A silence fell between them. Each occupied with his own gloomy thoughts, they resumed their walk. No doubt everyone will have recognised in these two men our proscribed and exiled heroes, Porthos and Aramis. Their hopes blighted by the downfall of Monsieur d'Herblay's gigantic schemes, they had fled for refuge to Belle-Isle-en-Mer.

'You may say what you will, my dear Aramis,' Porthos repeated, taking a deep breath of the salty air and expanding his powerful chest – 'you may say what you will, Aramis, but I'm sure that there is something extraordinary about this total disappearance, within the last two days, of all the fishing boats which left the harbour. There has been no storm at sea. The weather has remained calm all through – hardly a breeze – and even if we had had a tempest, *all* the boats wouldn't have sunk. I say once more, it is very strange; and this total disappearance astonishes me, let me tell you.'

'True,' muttered Aramis, 'you are right, friend Porthos. There is something at the bottom of this, I am convinced.'

'And then again,' added Porthos, whose ideas, after receiving the support of the Bishop of Vannes, seemed to expand, 'have you noticed that if the boats have gone down, not a single plank has been washed up on the shore?'

'I have noticed that also.'

'You may have remarked too that the only two boats remaining in the whole island, which I sent out to get news of the others – '

At this point Aramis interrupted his campanion by a cry and

movement so sharp that Porthos stopped short with his mouth open.

'What is that you say, Porthos! What! you have sent away the two boats – '

'To look for the others, yes, certainly,' replied Porthos with the utmost simplicity.

'Unhappy man! what have you done? Then we are lost!' cried Aramis.

'Lost? – what's that?' exclaimed Porthos, alarmed. 'Why *lost*, Aramis? How are we lost?'

Aramis bit his lip. 'Nothing – nothing at all. Forgive me – I meant to say – '

'What?'

'That if we had had an idea of taking a trip to sea this would prevent it.'

'Good! So that is what vexes you? A nice amusement, upon my word! For my part, I'm not at all sorry. What I regret is not a trifle of amusement more or less to be had in Belle-Isle. What I do regret, Aramis, is Pierrefonds, and Bracieux, and Le Vallon – my beautiful France. One is no longer in France, here, my dear friend. This is an outlandish place. Yes, Aramis, I may speak freely to you, and your affection will excuse my frankness. I feel that I must tell you I am not happy in Belle-Isle. No, truly, I am not happy here.'

Aramis stifled a sigh. 'Dear friend,' he said, 'that is why it is such a great pity you have sent away the last two boats to look for the others which have been missing for the last few days. If you had sent them to make discoveries, we could have gone away in them.'

'Gone away, Aramis? But what about our orders?'

'What orders?'

'Why, the orders you have so often repeated to me; that we are to hold Belle-Isle against the usurper. You know quite well.'

'True,' muttered Aramis again.

'Therefore you see, my dear Aramis, we cannot go away. So that we are no worse off because of those two boats being sent to look for the others.'

Aramis was silent. His glance, clear as that of a sea-bird, hovered long over the surface of the sea, interrogating space and trying to pierce the horizon.

'For all that, Aramis,' continued Porthos, who clung to his idea, the more tenaciously that the bishop had confirmed its soundness, 'for all that, you do not explain what has happened to those unfortunate boats. Whichever way I turn, I am greeted with shouts and complaints. Even the children begin crying when they see their mothers in grief. As if I could bring back their fathers – their absent husbands! What do you think is the cause of it, Aramis, and what am I to reply to them?'

'We may suppose anything, my good Porthos, but we must say nothing.'

Porthos was not at all satisfied with this reply. He turned away in ill-humour, growling to himself. Aramis stopped the valiant soldier before he had gone many paces. 'Do you remember,' he said, in a tone of gentle melancholy, clasping the giant's hands with affectionate cordiality in his own, 'do you remember, friend Porthos, in the glorious days of our youth, when we were strong and valiant, the other two and ourselves – do you remember, Porthos, what we should have done if we had ever had a strong wish to return to France – would this little strip of salt water have prevented us?'

'Oh!' cried Porthos, 'it is six leagues, don't forget!'

'If you had seen me get astride a plank, would you have remained on shore, Porthos?'

'No, by heavens! no, Aramis! But nowadays, what a big plank we should want, my dear friend; I, especially!' And the Lord of Bracieux, glancing proudly at his colossal figure, burst out laughing. 'And do you seriously tell me that you are not tired of Belle-Isle? Wouldn't you sooner be on your pleasant estate – in your episcopal palace at Vannes? Come, confess frankly.'

'No,' replied Aramis, but without daring to look at Porthos.

'We will stay where we are then,' said his friend, a loud sigh escaping from his breast in spite of his efforts to restrain it. 'Yes, we will stay. Still,' he added, 'if we really wished – if we decidedly wanted – well, if we had absolutely determined – quite made up our minds, if you understand me, to return to France, and there were no boats – '

'Have you noticed another thing, dear friend? I mean that during the last two days, since the fishing boats disappeared, not a single rowing boat has come ashore on the island.'

'Yes, it is true – you are right. I have noticed it also, for it is quite noticeable. Before these last two fatal days boats of every description kept arriving in shoals.'

'I must obtain information,' cried Aramis, suddenly, in a tone of decision. 'Perhaps it would be as well to have a raft built.'

'But we have one or two little rowing-boats, my dear Aramis. Would you like me to take one of them and go – '

'A little boat! Don't think of it, Porthos. It would be upset. No, no,' replied the Bishop of Vannes, 'you are not built for balancing yourself upon a knife blade. Let us wait a little.'

And Aramis continued to pace to and fro with every sign of increasing uneasiness.

Porthos grew weary of watching the nervous movements of his friend. Porthos, with his placid and trustful disposition, could understand nothing of his friend's apparent exasperation of nerves, which manifested itself by continual restlessness. 'Come and sit down on this rock, Aramis,' he said; 'come and sit here beside me, and let me ask you just once more to explain to me quietly, in such a way that I can understand it, what it is we are doing here.'

'Porthos – ' began Aramis, in a tone of constraint.

'I know that the false king wanted to dethrone the true king. So far, so good. I quite understand that.'

'Yes,' said Aramis.

'Then I know the false king had planned to sell Belle-Isle to the English. That, again, I understand perfectly.'

'Yes.'

'And, of course, I know that we engineers and captains came here to throw ourselves into Belle-Isle in order to superintend the works and take over the command of the ten companies of recruits who are in the pay of Monsieur Fouquet, or rather, the ten companies commanded by his daughter's husband. I am perfectly clear upon all that.' Aramis jumped up impatiently, like a lion worried by a gnat. Porthos held him back by the arm.'But what I can't understand, in spite of deep reflection, what I shall never understand – is why, instead of sending us reinforcements, instead of sending us fresh troops, stores and ammunition, they leave us without boats – they abandon Belle-Isle altogether – not a soul comes near us. Instead of keeping open the communications, either by signals or by written or verbal messages, they allow all our letters to be intercepted. Tell me what it means, Aramis, or rather, before you answer me, shall I tell you what I think myself? Shall I tell you the idea which has struck me – what I have imagined?' The bishop raised his head wearily. 'Well, Aramis,' continued Porthos, 'I thought, I had an idea, it struck me that something must have happened in France. I was dreaming about Monsieur Fouquet all last night, and I dreamed besides about dead fish and broken eggs and badly built and poorly furnished rooms. Bad dreams, my dear d'Herblay! You will admit that it is unlucky to have such dreams!'

'Porthos, what is that over yonder?' interrupted Aramis, rising to his feet suddenly and pointing out to his friend a black spot upon the purple line where sea and sky met.

'It is a boat!' said Porthos. 'Yes, it is undoubtedly a boat. Ah! now we shall have some news.'

'Two of them!' cried the bishop, pointing to another mast visible over the horizon. 'Two! three! four!'

'Five!' cried Porthos, in his turn. 'Six! – seven! Good heavens! it is a fleet!'

'Our fishing-boats returning, no doubt,' said Aramis, who, notwithstanding his affected composure, felt seriously uneasy.

'They are very large for fishing-boats,' observed Porthos, 'and then again, if you notice they are coming from the mouth of the Loire.'

'They are coming from the Loire – yes.'

'See, all the people here have seen them as well; here they come, women and children, flocking on the jetty to meet their husbands and fathers.'

An old fisherman went by.

'Are those our boats?' asked Aramis.

The old salt screwed up his eyes and looked hard at the horizon. 'No, your eminence,' he replied, 'they are cutters belonging to the royal service.'

'Ah!' cried Aramis, with a start, 'how do you know that?'

'By the flag.'

'But,' said Porthos, 'the boat itself is barely visible; then how the deuce can you distinguish the flag?'

'I see that there is one,' replied the old man; 'our own boats and the trading luggers carry no flag. Craft of the sort yonder are what they generally use for transporting troops.'

'Ah!' cried Aramis.

'Hurrah!' cried Porthos, 'they are sending us reinforcements. Isn't that it, Aramis?'

'It is very probable.'

'Unless perhaps it is the English coming.'

'By way of the Loire? That would be a grave misfortune for France, for they would have had to come by way of Paris!'

'You are right; then certainly they must be reinforcements – or supplies.'

Aramis rested his head in his hands and made no reply. After a moment's silence, he said suddenly – 'Porthos, have the alarm sounded.'

'The alarm? – Do you really think so?'

'Yes, and let the gunners take their stations in the batteries – let every man be at his gun, and especially in the forts along the coast.'

Porthos opened his eyes in astonishment. He stared at his friend as though to convince himself that he had not taken leave of his senses.

'I will go myself, Porthos,' continued Aramis, in his gentlest tones; 'I will go and see to these orders myself if you don't wish to go, my dear friend.'

'Why, I'm going this very instant!' said Porthos, and went off to give the necessary directions, not, however, without some backward glances to ascertain if the Bishop of Vannes had been mistaken, or to see if, having returned to his right senses, Aramis would call him back.

The alarm was raised. The air was pierced by the notes of bugles; drums sounded, and the great bell began tolling clamorously. A crowd of soldiers and idlers promptly gathered on the mole. Artillerymen, stationed behind their big guns whose grinning muzzles peeped through their emplacements of solid masonry, held their matches ready lit. When at last every man was at his post, when every preparation for the defence had been completed, Porthos returned beside Aramis and murmured timidly in the bishop's ear – 'Will you permit me now, my dear friend, to try if I can understand?'

'Nay, Porthos, my dear fellow, you will understand only too soon,' was the bishop's reply to the question of his lieutenant.

'The fleet which is approaching yonder – those ships under full sail which are heading straight for the harbour – it is a royal fleet, is it not?'

'Yes, but as there are two kings in France, Porthos, to which of the two do you suppose this fleet belongs?'

'Ah! now you open my eyes,' replied the giant, quite satisfied by this argument. And Porthos, thus enlightened – or rather, still further plunged into the dark by his friend – hurried off to the batteries to direct the defences, and to exhort every man to do his duty.

Meanwhile, Aramis, his eye constantly fixed on the horizon, watched the vessels approaching. The populace and the soldiers, whose duties did not call them elsewhere, climbed to the tops of the hills and clambered upon every pinnacle of rock, whence they could distinguish the masts of the vessels. Soon the hulls rose into view, with the royal standard of France flying at the peak. Night had already fallen when the foremost vessel of the fleet, whose approach had caused so great a stir among the inhabitants of Belle-Isle, came within gunshot, and lay to, broadside on to the fortress. In spite of the gathering gloom, figures could be discerned in brisk movement on board the vessel. Soon a boat was lowered and pushed off from the ship's side, and the sailors, leaning to their oars, pulled away in the direction of the harbour. A few moments more and the boat was beached beneath the fortress. One of the men sprang upon the mole, and came forward with a letter in his hand, which he waved in the air, as though asking to whom he was to deliver it. The man was promptly recognised by the soldiers. He was one of the pilots belonging to the island – the owner of one of the two boats retained by Aramis, but which Porthos, in his anxiety respecting the fate of the fishermen who had disappeared two days before, had sent in search of the missing boats.

He asked to be taken to Monsieur d'Herblay. At a sign from the sergeant, he was placed between two soldiers and escorted to where Aramis was standing upon the quay. It was now almost dark, in spite of torches carried by the soldiers, who were following some little distance behind Aramis as he went his rounds.

'What! is that you, Jonathan? whom do you come from?'

'Your eminence, I have been sent by those people over there who captured me.'

'Who was it captured you?'

'Well, your eminence, you know we was sent to look for our mates?'

'Yes, well?'

'Well, your eminence, we was scarce a league off shore before we was caught by one of the king's cutters.'

'Which king?' asked Porthos. Jonathan the pilot stared.

'Go on, what next?' said the bishop.

'As I was saying, your eminence, we was took, and put among those men what was caught yesterday morning.'

'They seem to have quite a mania for capturing people,' interrupted Porthos.

'It was so as we shouldn't come and tell you, sir.'

Porthos was no further enlightened by this answer – 'And so they are releasing you today?' he asked.

'Just so as I can come and tell you we was took.'

'Things are getting worse and worse,' thought honest Porthos.

Meanwhile, Aramis had been thinking. 'Then a royal fleet is blockading the coast?' he said.

'Yes, your eminence.'

'Under whose command?'

'Under the command of the captain of the king's musketeers.'

'D'Artagnan?'

'D'Artagnan!' echoed Porthos.

'I think that's what the gentleman was called.'

'And it was he who gave you this letter?'

'Yes, your eminence.'

'Bring your torches nearer.'

'It is d'Artagnan's handwriting,' said Porthos.

Aramis read with one glance the following words:

> Order of the king to take Belle-Isle; to secure the garrison or to put every man to the sword in case of resistance. Signed, D'ARTAGNAN, who, two days ago, arrested Monsieur Fouquet, now in the Bastille.

Aramis grew pale and crumpled the paper in his hand.

'What is it?' asked Porthos.

'Nothing, my friend, nothing!'

'I say, Jonathan – '

'Sir!'

'Have you spoken to Monsieur d'Artagnan?'

'Yes, your honour,'

'What did he say?'

'He said he would tell you more about it when he saw you himself.'

'Where does he wish to see me?'

'On board.'

'On board?' repeated Porthos.

'The captain, he says, I was to put you in my boat and take you aboard.'

'Come on, then,' said Porthos. 'Dear old d'Artagnan.'

Aramis stopped him. 'Are you mad?' he cried. 'How do you know this is not a trap?'

'Of the other king?' said Porthos sagaciously.

'A trap, anyhow! no more need be said, friend Porthos.'

'H'm! it is possible. What are we to do, then? But still, if d'Artagnan asks us to go – '

'How do you know it is d'Artagnan?'

'Ah! then you – but his handwriting – '

'Handwriting can be imitated. I am sure this is a forgery; see, it is shaky.'

'You are always right; but still, we don't really know anything.'

Aramis was silent.

'True,' said the excellent Porthos, 'we don't need to know anything.'

'What am I to do, your honours?' asked Jonathan.

'You will go back to the captain, and you will tell him that we shall be glad if he will come here himself.'

'I understand,' said Porthos.

'Yes, your eminence, but supposing the captain won't come to Belle-Isle?'

'If he refuses, we have guns, and we will make use of them.'

'Against d'Artagnan?'

'If it be d'Artagnan, he will come, Porthos. You may go, Jonathan, you may go.'

'Upon my honour, I can't understand anything at all about it,' murmured Porthos, plaintively.

'You shall understand all, dear friend, the moment has come. Take a seat on this gun carriage, and give me your whole attention.'

'Oh! I am listening, *pardieu*. Leave that to me!'

'Am I to go, then, your honours?' asked Jonathan.

'Yes, go; and come back with an answer. Let the boat pass, you men!'

The boat pulled off to rejoin the vessel. Aramis took Porthos by the hand, and began his explanations.

CHAPTER 71

## *Aramis explains*

'WHAT I HAVE TO TELL YOU, friend Porthos, will probably surprise you, but will instruct you also.'

'I love being surprised,' said Porthos, with placid good-humour. 'You can't overdo it. I can stand a great deal of emotion, so don't be afraid – speak out.'

'It is not easy, Porthos, it is far from easy; for, in truth, I warn you a second time, I have very strange – very extraordinary things to tell you.'

'Oh! you speak so well, my dear friend; I could listen to you for whole days. Then pray speak out, and – stay, I have an idea; to render it easier for you – to help you to tell these strange things you speak about, I will ask you questions.'

'I shall be very pleased.'

'Why are we going to fight, dear Aramis?'

'If you ask many questions of that sort – if this is your way of rendering my task of confession easier for me, Porthos, you will not help me at all. On the contrary, you have exactly hit upon the difficulty. Ah! I perceive that, with a kind-hearted, generous and devoted man such as you are, I owe it to such a friend as well as to myself, to confess my fault bravely. My good friend Porthos, I have deceived you.'

'You have deceived me?'

'To my sorrow, it is true.'

'Was it for my good, Aramis.'

'I sincerely believed so, Porthos.'

'In that case,' cried the worthy Lord of Bracieux, 'you have rendered me a service, and I thank you. If you had not deceived me, I should probably have deceived myself. But how have you deceived me? Tell me.'

'Inasmuch as I was serving the usurper, against whom Louis XIV is directing all his efforts at this moment.'

'The usurper?' said Porthos, scratching his head, 'that is – I don't understand any too well, even now.'

'He is one of the two kings who were disputing the crown of France.

'Very good! – Then you are serving the one who is not Louis XIV.'

'You have hit upon the truth at the first word.'

'And the result is – ?'

'The result is that we are rebels, my poor friend.'

'The deuce we are!' cried Porthos, considerably crestfallen.

'Oh! but, do not be alarmed, my dear Porthos, we will yet find a means of putting ourselves right, trust me.'

'That is not what troubles me,' replied Porthos; 'it is that ugly word *rebels* – that's where I feel the rub.'

'Oh! as to that – '

'And then again, that dukedom I was promised – '

'It was the usurper who would have bestowed it.'

'It is not the same thing, Aramis,' said Porthos, with dignity.

'My dear friend, if it only rested with me, you should be a prince.'

Porthos began gloomily biting his nails. 'That is where you did wrong to deceive me; for having been promised this dukedom, I was counting upon it. Oh! yes, I counted upon it seriously, knowing you to be a man of your word, my dear Aramis.'

'Poor Porthos! Forgive me, I implore you.'

'So then,' continued Porthos, without replying to the bishop's prayer, 'so then I have quite broken with King Louis XIV.'

'Oh! I will arrange all that, my excellent Porthos, I will arrange all that.'

'Aramis, my dear fellow!'

'No, no, Porthos, I beg you, let me act first. No false generosity, Porthos! This is no time to show your devotion to me! You know nothing of my plans. You have done nothing of your own accord. With me it is different. I alone am the instigator of the plot. I needed my inseparable companion. I called upon you and you came to me at once, remembering our old compact, "Each for all, and all for each". Where I have committed the crime is in having been egotistical.'

'Now that is a word I like,' said Porthos. 'Since you have acted solely for yourself, it is impossible to blame you for what has happened to me. It is natural!' And with sublime self-forgetfulness, Porthos pressed his friend's hand warmly. In contrast with such simple greatness of soul, Aramis realised his own meanness. For the second time he was obliged to bend before this manifest superiority of heart, so much more powerful in human affairs than mere brilliance of intellect. He cordially responded to his friend's hearty grip, but found no words to reply.

'And now,' said Porthos, 'that our explanation has been made – now that I know the exact position in which we stand with regard to King Louis, I think, my dear friend, it is time for you to try to make me understand the political intrigue of which we are the victims; for I see quite plainly that there is some political intrigue at the bottom of it all.'

'My good Porthos, d'Artagnan will be here soon, and he will give you all the details. You will excuse me if I say no more – I am overwhelmed with grief, and I have need of all my acumen and presence of mind to extricate you from the serious position into which I have unwisely led you. Louis XIV has henceforth but one enemy – myself. I have made you a prisoner; you followed me, but today I set you free. You will return to your allegiance. You may see for yourself, Porthos, that there is no difficulty standing in the way to prevent you.'

'Do you think so?' said Porthos.

'I am certain of it.'

'Then why,' said Porthos, and here spoke his sound common-sense, 'then why, if the position is so simple, why, my dear friend, are we preparing guns, muskets and warlike engines of all sorts? It would be far simpler, it seems to me, to say to Captain d'Artagnan – "My dear friend, we have made a mistake, but it can be rectified; open the door to us, let us pass, and good-day to you!" '

'H'm!' muttered Aramis, shaking his head.

'What! you don't approve of my plan?'

'I certainly see one obstacle.'

'What is that?'

'Suppose d'Artagnan is acting under orders which will force us to defend ourselves?'

'What! defend ourselves against d'Artagnan? Nonsense! Dear old d'Artagnan!'

Again Aramis shook his head. 'Porthos,' said he, 'if I have had the matches lighted and the guns laid – if I have ordered the tocsin to be sounded and summoned every man to his post upon the ramparts – these splendid ramparts of Belle-Isle, which you have so well fortified – you may rest assured it was for some good reason. Wait, and judge for yourself. Or rather, do not wait – '

'What is to be done?'

'If I knew, friend Porthos, I should have told you.'

'But there is something we can do far more simple than holding this place. We can take a boat, and hey! for France!'

'My dear friend,' said Aramis, smiling sadly, 'let us not reason like children. Let us show ourselves men both in our plans and in their execution. Stay; someone is hailing the quay. Steady now, Porthos, steady!'

Porthos approached the parapet. 'It is d'Artagnan, no doubt,' he roared in a voice of thunder.

'It is I!' replied the captain of the musketeers, springing lightly upon the steps of the mole. And he ran up the steps quickly towards the little esplanade where his two friends were awaiting him. As he came towards them, Porthos and Aramis could distinguish an officer following immediately behind d'Artagnan. Halfway up the stairs leading to the esplanade, d'Artagnan stopped. His companion stopped also – 'Order your people to draw back out of earshot,' cried d'Artagnan to Porthos and Aramis.

The order, given by Porthos, was immediately executed. Then d'Artagnan, turning to the man who followed him, said, 'Monsieur, we are no longer on board the king's ships where, relying upon your orders, you spoke to me so impertinently just now.'

'Sir,' replied the officer, 'I am very far from wishing to be impertinent. I was simply, if strictly, obeying commands. I was ordered to follow you, and I am following you. I was told not to allow you to communicate with anybody without full knowledge on my part. That is why I interfere in your negotiations with the enemy.'

D'Artagnan trembled with rage, and Porthos and Aramis, who had heard this dialogue, trembled also, but with apprehension. D'Artagnan gnawed his moustaches, with him a sure sign that he was exasperated almost beyond bounds. He retraced his steps and drew close to the officer. 'Sir,' he said, in a quiet tone which from its very restraint was all the more impressive and threatened a formidable explosion of wrath, 'Sir, when I sent off a boat, you wished to know what I was writing to the defenders of Belle-Isle. You showed me your authorisation, and I instantly showed you the note I had written. When the boatman returned, you heard every word of the reply sent me by those two gentlemen yonder. All that was well within your orders, and I threw no obstacle in the way of your following out your instructions. Is that not the case?'

'Yes, sir,' stammered the officer, 'yes, no doubt, sir; but – '

'Sir,' continued d'Artagnan, with rising anger, 'when I expressed my intention of leaving my vessel to come across to Belle-Isle, you insisted upon accompanying me. You are in Belle-Isle, are you not?'

'Yes, sir, but – '

'I will hear no *buts*! It is no longer a question of Monsieur Colbert or of anybody else alive who may have given you these orders. It is only a question of a man getting in the way of Monsieur d'Artagnan – and who finds himself alone with Monsieur d'Artagnan on a flight of slippery steps with six fathoms of salt water below them. An awkward position for such a man, sir, an awkward position, let me tell you!'

'But, sir, if I am in your way,' expostulated the officer timidly, his voice shaking with fear, 'it is my duty which – '

'Sir, you have had the misfortune – you, or those who send you – to insult me. That is done. I cannot seek redress from your employers. They are unknown to me, or are out of my reach. But I have you under my hands, and I swear that if you lift a foot to follow me when I mount these stairs – as my name is d'Artagnan, I will run you through and throw your body into the sea. Now I have warned you. I have been angry only six times in my life, and on the other five occasions I have killed my man.'

The officer made no movement. He grew pale under this formidable threat, but replied simply – 'you do wrong, sir, to go against my orders.'

Porthos and Aramis on the parapet above, who had listened to this dialogue with keen interest, shouted to the musketeer – 'Take care, d'Artagnan, take care!'

D'Artagnan silenced them with a gesture, then with terrifying calmness took a step forward, and turned round, sword in hand, to see if the officer would follow him. The latter crossed himself and stepped forward also. Porthos and Aramis, who knew their d'Artagnan, gave a cry and rushed down to try to stop the blow which they believed they could already hear.

But d'Artagnan, slipping his sword into his left hand, said to the officer with a ring of genuine emotion in his voice – 'Sir, you are a brave man. You should better understand what I am about to tell you than what I have just been saying.'

'Speak, Monsieur d'Artagnan, speak,' replied the gallant officer.

'Those gentlemen whom you see, and against whom your orders are directed, are my friends.'

'I know it.'

'You will judge then if I can act towards them as your orders direct.'

'I appreciate your reservations.'

'Then permit me to speak to them without witnesses.'

'Monsieur d'Artagnan, were I to do as you ask, I should be breaking my word; but were I to refuse, I should be disobliging you. I prefer the former alternative. Speak with your friends, and do not think the worse of me if I consent, for the sake of a man whom I admire and esteem, and for his sake alone, to neglect my plain duty.'

D'Artagnan was touched by the officer's generosity. He thanked him with a hearty clasp of the hand and went up to his friends, while the officer, wrapped in his cloak, sat down upon the steps overgrown with damp seaweed.

'Well,' said d'Artagnan to his friends, 'you see the position I am in.' All three embraced one another with the ardour of days long gone by – the golden days of youth, when life was sweet and friendship sacred.

'What do all these precautions signify?' asked Porthos.

'You ought to have some inkling of their meaning, my dear friend,' replied d'Artagnan.

'Very little, I assure you, my dear captain, for really, I have done nothing – nor Aramis either,' the excellent fellow hastened to add.

D'Artagnan darted a look of reproach at the prelate, which penetrated that hardened heart. 'Dear good fellow, Porthos,' murmured the Bishop of Vannes.

'You see what has been done,' said d'Artagnan. 'Everybody and everything coming from or going to Belle-Isle has been intercepted. All your boats have been seized. If you had attempted flight you would have been captured by one of the cruisers which are sailing about in all directions on the lookout for you. The king has made up his mind to have you, and have you he will.' And d'Artagnan tugged at his grey moustaches savagely. Aramis became gloomy and Porthos angry. 'My idea was this,' continued d'Artagnan: 'to get you both on board my vessel, to have you near me, and then set you at liberty. But now, how am I to know that when I return on board, I shall not be superseded by the king's orders, and that the man who takes over the command will not dispose of you in such a way as to leave me no chance of helping you?'

'We must remain in Belle-Isle,' said Aramis with decision, 'and I warn you, we shall give a good account of ourselves.'

Porthos said nothing. D'Artagnan noticed his friend's silence. 'I must see what can be done with this officer – this brave fellow who accompanies me. His plucky resistance pleases me greatly, for it proves he is a man of honour, and although he is opposed to us, he is infinitely more to be trusted than a coward, however accommodating he might have shown himself. We can try, and at any rate we shall learn how far his orders permit him to use his own discretion.'

'Try,' said Aramis.

D'Artagnan walked to the parapet, and leaning over, called to the officer, who at once came up.

'Sir,' said the captain, after the cordial exchange of compliments natural between gentlemen who know and appreciate each other's worth; 'Sir, if I were to take these two gentlemen back with me, what would you do?'

'I should have no personal objection to raise, sir, but as I have formal and precise orders to guard them carefully, I should be compelled to treat them as prisoners.'

'Ah!' cried d'Artagnan.

'That clinches it,' said Aramis gloomily.

Porthos made no remark.

'However, you can take Porthos with you,' said the Bishop of Vannes. 'He will find a means of convincing the king – with my help and your own, d'Artagnan, that he had nothing to do with this affair.'

'H'm!' muttered d'Artagnan. 'Will you come, Porthos? Will you trust yourself with me? The king's clemency is great.'

'I ask time to reflect,' said Porthos, nobly.

'You mean to stay here, then?'

'Until you have fresh orders,' interposed the bishop, quickly.

'Until some fresh idea strikes us,' replied d'Artagnan. 'I don't think it will be long, for I have an idea already.'

'Well, we must say farewell,' rejoined Aramis. 'But really, my dear Porthos, you ought to go.'

'No!' replied Porthos, laconically.

'As you please,' replied Aramis, upon whom his companion's

morose tone jarred slightly, for he was in a nervously irritable state. 'Only I am reassured by the promise of an idea from d'Artagnan – an idea which I fancy I have guessed.'

'Let's see,' said the musketeer, inclining his ear, into which the bishop spoke a few rapid words. 'You have hit it exactly.'

'Then it can hardly fail,' cried Aramis, cheerfully.

'Take care of yourself during the first excitement which this plan will cause, Aramis.'

'Oh! don't be alarmed!'

'And now, sir,' said d'Artagnan, turning to the officer, 'accept my sincere thanks. You have made three friends for life, whatever happens.'

'Yes,' said Aramis. Porthos alone said nothing, but testified his concurrence by a nod.

Having tenderly embraced his two old friends, d'Artagnan quitted Belle-Isle with the inseparable companion with whom Colbert had provided him. Except for the partial explanation with which the worthy Porthos had been willing to remain satisfied, there was no apparent change in the situation with regard to either party. But, as Aramis had said, there was always d'Artagnan's idea to be counted upon. The captain of musketeers did not return on board without elaborating in his mind the scheme he had hit upon. Now, we know that when d'Artagnan gave his mind to a problem, he was accustomed to find a solution to it. His friend the officer maintained a respectful silence, and left him full leisure for meditation. As a result, by the time the captain had set foot on board his vessel anchored within gunshot of Belle-Isle, he had thoroughly matured his plans. He immediately called a council of war, composed of the officers who were serving under his orders. These officers were eight in number, viz., a captain of the fleet; a major in charge of the artillery; an engineer; the officer of whom we have spoken, and four lieutenants. The council being assembled in the aftercabin, d'Artagnan rose, took off his hat, and began in these terms: 'Gentlemen, I have been to reconnoitre Belle-Isle-en-Mer and I found the garrison in considerable strength. More than that, they are well supplied and are prepared to offer a resistance which may give us some trouble. I therefore intend sending for two of the principal officers of the garrison to discuss the matter with us. By having them separated from their troops and their guns we shall be able to make a better bargain with them, especially with the arguments we are in a position to use. Do you agree with me, gentlemen?'

The major of artillery got upon his feet. 'Sir,' he began, respectfully but firmly, after a preliminary cough, 'you have just said that the place is disposed to offer a troublesome resistance. That is to say the garrison has decided upon open rebellion.'

D'Artagnan was visibly put out by this reply. However, he was not the man to be checked by a trifle, so he resumed. 'Sir,' he said, 'your observation is a just one. But you must not forget that Monsieur Fouquet is feudal lord of Belle-Isle-en-Mer, and that the lords of Belle-Isle have the privilege, conferred upon them by the ancient kings, of arming their vassals.' The major made a movement. 'Oh! do not interrupt me,' continued d'Artagnan. 'You were going to say that the right of arming against the English is no excuse for taking up arms against the king. But I am at liberty to suppose that it is not Monsieur Fouquet who is holding Belle-Isle at the present moment, since I arrested Monsieur Fouquet the day before yesterday. Now, the people of Belle-Isle and the garrison have heard nothing of his arrest. It would be quite useless for you to announce it to them. It is a thing so unheard of, so extraordinary and unexpected, that they would never believe you. A Breton serves but one master – his feudal lord – and he serves that master until he has seen him dead. Now, so far as I am aware, the Bretons have not yet seen Monsieur Fouquet's corpse. Therefore it is not surprising that they hold the place against everybody who is not Monsieur Fouquet or who does not hold his signature.' The major bowed in token of assent. 'That is why,' continued d'Artagnan, 'that is why I propose to bring two of the principal officers of the garrison on board this vessel. They will meet you gentlemen – they will see the strong force we have at our disposal – and consequently they will be able to judge of the fate in store for them in case of contumacy. We can convince them of the fact that Monsieur Fouquet is a prisoner, and we can point out to them that any resistance on their part would only serve to prejudice his cause. We shall remind them that, after the first shot is fired, no mercy is to be expected from the king. Then they will abandon the idea of resistance – at least, that is what I anticipate. They will surrender the place without bloodshed, and we shall obtain in a friendly way what in all probability would otherwise have entailed serious loss.' The officer who had accompanied d'Artagnan was about to speak, but the captain continued quickly – 'Yes, I know what you are going to say, sir; I know that the king's orders forbid all secret communications with the defenders of Belle-Isle. It is for that very reason that I propose to negotiate with them only in the presence of my staff.' And d'Artagnan nodded pleasantly to his officers by way of impressing them with a due sense of his condescension towards them.

The officers looked at one another to see if their opinions were unanimous, and were evidently ready to fall in with d'Artagnan's wishes. The latter was delighted to perceive that their reply would be favourable, and was already deciding to send off a boat at once for Porthos and Aramis, when the king's officer produced from his breast-pocket a sealed document, which he handed to d'Artagnan. The paper was superscribed with the number 1.

'What is this, then?' murmured the surprised captain.

'Read it, sir,' replied the officer in a tone of politeness which was not free from a shade of compunction.

D'Artagnan fingered the paper mistrustfully, then breaking the seal he read these words:

> Monsieur d'Artagnan is forbidden to hold any council whatsoever or to discuss measures until Belle-Isle has surrendered and the prisoners have been executed.          Louis

D'Artagnan repressed any outward manifestation of his extreme annoyance. Turning to the officer he said with a gracious smile – 'Very well, monsieur, the king's orders shall be complied with.'

### CHAPTER 72

## *D'Artagnan's ideas fail to agree with the king's*

IT WAS A STAGGERING BLOW. D'Artagnan was intensely disgusted to find that the king had forestalled his design; still, he was by no means inclined to abandon hope. Whilst turning over in his mind the idea he had conceived in Belle-Isle, there occurred to him a fresh means of ensuring the safety of his friends. 'Gentlemen,' he resumed, suddenly, 'since the king has seen fit to confide his secret orders to some other officer than myself, it is evident that I no longer enjoy his confidence. I should indeed be unworthy of it were I willing to retain a command subject to so many galling restrictions. I will therefore return at once and hand my resignation to the king. I announce my intention before you all and I shall direct you to return with me towards the French coast in order that the forces which his majesty confided to me shall in no way be endangered. Return to your posts, gentlemen, and let orders be given to fall back upon the coast. The tide will serve in an hour. To your stations, gentlemen! – I suppose,' he added, seeing that all were preparing to obey him with the exception of the officer set to watch him, 'I suppose you have no orders to the contrary this time?'

D'Artagnan was enjoying his triumph even as he uttered these words. In this plan lay the safety of his friends. Once the blockade was raised, they could immediately set sail for England or for Spain without fear of being molested. Whilst they were making their escape, d'Artagnan would return to the king, justifying his return by the indignation he felt against Colbert at the scurvy treatment he had received. He would be sent back armed with full powers, and he would capture Belle-Isle, the cage from which the birds had flown. But this plan was frustrated by the officer producing a second order from the king in these terms: 'Should Monsieur d'Artagnan manifest a desire to resign the command, he ceases from that moment to be the leader of the expedition, and every officer placed under his command is hereby instructed to disregard his orders. Furthermore, the said Sieur d'Artagnan, having forfeited the chief command of the Army sent against Belle-Isle, must leave the colours and return to France immediately, in company with the officer who has remitted this dispatch to him, and who is to regard him as a prisoner for whom he will be held responsible.'

Brave and high-spirited as he was, d'Artagnan grew pale. All these measures had been calculated with such far-seeing astuteness and precision that the captain was reminded, for the first time within thirty years, of the hard-headed logic of the Great cardinal. He rested his head upon his hand, thinking hard and scarcely breathing. 'If I were to put this letter in my pocket,' he thought, 'who could prevent me, and who would be any the wiser? Before the king could hear of it I should take Belle-Isle and save those two poor fellows. Come, let us adopt the bold course! I am not the sort of man who is likely to have his head cut off for disobedience. I will disobey!'

But as he was about to put his resolution into effect, he noticed that the officers about him were reading similar letters, which had just been distributed by Colbert's *âme damnée*.[186] The possibility of d'Artagnan's disobedience had also been foreseen. The officer approached him, saying, 'Sir, I await your good pleasure to depart.'

'I am ready,' replied the captain, grinding his teeth. The officer immediately ordered a boat to be lowered. The sight was maddening to d'Artagnan. 'What arrangements are to be made here,' he stammered, 'for the command of the different corps?'

'When you are gone, sir,' replied the officer in command of the fleet, 'it is to me that the direction of affairs has been entrusted.'

'In that case, sir,' rejoined Colbert's agent, addressing the new leader, 'this last order which I carry is intended for you. Will you show me your authority?'

'Here it is,' said the sailor, exhibiting a document bearing the royal signature.

'And here are your instructions,' replied the officer, handing him the envelope. Then, turning towards d'Artagnan, 'Come, sir,' he said, not without some emotion at the sight of a strong man's despair, 'do me the favour to step into this boat.'

'In one moment,' replied d'Artagnan, in a voice very different from his usual brisk tone. He was crushed and subdued by the unexpected and almost incredible calamity which had fallen upon him. And he went and took his place in the boat. A sail was hoisted and the little boat ran before the wind in the direction of France, assisted also by the tide.

An idea occurred to d'Artagnan which brought him some consolation. He hoped to reach Nantes quickly and trusted that his eloquence in pleading the cause of his friends would cause the king to abate his rigour. The boat skimmed across the sea like a swallow. D'Artagnan could distinctly see the coast of France rising up black out of the grey night mist. 'Ah! Sir,' said he in a low tone to the officer, to whom he had not spoken a word for the last hour, 'what would I not give to know the tenour of the new commander's instructions! They are of a peaceful character, are they not? And – ' He did not finish what he was about to say, for the hollow rumbling of a distant gun could be heard across the water. It was answered by another, then another, followed a moment later by several louder rumblings.

'They have opened fire upon Belle-Isle,' replied the officer.

At the same moment the boat ran in shore and touched the mainland of France.

CHAPTER 73

## Porthos and his ancestors

As soon as d'Artagnan had taken leave of Aramis and Porthos, these latter betook themselves to the principal fort in order to converse more at their ease. Porthos's moody abstraction began to wear upon Aramis's nerves, for his own mind had never been clearer or more vigorous. 'My dear Porthos,' said the latter, suddenly breaking the silence, 'I am going to explain d'Artagnan's idea to you.'

'What idea, Aramis?'

'An idea to which we shall owe our liberty before twelve hours are past.'

'Really now?' cried Porthos in astonishment. 'Well then, let us hear.'

'You noticed from the altercation which took place between d'Artagnan and the officer that there were certain orders which impeded our friend's actions with regard to ourselves.'

'Yes, I noticed that.'

'Well, d'Artagnan has resolved to hand in his resignation to the king, and during the confusion which will result from his absence, we can make our escape – or at least you, Porthos, will be able to get away should it happen that the flight of only one of us is possible.'

At this point Porthos shook his head and replied, 'We will escape together, Aramis, or not at all.'

'This generosity is only what I should have expected from you,' said Aramis. 'The only thing that saddens me is your melancholy air of uneasiness.'

'I am not uneasy,' said Porthos.

'Then you are angry with me?'

'Not at all.'

'My dear friend, then why this dismal expression?'

'I will tell you. I am making my will.' And as he uttered these words, the good Porthos looked at his friend with a face of woe.

'Making your will?' cried the bishop. 'What! have you given yourself up for lost?'

'I feel tired. It is the first time I have ever felt that way, and it is a warning in our family.'

'A warning?'

'My grandfather was twice as strong a man as I am.'

'Oh! come! If that's true, your grandfather must have been Samson himself.'

'No. His name was Antoine. Well, he was the same age as I when one morning, as he was going off to the hunt, he felt his legs weak, a thing which had never happened before.'

'And what was the meaning of that, friend Porthos?'

'It was a bad sign, as you shall hear. He went out, as I say – always complaining of his legs – and started a boar and brought him to bay, took a shot at him with his arquebuse and missed and was ripped up by the beast and died on the spot.'

'That is no reason why you should alarm yourself, my dear Porthos.'

'Oh! wait a moment. My father was as strong again as I am. He was a soldier under Henri III and Henri IV, and his name was not Antoine, but Gaspard, after Monsieur de Coligny.[187] Always on horseback, he never knew what it was to feel tired. One day he was rising from table when he felt his legs give under him.'

'He had dined rather well, perhaps?' said Aramis. 'That is what made him stagger.'

'What! a friend of Monsieur de Bassompierre? Nonsense! No, he was astonished at feeling tired, and said to my mother, who was by way of making fun of him, "One would think I was going to meet a boar, like my father, the late Monsieur Du Vallon."'

'Well?' said Aramis.

'Well, in spite of this weakness, my father insisted upon walking down to the garden instead of going to bed. His foot slipped on the first step; the staircase was rather steep; my father fell against a corner of the buttress in which an iron hinge was fixed. The hinge cut open his temple and killed him on the spot.'

Aramis looked up at his friend quickly. 'Two very strange circumstances, certainly,' he said, 'but there is no reason to suppose they will be followed by a third. It does not become a man of your calibre to be superstitious, my good Porthos. Besides, there are no indications of any weakness in your legs. Never have I seen you look more massive and upstanding; you look as though you could walk off with a house on your shoulders.'

'Oh! I am right enough for the present moment, but a few minutes ago I felt myself sinking, and indeed I have experienced this phe–phenomenon, I think you called it, three or four times lately. I don't say that it makes me afraid, exactly, but it troubles me. Life is very pleasant. I have money and fine estates; I have horses I am fond of, and friends whom I love; d'Artagnan, Athos, Raoul and yourself.' The excellent Porthos did not even take the trouble to hide from Aramis the order in which he placed him among his friends.

Aramis pressed his hand – 'We will both live to a good old age,' he said, 'if only to preserve in the world rare specimens of manhood. Trust yourself to me, my friend. We have had no reply from d'Artagnan, and that is a good sign. No doubt he has given orders for the fleet to get together and clear the seas. For my part, I have ordered a boat to be moved on rollers to the passage which leads out of the great cave of Locmaria – you know the place – where we have so often gone fox-hunting.'

'Yes, the passage which opens out on to a little creek through that gulley we discovered the day that fine dog-fox went to earth down there.'

'Exactly. The boat is to be hidden in the cave in case of necessity; no doubt it is there by this time. We will wait for a favourable opportunity, and one night we will slip the boat into the sea and sail off.'

'That is a capital idea.'

'You are right, for, in the first place, nobody knows of this cave – or rather, of the passage leading from it – except, perhaps, two or three sportsmen. Moreover, if the island is occupied by troops, their scouts, seeing no boat on the beach, will believe it impossible for anyone to escape, and will relax their vigilance.'

'I understand.'

'Well, and how are your legs?'

'First rate, at the present moment.'

'You see then that everything conspires to render our minds easy. D'Artagnan will clear the sea and leave the road to freedom open. No fleet to be dreaded, and no attempt to land troops to be expected. *Vive Dieu!* Porthos, we have still a good fifty years of adventures in store for us, and, once I reach Spain, I swear to you,' added the bishop with terrific energy, 'that your dukedom is not so far off as some people choose to suppose.'

'We will hope for the best,' cried Porthos, rendered somewhat more cheerful by his companion's unusual warmth.

Suddenly a shout was heard – 'To arms!' This cry, repeated by a hundred throats, penetrated to the room where the two friends were conversing, causing surprise to the one and uneasiness to the other. Aramis flung open the window. He saw a crowd of people running with torches in their hands. Women were hurrying to seek shelter and armed men hastening to their stations.

'The fleet! the fleet!' cried a soldier, recognising Aramis.

'The fleet?' repeated the latter.

'Within half a cannon shot,' added the soldier.

'To arms!' cried Aramis.

'To arms!' roared Porthos, in his formidable bass. And both rushed towards the mole, to place themselves behind the shelter of the batteries. Boats, filled with soldiers, were seen approaching in three directions in order to deliver the attack simultaneously upon three points.

'What steps are to be taken?' asked the Officer of the Guard.

'Prevent their landing, and if they persist, fire upon them!' said Aramis. Five minutes later the cannonade commenced. This was the firing d'Artagnan had heard as he landed in France. But the boats were too close to the mole to permit of the guns being effectually trained upon them. The attacking party landed, and an almost hand-to-hand combat ensued.

'What is the matter?' asked Aramis of his friend.

'Nothing – my legs – really, it's most extraordinary, but they will be better when we charge.' And in fact Porthos and Aramis flung themselves into the charge with so much vigour and heartened the defence so well that the king's troops returned to their boats precipitately; the only result of their attack being a number of wounded men whom they carried away with them.

'Quick, Porthos!' cried Aramis. 'We want a prisoner captured. Quick!' Porthos leaned over the steps of the mole and seized one of the officers of the royal army by the nape of the neck as he was about to step into the boat after having seen all his men embarked. The giant carried off his prey under his arm, holding him in such a way as to act as a shield for his own protection, and returned without a shot having been fired at him.

'Here is a prisoner for you,' said Porthos to Aramis.

'Well now,' cried the latter, laughing, 'do you still complain of your legs?'

'But I did not take him with my legs,' replied Porthos, gloomily, 'it was with my arm.'

CHAPTER 74

## *The son of Biscarrat*[188]

THE BRETONS of the island were very proud of their victory, but Aramis was not inclined to encourage the feeling. 'What will happen,' said he to Porthos, when quiet was once more restored, 'will be that the king's anger will be aroused when he hears of our resistance, and these brave men will be shot in hundreds when the island is taken – an event which cannot fail to take place.'

'You mean to say then,' said Porthos, 'that we have acted to no purpose?'

'Not altogether, since we have a prisoner from whom we can learn the enemy's intentions.'

'Yes, let us interrogate the prisoner,' cried Porthos. 'There is a simple means of getting him to speak: we are going to have supper and we will invite him. When he has drunk a little it will loosen his tongue.'

Porthos's suggestion was adopted. The officer, somewhat mistrustful at first, was promptly reassured when he saw the people with whom he had to deal. Having no occasion to fear compromising himself, he gave the fullest possible details as to d'Artagnan's resignation and subsequent departure. He explained how the new commander, after d'Artagnan had left, had ordered a surprise attack upon Belle-Isle, but beyond that he would say nothing. Porthos and Aramis exchanged a glance which confessed their extreme disappointment. No longer could they rely upon d'Artagnan's fertile imagination. Consequently, in the event of their sustaining a defeat, they would be left without resources. Aramis questioned the prisoner as to what his chiefs contemplated doing with the principal officers of Belle-Isle.

'The orders are,' replied the prisoner, 'to kill the leaders during the fighting or to hang them afterwards.'

Again Aramis and Porthos looked at one another. The colour mounted to the faces of both.

'I am scarcely heavy enough for the gallows,' replied Aramis. 'People like me are not hanged.'

'And as for me,' said Porthos, 'I am *too* heavy. People of my sort break the rope.'

'I am sure,' said the prisoner politely, 'that we ought to have obtained for you the favour of death by whatever means you prefer.'

'A thousand thanks,' said Aramis, seriously.

Porthos bowed his acknowledgments – 'Another glass of wine to your health,' he cried, and duly honoured the toast. Chatting about various matters, the supper was prolonged. The officer was a man of intelligence and an amusing companion, and he surrendered to the charm of Aramis's wit and the cordial good-fellowship of Porthos.

'You will forgive me, I am sure, if I address a question to you – for when a man is at his sixth bottle he certainly has the right to forget himself a little.'

'Address it! by all means, address it!' said Porthos, affably.

'Any question you please,' said Aramis, courteously.

'Were you not, gentlemen, both in the late king's musketeers?'

'Yes, sir, we were, and among the best of 'em, if you please,' replied Porthos.

'I am sure of it – indeed, I would even say the two most gallant soldiers of the time, did I not fear to wrong my father's memory.'

'Your father?' cried Aramis.

'Do you know my name, monsieur?'

'Faith, no; but you will tell me, and – '

'My name is Georges de Biscarrat.'

'Oh!' cried Porthos in his turn, 'Biscarrat! You remember that name, Aramis?'

'Biscarrat – ?' mused the bishop. 'It seems to me – '

'Search your memory, sir,' said the officer.

'*Pardieu!* that's easily done,' cried Porthos. 'Biscarrat, whom they used to call the Cardinal – one of those four who came and interrupted us the day we first made d'Artagnan's acquaintance, sword in hand.'

'Exactly, gentlemen.'

'The only one whom we failed to wound,' said Aramis, quickly.

'A notable swordsman, consequently,' said the prisoner.

'That is true – very true!' cried the two friends together. 'Faith! Monsieur de Biscarrat, we are delighted to make the acquaintance of so brave a man.'

Biscarrat grasped the hands of the two old musketeers with the heartiest good-feeling. Aramis looked at Porthos as much as to say, 'Here is a man who may be of use to us.' To Biscarrat he said, 'Confess, monsieur, that it is a fine thing to have earned an honourable reputation.'

'That is what my father always said, monsieur.'

'Confess also that it is a melancholy circumstance when one meets people who are condemned to be shot or hanged, and discovers that these people are old acquaintances – old hereditary acquaintances.'

'Oh! you are not reserved for so dreadful an end, gentlemen,' said the young man, with confidence.

'Why, you declared it yourself.'

'If I said it, it was before I knew who you were; but now I know you, I say that, if you wish it, you can avoid this dismal fate.'

'How, if we wish it?' cried Aramis, whose eyes sparkled with intelligence as he looked alternately at his prisoner and at Porthos.

'Always provided,' Porthos interposed, glancing at the bishop and Monsieur de Biscarrat with noble fearlessness, 'always provided that we are not required to act in any manner which might be considered disgraceful.'

'Nothing at all will be required of you, gentlemen,' replied the officer of the royal army; 'what would you expect them to ask? If they find you, they will kill you – that is unquestionable; see to it, then, that they do not find you.'

'I may, perhaps, be mistaken,' said Porthos, with dignity, 'but it seems to me that if they want to find us, they will have to seek us here.'

'In that you are perfectly right, my dear friend,' rejoined Aramis, still keeping his enquiring glance directed upon Biscarrat, who had become silent and constrained. 'You would like to tell us something, Monsieur de Biscarrat, to make some proposal to us, would you not? but you do not feel yourself at liberty.'

'Ah! gentlemen – friends, since you permit me to call you friends – were I to say anything it would be betraying our plans. But hark, I hear a master-voice which sets me at liberty to speak.'

'Guns!' exclaimed Porthos. A low, distant roar was heard, the sinister announcement of an engagement in progress under the rocky cliffs. Soon the roar of the guns ceased altogether.

'What is that?' asked Porthos.

'Eh! *Pardieu!* it is as I feared,' cried Aramis.

'What did you fear?'

'The attack in which you were engaged was only a feint, was it not, monsieur? Whilst your troops allowed themselves to be repulsed you were enabled to effect a landing on the other side of the island.'

'In several places, monsieur.'

'Then it is all over with us,' said the Bishop of Vannes, coolly.

'It may be so,' replied the Seigneur of Pierrefonds, 'but they haven't caught and hanged us yet.' And, saying this, he rose from the table, crossed the room and took down his sword and pistols from the wall. He examined them carefully, like an old soldier preparing for battle who feels that his life in great measure depends upon the excellence and the good condition of his weapons.

Hearing the cannonade, and learning that a surprise had been effected which would, in all probability, put the royal troops in possession of the island, a crowd of terrified inhabitants streamed into the fort. They had come to obtain advice and assistance from their leaders. Aramis, pale and dejected, stepped to a window which overlooked the main courtyard and showed himself between two torches to the crowd of soldiers who had come for orders and the crowd of frantic civilians who implored his help.

'My friends,' said d'Herblay, in a grave and sonorous voice, 'it is my duty to tell you that Monsieur Fouquet, your protector, your father and friend, has been arrested by order of the king and thrown into the Bastille.' A long cry of rage and menace rose to the window where the bishop was standing. 'Vengeance on his enemies! Death to the king's troops!' cried the more excited among the throng. 'No, my friends,' replied Aramis solemnly, 'let there be no resistance. The king is master in his kingdom. The king is God's chosen instrument. God and the king have smitten Monsieur Fouquet. Humble yourselves before the hand of God. Fear the God and honour the king who have struck down Monsieur Fouquet. Think not to avenge your seigneur. It would be throwing away your property and your liberty, and that of your wives and children. Lay down your arms, my friends, lay down your arms, since such is the king's command, and retire quietly to your own homes. I ask you to do this – nay, I beg you, and if necessary, order you in Monsieur Fouquet's name.' The crowd assembled under the window replied by a long, hoarse roar of anger and fear. 'The troops of Louis XIV have landed in the island,' continued Aramis. 'From this moment it would no longer be a question of fighting – it would be a massacre. Away with you, then! disperse! and this time I command you in the name of the Lord!'

The insurgents slowly retired, for the most part in submissive silence.

'What is all this you have been saying, my friend?' said Porthos.

'Monseigneur,' said Biscarrat to the bishop, 'this will save the inhabitants, but it will save neither you nor your friend.'

'Monsieur de Biscarrat,' said the Bishop of Vannes with noble courtesy, 'pray be good enough to accept your freedom.'

'With great pleasure, monsieur, but – '

'You will thereby render us a service, for in announcing to the king's lieutenant the islanders' submission, you will perhaps be able, by informing him of the manner in which their submission has been effected, to obtain mercy for us.'

'*Mercy!*' cried Porthos, scandalised. 'Mercy indeed! I don't recognise the word!'

Aramis jerked his friend's elbow as he had been accustomed to do in the old days when he wished to apprise Porthos that he had committed or was about to commit a blunder. Porthos took the hint and said no more.

'I will go then, gentlemen,' replied Biscarrat, a trifle surprised to hear the word "mercy" in the mouth of the fire-eating musketeer whose heroic exploits he had, a few moments before, been relating with so much enthusiasm.

'I will wish you farewell, Monsieur Biscarrat,' said Aramis, bowing, 'and beg you to accept the expression of our gratitude.'

'But, gentlemen – you whom I am proud to call my friends, since you are kind enough to permit me to use this title – what will become of you in the meantime?' rejoined the officer, not without some emotion, as he took leave of the two old adversaries of his father.

'Oh! we shall remain here.'

'But – good Lord! the order is precise!'

'I am the Bishop of Vannes, Monsieur de Biscarrat, and it is no more customary to execute bishops than it is to hang gentlemen.'

'Ah! yes, monsieur, yes monseigneur,' replied Biscarrat, 'yes, you are right. There is still this chance for you. Well then, I will go. I will go straight to the leader of the expedition. Farewell, then, gentlemen – or rather, *au revoir!*' And the good fellow, mounting the horse which Aramis had had brought for him, rode off in the direction whence the firing had been heard which, causing the crowd to gather in the fort, had interrupted the conversation of the two friends with their prisoner. Aramis watched him depart, and when he was again alone with Porthos, 'Well, do you understand?' he asked.

'Faith! not I!'

'Did you not find Biscarrat rather in the way here?'

'No. He is a decent lad.'

'Yes, but the cave of Locmaria? – There is no reason why everybody should know of it.'

'Ah, very true, very true. I understand. We are going to slip away by way of this cavern?'

'Why, to be sure!' replied Aramis, briskly. 'Forward, friend Porthos! Our boat awaits us, and the king has not caught us yet.'

## CHAPTER 75

## *The grotto of Locmaria*

THE CAVERN OF LOCMARIA was far enough away from the mole to render it necessary for the two friends to husband their strength to reach it. Besides, it was night – midnight had just struck – and Porthos and Aramis were weighed down by their weapons, and the money they carried. They were making their way across the open moorland between the cavern and the mole, stopping to listen to every sound in order to avoid falling into any ambush. Carefully keeping clear of the road which lay to their left, they could see from time to time parties of fugitives passing along it from the interior of the island, hurrying to take refuge in the fort at the news of the landing of the king's troops. Aramis and Porthos, hidden behind some boulder, could catch the words uttered by these poor people, fleeing in fear and trembling, dragging with them whatever they possessed of most value; and tried to gather some information which might be of service to themselves. At length, after a rapid journey, often interrupted, however, by stoppages counselled by prudence, they reached those extensive grottoes within which the far-seeing Bishop of Vannes had taken the precaution of having a serviceable boat moved on rollers – a boat sufficiently large to be capable of keeping the sea at this open season of the year. 'Here we are at last,' said Porthos, blowing noisily. 'But, my dear Aramis, I thought you spoke of three men – three servants who were to go with us. I don't see them: where have they got to?'

'Why should you expect to see them, my dear Porthos? No doubt they are waiting for us in the cavern, and are probably resting after their heavy labour in bringing the boat here.' Aramis stopped Porthos, who was about to enter the cave. 'Will you allow me to go in first?' said he to the giant. 'I know the signal which I gave these men, who, not hearing it, would be very likely to shoot at you or throw a knife at you in the darkness.'

'Go on then, Aramis, go on ahead. You are wisdom and prudence itself. And then, I feel that tired feeling of which I spoke to you coming on again.'

Aramis left Porthos seated on a rock at the mouth of the cave, and bending his head, he made his way into the depths of the grotto, imitating the cry of an owl. A faint hoot, scarcely audible, replied to him from within. Aramis continued to advance cautiously, and soon he was stopped by a similar cry which proceeded from within ten paces of him. 'Are you there, Yves?' cried the bishop.

'Aye, aye! your eminence. Goennec is here too, and his son is with him.'

'Good. Is everything in order?'

'Yes, your eminence.'

'Just go to the entrance of the cave, my good men, where you will find the Seigneur of Pierrefonds resting, for the journey has fatigued him. And if you should find that he cannot walk, you must carry him here to me.'

The three Bretons hastened to obey. However, Aramis's recommendation was needless. Porthos, having rested, had already begun to cross the cave, his heavy tread echoing in the recesses of the grotto among the natural pillars which supported the roof. As soon as the Lord of Bracieux and Pierrefonds had rejoined the bishop, the sailors lighted a lantern with which they had provided themselves, and Porthos assured his friend that he felt as strong again as ever.

'Let us see the boat,' said Aramis, 'and make sure she has everything needful in her.'

'Don't get too close with the light,' said Yves the skipper. 'Because, as you told me, monseigneur, I shoved that chest under the thwarts at the stern, and as you know, there's that keg of gunpowder in it and the loaded muskets you sent down from the fort.'

'Very well,' said Aramis. He took the lantern, and examined the boat thoroughly, with all the care of a man who well understands the danger which he faces without shrinking. The boat was long and light, with fine lines and drawing little water – in fact, one of those excellent little vessels for which Belle-Isle has always been noted – a trifle high in the gunwale, but steady in a seaway, handy to steer and furnished with raised planks abaft the forecastle which serve in rough weather to keep the waves which wash over the bows out of the steerage and to protect the rowers from the sharp spray. In two lockers, one in the bows and the other at the stern, Aramis found bread, biscuits, dried fruit, a quarter of bacon and some leathern bottles containing water; the whole forming ample rations for people who had no intention of sailing far from the coast and were in a position to revictual their craft when required.

With regard to the armoury department, there were eight muskets and as many horse-pistols, all in good condition and ready loaded.

Spare oars were provided in case of accident, and the boat was furnished with a mast and a small lug-sail, which, used in conjunction with the oars, is so useful in assisting the boat's progress when the breeze serves, whilst adding practically nothing to the vessel's burden.

Having completed his inspection and expressed himself satisfied, Aramis turned to his friend, saying – 'Now, my dear Porthos, let us consult as to whether we ought to attempt to get the boat down the slope to the unknown passage at the far end of the cave, or whether it would be better to take her out openly by the mouth of the cave, slipping her over the rollers through the thicket and smoothing a path down the cliff. The cliff is not more than twenty feet high, and beneath it there are three or four fathoms of smooth water at high tide, with a good bottom.'

'Begging your pardon, monseigneur,' said the skipper Yves respectfully, 'I don't think it would be so easy to take her through the cave in the dark as it would be to get her over the cliff. I know the cliff well and I'll warrant it's as smooth as a lawn, whereas the floor of this here cave is wonderfully knobbly – to say nothing of the gully at the other end leading on to the sea, where very likely the boat will get stuck fast.'

'I have made my calculations,' replied the bishop, 'and I am positive the boat could be hauled through.'

'Very good, your eminence, your pleasure is mine, but your highness knows,' persisted the skipper, 'that to get her to the far end of the gully, we've got to shift a big rock – that rock the fox always dives underneath and which shuts up the gully like a door.'

'Never mind that,' said Porthos, 'I'll soon shift it.'

'Oh! yes, I know your honour is as strong as ten ordinary men,' replied Yves, 'only it's giving your honour a deal of trouble.'

'I fancy the skipper is right,' said Aramis. 'We will try the open way.'

'All the more reason,' continued the fisherman, 'because anyhow we shan't be able to get her afloat before daybreak. It won't be anyways easy to get her launched. And then, as soon as it begins to get light, we shall have to keep a good lookout aloft – at the mouth of the cave, I mean; that we can't do without, for we must keep an eye on those cruisers that are on the watch to snap us up.'

'Yes, yes, Yves, your arguments are sound. We will take the boat over the cliff.' And the three sturdy Bretons were about to place the rollers under their boat in order to put it in motion, when all at once the baying of hounds could be heard in the distance. Aramis ran to the mouth of the cavern followed by Porthos. The pearly hues of dawn threw a faint glimmer over sea and plain; in the half-light one could distinguish stunted, melancholy-looking pine trees rising like spectres from the rugged soil; long flights of crows sailed slowly, with much flapping of sooty wings, over the sparsely cultivated fields of buckwheat. In a quarter of an hour it would be broad daylight; birds were awake and joyously chirping the good news to their kindly mother Nature. The distant baying, which had caused the three fishermen to stop and had drawn Aramis and Porthos out of the cavern, became more clearly audible as the hounds were in a deep gorge about a league's distance from the grotto.

'It is a pack of hounds,' said Porthos, 'and they seem to be on a burning scent.'

'What can it mean? Who would be hunting at such a time as this?' thought Aramis.

'Coming this way, too,' continued Porthos, 'where they may expect to encounter the royalists!'

The sound grew more distinct.

'Yes, you are right, Porthos; the hounds have caught a scent. Why! what – Yves! Yves! come here quickly!'

Yves came up at a run, dropping the roller which he was about to place under the boat when the bishop's exclamation had interrupted him.

'What is the meaning of this hunt, skipper?' asked Porthos.

'Eh! your honour, I don't know what it means at all,' replied the Breton. 'The Seigneur of Locmaria would not be hunting at such a time as this. And besides, the hounds – '

'Unless, perhaps, they have escaped from the kennels.'

'Oh, no,' said Goennec, 'these are not the Seigneur of Locmaria's hounds.'

'Well, let us return to the grotto as a precaution,' said Aramis. 'They are evidently coming this way and we shall soon know what they are after.'

They all re-entered the cave, but hardly had they gone a hundred paces in the gloom ere a fox panting and terrified, dashed past the fugitives with the rapidity of lightning, leapt over the boat and disappeared, leaving behind him the delightful odour peculiar to that animal, which remained perceptible for some seconds under the low, vaulted roof.

'Yoicks! a fox!' shouted the Bretons, with all the glee of inveterate sportsmen.

'Accursed chance!' cried the bishop, furiously, 'our retreat is discovered.'

'How so?' asked Porthos. 'Are you afraid of a fox?'

'What! do you think it is anything to do with the fox? It is not a question of a fox, *pardieu!* Don't you know, Porthos, that after the fox come the hounds, and after the hounds, the huntsmen?'

Porthos felt snubbed and hung his head. As though to confirm Aramis's words, they heard the pack in full cry, following with frightful swiftness the trail of the animal. Three couple of hounds burst out together upon the little clearing and gave tongue vociferously.

'Here we have the hounds,' said Aramis, who had posted himself in a place of observation behind a cleft between two boulders; 'now what of the huntsmen?'

'If it is the Seigneur of Locmaria,' replied the fisherman, 'he will let the hounds draw the cavern, for he knows them, but he will not enter himself. He knows quite well that the fox will have gone away at the other side, and that's where he will make his next cast.'

'It is not the Seigneur of Locmaria who is hunting,' replied Aramis, growing pale in spite of himself.

'Who is it then?' asked Porthos.

'Look!'

Porthos applied his eye to the cleft, and saw upon the top of the hillock some dozen mounted men, who were following and cheering the hounds – 'Guardsmen!' he said.

'Yes, friend Porthos, the king's guards.'

'The king's guards,' repeated the boatmen, growing pale in their turn.

'With Biscarrat at their head, mounted on a grey horse,' continued Aramis. At the same moment, the hounds dashed into the cave like an avalanche, filling the place with their deafening uproar. 'It's the very deuce!' cried Aramis, regaining his natural coolness in face of a tangible, inevitable danger. 'No doubt we are done for, but at least we have one chance left. If these men who are following the hounds discover the entrance to this cave there is no hope for us, for if they come in, they will see us and the boat as well. Not a single hound must be allowed to get out of here – not a single man must enter – you understand?'

'I see,' said Porthos.

'There are six hounds,' added the bishop, with the quick decision of a man accustomed to command. 'They will come to a check at the big rock under which the fox has gone to earth. The opening is very narrow and there they must be taken and killed.'

The Bretons opened their knives and dashed forward. A few

moments later, there was a frightful din of agonised yelping, followed by silence.

'Good!' said Aramis, coolly. 'Now we must attend to their masters!'

'What are we to do?' said Porthos.

'Wait until they come close, keep ourselves hidden and kill them!'

'Kill them?' repeated Porthos incredulously.

'There are sixteen of them,' said Aramis; 'at least, that is all at present.'

'And well armed,' added Porthos, feeling somewhat consoled.

'It will take us ten minutes,' said Aramis, 'Come along Porthos.' And with that he resolutely seized a musket and placed his hunting-knife between his teeth – 'Yves, Goennec and his son,' mumbled Aramis between his fixed jaws, 'will pass the muskets to us. We can easily account for eight before the others know what is happening. And then the five of us will fall upon the other eight knife in hand and dispatch them.'

'And poor Biscarrat?' said Porthos.

Aramis paused for an instant and reflected – 'Biscarrat first of all,' he said coldly. 'He would recognise us.'


CHAPTER 76

## The Cavern


IN SPITE OF Aramis's habitual accuracy in forecasting events, which almost amounted to a faculty of divination, the thing which actually happened, as is usual with matters decided by pure chance, was not quite in accordance with the Bishop of Vannes's prediction. Biscarrat, who was better mounted than his companions, was the first to arrive at the mouth of the cave. He instantly grasped the fact that both fox and hounds had passed through into the cave, but feeling that superstitious dread natural to most men at the sight of a gloomy cavern, he stopped short outside the grotto to wait until he was joined by his companions.

'What is it?' cried the young men, hot and out of breath and unable to understand the reason of his inaction.

'I can't hear the hounds – I think Master Reynard and the dogs to boot have all disappeared in this chasm.'

'They are too well broken,' said one of the guards, 'to have lost the view entirely. Besides, we should hear them yelping, yelping from one side to another. It must be as Biscarrat says – they are inside this grotto.'

'Then how is it,' said another of the guardsmen, 'we don't hear them give tongue?'

'It is certainly very strange,' said another.

'Well, suppose we enter the cave,' said a fourth. 'Are we, by any chance, forbidden to go in?'

'No,' replied Biscarrat, 'only it is dark as a wolf's throat and we might easily break our necks.'

'Witness the hounds,' said one, 'who seem to me to have broken theirs.'

'What the devil can have got the brutes?' – The master of the hounds called each animal by its own name, whistled his favourite call, but not a sound replied, not a bark, not a whimper.

'An enchanted grotto, evidently,' said Biscarrat. 'Let us go in and see.' And, dismounting from his horse he stepped into the grotto.

'Wait! – wait a moment, I'll go with you,' cried another officer, seeing Biscarrat about to disappear into the semi-darkness.

'No,' replied Biscarrat, 'there's something very queer about this place. We must not all of us run the risk at once. If you hear nothing of me in ten minutes' time, you can enter, but all together then.'

'Very well,' said the sportsmen, thinking, of course, that Biscarrat ran no great risk from such an enterprise. 'We will wait for you' – and without dismounting, they formed a circle round the mouth of the cavern.

Biscarrat accordingly entered alone, and walked on in the darkness until he suddenly encountered Porthos's musket. This obstacle to his progress astonished him; he put his hand out and gripped the cold barrel. At the same moment, Yves sprang upon the young man with lifted knife, and was about to plunge it into Biscarrat's chest with all the strength of his arm; but his wrist was seized halfway in Porthos's iron grip. Biscarrat heard a hollow, rumbling voice utter the words – 'I won't have him killed.' He felt himself threatened and protected at the same time, and the one appeared almost as terrible as the other. Brave though the young man was, he could not repress a cry, which Aramis instantly smothered by cramming his handkerchief into his mouth – 'Monsieur de Biscarrat,' said Aramis in a low voice, 'we wish you no harm, as you should know if you have recognised us; but at the first word – the first sound – we shall be obliged to kill you as we have killed your hounds.'

'Oh! I recognise you, gentlemen,' said Biscarrat in a whisper, when Aramis had removed the gag – 'But how is it you are here? What are you doing? Unfortunate men! I thought you were in the fort.'

'And you, sir, you were to obtain conditions for us, I think?'

'I did what I could, gentlemen, but – '

'But?'

'The orders are strict.'

'To kill us?'

Biscarrat made no reply. To speak to gentlemen of the gallows would have been too painful. Aramis understood the prisoner's silence. 'Monsieur de Biscarrat,' said he, 'you would have been a dead man at this moment if we had not had regard for your youth and the ties of old acquaintance with your father. You may yet escape from here if you swear to us not to speak to your companions of what you have seen.'

'Very readily, and not only will I say nothing of what I have seen, but I swear I will do my utmost to prevent my companions setting foot in this grotto.'

'Biscarrat! Biscarrat!' shouted several voices from inside the mouth of the cave. The sounds echoed strangely through the subterranean vault.

'Answer them,' said Aramis.

'Here I am!' cried Biscarrat.

'Now go, and remember we depend upon your good faith.' Aramis released the young man, who made towards the patch of daylight.

'Biscarrat! Biscarrat! where are you?' cried the voices still nearer, and several moving shadows appeared in the gloom. Biscarrat sprang towards his friends in order to stop them, and met them just as they were adventuring into the grotto. Aramis and Porthos strained their ears like men whose life depends upon a breath of wind. Biscarrat had regained the mouth of the grotto, followed by his friends.

'Oho!' cried one of them, as they reached daylight. 'Why, man, you are as white as a ghost!'

'White!' said another, 'you mean *green*!'

'Who? – I?' said the young man, trying to regain his self-control.

'What in the name of heaven has happened to him?' asked several voices.

'Poor dear fellow! you seem to have lost every drop of blood you ever had,' cried another with a laugh.

'Gentlemen! gentlemen! it is a serious matter,' said another. 'He feels poorly, does anyone happen to have a bottle of salts about him?' – And they all laughed consumedly.

A running fire of questions, mingled with laughter and jests, assailed poor Biscarrat's ears; but, like a good soldier, he soon recovered his coolness in the heat of the mêlée – 'What do you suppose I saw?' he asked. 'I was in a perspiration when I entered the cave, and I have taken a chill, that's all.'

'But the hounds! the hounds! Did you find them? Did you hear them speak? What's the news of them?'

'I'm obliged to suppose they have taken another direction,' said Biscarrat.

'Gentlemen,' said one of the young men, 'it seems to me that our friend's interesting paleness and silence betoken some mystery which either he can't reveal or else he doesn't wish to. I'll lay odds Biscarrat has seen something inside this cave. Well, I'm naturally inquisitive, and hang me if I don't see it too, even if it be the Devil! To the cavern, gentlemen! Yoicks! Hark for'rard!'

'To the grotto!' they all shouted in chorus, and the echoes repeated to Aramis and Porthos the sinister threat – 'To the grotto! To the grotto!'

Biscarrat threw himself in front of his friends. 'Gentlemen! gentlemen!' he cried, 'for God's sake, do not go in!'

'Why, what is there so awe-inspiring about your confounded drain?' someone asked. 'Come, speak up, Biscarrat, my game old rooster!'

'I'll swear the lad has seen old Nick,' repeated the young man who had already advanced this hypothesis.

'Well, suppose he has,' cried another, 'that's no reason why he should keep the thing all to himself.'

'Why shouldn't we have a peep too?'

'Gentlemen, I beg you!' insisted Biscarrat.

'Oh! come now, don't block up the way!'

'Gentlemen, do not go in, I entreat you!'

'But, hang it, *you* went in!'

At that moment one of the officers, older and more staid than the others, who, until now, had remained silent in the background, advanced towards the group. 'Gentlemen,' said he, his calm voice contrasting with the lively tones of the youngsters, 'there is something – or someone – in there who is not the Devil but yet has had the power to silence our hounds. We must find out who or what this somebody or something is.'

Biscarrat made a last attempt to restrain his friends, but his effort was fruitless. In vain did he throw himself in front of the bolder spirits – in vain he clung to the rocks and tried to bar their passage.

The young men crowded into the cave behind the officer who had been the last to speak but was the first to plunge forward, sword in hand, to confront the unknown danger. Pushed aside by his friends – unable to accompany them himself, under penalty of appearing as a perjured traitor in the eyes of Porthos and Aramis – Biscarrat leant against a rugged wall of rock with his ears on the stretch and his hand still in the attitude of supplication, in a position which he judged most exposed to the fire of the two old musketeers. As for the officers, they penetrated ever deeper into the cave, their voices becoming less and less distinct as they advanced. Suddenly there was a discharge of musketry, with a roar like thunder echoing beneath the vaults. Two or three bullets flattened themselves on the rock against which Biscarrat was leaning. Next moment there arose a chorus of shouts, groans and curses, and the little troop of gentlemen reappeared – some pale, some bleeding – all enveloped in a haze of smoke which seemed to be drawn up from the depths of the cavern by the air outside – 'Biscarrat! Biscarrat!' cried the fugitives, 'you knew there was an ambuscade in the cavern, and you did not warn us!' 'Biscarrat, you are the cause of our deaths – four of us are killed – black shame upon you, Biscarrat!'

'I am mortally wounded, and it is your fault,' cried one of the young men, dashing the blood from his hand into the face of Biscarrat. 'My blood be upon your head!' And he rolled at the young man's feet in the agony of death.

'But, at least, you will tell us who is there?' cried several furious voices. Biscarrat was silent.

'Speak, or you die!' cried the wounded man, raising himself upon one knee, and feebly raising his ineffectual blade. Biscarrat bent down and bared his breast to the blow, but the wounded man fell back never to rise again and breathed his last sigh. Mad with grief, with haggard eyes, Biscarrat advanced to the interior of the cavern, saying, 'You are right – let me die, since I have allowed my companions to be murdered! I am a coward!' And, flinging away his sword, for he wished to die without defending himself, he plunged on into the cave. The others followed him. Eleven, all that remained of the sixteen, dashed with him into the gulf. But they advanced no farther than before. A second discharge stretched five of them upon the smooth sand, and as it was impossible to see whence proceeded this murderous thunder, the survivors retreated in a panic. But instead of giving ground as the others had done, Biscarrat, who had not received a scratch, sat down upon a fragment of rock and waited. No more than six of the gentlemen now remained uninjured.

'In sober earnest, I ask now,' said one of the survivors, 'is it the Devil?'

'Faith! it's a deal worse,' replied another. 'Ask Biscarrat – he knows.'

'Where is Biscarrat?'

The young men looked round, and saw that Biscarrat was missing.

'He is killed!' cried three or four voices.

'No,' replied another, 'I saw him in the very middle of all the smoke calmly seated on a rock. He is in the cavern, waiting for us.'

'He must know who our enemies are.'

'How should he know?'

'He was a prisoner among the rebels.'

'Ah! true. Well, call him, and let us find out from him with whom we have to deal.'

And, raising their voices, they shouted, 'Biscarrat!'

There was no reply.

'Good!' said the officer who had exhibited so much coolness throughout the affair, 'we shall not need him now; here come reinforcements.'

A company of guards, left in the rear by their officers, whom the excitement of the hunt had carried away, a company about seventy-five or eighty strong marched up in good order, led by a captain and a lieutenant. The five remaining officers ran to meet their men, and pointed out to them their desperate position with all the eloquence which the facts merited. The captain interrupted them. 'Where are your companions?' he asked.

'Dead!'

'But there were sixteen of you!'

'Ten are killed, Biscarrat is in the cave, and we are the remaining five.'

'Then Biscarrat is a prisoner?'

'Most likely.'

'No, for here he comes – look.' And, indeed, Biscarrat at that moment appeared at the mouth of the cavern.

'He is signalling us to approach,' said the officers. 'Come on!'

'Forward!' cried the whole troop. And they ran forward to meet Biscarrat.

'Sir,' said the captain to Biscarrat, 'I am told that you know who the men are who are in this cave and making such a desperate defence. In the king's name I summon you to declare what you know.'

'Captain,' said Biscarrat, 'I have this moment been released from my parole, and I come to you in the name of these men.'

'To tell me that they have decided to surrender?'

'To tell you that they have decided to defend themselves to the last breath unless you grant them good terms.'

'What is their number?'

'There are two of them,' said Biscarrat.

'*Two!* – and they talk of imposing conditions!'

'Two men, but they have already killed ten,' said Biscarrat.

'Why, what sort of people are they? – Giants?'

'More formidable still. Do you remember the story of the Bastion Saint-Gervais,[189] captain?'

'Yes; where four of the king's musketeers held the place against an army.'

'Well, these two men were of those four musketeers.'

'What are their names?'

'At that time, they were known as Porthos and Aramis. At present they are called Messieurs d'Herblay and Du Vallon.'

'And what is their object in all this?'

'They are the men who were holding Belle-Isle for Monsieur Fouquet.'

A murmur ran through the group of soldiers as they heard the names Porthos and Aramis.

'The musketeers! the famous musketeers!' passed from one mouth to another, and among all these brave young fellows, the idea that they were about to contend against two of the most redoubtable paladins who had ever done honour to French arms caused a thrill, partly of enthusiasm, partly of dread. Those four names, d'Artagnan, Athos, Porthos and Aramis were held in veneration by all who wore a sword; just as in ancient times the names of Hercules, Theseus, Castor and Pollux[190] were venerated.

'Two men!' cried the captain; 'and they have killed ten officers in a couple of discharges. Impossible!'

'I don't say, captain, that they have not two or three men with them, as the musketeers had their three or four lackeys at the Bastion Saint-Gervais; but believe me when I tell you – I who have seen these men – believe me, they are capable by themselves of destroying a whole army corps.'

'That remains to be seen,' said the captain, 'and that without delay.'

At this reply, no one stirred, but all awaited the word of command. Biscarrat alone attempted to change the captain's resolution.

'Sir,' he said, in a low tone, 'take my advice – leave these two men, two lions, unmolested. If you attack them they will fight to the death.

They have already killed ten men; they will kill twice as many more, and will finish by killing themselves rather than surrender. What should we gain by fighting?'

'It is not a question of advantage, but of avoiding the shame of seeing eighty of the king's Guards retire before two rebels. If I were to listen to your advice, sir, I should forfeit the esteem of every man of honour, and my shame would be reflected upon the whole army. Forward, my lads.' And, at the head of his company, the captain marched to the mouth of the cave. There he called a halt, in order to obtain from Biscarrat and his companions a description of the interior of the grotto. Then, when he believed he had sufficiently mastered the topography of the disputed stronghold, he divided his company into three sections, with orders to enter successively, and to keep up a sustained fire in every direction. By this mode of attack, he reckoned upon losing perhaps another five men, or even ten; but unquestionably they would end by capturing the rebels, since the cave had no other issue, and, at the very worst, two men could not possibly kill eighty.'

'Captain,' said Biscarrat, 'I ask you to grant me the privilege of marching at the head of the first attack.'

'So be it,' replied the captain. 'You shall have that honour. I make you a present of it.'

'I thank you,' replied the young man, with steadfast courage worthy of his brave father.

'But don't go without your sword! You may find it useful.'

'I will go unarmed, captain,' said Biscarrat. 'I am not going with the intention of killing, but of being killed.' And, putting himself at the head of his men, with head uncovered and folded arms, he gave the word to advance.

CHAPTER 77

## A Homeric[191] combat

IT IS TIME to pass into the other camp and to describe both the combatants and the field of battle.

Aramis and Porthos had gone to the Grotto of Locmaria with the certainty of finding the boat hidden there by their helpers, the three Breton fishermen. At first they had hoped to get the boat down to the sea by way of the smaller passage which Aramis had discovered. This passage opened into a gully which led directly on to the beach, and by passing the boat through this defile, all traces of their labour, and consequently, of their flight, would be concealed. The inopportune arrival of the fox and the pack of hounds had compelled them to remain hidden. The cave extended for a length of some two hundred yards, and, a short distance from the mouth, the ground fell suddenly, forming a cliff overlooking a creek. No doubt the grotto had formerly served as a druidical temple in the remote period when Belle-Isle was known as Calonesa, and probably it had seen more than one human sacrifice accomplished in its mysterious depths. From its landward entrance, the cavern extended by a gentle downward slope; the low, vaulted roof sustained by rocky pillars. The floor was extremely uneven, and a passage through the cave was rendered dangerous by the masses of rock which hung from the low vault. The interior was divided into several minor caverns leading one into the other by means of several steps, broken and precipitous, between enormous natural pillars. In the passage leading to the third chamber the roof was so low, the pillars so close together, that the boat had with great difficulty been dragged through, scraping both walls; however, in desperate circumstances, the hardest wood will yield a little, and even the native rock grow compliant to the dominating power of the human will.

Such was Aramis's thought when, after twice over repulsing his assailants, he decided upon flight – a hazardous enterprise certainly, since all his assailants had not been killed. Nay, admitting the possibility of getting the boat launched, he and his friends would have been obliged to put to sea in broad daylight in full view of their enemies, who, seeing the small number they had to deal with, would be more than ever determined to avenge their defeat. After the two volleys had killed ten of the attacking party, Aramis, who was well acquainted with the windings of the cavern, went off to reconnoitre, counting the twists and turns one by one, for the smoke with which the cave was filled rendered it impossible either to see or to be seen. Returning to his companions, he ordered that the boat should be moved forward as far as the big rock which barred the passage to freedom. Porthos collected his strength and lifted up the boat in his arms whilst the fishermen placed the rollers in position and helped to run the boat along. The third chamber was reached and passed; the boat was brought to a stop by the rock which walled up the outlet. Porthos seized the huge stone round the base, applied his mighty shoulder to it, and gave a heave which made the rock crack. A cloud of dust fell from the roof, together with the remains of the nests of ten thousand generations of sea-birds which covered the rock like cement. At the third heave, the stone began to give; it rocked for a moment upon its base. Porthos put his broad back against the adjacent rocks, and with a vigorous thrust of his foot forced the stone away from the concretion of limestone which had for ages held it immoveable. The stone having fallen, daylight streamed into the cavern through the opening thus made – daylight brilliant and dazzling – and the blue sea appeared before the eyes of the delighted Bretons. They began hoisting the boat over the stone which formed a barricade. Fifty yards more, and their boat would be afloat. It was during this time that the company of Guards arrived to reinforce the attacking party, and was formed up by the captain for the escalade, or perhaps it would be more correct to say the assault.

Aramis superintended everything and directed the labours of his friends. He saw the reinforcements and counted their number. A glance convinced him that renewed combat was out of the question. But to put to sea at the moment the cavern was about to be invaded was hardly to be thought of. Indeed, by the daylight which now illumined the last two chambers of the grotto, the soldiers would be able to see the boat being rolled towards the sea, and the two rebels within musket-shot; and by a volley they might riddle the boat with holes even if they did not succeed in killing the five navigators. Moreover, allowing that the boat was launched with the five men on board unhurt, it was evident that the alarm would be raised and their retreat cut off by the royal cruisers. How was it possible that the ill-fated craft, watched by the soldiers on shore and chased on the sea, could avoid being captured before the end of the day? Aramis, with rage in his heart, was ready to call upon any god or devil who might be willing to extricate him from his perilous plight. Beckoning to Porthos, whose single exertions were of far greater efficacy in moving the boat forward than all the rollers or the men who used them – 'My friend,' said he, dropping his voice, 'our enemies have just received reinforcements.'

'Ah!' said Porthos imperturbably, 'what shall we do next?'

'To resume the fight,' said Aramis, 'would be too great a risk.'

'Yes,' said Porthos, 'for it would be pretty strange, with only two of us, if they couldn't contrive to kill one or the other; and, of course, if one of us were killed, the other would get himself killed too.' The excellent Porthos, whose vast bodily strength seemed but to enhance the great-hearted simplicity of his nature, took it as a matter of course that one friend would never consent to survive the other.

Aramis was stung by the contrast between his own self-seeking nature and the loyalty of his friend.

'Neither of us need be killed, if you will do what I tell you, friend Porthos.'

'Tell me what to do.'

'Those men are going to enter the grotto.'

'Yes.'

'We might kill fifteen of them, but hardly more.'

'How many are there of them?' asked Porthos.

'They have just been reinforced by seventy-five men.'

'H'm – seventy-five and five – eighty,' said Porthos. 'If they fire a volley, we shall be riddled with bullets.'

'Undoubtedly.'

'Without reckoning that the concussion might bring down the roof on our heads.'

'As a matter of fact,' said Porthos, 'a rock which fell just now knocked some of the skin off my shoulder.'

'What! you are – '

'Pooh! that's nothing at all.'

'Well, we must decide quickly. Our men can be left to get the boat down to the sea.'

'Very well.'

'We two will stay here and look after the muskets and ammunition.'

'But we two can never keep up a sustained musket fire,' said Porthos, naïvely. 'I don't think it would be much use to rely on the muskets alone.'

'Suggest a better means of defence.'

'I have it!' cried the giant, suddenly. 'I will go and hide myself behind the pillar with this iron bar – they can't see me, and they won't be able to get at me – and I'll wait till they have all swarmed into the cave, and then I'll play upon their skulls with my crowbar thirty beats to the minute! – Well? How does that strike you? Isn't it a beautiful idea?'

'Excellent! my dear friend – perfect! I approve of it most heartily. Only I am afraid you will scare them, and half of them will remain outside to reduce us by famine. What we need, my dear friend, is the total annihilation of the whole force – one man left alive would ruin us.'

'You are right, my dear friend, but how are we to entice them inside I should like to know?'

'By not stirring, my good Porthos.'

'Very well, we won't stir. But when they are all inside the cave – ?'

'Leave it to me. I have an idea.'

'In that case, if your idea is a good one – and it is sure to be good if it is yours – I am quite satisfied.'

'To your ambuscade, Porthos, and count how many enter.'

'But what will you do?'

'Do not be uneasy on my account, I have a piece of work to do.'

'I fancy I can hear their voices.'

'They are coming! To your post! – Keep within sound of my voice and where I can reach you myself.'

Porthos took up his position in the second chamber, which was in pitch darkness. Aramis slipped into the third. The crowbar which the giant held had been provided for the purpose of assisting the operation of shifting the boat. Although it weighed fully fifty pounds, Porthos wielded it as though it had been a walking-stick.

Meanwhile, the fishermen had pushed the boat forward almost to the beach.

Aramis, in the third cave, into which the daylight entered, keeping well out of sight, was kneeling on the ground engaged in some mysterious operation.

A word of command was uttered in a ringing voice. It was the final order of the captain to the men of the first storming party. Five-and-twenty men dropped into the outer chamber of the grotto, and having landed on their feet, formed up and fired a volley. The echoes resounded; the whistling of the bullets cut the air; a dense smoke filled the whole cave – 'To the left! To the left!' cried Biscarrat, who had seen the passage leading to the second cave where he entered previously. The men accordingly rushed to the left; the cave gradually narrowed; Biscarrat, devoted to death, marched at the head of his men, feeling the walls with outstretched hand – 'This way! this way!' he cried. 'I see daylight!'

'Strike, Porthos!' cried the sepulchral voice of Aramis.

Porthos gave vent to a sigh, but he obeyed. The crowbar fell with deadly precision upon Biscarrat's head, killing him before he could utter a cry. Ten times in as many seconds did the tremendous weapon rise and fall, and each time it fell another corpse was added to the number of the slain. The soldiers could see nothing; they heard cries and groans, but they had not yet understood. They still advanced, stumbling against one another. Still the heavy bar rose and fell, and soon the whole of the first party was annihilated. The second section advanced quietly, not having heard a sound. However, this second party, under the command of the captain, had broken a branch from a stunted fir tree which grew at the edge of the cliff and twisting the resinous twigs together had made a torch, which was carried by the captain. As they reached the chamber where Porthos, like a Destroying Angel, had exterminated everything he had touched, the leading rank recoiled in horror. There had been no answering volley to that of the Guards, yet they found themselves stumbling over a heap of dead bodies and literally wading in blood.

Porthos still remained concealed behind his pillar. The captain, illuminating this scene of carnage with his feeble, flickering torch, and vainly endeavouring to discover the cause of the massacre, backed towards the pillar behind which the terrible Porthos lay in ambush. A gigantic hand issued from the gloom and gripped the captain by the throat. He gave vent to a hoarse rattle, beating the air with his hands; the torch dropped from his fingers and was extinguished in blood. A moment later, the dead body of the captain fell beside his extinguished torch to add to the number which encumbered the passage. All this had taken place mysteriously, as if by black magic. Hearing the ghastly rattle from the throat of the strangled captain, his men had turned; they had seen his arms waving convulsively – his eyes starting from their sockets. Then, the torch having fallen to the ground, all was plunged into profound darkness once more. Mechanically, without reflection, the lieutenant yelled – 'Fire!' Next moment a scattered volley thundered through the cavern, bringing down enormous fragments of the roof. The cavern was lit up for a moment by this fusillade, then instantly darkness fell, rendered more impenetrable still by the dense smoke.

A deathly silence followed, broken a moment later by the footsteps of the third brigade, which had now entered the grotto.

CHAPTER 78

## The death of a Titan

JUST AS PORTHOS, more habituated to the darkness than the men coming directly out of the daylight, was looking round to see whether Aramis might have any signal to make, he felt a gentle touch upon the arm, and a voice, low as a breath, murmured in his ear – 'Come,'

'Oh!' cried Porthos, startled.

'Sh,' breathed Aramis. And, whilst the third brigade was continuing to advance, in the midst of the savage curses of the Guards still unwounded and the groans of the dying, Aramis and Porthos slipped unnoticed along the granite wall of the cavern. Aramis led Porthos into the third cave, and showed him in a hollow of the wall a barrel of gunpowder weighing from sixty to eighty pounds, to which he had just attached a slow match – 'Friend Porthos,' said he, 'you will take this barrel, of which I am now going to light the fuse, and you will fling it right into the midst of our enemies; do you think you can?

'I should rather think so!' replied Porthos, lifting the barrel with one hand – 'Light the match.'

'Wait until they are all together,' said Aramis, 'and then, my own Jupiter,[192] hurl your thunderbolt into the midst of them.'

'Light it,' repeated Porthos.

'For my part,' continued Aramis, 'I will go and join our men and help them to launch the boat. I will wait for you on the beach. Throw it well into the middle of them and then run for the boat.'

'Light it,' said Porthos, for the third time.

'You quite understand?' said Aramis.

'*Parbleu!*' said Porthos, with a boisterous laugh which he made no effort to check, 'I understand well enough when a thing is explained to me. Off you go, and give me the light.'

Aramis gave the burning tinder to Porthos, who held out his elbow for his friend to shake, his hand being otherwise occupied. Aramis squeezed Porthos's arm between his two hands and returned to the opening of the cavern, where the three fishermen awaited him.

Porthos, left to himself, unflinchingly applied the tinder to the slow-match. The feeble spark, germ of a mighty conflagration, glowed in the semi-darkness like a fire-fly; then touching the fuse, it ignited it, and Porthos fanned the spark with his breath. The smoke had, by this time, partially cleared, and by the glimmer of the fuse, surrounding objects could be dimly discerned for the few moments that the match burned. It was a brief, but awe-inspiring sight, the giant, his face and hands smeared with blood, standing there in the gleam of the burning slow-match. The soldiers perceived him, saw the barrel he was holding in his hand. Suddenly they understood what was a-foot. Already terrified by what had been accomplished, and mad with fear of the hideous danger before them, the men gave vent to a simultaneous yell of agony. Some attempted flight, but they met the third brigade who barred their exit. Others raised their muskets mechanically, forgetting that they had not been reloaded. Others again fell upon their knees. Two or three of the officers shouted to Porthos promising him liberty in exchange for their lives.

The lieutenant commanding the third brigade ordered his men to fire, but the Guards were impeded by their terrified companions, who formed a living rampart for Porthos's protection.

As we have said, the light from the glowing tinder and the slow-match lasted but a few seconds; but during those few seconds this is what it revealed: a gigantic form looming out of the darkness; then, ten paces farther, a heap of bodies, crushed, mangled and bleeding, amongst them some still writhing and groaning in the death agony, causing the whole mass to stir like the heaving of some vast, shapeless monster expiring in the night. Every time Porthos breathed upon the match, this mass of bodies took on hues of sulphur flecked with purple. Beyond this principal group lay corpses scattered, as they had fallen, in various parts of the cavern. From the ground all reeking with blood rose the massive pillars of the cavern, their angles standing out sharply from the surrounding gloom. All these objects were rendered visible by the glimmering light of a fuse attached to a barrel of gunpowder, a beacon fire, as it were, which at one and the same time revealed the havoc which was completed and gave warning of the catastrophe to follow.

During those few moments, an officer of the third brigade collected eight guards armed with muskets and ordered them to fire upon Porthos over their companions' shoulders. But, in their terror, they aimed at random. Three of the men in front fell, the other five bullets tore up the ground or flattened themselves against the walls of the cavern.

The thunder of the musketry was followed by a burst of laughter. Then the giant raised his arm, and a train of fire flashed across the cavern, like a shooting star across the heavens.

The barrel, hurled a full thirty paces, cleared the barricade of corpses and fell among a yelling crowd of soldiers, who threw themselves flat on the ground.

The officer had followed the course of the train of fire, and dashed forward to fling himself on the barrel to tear out the match before it reached the powder. Unavailing his act of self-devotion! The air had quickened the fuse. Left to itself it would have burned another five minutes, as it was, it was consumed in thirty seconds; and the infernal engine exploded.

In an instant the cavern was full of wild, whirling eddies of flame, the mad spitting and spluttering of sulphur and saltpetre, the devouring ravages of fierce, fervent heat, the deafening thundering of explosion, and became as the very pit of hell.

The rocks split asunder like fir-logs under the hatchet. A fountain of fire and smoke and fragments shot up from the grotto, broadening and widening as it rose. The massive walls of granite toppled and fell in upon the sandy floor, while the sand itself, torn up from its hardened bed, was turned into an instrument of torment and struck and pitted the faces of the dying with its myriads of torturing particles.

Cries, yells and curses, all were drowned in the appalling crash, as life fell lifeless at the shock. The three chambers of the cave formed one yawning abyss, into which rained, one by one, the torn and mangled vestiges of vegetable and mineral and man.

Then came lighter layers of sand and still smoking ashes, descending softly and laying a grey winding-sheet over these sad wrecks of humanity.

Where now, in this seething sepulchre, this burning crater, where are the king's guards with their blue coats and silver facings? Where are their officers, glittering with their gold lace? Where are the arms that should have defended them? These, and the stones which slew them, and the very ground on which they stood – are utterly vanished and gone.

One man had made all this chaos, worse confounded than the chaos that reigned ere ever God spake the word and brought forth light out of darkness.

Of the three first divisions of the cavern not a vestige was left; not a thing remained that the Creator Himself could have claimed as his handiwork.

As for Porthos, after he had hurled his thunderbolt, he had fled towards the opening of the cave. On reaching the last chamber he perceived the boat a few hundred yards away, floating calmly upon the water. There lay life and liberty; there his friends awaited him. Six more of his huge strides and he would be out of the cavern; two or three vigorous leaps and he would reach safety. Suddenly he felt his limbs give way and his knees become powerless – 'Oho!' he muttered, 'this weakness is come on again – I cannot walk now. What's the meaning of this?'

Aramis had seen him approaching and was unable to understand the reason of his halt. 'Come, Porthos!' he shouted, 'quick, quick!'

'Oh!' groaned the giant, making a tremendous effort, 'I cannot move.' With these words, he fell forward upon his knees; but, gripping the rocks with his strong hands, he pulled himself upright again.

'Quick! Quick!' cried Aramis excitedly.

'Here I am,' stammered Porthos, collecting all his strength to make one step more.

'In heaven's name, make haste, Porthos! make haste! The barrel is going to explode!'

'Make haste! oh, make haste! your honour!' yelled the boatmen to Porthos, who was struggling as though in the grip of a nightmare.

Too late! the roar of the explosion filled their ears; the earth shook; smoke issued from fissures in the rock and obscured the sky; the sea receded, driven back before the blast of flame which spouted from the grotto as from the throat of some gigantic fiery dragon; the reflux swept the boat twenty yards from the shore; solid rocks cracked to their bases like timber split by a wedge; the roof of the cavern sprang towards the sky in a burst of lambent flame and hurtling rocks, surmounted by a majestic dome of smoke. The four spectators saw tall rocks, which the force of the explosion had not been able to uproot from the beds where for untold ages they had lain, oscillate and nod to one another like old men, slow and deliberate, and then fall crashing, to lie for ever prostrate.

This terrific shock seemed to restore to Porthos his lost strength. He pulled himself up, a giant in the midst of giants. But as he started to run between the double row of granite monoliths, these, no longer sustained by their connecting lintels, began to fall around the Titan,[193] who might have been hurled from Olympus amidst the boulders with which he had been assailing the Father of the Gods.

Porthos felt the earth trembling beneath his feet. He stretched his hands to right and left to push back the tottering pillars. A gigantic stone was held back by each of his extended hands; he bowed his head, and a third mass of granite sank between his shoulders.

For an instant his arms gave way; but exerting his Herculean strength, the two walls which held him prisoner fell slowly back, as though to make way for him. For one moment he appeared framed in granite like the genius of ancient chaos;[194] but in pushing back the lateral rocks he had deprived of its support the boulder which weighed upon his strong shoulders, and, receiving its full weight, the giant was forced to his knees. The lateral rocks, separated a moment before, fell together again, adding their weight to that of the stone upon his shoulders, which by itself would have been sufficient to crush ten ordinary men.

The giant fell without a cry for help; he fell in the act of answering Aramis with words of hope and encouragement. He may have thought for a moment that, thanks to the puissant flying-buttress of his arms, he could shake off, like Enceladus,[195] the triple load. But gradually, almost imperceptibly, Aramis saw the stones sink together; the mighty arms, extended for a last effort, give way; the Herculean shoulders, unable to sustain the prodigious weight upon them, slowly yield as the rock sank lower and lower and lower by degrees – 'Porthos! Porthos!' cried Aramis, wildly, 'where are you? Speak!'

'There, there!' gasped Porthos, his voice barely audible. 'Steady! One moment!'

Scarce had he time to utter the last word; the huge stone sank with increasing swiftness, pressed downwards by the two others falling in from the sides, and buried Porthos in a sepulchre of broken and crumbling rock. Hearing the dying voice of his friend, Aramis had sprung ashore, followed by two of the Breton fishermen with a crowbar, whilst the third remained to guard the boat. The last choking sighs of the vanquished champion guided them through the ruins to the spot where the Titanic struggle had taken place.

Active and alert as a young man of twenty, Aramis dashed towards the triple mass; and with his small, white hands, delicate as those of a woman, he contrived, by a miracle of desperate strength, to raise a corner of the vast granite sepulchre. He caught a glimpse of his friend's eyes, still bright with life, for the momentary easing of the mass had allowed him to breathe once more. The two men rushed up, inserted their iron lever beneath the stone, and all three, uniting their efforts, bent their whole strength to the task – not of lifting it, but of keeping it in place. In vain; the three men bent and bowed slowly but surely, with groans of bitter grief as they realised that their best efforts were in vain. Seeing them exhausting themselves in a useless struggle, Porthos, to whose simple mind the puny strength of lesser men had always been a source of good-humoured amusement, chuckled out with his last gasp the final words, 'Too heavy!'

Then his eyes grew dull and closed, his face paled, his hands grew white, and the Titan collapsed, expiring a last sigh.

The masses of rock which, even in his death agony, he had sustained, sank with him. The lever dropped from the other's hands upon the stones which formed his tomb.

Then pale, panting, with streaming brow, Aramis listened, his heart like to burst within his breast. Not a sound.

The giant was sleeping his eternal sleep in the sepulchre which God had fashioned him – a giant's sepulchre befitting his gigantic frame.

CHAPTER 79

## *Porthos's epitaph*

SILENT, CHILLED, trembling like a frightened child, Aramis shudderingly rose from off the stone. A Christian loves not to walk upon a tomb.

Although able to stand, he was incapable of walking. It seemed as though something of his dead friend had just died within him. His men gathered round him, and Aramis, yielding like a child, allowed the three sailors to raise him in their arms and carry him to the boat. Seating him on a thwart in the stern-sheets, they got out their oars and rowed away from the shore, for they were afraid of attracting attention by hoisting the sail.

Above all the levelled surface of the ancient grotto of Locmaria, a single hillock stood out against the sky. Aramis was unable to take his eyes off it; and from the sea, this rock loomed up portentously upon the ever-receding shore, seeming to draw itself up proudly, as Porthos used to draw *himself* up; lifting its serene and invincible head towards heaven, like that of the staunch and valiant friend – the strongest of the four, and yet the first to die. A strange destiny for these men of iron! Porthos, the simple-hearted, allied to the most astute of the four; his bodily strength directed by Aramis's subtlety of mind; and then, at the decisive moment, when strength alone could save both mind and body, a stone, a rock, a mere dead mass, had triumphed over muscular vigour and, crushing down upon the body, had forced the spirit out of it.

Good, honest Porthos! born to help others, always ready to sacrifice himself on behalf of the weak – as though God had endowed him with strength but for that purpose – and dying in the belief that he was only carrying out the conditions of his compact with Aramis; a compact which, however, Aramis alone had devised, and which Porthos had reaped nothing but calamity from. Noble Porthos! of what avail now are all thy châteaux filled to overflowing with costly furniture and pictures, thy forests teeming with game and lakes with fish; of what avail thy piled-up wealth? Can all thy servants in their gorgeous liveries avail thee now? Or Mousqueton, proud of the power with which he was invested by thee? Noble Porthos! careful heaper up of treasures, was it necessary to labour so hard to sweeten and gild life, only to lay thy mangled bones beneath a cold stone on a desolate shore, silent save for the cries of sea-birds! To what end, noble Porthos, didst thou amass gold, who canst not now command even the poor meed of an epitaph engraven upon thy monument?

Valiant Porthos! He yet sleeps, no doubt, unknown and forgotten, beneath the rock which the shepherds of the upland take for the mighty roof-stone of a sunken cromlech.

But so well have the heather and the moss and the lichen, quickened by the salt sea breezes, welded the boulder to mother earth, no passer-by could ever dream so ponderous a mass of granite could ever have been supported by the shoulder of a mortal man!

Aramis, still pale and cold, gazed shorewards with fluttering heart, until, with the last ray of daylight, the land faded from the horizon. Not a word escaped from his lips, not a sigh rose from his breast. The superstitious Breton sailors looked at him with awe. Such silence seemed hardly human – it was the silence of a statue.

Meanwhile, with the first streaks of grey which descended from the sky, the little sail had been hoisted and, swelling with the breeze, had borne them rapidly from the coast. The boat's nose was pointed for Spain, and she bounded forward gallantly across the Bay of Biscay, dreaded by sailors for its sudden and terrible tempests. Half an hour after setting the sail, the men ceased rowing. Bending over their thwarts, and shading their eyes with their hands, they pointed out to each other a white point which appeared upon the horizon, as motionless in appearance as a gull cradled by the insensible swell of the sea. But what appeared stationary to the ordinary eye was, to the practised eye of a sailor, in rapid motion. For some time, seeing the profound torpor in which Aramis was plunged, they did not venture to rouse him, but contented themselves with exchanging uneasy conjectures in a low tone. For indeed Aramis, the active and vigilant – Aramis, whose lynx eye was perpetually on the watch and, one might almost say, could, like that of the lynx, see as well by night as by day – Aramis's faculties lay dormant under the spell of a despair which filled his soul.

Thus an hour passed, during which the last rays of departing day gave place to twilight and the vessel which the boatmen had sighted gained so rapidly upon them that Goennec, one of the three, ventured to raise his voice and say – 'Monseigneur, we are being chased.'

Aramis made no reply. The vessel continued to overhaul them. Then, of their own accord, the sailors lowered the sail, in order that the only point which could be distinguished by their pursuer should cease to direct their enemy. The vessel in question meanwhile shook out more canvas. Unfortunately, it was the time of the year when days are longest, and a brilliant moon succeeded the unwelcome daylight. The corvette which, with a poop wind, was chasing the tiny lugger could therefore reckon upon a whole night of bright moonlight after another half-hour's twilight.

'Your eminence! Monseigneur! we are done for!' said the skipper Yves. 'Look, they can still see us for all we have hauled down the sail.'

'No wonder,' growled one of the sailors, 'for I've heard say the clever folk who live in cities have made a sort of pipe, with the devil's help, and when they spy through it they can see as well at a distance as they can close to, by night or by day.'

Aramis took from the bottom of the locker a telescope which he had provided, and handing it to the sailor – 'Take this,' he said, 'and look through it.'

The sailor hesitated.

'Set your mind at rest,' said the bishop, 'you will commit no sin – whatever sin there may be I will take upon my own shoulders.'

The sailor applied the glass to his eye, and gave a startled exclamation. He fancied that the corvette, which appeared through the telescope to be within cannon-shot had miraculously covered the distance with a single bound. But, on taking the glass from his eye, he saw that the vessel was still at the same distance as before.

'So then,' muttered the sailor, 'they can see us just as we can see them?'

'Yes, they can see us,' replied Aramis. And he resumed his former impassivity.

'What! they can see us? How can that be?' asked the skipper.

'Take hold of this, skipper, and see for yourself,' said the sailor, passing the telescope.

'Will your eminence vouch for it,' asked Yves, 'that the devil has nothing to do with all this?'

Aramis shrugged his shoulders. The skipper put the glass to his eye.

'Why! it is a miracle!' he exclaimed. 'There they are – I can almost touch them. Five-and-twenty men if not more! Ah! I can see the captain on the fo'castle. He's got a thing like this against his eye and he's looking at us. Now he's turned round – he's giving an order. They are casting loose the bow chaser – they are loading her – now they are taking aim. Holy Virgin! they are firing on us!'

And mechanically the skipper took the glass from his eye, and the objects seen, springing back to the horizon, resumed their normal aspect. The vessel was still nearly a league behind, but the manoeuvre which Yves had described was none the less real. A tiny patch of smoke appeared beneath the sails, opening out like a blue flower; then, about a mile astern, they saw the ball cut the heads off two or three waves and plough a white furrow in the sea, disappearing at the end of the furrow as inoffensively as the stone with which a school-boy makes 'ducks and drakes' upon the surface of a pond.

The shot was at the same time a warning and a threat – 'What are we to do?' asked the skipper.

'They are going to sink us,' said Goennec. 'Give us absolution, monseigneur.' The sailors fell on their knees in front of the bishop.

'You forget that they can see us,' said the latter.

'That is true,' said the sailors, ashamed of their weakness. 'Tell us what to do, monseigneur; we are ready to die if you give the word.'

'Wait,' said Aramis. 'Don't you understand that, as you said just now, they will sink us if we attempt to run?'

'But perhaps,' the skipper ventured to suggest, 'perhaps we might be able to give them the slip during the night.'

'Oh!' said Aramis, 'they are sure to be provided with Greek fire,[196] or flares of some sort, to light up their way – and ours.'

As though to illustrate Aramis's remark, a second puff of smoke appeared at the vessel's side and rose slowly towards the sky. From the midst of this cloud sprang a streak of fire which described a curve like a rainbow, then plunged into the sea, where it continued to burn, lighting up a circle a quarter of a league in diameter. The fishermen looked at each other with terrified eyes.

'You see,' said Aramis, 'that it will be best to wait for them.'

The sailors unshipped their oars, allowing them to trail from the thole-pins, and the little boat, losing her way, gently rose and fell upon the bosom of the waves. Night advanced, but the cruiser still continued to approach. It almost seemed as though her speed had increased with the darkness. From time to time the terrible Greek fire leapt from the ship's side, like a red-necked vulture darting its head out of its nest, and launched its flame into the middle of the ocean, where it burned with an incandescent glare. Soon the corvette had arrived within musket shot. The whole crew was on deck, marines with shouldered muskets, gunners standing to their pieces, linstock in hand. One would have said they were preparing to board a frigate manned by a crew superior to their own, and not merely to capture a tiny boat with only four men on board.

'Surrender!' shouted the captain of the ship through his speaking-trumpet. The sailors looked at Aramis, who nodded in token of assent. The skipper Yves raised a white cloth at the end of a boat hook. This was equivalent to striking their flag. The corvette came thrashing along like a racehorse, and hove-to all standing within biscuit-toss. Another rocket of Greek fire spurted forth, and fell within yards of the boat, illuminating it more brilliantly than the sun at noonday.

'At the first sign of resistance we fire!' cried the commander of the corvette. The marines brought their muskets to the present.

'Haven't we said we would surrender?' shouted Yves.

'Alive, captain!' cried several officers excitedly. 'We must take them alive!'

'Very well, we'll take them alive,' said the captain. Then, hailing the three Breton fishermen, 'Your lives shall all be spared, my men,' he cried, 'with the one exception of that of the Chevalier d'Herblay.'

Aramis shuddered involuntarily. For an instant he fixed his gaze upon the depths of the ocean whose surface was lit up by the last rays of the Greek fire which flashed upon the sides of the waves and sharply outlined their crests against the black hollows, rendering still most terrible and mysterious the abysses beneath them.

'Do you hear that, your eminence? asked the skipper. – 'Yes.' – 'What orders do you give us?' – 'You are to accept the conditions.' – 'But you, you eminence?' – Aramis leaned still farther over the boat's side, and his slender white hand playing with the green water, to which he smiled as to a friend, 'Accept!' he repeated.

'We agree,' shouted the man,' but how do we know you will keep the terms?'

'You have my word as a gentleman,' said the officer. 'I swear by my name and rank that all of you shall have your lives spared, with the exception of Monsieur d'Herblay. I am lieutenant of her majesty's frigate *Pomona*, and my name is Louis-Constant de Pressigny.'

With a swift gesture, Aramis, already bending over the sea – already half out of the boat – Aramis raised his head, then rose to his feet and with flashing eye and smile upon his lips – 'Let down the ladder, gentlemen,' he said, in a tone of authority, as though it were he who commanded the cutter. The ladder was swung over the ship's side, and Aramis, seizing the rope guard-rail, mounted first – but instead of the terror which one might have expected him to display upon his countenance, the sailors on board the king's ship, to their extreme surprise, saw him, on reaching the gangway, walk straight up to the commander with an assured step, look him full in the face and make a mysterious sign with his hand, at the sight of which the officer grew pale, trembled and bowed his head. Without uttering a word, Aramis raised his hand level with the commander's eyes, allowing him to see the bezel of a ring which he wore upon the third finger of his left hand. And, as he made this sign, Aramis's mien was so imposing and majestic, so cold and haughty, that one would have said he was an emperor giving his hand to be kissed. The commander, who had for a moment raised his head, bowed a second time with every mark of profound respect. Then, pointing towards the aftercabin – that is to say, his own quarters – he stood aside for Aramis to go first.

The three Bretons, who had mounted the ladder behind their bishop, looked at one another in amazement. The whole crew were struck silent. Five minutes later, the captain summoned the quartermaster and gave him directions to lay the ship's course for Corunna. Whilst the ship was being put about in conformity with this order, Aramis reappeared on deck, and seated himself beside the bulwarks on the port quarter. Night had fallen, but the moon had not yet appeared; nevertheless he remained gazing fixedly in the direction of Belle-Isle.

The captain had resumed his station upon the quarter-deck. Yves climbed the companion ladder, and approaching him cap in hand, ventured to ask respectfully – 'Where are we bound for, your honour?'

'We are bound for whatever port his eminence pleases,' replied the officer.

Aramis passed the night in the same attitude, with his elbow resting on the bulwarks. Next morning, as Yves was passing him, it struck him that there must have been a heavy mist during the night, for the woodwork upon which the bishop's head had been resting was wet, as if with dew.

Who shall say? – It may be that these were the first tears which Aramis had ever shed. Oh, Porthos, good and brave! could any epitaph have been so eloquent as this?'

## CHAPTER 80

## *Monsieur de Gesvres makes his rounds*

D'ARTAGNAN had not been accustomed to meet with obstructions like those he had just encountered. He returned to Nantes in a state of extreme irritation. In the case of d'Artagnan's vigorous temperament, to say that he was irritated is equivalent to saying that he was about to take prompt reprisals; and few persons hitherto had been able to resist his attack, even were they kings or giants. Shaking with fury, the captain went straight to the château and asked to be admitted to the king's presence. It was then about seven o'clock in the morning, and since his arrival at Nantes, the king had been an early riser. However, on reaching the little corridor of which we have already spoken, d'Artagnan encountered Monsieur de Gesvres, who stopped him with great politeness and begged him not to raise his voice as the king was resting.

'Is the king asleep?' asked d'Artagnan. 'In that case I will let him sleep on. About what o'clock do you suppose he will rise?'

'Oh! in about a couple of hours' time. The king has been awake all night.'

D'Artagnan clapped on his hat, saluted Monsieur de Gesvres and went to his own quarters. About half-past nine he returned. He was informed that the king was at breakfast – 'Very well,' said he, 'I will talk to his majesty as he is breakfasting.'

Monsieur de Brienne reminded d'Artagnan that the king received nobody whilst he was at meals.

'But,' said d'Artagnan, looking askance at Brienne, 'perhaps you are not aware, Mr Secretary, that I have permission to enter whenever and wherever I please.'

Brienne took the hand of the captain kindly, and replied – 'Not at Nantes, dear Monsieur d'Artagnan – the king on this journey has changed the order of his household.'

D'Artagnan, somewhat mollified, asked when the king would have finished breakfast.

'We don't know,' replied Brienne.

'What! you don't know? What is the meaning of this? You don't know how long the king takes over his breakfast? He usually takes an hour, and allowing that the air of the Loire gives one a good appetite, we will call it an hour and a half – that ought to be long enough, I think. I will wait here.'

'Oh! but my dear Monsieur d'Artagnan, the orders are to allow nobody to remain in the corridor: I am on guard for that purpose.'

For the second time d'Artagnan felt his anger rising to his head. He went out hurriedly for fear of complicating matters by a display of ill-humour. Once outside the château he began to reflect. 'The king,' he thought, 'evidently does not wish to see me. The young man is angry, and is afraid to hear what I have to say to him. Yes; but in the meantime Belle-Isle is being besieged, and my two friends will be taken and perhaps killed – Poor Porthos! But as for Master Aramis, I am quite easy on his account; he is full of resources. No, no! Porthos has not yet lost his strength, nor is Aramis quite an imbecile. The one with his arm and the other with his head will provide plenty of work and amusement for his majesty's soldiers yet! Who knows but these two good men may devise some little Bastion Saint-Gervais for the edification of his most Christian majesty? I shouldn't be surprised – they have guns, and men to work them. And yet,' continued d'Artagnan, shaking his head thoughtfully, 'I fancy it would be better to put an end to the fighting. If it only concerned myself, I would not put up with any shiftiness or black looks from the king; but for the sake of my friends I am prepared to endure snubs or even insults. Suppose I go and call upon Monsieur Colbert. There is a man into whom I must instil habits of wholesome dread, and the sooner I begin the better. So here goes for Monsieur Colbert.' And d'Artagnan marched boldly to Monsieur Colbert's rooms, only to be informed that the new minister was at the château, engaged with the king. 'Good!' growled the captain; 'it appears we are back in the times when I used to tramp backwards and forwards from pillar to post, wearing out the pavement between Monsieur de Tréville's quarters and the cardinal's lodgings, from the cardinal's to the queen's, and from the queen to Louis XIII. It is a true saying that men as they grow old become children again. Well, back we go to the château!'

On returning, he found Monsieur de Lyonne going out. He took d'Artagnan by both hands, and told him that the king would be engaged all the afternoon and most probably all night too, and that he had given orders that no one was to be allowed to enter.

'Not even the captain whose duty it is to take the order of the day?' cried d'Artagnan. 'This is too much!'

'Without any exception,' said Monsieur de Lyonne.

'Since this is the state of affairs,' replied d'Artagnan, cut to the heart, 'since the captain of the musketeers, who has always had the privilege of entering the king's bedroom, cannot enter his cabinet or where he takes his meals, it means either that the king is dead or that his captain is in disgrace. In either case he has no further need of me. Do me the favour of returning to his majesty – you, Monsieur de Lyonne, who are in favour – and telling the king point blank that I resign my commission.'

'D'Artagnan, be careful!' cried de Lyonne.

'For friendship's sake, do as I ask.' And he pushed him gently towards the king's cabinet.

D'Artagnan strode up and down in the corridor until Lyonne returned.

'Well, what did the king say?'

'The king answered, "Very well," ' replied Lyonne.

' "Very well", indeed!' burst out the captain. 'Then he accepts my resignation. Good! now I am free. I am a plain civilian, Monsieur de Lyonne, at your service! Farewell château, farewell corridor and antechamber! A citizen who has regained his liberty takes his leave of you.' And, without more ado, the captain turned on his heel, left the terrace and descended the staircase where he had picked up the pieces of Gourville's letter. Five minutes later he had re-entered the inn where, in accordance with the custom of the chief officers who had quarters in the château, he had taken what he called lodgings in town. Having arrived there, instead of removing his sword and cloak, he took his pistols, put his money into a large leathern purse, sent a man to fetch his horses from the stables of the château and gave directions for reaching Vannes during the night.

Everything went forward in accordance with his wishes. At eight o'clock that evening, as he was putting his foot in the stirrup, Monsieur de Gesvres made his appearance in front of the inn at the head of a dozen troopers of the Guard. D'Artagnan saw this out of the corner of his eye, for indeed, he could scarcely fail to be aware of the presence of thirteen mounted men; but he pretended to have noticed nothing, and swung himself astride his horse. Gesvres rode up to him.

'Monsieur d'Artagnan!' said he, loudly.

'Ah! Monsieur de Gesvres, good-evening!'

'One would say you are getting on horseback.'

'More than that, I am already mounted, as you see.'

'It is fortunate I have met you.'

'Were you looking for me?'

'Indeed, I was.'

'You've been sent by the king, I'll wager.'

'Yes.'

'In the same way that I looked for Monsieur Fouquet, two or three days ago?'

'Oh!'

'Come, there's no occasion for excessive delicacy with me! Trouble thrown away, man! Say at once that you have come to arrest me.'

'To arrest you? Good heavens, no!'

'Then why do you come to "look for me" with a dozen troopers?'

'I am making my rounds.'

'That's pretty good! and so you just pick me up on your rounds, I suppose?'

'Not at all. I meet you, and I beg you to come with me.'

'Where?'

'To the king.'

'Good!' said d'Artagnan, sarcastically. 'So then his majesty is quite disengaged now?'

'For heaven's sake, captain,' said Monsieur de Gesvres, seriously, in a low tone, 'be careful what you say. These men can hear you!'

D'Artagnan laughed carelessly.

'March!' he cried. 'People when they are arrested are placed between the six first and the six last guards.'

'But as I am not arresting you, you will please to ride behind me,' replied de Gesvres.

'Well, duke,' said d'Artagnan, 'you arrange the thing very nicely, and you are quite right; for if I had occasion to make my rounds in the neighbourhood of *your* lodgings in town, I should have acted just as politely towards you, I assure you on my honour! Now do me one more favour. Tell me what the king wants with me.'

'Oh! the king is furious!'

'Well, if he has taken the trouble to get into a fury, he must take the trouble to calm down again, that's all. I shall not die of it, I swear.'

'No, but –'

'But I shall be sent to keep poor Monsieur Fouquet company? Faith! he is a gentleman. We will live together, and very agreeably, too, I am sure.'

'Here we are,' said the duke. 'For heaven's sake, captain, don't anger the king.'

'Oho! you are wondrous civil to me, duke,' said d'Artagnan, with a sharp glance at Monsieur de Gesvres. 'I was told you had an ambition to add the musketeers to your Guards – this would be a splendid opportunity, I fancy.'

'An opportunity of which I shall take particular care not to avail myself, captain!'

'Why?'

'Oh, for several reasons. If I were to take your place in the musketeers, after having arrested you – '

'Then you admit you have arrested me?'

'By no means!'

'We will say *met* me, then. You were saying, if you were to succeed me after having met me – ?'

'Your musketeers, the first time I took them out for firing practice, would shoot me by accident.'

'Ah! as to that I won't contradict you. My rascals are very fond of me.'

De Gesvres made d'Artagnan pass in first, took him straight to the cabinet where the king was awaiting his captain of musketeers, and stationed himself behind his colleague in the antechamber. The king's voice could be very distinctly heard speaking to Colbert, in the same cabinet where Colbert might have heard, a few days before, the king speaking to d'Artagnan. The Guards remained as a mounted picket before the principal gateway; and the report was gradually spread through the town that the captain of the musketeers had been arrested by order of the king. The news caused a ferment among the townspeople. It seemed as though the good old days of Louis XIII and Monsieur de Tréville had returned. The people formed in groups to discuss the news, and crowded on the staircases; vague murmurs, proceeding from the courtyard, could be heard above, like the hoarse moanings of the sea at flood-tide. Monsieur de Gesvres became fidgety. He looked at his Guards, who were being plied with eager questions by the musketeers who had broken through their ranks. They began to draw together apart from the musketeers and to show some signs of uneasiness. D'Artagnan was indeed far more self-possessed than Monsieur de Gesvres, the captain of the Guards. He had seated himself on entering the room in the embrasure of a window, whence his eagle glance could see everything that went on, though he did not move a muscle of his countenance. Not a single detail had escaped him of the excitement manifested below at the rumour of his arrest. He foresaw that there would be an explosion before long, and, as we know, his judgment was very rarely at fault. 'It would be rather quaint,' he thought, 'if my praetorians were to make me King of France this evening. How I should laugh!'

But at the moment when matters seemed ripe for a disturbance, quiet was suddenly restored. Guards, musketeers, officers and troopers dispersed; murmurs were silenced and calmness restored. Every sign of storm or mutiny vanished. A single word had quelled the tumult; the king had sent Brienne out to say – 'Silence, gentlemen, you are disturbing his majesty.'

D'Artagnan heaved a sigh. 'It is all over,' he said to himself. 'The musketeers of the present day are not the musketeers of his majesty Louis XIII. It is all over, all over!'

'The king will receive Monsieur d'Artagnan!' cried an usher.

## CHAPTER 81

## King Louis XIV

THE KING was seated in his private cabinet, with his back towards the door of entrance. In front of him was a mirror in which he only needed to glance as he was turning over his papers in order to see those who came in. Louis did not turn as d'Artagnan entered, but covered his letters and plans with a large green silk cloth which he made use of to conceal his secrets from inquisitive eyes. D'Artagnan understood the byplay, and remained at the door, so that after a moment's pause, the king, who could hear nothing and could see only with the corner of his eye, was obliged to enquire, 'Has Monsieur d'Artagnan not come yet?'

'Here I am, sire,' cried the musketeer, coming forward.

'Well,' said the king, fixing his clear glance upon d'Artagnan, 'and what have you to say to me?'

'I, sire?' replied the latter, who had waited for the king to open the attack in order to parry the thrust effectively. 'I have nothing to say to your majesty – unless it be that you have had me arrested, and here I am.'

The king was about to reply he had not ordered d'Artagnan's arrest; but it would have seemed too like an excuse, and he remained silent. D'Artagnan was determined not to be the first to speak again.

'Monsieur d'Artagnan, what was the commission I gave you at Belle-Isle? Tell me, if you please,' resumed the king at length, looking his captain steadily in the face.

D'Artagnan felt that he was in luck. This was the very chance he had been hoping for. 'I think your majesty did me the honour of asking me for what purpose I went to Belle-Isle?' he said.

'Yes.'

'Well, sire, I am entirely ignorant of the purpose of my going; it is not I whom you should ask, but one of those innumerable officers of all ranks and every service who received a number of orders of all kinds, whilst I, the leader of the expedition, had received no definite orders at all.'

The king felt the thrust, as his reply showed.

'Monsieur,' he answered, 'orders were given only to those who were judged trustworthy.'

'I find it surprising,' retorted d'Artagnan, 'that a captain of musketeers, who ranks with a Marshal of France, should be placed under the orders of five or six lieutenants or majors – excellent as spies, perhaps, but scarcely competent to conduct a campaign. It was about this I came to ask an explanation of your majesty when I was denied admittance; and this last insult to a brave man has led me to quit your majesty's service.'

'Monsieur d'Artagnan,' replied the king, 'you seem to think you are still living in an age when kings were in the position of which you yourself are complaining – under the orders and at the mercy of their inferiors. I think you are apt to forget that a king owes an account of his actions to none but God.'

'I forget nothing, sire,' cried the musketeer, wounded in his turn by this admonition. 'Besides, I do not see how an honest man can commit an offence by asking his king in what way he has served him ill.'

'You have served me badly, monsieur, by taking the part of my enemies.'

'Who are your enemies, sire?'

'Those men against whom I sent you.'

'Two men the enemies of your majesty's whole army! It is incredible, sire.'

'It is not for you to judge my actions.'

'But I have to consider my old friendships, sire.'

'A man who serves his friends cannot serve his master.'

'I have so well understood that, sire, that I have respectfully tendered your majesty my resignation.'

'Which I have accepted,' said the king. 'Only, before losing sight of you, I wished to show you that I know how to keep my word.'

'Your majesty has more than kept your word – you have had me arrested,' said d'Artagnan, with provoking coolness. 'You had not promised me that.'

The king disdained to notice this pleasantry. 'You see, monsieur,' he said in a tone of severity, 'to what your disobedience has forced me.'

'My disobedience?' repeated d'Artagnan, flushing angrily.

'That is the mildest term I can find,' pursued the king. 'My own idea was to have the rebels caught and punished; was I to enquire if these rebels were your friends?'

'But it was a question *I* could not neglect,' replied d'Artagnan. 'It was cruel of your majesty to send me to seize my friends in order to hand them over to your hangman.'

'I wished to make trial, monsieur, of those who pretend to serve me – who eat my bread, and whose duty it is to defend my person. The result has disappointed me, Monsieur d'Artagnan.'

'In place of the one bad servant whom your majesty is losing,' said the musketeer bitterly, 'you can find ten more who have, this very day, proved their worth. Listen to me, sire; *I* am not accustomed to such service – I am but an unwilling tool when I am required to do ill. It was a painful task for me to have to hunt to the death two men whom Monsieur Fouquet – your majesty's preserver – had begged you to spare. Moreover, these two men were my friends. They were not attacking your majesty; they were already yielding beneath the weight of your anger. Then why not have allowed them to escape? What crime have they committed? I admit you will dispute my right to judge their conduct. But why suspect me beforehand? Why surround me with spies? Why dishonour me before the army? I, in whom you have hitherto shown entire confidence – I who have been attached to your person for the last thirty years and have given you a thousand proofs of my devotion. I am forced to remind your majesty of this, now that I am accused. Why put me under the shameful necessity of seeing three thousand of the king's soldiers march against two men?'

'One would suppose you had forgotten the treason these men have been guilty of,' said the king grimly. 'If it had rested only with them, I should not be here now.'

'Sire, one would say you had forgotten that I was there!'

'Enough, Monsieur d'Artagnan, enough of these side issues which interfere with the development of my interests. I am founding a state in which there shall be but one master. I promised you this long ago, and the moment has come for the promise to be kept. You think you can be allowed to thwart my plans and shield my enemies according to your own preferences or friendships? I will break you or I will get rid of you. Perhaps you would seek a master less exacting? Oh! yes, I am well aware that another king would not deal with you as I am doing – he would allow himself to be guided by you until one day he would find it necessary to send you to keep Monsieur Fouquet company. But I have a good memory, and I never forget those who render me a service – in the case of those who have served me well, I can overlook grave faults. I read you this lesson then, Monsieur d'Artagnan, and it shall be the sole punishment for your indiscretion. I will no more imitate my predecessors in their anger than I have imitated them in showing favour. There are other considerations which induce me to act leniently towards you: in the first place because you are a man of sense – a man of sound common sense as well as a man of heart – and you will be a good servant when you have been forced to recognise your master; and then again, you will no longer have any motives for insubordination. Your friends have been destroyed or ruined by me. I have removed those considerations which tended, in spite of yourself, to undermine your loyalty. By this time my troops have captured or killed the rebels at Belle-Isle.'

D'Artagnan changed colour. 'Captured or killed?' he cried. 'Oh! Sire, if you meant what you say, and if you were certain of the truth of it, I should forget how much there is that is just – nay, generous – in the words you have spoken, and I should call you a barbarous king and a man without bowels. But I pay no regard to those words,' he continued, smiling proudly; 'I can forgive such words from a prince who does not know, who cannot understand what such men as Monsieur d'Herblay, Monsieur Du Vallon and myself are. Captured or killed! Ha! Ha! Tell me, sire, if this news is true, how many men and how much money it has cost you? We can calculate afterwards if the game was worth the candle.'

'Monsieur d'Artagnan, now you are talking like a rebel. Who is King of France? If you know of another king, pray tell me!'

'Sire,' replied the captain of the musketeers, coldly, 'I remember one morning at Vaux when you addressed that same question to a number of people who were at a loss to answer it, whilst I alone did not hesitate. If I recognised the king that day, when it was no easy matter to recognise him, it seems to me unnecessary to repeat the question now that your majesty is alone with me.'

At these words, Louis XIV cast down his eyes. It seemed to him that the spectre of the ill-fated Philippe had passed between d'Artagnan and himself in order to recall to him that terrible adventure. Almost at the same moment an officer entered and handed a dispatch to the king, who, in his turn, changed colour as he read it. D'Artagnan noticed the king's annoyance. After having read the letter a second time, Louis remained for some moments silent and motionless. Then, having made his decision, he said suddenly, 'Monsieur, the news I have just received you will learn later in any case; it is better that I should tell you, that you should learn it from the mouth of the king. There has been an engagement at Belle-Isle.'

'Ha!' said d'Artagnan, calmly, although his heart was beating fast. 'Well, sire?'

'Well, Monsieur d'Artagnan, I have lost a hundred and six men.'

D'Artagnan's eye flashed with joy and pride. 'And the rebels?' he asked.

'The rebels have escaped,' said the king. The captain could not repress an exclamation of triumph. 'However,' added Louis, 'my fleet is keeping Belle-Isle strictly blockaded, and I am certain no boat will succeed in evading my cruisers.'

'So that if these two gentlemen are caught – ?' said the musketeer, his hopes somewhat dashed by the king's words.

'They will be hanged,' said the king, quietly.

'And do they know that?' asked d'Artagnan, repressing a shudder.

'They know it, since you must have told them, and besides, it is common knowledge.'

'Then, sire, you will never have them alive, I will answer for it.'

'Indeed!' said the king indifferently, as he took up the letter again. 'Well then, we must have them *dead*, Monsieur d'Artagnan; and it will amount to the same thing, because I should capture them only to have them hanged.' D'Artagnan wiped the sweat from his forehead. 'I have told you,' pursued Louis XIV, 'that one day I would prove myself a kind, considerate and constant master. At the present day you are the only man of the older generation who is worthy of my anger or of my goodwill. I will not be sparing of either in my treatment of you, according as you behave. Would you be content, Monsieur d'Artagnan, to serve a king if there were a hundred other kings equal to him in the realm? Tell me, do you think it would be possible for me, if my power were thus divided, to accomplish the great schemes I have in mind? Have you ever known an artist produce good work with indifferent tools? We must make a clean sweep of all survivals of old feudal abuses! The Fronde, which threatened to overthrow the monarchy, has given it a new lease of life. Yes, Captain d'Artagnan, I am master here, and I will have servants who will set no limits to their obedience, though they may perhaps lack your capacity. But one does not require the limbs to be endowed with intelligence. It is for the head to direct, and the limbs to obey; and it is I who am the head.' D'Artagnan stirred uneasily.

Louis XIV continued as though he had not seen the gesture, although it had not escaped him. 'Now, let us ratify the bargain we made one day at Blois,[197] when I was a boy. You will at least allow, monsieur, that I have never sought to make anyone pay for the tears of shame I was forced to shed at that time. Look around you; you will see that powerful heads have been obliged to bend. You also must humble your pride, or else choose such exile as will suit you best. Perhaps, on reflection, you will recognise that this king is not wanting in generosity who places sufficient reliance upon your loyalty to permit you to leave him when you are dissatisfied, and when you possess the knowledge of an important secret of state. You are a brave man – that I know full well. Why have you judged prematurely? Judge of me from this day forward, d'Artagnan, and with as much severity as you please.'

D'Artagnan remained lost in mute bewilderment, and, for the first time in his life, was unable to come to a decision. He had at last found an adversary worthy of his steel. He recognised that this was no longer cunning, but the calculated foresight of a master mind; no longer violence, but strength; in place of petulance and empty boasting, he found determination and method. This young man, who had caused Fouquet's downfall and who could very well do without d'Artagnan, upset all the captain's somewhat over-confident calculations.

'Come now, what is your difficulty?' said the king, kindly. 'You have given in your resignation; if you like, I will refuse to accept it. I understand that it is hard for an old soldier to admit that he has been too hasty.'

'Oh!' replied d'Artagnan sadly, 'it is not that which troubles me greatly. I hesitate to revoke my resignation because I am an old man compared with you, and I have formed habits which are hard to break. Henceforth you will require courtiers who understand how to amuse you, or fools who will kill themselves in carrying out what you are pleased to call your great schemes. Not that I have any doubt of their greatness, but suppose I were to find that they did not appeal to me? Sire, I have seen war and I have lived in times of peace. I have served Richelieu and Mazarin; I have been scorched with your father at the fire of La Rochelle;[198] I have been stuck as full of holes as a sieve, and have grown a fresh skin ten times over, like the serpents. After putting up with slights and injustice, I have obtained a command which at one time was not inconsiderable, since it carried with it the privilege of speaking freely to the king. But in future your captain of musketeers will be a sort of superior doorkeeper. Sire, if such are the duties one may henceforward expect, take this opportunity of our being on good terms to relieve me of my command. Never believe that I bear malice; no, you have mastered me, as you said; but I am fain to confess that in taming me, you have at the same time lessened my self-esteem, in forcing me to bend, you have convicted me of weakness. Ah! if you knew the satisfaction I felt in being able to carry my head high, and what a pitiful figure I should cut as a sort of tame spaniel! Oh! Sire, I look back with regret to the times – and you also will have cause to regret them – when the King of France had his vestibules filled with gentlemen, hardy, hungry, growling and surly mastiffs whose bite was mortal when they were loosed upon the king's enemies. They would lick the hand which fed them, but the hand that struck them, ah! they would very soon make their fangs meet in it! A trifle of gold embroidery on the edges of their cloaks, a fine, upstanding figure, a dash of grey in their hair, and there you have your finest dukes and Peers, your gallant Marshals of France! But what use to speak of all this? The king is my master, he decides that I am to string rhymes – to polish the mosaic floors of his antechambers with my satin shoes. Deuce take me if I find it easy! But I have done even more difficult things. It shall be done. Why do I do it? Because I am fond of money? – I have enough. Because I am ambitious? – My career has reached its limit. Because I should mope if I were not at court? – Certainly not. No, if I remain, it is because I have grown accustomed this last thirty years to go and take the password of the king and to hear him say – "Good-morning, d'Artagnan," with a smile which I had no need to beg. If necessary, I will beg for that smile. Are you satisfied, sire?'

So saying, d'Artagnan gently bowed his silvery head, upon which the king laid his hand with pride, whilst he said as he smiled kindly – 'Thanks! thanks! my old servant, my faithful friend. Since, from this day forward, I have no more enemies in France, it only remains for me to send you to some field abroad where you can pick up your marshal's baton. Depend upon me to find the occasion. Meanwhile, eat of my best bread and sleep in peace.'

D'Artagnan was greatly moved, but he only said – 'That is all very fine, sire, but what about those poor friends of mine at Belle-Isle? One of them especially, so good, so simple and true!'

'Do you ask me to grant their pardon?'

'On my knees, sire.'

'Very well, you shall take it to them, if it be not too late. But you will answer for them?'

'I will answer for them with my life.'

'Go, then. Tomorrow, I am returning to Paris. Return here by tomorrow: for I wish to keep you beside me.'

'Rest assured of that, sire,' cried d'Artagnan, kissing his royal Master's hand. Then, with a heart swelling with joy, he hastened from the château and took the direction of Belle-Isle.

CHAPTER 82

## Monsieur Fouquet's friends

THE KING had returned to Paris, and with him d'Artagnan, who, in the twenty-four hours at his disposal, having made all possible enquiries at Belle-Isle, had learned nothing of the secret so well concealed by that ponderous rock at Locmaria, fit tomb for the valiant Porthos. The captain of the musketeers knew only what those two valiant men – those two friends, whose defence he had undertaken, and whose lives he had endeavoured to save – had accomplished, with the assistance of three faithful Bretons, against a whole army. He had seen the havoc wrought by the frightful explosion in the cavern of Locmaria. He had also gathered that a boat had been seen far out at sea; one of the royal cruisers, like a bird of prey, had given chase, had swooped down upon and devoured that poor little bird in full flight. But this was all the captain had been able to verify; and beyond this limit opened out the wide domain of conjecture. For his own part he knew not what to think. The cruiser had not returned. True, a gale of wind had been blowing for three days past; but the corvette was known to be a good sea boat and well-found in every respect; she had no reason to lie-to on account of a mere capful of wind, and should, according to d'Artagnan's calculations, have returned by that time to Brest or have entered the Loire.

Such was the news he was able to collect – incomplete, it is true – but to a certain extent reassuring to him personally. D'Artagnan returned with these tidings to Louis XIV; and immediately afterwards, the king, followed by the whole court, set out to return to Paris. Satisfied with his success, and become more affable and considerate in manner since he had begun to feel his own power, Louis had not for a moment quitted the door of the carriage in which La Vallière was riding. All the courtiers had done their utmost to amuse the two queens, in order to make them forget this neglect on the part of husband and son. Everything breathed of the future; all thoughts of the past seemed to have been put aside. Still, that past had left painful wounds, not yet healed, in the hearts of more than one sensitive and devoted spirit. Of this the king received a touching proof as soon as he was reinstalled in Paris.

Louis XIV had just risen, and taken some refreshment, when his captain of musketeers presented himself before him. d'Artagnan was a trifle pale and wore an air of constraint. At the first glance, the king perceived this expression on the musketeer's countenance, usually so equable. 'What is the matter, d'Artagnan?' he asked.

'Sire, a great misfortune has happened to me.'

'Good heavens! what is it?'

'Sire, I have lost one of my friends – Monsieur Du Vallon – in the affair at Belle-Isle.' As he said these words, d'Artagnan glanced keenly at Louis XIV to ascertain what would be the first feeling he would manifest.

'I was aware of it,' replied the king.

'You knew it, and said nothing to me!' cried the musketeer.

'What good would it have done to tell you? Your sorrow, my good friend, is worthy of all respect! I could not do otherwise than treat it with consideration. To have informed you of this misfortune, so painful to you, d'Artagnan, would have seemed like rejoicing over your grief. Yes, I knew that Monsieur Du Vallon lies buried beneath the rocks at Locmaria; I was also aware that Monsieur d'Herblay has seized one of my vessels with its crew in order to pass over to Bayonne. But I wished you to learn these facts from other sources, that you might be convinced that I hold sacred whatever affects my friends – that, as a man, I am always willing to sacrifice myself on behalf of my fellow-men, although the king is so often forced to disregard his private feelings and sacrifice men for the sake of his majesty and power.'

'But, sire, how did you know – ?'

'How did you know yourself, d'Artagnan?'

'Through this letter, which Aramis has sent me from Bayonne, where he is in freedom and safety.'

'Stay a moment,' said the king. And he drew a paper from a casket which stood upon a table close by d'Artagnan's elbow – 'Here is an exact copy of Aramis's letter to you, which Colbert placed in my hands eight hours before you received the original. I am well served, am I not?'

'Yes, sire,' murmured the musketeer; 'you were the only other man whose star could prevail over the fortunes of my two friends. You have used your power, sire; but you will not abuse it, I am confident.'

'D'Artagnan,' said the king, smiling kindly, 'I could, if I wished, have Monsieur d'Herblay seized upon the territory of the King of Spain and have him brought here alive to submit to justice. But you may rest assured I will not yield to this first very natural impulse. He is free, and he shall remain unmolested.'

'Oh! Sire, you will not always remain so merciful, so noble and generous as you have just shown yourself towards me and towards Monsieur d'Herblay; you will find counsellors who will cure you of these weaknesses.'

'No, d'Artagnan, you are wrong if you think my advisers are likely or willing to influence me on the side of severity. The recommendation to spare Monsieur d'Herblay comes from Colbert himself.'

'Ah! exclaimed d'Artagnan, taken aback.

'With regard to yourself,' continued the king with unwonted kindliness, 'I have some good news for you, but I will defer entering into particulars until I have made all necessary arrangements. I told you, my dear captain, that I intended to make your fortune. The promise is about to be realised.'

'A thousand thanks, sire; but I can afford to wait. But I beg that your majesty, whilst I am practising patience, will deign to notice those poor fellows who have long been besieging your antechamber, and who have come humbly to lay a petition at the king's feet.'

'Who are they?'

'Some of your majesty's enemies.' – The king looked up quickly – 'Friends of Monsieur Fouquet,' added d'Artagnan.

'Their names?'

'Monsieur Gourville, Monsieur Pélisson and a poet named Monsieur Jean de La Fontaine.'

The king paused a moment to consider, and then asked, 'What is their object?'

'I do not know.'

'Well, what sort of figure do they cut?'

'They seem to be in great affliction.'

'Do they say anything?'

'Nothing at all.'

'What are they doing?'

'They are in tears.'

'Let them come in,' said the king, his face hardening.

D'Artagnan turned quickly towards the door, and raising the tapestry which screened the entrance to the king's apartment, called into the adjoining room, 'Let these gentlemen be introduced.' The three men whom d'Artagnan had named appeared at the door of the cabinet where the king was engaged with his captain of musketeers. Around them a deep silence prevailed. The courtiers, when the friends of the ex-minister of Finance made their appearance – the courtiers, we say, drew back as though they feared the contagion of his disgrace and misfortune. D'Artagnan stepped forward to take the poor fellows by the hand who were hesitating timidly before the door of the royal cabinet; he led them before the chair beside which the king was standing in the embrasure of a window, in expectation of their being presented to him, and prepared to give them a severely diplomatic reception. The first to advance was Pélisson. He had ceased to weep, but his tears were restrained only that he might be the better able to make his supplication to the king. Out of respect for his majesty, Gourville was biting his lips in order to check the tears. La Fontaine's face was hidden in his handkerchief, and one could see his shoulders heaving with convulsive sobs.

The king had preserved all his dignity. His face still wore the frown which had appeared when d'Artagnan announced to him the presence of his enemies. He made a gesture which signified permission to speak, and remained standing with his eyes fixed searchingly upon the three unhappy men. Pélisson bowed almost to the ground, and La Fontaine knelt humbly at the king's feet. Still no one spoke, and the silence was only broken by sighs and groans, so mournful that the king was stirred, not to pity, but to impatience.

'Monsieur Pélisson,' began Louis abruptly, 'Monsieur Pélisson, and you, monsieur' – indicating La Fontaine, whom he did not name – 'I observe with lively displeasure that you have come to plead on behalf of one of the greatest criminals whom our justice has ever overtaken. A king cannot permit himself to be moved by tears or by remorse – tears of the innocent or remorse of the guilty. I attach no faith either to the remorse of Monsieur Fouquet or to the tears of his friends, because the one is too callous and the others have cause to dread my resentment if they venture to cross me here in my own palace. Therefore, Monsieur Pélisson, and you, monsieur ... I recommend you to be careful how you utter any words which may seem to be in the slightest degree incompatible with absolute submission to my will.'

'Sire,' replied Pélisson, trembling at these terrible words, 'we are come to say nothing to your majesty which could be for a moment considered wanting in the most profound respect and sincere devotion which are due to the king from all his subjects. Your majesty's justice strikes hard, but it is the duty of every man to accept with respect its decrees, and we bow before them in all humility. Far be it from us to think of defending him who has the misfortune to incur your majesty's displeasure. The man who has fallen may indeed be our friend, but he is an enemy to the state. We abandon him sorrowfully to the severity of a justly offended king.'

'He will be judged by my Parlement,' interrupted the king, mollified by Pélisson's persuasive words no less than by his tone of resignation. 'I do not strike without duly weighing the crime. If Justice is armed with the sword, she also bears the scales.'

'Therefore we have entire confidence in the king's impartiality, and we may hope, with your majesty's consent, to make our feeble voices heard on behalf of our friend when, in due season, he is impeached before the Parlement.'

'Then what is it you are here to request?' asked the king, coldly.

'Sire,' replied Pélisson, 'the accused leaves a wife and family. What few effects he had were barely sufficient to pay his debts; and Madame Fouquet, since her husband's arrest, has been abandoned by everybody. When your majesty strikes, it is as though it were the hand of God. When God afflicts a family with the scourge of leprosy or plague, the dwelling of those who are stricken is shunned by all. Sometimes, but rarely, a generous physician alone dares to approach the accursed threshold, enters courageously and risks his life in a struggle with death. Such a man is the last resource of the dying; he is the instrument of divine mercy. Sire, we implore you on our knees to have mercy upon Madame Fouquet. Her friends have deserted her; she has no longer the means of support; she is left alone to weep by all those who besieged her doors during the time of her prosperity; her credit is gone and she is without hope! The unhappy man who has been visited by your anger, receives from you, culpable though he may be, his daily bread, which is moistened by his tears; equally afflicted, though more destitute than her husband, Madame Fouquet – she who had the honour of receiving your majesty at her table – Madame Fouquet, the wife of the former minister of your majesty's Finances, is now in want of bread.'

At this point the tears of Pélisson's friends burst forth afresh, and d'Artagnan, who felt a lump rising in his throat, turned round sharply into a corner of the room, where he bit his moustaches with unwonted vigour.

The king's expression still remained severe, but the colour had mounted to his cheeks, and his look had lost something of its harshness. 'What is it you wish?' he asked, with a trace of compunction in his voice.

'We are here to ask humbly of your majesty,' replied Pélisson, his voice breaking with rising emotion, 'to permit us, without incurring your displeasure, to lend Madame Fouquet a sum of two thousand pistoles collected amongst her husband's old friends, in order that the widow may not lack the simple necessities of life.'

This word 'widow' applied to the wife of a man who was still living, caused the king to grow extremely pale; his pride gave way and his heart was touched with pity. He glanced almost kindly at the poor fellows who were sobbing at his feet.

'God forbid,' he said, in a softened tone, 'that I should confound the innocent with the guilty! They little know me who can doubt of my compassion for the weak. I strike none but the powerful who abuse their power. Gentlemen, I authorise you to act according to the dictates of your hearts in whatever way you think proper to relieve Madame Fouquet's distress. You may retire, gentlemen.'

In silence the three men rose. Their eyes were dry, for their capacity for tears was exhausted. They lacked the strength even to express their thanks to the king, who, moreover, in his anxiety to cut short this harrowing scene, had retreated behind his armchair almost before they had time to make their grateful bows.

D'Artagnan alone remained with the king.

'Good!' said he, in reply to Louis's enquiring look. 'If you were not already provided with a motto – the motto which goes with the device of the sun – I would suggest one, which Monsieur Conrart might do into Latin: "Gentle towards the weak, but terrible to the strong." '

The king smiled, then, as he was about to pass into the next room, he paused and said – 'I give you leave of absence, which no doubt you will need in order to arrange the affairs of your friend, the late Monsieur Du Vallon.'

## CHAPTER 83

### Porthos's last will and testament

AT PIERREFONDS everything showed signs of mourning. The court-yards were deserted, the stables shut up, the flower-beds neglected. The fountains, whose sparkling jets of water had formerly flashed noisily and incessantly into the marble basins, had ceased to flow. On all the roads in the neighbourhood certain persons, wearing a subdued air, might have been seen mounted upon mules or rough country nags ambling along in the direction of the château. They were neighbours, bailiffs of adjacent estates or curés from the surrounding villages. As they reached the château, all these people entered silently, gave their animals into the charge of a sad-faced groom and were conducted by a footman clothed in black towards the great hall, where Mousqueton received them at the door. Mousqueton had lost flesh so much during the last two days that his clothes hung upon him loosely. His cherubic pink and white face, like that of Vandyck's Madonna,[199] was furrowed by two silvery streams which ran down his cheeks, formerly round and plump, but now slightly fallen in from the effects of his grief. At every fresh arrival, his tears flowed afresh, and it was pitiful to see how he squeezed his throat with his fat hand in order to keep from bursting openly into sobs.

All these visitors had arrived to hear the reading of Porthos's will, announced to take place that day, and, whether animated by cupidity or by regard for the deceased nobleman – who was the last of his race – all the neighbours were anxious to be present. As each visitor arrived he took his place and, as the clock struck the hour of twelve – the time appointed for the reading – the doors of the great hall were closed. Porthos's attorney, who, as might have been expected, was the successor of Mâitre Coquenard, began by unrolling the vast parchment upon which Porthos's powerful hand had traced his final testamentary wishes. Having adjusted his spectacles and broken the seals, the attorney cleared his throat loudly by way of ensuring attention. Poor Mousqueton had effaced himself in a corner where he could hear less and could give freer vent to his tears. Suddenly, the folding-doors of the great room, which, as we have said, had been closed, were thrown open as though by a prodigy, and a manly figure appeared, in the full blaze of the sun, upon the threshold. It was d'Artagnan, who, having ridden up to the hall door and having found nobody to hold his stirrup, had fastened his horse to the knocker and announced himself. The hall was invaded by a flood of daylight; and Mousqueton was aroused from his melancholy abstraction by the murmur which passed round the company and still more by the dog-like instinct of a faithful servant. He raised his head, recognised his master's old friend and with a cry of grief flung himself forward and embraced d'Artagnan's knees. The captain raised the poor fellow and embraced him as if he had been a brother, then, after acknowledging with a dignified salute the bows of the whole company, among whom his name passed from mouth to mouth, he took a seat at the upper end of the great hall wainscoted with carved oak, still holding by the hand poor Mousqueton, who sank down upon the step of the dais, almost choked by his sobs. The lawyer was affected like the rest, and his voice shook slightly as he began reading.

After a pious and sincere profession of his faithful adherences to the Christian faith, Porthos asked forgiveness of his enemies for any wrong he might have done them. As this paragraph was read, d'Artagnan's eye beamed with a ray of inexpressible pride. In his mind's eye he saw the old soldier, whose terrible hand had brought all his enemies low; he reckoned up the number of them, and told himself that Porthos had acted wisely not to mention his enemies in detail or the injuries he had inflicted on them, else the reading would have been interminable.

The lawyer continued reading:

'I stand possessed at this present time, by God's grace, of the following properties:
1 – The demesne known as Pierrefonds, including ploughed lands, woods, meadows, waters and forests; the whole surrounded by good walls.
2 – The demesne known as Bracieux, including the château and forests, together with arable land distributed among three farms.
3 – The small estate known as Du Vallon, so called, because it lies in a valley. [Dear old Porthos!]
4 – Fifty farms in Touraine, together amounting to seven hundred acres.
5 – Three mills upon the Cher, each bringing in six hundred livres yearly.
6 – Three fishponds in Berry, yielding together two hundred livres yearly.
As regards moveable property, so called, because it is not fixed – as I have my learned friend the Bishop of Vannes's authority for stating – '

D'Artagnan shuddered as he remembered the fatal connection of poor Porthos with the man just named. The attorney continued without a smile:

'My moveable property consists of the following:
1 – Furniture, etc., which I cannot detail here for want of room, and which is to be found in all my châteaux or houses, but of which an inventory has been drawn up by my steward – [All eyes were turned upon Mousqueton, who, however, was absorbed in his grief.]

2 – Twenty horses, for saddle or draught, which I keep usually in my stables at Pierrefonds, and which are called: Bayard, Roland, Charlemagne, Pepin, Dunois, La Hire, Ogier, Samson, Milo, Nimrod, Urgande, Armida, Falstrade, Delilah, Rebecca, Yolande, Finette, Grisette, Lisette and Musette.

3 – Four packs of hounds, viz.: stag-hounds, wolf-hounds, boar-hounds and beagles; besides pointers and setters and watchdogs, twenty in all.

4 – Weapons, both for war and for the chase, contained in my gallery of arms.

5 – My wines of Anjou, selected for the Comte de la Fère, who was fond of them in old days; Burgundies, Champagnes, Bordeaux and Spanish wines, stocking eight cellars and twelve vaults in my various houses.

6 – Pictures and statues, which I am told are of great value and which are sufficiently numerous to tire the eye.

7 – My library, composed of six thousand volumes, quite new, never having been opened.

8 – Silver plate, a trifle worn, perhaps, but ought to weigh nine or ten hundredweight, for I can scarcely lift the chest which contains it and can only carry it six times round the room.

9 – All these effects, besides table and house-linen, are distributed amongst those houses of which I was most fond – '

At this point the reader stopped to take breath. The listeners coughed, moved in their seats, and then settled down to listen with even keener attention. The lawyer continued:

'I have hitherto been childless, and it is probable I shall never have any children, which is a great grief to me. I am mistaken, though, for I have a son in common with the rest of my friends, viz.: Raoul-Auguste-Jules de Bragelonne, the true son of the Comte de la Fère.

This young nobleman I have judged worthy to follow in the footsteps of the three valiant gentlemen whose friend and very humble servant I have the honour to be.'

Here the reading was interrupted by a ringing clatter. It was caused by d'Artagnan's sword, which, slipping from the hilt, had fallen upon the oaken floor. All eyes were turned in his direction and they saw that a large tear had trickled down his aquiline nose, the curve of which threw out a sharp glint like a crescent shining in the sun.

'For this reason [continued the lawyer] I hereby bequeath the whole of my estates, real and personal, included in the above enumeration, to the Vicomte Raoul-Auguste-Jules de Bragelonne, son of the Comte de la Fère, in order to console him for the trouble of mind he appears to be in, and to enable him to support with fitting dignity the illustrious name he bears – '

A prolonged murmur ran through the audience. Supported by d'Artagnan's flashing glance, which, running over the assembly, restored the interrupted silence, the lawyer continued his reading.

'Subject only to the following charges:

1 – The said Vicomte de Bragelonne to give to the Chevalier d'Artagnan, captain of the king's musketeers, whatever the said Chevalier d'Artagnan may see fit to ask of my property.

2 – The said Vicomte de Bragelonne to provide a handsome pension for my friend, the Chevalier d'Herblay, should he be compelled to live in exile.

3 – The said Vicomte de Bragelonne to retain those of my servants who have been in my service for over ten years, and to present each of the others with five hundred livres.

I leave to Mousqueton, my steward, all my clothes, both sporting and campaigning suits and my clothes for town wear, to the number of forty-seven complete suits, feeling assured that he will wear them in love and remembrance of me until they are worn out.

Moreover, I commend to the care of the Vicomte de Bragelonne my faithful friend Mousqueton, before-named, charging the said Vicomte de Bragelonne to act in such a way that Mousqueton may declare, on the day of his death, that he has never ceased to be happy.'

On hearing these words, Mousqueton, pale and trembling, rose to his feet and bowed; his broad shoulders heaved convulsively; his countenance distorted with grief, appeared from between his hands, and the spectators saw him stagger – hesitate – as though wishing to leave the hall, but unable to find the way.

'Mousqueton, my good friend,' said d'Artagnan; 'this way. Go and pack up your things – I will take you to Athos. I am going to him as soon as I leave Pierrefonds.'

Mousqueton could make no reply. With the oppression at his heart he could scarcely breathe, and it seemed to him that henceforth all those about him in that hall would be strangers. He groped blindly for the door, opened it and disappeared with tottering steps.

The lawyer finished reading the will; after which the greater number of those who had come to hear how Porthos had disposed of his property dispersed. They were perhaps disappointed, nevertheless they were filled with respect.

As for d'Artagnan, who had remained alone, after receiving a ceremonious bow from the lawyer, he fell to admiring the true wisdom of the testator, who had so justly bestowed his wealth upon the most worthy and upon those who had most need of it, and that with a rare tact such as none, even among the most refined courtiers and the most noble-hearted, could have exceeded. When he enjoined Raoul de Bragelonne to give d'Artagnan whatever he should ask, worthy Porthos well knew that d'Artagnan would ask nothing; and, if he were to ask for anything, no one, himself excepted, would ever know the amount. Then again, in leaving a pension to Aramis, the latter, were he tempted to ask too much, would be checked by d'Artagnan's example. And the word 'exile', which the testator dropped apparently without intention, was it not the mildest, the most exquisite criticism of Aramis's conduct, which had been the cause of Porthos's death?

Lastly, there was no specific mention of Athos in the will. For, indeed, could Porthos have supposed that the son would not offer his father the greater part? – The simple mind of Porthos, with the instinctive delicacy of a true heart, had weighed all these possibilities, had seized all these shades of meaning, better than law or custom, better than good-taste itself when unenlightened by good-feeling – 'Great-hearted Porthos!' said d'Artagnan to himself with a sigh.

At that moment the captain's thoughts were diverted by a groan which seemed to come from above. Suddenly he remembered poor Mousqueton, who needed a friendly face in his affliction. Thinking to cheer the poor fellow, d'Artagnan hurried from the hall and went to look for the steward, since the latter had not returned. He ran up the staircase to the first floor, and there, in Porthos's room, he saw a mass of clothing of every colour and every variety of material, upon which Mousqueton was lying, after having heaped them together. It was the legacy left to the faithful friend. These clothes were truly his own, having been specially mentioned by his master. Mousqueton's arm was stretched out over these relics as if to embrace them. D'Artagnan went up to the poor old servant with words of consolation.

'Great heavens! What's this? – He doesn't stir – he must have swooned!'

But d'Artagnan was mistaken; Mousqueton was dead.

Dead – like a faithful dog who, having lost his master, crawls home to die upon his cloak.

CHAPTER 84

*Athos grows old*

DURING THIS TIME, whilst all these events were occurring to separate for ever the four musketeers who had formerly been bound to one another by ties which appeared indissoluble, Athos, after Raoul's departure, began to experience that desolate sense of lone-liness – that living death which numbs the faculties of those who are parted from all whom they love.

After reaching his home near Blois, Athos could feel his natural vigour, which for so long had seemed to defy the infirmities of approaching age, every day diminishing. Even Grimaud was no longer there to receive a wan smile as he passed his master in the garden. The society of the son whom he loved so dearly had prevented him from growing old; but now old age came upon him with its attendant pains and troubles, which made themselves felt only the more remorselessly for having been delayed. Athos no longer had the inducement of Raoul's presence to pay attention to the way he carried himself, to hold his head erect by way of example; he missed the young man's bright eyes, the fire of which had brought a reflected brightness to his own. And then we cannot but admit that his sensitive and reserved nature, shrinking from such consolation as others could offer, lacked something of the same balance common to temperaments less highly organised; he gave way to grief with all the abandonment with which vulgar minds throw themselves into their pleasures. The Comte de la Fére, in his sixty-second year,[200] was still young – the tried soldier had preserved his strength in spite of his arduous compaigns; in spite of his misfortunes he had retained his freshness of mind and his calm serenity of soul and body – in spite of Mazarin, in spite of Mylady and of La Vallière. But in a single week Athos had become an old man, from the day when he had lost the support of his son, thanks to whom he had prolonged his youth, as it were the St Martin's summer[201] of his declining days.

Still handsome, though bent; his expression noble as always, even in its sadness, gentle and patient; in these days of loneliness, he would seek with feeble steps those glades in the avenues of the park where the sun penetrates through the foliage. Now that Raoul was no longer with him, he had discontinued the vigorous exercise which was the habit of a lifetime. These summer mornings the servants, accustomed to see him rise with the dawn at all seasons, were astonished to hear seven o'clock strike before their master had quitted his bed. Athos would lie awake with a book under his pillow which he lacked the energy to open. Remaining in bed because he had neither the will nor the strength to bear the fatigue of walking, he allowed his soul to wander from its prison of clay to return to God or to his son Raoul. At times his people, with real alarm, saw him for hours together absorbed in silent reverie, unconscious of the presence of the servant in the doorway watching with anxiety over his master's sleep or waiting for the moment of his awakening. It would sometimes happen that he forgot that the day had half slipped away, that the hours for the first two meals were past. Then they would rouse him, and he would get up and go out beneath the shady avenue, and then come out for a little while into the sunshine as if to share the warmth for a moment with his absent son. And afterwards the sad, monotonous walk would recommence until he was exhausted, when he would return to his room and to his bed as to a welcome refuge. For several days the comte did not utter a single word. He refused to see visitors who came, and during the night he was observed to get up and light his lamp and pass long hours in writing and turning over his parchments.

One of these letters the comte wrote to Vannes, and another to Fontainebleau: they remained unanswered. We know why – Aramis was no longer in France, and d'Artagnan was travelling from Nantes to Paris, and from Paris to Pierrefonds. His valet noticed that he shortened his walk every day by several turns. The long avenue of lime trees at length became too great a distance for the feet which formerly had traversed it a hundred times a day. The comte would drag himself painfully as far as the middle of the walk and sit down upon a mossy seat at the corner of a side-path, there to gather strength, or rather to wait for the return of night. Very soon, a hundred steps exhausted him. Finally, Athos kept his bed all day; he refused nourishment, and, though he made no complaint, though he still had a smile upon his lips and a kind word for those who approached him, his servants became so alarmed that they sent to Blois for an old physician who had attended Monsieur, the late king's eldest brother, and introduced him to the comte's rooms in such a way that he could see Athos without the latter seeing him. For this purpose they placed him in a closet adjoining the patient's bedroom, begging him not to show himself lest their master, who had not asked for a doctor, should be displeased.

Athos was held up as a sort of model for the neighbouring country gentlemen. The people of Blois were proud of possessing this sacred relic of the ancient glories of France, for Athos was indeed a *grand seigneur* in comparison with the new nobility which sprang from the decaying trunks of the provincial heraldic trees at the life-giving touch of the young king's sceptre. We say then that Athos was respected as well as beloved. The old doctor could not bear to see the comte's people inconsolable, and he wished to relieve the anxiety of the poor folk of the countryside, who loved Athos for his kind words and charitable deeds and flocked to him for news of their benefactor. From where he was hidden he watched the mysterious malady which had stricken down so swiftly a man who had always been so full of life and of desire to live. He noticed the dark hue of fever upon Athos's cheeks – that slow and pitiless fever engendered within the heart and sheltering itself behind that rampart, nourished by the suffering to which it gives rise, at the same time both the cause and the symptom of a dangerous illness.

As we have said, the comte spoke to no one, not even to himself. His thoughts shrank from the slightest sound and had reached that state of over-excitation which borders upon hallucination. A man who is thus absorbed, if he has not yet entered into God's keeping, has already severed the ties which bind him to earth. The doctor remained for several hours studying this painful struggle of the will against a superior power. With increasing alarm he noticed the eyes fixed always upon some faraway, invisible object – he was terrified to observe the same monotonous pulsation of the heart, never varied by even a sigh; for often sharp pain forms one of the most hopeful symptoms to the eyes of a physician. Thus passed half the day. Then, like a brave man, the doctor formed a resolution and carried it into effect boldly. He issued suddenly from his place of retreat and went straight up to Athos, who looked at him without testifying any more surprise than if the doctor's appearance had made no impression on his senses.

'Pardon me, comte,' said the doctor, approaching the invalid with open arms, 'but I am going to reproach you. You will listen to what I have to say, will you not?' And he sat down by the bedside of the sick man, who with great difficulty roused himself from his preoccupation.

'What is it, doctor?' asked Athos, at length.

'You are ill, comte, and you do not seek advice.'

'Am I ill?' asked Athos, with a smile.

'Fever, consumption, weakness and wasting, comte!'

'Weakness!' replied Athos; 'is it possible? Why, I do not get up.'

'Come, come, comte, no evasions! You are a good Christian?'

'I trust so,' said Athos.

'Do you mean to kill yourself?'

'Never, doctor.'

'Well, you are not unlikely to die as you are going on at present. To remain in this condition is nothing less than suicide – this will never do, comte; you must get well!'

'Of what? Find the malady, first of all. Indeed, I have never felt better – never has the sky appeared more beautiful to me, never have I taken more interest in my flowers.'

'You have some secret grief.'

'Secret? No, no; it is my son's absence, doctor; that is all that is the matter with me. I make no secret of it.'

'Nay! Comte, your son is alive and strong; he has a future worthy of his merit and of his lineage; live for him – '

'But I am living, doctor. Oh! you may rest assured,' he added, with a sad smile, 'that so long as Raoul lives, all will know that he is alive; for so long as he lives, I shall live also.'

'What are you saying?'

'It is very simple. At this moment, doctor, I am in a state almost of suspended animation. To live a life of forgetfulness and careless indifference whilst Raoul is no longer with me would be a task beyond my powers. You do not expect the lamp to burn before a light has been applied to the wick; then do not expect me to leave my retirement and lead an active life. I merely exist, waiting and preparing myself – like those soldiers we used so often to see at the ports where they were waiting to be embarked; lying without paying heed to anything by the water's edge, neither having reached their destination nor yet in the country they were about to quit; baggage packed, their thoughts suspended and their eyes fixed, they were waiting. Like those soldiers, I lie here with my ears stretched to catch the sound of the summons in obedience to which I am ready to depart at once. What will this summons be? Will it be that of life or of death? My baggage is ready, my soul is prepared, I await the signal – I am waiting, doctor, waiting!'

The doctor understood the highly strung temperament of the comte, and he appreciated the soundness of his constitution. After a moment's reflection he told himself that his words were useless, his remedies absurd; and he went away after enjoining upon the servants of Athos not to leave their master for a moment.

The doctor having gone, Athos showed neither anger nor annoyance at having been disturbed. He did not even request his servants to bring him directly they arrived any letters which might come for him, for he well knew that they would joyfully have shed their blood to procure for him any distraction which might tend to ease his mind.

Sleep now rarely visited his pillow. By intense thinking, Athos forgot himself, for a few hours at most, in a waking reverie more profound and obscure than the dreams of slumber. The momentary repose which this forgetfulness afforded the body was at the expense of fatigue to the soul; for Athos lived a double life during these flights of his intelligence. One night he seemed to see Raoul dressing in his tent in order to take part in an expedition under the command of Monsieur de Beaufort in person. The young man appeared sad, he buckled on his cuirass slowly – slowly he girded on his sword. 'What is the matter, Raoul?' asked his father, tenderly.

'I am grieved at Porthos's death – our dear old friend Porthos,' replied Raoul. 'I am suffering over here the same grief you will feel at home.'

The vision disappeared and Athos awoke. At daybreak, a valet entered his master's room bearing a letter which had arrived from Spain. 'It is in Aramis's writing,' thought the comte. He opened it and read.

'Porthos is dead!' he cried, after he had read the first few lines. 'Oh! Raoul, Raoul, I thank thee! thou keepest thy promise to warn me!'

And, breaking into a mortal sweat, Athos swooned in his bed from no other cause but sheer weakness.

CHAPTER 85

## *Athos sees a vision*

HAVING RECOVERED from his faint, the comte, with a feeling almost of shame at having been so strongly affected by the supernatural occurrence, got up and dressed; then ordered a horse to be saddled, fully determined to ride to Blois to make more certain arrangements for correspondence, either with Africa or with d'Artagnan or Aramis. For indeed the letter he had received from Aramis had contained news of the failure of the expedition sent by the king against Belle-Isle, and gave the comte sufficiently full details of the death of Porthos to move Athos's tender and devoted heart to its very depths. Athos wished to pay a last visit to Porthos's resting-place, in order to do honour to his old companion-in-arms. He decided to write to d'Artagnan and ask him to recommence in his company the painful journey to Belle-Isle – to make this melancholy pilgrimage to the tomb where the giant whom he had loved so well lay sleeping. Afterwards Athos would return home in obedience to the secret influence which was leading him, by paths unknown and mysterious, towards the goal of eternity.

But scarcely had the servants dressed their master, whom they were delighted to see about to undertake a journey which might help him to throw off his melancholy; scarcely had the horse – the easiest-paced animal in the stables – been saddled and led to the door than Raoul's father felt his head become confused, his limbs give way. He understood that, in his present state, it was impossible for him to go one step farther. He asked to be taken out into the sunshine. They carried him and laid him upon the mossy bank, where he passed a full hour before he recovered his energies. This weakness was very natural after having remained inert for some days. In order to recover his strength, Athos took a basin of soup, and moistened his parched lips in a brimming glass of his favourite wine – that old wine of Anjou mentioned by poor Porthos in his admirable will. Then, feeling refreshed both in body and mind, he had his horse brought round; but it was only by the aid of his servants that he succeeded, with difficulty, in reaching the saddle. Scarcely had he ridden a hundred paces when, at the turn of the road, he was seized with the same giddiness. 'This is very strange,' said he to his body-servant who accompanied him.

'Do not go on, monsieur, I entreat you!' replied the faithful servant. 'You have grown quite pale.'

'Oh! that shall not prevent me from continuing my journey now that I have started,' rejoined the comte. And he gave his horse his head. But suddenly the animal, instead of obeying his master's wishes, stopped short. The bit had been drawn tight by a movement of which Athos was unconscious.

'Something wills that I shall go no farther,' said Athos. 'Support me,' he added, stretching out his arms; 'come here, quick! I feel all my strength oozing away, and I am going to fall.'

The man had seen his master reeling almost before he received the order. He hastened forward to receive the comte in his arms; and as they were still close to the house, the servants, who had remained in the doorway watching the departure of the Comte de la Fère, noticed the unwonted interruption of their master's progress, usually so orderly. The servant who was supporting Athos called his companions with voice and gesture, and they came running up to his assistance. Athos returned towards the house, but before he had gone many steps he began to feel better. His strength seemed to revive, and with it the desire to reach Blois. He turned his horse round. At the animal's first step, however, the comte fell back into the same state of anguished torpor. 'Unquestionably,' he murmured, 'some power *wills* that I should remain at home.'

The servants approached and helped the comte from his horse, then carried him as quickly as possible into the house, where he was immediately put to bed.

'You will not forget,' he said, as he was preparing to go to sleep, 'that I am expecting letters from Africa this very day.'

'Monsieur will no doubt hear with pleasure that Blaisois's son has gone off on horseback to gain an hour over the courier from Blois,' replied the valet.

'Thank you,' replied Athos, with his pleasant smile.

The comte fell asleep, but his troubled slumber was that of suffering rather than repose. The man who watched him saw several times upon his features the expression of torture within him. Perhaps Athos was dreaming.

The day wore on; Blaisois's son returned with the news that the courier had not brought a letter. The comte had counted the minutes with a presentiment of this disappointment; when the minutes had mounted up to an hour he could not repress a despairing groan. Once the idea that he had been forgotten occurred to him, wringing his heart with anguish. Nobody in the house expected that the courier would come as it was now long past his time. Four times had the messenger repeated his journey to Blois, but each time found there was nothing for the comte's address. Athos knew that the courier arrived only once a week; and consequently he would have to endure the distress of hope deferred for another eight days. With this sad conviction in his mind he entered upon another long night. Every foreboding of calamity which a man, sick in mind and body, can add to facts and probabilities already sufficiently grave, obsessed the brain of Athos during the early hours of that terrible night. The fever increased; it mounted to his chest, where, in the words of the physician who had been sent for from Blois, the fire soon caught. Before long it had reached the head. The doctor bled the patient twice in succession, and, although the fever yielded to this treatment, the patient was left so weak that he had no power to move a muscle; his brain alone was capable of activity. However, the dangerous symptoms of fever had abated. For some time the fever held out in the comte's hands and feet, which had lost all feeling; but it was eventually driven away completely before midnight struck. The physician, seeing this undoubted improvement, returned to Blois after having prescribed for his patient, whom he declared to be out of danger.

Then it was that the mind of Athos began to float in a strange, ethereal medium. Free to think, his mind reverted to Raoul, the son whom he loved so tenderly. He saw in imagination the African landscape bordering upon Jijeli, where Monsieur de Beaufort had disembarked his army. He had an impression of grey rocks covered in places with green seaweed where the sea beat against the shore when the waves ran high under the lash of the tempest. Away inland at a short distance from the shore, dotted with boulders resembling tombs, rose a straggling, white-walled village, like an amphitheatre, amidst cactus and dingy mastic trees. The village was filled with smoke, confused noise and terrified movement. Suddenly, from the midst of the smoke sprang up a flame which soon enveloped the whole village like a fiery rampart and, gaining rapidly, at length embraced in its withering grasp the arms impotently stretched out towards heaven with shrieks and groans. For a moment there was a frightful confusion of falling joists and red-hot walls, of trees disappearing in a burst of writhing flame. Strange circumstance! In the midst of this chaos, where Athos could distinguish arms raised and could hear agonised yells, he saw not a single human figure.

From beyond the village could be heard the crackling splutter of musketry with the deeper note of cannon rising above the monotonous ground-bass of the surf. Flocks of goats made their escape, bounding away over the grassy slope. But never a soldier appeared to apply his match to the guns in the batteries – never a sailor to assist the manoeuvres of the fleet nor a goat-herd to attend to the flocks.

After the demolition of the village and of the forts which dominated it – a destruction operated magically, without the cooperation of a single human being – the flames died away, the smoke again began to rise, then, diminishing in volume, at length faded and evaporated completely. Night fell over the landscape, a night of intense blackness on the earth, beneath a brilliant firmament; the blazing stars which scintillated in the African sky shone without illuminating anything but the sky itself. A long silence ensued, giving a moment's repose to Athos's troubled imagination; but as he had a feeling that the vision was not ended, he bent his mind's eye yet more attentively upon the strange spectacle which his imagination had presented to him.

This spectacle was soon resumed. The moon rose, mild and pale, behind the precipitous rocks which bordered the coast, streaking with eddying ripples of light the broad surface of the waters, and touching the rough thickets on the hillside with a shimmer of diamonds and opals. The thunder of the surf had ceased. Like silent and attentive phantoms, the grey rocks raised their moss-grown heads as though to examine the battlefield by the light of the moon; and Athos perceived that the plain, entirely deserted during the fight, was now strewn with the bodies of the slain. A shudder of inexpressible horror shook his very soul when he examined these inert figures. He recognised the white and blue uniform of the soldiers of the Picardy regiment, their long pikes with blue staves and their muskets with the fleur-de-lis branded on the stock. He saw the cold, gaping wounds open to the violet sky as though to demand again the souls to which they had given passage. Disembowelled horses lay stark, with tongues hanging from between their bared teeth, the blood stiffening in their manes and staining their housings. He saw Monsieur de Beaufort's white horse stretched in the front rank of the dead with its head shattered. Athos passed a cold hand over his brow, and was astonished to find that it was not burning. This convinced him that he was witnessing, not a feverish dream, but a vision of the battlefield the day after the assault upon the town of Jijeli by the army which he had seen leave the coast of France and disappear beneath the horizon, and whose last cannon-shot, in token of farewell to the country of their birth, he had saluted with thought and gesture.

Who shall depict the mortal agony with which his soul was torn as it wandered from group to group of these corpses, regarding them one by one in order to find if Raoul lay sleeping among them? Who could express the divine, delirious joy with which Athos rendered thanks to God for not having found what he had been seeking with such exquisite dread among the slain? For indeed, all these men who lay stiff and cold where they had fallen were easily to be recognised, and seemed to turn their faces with pity and respect towards the Comte de la Fère in order to assist him in his mournful inspection. Yet he was astonished, whilst he passed through the ranks of the dead, to perceive no trace of the survivors.

The illusion had reached such a point of actuality that this vision had become for him a real journey which the father was making to Africa to obtain more exact tidings of his son. Fatigued by his travels over seas and continents, he sought to repose himself in one of the tents raised behind the shelter of a rock. Above the encampment floated the white banner with golden fleur-de-lis. He looked around to find a soldier who could direct him to Monsieur de Beaufort's tent. Then, whilst his glance wandered over the plain in every direction, he saw a white form appear from behind a cluster of fragrant myrtle-bushes. This figure wore the dress of an officer; it held in its hand a broken sword; it advanced slowly towards Athos, who, stopping short and fixing his eyes upon it, was unable to speak or move, though he struggled to open his arms, for, in that pale and silent officer, he had recognised Raoul. The comte attempted to utter a cry, but it was stifled in his throat. Raoul enjoined silence by placing a finger on his lips, then drew back slowly, without Athos being able to perceive any motion of the limbs. The comte, more pale than Raoul, followed his son tremblingly, painfully traversing briars and bushes, over stony and broken ground. Raoul appeared not to touch the earth, and no obstacle impeded his gliding progress. The comte, fatigued by the roughness of the ground, was soon exhausted and compelled to stop. Still Raoul beckoned him to follow. The tender father, to whom love restored strength, made a last effort and climbed the mountainside after the young man, who encouraged him with smiles and gestures.

At length he reached the crest of the hill and saw thrown out in black against the wan horizon the aerial form, perfected and purified, of Raoul. Athos stretched forth his hand to reach the son whom he loved so dearly; but suddenly, as if the young man had been drawn away in spite of himself, still retreating, he rose from the earth, and Athos could see between the feet of his child and the crest of the hill a breadth of sparkling sky. Insensibly Raoul rose into the void, still with a smile upon his lips – still beckoning his father to follow – and departed into the sky. Athos gave vent to a cry of anguished tenderness. He turned his glance downward. Beneath him lay the stricken camp, and the white, motionless forms of the dead soldiers of the royal army. Then, raising his head, he saw his son ever rising, ever motioning him to ascend with him to heaven.

## CHAPTER 86

### The Angel of Death

ATHOS'S VISION had reached this point when suddenly the spell was broken by an uproar which came from outside the house. The clatter of a horse galloping upon the hard gravel of the great avenue and the confused sound of many people in excited conversation reached the room in which the comte was dreaming. Athos hardly stirred, merely turning his head towards the door that he might the sooner catch the import of the noises which had awakened him. A heavy step ascended the stairs to the hall. The horse, which had arrived at a gallop, was led slowly towards the stables. A certain faltering hesitation was noticeable in the footsteps which gradually approached the chamber of Athos. Then a door was opened, and the comte, turning slightly towards the side whence the sound proceeded, cried in a feeble voice, 'It is a courier from Africa, is it not?'

'No, comte,' replied a voice which sent a shiver through Raoul's father.

'Grimaud!' he murmured. And the sweat began to pour down his wasted cheeks.

Grimaud appeared in the doorway, but no longer the same Grimaud we have seen, still young in his courage and devotion, when he sprang into the boat destined to carry Raoul de Bragelonne to the royal fleet. A pale, haggard and grim-featured old man, his clothes covered with dust, his scanty hair bleached by age and grief, stood before his master. He supported his trembling limbs by holding the doorpost, and was nearly falling when, across the breadth of the room, he caught sight of the comte's face in the lamplight. These two men, who had lived together so long in community of intelligence and in the habit of economising speech, knew so well how to speak to one another with a glance – these two old friends, equal in nobility of heart, if unequal in fortune and birth – remained each gazing in the other's face without a word uttered. Mutually they read each other's hearts. Grimaud bore upon his countenance the imprint of a grief already old – an impression stamped indelibly by an ever-present sorrow. Long accustomed to be silent, he had now lost the habit of smiling.

Athos read all these indications in the face of his faithful servant; then, in the same tone with which, in his dream, he had spoken to Raoul – 'Grimaud,' he said, 'Raoul is dead, is he not?'

Behind Grimaud stood the other servants listening, with beating hearts, their eyes fixed upon the bed of their sick master. They heard this terrible question, followed by a strained silence.

'Aye,' answered the old man in a hoarse whisper which seemed to tear his breast. Loud groans and lamentations from the servants filled the room with regrets and prayers, whilst the poor father in agony sought his son's portrait with his eyes. For Athos this was the transition leading him back to his dream. Without a cry, without a tear – patient, gentle and resigned as a martyr, he raised his eyes to heaven, there to see once more, rising above the mountain at Jijeli, the beloved shade that was departing from him at the moment when Grimaud arrived. Without doubt, as he looked upward and resumed his dream, he passed by the same road by which the vision, at once sweet and terrible, had led him before. After gently closing his eyes he opened them again and smiled; he had seen Raoul, who smiled upon him. His hands clasped upon his breast, his face turned towards the window and fanned by the fresh night air laden with the scents of the flowers and of the woods, Athos entered, nevermore to return, into the contemplation of that paradise which lies beyond the ken of the living – beyond the gates of death. At that solemn hour when other men think tremblingly upon the Judgment of the Lord, and cling to the existence which they know, in terror of that other life to which they are about to be summoned – at that solemn moment, God willed, no doubt, that the treasures of eternal bliss should be opened to this, His elect. Athos was guided by the pure, transfigured soul of Raoul which inspired that of the father. For this righteous man, the rough road which the souls of men must tread ere they reach their celestial home was a path of melody and perfume. For an hour Athos remained absorbed in ecstasy, then, with the smile still upon his lips, he slowly raised his waxen hands and murmured in a whisper, so low that it was scarce audible, these words addressed to God or to Raoul – '*I am ready*,' and his hands sank back upon his breast slowly, as if he himself had still controlled them.

Death had worn a mild and caressing aspect for this noble being. The Angel of Death had spared him the last pang of a departing spirit, and had opened with indulgent finger the gates of eternity for that grand soul, worthy of the angel's entire respect. It may be that God had willed it thus in order that the pious remembrance of this peaceful passing away should remain in the hearts of those present and in the memory of others, to rob the grave of its victory and death of its sting for those whose life on this earth has been such that they have no cause to dread their reception at the judgment seat.

Even in his eternal sleep the features of Athos retained a sweet and placid smile, destined to accompany him even to the tomb. This peaceful expression led his servants for a long time to remain uncertain if he were really dead. They wished to lead Grimaud away, who from a distance regarded with fixed gaze that face growing pale, fearful lest in approaching he should bring with him the rustle of death's wings. But, weary as he was, Grimaud refused to stir. He sat down by the door, guarding his master with the vigilance of a sentinel and jealous of sharing his first glance on awakening or his last dying sigh. Every sound was hushed throughout the house, for all respected the sleep of their seigneur. Grimaud, listening intently, perceived that the comte no longer breathed. He raised himself upon his hands, and from where he was, looked eagerly to see if he could detect any slight motion on the part of his master. Not a tremor! Fear seized him; he rose to his feet but at the same moment he heard footsteps upon the stairs – a rattle of spurs against a sword, a martial sound familiar to his ears – which checked him as he was about to advance to the bedside. A voice, more sonorous than brass or steel, resounded within three paces of him.

'Athos! Athos my friend!' cried this voice, agitated even to tears.

'The Chevalier d'Artagnan!' faltered Grimaud.

'Where is he?' demanded the musketeer.

Grimaud seized the captain's arm in his bony fingers and pointed to the bed, against the sheets of which were already to be seen the livid hues of death.

D'Artagnan choked, unable to utter a cry. He advanced on tiptoe to the bed, frightened by the sound of his footsteps upon the floor, his face twitching, his heart wrung by intolerable agony. Bending over the comte he listened intently, but not a movement, not a sound came to reassure him. D'Artagnan drew back. Grimaud, who had followed with his eyes the captain's movements, each of which had been a revelation to him, went timidly and sat down at the foot of the bed; then pressed his lips to the coverlet over the cold feet of his dead master. Slow, difficult tears welled from the old man's red-rimmed eyes. This poor old fellow, despairingly bent over the still form of the comte and silently weeping, presented to d'Artagnan the most pathetic sight he had ever met with in a life full of varied emotions. D'Artagnan remained standing in contemplation of the smiling face of the dead, whose last thought one would have said had been to keep a kind welcome for his best friend – the man whom, after Raoul, he had loved best in all the world. Even from beyond the portals of life he welcomed him; and, as though to repay this touching hospitality, d'Artagnan stooped and kissed Athos on the brow, and with trembling fingers, closed his eyes. Then he seated himself beside the pillow, feeling no dread of that dead man who, in life, for five and thirty years, had been to him so loyal and affectionate a friend. A crowd of recollections recurred to his mind at the sight of the comte's noble visage; some sweet and charming as the dead man's smile, some chilling and sombre as that figure whose eyes were closed in eternal sleep. At length the tide of bitter sorrow which surged in his heart overflowed, swelling his breast almost to bursting. Unable to master his emotion, he rose, and, tearing himself blindly from the room he had just entered to bring to Athos the news of Porthos's death, only to find that the spirit of Athos had departed, this strong man burst into sobs so heartrending that the servants, who seemed but to have waited for an explosion of grief, answered him with loud lamentations, in which the dogs of the late comte joined by dismal howlings. Grimaud alone uttered no sound. Even in the paroxysm of his grief he would not profane the dead, nor for the first time disturb the slumber of his master.

At daybreak d'Artagnan, who had been wandering about the hall biting his fingers to stifle his sobs, again mounted the stairs, and awaiting the moment when Grimaud turned his head towards him, made him a sign to come to him. The faithful servant obeyed without making more sound than if he had been a shadow. D'Artagnan went down again, followed by Grimaud. Having reached the vestibule, he took the old man's hands and said – 'Grimaud, I have seen how the father died; tell me now in what manner the son met his end.'

Grimaud drew from his pocket a large envelope, upon which the address of Athos was inscribed. D'Artagnan recognised Monsieur de Beaufort's handwriting. Breaking the seal, he read it in the wan light of early dawn, as he walked to and fro in the avenue of ancient lime trees along which could still be traced the footprints of the comte who now lay dead.

CHAPTER 87

*News from the field of battle*

THE DUC DE BEAUFORT had written to Athos; but the letter destined for the living had only reached the dead. God had changed the address.

In his large, awkward schoolboy hand the prince had written as follows:

> MY DEAR COMTE – A great misfortune has happened to us in the midst of a great triumph. The king loses one of the bravest of his soldiers. I deplore the loss of a friend. You, Comte, have lost Monsieur de Bragelonne. He died a glorious death – so glorious, that I cannot find it in my heart to mourn. Pray accept, my dear Comte, my heartfelt condolences. Heaven tries us each according to our strength. This is a grievous trial, but not beyond your courage to support. Your good friend –          BEAUFORT

Enclosed in the same envelope was an account of the fight from the hand of one of the prince's secretaries. It was a true and touching recital of that disastrous episode which had cut the thread of two existences. D'Artagnan, who was accustomed to the emotions of the battlefield and whose heart was steeled against tenderness, could not repress a start as he read the name of Raoul, whom he had loved like a son, and who, like Athos, had become a shade. This is what he read:

> This morning, his highness ordered an attack to be delivered in force. The Normandy and Picardy regiments had taken up a position in open order on the rocky plain at the base of the hill crowned by the bastions of Jijeli. The action was opened by the artillery. The two regiments were then formed in column, and upon the word of command, advanced with a cheer, the halberdiers with pikes at the carry, the musketeers with their weapons at the trail. The prince watched the advance of the troops, ready to support them in case of need with a strong

reserve. His highness was attended by the senior officers and by his aides-de-camp. The Vicomte de Bragelonne had received orders not to quit the prince's side. Meanwhile, the enemy's guns, which had been served with little skill against our massed troops, now began to get the range, and the balls, aimed with more precision, had killed several men in the prince's immediate neighbourhood. The regiments which were advancing in column to storm the ramparts were also rather roughly handled. Our troops, finding themselves badly supported by the artillery, began to waver. Indeed, the batteries which had been thrown up the night before could render little assistance, on account of their position. The high elevation at which it was necessary to lay the guns in order to engage the forts was unfavourable both for the range and for the accuracy of their fire.

His highness, noticing the small effect of the bombardment of the heavy artillery, commanded the frigates standing off in the roads to concentrate their fire upon the hill-forts. Monsieur de Bragelonne was the first to volunteer to carry the order to the ships; but the prince refused the vicomte's request. His highness had a strong personal regard for Monsieur de Bragelonne, and was unwilling to allow him to incur unnecessary danger. The event justified his foresight, for scarcely had the sergeant to whom the dispatch had been entrusted reached the shore than he was struck down by a couple of bullets from the long carbines of the enemy's skirmishers. The sergeant fell, bleeding from a mortal wound. As he observed this, the prince turned to Monsieur de Bragelonne, and said, with a smile – 'There now, vicomte, you see I have saved your life. When you write again to the Comte de la Fère, tell him this, in order that learning it from *you*, he may be duly grateful to *me*.' The young man smiled sadly, and replied to the duke, 'True it is, monseigneur, that, but for your kindness, I should have been killed yonder in place of that poor sergeant and should now be done for and at rest.' Something in the tone in which Monsieur de Bragelonne made this answer caused his highness to reply sharply, ' 'Pon my soul! young man, you seem to be a glutton for wounds; but ecod! by the Lord's help 'twill go hard if I don't baulk your little propensity and carry you home alive to your father, as I promised him.' Monsieur de Bragelonne coloured, and said in a lower tone, 'Pray forgive me, monseigneur, if I have seemed importunate, and attribute it to my eagerness to find an opportunity of distinguishing myself before the general – more especially when the general is his highness the Duc de

Beaufort.' The duke was somewhat mollified, and turning to the officers who surrounded him, gave several orders.

The grenadiers attached to the two regiments penetrated near enough to the enemy's advanced earthworks to throw their grenades; these however did slight execution. Monsieur d'Estrées,[202] who was in command of the fleet, had noticed the sergeant's attempt to reach the ships, and understanding that it would be expedient to support the attack, opened fire upon the forts without waiting for orders. The Arabs, finding their men dropping under the balls from the fleet and their flimsy walls crumbling about their ears, gave vent to vociferous yells. Their light horsemen swept down the hill at a furious gallop, bent low in their saddles, and charged full tilt upon the leading columns of infantry, who, standing firm with serried pikes, succeeded in checking the desperate assault. Finding they could make no impression on the solid ranks of the pikemen, the Arabs turned, and brandishing their weapons, charged furiously in the direction of the general staff, who, at that moment, were in an isolated position.

The danger was extreme. The prince drew his sword; his secretaries and staff imitated him, and were soon engaged in a hand-to-hand scuffle with the fanatical horsemen.

Monsieur de Bragelonne now had an opportunity of satisfying the desire he had manifested from the commencement of the action. He fought by the prince's side with the greatest intrepidity and killed three of the Arabs with his small sword. But it was evident that his courage was not due merely to the soldierly pride, natural in the circumstances, by which the others were animated. He attacked impetuously, even with rashness; it seemed as though he wished to heat his blood by plunging into the thick of the noise and the carnage. He was so far carried away by his lust for fighting that his highness found it necessary to order him to desist. Monsieur de Bragelonne must have heard the prince's voice, since we all heard it who were near him. However, he continued as though he had heard nothing, still engaged with the enemy, who were retreating towards their entrenchments. As Monsieur de Bragelonne was known to be a well-disciplined officer, his disobedience to the prince's orders caused astonishment to everybody, and Monsieur de Beaufort shouted to him still more insistently to stop. Imitating the prince's gesture we all raised our hands, expecting to see the vicomte turn his horse; but still he rode on towards the enemy's defences. 'Stop, Bragelonne!'

shouted his highness at the top of his voice; 'remember your father – come back!'

At these words, Monsieur de Bragelonne turned his head; his face wore an expression of grief, but still he did not stop. We came to the conclusion that his horse had got out of hand. In this persuasion, his highness, seeing that the vicomte had advanced beyond the first line of grenadiers, shouted – 'Shoot his horse, musketeers! A hundred pistoles to the man who brings him down!' – But none of the grenadiers dared to shoot lest they should hit the rider. A sharp-shooter of the Picardy regiment named Luzerne left the ranks, took a careful aim, fired and struck the vicomte's horse in the quarters; for, the horse being a grey, we could see where the blood flowed from the wound. However, instead of dropping, the cursed beast galloped on still more furiously. Seeing the young man's imminent peril, the Picardies raised a shout which might have been heard a mile away – 'Throw yourself off, sir! – throw yourself off!' – Monsieur de Bragelonne was an officer well known and esteemed throughout the army.

The vicomte was now within pistol-shot of the ramparts. A volley was fired and for a moment he was enveloped in smoke. We lost sight of him, but when the smoke cleared away, he re-appeared, now on foot. His horse had just been killed. The Arabs summoned the vicomte to surrender, but he shook his head and continued to advance. It was the height of rashness; still the whole army wildly applauded his resolution. Before he had advanced many paces a second volley shook the walls, and again the Vicomte de Bragelonne disappeared in the cloud; but this time he no longer appeared standing when the smoke dispersed. He was down, lying amidst a clump of brushwood, and the Arabs began to leave their entrenchments in order to seize the body or to cut off the head, as is the custom among these savages. But his highness the Duc de Beaufort, who had watched this sad spectacle with painful interest, shouted, as he saw the Arabs gliding like white phantoms through the mastic trees – 'Grenadiers! pikemen! you will never let them carry off the body?' – With these words, he waved his sword and galloped to the front. The regiments charged behind him at the double, yelling as frantically as the Arabs themselves. The engagement began over the body of Monsieur de Bragelonne and was sustained with such heat that a hundred and sixty of the Arabs were left upon the field, besides at least fifty of our men. It was a lieutenant of the Normandies who finally took the body of the vicomte upon his shoulders and brought it back within our lines.

The advantage thus gained was followed up; the reserves were thrown into the fighting line and the enemy's palisades were destroyed. By three o'clock the Arabs' fire had ceased; the remainder of the fight was with cold steel and lasted two hours – it was a massacre. At five o'clock every position had been gained; all resistance was at an end and the prince had ordered the flag to be planted upon the crest of the hill. We then had leisure to think of Monsieur de Bragelonne, who had eight large wounds through his body, by which most of his blood had drained away. However, he still breathed, and this news afforded the prince lively satisfaction. He insisted upon being present at the first dressing of the wounds and at the consultation of the surgeons. Two of the latter declared that Monsieur de Bragelonne would live. His highness promised them each a thousand louis if their prediction was made good.

The vicomte heard this discussion. Whether it was that he despaired of his life, or whether the pain of his wounds caused him to take a gloomy view, cannot be known; but, at any rate, his countenance expressed a conviction contrary to that of the surgeons. This idea of the wounded man gave cause for reflection to one of the secretaries, more especially when he became aware of what followed.

The third surgeon who was in attendance was Brother Sylvain, of the Hospitallers of Saint-Cosmo – the most expert of all our medical staff. He probed the wounds in his turn, and said nothing. During this examination Monsieur de Bragelonne appeared to follow the surgeon's every move with an expression of anxious enquiry in his eyes. The latter, in answer to a question from the prince, replied that three of the eight wounds would, in ordinary circumstances, be mortal; but that with the vicomte's youth and vigorous constitution, and God's blessing, Monsieur de Bragelonne might recover. He added that the slightest movement would prove fatal. We all left the tent feeling very little hope as to the result. The secretary who has been mentioned fancied he noticed, as he went out, a mournful smile upon the vicomte's lips when the duke said to him kindly – 'Cheer up, young man, we'll pull you through!'

Later in the evening, when we thought the wounded man had, in all probability, been reposing, one of the aides-de-camp entered his tent; then immediately ran out, calling us loudly. We hurried to the tent, the duke among us, and saw the body of Monsieur de Bragelonne extended on the ground by the bed, weltering in what little blood had remained in him. Apparently he had had a convulsion, or had made an unconscious movement in his fever and had fallen. As Brother Sylvain had predicted, this accident had hastened his end. We raised the vicomte; he was dead and quite cold. His right hand was pressed to his heart, and grasped a lock of fair hair.

Further details of the expedition followed, and of the victory obtained over the Arabs. D'Artagnan did not read beyond the account of Raoul's death. Shaking his head he murmured – 'Unhappy lad! – a suicide.'

Then, turning his eyes towards the room in the château where Athos lay sleeping his eternal sleep – 'They have kept their promises to one another,' he said, in a low tone. 'Now at last they are happy, for their souls are united.'

D'Artagnan returned slowly towards the château by the path through the flower-beds. The people of the neighbourhood were already arriving to pay their last respects to the dead, and were discussing in subdued tones the double catastrophe.

## CHAPTER 88

### *Being the last of this epic history*

ON THE MORROW representatives of all the neighbouring families of distinction, and indeed, all the nobility of the province, so far as messengers had been able to spread the news, began to arrive. D'Artagnan had retired into seclusion, having no inclination to talk to anybody. These two crushing blows, falling upon the captain so soon after Porthos's death, weighed heavily upon his spirit, and it would be long before he would have the courage to speak of his grief. D'Artagnan saw no one, neither servants, nor guests, Grimaud alone excepted, who entered his room once. By the sounds in the house and by the continual arrivals, he was able to gather that the preparations for the comte's funeral were in progress. He wrote to the king, asking for his leave of absence to be extended. Grimaud, as we have said, had entered d'Artagnan's room, and had sat down upon a stool close to the door like a man deep in meditation; then rising, he had made a sign to the captain to follow him. The latter obeyed in silence. Grimaud led him to the comte's bedroom, pointed with his finger to the empty bed and raised his eyes eloquently towards heaven.

'Yes,' said d'Artagnan, 'yes, Grimaud, he is with the son whom he loved.'

Grimaud left the bedroom and led the way to the hall, where, according to country custom, the body was lying in state before burial. D'Artagnan was astonished to see two open coffins in the hall; in reply to Grimaud's mute invitation he approached, and saw in one of them Athos, still handsome in death, and in the other Raoul, with a smile upon his violet lips. He shuddered at the sight of father and son, two departed souls, represented on earth by their discarded tenements of clay. 'Raoul here!' he murmured. 'You did not tell me this, Grimaud.'

Grimaud shook his head and made no reply, but taking d'Artagnan by the hand, he led him to the coffin and showed him through the thin cerements the black wounds by which the spirit had escaped. The captain turned away his head, and judging it useless to question Grimaud, who answered nothing, he remembered that Monsieur de Beaufort's secretary had written more than he, d'Artagnan, had had courage to read. Looking again at the account of the affair which had cost Raoul his life, he found these words forming the last paragraph of the letter: 'The duke gave orders that the vicomte's body should be embalmed, according to the method in practice among the Arabs when they are desirous of being buried in their native land. The prince has also made arrangements for relays of horses, to enable a confidential servant who accompanied the young man to convey the coffin to the Comte de la Fère.'

'And so,' thought d'Artagnan, 'I am left to follow thy funeral, dear lad – I, an old man, of little value on this earth – and I am to sprinkle dust upon the brow I kissed only two months agone. It is God's will. It was thy own wish also. I have not even the right to weep, since death was of thy own choosing.'

At length the moment arrived for the last solemn rites to be performed. So large a number of gentlemen – many of whom had been comrades-in-arms of the deceased – had come to the funeral that the road from the town to the place of burial, a chapel in the plain, was filled with people on horseback and people on foot clad in habits of mourning. Athos had chosen for his last resting-place the little enclosure round this chapel, erected by himself upon the boundary of his estate. He had caused to be transported hither the stones, cut in the year 1550, of an old Gothic manor-house, situated in Berry, where he had spent his early youth. The chapel, thus re-edified, stood pleasantly beneath a clump of tall poplars and sycamores. There, every Sunday, mass was celebrated by the curé from the neighbouring village, to whom Athos had left an endowment of two hundred livres yearly for this service. All the vassals of his demesne, to the number of about forty, the farmers and farm-labourers, with their families, attended mass there in preference to going to the town.

Behind the chapel, enclosed between two tall hedges of nut trees, elder and hawthorn and surrounded by a deep ditch, extended the little enclosure, uncultivated, yet gay in its very wildness, for there the moss was thick and the wild heliotropes and wallflowers mingled their perfumes. There beneath the chestnut trees issued a spring which poured its waters into a marble cistern; there grew the wild thyme, visited by myriads of bees from far and wide, and the finches and red-breasts warbled their glad songs amidst the flowering hedges.

Hither the two coffins were borne, attended by a crowd in subdued silence.

The office of the dead having been celebrated, the last farewells paid to the noble dead, the assembly dispersed, talking as they went of the virtues and of the peaceful death of the father, and of the bright hopes he had had for his son, doomed to a melancholy end upon the shores of Africa. Gradually these sounds were extinguished like the lamps which had been lit in the little chapel. The curé bowed once more to the altar and to the still fresh graves; then followed by his acolyte carrying the shrill-toned bell, he slowly made his way toward the presbytery.

D'Artagnan, thus left alone, perceived that night was falling. Wrapped in thoughts of the dead, he had forgotten the flight of time. He rose from the oaken bench upon which he had been seated in the chapel, with the intention of bidding a last farewell to the double grave which held the remains of his lost friends. A woman was kneeling upon the damp earth in prayer. D'Artagnan stopped in the doorway of the chapel to avoid disturbing her and also to find out who this pious friend might be who had come to fulfil this sacred duty with so much zeal and perseverence. The unknown hid her face in her hands, white as alabaster. It was manifest from the noble simplicity of her costume that she was a woman of distinction. A little way off a carriage and horses, with several mounted servants, were waiting for the lady. In vain d'Artagnan sought to make out what brought her there. She continued praying and often she pressed her handkerchief to her eyes. D'Artagnan saw her strike her breast in pitiless self-abhorrence. Several times he heard her murmur – 'Forgive me!' as from a heart overflowing with anguish. And, as she appeared to abandon herself utterly to her grief, d'Artagnan, touched by these signs of mourning for the friends whose loss he himself felt so keenly, made a few steps towards the grave to interrupt the melancholy communion of this living penitent with the dead. But, as his foot crunched upon the gravel, the unknown raised her head and revealed to d'Artagnan a well-remembered face, bathed in tears. It was Mademoiselle de la Vallière.

'Monsieur d'Artagnan!' she murmured.

'You!' replied the captain in a stern voice; 'you here! Ah! Madame, far rather would I have seen you decked with bridal flowers in the manor-house of the Comte de la Fère. You would have had less cause to weep – and they – and I!'

'Monsieur!' she sobbed.

'It is you,' continued d'Artagnan, pitiless from his sense of bitter loss, 'it is you who have brought these two men to the grave.'

'Oh! spare me!'

'God forbid that I should deal harshly with a woman, or that I should make anyone weep without cause; but I must say that the place of a murderer is not upon the grave of her victims.'

She would have replied, but d'Artagnan added, coldly, 'What I am saying to you now, I have already said to the king.'

La Vallière clasped her hands.

'I know,' she said, 'that I am the cause of the Vicomte de Bragelonne's death.'

'Ah! you know it?'

'The news reached the court yesterday. Since two o'clock last night I have travelled forty leagues to come here to ask forgiveness of the comte, whom I believed to be still living, and to beseech God, upon Raoul's grave, to visit me with all the misfortunes I deserve, save one alone. And now I learn that the son's death has killed the father – I have two crimes upon my conscience – I have double punishment to expect from God.'

'I will repeat to you, mademoiselle,' said d'Artagnan, 'the words spoken of you by Monsieur de Bragelonne at Antibes, when he already meditated death: "If she has been misled through pride or coquetry, I pardon her while despising her. If love has caused her to sin, I forgive her, swearing that none could have loved her as well as I." '

'You know,' interrupted Louise, 'that for my love I was ready to sacrifice myself; you know whether I suffered that day you met me lost, dying, abandoned. Yet, I declare to you that never have I suffered as I suffer today, for then I had hope – now, I have no longer anything to wish for, since this death engulfs all my joy in the tomb. I dare no longer love without remorse, and I feel – yes, it is the law of fate – oh! I feel that he whom I love will repay me with all the torture I have made others undergo.'

D'Artagnan answered nothing; he was too well convinced that she was not mistaken.

'Then do not crush me now, dear Monsieur d'Artagnan,' she continued, 'once more I implore you. I am like a branch torn from a tree trunk, I no longer have any ties to bind me to this earth, and a mighty wind carries me away, whither I know not. I love to distraction – I love so strongly that I dare to avow it here, over the ashes of the dead, without a blush, without remorse. Such love as mine is a religion. But, as you will see me hereafter despised and forgotten – as you will see me suffering my destined punishment – spare me in my short-lived happiness, leave it to me for those few days – those short moments. Perhaps, even now, at this moment I speak to you, it no longer exists. My God! perhaps this double murder is already expiated!'

Whilst she was still speaking, a sound of voices and of horses approaching drew the captain's attention. An officer of the king's household, Monsieur de Saint-Aignan, had come by the king's orders to seek La Vallière. Saint-Aignan explained that his majesty was consumed by jealous uneasiness. The courtier did not see d'Artagnan, who was half-hidden by the chestnut tree which grew beside the graves. Louise thanked him, and dismissed him with a gesture, and Saint-Aignan quitted the enclosure.

'You see,' said the captain, bitterly, to the young woman, 'you see, madame, that your happiness still lasts.'

Louise rose and in a solemn tone said, 'You will repent, one day, of having judged me so ill. On that day, monsieur, it is I who will pray God to forgive you for having wronged me. And then, I am about to suffer so much that you will be the first to pity my sufferings. Do not reproach me with this happiness, Monsieur d'Artagnan; it cost me dear, and I have not paid all my debt.' And with these words, she again knelt down. 'Again, for the last time, Raoul, my betrothed,' she murmured softly, 'again I crave thy forgiveness. It is I who broke the chain – we both are destined to die of grief. Thou art the first to depart – soon I shall follow thee. Allow only that I have not acted basely and see how I come here to bid thee this last farewell. The Lord is my witness, Raoul, that if I could have redeemed thy life at the cost of my own, I would have given my life gladly. My love I could not give. Once more, forgiveness!'

She plucked a branch and planted it in the ground; then, wiping the tears from her eyes, she bowed to d'Artagnan and disappeared.

The captain watched carriage and horses and horsemen depart; then, folding his arms upon his swelling breast – 'When will it be my turn to depart?' he thought. 'What is there left for a man after youth and love, after glory and friendship, after strength and riches are gone? Nothing but that rock, under which Porthos sleeps – Porthos who possessed all that I have named. Nothing save this moss, beneath which Athos and Raoul lie at rest, who possessed far more beside!' For a moment he stood in doubt, with drooping head and sunken eye; then, drawing himself up – 'Onward!' he said – 'forward and onward! In God's good time I shall be called, as He has called the others.'

With his fingers he touched the earth, moist with the dew of evening, then, making the holy sign, he turned away and took the road to Paris, alone – alone henceforward and for evermore.

## *Epilogue*

FOUR YEARS after the scene we have just described, two well-mounted horsemen rode through Blois, in the early morning, to make arrangements for a hawking party the king was about to give in the undulating plain which is bisected by the Loire and bounded by Meung in the one direction and Amboise in the other.

The horsemen in question were the master of the king's harriers, and the king's chief falconer, officers of high importance in the time of Louis XIII, although not held in such high esteem by his successor.

The two horsemen were returning, after making a survey of the country, when they observed several small parties of soldiers being posted by their sergeants here and there at the entrances to the various enclosures. These soldiers were the king's musketeers, under the command of their captain, a man with grey hair and grizzled beard, slightly bent it is true, but, none the less, evidently an accomplished horseman.

'Monsieur d'Artagnan does not age much,' remarked the master of the harriers to the chief falconer, 'he is a good ten years our senior, yet he sits his horse like a young man.'

'That is so,' replied the falconer, 'he has not changed an atom during the last twenty years;' but there he was wrong, for d'Artagnan in the last four years had lived a dozen.

The pitiless claws of age had left their marks at the corners of his eyes, his forehead had lost its hair, and his hands, once so brown and strong, had whitened as though the blood in their veins had frozen.

D'Artagnan rode up to the two officials and addressed them with well-bred courtesy, receiving in return their respectful acknowledgements.

'A fortunate chance, indeed, to meet you here, Monsieur d'Artagnan,' cried the falconer.

'I should rather say that to you, gentlemen,' replied the captain, 'for nowadays, the king makes more use of his musketeers than of his falcons.'

'Ah! it is not as it used to be in the good old times,' sighed the falconer. 'You remember the time, do you not, Monsieur d'Artagnan? – when the late king used to fly his hawks in the vineyards beyond

Beaugency. Ah! you were not captain of musketeers in those days, Monsieur d'Artagnan.'

'Neither were you chief falconer,' retorted d'Artagnan good humouredly. 'All the same, those were good times, for the time is always good when one is young. Good-morning, sir,' he added, addressing the master of the harriers.

'You do me much honour, comte,' said the latter.

D'Artagnan made no reply. The title of *comte* did not strike him; indeed, d'Artagnan, it should be stated, had become *comte* four years previously.

'Are you not tired after your long journey, captain?' continued the falconer. 'It must be quite two hundred leagues from here to Pignerol.'[203]

'Two hundred and sixty to get there, and as many to come back,' said d'Artagnan quietly.

'And,' said the falconer, lowering his voice, 'how is *he*?'

'Whom do you mean?' asked d'Artagnan.

'Why, poor Monsieur Fouquet,' said the falconer, whilst the master of the harriers discreetly moved away out of hearing.

'Ah! poor man, he is terribly depressed. He does not understand that imprisonment may be a favour; he says that, in banishing him, the Parlement absolved him, and that banishment means liberty. He cannot see that his death had been determined upon, and that to be saved from the clutches of the Parlement means infinite obligation to God.'

'Yes,' said the falconer, 'the poor fellow has been unpleasantly near the scaffold; they say that Monsieur Colbert had already given instructions to the governor of the Bastille, and that the execution was ordered.'

'Let us change the subject,' said d'Artagnan. But, here, the master of the harriers again approached them saying, 'Well, there is Monsieur Fouquet at Pignerol, where he richly deserves to be, and, moreover, he has had the honour of being conveyed thither by you. Well, he had robbed the king sufficiently.'

D'Artagnan gave him one of his most forbidding looks, as he said, 'Sir, if I were told that you had devoured your hounds' food, I should refuse to believe it, and if you were sentenced to undergo punishment for the offence, you would have my sympathy, and I would not allow anyone to speak ill of you in my hearing. However honourable a man you may be, you cannot be more so than is the unfortunate Monsieur Fouquet, and it is I, d'Artagnan, who tell you so.'

After receiving this sharp reproof, the master of his majesty's harriers hung down his head and allowed the falconer to take two steps in front of him in d'Artagnan's direction.

'He is satisfied,' said the falconer in a low tone to the musketeer; 'it is easy to see that harriers are in fashion just now; had he been falconer, he would not have spoken like that.'

D'Artagnan smiled sadly at seeing so important a political question solved by the discontent of so humble an interest; and he let his thoughts dwell for a moment longer upon the brilliant career of the minister, upon the decay of his fortunes and upon the miserable end which awaited him. Then he asked, 'Was Monsieur Fouquet fond of falconry?'

'Yes, passionately,' replied the falconer, in a tone of regret and with a sigh that was the funeral ovation of Monsieur Fouquet.

D'Artagnan took no notice either of the ill temper of the one nor of the regrets of the other, and continued his progress across the plain. They could already discern the huntsmen in the distance, issuing from the outlets of the woods, the plumes of the outriders flashing like shooting stars in the clearings and the apparitions of white horses glancing through the dark shelter of the underwood.

'Will this be a long business?' asked d'Artagnan presently. 'For heaven's sake find us a bird quick on the wing, for I am frightfully tired. Will it be a heron or a swan?'

'Both, sir,' answered the falconer, 'but pray don't distress yourself; the king is not much of a sportsman, and he is giving this party less for his own gratification than for that of *the ladies*,' the last two words being so emphasised as to make d'Artagnan prick up his ears.

'Indeed!' he said, looking at the falconer with an air of surprise, and the master of the harriers smiled, probably with the view of restoring himself to d'Artagnan's good graces.

'Oh! laugh away,' said the latter. 'I know nothing whatever of what is going on. I only arrived here yesterday after a month's absence. I left the court mourning for the death of the queenmother. The king was not in the humour for amusement, after having received the last sigh of Anne of Austria. Well, everything in this world comes to an end, and, if the times are no longer sad, why, so much the better.'

'And everything has a beginning, too,' said the master of the harriers with an unctuous chuckle.

'Ah! indeed' said d'Artagnan again. He was consumed with curiosity, but too dignified to ask for information from those beneath him in rank. 'Apparently something is soon to be doing now,' he added.

The master of the harriers winked significantly, but d'Artagnan still declined to ask any question of him.

'Will the king be here early?' he asked of the falconer.

'At seven o'clock I fly my falcons.'

'Who accompanies the king? How is Madame? How is the queen?'

'Better.'

'Better? has she been ill, then?'

'Since her last upset, her majesty has been somewhat out of sorts.'

'What upset? I beg you tell me the news. Remember I am but just arrived.'

'Well, it seems that the queen, since the death of her mother-in-law, has felt herself somewhat neglected. She accordingly complained to the king, who answered her, 'Do I not sleep with you every night, madame? What more would you have?'

'Ah!' said d'Artagnan, 'poor woman, how she must hate Mademoiselle de la Vallière.'

'Oh! no; not Mademoiselle de la Vallière,' replied the falconer.

'Whom, then – ?'

The sound of a horn here interrupted the conversation. It was a signal for the hounds and the falcons to be brought forward, and the falconer and his companion hurried off, without giving d'Artagnan time to complete his sentence. The king appeared in the distance surrounded by a group of ladies and gentlemen on horseback. In good order, they came on at a walk, the inspiring sounds of the hunting-horns quickening the blood of both hounds and horses. There was a sense of action, of noise and of bright light, of which nothing can convey an idea unless it be the fictitious splendour and majesty of a theatrical display.

D'Artagnan, notwithstanding his slightly failing eyesight, was able to distinguish, behind this party, three carriages, the first of which had been intended for the accommodation of the queen, but which was, however, empty.

D'Artagnan, who did not see Mademoiselle de la Vallière by the king's side, looked for her elsewhere, and found her seated, in the second carriage, with two other ladies, obviously as uninterested in the proceedings as she was herself.

On the king's left hand, upon a high-mettled horse which she held well in hand, rode a lady of conspicuous beauty, who smiled upon the king, as he smiled upon her, whilst her utterances appeared to be productive of unfailing merriment.

'I certainly ought to recognise that lady,' said the musketeer to himself, 'who the deuce is she?' and leaning over to his friend the falconer he asked him the question. Before the latter could answer, however, the king caught sight of d'Artagnan, and called out to him – 'Ah! Comte,' he said, 'so you are back again? How is it that I have not seen you?'

'Sire,' replied the captain, 'your majesty was asleep when I arrived, and had not awakened when I went on duty this morning.'

'Still the same,' said Louis in a satisfied tone of voice. 'Well, now I order you to take some rest, and you will dine with me today.'

D'Artagnan was at once surrounded by a crowd of admirers, for to dine with the king was an honour which his majesty conferred far more sparingly than did Henri IV. The king walked his horse on a few paces, and d'Artagnan found his own passage barred by a fresh group, in the centre of which was Colbert.

'Good-morning, Monsieur d'Artagnan,' said the minister politely, 'have you had a pleasant journey?'

'Very much so,' answered d'Artagnan, bowing to his horse's neck.

'I heard the king invite you to dinner for this evening,' continued the minister, 'you will meet an old friend there.'

'An old friend?' repeated d'Artagnan, plunging into a sea of sombre reminiscences – a sea which had engulfed so many of his friendships and dislikes.

'The Duke of Alameda, who arrived this morning from Spain,' replied Colbert.

'The Duke of Alameda!' cried d'Artagnan, looking round in search of him.

'Yes, I!' said an old man, white as snow, and sitting bent in his carriage, the door of which he opened in order to meet the musketeer.

'Aramis!' cried d'Artagnan in astonishment, as he felt the old man's feeble arm clasp him round the neck.

Colbert having looked on for a moment in silence, pushed on his horse and left the old comrades to have a confidential chat together.

'And is it really you?' said the musketeer, taking the other's arm, 'you, the exile, the rebel, once more in France?'

'And I meet you at dinner with the king,' said the Bishop of Vannes with a smile. 'Yes, and what use is fidelity in this world? you may well ask. Come, let us drive past poor La Vallière's carriage; see how troubled she is, and how with tearful eyes she follows every movement of the king.'

'Who is the lady with him?'

'Mademoiselle de Tonnay-Charente, now Madame de Montespan,' replied Aramis.

'Is La Vallière jealous? Has she been deserted?'

'Not yet, d'Artagnan, but she soon will be.'

They talked thus together whilst the hawking proceeded, and the coachman drove so skilfully that they arrived on the spot at the precise moment when the falcon, making a swoop, bore down the quarry to the earth.

The king dismounted and Madame de Montespan followed his example.

They had arrived in front of a chapel which stood solitary upon the plain, hidden by large trees from which the autumn winds had stripped most of the foliage. Behind the chapel was an enclosure, the entrance to which was through a trellised gate. Into this enclosure the falcon had descended with its prey, from which the king, according to custom, was desirous of plucking the first feather.

For this purpose, therefore, he entered the enclosure, the rest of the company forming a circle round about it.

D'Artagnan detained Aramis, who, like the rest, was about to leave his carriage, and said in a broken voice, 'Do you know, Aramis, whither fate has led us?'

'No,' replied the duke.

'Some friends of mine lie buried here,' said d'Artagnan, with emotion.

Aramis, without guessing his friend's meaning, entered with faltering step through the little door which d'Artagnan held open for him.

'Where are they buried?' he asked.

'There, in the enclosure. There is a cross, you see, under the little cypress, and the cypress is planted over their tomb. Don't go that way; the heron has fallen there, and the king will be going to it in a moment.' Aramis stopped, and concealed himself in the shadow. Then they observed, without being seen, the pale face of La Vallière, who, observed by everyone, had at first surveyed the scene from her carriage, but who presently, moved by jealousy, had made her way into the chapel, from whence, supporting herself against a pillar, she could see the king in the enclosure as he smilingly assured Madame de Montespan that there was no danger and encouraged her to approach.

Madame de Montespan, accepting the king's outstretched hand, approached accordingly, and Louis, plucking a feather from the dead heron, placed it in the hat of his beautiful companion, who, smiling, in her turn, tenderly kissed the hand which had conferred upon her so much distinction. The king coloured up with pleasure and looked at Madame de Montespan with ardent and admiring eyes.

'What will you give me in exchange for my feather?' he asked her. She broke off a sprig of cypress and offered it to the king, who seemed to be half intoxicated with hope.

'A rather grim kind of offering,' whispered Aramis to d'Artagnan, 'seeing that the cypress o'ershadows a tomb.'

'Yes, and the tomb, moreover, is that of Raoul de Bragelonne,' said d'Artagnan aloud, 'poor Raoul who sleeps beneath that cross by his father's side.'

A groan was heard behind them, and, turning round, they perceived that a woman had swooned. It was Mademoiselle de la Vallière, who had seen and heard everything.

'Poor thing!' murmured d'Artagnan as he lent a hand in assisting to her carriage the woman who henceforward was destined to suffer so much.

The same evening, d'Artagnan, together with Monsieur Colbert and the Duke of Alameda, found himself seated at the royal dinner-table.

The king was in excellent spirits. He paid a thousand attentions both to the queen, and to Madame, who sat at his left hand and seemed to be somewhat depressed. The moment was reminiscent of the tranquil time when the king was wont to seek, in his mother's eyes, approval or disapprobation of something he had said or done.

The question of mistresses was, naturally, not discussed at this dinner. The king occasionally addressed a few words to Aramis, calling him 'Monsieur l'Ambassadeur', which increased the surprise already felt by d'Artagnan at seeing his friend, lately stigmatised as *a rebel*, so marvellously well received at court.

Upon rising from table the king offered his hand to the queen, making, at the same time, a sign to Colbert, whose eye never left that of his master. Colbert drew d'Artagnan and Aramis on one side; the king entered into conversation with his sister-in-law, whilst Monsieur, in an unenviable frame of mind, did his best to entertain the queen, taking care, at the same time, to watch his wife and his brother out of the corner of his eye. The conversation between Aramis and d'Artagnan and Colbert turned upon everyday subjects, upon preceding ministers amongst others, and they ex-changed reminiscences of Mazarin and of Richelieu. D'Artagnan was surprised to find this man, with the thick eyebrows and low forehead, so full of information and in such a genial humour, and Aramis was no less astonished at the easy way in which he contrived to postpone the serious conversation which each of them felt to be inevitable.

It was obvious, from his uneasy manner, how greatly Monsieur was bored at having to make conversation with the queen. He observed that his wife was on the point of shedding tears; was she about to complain to the king and create a scene before the court?

The king drew her aside, and spoke to her so tenderly as to remind her of the days when she was loved for herself alone.

'My dear sister,' said he, 'why are your beautiful eyes so tearful?'

'Ah! Sire – ' she said.

'Monsieur is jealous, is he not?'

She threw a glance at her husband, which was sufficient to assure him that he formed the subject of her conversation with the king.

'Yes,' she answered.

'Listen to me,' said the king, 'if your friends compromise you, it is through no fault of Monsieur's.'

He spoke so tenderly that Madame, who had lately undergone so many trying ordeals, could no longer restrain her tears.

'Tut, tut! little sister,' said the king, 'tell me your troubles; on my word as a brother, you shall have my sympathy, and on my word as a king, your sorrow shall come to an end.'

She raised her fine eyes and said, sadly, 'It is not my friends who compromise me, for they are absent or in hiding; they have been made to incur your majesty's displeasure, they who are so devoted, so loyal and so true.'

'You allude to de Guiche, whom I have sent into exile at Monsieur's request?'

'And who, since his unjust banishment, has, every day, sought to take his own life.'

'*Unjust* banishment, did you say, sister?'

'So much so that did I not entertain for your majesty the respect, coupled with friendship, which I have ever – '

'Well?'

'I would ask my brother Charles upon whom I can always – '

The king started. 'What then?' he said sharply.

'I would have asked him to represent to your majesty that Monsieur and his favourite, the Chevalier de Lorraine,[204] should not be permitted to trample with impunity upon my honour and happiness.'

'The Chevalier de Lorraine!' said the king. 'What! that dismal-faced fellow?'

'He is my mortal enemy. So long as that man remains under the same roof with me, or Monsieur retains him in his service and confers power upon him, so long shall I be the most maligned and least considered woman in the kingdom.'

'So,' said the king deliberately, 'you look upon your brother Charles of England as a better friend to you than I am?'

'I can judge only by actions, sire.'

'And you would prefer to ask help from – '

'From my own country,' she said proudly. 'Yes, sire.'

'You,' replied the king, 'like myself, are a grandchild of Henri IV; and do you not think that the relationship of cousin and brother-in-law is as binding as that of brother-german?'[205]

'Then,' said Henrietta, 'act.'

'Let us make a compact.'

'Begin then.'

'You say that I exiled de Guiche unjustly?'

'Yes,' she said, with a blush.

'He shall be recalled.'

'That is excellent.'

'And next, you complain that I am wrong in allowing the Chevalier de Lorraine to live in the same house with you, and you allege that he advises Monsieur to your detriment?'

'Mark well what I am about to say, sire; the Chevalier de Lorraine someday – well, if ever I meet with an untimely end, remember that I accuse beforehand the Chevalier de Lorraine. He is capable of any villainy.'

'You may take it from me that the Chevalier de Lorraine shall no longer be a menace to you.'

'Then, this will be a true preliminary treaty of alliance, sire, and I sign it. But, since you are ready to perform your part of the contract, tell me how I am to fulfil mine.'

'Well, then, instead of sowing discord between me and your brother Charles, you must do your best to cement the friendship which already exists between us.'

'That is easily done.'

'Not so easily as you seem to imagine, for whereas in ordinary friendship an embrace and the exchange of simple and inexpensive courtesies suffice, when it becomes a question of political friendship – '

'Ah! you are thinking of a political friendship?'

'Yes; and then, instead of embraces and hospitality, you must place at your ally's disposal troops and ships in efficient condition, and it does not always happen that you are financially strong enough to enable you to make such an offer.'

'You are right,' said Madame, 'and England's coffers have been sounding very hollow for a long time.'

'But you, my dear sister, whose influence with your brother is so great, might, nevertheless, contrive to bring about what an ordinary ambassador would never accomplish.'

'In that case, my dear brother, it would be necessary for me to go to London.'

'I have thought of that,' replied the king quickly; 'and I think, moreover, that the change would do you good.'

'It must not be forgotten, however,' said Madame, 'that it is quite possible that I may fail. The King of England's advisers have to be reckoned with.'

'When you say advisers, I presume you include ladies?'

'Certainly. Suppose, for example, that your majesty had it in contemplation – mind, I am only supposing – to suggest to Charles the formation of an alliance for the purposes of war – '

'For war?'

'Yes; well, then, the king's advisers,[206] who are seven in number, namely, the Mistresses Nell Gwynne, Winifred Wells, Lucy Walters, Margaret Hughes, Margaret Dairs, the Lady Frances Stewart and the Countess of Castlemaine, would point out to the king that the contemplated war would cost a large sum of money, which might be spent to much better advantage upon providing balls and suppers at Hampton Court than upon fitting out ships of the line at Portsmouth and Greenwich.'

'And then your negotiation would fall through?'

'Oh! these ladies would infallibly upset any negotiation in which they had no personal interest.'

'I have an idea, sister.'

'Let me hear what it is.'

'It is that by looking about you, you might be able to find an eighth adviser whom you could take with you, and whose eloquence might be powerful enough to counteract the malign influence of the seven others.'

'That is a grand idea, sire; I will look about me.'

'You will find her.'

'I hope so.'

'She must be good-looking. A pretty face is better than a plain one, is it not?'

'Of course, it is.'

'And she must be quick-witted, amusing and daring.'

'Just so.'

'As to her nobility, she should be highly-born enough to enable her to approach the king without too much diffidence, but not sufficiently so to cause her to be restrained unduly by the dignity of her race. Moreover, she should be able to speak a little English.'

'Just so, and I think I know the very woman!' cried Madame. 'What should you say to Mademoiselle de Kéroualle,[207] for instance?'

'Yes!' exclaimed the king, 'the very woman we want! You have found her at once, my dear sister.'

'I will take her. You will make it worth her while, I suppose?'

'Of course,' said the king. 'I will confer on her the style of "Charmer Plenipotentiary", and the title shall carry with it an appropriate endowment.'

'That is excellent.'

'I fancy I already see you on your way, my dear sister, and free from all your troubles.'

'I will go, upon two conditions, the first of which is that I am informed of the object of my negotiations.'

'Here it is, then. The Dutch, as you know, insult me daily in their gazettes, and by their leaning towards republicanism. Well, I hate republics.'

'It is only natural that you should, sire.'

'It annoys me to see that these self-styled kings of the sea bar the commerce of France from the Indies and to know that their ships will soon occupy all the ports of Europe. A power like that is too near me, my sister.'

'They are your allies, nevertheless.'

'For which reason they had no business to have that medal[208] struck, of which you have heard, representing Holland, as Joshua, arresting the course of the sun, and bearing this legend: *The sun has stopped before me*. That does not show a very fraternal spirit, does it?'

'I thought you had forgotten that nonsense.'

'I never forget anything, my dear sister; and, if my real friends, such as your brother Charles, are willing to support me – '

The king paused, but the princess was silent, and appeared to be wrapped in thought.

'Listen,' continued Louis XIV, 'there is the empire of the seas to be shared, and could I not divide it with England, as well as the Dutch?'

'We had better leave Mademoiselle de Kéroualle to deal with that question,' replied Madame.

'Well, then, tell me the second condition to which you alluded just now.'

'My husband's consent to my going to England.'

'You shall have it.'

'Then you may consider the matter settled, and I go, my dear brother.'

On hearing these words, Louis XIV turned towards the corner of the room where Colbert and Aramis were conversing with d'Artagnan, and made an affirmative signal to his minister.

Colbert immediately interrupted the discussion in which the three were engaged, and, addressing Aramis, said, 'Monsieur l'Ambassadeur, with your permission, we will proceed to business.'

Upon hearing this, d'Artagnan discreetly walked away towards the fireplace, where he took up such a position as would enable him to overhear what the king was about to say to Monsieur, who, obviously ill at ease, advanced to meet his majesty. The king wore an animated expression, and his look indicated that indomitable resolution which had already made itself felt in France, and was destined soon to exercise an influence over the whole of Europe.

'I do not approve of the Chevalier de Lorraine,' said the king, turning to his brother, 'and I will thank you, who appear to take so great an interest in him, to suggest that it would be well for him to travel for a few months.'

These words fell upon Monsieur with the crash of an avalanche, for he had the highest regard for his favourite and concentrated upon him nearly all the affection of which he was possessed.

'May I ask,' he said, 'in what way the chevalier has had the misfortune to displease your majesty?' and he threw a furious look at Madame.

'I will tell you that when he has gone,' replied the king quietly; 'and also when Madame, here, has left for England.'

'Madame left for England?' repeated Monsieur, who seemed amazed at the idea.

'She will go within a week,' continued the king, 'and we two will go whither I will acquaint you at the proper time;' saying which, the king turned upon his heel, after bestowing upon his brother a smile intended to sweeten the unpalatable news he had just conveyed to him. Whilst all this was taking place, Colbert had been talking with the Duke of Alameda.

'It is high time,' he now said to the latter, 'for us to come to an understanding. I have restored to you the king's favour, as, indeed, a man of your merit deserves to be restored; I have already received from you the assurance of your goodwill, and the time has now arrived for putting it to the proof. You are, moreover, more French than Spanish. Now, answer me frankly, in the event of our taking arms against the United Provinces, can we depend upon the neutrality of Spain?'

'Sir,' replied Aramis, 'the interest of Spain is very clearly defined. It lies in the embroiling of Europe with the United Provinces, against which the old feeling of jealousy and resentment still exists in respect of the freedom which they have won for themselves. That is our policy; but the King of France has allied himself with the United Provinces. You cannot be ignorant that the result of any action would be a maritime war, and that France is in no condition to undertake such a war with any hope of success.'

At this point, Colbert, happening to turn his head, observed d'Artagnan, who, during the private confabulation of the king with Monsieur was looking about for someone to talk to.

Colbert beckoned to him, saying at the same time to Aramis, 'Suppose we hear what Monsieur d'Artagnan has to say on the subject?'

'Oh! by all means,' replied the ambassador.

'We were just saying, the duke and I,' said Colbert to d'Artagnan, 'that a conflict with the United Provinces would mean a maritime war.'

'Of that, there can be no doubt,' replied the musketeer.

'And what is your opinion of the matter, Monsieur d'Artagnan?'

'I think that, in the event of a maritime war, it will be necessary for us to have a large land force.'

'I beg your pardon?' said Colbert, who thought that he had not rightly understood.

'Why a large land force?' asked Aramis.

'Because, if the English don't help him, the king is sure to be beaten at sea, in which case the Dutch would attack his ports and the Spanish invade his territory.'

'With Spain preserving a neutrality?' said Aramis.

'A neutrality, so long as the king remains the stronger,' replied d'Artagnan.

Colbert looked with undisguised admiration at this man who never brought his intelligence to bear upon any question without fathoming it to the very bottom.

Aramis smiled too. He knew full well that in matters connected with diplomacy, d'Artagnan had few equals.

Colbert, who had unbounded confidence in his own wisdom, was the next to speak.

'Who has told you, Monsieur d'Artagnan,' he said, 'that the king has no navy?'

'Oh! I have not considered all the details,' replied the captain. 'I am but a poor sailor, and, like most men of nervous temperament, I dislike the sea.'

'Nevertheless, I have an idea that, France being a hydra-headed monster in the matter of seaports, if only we have the ships, we shall soon find sailors to man them.'

Colbert drew from his pocket an oblong pocket-book divided into two columns. The first of these showed the names of the various ships, and the second, an array of figures representing the number of men and guns with which those vessels were to be equipped.

'The same idea has occurred to me, you see,' he said to d'Artagnan, 'and therefore, I have had our navy reinforced. We have now, altogether, thirty-five ships.'

'Thirty-five ships! Impossible!' cried d'Artagnan.

'Somewhere about two thousand pieces of cannon,' continued Colbert. 'That is what the king possesses at the present moment. With thirty-five ships, we could form three squadrons; but I want five.'

'Five!' cried Aramis.

'They will be afloat before the end of the year, gentlemen, and the king will have fifty-five ships of the line. We ought to be able to make a fight with a navy like that; don't you think so?'

'To build ships,' remarked d'Artagnan, 'is difficult, though not indeed impossible. But how are they to be armed? In France, we have neither foundries nor military dockyards.'

'Bah!' said Colbert good humouredly, 'for the last year and half I have been providing for all that. And you did not know it? Do you happen to be acquainted with Monsieur d'Infreville?'[209]

'D'Infreville?' replied d'Artagnan, 'no.'

He is a man whom I have discovered. He has a genius for making people work, and he has forged cannon at Toulon and cut down timber in Burgundy. And then – but, perhaps, you will hardly believe what I am going to say now – I have yet another idea in my head.'

'I am not in the least surprised,' said Aramis graciously.

'It gratifies me to hear you say so,' replied Colbert. 'Well, then, when I consider the national characteristics of our friends the Dutch, I say to myself, "They are merchants, and well-disposed towards the king, and surely, they will not be unwilling to sell to his majesty things which they make for themselves, and the more we can buy – " and that again, reminds me that I have Forant. Do you know Forant, d'Artagnan?'

Here Colbert had made a slight slip. He had addressed the captain as plain 'd'Artagnan', as did the king. The captain, however, merely smiled at the omission of the prefix as he answered, 'No, I do not know him.'

'Well, here, again, is a man whom I have unearthed, and whose speciality is *buying*. He has bought for me 350,000 lbs of iron for bullets and 200,000 lbs of powder, twelve cargoes of Norway timber, besides matches, grenades, pitch, tar and I know not what else, for seven per cent less than it would have cost to buy the things in France.'

'A good idea, that,' said d'Artagnan, 'to get from Holland bullets which will be returned to the Dutch.'

'Yes, and with a loss too,' returned Colbert chuckling at the joke.

'And besides,' he added, 'these same Dutchmen, at this very moment, are building six ships upon the most approved lines in their own navy. Destouches – Ah! I am forgetting; perhaps you don't know Destouches either?'

'No, I do not.'

'Well, he is a man with the singular gift of being able to tell at a glance the merits and defects of any ship afloat. That is a very remarkable gift, you know. Nature is very unaccountable in her caprices and whims. Well, this Destouches is, in my opinion, a very valuable man; he is superintending the construction of six ships of seventy-eight guns, which the Provinces are building for his majesty. So you see, my dear Monsieur d'Artagnan, that, should the king come into conflict with the Provinces, he will have no reason to be ashamed of his navy. As regards his army, no one is better qualified to express an opinion than yourself.'

D'Artagnan and Aramis exchanged glances of admiration at the marvellous work which this man had accomplished in a few short years, and Colbert, who intercepted their signals, fully appreciated the delicate flattery which they conveyed.

'If we knew nothing of all this in France,' said d'Artagnan, 'still less must be known outside the kingdom.'

'Now, Monsieur l'Ambassadeur, you can understand why I said what I did, that, with Spain neutral and England assisting us – '

'Oh! if England helps you,' said Aramis, 'I will answer for the neutrality of Spain.'

'Shake hands on that bargain,' cried Colbert with bluff good-humour. 'And the thought of Spain reminds me that you have not the order of the Golden Fleece, Monsieur d'Alameda. I heard the king say, only the other day, that he should be pleased to see you decorated with the Grand Cordon of St Michael.'[210] Aramis bowed.

'Oh!' said d'Artagnan to himself, 'and to think that Porthos is no longer here! What yards of ribbon he would get out of all these decorations! Dear Porthos!'

'And, Monsieur d'Artagnan,' continued Colbert, 'you, I would venture to wager, would have no objection to leading your musketeers into Holland. By the by, can you swim?' and he laughed with the air of a man who is on the best of good terms with himself.

'I can swim like a fish,' replied d'Artagnan.

'Because there is plenty of water there, as you know, Monsieur d'Artagnan, canals, swamps and all the rest of it – but even the best swimmers are drowned occasionally.'

'My life,' replied the musketeer, 'belongs to the king. Only, in war, one rarely finds much water without a little fire, and I declare to you beforehand that I shall do my best to choose the fire. I am not so young as I was, and water freezes me, whereas fire warms, Monsieur Colbert,' and d'Artagnan looked so strong and handsome as he said this, that Colbert, in his turn, could not help staring at him in admiration.

D'Artagnan was by no means unconscious of the effect he had produced. He remembered that a good merchant does not underrate the value of what he has to sell, and he determined upon the price he meant to ask, accordingly.

'So then,' said Colbert, 'we go to Holland?'

'Yes,' replied d'Artagnan, 'only – '

'Only?' said Colbert.

'Only,' repeated d'Artagnan, 'of course the questions of self-interest and of self-respect have to be taken into consideration. It is a fine thing, no doubt, to be captain of the musketeers, but you will please to observe that we have now the guards and the military household of the king, as well. Now, a captain of musketeers ought either to have sole command of them all, which would entail upon him the expenditure of some hundred thousand livres a year for mess and other regimental expenses – '

'Do you suppose,' interrupted Colbert, 'that the king would haggle over trifles of that kind?'

'Perhaps you do not quite understand me, sir,' said d'Artagnan, feeling pretty sure that he had carried the question at issue. 'I desired to point out that I, a veteran, formerly in command of the king's guard, and having precedence of the Marshals of France, once found myself in the trenches with two officers of rank equal to my own, namely the captain of the guards and the colonel commanding the Swiss. Now, I am not going to stand that at any price. I have old habits to which I remain firm.'

Colbert felt the blow, which, however, he was quite prepared to meet.

'I have been thinking about what you said not long ago,' he replied.

'What was that?'

'We were speaking of canals and swamps in which people are sometimes drowned.'

'Well?'

'Well, when they drown, it is often from the want of a boat, a plank or even a stick to cling to.'

'Aye, of a stick, even though it be no longer than a baton,'[211] assented d'Artagnan.

'Precisely so,' said Colbert; 'and, now I come to think of it, I cannot call to mind any occasion upon which a Marshal of France was drowned.'

D'Artagnan turned pale with joy, and said, in a voice which was not quite steady. 'They would be very proud of me in my country were I to become a Marshal of France; but, in order to obtain that distinction, one must previously have been in command of an expedition.'

'Well, sir,' said Colbert, 'you will find in this portfolio, to which I beg leave to invite your attention, the plan of campaign of an expedition of which it is the king's intention to place you in command sometime in the early part of next spring.'

D'Artagnan received the book tremblingly, and as his fingers met those of Colbert, the minister cordially grasped the hand of the musketeer.

'Why, sir,' he said, 'each of us has to be revenged upon the other. I have had my opportunity; your turn has to come.'

'I shall not be found wanting,' replied d'Artagnan, 'and, meanwhile, I would beg of you to tell the king that at the first opportunity either he will be the gainer of a victory or I shall be the loser of a life.'

'I will see to it,' said Colbert, 'that the fleurs-de-lis for your marshal's baton are put in hand at once.'

On the following day, Aramis, who was starting for Madrid in order to negotiate the neutrality of Spain, went to take leave of d'Artagnan at his lodging.

'There are but two of us left now,' said d'Artagnan, 'we must love each other enough for four.'

'And perhaps, my dear d'Artagnan, we may never meet again,' said Aramis. 'I wish you could realise the strength of my affection for you! I am old; I am worn out; virtually, I am dead.'

'My friend,' said d'Artagnan, 'you will outlive me; diplomacy commands you to live; but, as for me, honour condemns me to die.'

'Bah! men like you, Monsieur le Maréchal,' said Aramis, 'die only through excess of joy or glory.'

'Ah!' said d'Artagnan sadly, 'but, just now, I have little appetite for either.'

They embraced once more, and two hours afterwards each went on his separate way.

## The death of d'Artagnan

IN PLEASING CONTRAST to what the common experience of life might well have led us to expect, the promises recorded in our last few pages were all faithfully kept by the persons who made them.

The king recalled Monsieur de Guiche and banished the Chevalier de Lorraine, to Monsieur's extreme grief and discontent.

Madame went to London, where she so successfully inclined the ear of Charles II to the promptings of Mademoiselle de Kéroualle, that an alliance between France and England was entered into, and a treaty duly signed, under the conditions of which the English men-of-war, equipped at the expense of France, made a vigorous attack upon the fleet of the United Provinces; whilst, in recognition of the value of Mademoiselle de Kéroualle's advice, the King of England created her Duchess of Portsmouth.

The promises of ships, munitions of war and victories which Monsieur Colbert had made to Louis XIV were, as is known to all readers of history, duly fulfilled; whilst Aramis, whose undertakings were the most risky of all, wrote to the French Minister the following letter with regard to the negotiations which he had undertaken at Madrid.

MONSIEUR COLBERT – I have the honour to present to you the bearer of this letter, the Reverend Father d'Oliva,[212] general, for the time being, of the Society of Jesus, and my provisional successor.

The reverend father will explain to you, Monsieur Colbert, that I still reserve to myself the direction of all those affairs of the order which relate to France and Spain. I do not, however, desire to retain the title of *general*, since too much light might, thereby, be thrown upon the progress of the negotiations with which His Catholic Majesty has entrusted me. I shall, by command of his majesty, resume that title upon the accomplishment of the work, which, in concert with you, I have undertaken for the greater glory of God, and of His church.

The Reverend Father d'Oliva will inform you of the consent which has been given by His Catholic Majesty to the signature of a treaty assuring the neutrality of Spain in the event of war breaking out between France and the United Provinces.

This treaty will stand good, even if England, instead of taking any active part in the hostilities, should be content to remain neutral.

With regard to Portugal, which has already formed the subject of conversation between us, you may accept my assurance that this power will, to the utmost of her resources, give her support to the Most Christian King[213] in his war.

I have the honour to assure you of my profound consideration, and to lay my respect at the feet of his Most Christian Majesty.

D'ALAMEDA

Aramis, then, having more than carried out his promise, it remains to be seen how the king, Monsieur Colbert and d'Artagnan fulfilled their respective obligations. In the spring, as Colbert had foretold, the land forces of the king entered upon their campaign. The army preceded, in grand array, Louis XIV, who, mounted on horseback and surrounded by carriages full of ladies and courtiers, brought with him the élite of the kingdom to this sanguinary fête.

The officers of his army had, it is true, no other music than the artillery of the Dutch forts, but this was enough for a great number of them, who found in this war honours, promotion, fortune or death. Monsieur d'Artagnan found himself in command of a body of cavalry and infantry, twelve thousand strong, with which he had orders to lay siege to a number of places which represented the knots in that strategic network known as Friesland.

Never did a more gallantly conducted army set forth upon an expedition. The officers knew that their commander, cautious and skilful as he was brave, would neither sacrifice a single life, nor yield an inch of ground, except of sheer necessity.

He adopted the old fashion of warfare, which was to live on the invaded country and to keep his soldiers singing whilst the enemy wept.

The captain of the king's musketeers put himself on his mettle to show that he was equal to the emergencies of every situation. Never were his moments for action ill-timed or his attacks ill-supported, whilst no one knew better than he how to use to the best advantage any weakness disclosed by the enemy. D'Artagnan's army had taken twelve small places in the course of a month, and he was now besieging a thirteenth, which had held out for five days. D'Artagnan opened his trenches, as though he had no idea that the enemy would ever capitulate. The corps of pioneers attached to this man's army were zealous and filled with the spirit of emulation because he treated them like soldiers, knew how to make their work glorious and never exposed them to unnecessary risk. It was good to see with what readiness they attacked the obstacles to their progress which the marshy lands of Holland presented; huge mounds of turf and clay melted away, as the soldiers said, like butter in the huge frying-pans of the Friesland housewives.

D'Artagnan constantly dispatched couriers to the king with news of his latest successes, and this had the effect of increasing his majesty's good humour, and of making him more eager than ever to improvise entertainments for the amusement of the ladies of the court.

D'Artagnan's victories, indeed, invested the king with so much majesty, that Madame de Montespan thenceforth called him Louis the Invincible, whilst Mademoiselle de la Vallière, who had called him merely Louis the Victorious, fell into comparative disfavour. Besides, her eyes were frequently red, and for an 'Invincible', nothing could be more out of character than a tearful mistress when everyone else around him wore a smiling face. The star of Mademoiselle de la Vallière was lost in a horizon of clouds and tears, but the gaiety of Madame de Montespan redoubled with the king's success and amply consoled him for the loss. And it was d'Artagnan to whom the king was indebted for all his happiness. His majesty did not fail to recognise that this was the case, and being anxious to show his appreciation of d'Artagnan's services, he wrote to Monsieur Colbert in the following terms:

MONSIEUR COLBERT – We have a promise to redeem as regards Monsieur d'Artagnan, who has so faithfully fulfilled his own, and now is the time to redeem it. You will receive the necessary instructions in due course.         LOUIS

Upon receipt of this communication, Colbert at once dispatched, by messenger, a letter to d'Artagnan, together with a box of ebony inlaid with gold, which, although not very bulky, must have been of considerable weight, since an escort of five men was sent with the messenger to help him carry it. They reached their destination at daybreak and at once presented themselves at d'Artagnan's headquarters.

They learnt there that, on the previous evening, the governor of the besieged town had made a sortie in the course of which d'Artagnan's works had been considerably damaged and seventy-seven of his men killed, whilst the enemy had taken advantage of the occasion to repair a breach in their own walls, and that d'Artagnan himself, at the head of twelve companies of grenadiers, had just left for the scene of disaster. Monsieur Colbert's messenger, having received orders to find d'Artagnan wherever he might be, either by day or night, lost no time in making his way to the trenches, accompanied by his mounted escort.

They found d'Artagnan in the open plain, where his long cane and gold-laced hat and uniform rendered him a conspicuous object. He was gnawing his white moustaches, and, from time to time, brushing from his uniform the dust thrown upon it by the balls which ploughed up the ground round about him.

Notwithstanding the terrific hail of bullets which filled the air, officers were to be seen handling the spade and men wheeling barrows; whilst huge fascines were carried or dragged by detachments of soldiers and placed in position to protect the trenches, which the frantic energy of the men, cheered on by their general, had by this time reopened.

In the space of three hours everything had been got into working order. D'Artagnan's voice became milder and he had quite calmed down by the time the captain of the pioneers came to report to him that the trenches were, once more, habitable. The unfortunate man, however, had scarcely opened his mouth when a cannon-ball carried off one of his legs and he fell into the arms of d'Artagnan, who, with sympathetic words, carried him down under cover amidst the cheers of the soldiers. Thenceforward delirium, not enthusiasm, reigned, and two companies, stealing away, charged the enemy's outposts, which they carried with a cheer. When their comrades, whom d'Artagnan found the greatest difficulty in keeping in hand, saw them on the bastions, they were to be withheld no longer, and, dashing forward, commenced a furious attack upon the counterscarp, upon which the safety of the place mainly depended.

D'Artagnan now saw that the only way of stopping his soldiers was by taking the place by storm, and he, accordingly, brought a strong force to bear upon the two breaches which the enemy were attempting to repair. The assault, in which eighteen companies took part, was terrific; and was supported by d'Artagnan, at a distance of half a cannon-shot, with the remainder of his troops arranged *en échelon*.[214]

The cries of the Dutch were distinctly audible as they were poniarded at their guns by d'Artagnan's grenadiers, and as the fight waxed fiercer, so greater waxed the despair of the governor of the town, who disputed his position inch by inch. D'Artagnan, in order to put an end to the affair and to silence the fire which was still being kept up, ordered the advance of another column. This quickly bored its way like a gimlet through the gates of the town, which were still standing, and the enemy were soon in full flight, hotly pursued by the besiegers.

It was at this moment of triumph that the exultant general heard, at his side, a voice saying, 'A dispatch, if you please, from Monsieur Colbert.'

He opened a letter which contained these words:

> MONSIEUR D'ARTAGNAN – I am commanded by the king to inform you that he has appointed you a Marshal of France in consideration of your distinguished services and the honour you confer upon his arms.
>
> The king is much gratified with the captures you have made, and he trusts that the business which you have now in hand will be attended by good fortune to you and success for him!

D'Artagnan paused here, and with heightened colour and sparkling eye, watched the progress of his troops towards the walls, which were still enveloped in clouds of smoke.

'It is all over,' he said to the messenger, 'the town will have surrendered in a quarter of a hour.' He then resumed the perusal of the letter.

> The accompanying box is an offering from myself, and will perhaps remind you that, whilst your warriors are drawing the sword in defence of the king, I am encouraging pacific art in ornamenting the rewards which are so justly your due.
>
> I commend myself to your friendship, Monsieur le Maréchal, and beg you to believe most thoroughly in my own.
>
> COLBERT

D'Artagnan, overcome with joy, made a sign to the messenger, who approached him bearing a box in his hand, but, at the moment when the marshal was about to examine it, a terrific explosion upon the ramparts called his attention in the direction of the town. 'It is strange,' he said, 'that I don't see the king's standard flying upon the walls yet, nor hear the beat of the drums,' and he ordered a fresh body of three hundred men to effect another breach in the wall.

Having thus eased his mind, he once more turned his attention to the box which Monsieur Colbert's messenger presented to him. It was his prize; he had fairly won it.

D'Artagnan had just raised his hand to open the box when it was smashed by a bullet from the town which then buried itself in d'Artagnan's breast, knocking him down upon a mound of earth, whilst the marshal's baton, ornamented with fleurs-de-lis, escaped from the shattered casket and rolled beneath the marshal's inert hand.

D'Artagnan made an effort to rise and it was at first hoped that although knocked over he was otherwise uninjured, but a cry of dismay from the surrounding officers presently showed it was not so. The marshal was found to be bathed in blood and the pale hue of death quickly overspread his noble features. Reclining upon the arms which were stretched out on all sides to receive him, d'Artagnan was able once more to direct his gaze upon the conquered town, and to distinguish the white flag[215] which now floated over the chief bastion, and his ears, already deaf to the ordinary sounds of life, could yet catch the roll of the drums which announced the victory.

Then, taking in his feeble grasp the baton, adorned with the golden fleurs-de-lis of France, he bent upon it the eyes which he had no longer the strength to raise to heaven, and fell back, murmuring these strange words, the significance and pathos of which none but himself could understand.

'Athos, Porthos, *au revoir* – Aramis, *adieu* for ever.'

Of the four gallant men whose history we have related, but one now remained; the others God had taken to Himself.

# NOTES

NB Many of these notes gloss characters and events that figure in the previous novels of the *Musketeers* cycle. I therefore recommend that they be used sparingly on a first reading of the text, in order not to slow the pace of the narrative. For convenience, I have abbreviated the previous novels as follows:

TM    *The Three Musketeers*, ed. K. Wren, Wordsworth, Ware 2001

TYA   *Twenty Years After*, ed. D. Coward, World's Classics, Oxford 1993

VB    *The Vicomte de Bragelonne*, ed. D. Coward, World's Classics, Oxford 1995

LV    *Louise de la Vallière*, ed. D. Coward, World's Classics, Oxford 1995

1 (p. 3) *as elsewhere recorded* In *VB* (Ch. 61–2) d'Artagnan and Raoul de Bragelonne quell a riot provoked by Fouquet's supporters to facilitate the rescue of Lyodot and d'Emerys, two of the superintendent's subordinates who have been condemned to death.

2 (p. 3) *Ninon de l'Enclos* (1620–1705) a celebrated French beauty who retained her looks until an advanced age

3 (p. 3) *duchess* Marie de Rohan-Montbazon, Duchesse de Chevreuse (1600–79), in *TM* the confidante of the queen, Anne of Austria, and Aramis's mistress, now based in Brussels with the Marquis de Laicques (1614–74), who may or may not have been her husband. She had previously been married briefly to the Duc de Luynes (1578–1621), the favourite of Louis XIII, and subsequently to the Duc de Chevreuse (1578–1657). It appears to be the Luynes contingent that is causing her grief later in the chapter.

4 (p. 4) *Fontainebleau* Aramis and the duchess have previously encountered each other and had an extended conversation (witnessed by d'Artagnan) in the cemetery here (*LV*, Ch. 53).

5 (p. 4) *that tomb so recently filled in*   that of the Franciscan monk, otherwise General of the Jesuits, whom Aramis has now succeeded (*LV*, Ch. 35). It is implied that the general has been poisoned on the orders of the Jesuit Grand Council, and that Aramis is aware of and probably implicated in it.

6 (p. 4) *Madame de Longueville*   The Duchesse de Longueville (1619–79) resembles Mme de Chevreuse in her passion for intrigue; she does not appear in *The Man in the Iron Mask*, but is Aramis's mistress in *TYA*, where she plays a major role in the Fronde rebellion. It is strongly hinted there (Ch. 115 and Conclusion) that Aramis is the father of her son.

7 (p. 5) *Marie Michon*   an assumed identity of Mme de Chevreuse in *TM*

8 (p. 5) *Belle-Isle-en-Mer*   Fouquet's island fortress, off the coast of Brittany; in *VB*, Aramis fortifies it with the assistance of Porthos

9 (p. 5) *grievance*   Anne of Austria fell out with Mme de Chevreuse over the part played by the latter in the Fronde in opposition to Mazarin and the royal party.

10 (p. 6) *Baisemeaux*   The Marquis de Baisemeaux (1613–97) is indebted to Aramis for the money lent him to buy his post of governor of the Bastille (*LV*, Ch. 3).

11 (p. 8) *affiliated travellers*   refers to the meeting (*LV*, Ch. 35) at which the dying Franciscan monk nominates Aramis as General of the Jesuits

12 (p. 8) *livres*   A livre was divided into twenty sous, each sou being subdivided into four liards or twelve deniers. Three livres constituted an écu (crown), ten livres a pistole.

13 (p. 9) *Flanders*   still at this time a Spanish possession, more or less equivalent to the modern Belgium. The United Provinces (the present-day Netherlands) had gained independence from Spain by the Treaty of Westphalia (1648).

14 (p. 10) *Fouquet*   Much of *VB* and *LV* concerns itself with Louis XIV's determination to discredit and ruin Nicolas Fouquet (1615–80), his Minister of Finance.

15 (p. 10) *Signor Mazarini*   a contemptuous designation of Cardinal Mazarin (1602–61), whose death is narrated in *VB*. He also features in *TYA*, where he has secretly married Anne of Austria after the death of her husband Louis XIII.

16 (p. 16) *Colbert*   Jean-Baptiste Colbert (1619–83) became Louis XIV's Controller of Finances late in 1665.

17 (p. 18) *Voiture*   Vincent Voiture (1597–1648), French writer, grammarian and wit

18 (p. 18) *Conrart* Valentin Conrart (1603–75), first secretary of Richelieu's French Academy

19 (p. 18) *Cinq-Mars* Henri d'Effiat, Marquis de Cinq-Mars (1620–42), the favourite of Louis XIII, executed for conspiring with Spain to overthrow Richelieu. He was the eponymous hero (in 1826) of a not very good historical novel by Dumas's contemporary, Alfred de Vigny (1797–1863).

20 (p. 22) *Béguines* a lay religious order particularly strong in the Low Countries

21 (p. 26) *unfaithful wife* in defiance of historical veracity, Dumas makes Vanel's wife into one of Fouquet's former mistresses

22 (p. 28) *Gourville, Pélisson* Jean Hérault de Gourville (1625–1703) and Paul Pellisson (1624–93), part of Fouquet's inner circle (the Epicureans). Fouquet, strapped for cash, is selling off his post of Procureur-Général, a high-risk strategy as the job confers immunity from prosecution.

23 (p. 31) *Monsieur, Madame* Monsieur was the honorific title always given to the eldest of the king's brothers, Madame the title given to his wife.

24 (p. 32) *Monsieur Valot* Antoine Valot (1594–1671) was Louis XIV's principal doctor.

25 (p. 37) *Péronne, Laporte* Péronne (or Péronnette) has not been previously mentioned, but Pierre de La Porte (1603–80), who really existed, figures quite prominently in both *TM* (as Anne of Austria's valet) and *TYA* (where his services have been transferred to Louis XIV).

26 (p. 45) *three canvasses* It is not quite clear what Dumas means here, since of the key plot-lines only the love triangle between Louis XIV, Louise and Raoul has arguably run its course, and Dumas is only just beginning to exploit the 'Iron Mask' intrigue.

27 (p. 45) *Saint-Mandé* at the time a small village close to Paris where Fouquet had his country house

28 (p. 46) *Vatel . . . Abbé Fouquet . . . Loret . . . La Fontaine* François Vatel (d. 1671) was head of Fouquet's household; Basile Fouquet (1622–80) was in minor orders; Jean Loret (1600–65) was a (rather bad) poet and early gossip columnist; Jean de La Fontaine (1621–95), one of the great literary luminaries of seventeenth-century France, wrote stories and fables.

29 (p. 48) *Boccaccio and Aretino* The first (1313–75) is the author of the *Decameron*, the second (1492–1556) a noted satirist: they have in common the fact that both write in a style somewhat equivalent to the tale La Fontaine tells in this chapter.

30 (p. 48) *the spurious coin*   an inaccurate reference to the biblical story of the widow's mite (Mark 12:42, Luke 21:2). Neither evangelist mentions the presence of a Pharisee.

31 (p. 50) *Gascon*   Gascons were proverbial for being boastful.

32 (p. 50) *Fugiunt risus leporesque*   a rather feeble pun on the two possible meanings of *lepores* in Latin (graces or hares). *Fugiunt* = they flee.

33 (p. 51) *Rara avis in terra*   'a rare bird on earth'

34 (p. 53) *Semper ad adventum*   Fouquet is misquoting the Latin poet Horace, whose advice to other poets was always to hurry on towards the conclusion (*eventum* not *adventum*).

35 (p. 54) *the minister's cabinet*   described in *VB*, Ch. 54

36 (p. 54) *Madame de Bellière*   Elise, Marquise de Bellière (1608–75), one of Fouquet's mistresses, who has previously sold her jewels and plate (*LV*, Ch. 9) to stave off impending financial meltdown

37 (p. 61) *the Valtellina*   occupied in 1626 by Richelieu during the Thirty Years' War (1618–48) owing to its strategic situation between Lombardy and Southern Germany

38 (p. 62) *Montfaucon, Marigny, Samblançay*   Montfaucon was a celebrated gallows and place of execution situated just outside Paris. Marigny, the Finance Minister of Philip IV of France, was hanged there in 1315. Samblançay (more usually Semblançay), François I's Finance Minister, was executed in 1527.

39 (p. 72) *a fête at Vaux*   In *LV*, Ch. 28, Colbert, with a view to ruining Fouquet, has persuaded him to invite the king to an entertainment at his (Fouquet's) château of Vaux-le-Vicomte.

40 (p. 75) *Ruysdael*   Jacob van Ruysdael (1629–82), Dutch landscape painter

41 (p. 75) *where we last left Raoul*   in fact at the end of *LV*. Sent by Louis XIV to the court of Charles II, so that Louis can pursue his amours with Louise, Raoul has been recalled by a letter from his friend Guiche, ostensibly because the latter has been seriously wounded in a duel. Henriette (Madame) has also requested his return by way of a despatch to Charles, her brother. In company with Aure de Montalais, he goes to see Louise, but finds her in a compromising position with Louis.

42 (p. 78) *oak tree*   This refers to the episode (*LV*, Ch. 23) in which Louise avows her love for the king, not suspecting that he overhears her.

43 (p. 83) *carpenter*   In *LV*, Ch. 80, Saint-Aignan, the king's confidant, having exchanged his prestigious suite of rooms at Fontainebleau for a much inferior set immediately below those occupied by Louise,

employs a carpenter to install a connecting secret staircase, so that Louise may descend to meet the king in Saint-Aignan's apartment.

44 (p. 86) *de Wardes*   François-René, Marquis de Wardes (or Vardes) (1620–88), son of the Comte de Wardes whom d'Artagnan wounds in a duel at Calais (*TM*) and whom he subsequently replaces in Milady's bed. De Wardes junior tries to provoke Raoul to a duel (*VB*, Ch. 87), but d'Artagnan intervenes to prevent this.

45 (p. 86) *Madame had been immensely flattered*   Louis XIV's flirtation with his sister-in-law (recounted in *LV*) was particularly welcome to her because her husband was homosexual

46 (p. 88) *flight to Chaillot*   Louise flees to Chaillot (followed/escorted by d'Artagnan) when she believes herself abandoned by the king (*LV*, Ch. 73).

47 (p. 90) *Saint-Aignan*   François, Comte de Saint-Aignan (1610–87) is the royal courtier who facilitates the liaison between Louis XIV and Louise de la Vallière.

48 (p. 94) *Tonnay-Charente*   Athénaïs de Tonnay-Charente, subsequently Marquise de Montespan (1641–1707), was the king's mistress after he tired of Louise de la Vallière.

49 (p. 96) *Porthos*   In *LV*, Ch. 55, d'Artagnan has presented Porthos to the king: invited to supper, Porthos's gargantuan appetite makes him a huge success (*LV*, Ch. 61).

50 (p. 96) *Mouston*   Porthos's valet appears in *TM* as Mousqueton, but changes his name to Mouston in *TYA*.

51 (p. 96) *Engineer*   Porthos takes to himself the credit for fortifying Belle-Isle-en-Mer, even though the technical expertise belongs to Aramis.

52 (p. 96) *Trüchen and Planchet*   Planchet first appears in *TM* as d'Artagnan's valet, but is now set up as a prosperous grocer in Paris. Trüchen is his mistress, whom he has discreetly installed at Fontainebleau.

53 (p. 102) *Minimes*   a convent and preferred venue for duellists

54 (p. 103) *cartel*   a challenge to a duel

55 (p. 103) *Apollo*   In classical mythology, Apollo is (among other things) the god of poetry and the fine arts.

56 (p. 104) *Ronsard or Malherbe*   Pierre de Ronsard (1524–85) was the most celebrated French poet of the sixteenth century; François de Malherbe (1555–1628), also a poet, was arguably better known as a stylist and grammarian.

57 (p. 117) *the royal Mercury*   In classical mythology, Mercury was the messenger of the gods.

58 (p. 118) *Styx*   in classical mythology, the river marking the boundary of the Underworld (Hades), around which it flowed seven times

59 (p. 118) *Apollo with Phoebus* For Apollo, see above, Note 55. This is a rather feeble pun on the meaning in French of Phoebus: either another name for Apollo or (*phébus*) bombastic and exaggerated language. Louis is suggesting that Saint-Aignan is overdoing the prophecies of doom.

60 (p. 118) *the famous 'four'* i.e., the musketeers – Athos, Porthos, Aramis and d'Artagnan

61 (p. 119) *My uncle, Henri IV* translator's error – the French gives *aïeul*, meaning grandfather, which is genealogically correct

62 (p. 122) *Ovid* The Latin poet Ovid (43BC–AD18) was banished by the Emperor Augustus for reasons that remain obscure – possibly because he witnessed the emperor committing incest with his daughter Julia.

63 (p. 123) *old grievances* this may be Louis referring to the humiliating events of the Fronde (*TYA*, Ch. 53), or to his impatience at being held so long in check by Mazarin

64 (p. 123) *allow the Comte de la Fère to pass* Athos's reward for the role he played in restoring Charles II to the throne of England

65 (p. 125) *Buckingham's departure* George Villiers, Duke of Buckingham (1627–87) was the son of the duke assassinated in 1628 through the machinations of Milady (*TM*). He features in *VB* and *LV*: himself in love with Madame, he escorts her to France for her marriage to the king's brother, and is subsequently sent home by the queen mother.

66 (p. 129) *kings have been under obligations* certainly Charles II, restored to the English throne by the efforts of d'Artagnan and Athos (*VB*); possibly Charles I, whom the musketeers fail by a whisker to save from the scaffold (*TYA*)

67 (p. 130) *the vaults of St Denis* In *TYA*, Ch. 24, Athos tells Raoul: 'learn ever to separate the king and the principle of royalty. The king is but man; royalty is the spirit of God.' Raoul swears to devote himself to the latter.

68 (p. 137) *Manicamp* Louis, Comte de Manicamp (1630–1708), a close confederate of Guiche and Malicorne

69 (p. 145) *Grimaud* Athos's devoted servant, a man of few words, Grimaud features prominently both in *TM* and *TYA*.

70 (p. 146) *General Monk* In *VB*, at the Restoration of Charles II (in which d'Artagnan has been instrumental), Monk presents the musketeer with a keepsake in the shape of 'a little house in a grove, a cottage as it is called here'. Most cottages, then as now, were not set in a hundred acres of land (as this one is). Improbably, it is situated on the banks of the Clyde, which Dumas seems to think is in England.

71 (p. 153) *the old dowager duchess* the second wife of Gaston d'Orléans, the king's late uncle

72 (p. 154) *Baradas and Cinq-Mars* For Cinq-Mars, see above, Note 19. François de Barradat (1604–82) also plotted against Richelieu, but was pardoned and disgraced in 1626. The reference to 'weary days and years' seems odd, as Cinq-Mars was only twenty-two when he was beheaded.

73 (p. 157) *your Majesty refused to King Charles* At the beginning of *VB*, Mazarin refuses Louis XIV's request for money to fund the restoration of Charles to the English throne.

74 (p. 162) *the thirty-livres prisoners* Baisemeaux's income as governor of the Bastille depends on the number of his prisoners and their status, different categories of inmate attracting different amounts (*LV*, Ch. 5).

75 (p. 163) *The pigeon which stays at home* a reference to La Fontaine's fable of 'The Two Pigeons', the more adventurous of which decides to go travelling and is lucky to get home alive. The moral is, if you're well off somewhere, stay put.

76 (p. 177) *Watch . . . the hour* 'Watch therefore: for ye know not what hour your Lord doth come' (Matthew 24:42)

77 (p. 179) *Aramis's first visit* Aramis has previously visited the Bastille (*LV*, Ch. 7) and briefly encountered the prisoner under the name of Marchiali.

78 (p. 184) *monseigneur* The change of title is significant, since it was used only in addressing princes, members of the high aristocracy, and bishops.

79 (p. 194) *St Louis . . . François I* St Louis is Louis IX, King of France from 1226 to 1270. François I reigned from 1515 until 1547.

80 (p. 195) *Monsieur was only born* Anne of Austria's second son, Philippe d'Orléans, was born two years after Louis XIV, in 1640.

81 (p. 202) *a receipt for one hundred and fifty thousand livres* Aramis has previously (*VB*) lent Baisemeaux this sum to enable him to purchase the governorship of the Bastille.

82 (p. 203) *La Fontaine's hare* In 'The Hare and the Frogs', however, the hare is sad and preoccupied because he is so timid that everything terrifies him.

83 (p. 207) *Costar* Pierre Costart (1603–60), another minor literary luminary of the period

84 (p. 210) *the time of Charles IX* about a century previous to this, Charles IX having reigned from 1560 to 1574

85 (p. 210) *Ambroise Paré* celebrated French surgeon, lived *c.*1509–90

86  (p. 210) *la belle Margot*   Queen Marguerite of Navarre (1492–1549), a protector of the Protestants (Huguenots)

87  (p. 210) *Queen Catherine*   Catherine de Médicis (1519–89), wife of Henri II, mother of Charles IX, also of François II (1559–60) and Henri III (1574–89)

88  (p. 211) *Marie de Medici*   Marie de Médicis (1573–1642), married Henri IV in 1600. She was the grandmother of Louis XIV.

89  (p. 211) *Bassompierre*   François de Bassompierre (1579–1646), subsequently imprisoned by Richelieu (in 1631)

90  (p. 211) *Concini . . . Galigaï*   Concino Concini, assassinated at Louis XIII's behest in 1617 by the Marquis de Vitry, was the favourite of the regent, Marie de Médicis; his wife Leonora, known as Galigaï, was burnt at the stake as a witch in the same year.

91  (p. 211) *Richelieu*   Armand Duplessis, Cardinal de Richelieu (1585–1642), first minister of France from 1624 until his death. He is one of the major characters in *TM*. The implausible story of him dancing a saraband in a clown's costume in the presence of Anne of Austria is also mentioned in the earlier novel, as is the story of Buckingham's pearls.

92  (p. 211) *Mirame*   a play supposedly written, at least in part, by Richelieu himself, dating from 1641

93  (p. 211) *Beaufort*   François, Duc de Beaufort (1616–69) reappears later in the novel when Raoul joins his Algerian expedition. His famous escape from Vincennes prison (1648), aided by Athos and Grimaud, is one of the major episodes in *TYA*. He was one of the prime movers of the Fronde.

94  (p. 211) *Marion de Lorme*   a famous French courtesan who lived from 1611 to 1650. Dumas would have been familiar with Victor Hugo's verse drama (1829) of which she is the eponymous heroine.

95  (p. 212) *de Lyonne, Letellier*   Hugues de Lyonne (1611–71) and Michel Le Tellier (1603–85) were responsible for foreign affairs and war respectively in Louis XIV's government.

96  (p. 213) *Hôtel de Bourgogne*   a famous Paris theatre, founded in 1629. The translator misrenders *comédien* as 'comedian': it means 'actor'.

97  (p. 214) *cordons bleus*   refers to the blue sash worn by the Knights of the Order of the Holy Spirit

98  (p. 215) *Molière*   Jean-Baptiste Poquelin, known as Molière (1622–73), was the major French comic dramatist of the seventeenth century

99  (p. 220) *Le Brun*   Charles Le Brun (1619–90), responsible for the décor of Vaux-le-Vicomte

100 (p. 220) *Marco Antonio* the Italian engraver, Marco Antonio Raimondi (1488–1546)

101 (p. 223) *lay figures* wickerwork cage structures on which tailors put together clothes

102 (p. 225) *Le Bourgeois Gentilhomme* not produced until 1670, so rather long in gestation if Porthos was indeed its inspiration. The play satirises the aristocratic pretensions and aspirations of the middle classes.

103 (p. 226) *Volière* an aviary

104 (p. 228) *Coquenard* the name of Porthos's deceased wife, widow of a rich lawyer. Both characters appear in *TM*.

105 (p. 231) *Les Fâcheux* a three-act verse comedy by Molière, first performed in 1661 and portraying a series of bores

106 (p. 231) *lumière* light

107 (p. 233) *Molière . . . no philosopher* almost certainly a reference to Molière's own marital difficulties, even though he did not in fact marry Armande Béjart until the following year

108 (p. 234) *La Pucelle* Joan of Arc, the maid (*pucelle*) of Orléans. Chapelain published the first twelve cantos of his epic poem in 1656 (the last twelve did not appear until 1682).

109 (p. 234) *légume* vegetable; *posthume* posthumous; *rivage* bank (of a river); *herbage* grassland; *heureux* happy; *fâcheux* annoying; *capricieux* capricious

110 (p. 236) *Xenocrates* Greek philosopher (406–314 BC), a disciple of Plato. The allusion is somewhat obscure, as Xenocrates had a reputation as a sobersides who did not go in for this sort of malarkey.

111 (p. 238) *lettre de cachet* a royal warrant authorising arrest and detention without trial for an indefinite period (familiar to English readers through the fate of Alexandre Manette in Dickens's *A Tale of Two Cities*)

112 (p. 249) *AMDG* i.e., *Ad Majorem Dei Gloriam* (to the greater glory of God), the motto of the Jesuit Order

113 (p. 252) *water-kennel* a water course, 'kennel' being here a variant on the word 'channel'

114 (p. 255) *Louis XI or Charles IX* oddly paired: Louis XI (1461–83), ruthless and cruel in his pursuit of power, was none the less one of the founders of the French monarchy; Charles IX (1560–74) provoked the St Bartholomew's Day Massacre of the Huguenots in 1572

115 (p. 255) *Patiens quia aeternus* St Augustine's description of God, 'patient because he is eternal'

116 (p. 258) *alone in the world*   not strictly true; see above, Note 6

117 (p. 266) *Charles V*   King of Spain (from 1516) and Holy Roman Emperor (1519–56), featured in Hugo's Romantic drama *Hernani* (1830), in which he has a 200-line soliloquy in which he envisions carving up the governance of the world between himself and the Pope

118 (p. 266) *Charlemagne*   the claims are exaggerated: Charlemagne was Holy Roman Emperor from 800 until 814, but his lands were restricted to France, part of Germany and part of Italy. However, Dumas is probably recalling here Charles V's invocation to Charlemagne in the Act IV soliloquy in *Hernani* (see previous Note).

119 (p. 267) *1635*   The date is incorrect and should be 1653, as the subsequent reference to 'the park, which has only existed eight years' makes clear.

120 (p. 267) *Levau . . . the interior*   Louis Levau (1612–70) built Vaux; André Le Nôtre (1613–1700) designed the gardens. For Le Brun, see above, Note 99.

121 (p. 268) *caryatides*   A caryatid in architecture is a supporting pillar carved in the shape of a female form.

122 (p. 268) *Wolsey*   Thomas Wolsey (1471–1530), Lord Chancellor to Henry VIII, built Hampton Court Palace for himself, then thought better of it and gave it to the king.

123 (p. 268) *Boileau, Despréaux*   The names refer to the same person, Nicolas Boileau-Despréaux (1636–1711), a celebrated poet and literary critic.

124 (p. 269) *Maecenas*   minister and patron of the arts under the Emperor Augustus, lived from 69 BC to 8 BC. The word *mécène* is current in French, meaning a patron or benefactor.

125 (p. 269) *Scudéry*   Georges de Scudéry (1601–67). *Clélie* was an immensely long novel of which the tenth (and mercifully final) volume had appeared in 1660.

126 (p. 271) *Abbé Terray*   Joseph-Marie de Terray (1715–78), Controller of Finances under Louis XV

127 (p. 272) *Calypso, Ulysses*   In Homer's *Odyssey*, Calypso welcomes the shipwrecked Ulysses on his return from the Trojan War and detains him for seven years.

128 (p. 273) *stole*   a reference to Aramis's clerical status as Bishop of Vannes

129 (p. 273) *The oath of long ago*   'all for one – one for all', the famous oath of the musketeers (*TM*, Ch. 9)

130 (p. 279) *Juno . . . Jupiter*   In classical mythology, Juno, queen of the gods, was regularly portrayed as arrogant and haughty (her

favoured bird was the peacock). The reference to her husband Jupiter is less clear.

131 (p. 280) *Morpheus*   In classical mythology, Morpheus was the god of sleep or dreams.

132 (p. 280) *A Roland for an Oliver*   the reference is to the inseparable friends Roland and Oliver, central characters in the Old French epic, *The Song of Roland*. It is not a good translation of the French chapter title, 'A Gascon, Gascon et demi', meaning that the Gascon d'Artagnan, wily as are all Gascons, is none the less outfoxed by Aramis.

133 (p. 291) *the cascade and the fountain*   two of the spectacular entertainments laid on by Fouquet for the king at Vaux

134 (p. 291) *Maucrou*   François de Maucroix (*sic*) (1619–1708), a great friend of La Fontaine

135 (p. 293) *a hundred and ninety thousand livres*   Dumas's mathematics appear to have let him down. A pistole is worth ten livres, so the correct figure would be ninety thousand livres.

136 (p. 294) *Titan*   In classical mythology, in the war between the gods of Olympus and the Titans, a terrestrial race of giants, the latter attempted to scale the heights of Olympus by piling mountains one on top of the other.

137 (p. 298) *Toby*   a double agent, Fouquet's lackey, but in Colbert's pay; in *VB*, he hands over to Colbert an undated love-letter written by Fouquet to Louise de la Vallière

138 (p. 298) *Maréchal d'Ancre*   another name for Concini (see above, Note 90)

139 (p. 301) *Fons et origo*   Latin for 'source and origin'. The original French gives the legal term *corps du délit* (*corpus delicti*), i.e., the cause of the trouble or offence.

140 (p. 302) *Prometheus*   In classical mythology, Prometheus was punished by the gods for his theft of fire by being chained to Mount Caucasus and having a vulture devour his self-renewing liver.

141 (p. 305) *Milo of Crotona*   a great athlete of antiquity whose hand became wedged in a tree he was trying (for no immediately apparent reason) to split. Unable to escape, he was eaten by wild beasts.

142 (p. 305) *Mrs Radcliffe*   Anne Radcliffe (1764–1823), author of such enormously successful Gothic romances as *The Mysteries of Udolpho* (1794) and *The Italian* (1797)

143 (p. 305) *decrees of Minos*   Minos, King of Crete, was rewarded for the justice of his rule by being made, after his death, one of the three Judges of the Underworld (Hades).

144 (p. 307) *Seldon*   an invented character (though based on fact) of indeterminate nationality. Earlier, in Ch. 36, he is Irish.

145 (p. 309) *six long years*   In Ch. 29, it is indicated that the period of time involved is nearer eight years.

146 (p. 310) *Caeteris paribus*   (Latin) 'all other things being equal'

147 (p. 311) *Jeanne d'Albret*   (?1528–1572) Queen of Navarre, supposedly poisoned by Catherine de Médicis at the court of France

148 (p. 316) *Luynes*   See above, Note 3.

149 (p. 316) *Ahasuerus . . . Haman*   in the Book of Esther, Haman, the chief minister of Ahasuerus, King of the Medes and Persians, is hanged by the King on the gallows prepared for Mordecai the Jew. For Marigny, see above, Note 38.

150 (p. 324) *Cinq-Mars . . . Chalais . . . Condé . . . Retz . . . Broussel*   for Cinq-Mars, see above, Note 19. Henri, Marquis de Chalais (1599–1626) conspired with Louis XIII's brother Gaston against Richelieu and was executed for his pains. Condé (referred to elsewhere as M. le Prince), Retz and Broussel all took a prominent role in the Fronde; Retz and Broussel play minor parts in *TYA*.

151 (p. 326) *the end crowns the work*   The Latin proverb is *Finis coronat opus.*

152 (p. 343) *Mithridates*   Mithridates VI Eupator, King of Pontus in the first century BC, developed a resistance to poison by taking quantities of it himself over a long period of time. The last section of A. E. Housman's poem 'Terence, this is stupid stuff', narrates the story.

153 (p. 355) *the whole populace of Paris*   a rather facile prefiguration of the storming of the Bastille (14 July 1789) by the Parisian mob, in the course of which the prison governor was killed

154 (p. 364) *petit lever*   A small number of chosen courtiers and family members would normally attend the rising of the monarch after sleep. It would be followed by the more ceremonial *grand lever*.

155 (p. 368) *eight long years of agony*   or possibly six, depending on which version you believe. See above, Note 145.

156 (p. 373) *a mask of iron*   although in Ch.105 Dumas unaccountably refers to it as 'a mask of burnished steel'

157 (p. 378) *no greater than other men*   a somewhat oblique remark, possibly pertaining to the execution of Louis XVI in 1793, or to the bourgeois monarchy of 1830–48. Louis-Philippe prided himself on strolling the streets of the capital carrying an umbrella.

158 (p. 379) *the mills of God*   in the French, *meule immense*, implying some huge mechanism such as the Juggernaut. The translator appears to be remembering lines from Longfellow's poem 'Retribution': 'Though the mills of God grind slowly, yet they grind exceeding small.'

159 (p. 380) *who is also an Infante* slightly obscure, though presumably intended to stress that Philippe is the son of a Spanish princess (Anne of Austria) as well as of a French king

160 (p. 380) *since you are already a grandee of Spain* also rather obscure: possibly referring to the fact that at the end of *TM*, Athos inherits property in Roussillon, which was part of Spain until finally conquered by France in 1642

161 (p. 383) *Roi des Halles* Beaufort was adored by the population of Paris; the nickname refers to the market area of the city

162 (p. 383) *Jijeli* in Algeria, a coastal village some eighty miles northwest of Constantine, captured by the French in 1664 in an expedition against the Barbary pirates

163 (p. 384) *Turenne* Henri, Vicomte de Turenne (1611–75) one of Louis XIV's most successful generals

164 (p. 385) *Vincennes* See above, Note 93.

165 (p. 385) *Vaugrimand* Dumas's mistake: one of his sources provided him with the name Vaugrimont as someone who assisted with Beaufort's escape from Vincennes (*TYA*), but Grimaud only ever uses his own name.

166 (p. 388) *a Knight of Malta* the Knights of Malta were a military order devoted to fighting the infidel. As they were subject to monastic vows, the implication is that Athos's line will die out.

167 (p. 391) *Malicorne* Germain, Baron de Malicorne (1626–94), the lover of Aure de Montalais, who in *LV* helps to foster Louis XIV's relationship with Louise de la Vallière

168 (p. 399) *Longus* Ancient Greek author of uncertain date, who wrote the pastoral idyll *Daphnis and Chloë*

169 (p. 400) *Ruth . . . Boaz* The reference is to the Book of Ruth, where Ruth the Moabitess, stranded 'amid the alien corn', finds a husband in the elderly Boaz, 'a mighty man of wealth'.

170 (p. 400) *Rochefort* The Comte de Rochefort is d'Artagnan's enemy in *TM*, an ally of Richelieu, but his friend in *TYA*. However, they are on opposite sides, and d'Artagnan inadvertently kills him at the end of the novel.

171 (p. 400) *speculation* Planchet had largely financed d'Artagnan's expedition to England to restore Charles II to the throne (*VB*).

172 (p. 402) *decree of the people* a reference to the execution of Louis XVI in 1793, subsequent to his trial and condemnation by the Revolutionary Convention

173 (p. 404) *Corsairs, Lepanto* As readers of G. K. Chesterton's poem 'Lepanto' will know, Don John (Juan) of Austria defeated the Turks at Lepanto in 1571. The destruction of Turkish sea power resulted in an increase in piracy in the Mediterranean.

174 (p. 416) *Saint-Mars*  Not to be confused with Cinq-Mars (see above, Note 19), Bénigne d'Auvergne de Saint-Mars (1622–1708) was initially Fouquet's gaoler at the fortress of Pignerol in 1665, and subsequently in charge of the masked prisoner at Sainte-Marguerite from 1687 onwards.

175 (p. 433) *Rabaud*  d'Artagnan's servant – the one and only appearance of the character

176 (p. 434) *genius for intrigue*  This is not clear in the French – does it mean two people in addition to Aramis, or two including Aramis? On the latter assumption, the reference is to the Cardinal de Retz.

177 (p. 438) *States-General*  Mistranslated: the reference is to the provincial estates of Brittany. The States-General did not in fact meet between 1614 and 1789.

178 (p. 439) *Brienne*  Henri-Auguste de Loménie de Brienne (1596–1666), Louis XIV's Secretary for Foreign Affairs

179 (p. 439) *Gesvres*  Léon, Duc de Gesvres (1620–1704), captain of the king's guard since 1646

180 (p. 442) *tertian fever*  intermittent, in the sense that the paroxysms occur only every other day

181 (p. 452) *Philip III*  Dumas's mistake. Philip III was King of Spain between 1598 and 1621. At the time of the action, Philip IV (1621–65) rules in Spain.

182 (p. 454) *Notables*  the aristocratic members of the Breton estates

183 (p. 462) *Montmorency*  Henri, Duc de Montmorency (1595–1632), executed for collaboration in another of Gaston d'Orléans' (many) conspiracies against Richelieu

184 (p. 465) *Rose*  Toussaint Rose (1613–1701), private secretary to the king since 1657

185 (p. 474) *Daedalus*  in classical mythology, the inventor of (among other things) the Cretan labyrinth, in which he was imprisoned, but from which he subsequently escaped by making wings for himself out of wax and feathers

186 (p. 505) *âme damnée*  The French gives 'infernal agent' (which means exactly what it says). An *âme damnée* is someone totally devoted to the interests of someone else, hardly the same thing.

187 (p. 508) *Coligny*  Gaspard de Coligny (1517–72), Admiral of France, murdered in the Massacre of St Bartholomew's Day. It is not at all obvious why Porthos's father, presumably a good Catholic, should have been named after the head of the Protestant faction.

188 (p. 511) *Biscarrat*  In *TM*, Biscarrat's father is one of the opponents of d'Artagnan and the musketeers in the first duel they ever fight together, and the only one to remain undefeated.

189 (p. 527) *Bastion Saint-Gervais*   reference to a famous episode in
   *TM* when d'Artagnan and the musketeers capture an outpost of the
   besieged town of La Rochelle and proceed to eat their breakfast
   there, under constant fire from the enemy

190 (p. 527) *Hercules, Theseus, Castor and Pollux*   These names of
   mythological heroes seem to be chosen largely at random, although
   Hercules clearly stands for Porthos. Theseus, King of Athens,
   conqueror of the Minotaur, both wily and amorous, could be
   Aramis. Castor and Pollux were twin brothers, one immortal, one
   not: when Castor, the mortal twin, was killed, Pollux begged to be
   stripped of his immortality so as to die with his brother. Perhaps
   Dumas uses them to illustrate the spirit of comradeship that once
   prevailed among the four.

191 (p. 528) *Homeric*   heroic. Frequent references to classical antiquity
   underline the superhuman nature of Porthos's last exploit.

192 (p. 534) *my own Jupiter*   The thunderbolt was the preferred
   weapon of Jupiter, king of the gods.

193 (p. 537) *Titan*   Dumas's fields of reference get very confused here,
   since Porthos is also compared to Jupiter, the (im)mortal foe of the
   Titans (see previous Note). There is further confusion between the
   Titans and the Giants – in classical mythology it was the Giants who
   plotted against Jupiter and tried to scale the heights of Olympus.

194 (p. 537) *genius of ancient chaos*   a vaguely epic-sounding attribution
   that does not seem to refer to anything in particular. Dumas uses
   the word *ange* (angel), which suggests a (somewhat unspecific) link
   to the metaphysical epic poetry popular at the time.

195 (p. 537) *Enceladus*   the most powerful of the Giants, struck down
   by Jupiter's thunderbolt and buried under Mount Etna

196 (p. 542) *Greek fire*   an inflammable mixture shot from tubes on
   board warships that caught fire when it touched the water

197 (p. 555) *the bargain we made one day at Blois*   In *VB* d'Artagnan
   resigns his commission as captain of the musketeers in dissatisfaction with Louis XIV's abandonment of his beloved Marie
   Mancini for reasons of state, at which point the king, sobbing with
   rage and frustration, predicts his future dominance, which is demonstrated here.

198 (p. 555) *La Rochelle*   The story of the siege of La Rochelle figures
   prominently in *TM*.

199 (p. 563) *Vandyck's Madonna*   A number of religious paintings by Sir
   Anthony Vandyke (1599–1641) were on display in the Louvre at the
   time Dumas was writing.

200 (p. 568) *in his sixty-second year*   probably not. Evidence internal to the text of the *Musketeers* novels suggests that Athos was born *c.*1595, so he would now be sixty-six.

201 (p. 568) *St Martin's summer*   The Feast of St Martin is on 11 November, so the expression is equivalent to 'Indian summer'.

202 (p. 584) *d'Estrées*   Jean d'Estrées (1624–1707), admiral of the French fleet

203 (p. 594) *Pignerol*   the fortress in which Fouquet was imprisoned early in 1665

204 (p. 600) *Chevalier de Lorraine*   Philippe, Chevalier de Lorraine (1643–1702) is the favourite of Louis XIV's homosexual brother, Philippe d'Orléans (who, despite his lack of interest in women, was jealous of the king's attention to his newly married wife). Dumas develops these relationships in *VB* and *LV*.

205 (p. 601) *brother-german*   i.e., brother by blood, not by marriage

206 (p. 602) *the king's advisers*   The translator has changed some of Dumas's (invented) names in the original French: the Merry Monarch is not known to have had any paramours rejoicing in the name of Miss Orchay or Mademoiselle Zunga.

207 (p. 603) *Mademoiselle de Kéroualle*   Louise de Kéroualle (1649–1734), subsequently created Duchess of Portsmouth by Charles II

208 (p. 603) *that medal*   The incident is mentioned in *LV*, Ch. 75.

209 (p. 606) *d'Infreville, Forant, Destouches*   all naval engineers employed by Colbert

210 (p. 607) *Golden Fleece, Grand Cordon of St Michael*   The Golden Fleece was the highest order of Spanish chivalry, whereas the Order of St Michael was French, created by Louis XI in 1469.

211 (p. 609) *baton*   the insignia of a Marshal of France

212 (p. 611) *Father d'Oliva*   Jean-Paul Oliva was General of the Jesuits from 1664 until 1681, in succession to Aramis's (entirely fictitious) tenure. Since 1661, he had been deputy to the previous general, Father Nickel.

213 (p. 612) *His Catholic Majesty . . . the Most Christian King*   papal accolades bestowed on the Kings of Spain and France respectively

214 (p. 614) *en échelon*   in stepped formation

215 (p. 616) *white flag*   The white flag (with or without the fleur-de-lis) was the emblem of the Bourbons, the royal family of France, i.e., it is not here intended to signify surrender as such.